SLAYING THE JABBERWOCK

Book One of the Sutherland-Roberts Novels

Jean Kehoe Van Dyke

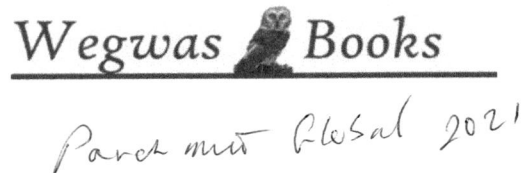

Parchment Global 2021

Copyright © 2021 by Jean Kehoe Van Dyke

All rights reserved. No part of this book may be reproduced or transmitted in any form or by any means, electronic or mechanical, including photocopying, recording, or by any information storage and retrieval, system, without permission in writing from the copyright owner.

This is a work of fiction. Names, characters, places and incidents are either the product of the author's imagination or are used fictitiously. Any resemblances to any actual persons, living or dead are entirely coincidental.

ISBN: 978-1-952302-46-6 (sc)

Library of Congress Control Number: 2021906362

Parchment

Author's Notes:

Slaying the Jabberwock is a character driven novel—to the point that I feel they wrote the book and I came along for the laughs and the privilege of sharing their experiences. There were many times I confidently sat down at the computer, knowing exactly what was supposed to happen, and ended up being totally wrong and thoroughly upstaged by the actions, antics and ambitions of people so real I expected them to walk in my door and swap stories with me.

They did, however, allow me to edit, or at least they let me think I did. They made me react to them and taught me about themselves through both their despairs and triumphs. But mostly, they entertained me, made me laugh and want to know more about them, which explains why there are two more books in the works: *Taming the Muse* and *Seeking Rigoletto*.

I've been writing tales about fictional people I would like to know in physical reality since I was a child. They live in my mind, but relate to the world in their own peculiar ways. As for genre, I don't think about it much. If pressed to come up with a description for this novel, I would call it psychological fiction about good families coping with life and love. There's a lot of tongue-in-cheek narrative, as well as very human misinterpretations and imagined assumptions that make the characters feel real in a story that runs the gamut from disastrous to hilarious.

The only writing style I lay claim to is that of an observant and all-seeing narrator, who says: "Meet my people and let them tell you their stories…"

My dedication is to the friends and patient souls who endured my babbling obsession throughout an extensive rewrite of a manuscript that took hold of me for longer than I ever expected. I give sincere thanks and appreciation for their suggestions and encouragements. Especially big thanks go to my husband John for putting up with me and to my good friends Laurey Simpson and Deb Newland, who read the manuscript with insights that encouraged me to find hidden stories that give my characters full, believable lives.

And most of all: to my readers—thanks for laughing out loud!

JABBERWOCKY
Lewis Carroll
(Through the Looking-Glass and What Alice Found There, 1872)

'Twas brillig, and the slithy toves
Did gyre and gimble in the wabe:
All mimsy were the borogoves,
And the mome raths outgrabe.

"Beware the Jabberwock, my son!
The jaws that bite, the claws that catch!
Beware the Jubjub bird, and shun
The frumious Bandersnatch!

He took his vorpal sword in hand:
Long time the manxome foe he sought—
So rested he by the Tumtum tree,
And stood awhile in thought.

And, as in uffish thought he stood,
The Jabberwock, with eyes of flame,
Came whiffling through the tulgey wood,
And burbled as it came!

One, two! One, two! And through and through
The vorpal blade went snicker-snack!
He left it dead, and with its head
He went galumphing back.

"And, has thou slain the Jabberwock?
Come to my arms, my beamish boy!
O frabjous day! Callooh! Callay!'
He chortled in his joy.

'Twas brillig, and the slithy toves
Did gyre and gimble in the wabe;
All mimsy were the borogoves,
And the mome raths outgrabe.

Chapter One

"Appassionato, Andrew! Appassionato!" The resonant voice of Maestro Vittorio Luciani boomed across the bare practice room. Its rudeness crashed through Drew Sutherland's concentration, froze his voice, ripped away the music in his head as it continued to hammer at him. "*Fieramente! Fieramente! Impetuoso!*"

"*Taci!*" With a swing of his arm, Drew smashed the upright supporting the slanted top of the piano beside him. The lid banged down with a discordant crash and he shouted, "*Taci!*" again, as if the vehemence of the word itself could make the badgering man shut up.

"*Silenzio!*" Vittorio continued his tirade in vehement Italian: "Listen when I speak! I am master! When I ask for passion, I want passion. Perfection is useless. Give me feeling. Give me Figaro! Not Andrew, Andrew, Andrew. I'm sick of Andrew!"

"I'm sick of your inflated opinion of yourself." Drew shouted at the wiry stick of a man, whose tempestuous anger raged with the awesome power of a firestorm, and shot his hand up in an obscene gesture of defiance. "Take your fucking passion and shove it!"

"Arrogant jackass!" Rising, Vittorio swept his hand across a paper cluttered table and hurled a tumbler in a wild, sidearm throw that sent it flying past his student.

Drew heard a startled scream, twisted to see the missile hit the woman playing the piano. He saw glass shatter against dark hair, watched pale liquid turn red as it mingled with blood, ran down an ashen face. A wave of red fury blotted out Drew's awareness before he stiffened, threw his head up and bellowed, "Do not hurt her!" as he charged forward, knocked a shouting Vittorio out of his way then froze when the woman looked at him in innocent surprise.

When powerful arms circled his chest and hauled him backwards, Drew shuddered, snapped his head, up and shattered the darkness in his mind. Growling, "*Imbecille*," he bent forward, twisted his shoulders to roll a heavy man across his back.

When the crushing hold released, Drew swung his right leg in an arc that swept the man's feet out from under him as his own straight-armed shove on the shoulder sent the attacker skidding across the floorboards. When a second pair of hands closed on his arms, he spun away from them, ducked, shot his foot at an unprotected chest. The assailant staggered backwards into a beverage cart that reared up on two wheels, crashed onto its side. Whirling, Drew saw the first man charging toward him. He dodged left and came up under the man's guard. The heel of his right hand slammed against hard jawbone. The man collapsed.

Ignoring the groaning form at his feet, Drew swept his gaze around the room. Vittorio sat on the floor, gaping at him from round eyes in a bloodied face. Drew started to ask what had happened then saw blood on his own arm, shirt and pant leg. He heard movement behind him and bolted for the door beyond where the smaller assailant was trying to push himself to his feet by leaning on the smashed serving cart.

"*Buono! Furioso! Fervente!*" Drew heard Vittorio shouting behind him, but it made no sense. Nothing could be good here. Nothing.

In the parking lot beyond the conservatory's sweeping lawn, Drew leaned on a fender of his car and concentrated on the flickering play of sun and shade on the deep blue finish. Shuddering, he shook himself free of the hypnotic flashes, fought to control the whirling chaos in his mind by focusing on tense hands and hard forearms, spatters of blood on the sleeve of his white shirt.

"Oh God, what did I do?"

Drew remembered Vittorio's shouts pounding at him until he didn't know what he was doing, didn't know where he was. He remembered a scream, a searing wave of rage. He remembered breaking away from two men who attacked him. He remembered staring at Vittorio, wondering why someone had assaulted his teacher. He remembered blood. Vittorio's blood? He tried to make sense of it, but there were no answers, only a desperate sense of wrong that drove him to the edge of panic, told him to run away and find refuge where he could think.

As Drew sped away from the conservatory, the decision to go to the only person he could trust to help him calmed the panic. He forced himself to focus beyond irrational chaos, took control of his racing anxiety and turned away from Genoa and its shimmering vista of the sun-drenched Mediterranean Sea.

Northwest of Paris, at the end of a long drive that curled uphill between dark masses of shade trees, a stone, French Provincial country house carved a black hole out of the dusty swath of the milky way. The house was unlit, except for a splash of light on stone steps to the front portico entrance, a faint golden glow beyond stained glass sidelights and the beckoning illumination of a triple-wide, multi-paned window at the right corner of the first floor.

Drew parked in the drive then shivered when, still wearing the open collar shirt that had been comfortable on the Mediterranean coast, he stepped into the chill of a December night in northern France. Beyond the unlocked front door, he paused on the slate floor of a silent entry hall and pulled in a steadying breath. The comforting scent of leather furniture and Old Spice led him through a dark sitting room toward the lighted corner office, where a trim, fit man, wearing a worn, *Le Mans Grand Prix* sweatshirt and khaki pants, sat sideways behind an antique, table-desk—watching him.

Drew stopped inside the office door and met Andy Sutherland's steady blue stare. "Why are you still up?"

"I've been expecting you. I had a call from Genoa."

"The police?" Drew walked to a russet leather sofa that faced his father's desk and sat astride its rolled arm. "That means you'll tell me I have to turn myself in."

"I don't think there would be much choice. If Genoa put out a warrant for you, you would have already been picked up by the Italians, or the French. There aren't many Lamborghinis like yours on the road and few places to hide it and keep moving between there and here."

"Then who called?"

"Vittorio Luciani."

Drew felt the name more than heard it. A cold fist clenched in his gut, turned his voice cynical. "He'd like to see me dead. Or at least flogged in the town square."

"Not the first; probably the second." Andy's hands tightened on the arms of the chair. He didn't raise his voice but it was hard enough to split rock. "Believe me, Drew; when I heard what you did, my primal desires were to slam you against a wall and flog you myself. Your behavior was inexcusable. However, I've had a few hours to harness those urges and think about what he said, which means there's a chance we may be able to talk about this like civilized people who respect each other."

"Right now, I don't think I'd blame you." Drew stared at the dried stains that marked his sleeve. "I have no acceptable excuses."

"Why do you think the police want you?"

"I beat up an old man, Dad." Drew lifted his gaze and faced his guilt, felt the fist relax.

"He's only fifty-eight. I'd appreciate it if you weren't so loose with your adjectives." Andy's eyes locked their two blue stares together. "He said you had provocation."

"He threw a glass of wine at Elise. It cut her and I lost my temper."

"He threw a plastic water tumbler at you. It hit her by mistake. She got wet; she wasn't cut."

"I saw the blood. It was mixed with the wine and ran out of her hair." Drew was confused, unable to accept what he was hearing. "I saw it. Why are you denying the truth?"

"Because if you're right, Vittorio is wrong."

Drew recoiled with dramatic cynicism. "Maestro Luciani, God's perfect man, wrong?"

"Drew, one of you isn't telling the right story. How do you know you beat him?"

"He was bloody. I have blood on me." He glanced back at the spattered stains.

"When he approached Elise, you gave him a bloody nose by knocking him aside with your forearm—an action he described as sweeping a bug out of your way. He said he kept shouting at you, trying to get through to you, but you weren't listening. Do you remember that?"

"That's not what I saw." The vision of blood-soaked dark hair loomed vivid in Drew's mind, making him wonder why Vittorio had lied about what seemed so real."

"Two carpenters ran in and pulled you away. You did more to them than to Vittorio."

"I didn't know who they were. I thought they were attacking me."

"They were trying to stop you."

"I didn't know that. Someone was squeezing the breath out of me. I threw him away, but they kept coming after me. All I did was defend myself."

"Your skills go beyond defense. You can be dangerous if you don't know what you're doing. You've been taught that for years."

"All I did was stop them from attacking me."

"You just said you didn't know what happened."

"I knew what I was doing then. I didn't know why they attacked me." He paused, searched for any memory that would verify what his father told him. There was nothing but the blood and deep red rage. "Why would Vittorio tell you all that?"

"I asked him to. I get very upset when someone tells me you don't act like yourself and don't listen to someone you should respect. I get more upset when you tell me you don't remember what happened."

"I got mad."

"You checked out."

"I got very mad." Drew's hands tightened into fists he pressed on his thighs. "He's an egomaniac. I can't take it when he starts badgering and won't let me think."

"Why you got mad is not what concerns me right now. I want to know why you dissociated."

"I didn't dissociate." Drew stiffened.

"You weren't responding as yourself. You had no memory of what you did, or where you were. What else do you call it?"

"All right!" Drew threw up his hands and broke away from the steady stare that could rip truth out of him no matter how much he wanted to keep it hidden. "Believe what you want."

"Why did it happen?"

"I don't know."

Drew stood facing the front window. He saw reflections of his father's sharp features, a gleam of light on strands of silvering blond hair. The darkness of his own cropped curls disappeared in the black of the night as the window threw the distraught reflection of similar features back in his face. He turned away from it and looked below his father's eyes at a stack of mail on the desk. "When I blow up, I don't think very well. You battled enough of my temper tantrums to know that. I feel like hell about it."

There was a long silence while Andy waited until Drew sat astride the arm of the couch. When his son met his probing stare, he asked, "What about the blood on Elise? Where did that come from?"

"I saw him throw the glass. I heard her scream and saw blood and wine running down a terrified face."

"There was no blood and no wine. How could you see it?"

"Maybe I imagined it."

"Or remembered it."

"What do you mean?" Drew reared back in rejection of what he heard.

"I think it was an abreaction," Andy stated flatly.

"How can you know that?"

"I don't know it. I think it. But I have experience on my side. I went through a lot of them with you."

"That's all over. I blew my temper. That's all." Drew forced himself to relax his clenched hands, the tightness in his neck and shoulders. All he'd done was lose control for an instant or two. His father was seeing ghosts. "I was a kid for shit sake. Let it go."

"If you agree to see Dr. Reynard."

"Sure. I like Paul." The eyes released him when his father leaned back in the chair, crossed his right ankle over his left knee, straightened the top of an argyle sock.

"Drew, you're not supposed to call your psychiatrist by his first name."

"He was my psychiatrist when I was a messed-up kid. We've mostly been friends lately. I took him sailing three weeks ago. We caught some nice Bonito and Dolphinfish." Drew shrugged, then looked across the room at a framed photograph. He was in Milan with his grandmother, standing in the plaza in front of La Scala. "How am I going to tell Gram about this?"

"My mother can handle disappointment," Andy said. "She's had to do it a lot in her life."

"She always finds a way to overcome it, but it leaves scars I don't want to cause." When Drew looked back, the lines of his father's chiseled features were softer, the eyes just as blue but less intently focused. "I failed her."

"Not yet."

"Dad, I told him to shove it and walked out on him. Nobody crawls back to Vittorio Luciani. Once he throws a student out, it's over. Singers have tried to bribe or threaten their way back into his favor. He scoffs at them."

"He didn't throw you out."

"Only because I quit first."

"He's offering you a chance to reconsider—a sabbatical of sorts—while you think it over."

"Vittorio said that?" Drew's eyes widened.

"There's a possibility he'll take you back next November. If you agree to his terms."

"What are his terms?"

"He didn't say, but he invited me to Genoa for a talk in the spring—after he's had time to think about it."

"Why you?"

"He doesn't want to talk to you until you grow up and develop enough sense of responsibility to live up to your commitment. He doesn't think three months is long enough."

"Are you sure he said that?" Drew studied the controlled expression on his father's face. "It sounds more like you."

"Well," Andy answered with a shrug, "he said it in an eruption of impassioned Italian, but that's an accurate interpretation put into watered down American English. It's a point Maestro Luciani and I agree on. You'll be twenty-six in two months. It's about time you decided what you want to do with the rest of your life."

"You always told me I could do anything I wanted."

"Don't be flip." The swift thrust of a rapier sharp voice set Drew back, then added quietly, "I said you could have any career you wanted. I didn't suggest you play at trying careers for the rest of your life. You graduated from college at twenty with the idea of going to law school. That lasted one semester before you gave it up for police training in a canine unit, which your grandmother strongly disapproved of."

"She disapproved of most everything I did for about three years."

"Not that it mattered." Andy said. "You used it as a job for less than three years before you quit to go to veterinary school."

"I took a leave of absence to go to vet school."

"Which lasted two semesters before you decided to use the talent you always saw as an entertaining diversion and became obsessed with music and theater. And then, it was opera training, which you insisted was the true calling of your life. Drew, you have more intelligence than the Pope has faith. Use some of it, for God's sake. Make a sensible decision about who you want to be and see it through. Find an anchor and stick to it."

"I thought I wanted to do all those things when I started them. It's just that something else always seemed better. What if I don't like what I choose?"

"You never stick with anything long enough to find out if you like it or not. Finish something and work at it until it becomes a career. It's all right to change careers, but it helps to have one first. Life isn't a smorgasbord of wild escapades and fleeting love affairs."

"Why not? I can afford it."

"Because it has no purpose." Andy rocked the chair forward and smacked his hand on the desk, making Drew recoil. "What the hell are you looking for?"

"I don't know. I don't even know what I want any more. How can I make a decision when I don't know what the choices are?" He gave his father an exasperated look. "You make them. You're very good at making decisions then telling me what to do."

"I made the rules for living in my household and insisted you behave according to the standards I believe in. Your education and personal goals were always yours. Do you still want to be an opera singer?"

"I don't know." Drew punched the padded leather between his thighs. "Just tell me what I want to do and I'll do it. Stop badgering me to make decisions I can't make."

"I won't make decisions like that for you, but I will make suggestions. You have other offers. You turned down excellent musical roles to do this opera thing. Why don't you take one of them and do what you know you're good at?"

"It would only remind me of my failure to live up to the dream Gram and I shared. I let her down."

"You ran into a road block. Don't give up because you found it isn't easy. You're tougher than that. You've made yourself go on to win before."

"When I knew I could do it." Drew shifted uncomfortably before he looked into his father's eyes and admitted what had been gnawing at his mind. "I blew up at Vittorio. But it was mostly against myself because I don't have what it takes to be what he and Gram want."

"You have a magnificent voice."

"Damn the voice. Voice is a tool." Drew broke from his father's pokerfaced stare and looked back at the photo. "Vittorio is right. I don't have the passion to make myself a great performer."

"And you have to be great?"

"I wanted to be a Domingo, Merrill, Bruson, Cappuccilli." Drew threw his hands up in frustration. "But I don't have what they had."

"Did they have it when they were twenty-five?"

"They must have because they made it and I can't." He eyed his father curiously. "Why would Vittorio take me back when he's rejected other good singers who possess the passion he says I don't have?"

"Maybe he believes in you, too."

"That's not what I hear him saying." Drew shot to his feet and released the energy of building frustration by pacing from couch to window, window to couch. "I'm pampered and arrogant and bullheaded. I'm a rich, spoiled *birichino*, who expects fame for tiny efforts. And get this!" He whirled to rant at his father. "I was never made to show proper respect for my superiors. He sure as hell doesn't know much about Sutherlands."

When Andy calmly stared at him with a reserved expression on his face, Drew made a weak attempt to stem the vehement tirade that shattered against the unyielding wall of his father's silence. A flashflood of indignant fury overpowered his control and sent him pacing again.

"He doesn't want proper respect. He wants me to take shit and say thank you, sir, for insulting me so you can inflate your own ego. He says I don't know anything—that I was never taught anything— that I don't have the drive to be what he wants to make me. He sees himself as a few steps above God on the operatic divinity scale and I'm sick of it."

Drew strode back from the, window, "I almost walked out on him twice last week—"

"Vittorio has a few good points." Andy's firm voice stopped Drew cold. "Arrogant and bullheaded come to mind. You used to walk out on me, too. But you always came back to face my—" a slanted smile twisted his lips— "I believe you called it pigheaded tyranny. I do think Vittorio makes some false assumptions about you based on his bias against rich Americans who want to buy instead of earn admiration. But he is not so different from me as he thinks. We both expect you to earn success, not buy it. You're having a little trouble with that, aren't you?"

"I don't want to buy it."

"Then earn it." The firm, but simple statement jolted Drew from anger to perplexity. "And think about this: buying does not always involve money."

"I don't know what you mean."

"When you figure that out, you should be able to make the right decision." Andy looked at his watch, then back at Drew. "It's almost two. I have an important meeting in the morning. Your rampage is not without cost. I have the names and phone numbers of the two carpenters you flattened. Maestro Luciani agreed to send you a bill for damages. There is no intent to involve the police, but I will suggest you offer apologies immediately and pay whatever compensation is expected. Write your apology to Vittorio. Don't call him."

"Is that all you're going to say?"

"It is for tonight." Andy stood, started for the door then stopped in front of Drew. He slid a hand across his son's shoulder to the back of his neck, then tightened it until Drew met his absorbing stare. "Do I have your full agreement that you will call Paul Reynard tomorrow morning? It's important to me."

"Yes." When his father's hand massaged away the tension at the base of his neck, Drew dropped his forehead to a sweatshirt covered arm. A tight knot unwound in his chest then released in a convulsive shudder. "I don't like myself right now."

"It isn't as bad as you think."

"Yes, it is. How can you accept what I did?"

"I don't condone it if that's what you mean. I love you and nothing ever changes that. Understanding what you did and forgiving will take longer. We need to do a lot of talking about that. But not tonight."

Drew felt his father's hand squeeze his neck before it released. He still felt wrong, but he no longer felt alone.

Chapter Two

Sitting alone in the early morning quiet of her family's farmhouse kitchen, Willow Roberts mulled over the most miserable Christmas in her life. She had arrived home three days ago, eager to share good news about being accepted as a working student under a world-famous dressage rider and trainer. In less than an hour, her excitement had been smothered under an avalanche of outraged reproach over how she had, without consulting her family, broken her engagement to a man as kind, successful and dependable as Tom Sorensen.

Since in Willow's mind, the onslaught of disapproval had more to do with her rejection of a match her family saw as perfect than why she'd done it, the angry assault irritated her until she lost her temper, as well as any hope of sympathy, by telling her brother Todd, in a shout loud enough to be heard by everyone in the house, that what she did with her future was none of his or anyone else's goddamn business—the engagement was over. She was taking a new job in Parsons Glen, Pennsylvania in the spring and had no intention of discussing it.

The next three days had passed in a prickly standoff of injured feelings and simmering anger. Since no one wanted to be the one to make a complete disaster of the holiday, a tenuous ceasefire created a semblance of peace that made her feel like a shamed outcast—a pariah, who dared to think there could be success, even happiness, beyond the stubborn mindset of Cottonwood Forks, Iowa.

Sighing at a twinge of remorse for her behavior, Willow closed her hands around a mug of hot coffee and glumly accepted that she'd created the crisis months ago by refusing to listen to her own misgivings and letting other people's enthusiasm push her into a relationship her family believed in more than she did.

Willow knew it would have been better if she'd seen more of Byron, the brother who shared her red hair and was close enough to her in temperament and spirit she often saw him as a twin born a year too early. But it was a busy season for Byron and he'd only been home for Christmas dinner. Her hopes of talking with the one person who understood how she felt had been dashed when, after devouring two pieces of pumpkin pie, Byron gave her a sympathetic hug and the succinct advice that following her heart was the only way to be true to herself before he rushed off on a weeklong holiday concert tour.

Last night, after Byron left, Willow actually listened to what her mother had to say. The reprimand for her burst of uncalled for profanity and cranky attitude that put a gloom on Christmas was expected. The realization that her mother not only understood her hurt but echoed Byron's advice to trust her feelings was surprising and appreciated. However, the insistence that she needed to come to some sort of immediate understanding with her father about the move east was not what Willow wanted to hear. When it concerned her, or Byron, clashes with their father only reached an understanding when *they* backed down and did what *he* wanted.

This morning Willow had awakened before dawn with the full intention of bearding her lion of a father about her determination to go to Pennsylvania. However, the thought of bringing up something else to fight about seemed to be an exceedingly dumb idea. Her car was already packed. All she had to do was walk out the back door and drive away. She wouldn't be going east until April, which gave him all winter to get used to the idea that, at twenty-four, his oldest daughter was mature enough to make her own decisions.

Ten minutes later, Willow wondered why she was still sitting at the table waiting for her father and youngest brother to return from tending to the farm's wintering herds of Angus cattle. She supposed her reluctance to leave had to do with the uncomfortable feeling that her father would see running away as cowardly rather than independent.

Sighing, Willow moved her chair closer to the warmth of the black cast iron woodstove that squatted in front of an old brick chimney. For as long as she could remember, the large wood rack beside the stove had been kept full by her brothers while she and her two younger sisters shared cooking and cleanup chores in the big square kitchen that, except for necessary replacements of outdated appliances, had hardly changed over her lifetime.

Brown and cream ceramic canisters of flours, brown and white sugars, rice, noodles and macaroni lined the back of counters alongside open crocks bristling with spatulas, wooden spoons and numerous other utensils, both new and well used. Scattered among and behind a variety of small appliances, a mishmash of packets, boxes and bottles containing spices, seasonings, herbs and garnishes, bunched together like stacks of forgotten cargo containers.

To the eyes of a stranger, the kitchen was a clutter of inefficiency. To the Roberts women, it was a miracle of organized disarray, where needed ingredients were easy to spot, easy to reach. There was ample room for several people to work at the same time; and if one project remained unfinished when the next began, there was space to push it aside for a spell.

Smiling, Willow let her gaze stop at the marble counter where she and her sisters had learned to roll pie crusts, as well as knead and shape dough for every kind of bread, including hot plump rolls filled with butter, cinnamon and nutmeg and lavishly glazed with sticky icing. The cinnamon rolls had always been a special part of every Christmas breakfast; and when she pulled in a breath, Willow could still taste their delicious aroma mingling with the sharp tang of wood smoke from when her father stoked the stove before dawn.

The sound of heavy boots stomping off snow on the back porch interrupted Willow's thoughts. She gulped down the last of her coffee and looked through the open door to the mudroom where her father shrugged off heavy winter coveralls that made him look like a hulking grizzly bear. After scrubbing a hand through a rumpled thatch of silver-flecked dark hair, Lloyd tossed his wool cap on a peg beside the coveralls and strode into the kitchen wearing his Christmas bounty of a black and yellow flannel shirt, crisp new work jeans and red wool socks.

At fiftyfour, Lloyd Roberts was a solid bull of a man. When he pulled his shoulders back and tightened his block jaw, he became awesomely powerful. When his ruddy complexion reddened and his dark eyes hardened, someone was in trouble. Willow recognized the signs and, refusing to be intimidated, locked stares with him.

"Are you ready to tell me what this matter of taking a job halfway across the country is all about?" Lloyd plucked the acceptance letter Willow had mistakenly left with her mother out of his shirt pocket and tossed it on the table. "Or are you going to get your dander up and tell me it's none of my business either?"

"I can't see that it's your concern any more than Todd's." Willow's retort snapped out before she pulled in a breath and relaxed her death grip on the empty ceramic mug. "But I do feel you deserve more explanation than he does."

"What you do with your life does concern me, Willow. I see no sense in this sudden reversal of your own plans." Lloyd picked up her mug and walked to the coffeemaker. "I want a reasonable explanation for that before you leave."

Willow leaned back in the chair and scowled at his broad back. This wasn't going to be easy. In view of the arguments, she had used to convince her father a degree in equestrian studies was a worthwhile academic pursuit, she knew he saw that education with the narrow view of its agricultural merit. Breeding and training horses to sell not only made sense to him, it fit into his one-dimensional belief that he wanted nothing more from his children than the contentment of local agrarian accomplishment. In his mind, the sport of high-level equestrian competition, especially at the international level, was a money hungry pastime for the rich, or those with pretentions to be rich. Lloyd Roberts wanted nothing to do with either of them.

"The job is with Mae Sutherland, a dressage trainer and former member of the U.S. Equestrian Team." Willow took a swallow of fresh coffee while Lloyd moved to stand closer to the warm radiance of the stove. "Mae came to Penwarden two years ago and I rode in the clinic she taught. She understands and connects with horses as if she can read their minds. I want to learn how she does that and there's nothing you can do to change my mind."

"I plan to try."

Taking his flat statement as a challenging order, Willow squared her shoulders, lifted a determined chin and glared at a broad, gruff face, dominated by thick sable brows. "I'm taking the job and that's all there is to it."

"That isn't all there is to me." Her father shifted closer to the back door and cut off her chance of storming out on him. "Why is this job offer better than the one you have at the college now, or the one you turned down here in Iowa?"

"This is the one I dreamed about but never thought I would get. The one at the college was no more than a temporary supplement while I waited for a better offer. I applied to the Iowa one because my advisor suggested it. One of my classmates was their alternate choice. Since she wanted it and I didn't, I backed out before the final interview."

"Why didn't you want it?"

"They expected me to rush horses without teaching good basics so they can sell them to rich clients, who want to win immediate ribbons instead of develop sound horses with good futures. I can't be that kind of trainer."

"It certainly pays better than this one." Lloyd tossed the letter onto the table.

"That includes at least two lessons a week from Mae Sutherland. You have no idea how much that's worth to me."

"If you ask me, it sounds more like a way to get cheap labor."

"I'm not asking you. I also get my own house with this job and—"

"You don't need a house. The other job was close enough you could live here until you are married and move in with Tom."

"Stop bringing up Tom." Willow wanted to shout but forced her voice under control when his face hardened. "I'm not going to marry him."

"Does that have anything to do with the grandson mentioned in the letter?"

"What are you talking about?" After glancing at the open envelope, Willow gave him an indignant look. "You mean the one I'm supposed to groom for? He's a kid. She wants me to be his show nanny."

With his heavy brows lowered in a scowl, Lloyd knuckled his right ear and searched her face looking for a sign of uneasiness she didn't feel. "Are you sure of that?"

"Since the legal age for competing in combined training is twelve and Mrs. Sutherland called him a boy, I assume he is a teenager. Why would you even think I would be interested in a boy?"

"Interest in another man is the only way I can make sense out you jilting Tom."

"I didn't jilt Tom. Ending the engagement was my idea but we agreed that it wasn't going to work. I'm fond of Tom but I don't love him." She watched a flicker of hesitation cloud his expression before he looked down and lifted his cup from the table.

"Love is not always fireworks, Willow," Lloyd said, then cleared his throat and took a swallow of his coffee. "You need to rethink the value of fondness and kindness before you reject them out of hand."

"I'll marry when I love a man beyond life itself, not when it's the comfortable or sensible thing to do."

"And if you don't find a man you can love beyond life itself?"

"I won't get married."

"You're sounding as cantankerous as my sister Rhian." Lloyd's dark gaze lifted to hers. "And you know what happened to her."

"Rhian never married, but she took life in her own hands and saw the world."

"Squandered all her gains chasing damn fool pipe dreams is what she's done. Never found her perfect man or accepted she wasn't going to be discovered as a great artist."

"Well, I plan to be a great horse trainer." Willow barged on before he could remind her of how Aunt Rhian's refusal to accept reality had turned her into a self-centered and bossy irritant. "Right now, I have the chance to learn from someone who already is great and I'm not going to pass it up because you don't believe in me."

"I believe in you to be sensible and accept the limits of reality. If you want to train horses, Tom is more than willing to support that goal on his farm. But he wants a wife and doesn't want to wait much longer."

"Then he can look elsewhere because I don't want a husband. I have my own goals and marriage isn't one of them." Willow snatched the letter off the table and marched past him into the mud room with the melodramatic determination of Scarlett O'Hara facing down a Union cavalry charge.

Lloyd's broad, flannel-covered shoulders seemed to fill the kitchen doorway as he watched his oldest daughter jerk an oversized rubber muck boot over her shoe. "Maybe I can't stop you from taking that job, but I can ask you to promise me you will think about whether you are running toward opportunity or away from regrets."

Willow paused with the second boot dangling from her hand and looked at his stern, weathered face. He was not a man who let expressions reflect his feelings, and she knew he'd said all he was going to say about the matter. Supposing that meant they'd reached the understanding her mother had mentioned, Willow let go of her anger and nodded. "Mrs. Sutherland needs an answer by the end of January. I promise I'll think about what you said before I give it to her."

Outside, Willow noticed her youngest brother Matt lingering by the tractor shed and realized he'd been waiting in the cold to avoid the confrontation in the kitchen. After answering his questioning look with a grateful smile, she tromped through squeaky-cold snow to a fenced paddock beside the barn. Standing at a red hay rack decorated with wind sculpted humps of new snow, a tall, brown and white pinto gelding snorted out plumes of crystalline breath while he picked through a mound of fresh hay and selected the tastiest bits to chew first.

Packy had always been that way: careful and precise, always making sure he did the best he could for her. When Willow stopped beside him, he nuzzled her hands and coat looking for the treats he could smell in her pocket.

"Since nobody else cares about my news, I'll have to tell you." Willow held out a carrot and watched the length of it disappear into the horse's mouth. While he crunched contentedly, Willow straightened a windblown forelock and slid her hand over an ear to rub the inside of it with her thumb. "Do you remember the nice lady we had a clinic with two years ago? When I said you didn't like your ears touched, she laughed and said you just thought you didn't because someone had hurt you that way. And then Mae won your trust and showed me how much you really liked it."

When Packy tipped his head so she could reach farther inside and rub harder, she laughed at the way he twitched his nose with pleasure. "Can you believe it, Packy? I'm going to work for Mae Sutherland. And I want to do it so much I'm willing to be a show groom for her grandson. He's probably a rich, spoiled brat, but the good news is he lives in Europe and will only be visiting for a short time."

After snorting a warm wash of horse breath across her hand, the gelding plucked the remaining piece of apple off her palm. "My heart is safely yours, Packy, even if you do run around with my little sister while I'm away." Willow smiled when a soft, warm tongue licked the last traces of sweetness off her palm. "But Beth says you take good care of her, so I forgive you for it."

In early April, Drew Sutherland drove a classic Mercedes sports car that had once belonged to his father into the driveway of a brick, nineteen-fifties era ranch house on the outskirts of Philadelphia and opened the garage door with a remote he dug out of his glove box. Inside the garage, he closed the door, parked beside an old Buick sedan and thumped down the car's raised door.

After taking a pot shot with his index finger at a concealed surveillance camera, Drew walked to an alarm panel beside a steel door into the house and watched a digital display count down toward zero as he typed in a code that would let him unlock the door without setting off a silent alarm he knew would bring the Philadelphia Police down on him within minutes. When the indicator lights flashed green, he opened the door with a key and walked into his uncle's kitchen.

A scribbled note on the table mentioned beer in the fridge and pretzels in the unreadable, but it hardly mattered. By the time Drew opened a beer bottle and looked out the kitchen window, a grey sedan that was clearly a police car pulled in the driveway. The man who stepped out of the driver's door wore brown slacks and a bronze-green sport coat over a yellow shirt open at the neck. At six-four and two-hundred and sixty pounds he looked as if he were still a defensive linebacker for Penn State. The balanced alertness of his movements and the way he seemed to be observing everything around him at the same time indicated survival skills learned on the more dangerous gridiron of Philadelphia's narrow backstreets.

Antonio Vitale was eight years older than Drew, bigger and burlier with a broad-boned face. Although he lacked Drew's sharply defined Sutherland features, Antonio shared his nephew's dark curling hair, wide smile and rolling laugh. They also shared a playful ability to laugh at themselves and a cocky bravado that radiated a daring need for adventure and challenge.

When the front door opened, Drew leaned against the kitchen doorjamb with the beer in his hand. "That was fast. I didn't even have time to decode where the pretzels were."

Antonio started at the resonant voice then pushed the door closed and cancelled the alarm. "How did you get here?"

"I wasn't about to leave the Mercedes in your driveway. It would be an attractive nuisance to the neighborhood hoodlums. If anything happened to that car, it would give Gram an excuse to flay me with one of her lack of responsibility lectures."

"You could use one." Antonio followed Drew into the kitchen and tossed his jacket on the back of a chair.

"You've been talking to my father again." Drew pulled out a chrome and cranberry-red vinyl chair and sat astride it with his arms folded on the back. His uncle tossed him a bag of soft pretzels he dug out of a grocery sack on the counter.

"Andy called me when you told him you planned to spend the summer with his mother. He had a lot on his mind." Antonio stripped off a shoulder holster, set it and its hefty automatic on the table before he walked to the refrigerator. "Are you willing to talk about it?"

"I'd rather avoid it."

"That may not be possible." Twisting the cap off his beer, the big man sat facing Drew across a rounded corner of the table. "He's not happy with you right now."

"I know. But he came through when I needed him and took a lot of time off to be with me. After his first few blasting lectures, he didn't pressure. My life crashed and when I showed up at Dad's, I couldn't make any decisions." Drew felt uncertainty gnawing a hole in him and looked away from his uncle's penetrating gaze. He'd never been able to bullshit Uncle Antonio, who could cut through his charming evasions and rationalizations like a laser beam. "Dad can't put my life back together this time. I don't know what to do about that."

"Why did you go back to the old neighborhood? You don't belong there." The gruff voice snapped Drew's attention to his uncle and the dark stare absorbed him with an intensity he couldn't evade.

"That's the only way I know how to start."

"Start what?"

"Finding answers. I have until November to sort myself out. That means I have to go back to things I'd rather not face."

"It was a mistake to go there."

"It's where it all started. I can't keep saying it wasn't important."

"You should have listened to your father and come to me first. I know what goes on there and could have clued you in on a few things." Antonio set the bottle on the table with a decisive clunk. "It's changed since you left and not for the better. Most of the kids you knew who still hang out there do it for the wrong reasons."

"For shit sake, there's all the same crap in Europe. I haven't spent all my life in cultured refinement."

"As far as I know there's no one in Europe who wants to kill you."

"Did you say kill me?" Drew recoiled.

"Yes, I did. I do a lot of undercover work there because it's where I grew up and they talk to me because they don't know I'm a cop. When your name popped up, I got interested and started pumping for information. A lot of them know your father was married to my sister, but they don't know Andy and I speak to each other, or even like each other. I want it that way."

"I understand that. But who wants to kill me?"

"Do you remember your stepfather's nephew Mario Pisano?"

"I sure do. We have a long history of mutual hate. Mario was a sneaky kid with a crabby mother and a bitter grandfather who wouldn't forgive her for having a bastard. His Uncle Gino was his hero and my enemy." A shimmer of revulsion twisted Drew's face. "I used to torque Mario's tail by calling him Mary-Ann Pissface. He was about fourteen when I left to live with Dad."

"What is between you two that makes him hate you so much?"

"You don't want to know."

"I definitely want to know." Antonio's vehemence rocked Drew back on the chair seat. "Don't hold out on me. Don't tell me it's none of my business. It's very important to Mario, and Mario is important to me. He's one sick fucker and I want to put him in jail for a long time."

"Mario had a fascination with knives." Drew stared into deep brown eyes. "I watched him stick one into a kid's hand one day. When Mario saw me, I ran, but he caught me and held the bloody knife under my nose. He threatened to cut off my balls and play marbles with them if I told on him. I was only six and had no idea why they were so important to me, but I was definitely fond of them and wanted to keep them where they were. When his grandfather heard about him sticking the kid, he beat him bloody with a belt buckle. Mario was convinced it was my fault. When he came looking for me with his damn knife, I threw a pot of hot fat at him and left him screaming."

"Did you tell on him?"

"I don't know." Drew shrugged and took a long swallow of beer.

"That surprises me." Antonio arched a thick eyebrow. "You have the most perfect recall of anyone I know."

"Not always and definitely not from then." Drew thought about it, but there were too many blanks from that time in his life. "I could have let it slip out. I don't remember doing it. A couple of years later I saw Mario in an alley punching a girl who wouldn't let him get his hand in her pants. I grabbed a piece of broken pipe and smashed him in the knee. Some people who saw it said I was afraid of him and protected myself. I don't remember feeling anything. I didn't even remember what happened. They said I kept hitting Mario until Mr. Shapiro pulled me away and took me into his drug store. They took Mario to the hospital. Gino whaled the crap out of me."

"Is that all?" The question sounded more demanding than fishing.

"Mario didn't like losing to a kid and told everyone he'd get even with me. He didn't have the chance. Dad took me to France before Mario was recovered and back on the street. Five years ago, when I was in vet school at Penn, Mario and two other morons attacked me outside a pizza bar. When I defended myself, the two morons deserted at a dead run. Mario gave me a reminder." Drew turned his left arm up to show a long scar on the inside of his forearm. "After I chucked his knife in a dumpster, he wasn't much of a challenge. I, however, was pissed and bounced him around a little before the cops showed up."

"What happened then?"

"Not much happened to me. There were witnesses who said I was attacked. I was on leave status then and my police ID was a big help. At the time, I didn't want to remember my past and said he tried to rob me. I acted as if I didn't know him and had my lawyer handle it. The Police were already looking for Mario for something else. I heard he was carrying enough drugs he got some jail time for dealing."

"He did but he's out now and he still hates you. When he found out you showed up on his turf last week, he went ballistic. He wants a piece of you and he's been pretty loud about it."

"He's a bully with a big mouth." Drew scoffed. "He terrorized us little kids and ran from the big ones."

"He's one of the big ones now."

"So am I. He tried to run from me last time, but I bounced him off a brick wall and scrambled his sense of direction."

"Drew, Mario is a vindictive son of a bitch since he got out of prison and he still has an obsession with knives."

"At least it isn't guns." Drew plunked his empty bottle on the tabletop.

"He didn't like jail. If he gets caught carrying, he goes back for a long time, so he stays away from guns. I know he's still dealing, but he's too smart to keep it on him or do it on the street. If we can pick him up and find enough drugs on him, we should be able to put him away again."

"Sounds like you want to use me for bait?"

"You made yourself bait by letting him know you're here. If you cooperate, I may be able to get rid of him and protect you at the same time."

"I don't need—"

"Damn it, Drew." Antonio bounced his fist off the table, making his nephew grab the beer bottle before it fell over. "Don't get cocky and tell me you can handle this yourself. He doesn't play by your kind of rules."

"I expected you to tell me to stay away from him."

"It's too late for that." Antonio scowled. "I guess you didn't listen to what I was trying to say. Mario wants you. It's a vendetta thing with him. I don't want him to start looking for you and I don't think you want him anywhere near your grandmother."

"That convinced me." Drew sucked back the arrogance and hardened his features. "What do I do?"

"I want you to go to Sal's Sports Bar and let people in there know who you are and that you're looking for Ernie Romano. As I remember, he used to be a friend of yours."

"For a few years in grade school." Drew twisted his face into a look that implied his uncle was nuts. "What am I supposed to talk to him about? All I clearly remember about Ernie is the time we tried to steal money out of his mother's purse. She chased us around the living room screeching at us and walloping us with a wooden spoon.

Ernie was chubby and slow, so I kept cutting in front of him to make sure he got the most whacks. He was yowling; I was cussing; his mother was yelling; his older sister was blocking the doorway and laughing like a maniac. It must have sounded like an insane asylum."

When Antonio sputtered into laughter, Drew stopped his comical ranting and stared down an aristocratically lifted nose in pompous indignation. "I beg your pardon. It was a very traumatic experience." He held the condescending look until his uncle met his eyes then burst out laughing with him.

"If you start with that rendition, you'll get Ernie laughing and you'll both start to remember more. Ernie's okay. He has a drinking problem, but he talks to me. He hated Mario."

"We all hated Mario." Drew watched distorted reflections of the window as he tipped the brown bottle in his hand. "I was the grade school superman after I stood up to him. It gave me a hero complex and a big ego. I was totally obnoxious and went from hero to bully in two weeks."

"You aren't a very good bully."

"I was then. Or at least part of me was. The memories are all mixed together now, and I can't always sort them out." Drew righted the bottle before he looked at his uncle. "When do you want me to do this?"

"I'm not sure right now. Do you have a cell phone?"

"I mostly leave it in the car or sitting on my dresser to collect messages." Drew fished a card out of his wallet and handed it to Antonio. "I got it at Dad's insistence but see it as a means for my convenience not everyone else's."

"Do me a favor and consider my convenience just as important." Antonio handed him a few cards. "That's my cell number. Put it in your phone and scatter the cards around where you can find one when you misplace the phone. There's some chatter about Mario being out of town next week. I don't want either of them around when you do this, but I want the information spread a.s.a.p. If Mario knows you'll come back to Sal's looking for Ernie, it will keep him from going after you. He'd much rather meet you on his own turf."

"You sure he won't try to shoot me on sight?"

"I can't be sure of anything but it isn't the way he does things. He likes to torment his victims."

"Has he killed anyone?"

"There's no proof, but I suspect he's responsible for a dead addict we found cut up in an alley."

"That's real encouraging, Tonio. Makes me want to leap right in and see how his carving techniques have improved."

"I plan on making sure you have good backup." Antonio looked him over critically. "You look like you still work out. They haven't turned you into a fat opera singer yet."

"That's the wining and dining, not the vocation. It's only necessary to be fit enough not to pass out from lack of air. Gives us big chests and loud mouths."

"You already had the loud mouth. I never knew another kid who could bellow like you."

"I had a lot of practice." Drew huffed. "My mother and the pig bastard pounded the snot out of me regularly."

"I wish I'd known the truth about that sooner."

"What could you have done about it?"

"What I did when I was sixteen. Tell your father about it."

"Your father and big brothers would have pounded on you for consorting with the enemy. Everyone in your family hated Dad."

"I guess I did, too." Antonio frowned. "Or at least I felt I was supposed to. I was too young to remember much about him, or the divorce, but I always liked something about you and figured Andy couldn't be all bad. He did keep trying to get you away from my crazy sister and sent extra money whenever she said she needed it for you."

"Too bad she never used it for me." Drew shrugged. "But then, the hippy thing was still in. Worn-out clothes that didn't fit and uncut hair were the peak of style."

"You been keeping up the martial arts training?"

"I've been teaching it."

"That'll help." Antonio looked at his watch. "We better get to Veterans Field before Hennessy tries to scalp our tickets."

"You can always arrest him."

"Nah, nobody will buy them on a Wednesday night. The Phillies aren't exactly burning up the league this year."

Chapter Three

In 1746 James Alistair Sutherland, the third Earl of Glendoncroft, publicly proclaimed his second son, Andrew, a traitor to the British Crown and charged him with treason for openly aiding the Jacobites in the Forty-Five Rebellion by supporting Bonnie Prince Charlie, the last of the Stuart pretenders, in his ill-fated final attempt to restore the Stuarts to the British throne. With political expediency taken care of the Earl arranged an escape that smuggled his son out of the Highlands only hours before British soldiers arrived to escort him to his execution.

Two days later, nineteen-year-old Andrew Sutherland, still weak from wounds received in the carnage at the Battle of Culloden, and his Highland bride secretly boarded a merchant ship in Glasgow and sailed to Philadelphia with a large enough fortune to purchase three sturdy merchant ships and establish what would become the wealthy trading and shipbuilding firm of Sutherland Mercantile. Andrew later resumed his rebellion against British rule by supporting the American Revolution and declaring himself and his family loyal citizens of the Commonwealth of Pennsylvania.

More than two hundred years after the final ratification of the United States Constitution, Sutherland Manor still looked as if it had been lifted, in toto, from the Scottish Highlands and transplanted, along with its rambling gardens, lush lawns and stone carriage house, into the rolling hills of Bucks County, Pennsylvania.

❖

Totally unaware of the historical and social magnitude of her employer's lineage, Willow Roberts turned her dusty, hand-me-down station wagon off the county road then stopped abruptly between two stone pillars supporting opened wrought iron gates. Stunned, she gaped through an insect splattered windshield at the size and setting of the imposing structure on the far side of a narrow, exclamation point lake. Massive, square towers stood silent guard at the front corners of the three-story manor house and tall stone chimneys with decorative caps cast deep shadows across steeply angled slate roofs. With rainbow shards of refracted sunlight transforming leaded window panes into precious gems set in a tapestry of ivy vines and weathered stone, the mansion's overall message of age, power and mystic fantasy created the evocative sensation of a castle out of time—an unread tome of mysterious secrets and untold stories.

Guess what, Miss County Fair Queen? You aren't in Iowa anymore. Coming to grips with the realization that the photo she had been sent of the horse barn and indoor riding arena had in no way prepared her for this panoramic, postcard view of the three-hundred-acre Sutherland estate, Willow let out a long breath and gave the house a look of dismay. *They undoubtedly have more fricking forks than I have names for.*

While the grandeur of the scene soaked into her reality, Willow straightened with resolve and told herself she had no choice but to head on down the yellow brick road and find out if she really was in Oz.

The curving strip of blacktop passed a carriage light lamppost with a sign reading, Sutherland Manor, Private Drive, before it continued over an arched, fieldstone bridge below a stone and mortar dam where clear water skidded down a mossy spillway into the rocky bed of a turbulent stream. Beside a fork in a copse of hardwoods, a sign on a second lamppost indicated left for the house, right for the stable.

Willow followed the meandering black ribbon to the stable and turned into a graveled parking lot that faced an enclosed connector between a long indoor riding arena that stretched away from her on the left, a horse barn to the right. Both buildings were wood, stained a deep mahogany with darker trim around large, sliding doors, open stall windows and translucent light panels below the eaves.

There was no one in sight when Willow stepped out of the car, which gave her a moment to absorb the setting for her job. Shrubs and flowering bulbs, deeply bedded in fresh wood chips, flourished beside the buildings and parking area. A flagstone path led to a raised porch on the connector where jumbles of colorful blossoms spilled from hanging baskets.

The building in the photo had been a stark intrusion of new construction still at odds with the green lushness beyond its leveled site. Even though Mae's most recent letter said the picture was taken several years ago, Willow had assumed it would look the same now—perhaps less brazen, more used and weatherworn. Instead, the scene around her was a Technicolor explosion of natural vibrancy and cultivated beauty with no sign of neglect, no indication that Sutherland Stables had been in decline after Mae's retirement from competition three years ago.

When a horse snorted from a hidden pasture and Willow heard the familiar rattling start of a diesel tractor inside the barn, she grinned and the unreal sense of Oz vanished. This was a world she understood: horses, tractors, hay, manure and the hard work that went with them. She noticed a burly, white-haired man in denim overalls and a worn, tweed flat cap trimming one of the shrubs beside the arena and walked toward him.

"Hello. Do you know where John is? I'm supposed to find him."

"You must be Willow and that's just what you did," he answered with a rolling touch of Scottish brogue. A flicker of pleased recognition warmed his broad face as he crunched across fresh chips, surrounded by the scent of dark loamy soil and growing vegetation. "I'm John Fergusson, gardener, general handyman and all-around good guy."

"I know I'm early, but I was anxious to get here." A relieved smile tugged at the corners of Willow's mouth when she met a kind, smoky green gaze.

"No harm being early. It's something that doesn't happen anywhere near as often as it should now that we can get everywhere so much faster." John offered a work callused right hand that felt as secure and welcoming as an open kitchen door. "If you continue down the paved drive and bear left on the gravel lane just past the mill pond, you'll be at your cabin. I'll meet you there."

"Do you want a ride?" Willow glanced at the jumble of maps, fast food bags and other accumulated junk on the passenger seat and floor in front of it. "I can clear you a space. I think."

"There's no need. The footpath to your back door is shorter than the lane. Your driveway and front door are arse-backwards to the barn, but you have a pretty view of the stream that way."

Willow's cabin was tucked into a clearing beside a pine-covered hill, where a crystal stream hop-scotched from cataract to cataract in its zigzag course down a steep cut, then wrapped around the back of the cabin before it ducked under the gravel lane. Built of dark logs, tightly fitted and chinked in bright white stripes, the cabin had a bedroom and spacious living room with a front door between. A deep, shed-roofed porch ran across the entire face of the structure. By the time Willow backed into the cabin's driveway and opened the rear hatch, John arrived.

"That's a mountain of goods for such a wee lass." Eyeing the boxes and bags filling the car, John pulled a red and white handkerchief from a back pocket and blew his broad nose. "If you'll wait until I wash off the garden dirt, I'll gie ye a hand."

"Thank you. Some of those boxes are heavy," Willow answered as she leaned into the back of the car.

"It's all right, John. I'll help her."

The deep voice startled Willow and she forgot to back up before she straightened and banged her head on the lift gate bracket.

"Ow!" Grimacing, she stumbled back a few steps and bumped into a firm body. A hard, arm circled her waist to steady her and a large, wooly black dog bounded playfully around them.

"I'll be leaving you in Mr. Sutherland's hands, Ms. Roberts." John lifted a thick white eyebrow and chuckled at her confusion. "The work will do him good and if he gets too cocky, whack him with something. It always worked for me." He gave her a quick nod before he headed toward the vegetable garden near the barn.

The arm relaxed and Willow turned, found herself embarrassingly close to a navy polo shirt stretched across the broad chest of a stunningly attractive man, who snapped his fingers at the dog and pointed toward John. When the animal turned and trotted after the gardener, Willow resisted a reflexive urge to follow the obedient animal then blinked up at sharply carved features that belonged on a publicity photo—not here, less than a foot away, emitting a charge of dominate masculinity that stopped her breath.

"I didn't know there was a Mr. Sutherland." Willow tried to back away, but the warm hand lingered at her waist and prevented her withdrawal.

"There are two of us, but I'm the only one here." A crooked smile softened his features, eased the feeling she was being held captive. "My father is in France."

Willow stared into deep blue eyes framed by dark lashes below heavy slashes of eyebrows. The eyes were entrancing but she forced herself to break from them when the arm slid away letting her shift closer to her car.

"You're Mae Sutherland's grandson?"

"Is there a problem with that?" Drew cocked his head, lifted an eyebrow.

"You're supposed to be about thirteen with big feet and a cracking voice."

"Did Gram tell you that?" A laugh rumbled out of his chest with more of the baritone resonance.

"Well, no, but she called you the boy." Willow's gaze slid up his fit, muscular build.

"From Gram that doesn't surprise me. And if you count birthdays, she's right. I'm only six and a half."

"Six and a half of what?"

"I was born on February twenty-ninth." Drew smiled when her scoff turned to enlightenment. "I got in a terrible fight one year when some older kids told me I couldn't have a birthday because it wasn't on the calendar."

"Does that mean you may never have a legal drink?"

"I remember a somewhat inebriated argument at a party over whether I was legal on the twenty-eighth or had to wait until March first. The debate went on for at least a six-pack and way past midnight when it became a moot point."

"To be honest," Willow relaxed with a sigh, "I was panicked that you might be an obnoxious teenager. I was afraid I would have to be a governess of some sort."

"As a former obnoxious teenager, I think I would have enjoyed a redheaded governess as spicy as you." He smiled at her wary look. "You have no idea how thankful you should be that I'm no longer an awkward adolescent with a dreadful case of self-importance."

"Why?"

"I was a horrible child who played outrageous pranks on anyone put in charge of me. Shall we start over?" Intrigued by her directness, Drew straightened and offered his hand with exaggerated correctness. "Andrew Wayne Sutherland."

"Willow Anne Roberts."

"Do you live up to your initials? I would say a woman known as WAR presents an intriguing challenge."

"Or a warning." She tugged her hand away.

It wasn't until Drew shifted his attention to a layer of packed boxes in her station wagon that Willow was able to think of anything but the intensity of his blue gaze and the possessive firmness of the hand that had momentarily engulfed hers before retreating with a lingering caress that unbalanced her. A shaft of sunlight enhanced fiery highlights in dark hair, lightly curled and haphazardly ruffled. His face was sharply sculptured, yet expressively mobile, with a square chin marked by a crescent scar.

"Why don't you go inside and decide where you want to put things while I take them in?"

Jolting herself back to practical matters, Willow swept her purse off the rear bumper and hurried up the wooden steps to the porch, where she propped open the screen door with a porch chair and stepped into the first home that she could call hers alone.

In the living room, large multi-paned windows looked out from front and end walls, proving John right about the view of the stream. The furniture was mission style oak with rust and wheat upholstery—the coffee table sturdy enough to hold up her feet, the couch long enough to stretch out on and read a book. A cabinet with a television and DVR player angled across one corner near a desk and large bookcase as well as an oak library table and shelf unit for her stereo.

When she heard steps behind her, Willow turned to see a pair of blue jean clad legs carrying a large cardboard carton with smaller boxes stacked on top of it. "That's books and desk stuff. Just put it on the floor."

"Gladly. Did you pack that car?" Squatting, Drew lowered the boxes to the floor and gave her a scrutinizing look, as if he expected to see Wonder Woman in disguise.

"No, my brother Todd did." Willow decided not to add that Todd had spent the whole time grumbling like a Neanderthal about mule-brained women who didn't know what was good for them. "He takes great pride in throwing bales into the loft from a hay wagon."

"You're a farm girl?" Drew looked at her with absorbing scrutiny.

"Yes." Unsettled by an appraisal that was both complimentary and boldly provocative, Willow walked to the library table. "I started my horse career in 4-H with a round, hairy Shetland pony. I also showed Angus steers with my brothers but it was horses I loved." She turned to see him lift his gaze from her snug jeans. "Nothing else interested me."

"What about ardent lovers?"

"With four protective older brothers in an Iowa hick town? The local boys saw me as untouchable. In college, I spent too much time in the horse barns to be alluring." When Drew remained silent, Willow glanced back at a skeptically amused expression and added, "I dated. I even went out with a classmate for a few months. I found horses more exciting and he got tired of sitting on the fence watching me ride. Rest assured. Your horses will come before my pleasure."

"Actually, I was thinking of my pleasure. But one thing is certain." Drew met her gaze with a slow half-smile. "I wouldn't be caught sitting on a fence where you were concerned."

"What does that mean?"

"I'd show you there's something more exciting than horses."

"Oh, is there, Mr. Sutherland?" Squaring her shoulders, Willow lifted a defiant chin. "Or does this conversation put us on a first name basis?"

"Our first contact put us on a first name basis."

"I assumed the thirteen-year-old would go by the name of Andy. Or are you always Andrew?"

"No."

"Well, which is it?"

"Drew. My father is Andy. My grandfather's older brother was Andrew, but he was killed in the Pacific at Midway, so my grandfather passed the name to Dad to appease his still grieving mother."

"And your son will be?"

"Peter, after a much-admired friend. I think we've about worn out the name. You, I will call Willow, even though I suspect you've grown up as Willy."

"How did you know my nickname?" She started when, with a gentle brush of fingertips on the nape of her neck, he reached behind her head and caught the fall of her bound hair. With a teasing smile, he pulled it over her shoulder and let it slip from his hand.

"Willy fits the feisty tomboy in a boy's shirt and ponytail." He answered wryly. "Willow is a woman of alluring beauty, her hair free, falling like a rain of fiery embers across golden skin."

"Maybe you'd better stick with Willy." She wrinkled her nose. "I don't recognize the creature of fire and beauty."

"You will." He teased. "One day she'll be there."

"Right. With her mouth full of hair." Willow sidestepped around him to face the wall by the kitchen door. "Would the stereo be best here or where the shelves are now?"

"The shelves. The kitchen wall is too exposed to traffic."

"It's brand new. I don't even know how to set it up." She turned to see him crouched down examining the stereo box on top of the carton.

"I can handle that. It's a good system."

"I hope so. I bought it on my brother's advice."

"The bale thrower?"

"No, the one who convinced me I needed to get away from Iowa. Byron teaches music at Iowa State and spends his summers in Italy working toward a doctorate. He took me on a three-week European tour when I graduated from college last year."

"Interesting."

"Byron always did whistle his own tune. When everyone else was rocking at school parties, he was playing Mozart. While studying classical in college, he earned his way fiddling in a country bar and playing piano in a cocktail lounge. I have some of his CD's if you're interested."

"Very."

"Mozart, or 'Turkey in the Straw'?"

"Both. I'll even take a cocktail lounge torch song. I'm a sucker for sentimental ballads."

Smiling at his enthusiastic reply, Willow watched Drew stride from the house, whistling a familiar melody she was unable to place but suspected could be found in a work by Mozart.

While she unloaded a box of books into the bookcase, Willow tried to sort out her impressions of Drew. Wealth, artistic appreciation and cultured education resonated from his speech, self-assurance and relaxed manners. At the same time, he was casually comfortable in old jeans that would look right in a haying crew. He was deeply tanned, especially for April, his muscles hard and developed.

Yes, Willow decided, Drew would fit into an Iowa landscape: shirtless, with hay chaff clinging to the sweaty sheen of his bronze tan. But then, he would also fit into a seaside panorama—shirtless with a snowy towel tossed casually over one shoulder. Catching herself, Willow grounded her imagination with sober practicality. Daydreams were fun, but they had no relevance to reality. Unpacking did.

While the rest of her belongings piled up around her, Willow became too involved in sorting what he helped her unpack and then shuffling items into different rooms to think about Drew, who, without disturbing her, began setting up the stereo and sifting through compact disks. In the bedroom, she was relieved to see the footlocker of riding gear she'd shipped earlier sitting beneath an open window facing the pines. She hooked the curtains back and glanced outside. Two squirrels caught her attention as they spiraled up a thick trunk and leapt from tree to tree as casually as she walked from room to room.

"Three guesses what's on their minds." Drew's voice startled her.

"I think it's called the rites of spring." She felt warm breath on her hair, inhaled the spicy, woodsy scent of him.

"Do I get spring rights?"

"I don't remember reading about such rights in the job proposal."

"That's because I wasn't consulted. In fact, I found it a surprise when I arrived last week and Gram told me you were coming to live in my cabin."

"Your cabin?" Willow sidestepped and pivoted to face him. "That was certainly not mentioned."

"I thought it a splendid idea. Gram, however, put an immediate veto on my suggestion. She can be such a prig." Tossing his hands up, Drew twisted his face in a comic portrayal of disappointment, then shrugged and let it dissolve. "I lived here when I was going to the University and had your job."

"Are you claiming my house and my job?"

"I'm no threat to your job. We can discuss housing at a later date."

"I don't think so."

Entertained, even fascinated, by Willow's innocence of sexual inuendo, Drew asked, "Willow, do you even *know* how to flirt?"

"I guess not."

"It's a game men-people and women-people play—sort of like testing the sexual waters with a big toe."

"I don't know the rules."

"Since you seem to like the direct approach, they are very simple. My ultimate objective is to get you in bed; yours is to make the chase enjoyable, not cut me off at the knees." Drew held his hand out to her. "Come in and listen to your stereo. I found a recording I like."

Willow hesitated, then reached out and felt his hand close around hers.

In the living room, all the boxes were stacked against the wall by the front door. The coffee table and chairs were moved against the kitchen wall, leaving an expanse of hardwood flooring in the center of the room.

"Are you planning to wax the floor?"

"Of course not. We're going to dance."

"Are you always this crazy?"

"Actually, I'm usually *that* crazy, not *this* crazy," Drew answered nonsensically before he released her hand and pressed a button to start a CD. "The enjoyment of a Johann Strauss, Jr. waltz is greatly enhanced when you dance to his music."

"I've never danced to a waltz, at least not with anyone who knew how."

"Then I'll teach you." He took her hand in his and bowed with mock propriety. "Shall we enjoy an oldie but goodie, 'The Emperor Waltz,' my Lady?"

"With pleasure, my Lord," Willow returned his joking gallantry with an awkward curtsy.

When Willow rose, she was swept into a strong, encircling arm and twirled across the floor like a fallen leaf caught up by a dust devil. Drew's closeness took her breath away; the spinning room made her dizzy and she stumbled against him. She flushed when he smiled and lifted a dark eyebrow, but the feel of his steadying arm, the pressure of her breasts against his chest turned the flush from embarrassment to pleasure.

"You won't get dizzy if you look into my eyes and close out the moving walls."

"I'm not too sure about that." Willow wanted to say his eyes unbalanced her in a different way but held it in. "I don't know where to put my feet."

"Try trusting me to lead?"

"I feel like a klutz."

"You won't if you let go of absurd inhibitions and move with me." He laughed gently. "Willow, relax and enjoy the game. I'm not going to ravish you on your living room floor."

"You said you wanted to get me in bed."

"Not in the next ten minutes. Besides, a worthwhile seduction is an enjoyable pursuit and the decisions are yours, not mine."

"Is that a promise?" She looked up to watch his expression.

"Absolutely." The steady way Drew met her gaze was reassuring. One hand gently caressed the hand he held while the other cradled her back until she melted closer to him. "Dancing is like good riding, *Cherie*. Don't think it. Feel it. Follow my body language and soften to my hands until we're one moving body controlled by the music."

Relaxed by the rhythmic flow of his words, Willow stopped thinking about what she was doing and let his movements control her. She felt no less lightheaded, but it wasn't from spins she did with surprising ease. Fascinated by the blue depth of his eyes, she let his stimulating hands transport her into a pleasurable fantasy, while their melded bodies whirled in a featureless dimension. Music became reality, his touches and nearness the only sensations. Orchestral music surrounded her and became a part of her until its notes and his movements played on nerves and senses, lured her into the musical energy.

No longer Strauss, an orchestra and Drew, the intimacy of the dance became a blended, overwhelming force that wrapped around Willow and closed her in its embrace until she felt she was floating upward in a state of gently spinning vertigo steadied by a strong arm and hand. The depth of his gaze overpowered her then blurred when the warm invitation of his lips touched hers. She met them hesitantly, closed her eyes and continued to whirl in a soft darkness that drew her into a vortex of swirling heat and excitement.

When the waltz and the touch of the kiss ended, Drew stepped back, cradled her face in his hands. "Your first dance lesson was superb. I would enjoy teaching you *la valse de l'amour*."

"Do you have the music?"

"Everyone knows the music, *Cherie*." The deep, throaty way he said French words tantalized almost as much as the fingers tracing the lines of her features. "I'll leave so you can dress for dinner. Better than jeans, nothing fancy. Gram expects a certain respect for her cook's excellent fare. I'll come back for you in an hour."

The parting touch of his fingertips was a teasing reminder of the pleasure flirting with her senses. After he was gone, Willow swayed to the music of the next selection and tried to recapture the magic of his presence. But it was, once again, recorded music in an afternoon room with packing boxes and unfamiliar furniture. Dust motes failed to shimmer like diamond dust in a golden shaft of sunlight. Her feet were encased in dingy cloth and rubber shoes that felt heavy and squawked on the polished floor. She collapsed onto the couch, closed her eyes and wrapped her arms around herself, trying to hold onto the lingering thrill inside her.

Willow had never felt so confused or out of control. While she tried to hold on to the memory of Drew's eyes, as darkly blue and vivid as an evening sky reflected in a bottomless mountain lake, the thrill ebbed away and a bittersweet uncertainty told her she had proved herself a fool by falling into a crush on a man she hardly knew—a man who was more hokey fantasy than reality. Willow considered herself pragmatic and much too cynical for such adolescent illusions, which left her confused and distrustful of her own gullible reaction.

❖

Afternoon light slanting through the conservatory's French doors, brightened Mae Sutherland's short, silver-white hair, then reached across her shoulder to light the book she was reading. When Drew hesitated in the doorway from the west parlor, his grandmother looked up and set the open book on a glass-topped, rattan table.

"Are you interruptible?" he asked.

"Of course." She gestured toward a high-backed chair across the table. "Did you get Willow settled in?"

"I emptied her car and set up her stereo." Drew leaned over and kissed his grandmother's smooth cheek before he sat. "She's pretty, feisty, and fun to tease. And she's devoted to horses. She'll be a good rider in the way you like them."

"What do you mean?"

"Willow responds to shared movement and lets body language control her. She's sensitive to subtle changes in tempo and balance. When she relaxes and forgets her self-consciousness, tensions dissolve and it all comes together."

"Did you see her ride?"

"No."

"Then how…" When he smiled with a roguish lift of an eyebrow, Mae paused and gave him an accusing look. "Drew, you didn't—"

"Of course not. In fact, I found her a little skittish about that part of life." He chuckled at her probing look. "I tested her new stereo and danced with her. I've had enough dance experience to know how to feel a partner's responses. Willow learns naturally, through sensation and body language, not by rote. She may be nervous when you start to teach her, but once you get her to relax and she lets it happen, instead of tries to make it happen, you'll have an exceptional student."

"She certainly seems better than the one last summer."

"Brunnhilde the bellowing Valkyrie would be better." Frowning, Drew looked at the French mailing envelop on the table. "Is that mine?"

"It's from your father."

"Probably my mail for the last month. I told him to send it here. I wasn't in Genoa long enough to worry about it."

"Why were you in Genoa?"

"To sublet the apartment until my lease is up next fall." He stripped open the mailer, dumped a pile of letters out of it and started picking through them. "There were a few things I couldn't just walk out on or handle through the Internet."

"Such as the best opportunity you've ever had?"

"Marissa wasn't that great, but she did deserve the courtesy of a personal explanation before I left the continent for six months." He set aside what he knew were bills and opened an envelope from Genoa containing signed lease papers.

"That's not what I meant."

"But that's what I answered. I'm not talking about it right now."

"You could at least tell me what happened with Maestro Luciani."

"We didn't get along." Drew stuffed the envelopes back in the packet and picked up several more. He barely glanced at them before they landed in the wastebasket. "Dad could have sorted out the junk and saved some postage."

"Drew, Maestro Luciani has produced some of the world's best operatic performers. His work with Verdi baritones is legendary."

"Verdi is his god. And therefore..." Drew straightened and fixed her with a hard look. "...I'm not fit to utter his sacred tones."

"The man invited you to train under him." Her brow creased in disapproval. "He took you on as a prodigy. He said you were a natural for Verdi's greatest roles."

"Not in what's left of this century, maybe not for a good part of the next millennia. According to him, if I master Rossini, Bellini, Donizetti, Puccini, and who knows what else he'll throw in my way, I might be able to think about Verdi."

"You're too impatient. It takes years to fully develop the voice you need."

"I have sung Verdi and been well received."

"Not an entire opera."

"I don't want to perform an entire opera yet. I'd just like to work on what I expected to learn. Gram, you agreed to back off until I was ready to talk about it. So, back off."

"I'm just trying to understand it."

"For shit sake!" Drew crumpled the letter in his fist and stood up. "How the hell can you understand it when I can't?"

"Sit back down, young man." Mae stiffened, drilled him with a hard stare. "And I'll thank you to mend your attitude and language around me."

"Excuse me, Gram." Drew lowered himself into the chair. "I'm not ready to address it calmly. I would appreciate it if you respected my request not to talk about it."

"All right, but I expect you to behave in a respectful manner."

"Yes, Gram."

"Thank you for remembering your manners."

Drew smoothed the scrunched letter and skimmed through the few handwritten paragraphs of Italian. "My placating efforts seem to have been wasted. Marissa will be touring with a dance troupe in Russia this summer. I'm forgiven for deserting her."

"Is she the Swiss dancer I met in Bologna?"

"That was Margot."

"Oh. Is Willow coming for dinner?"

"I told her I'd pick her up in an hour." Drew slid the remaining letters back in the mailer. "Did you know she has a brother who teaches music at Iowa State University?"

"No, I didn't. What did she think of you singing opera?"

"I didn't tell her."

"Why not?"

"I don't want her to know. I don't want you to tell her either."

"Drew, that's absurd. Why do you want to hide your talent?"

"It's more that I want to forget it right now. I want to go back to before I was someone with an image to live up to. For the last few years, I buried myself in music with an intensity I'd never shown for anything else in my life. I was driven by it. I was fawned over and flattered because of it. I became Andrew Sutherland, the *wunderkind*, a celebrity so caught up in publicity I let it define me. Vittorio showed me reality. I need time to see if I want to accept it and it would help if I could find someone who can know me without that damn image getting in my way. I'd like Willow to be that person."

"How can you do that?"

"By getting you and John to help."

"You want us to deceive her?" Mae's face clouded.

Drew leaned forward, took her hands in his. "Gram, remember how much you like to plan surprise parties?" He smiled at the interest in her expression, the grin of a willing collaborator. "That's what I want to do. Can you keep the secret for a month?"

"That shouldn't be hard."

"It might be. She asks very direct questions."

"What can I say about you?"

"Anything you want as long as it has nothing to do with music, theater, or opera."

"At least you like her." Mae sighed. "You were here for six weeks last summer and grumphed about Irene the whole time."

"You were the one who fired her, not I."

"The horses didn't like her."

Drew stood and picked up his mail. "Does that mean you value my opinion less than that of the horses?"

"She wasn't hired to ride you."

"Thank God for that. I don't think I'd like the way she overused whips and spurs." Drew laughed at his grandmother's frown. "Oh, give in and laugh. It was funny." As he strode out the door, he heard Mae chuckling behind him.

Chapter Four

After a shower, Willow fussed over what to wear to dinner until she thought she would be late. Finally, she chose a moss green skirt, casual enough to show she wasn't overdressing for him, and an ivory blouse with enough softness in the curve of the collar that Drew couldn't call it a boy's shirt. She pulled a comb through a mane of fine hair she knew would turn into a hopeless cross between wayward curls and flyaway tangles at the first hint of a breeze and gathered it into a ponytail.

Remembering the way Drew smiled when her hair tumbled from his hand, Willow released it, shook her head, then frowned at a mirrored reflection that, in her mind, more closely resembled a ravaged hay bale than Drew's vision of fiery embers. Deciding there was no way she was going to spend the meal pushing hair out of her face, she compromised by taming some of the disarray with a clip at the back of her head and let the rest tumble behind her shoulders. She dug a pair of flat shoes out of a carton just before she heard two sharp raps on the front door.

"Come in," Willow shouted as she shoved the carton toward the closet. After a last check in the mirror on a closet door she hurried through the short hallway to the living room.

When she saw Drew a lingering sense of the magic made her pull in a quick breath. His blazer took the place of an autumn sky by enhancing the blue of his eyes. He wore it open over a light blue shirt tailored to fit his tapered build. His slacks were khaki, but the overall image was a study in blue, its effect more the searing heat of an arc than the icy chill of a glacier. When he met her eyes, she forced out the words, "Will I meet your grandmother's standards?"

"Certainly, and you more than meet mine."

"It's the only skirt I had that didn't look like it came out of a backpack." She glanced down and brushed a minute speck of lint off the material.

"Skirts aren't a requirement. It's just that Gram's old-fashioned enough to have a prejudice against what she insists are dungarees at the dinner table." Drew opened the door and stepped back to let her out. "She relates them to stable duty and prefers to keep horse odors in the barn."

"It's a long walk." Willow's eyes followed the twisting drive.

"It's shorter and nicer by the path through the gardens." Drew took her hand in a reassuring hold and led her across the drive to a worn path that passed an extensive vegetable garden before it led to the stable. "John's horticultural genius is worth admiring. Give the man a pile of horseshit and he'll create an Eden."

"The stable garden is sensational."

"That's only a small sample of his talents."

They turned onto a pine needle path and climbed a wooden stile over a crumbled stone wall and mossy zigzag of split rails. The path turned to gravel and led to a wooden bridge over the chortling creek.

"Starting next week this walk will be a stroll through paradise." Drew paused to send a flat stone skipping across a still pool in the rocky stream before they crossed the railed bridge and stepped through a swinging gate in a dark hedge.

With scents and sights of gardens exploding around them, they followed a path lined with budding lilac bushes and golden forsythia. Willow slowed to pull in a deep breath when they passed a slope of terraced tulip beds embroidered with rainbow drifts of flowering bulbs. "Spring is heady stuff around here."

"I guess it would be after a Midwest winter. After the Italian Riviera, spring's a little late."

"That explains your tan."

"I was living on the Mediterranean outside Genoa. I sailed the Greek Islands and circled back along the Riviera last winter."

"What do you do in Europe that gives you so much leisure time?"

"Many things, most of them nonproductive." His face clouded with a fleeting grimace. "According to my father, Gram has made it too easy for me to live comfortably without resorting to work."

"Doesn't that make you feel dependent?"

"She insists it's hers to dispense and believes I'm a worthy investment. I'm her only grandchild. My parents divorced when I was four. My mother died when I was eight. Dad never remarried."

Drew sat on a low wall that ringed a sunken rose garden. "I like to hear you talk about your family. In fact, I envy the relationship you have with them, especially your brother Byron."

"I haven't said much."

"It was more the way you said it than what you said. I never had to share anything or really compete with anyone on that kind of level. I'm spoiled. For most of my life I've been able to have what I want."

"You seem nicely spoiled."

"When I'm getting my way." Drew teased her with a sly smile.

"Is that a warning?"

"It could be." The smile spread to his eyes. "However, since Dad and Gram never allowed me to be a brat about it, your observation is astutely on target. I'm here this summer to rethink a few choices I've made. I wasn't coping with myself very well."

"Maybe what you need is a menial job to show you how the other half lives. Waiting on tables did me a lot of good."

"I wish it were that simple." A wistful smile lifted one corner of his mouth. "When it's been relatively easy to achieve everything you want, it's hard to accept that what you want most may be unattainable."

"And that is?"

"Nothing I can explain very well." Drew gazed at her with a deeply pensive expression then seemed to catch himself, shuddered and looked away. Recapturing her hand, he moved away from the wall and led her toward the house. "If we're late, I'll get a tongue-lashing when she catches me alone."

"But not in front of me?"

"No way. It's not proper. I can remember waiting in dread for hours when we were out or in front of company. Once she drilled me with her *wait until I get you alone* look, or worse yet, muttered the, 'your father is going to hear about this,' threat, I was in for an earful, no matter how charming and reformed I tried to be. There's no way to distract Gram when she sets her mind on something." He smiled when apprehension brushed across Willow's face. "You may want to remember that."

"My mother was too busy raising children, chickens and vegetables to dwell on what was proper in that regard. If she didn't give us hell right away, she was likely to forget which one of us was supposed to catch it."

"There were five of you?"

"There are nine of us. I'm right smack in the middle of six boys and three girls, but I'm the oldest girl."

"How many brothers will come after me if I mistreat you?"

"Probably all six. Matt, the youngest, has a scholarship to play football for the Iowa Hawkeyes next fall." Willow made a humorously threatening face and chuckled at Drew's clowning look of dismay. "But they raised their sisters tough, so I don't think I'll need to call in reinforcements."

When they reached the mansion and entered the front hall, Willow halted and gaped at the massive oak staircase in front of her. Tapering in gentle curves from a full eight feet wide at its base on the glowing parquet floor to five feet at the top step, the structure soared to a railed balcony that enclosed the spacious hall. Across the balcony, two smaller stairways climbed the wall beyond the main staircase to a narrower balcony on the third floor.

In the center of the hall between the first and second floors a large model of a sailing ship hung suspended from a sculpted plaster ceiling. Brass and crystal chandeliers ringed the ship model to illuminate it when natural light from the front windows faded. A larger three-tiered chandelier hung over the center of the main staircase. Polished oak banisters, supported by balusters carved to resemble the twisted pattern of rope hawsers, swept down the staircase in graceful arcs then curved back on themselves on top of two stout newel posts shaped like the capstans of sailing ships.

"Wow! That is impressive."

"What's really impressive is the speed you can build up sliding down those banisters." Drew laughed at her startled look. "Wanna race?"

"What about your grandmother?"

"I don't think she's up to it anymore, but she'd be willing to time us if you want."

"She doesn't mind?"

"As far as I know, Sutherlands have been sailing down those banisters for two hundred years. I don't know how to rate it as an architectural masterpiece, but it is definitely a fantastic piece of indoor playground equipment. When I grew bored with the banisters, I pretended I was Aladdin or Ali Baba and bruised my ass bumping down the stairs on a worn-out hunk of oriental carpet while I brandished a foil-wrapped cardboard scimitar." He waved his arm in a wide arc that made her pull back and laugh.

"We were into swinging out of the hay barn to descend on the wagon shed like pirates boarding captured prize ships."

"Since the first American Sutherlands were merchant shipbuilders and the house is crammed with nautical stuff, I chose to be a brave ship captain defending my cargo from attacking pirates like you." Drew snarled, then laughed when she wrinkled her nose like a miffed rabbit. "I tied a rope to the third-floor railing once and used it for a Tarzan vine. That got me in big trouble when I crashed into that." Drew pointed at an antique Queen Anne table below an ornately framed mirror. "I broke its leg and totaled a bowl of flowers. Gram went berserk. I was forbidden to do it again."

"What about the ship?" Willow studied the ship suspended above the hall.

"She's the *Bonnie Jennie O*, named for the wife of the original Andrew Sutherland. She was a bark—the first ship newly designed and built by Sutherland Mercantile in 1758."

"Has there always been an Andrew Sutherland?"

"It goes in and out of favor every few generations." Drew led her below the staircase to show her the supports that anchored it to the balcony. "These are sections of two of the three original masts from the *Jennie O*. They were damaged in a storm and replaced in 1765 while the house was under construction. In a colonial spirit of recycling, they were used to hold up the balcony and staircase. I understand Old Andrew originally wanted to use ropes for handrails. Silas Pratt, the architect, insisted on the structural integrity of the solid railings. I suspect his inspiration was the desire to slide down them himself."

"Scary." Willow eyed the railings, then grinned. "But fun."

"Especially sidesaddle because you can really fly off the end." Drew shot his hand out toward the front door. "But since Silas didn't leave enough landing strip, the tricky part was to stop running before I crashed into the front wall. Dad and I used to compete over which of us could stay airborne the farthest and the fastest. When I got big enough to win, he seemed to lose interest."

"You're starting to sound like my jerky brothers."

"Which ones are the jerks?"

"All of them."

"That's because damn foolery is a result of having a Y chromosome instead of a double niXX." Drew crossed his index fingers then chopped a hand across his throat before he pulled three belaying pins out of a rail on the mast beside him. He juggled them for a few seconds then flipped the last one higher and caught it behind his back. "My jerkiness may also be explained by the number of times I bonked myself on the head learning to do that."

"We usually bonked things off each other's heads. We got in a lot of squabbles with each other, but I can't imagine growing up having to play alone."

"I had kids to play with off and on. I played with Dad a lot, too. He grew up here and showed me a lot of the fun stuff he used to do." Drew slid his hand across her back, cupped it around her shoulder and guided her away from the staircase. "After you learn more about this house, you'll discover Silas was an architect with a sense of humor and more innovative imagination than formal training. Its style isn't really true to anything. Silas, who was young and reckless at the time, and Old Andrew designed it together. They didn't always agree. Gram has a journal Silas wrote during the eight years it took to build the house. Although hard to decipher, it's one of the funniest things I've ever read. Especially when he starts venting about Scottish hardheaded, tyrannical stubbornness, which as far as I can tell hasn't changed much in two-hundred and forty years."

"Would that be a reference to present company?"

"To me? Never. It's Gram and Dad who are stubborn, not I." Drew looked at her and burst out laughing. "You're not falling for that, are you?"

"Not for a minute."

"Why would you say that?"

"It has something to do with intuition, but in all fairness, I'll warn you that a Roberts can out stubborn anyone."

"Is that a challenge?"

"I didn't intend it that way."

"Then why did I hear it that way?"

"You said the decisions were mine."

"Absolutely. You'll just have to keep making them." Drew's hand moved to her waist, slid down her hip.

Willow shifted away and caught his hand in a firm grip. The sensation of Drew's touch spread through her in a flush she insisted was indignation over the realization that the unappealing aspect of her job hadn't gone away. Instead of Mae's grandson being an obnoxiously spoiled teen, he was a charmingly spoiled playboy and she had no idea how to deal with that—except by viewing him objectively and keeping her feelings at a safe distance. She was here to do a job and follow her dream of becoming a horse trainer, not make a fool of herself over a man whose sole objective was to get her in bed with him—even if he was the most gorgeous hunk of testosterone she'd ever met.

After walking through a formal dining room filled with massive, hand-carved walnut furniture, Willow was relieved to discover they would be eating at a round table in a smaller, more intimate, family dining room that had once been the servants' hall adjacent to the butler's pantry.

The table was set with bright yellow linen and earth-toned stoneware. A large vase of fresh daffodils brightened the center of the table. The blending of browns and oranges with yellow accents reflected Mae Sutherland, a tall, gracious woman in a yellow silk dress with an elegant, almost regal, bearing and short white hair that brightened the warmth of her complexion. Mae walked with a cane and was thinner than when Willow had seen her at the dressage clinic during her junior year of college, but there was no indication Mae was anything but the Lady of the Manor and fully in charge.

"Hello, Willow." Mae's resolve was clear in her strong gaze and the sure grip that took Willow's offered hand in both of hers. "It's good to see you again. I've been looking forward to having conversations in person instead of over the telephone. Is the cabin satisfactory?"

"It's wonderful, so is the stable. I'm anxious to meet the horses."

"Roy, the stableman, will be there at seven in the morning. He'll fill you in on what you need to do. Roy has some learning disabilities and very little education, but he has an excellent rapport with animals and is a willing and competent worker." Mae looked at Drew. "I'll tell Greyson we're ready for dinner. You may seat Willow." Mae nodded at a chair before she walked through a doorway to the kitchen.

"Like I need to be reminded," Drew muttered as he pulled out a chair for Willow. He straightened the fall of her hair with a gentle hand before he stepped around the table and held a chair for his grandmother.

During dinner, there was polite small talk about Willow's trip and Mae's latest magazine article. Mae gave Willow a history of each horse in the stable, then went on to outline a training program and schedule for the three horses she expected Willow to work with. By dessert and coffee, Drew and Willow had exchanged a few looks of exasperation at the nonstop horse lecture Willow was supposed to absorb along with her lamb chops and spinach soufflé.

While Mae talked with Drew about him riding Rigoletto, her former Olympic grand prix horse, Willow found herself staring at him with an absorption that pulled her away from the conversation. She thought back to what he'd said in the garden and found it difficult to believe anyone as attractive and self-assured as Drew Sutherland could have trouble coping with anything. And what was it he really wanted and saw as unattainable? He seemed to already have more of everything than she wanted.

"When you're handling that big half-draft of Drew's, you may need to put the stud chain across his nose. Willow?"

With a start, Willow snapped out of her reverie and swept her eyes to Mae's. "I'm sorry."

"I was cautioning you about Bold Venture..." Mae paused when Greyson, the stout English butler, stepped into the room to say Drew had a phone call.

By the time Drew left, Willow had pulled some of their previous conversation out of her memory. "You said Bold Venture is used to being handled by a man, and not easily deterred."

"That's exactly right. He's like his rider in that way." Mae held Willow's gaze with eyes as intensely blue as Drew's. "I think you'd better remember to handle him firmly, too."

"Who?" Willow started at the shift from impersonal horse talk to intimate counsel.

"Drew, of course." Mae set a sure hand on the back of Willow's wrist. "Forgive me for seeming to pry, but I did notice the way you've been looking at him. I don't know any other way to put it, except to say Drew is a natural actor and an incurable flirt."

"There really isn't anything—"

"I'm not assuming there's any more to it than fascination." Mae's cool hand pressed Willow's wrist before she lifted her coffee cup. "I'm responsible for bringing you here. I don't want you to feel Drew has anything to do with your relationship with me. He attracts women, and they seem to enjoy him." She gave Willow a thoughtful look. "In truth, you may be good for Drew. You're certainly more genuine than most women he takes out."

"Does he love them?" Willow flushed when the question slipped out of her thoughts.

"Drew isn't good at letting his deep feelings out, so I have no knowledge of that." Mae hesitated for a moment, then softened her voice. "I can best describe him as shielded. As a child, he had a lot of anxiety over his mother deserting him."

"He said she died."

"The circumstances were unusual. To a child of his age, I don't think there would be a difference. She was the only parent he knew at that time."

"What about his father?"

"Drew's parents divorced when he was four, not long after Andy took over the operation of Sutherland FiberForms in France. Drew stayed in Philadelphia with his mother until he was eight."

"Is FiberForms a family corporation?" Willow asked when she heard Drew returning.

"It is a subsidiary of Sutherland International, which is based in Scotland. Andy and I own a significant percentage of shares in the parent company but have nothing to do with its operation. Andy is CEO of Sutherland FiberForms and owns the majority of its stock. It is an American corporation but is mostly European based. There are only a few Sutherlands left in the American branch of the family. I was a Scottish Sutherland, a two-century removed relative of my husband."

"Excuse me, Gram," Drew interrupted. "I'm supposed to be in Philly by eight-thirty, so I have to run. I need to see Nicole tonight and don't know when I'll be back."

"When did she arrive from Paris? I know you've been anxious for her to get here."

"This morning. I'll bring her out to see you tomorrow." Drew finished his coffee without sitting and encouraged Willow to finish hers. "I'll give you a lift home."

"I'm sure I can find my way back." The name Nicole bounced around in Willow's mind. She wanted to ask who Nicole was then passed it off as a family matter of no concern to her.

"I would like to give you some instructions of my own about Bozo," Drew said.

"Bozo?" Willow wrinkled her nose at the name.

"Bold Venture can be quite a clown. You'll agree after you get to know him."

"It's all right, Willow." Mae casually dismissed the offer to stay. "Our discussion of family history can wait until another time."

After Mae remembered a few instructions about the abundance of horse trails available in the area, Drew was able to get Willow away from his grandmother with a minimum of departing chatter. He led her through the kitchen to a mudroom and pressed a button on a panel beside the door to a roofed colonnade connecting the mansion to a long carriage house that had been converted into a garage.

While they walked between white columns and trellises thickly covered with spreading creepers of wisteria vines, Willow looked at lighted windows above the garage doors. "Does someone live there?"

"John has lived there for more than forty years."

"He's been the gardener that long?"

"John's father was head gardener at Gram's home in Scotland. She hired John for here because she was homesick for the gardens she knew as a child. John recreated what he could and made the rest better."

"How old is he?"

"Sixty-three, four years younger than Gram. John is a Master Gardener with a graduate degree in horticulture from Penn. But he's much more than a gardener to Gram. He's a very old friend and makes it possible for her to stay on the estate alone."

"What about Mr. Greyson?"

"Greyson Winter, who prefers to be called Greyson, is married to Alice, who is cook and housekeeper. They have a house and family in town and are only here on weekdays or for special weekend occasions. John, Greyson and Alice arrange to hire all additional help. The stableman is Roy, who actually works under John. That's the permanent staff."

"What about me? Or did you fire me already?"

"I couldn't fire you if I wanted to. Only Gram can do that, and I don't see much chance of it."

"I hope you're right. I feel a little over my head."

"You impressed her when you were in a clinic she did at your college."

"She remembered me?"

"Yes. Gram always remembers the best."

"Thank you for telling me that. I've been as nervous as a calf in ice skates."

"I noticed. Don't sweat it. She likes you."

"Are you sure?"

"I know what my grandmother likes."

"Can I ask you about some things she didn't mention?"

"Sure, but don't be afraid to ask her anything. You can even argue with her; just be sure your arguments have sound reasoning behind them. Don't ever lie to her or try to deceive her."

"I couldn't. We Roberts don't do things like that."

"In that case," Drew gave her a thoughtful look, "you should have no trouble with her Sutherland code of honor."

"It's the formality that intimidates me."

"Gram does cling to certain traditions. The assumption is that if you adhere to proper etiquette at home, you will know how to comport yourself outside the home. I've heard all her lectures a great number of times." He made a wry face. "I really am well trained, even though she has a little trouble remembering I'm not an obnoxious adolescent anymore. But then, she isn't a whole lot better with my father. Gram has this idea that boys and men need constant monitoring, or they degenerate into feral animals."

"With six brothers for examples, I think she's right."

"You'll get along with her just fine."

When they reached the garage, one of the doors was open, exposing a silver sports car with a rich red interior. Willow started when she looked at the emblem. "A Mercedes?"

"300SL gull wing coupe, 1955. Eighty percent of the eleven hundred or so produced were imported into this country. It was my father's car." Drew opened the passenger door that swung upwards to resemble the lifted wing of an alighting sea bird. "It was designed to be a race car, so getting in is a bit tricky. It takes a slide across the door sill with your knees hugged in front of you then a short drop into the seat. A woman getting in or out can be a sight that men dream about, so you might want to watch your skirt to avoid embarrassment."

"Oh, shit." After what turned out to be an awkward pratfall instead of a short drop, Willow flailed her arm out in an attempt to keep from toppling onto the driver's seat and a firm hand caught her elbow to hold her upright. Jerking her skirt down over her legs, she looked up at Drew's laughing face and gave him a scathing glare. "You could have turned the other way."

"That would have left you flopping around like a belly-up turtle cussing me out for not helping. I've experienced it. It isn't a good thing." He closed the door, circled the front of the car and slid into the driver's seat.

"It's in excellent condition," Willow said to divert him from her flubbed entry. "You take good care of it."

"Gram takes good care of it. She had it inspected and fine-tuned when she heard I was coming for the summer. When I leave, she'll have it moth-balled."

"I don't think I've ever been in a car with real leather seats." Willow rubbed her hand along the surface of the red leather.

Drew started the car and listened to the deep throb of the engine before he slipped it into gear. "This car was not manufactured. It was crafted."

"I just realized it's way older than I am."

"The car was already destined to be a classic when Dad received it, secondhand, for a college graduation present from his parents. It was a bribe that failed." Drew pulled out of the garage, punch the door remote on the visor. "He married my mother anyway, which made me legitimate and him a disgrace to his father."

"His parents didn't want him to marry?"

"His father disapproved of her."

"Why?"

"She was poor and uneducated. She was an Italian immigrant, who sang, danced and, mostly, drank in the wrong places. My grandfather informed him that one didn't marry women like that, only purchased them for a while. Then he took back the car and threw Dad out."

"Did your grandmother feel that way?"

"Gram may have accepted the first part of his statement. She certainly wouldn't agree with the second. Since my grandfather died, she's put great effort into making amends for it."

"You hold it against her?"

"Not I. Gram's been wonderful to me." A spreading smile erased his frown. "I never saw my Sutherland grandfather until after my mother died. By then, he was a cranky old fart, who'd had a stroke and was watched over by big male nurses, who kept him away from my father and me. He died soon after that, but Dad was too well established in Europe to leave. Gram wanted us to live here, but it never lasted for more than short visits or part of a summer."

"But she kept his car for him?"

"When I was in college, I told Dad I was driving his car. He said I would be doing us all a favor if I let it roll off a very high cliff. Gram's trying to make me what he wasn't—sentimental and attached to Sutherland Manor."

"Is she succeeding?"

"More than she did with him."

"Is he bitter?"

"Not toward her. Dad enjoys living in Europe, where his business is. Right now, he's living with an American writer, who's crazy in a fun-loving way. Kate's more dedicated to living life than recording it."

In Willow's driveway, Drew slipped the gearshift into neutral and set the hand brake before he raised his door and stepped out. When he saw Willow stand and swing her door closed, he scowled at her over the hood. "I was going to open it for you."

"I decided to conquer the exiting part on my own." She smirked triumphantly. "Besides, the chivalry has gone far enough. I'm your horse groom. You can stop opening doors like Prince Charming."

"Can I walk you to the door?" Sarcasm edged his voice.

"Yes. And you can give me your instructions for Bold Venture."

"That was mostly a way to save you from Gram. If she got started on Sutherland history, you'd be there for hours while she dragged you through rooms of family heirlooms that have been lurking in dusty corners, both here and in Scotland, for centuries."

"Really?"

"It's one of her eccentricities. You don't want to get caught in that trap if you can avoid it. In regard to Bold Venture, if I can't get away from Philly tomorrow morning, I'd appreciate it if you would lunge him for me about ten. His equipment is marked. Let him go a few minutes in each direction with no side reins at any gait he chooses so he can get the bucks and farts out. Wear gloves and hang on hard. After that, he'll work sanely."

"Does he know voice commands?"

"A great number of them. Let him out when you're finished. He hates being caged." When she started to open the screen door, Drew closed a hand over hers and lifted it off the latch. "I stocked your kitchen with some basics so you won't have to worry about shopping right away."

"Thank you." Willow looked up at his face, felt his hands close around her waist, found herself staring at the enticing lines of his lips. For a moment that felt like an eternity, she wavered between the inviting abandon of the waltz and the comforting security of a control she'd learned to trust.

When Drew moved one hand to her back and the other tilted her jaw, the lure of the fantasy drew her toward him. With the force of a slammed door, reality reasserted itself. She placed flat hands on his chest and looked at her watch. "How fast does that car go?"

"Very fast. Why?" His face tightened and his fingers tensed, holding her face immobile.

"I read the mile signs on my way here. If you don't leave now, you'll have to fly to make it to Philadelphia by eight-thirty."

"Shit." Drew glanced at her watch, then jogged to his car.

After the silver car disappeared around the pine-shrouded hill, Willow leaned against a porch post and looked toward the manor house. The sun was setting beyond the mansion's walls, turning it into a dark, angular cutout of jutting geometric shapes against a flaming backdrop. Sutherland Manor was still impressive, but reality was toning down her enchantment. There were enigmas beyond the splendor—enigmas Willow wasn't sure she wanted to see in such a picture-perfect setting.

Right now, Drew was Willow's biggest enigma. He could be the worldly gentleman, propelling her along with his casual charisma, sweeping aside her apprehensions with his off-the-wall flirting, unbalancing her with sensations that both intrigued her and threatened her feeling of control. He could also be the scolded boy who, when told he is late for class, kicks at the dirt, grins sheepishly and runs for the schoolroom.

And Drew was vulnerable. She had felt it in his troubled expression when they talked in the rose garden. She felt uncomfortable with his vulnerability, but she wanted to mean enough to him that she could touch it. Experiencing a twinge of loneliness, Willow knew Byron would smile and remind her she could be spinning daydreams while Todd would snort and say it was better to enjoy beer than long for champagne.

Chapter Five

"You had dinner?" Antonio looked up from a plate of reheated stew. "There's some in the pot."

"I ate with Gram and her new working student three hours ago." Drew closed the garage door behind him. "But I will steal one of your beers and some pretzels."

"I had to work late. Grab me a beer while you're there." Antonio tossed him an empty bottle. "Stick it in the case by the door. Is this girl any better than the last one?"

"You must be referring to the one I called Broomhilde, the demented Valkyrie." Drew handed his uncle an opened beer before he sat at the table and tipped the tubular framed chair onto its back legs. "You couldn't have paid me enough to screw that one. She had a body like a coat tree, a disposition like a buzz saw and a shrill voice that set my teeth on edge. Gram ignored my gripes, then sent her packing when she found out the horses didn't like her any better than I did. I never met the last one. She came and went while I was away. Gram was so disgusted with her lack of scruples, she stopped taking what other professionals sent her and did her own searching. She remembered this one from a clinic. Then she researched her with the diligence of an FBI agent."

"Did she show you the dossier?"

"She mostly got on the phone and grilled everyone she could at the college Willow attended, as well as the references and Willow herself. All she told me was, 'Go help the girl and save John's back.' Willow's different, Zio."

"What does that mean?"

"I don't know how to describe her."

"Start throwing out some words. Maybe I'll get the drift."

"Intriguing, funny, spunky, packed with spice. Smart and sharp witted enough to be a challenge. She's a redhead with brown and gold eyes, adorably pointed wood sprite ears, and only about so high." Drew held his hand at chest height.

"That's less than four feet, which puts her nose in your belly."

"When I'm standing." Drew gave him a withering look. "Willow's a little thing but solid and compact, full of fun and energy. She has a body I want to get my hands all over, firm boobs I want to choke on and a lusciously rounded backside I'm itching to swat and fill my hands with." Drew emphasized his statement with a waving twist of a flattened hand, then cupped his hands in front of him, gave them a critical look and spread his fingers a little. "Yeah, like that."

"I'm glad you don't know how to describe her." Antonio cracked up at Drew's clowning look of lust. "I'm getting a vivid picture here."

"It doesn't even start to describe what I feel in Willow. She's unaffectedly real and determined. But she's a dreamer, too. Willow is like Verdi's music, as ethereal and tantalizing as the fantasies of the mind, yet as down-to-earth and robust as the practicality of the body. And she's enticingly contradictory. She makes a big show of being all business and tomboy. But when I helped her unpack the parts of her life, she brought with her, I felt a different side of her. She has about fifty pounds of cooking stuff and an old marked-up cookbook stuffed with extra recipes that are scribbled on cards and wrinkled scraps of paper. And she sews pretty stuff."

"Like clothes?"

"Like pretty pictures." Drew frowned at his uncle's blank stare. "She has a hunk of blue cloth in a wooden hoop with a piece of a flower garden, hovering fairies and half a wizard's cap on it. It's delicately beautiful and romantically whimsical. It makes me want to experience that side of her. I'm fascinated by her, Zio. She's a refreshing diversion and I need one right now. She doesn't know anything about me or what went wrong. I want to keep it that way."

"You blew your control. You didn't disgrace yourself."

"That's not the way I see it. I came here for a retreat to sort myself out. It will be refreshing to spend time with someone who only knows me as Drew Sutherland, irresponsible screwball, instead of Andrew Sutherland, colossal failure."

"You're not a failure."

"I feel like one. And if you don't mind, I don't want to talk about the subject. I get enough of it from Gram. It only makes it worse."

"I thought she agreed to leave it alone."

"She tries, but she won't let go of the dream and can't resist trying to revive it in me. She doesn't understand that failing her is what hurts most."

"And you think this Willow can make you forget that?"

"No. But when I'm with Willow, I feel different. She's makes me laugh. I can be silly with her and have fun. She's nothing like the other ones."

"What other ones? I can't keep track of your love affairs. They change faster than traffic lights."

"I wasn't referring to my currently boring sex life."

"Boring? If I hand you a phone, what will it take for you to get laid? Without paying."

"I don't pay, at least not in the professional sense." Drew twisted his mouth in thought. "On a week night? A phone call or two, the cost of a few drinks or a good dinner, then the usual wrangle of your place or mine, or do I have to shell out for a hotel room. I can get sex, but there's no challenge in it. Besides, I wasn't talking about that."

"What were you talking about?"

"I was comparing Willow to the other girls Gram's hired since the summer I kept her horses worked after she trashed her knee. They flocked to her because she won Olympic medals and they wanted bragging rights as Mae Sutherland's students. This is a job to Willow and she wants to do it well. The others were more interested in using Gram's name for status, or to help boost their chances of getting on the Equestrian Team, which anyone with half a brain knows is twenty percent talent and eighty percent money. From what I gathered listening to her at dinner, I'm not even sure Willow cares about the competition part. She loves dressage and working with horses. She wants to learn from Gram because she admires the way Gram relates to horses, not because she's famous and won medals. I like Willow. She makes me want to teach her things."

"Are you planning on seducing her or adopting her?"

"Seducing her, of course. But she's naive, Zio. I want to teach her how to make love and show her that sex isn't something to cringe from."

"Are you saying she's a virgin?"

"I don't know about that. But I find it hard to believe a girl as enticing and lusty as Willow could make it through college and be so sexually inexperienced. She has a bunch of excuses about being more interested in horses than men, but I don't buy them. I feel sexual passion like you wouldn't believe in her. She acts as if she's ashamed of it."

"Maybe she's saving it."

"For what?" Drew straightened and thumped the chair legs on the floor. "She's twenty-four years old."

"Like maybe for marriage?"

"That's absurd. More than that, it's just plain *stupido*."

"It's a moral ideal. Unrealistic? Yes." Antonio nodded, then looked perplexed. "But I don't know about stupid."

"Yeah, dumb. To say nothing of sexist. Doesn't it make sense to have sexual experience a marital prerequisite in a woman? Think about it. A virgin can get herself legally bound to some insensitive ass whose idea of sex is a few frantic minutes of pumping gratification. Worse yet, she has to endure grueling sessions as a sexual treadmill for a man more interested in achieving his orgasm than hers. What can she do?"

Drew shrugged his shoulders and scoffed, "She's stuck with him without the faintest chance of discovering how much better life can get. I've run into them. Most of them weren't virgins when they got married, just limited in experience."

"And you decided to completely ruin their marriages by showing them how much better life can get, right?"

"I never went after a married woman." Drew raised open hands in wide-eyed indignation before he chuckled. "I just let them catch me a few times. However, I've been damn careful since a drunk truck driver tried to shoot me five years ago."

"How come you never told me about that?"

"Feeling like an ass comes to mind." Drew frowned at his uncle's confirming nod. "It was back when I was hanging out with the rodeo crowd. I didn't know I could run that fast or drive a truck so well on a flat tire while bobbing my head up and down to keep it below the dashboard. You should have heard me trying to explain to Gram that the stable's pickup had a complete blowout on a brand-new tire, and

Slaying the Jabberwock

for some strange reason, both the back and a passenger side window shattered when I hit the pothole."

"A three-fifty-seven magnum pothole will do that."

"I don't know what it was, but it sounded like a damn cannon. Do you know bullets make noise when they go by close?"

"I could probably guess the caliber by ear."

"Yeah, I suppose you could. I'm just glad I was out of his range before he let loose with the rest of his ammo—or I ran into a tree."

"What did he do to his wife?"

"I don't care. She told me he was in Alabama when she damn well knew he wasn't. I have no sympathy for a liar who almost gets me killed." Drew made a sour face. "Willow said she had four older brothers, which made her untouchable in high school. I didn't think they raised them that way anymore, even on Iowa farms."

"What do you know about Iowa farms?" Antonio asked.

"They grow things like corn and beef. She told me she has six brothers who would come after me if I mistreated her." He laughed at his uncle's recoil. "She was joking."

"You better hope. I'm from an Italian family. If six brothers think you mistreated their sister, it's no joke."

"I learned about that in Italy when I was fourteen, and there were only two of them."

"You seduced a girl when you were fourteen?" Antonio looked stunned.

"No. They just said I looked like I wanted to. Which was true, but I hadn't figured out how to do it yet." Drew batted away a thrown napkin. "But I got the message, right along with the bruises."

"Maybe you better back off on this one and think about it."

"Och! Not to worry." Drew laughed it off, then looked reflective. "I thought Willow and I had a good thing going before dinner. We were having silly romantic fun. After dinner, I got the royal brush-off, which makes me think Gram is trying to protect her from me. Is my image so corrupt even my grandmother doesn't trust me?"

"You do have a fuck and run reputation."

"I'm not interested in everlasting love, but fornication is my favorite recreation. I've devoted a lot of my time to studying it and developing my erotic skills. I'm a clitoral virtuoso and maestro of cunnilinctus." Drew ducked his uncle's playful slap at his head.

"You're also a wise ass."

"I came up with that at one of Gram's Music Society cocktail parties. A couple of know-it-all assholes were trying to impress me by gassing about Italian opera. I said it with authoritative pomposity in an outrageously exaggerated Italian accent. It went right over their heads. Unfortunately, Gram was standing behind them. I didn't think she heard it, or understood it, until she glared at me and turned a livid shade of purple. Dad was there and didn't know whether to laugh or knock my head off. I thought he was going to explode before he shoved me out the terrace door. We ducked behind a chimney and laughed until we were weak. When the guests left, Gram ripped into both of us about inappropriate obscenities."

"What was she mad at Andy for?"

"Not knocking my head off."

"And you wonder why she's trying to protect the innocent?"

"Willow doesn't need protecting. I don't deceive women. I give them whatever they want whenever I want. I make that very clear."

"The problem is you get bored before they do. Women don't like to be shelved when a new one catches your interest. When you do it in your grandmother's social environment, she gets wind of it and doesn't like it."

"How do you know that? You hardly know Gram."

"She talks to your father. He talks to me."

"I didn't know they discussed my sex life."

"It's more him listening than they discussing."

"I can believe that." Drew rolled his eyes theatrically. "Gram's always telling me Dad should find an older woman he can settle down with. Gram actually likes Kate, but after what she sees as six years of blatant foolishness, she says he ought to get serious about a mature relationship and stop acting like a man with a midlife crisis."

"Andy's serious enough about that business of his. It gets him by the balls once in a while. I think Kate's wildness is his escape. She challenges him and kicks him into letting loose the way you always did." Antonio scraped out the stew pot then put his plate and utensils in it and carried it to the sink, where he filled it with hot water, squirted some dish washing liquid into it and sloshed it around a few times.

"I know what you mean about the business." Drew snapped a lid on the leftovers and put them in the refrigerator. "I used to think it owned him, not vice versa. It's been better lately. He's put together a good management team and can actually get away for a while without being on the phone all the time."

"You ready to experience Sal's smoke house? There are times the atmosphere in there puts tears in my eyes."

"Is that it with the dishes?" Drew eyed the pot in the sink.

"That's the soak cycle. I'll flood it with fresh hot water when I get home, which will take care of the wash and rinse cycles." Antonio picked up the gun and holster and strapped it on.

"Should I try to look a little less yuppie?" Drew looked at his clothes.

"No. I want you to stand out like a Bible Thumper in a whorehouse. Play up the rich brat role. Act a little snotty. Be arrogantly insulting about Mario and make sure people hear you."

"I can do that. But why?"

"Because if they like you, they won't blab to Mario. If you're a condescending snot, he'll hear all about it."

"I'm not taking the Mercedes down there."

"We'll take the city's car. I'll drop you off and give you a route. When you leave the bar, backtrack the same way. I'll find you and we'll have a few drinks."

"I can't. I told Nicole I'd stay at her hotel tonight. I think we'll need each other's support."

"How's she handling it?"

"She sounded a little shaky on the phone."

"Peter?"

"No change."

"Give her my regards, or whatever is appropriate in French. And get her to eat. She looks emaciated."

"It's called anorexia, but she adamantly denies it."

"Does she own any mirrors?"

"An interesting thing about the human mind is that it can see what it wants to believe, not what is."

❖

Sal's Bar was a dark narrow room, thick with smoke and peppered with television screens tuned to different sports channels. Walking from the door to a spot halfway down the bar, Drew glanced at a hockey game, two fights, a baseball game and a car race. He looked around for a soccer game, the only team sport he paid much attention to lately, but didn't see one. The sound was muted on the televisions, but not on a jukebox that was banging out a song that seemed to be pure noise.

Drew sat on a stool, facing away from the bar and slowly swiveled back and forth while he looked everyone over with a bold stare that didn't belong in a bar like Sal's. People here didn't want to be noticed by an outsider with a condescending sneer.

When he was sure the scattered patrons at the tables and booths had a fill of him, he spun the stool to face the bar, looked toward the street door and watched the bartender, who was talking animatedly with two men Drew assumed were regulars. Greying black hair outlined the bald center of a round head atop a short trunk of neck rooted to heavily muscled shoulders. In spite of a thickening waistline, the body under the white shirt and stained apron was fit with well-developed muscles. Drew didn't know if the bartender was Sal, but the man looked capable of serving as both bartender and bouncer.

A young woman with an untamed mane of curly black hair streaked with iridescent orange sat between Drew and the bartender. She wore a mostly unbuttoned blouse that showed bulges of uplifted breasts. Her short tight skirt was hitched high enough on the stool that only shadows concealed a clear view up an inner thigh. Drew knew she was a hooker and ignored her attempts to catch his attention. Looking at the bartender, he took a set of keys out of his pocket and began tapping them on the bar in a rhythm that was enough out of beat with the thumping music to be annoying. When the bartender glanced toward him, Drew rapped the keys harder, lifted his chin and twitched his head in a beckoning gesture.

"You want something?" The man walked toward Drew in the rolling gait of a muscle-bound weightlifter.

Drew scanned the clutter of bottles behind the bar. "Glendoncroft Single Malt Scotch, neat."

"Don't got it."

"Do you have Aberlour Single Highland Malt?" Drew asked in a loud carrying voice.

"I got J&B Scotch. Take it or leave it."

"I guess I'll have to take it," Drew answered with a look of disdain he didn't feel. In spite of his Highland ancestry and his father's and grandmother's preferences for Scotch whisky, he preferred American sour mash.

When the bartender returned with the drink, Drew asked, "Are you Sal?"

"Yeah?" The reply had a *what's it to you?* tone that Drew, in a show of disdain, failed to acknowledge.

"I was told I could find Ernie Romano here. I used to know him. In fact, I used to live around here. I'm Drew Sutherland." He lifted his glass and took a long sip. Sal's nostrils widened slightly; his jaw tensed. After rolling the whisky in his mouth, Drew swallowed it slowly. "I've been thinking about Ernie lately."

"He ain't here tonight."

"I heard he was always here."

"He comes in a lot."

"Tell him I'm interested in talking to him about old times. I've developed an interest in my roots and thought it would be exciting to see the old neighborhood."

"Might be more exciting than you think. I only been around a few years so I don't know much about you. But I been hearing your name from a guy who don't want to talk friendly about old times with you."

"Are you talking about Mary-Ann Piss-face?" Drew took another swallow of the Scotch. "When did he get out of jail? I thought he got five years."

"If you mean Mario Pisano, they paroled him last fall." Sal frowned. "My advice is to get the fuck back to wherever you belong and forget about the old neighborhood."

"I stopped being afraid of Mario when I was eight and smashed his knee with a piece of pipe. He turned into a crybaby then, and he was still full of shit last time we met. Tell Ernie I'll be back to see him soon. And tell Mario I'm not afraid of him. I let him off easy when he jumped me. I won't again." Drew finished the drink and thumped the glass onto the bar.

"You want another one?"

"I have no reason to hang around tonight." Drew pulled a ten-dollar bill off the money clip in his pocket and dropped it next to the empty glass. "Thanks for the information."

When Drew spun on the stool, a number of gazes dropped away, but a few stayed fixed on him while he walked to the door with balanced strides and an alert awareness of everything around him. His muscles tensed when he heard light steps hurrying to catch up to him. Stepping onto the sidewalk, he pivoted to face the door and moved close to the wall of the building. The dark-haired hooker stopped outside the door and looked confused until she saw him.

"I'm not buying," Drew said.

"I want to talk to you. I remember you."

"Who are you?"

"Milly Costello."

Drew cocked his head and thought for a minute before he laughed gently. "Silly Milly?"

"I haven't heard that in a long time." She flushed and darted her eyes to where Sal stood at the bar. "Can we get away from here?"

"Sure, but I'm still not buying." Drew caught her elbow and directed her around the corner and across the street. He flagged a cab at the end of the block. In a matter of minutes, they were blocks away on a street of upscale shops and hotels. He caught sight of a grey sedan and turned Milly to face him. "Button your blouse before you get me in trouble."

"What do you mean?"

"This place has single malt scotch and can be touchy about certain illicit activities." When his uncle drove by, Drew lifted a hand behind Milly's back and flashed his fingers a few times before he waved Antonio off. Milly looked up and he dropped his gaze to her better-concealed cleavage. "That's more acceptable."

Drew escorted Milly to an isolated corner table in the hotel cocktail lounge, seated her in front of a mirror that gave him a view of both the door and the bar. This time he ordered Jack Daniels, along with a gin and tonic for Milly. As expected, Antonio arrived before they received their drinks. His uncle glanced around the room, then met Drew's eyes in the mirror. When Antonio lifted his right hand in front of his chest in a quick, obscene gesture before he walked back outside, Drew lost his composure and laughed.

"Did I do something funny?" Milly blinked at him.

"No." Drew looked away from the mirror and smiled at a memory that surfaced in his mind. "I was thinking of when Silly Milly started."

"You called it Valentine poetry." She puckered her face and scowled at him. "I called it mean."

"I don't remember what I wrote, but I do remember you calling me nasty names."

"I remember it. 'Silly Milly, your hair is black, your feet are flat, so take this red heart cuz you smell like a fart.' I thought maybe you liked me until you did that."

Drew laughed at her angry scowl. "I couldn't think of anything else that rhymed."

"Now you'd say, you look like a tart." Milly eyed his expensive clothes and blushed.

"It's rather that you looked the part."

"You called me Silly Milly after that. I hated it."

"Can I apologize and make you stop hating it?" Drew held her gaze, watched the hurt slip from her face.

"I don't hate it anymore." She looked down and took a swallow of her drink.

"I'm sorry I hurt you. I don't think I meant to."

"Oh, you meant to." Milly frowned when he looked confused. "Drew, you could be real nice and fun sometimes. Most of the time, you were a rotten shit."

"The part of me who made me write it meant it. I don't think I did."

"You used to say your bad older brother made you do mean things." Her face soured. "Drew, you didn't have a brother."

"I thought I had one then." He made a show of shrugging it off. "I didn't want to admit to the rotten stuff and said he did it. Milly, I was a screwed-up kid."

"You lived with an insane mother. We thought you were crazy, too."

"It took an excellent psychiatrist to prove I wasn't crazy, just self-protective. I came back here to see if I can make sense of some of what happened back then."

"Stay away, Drew. It will only make Mario nastier. He's been picking me up sometimes. Now he's starting to act like I can't be with nobody else unless he gets some money for it. I can't afford that, but I'm afraid of him."

"Quit hooking, Milly. Somebody's going to give you more than you want."

"I keep a pack of condoms in my purse. They gotta use them or it's no deal."

"That's not what I meant. I'm talking about guys like Mario. Stay away from him."

"That's what I'm trying to tell you." Concern and warning scarred Milly's face. "Mario says he would've taken you down if the cops hadn't stopped him. He says he'll finish it this time."

"All the cops stopped him from doing was running away with his dick shriveled up and his tail between his legs."

"He hurts people, Drew. I've heard him brag about it. He sliced the tip off the end of a guy's finger when he wouldn't pay what he owed. It made me sick when he told me."

"Get another job. Get away from here."

"I can't. My sister works days and has a family of her own, but she can come over for a while at night, so I have to work nights. One of us has to be with Mamma all the time. Since I'm the tag-along kid, it kinda fell on me. She's got the Alzheimer's, and we don't want to send her to one of those Medicaid places. She still knows us most of the time. She'd be upset if we sent her away."

"Do you know where Mario gets his drugs? Do you know how and where he sells them?"

"No." Her eyes widening, Milly shook her head. "Are you a cop or something?"

When she started to push away from the table, Drew set his hand on her arm and held her back. "I told the truth, Milly. I'm trying to understand my past. I just thought it might be a way you could get Mario off your back."

Milly continued to shake her head. "I couldn't talk to cops, even if I had something to tell them."

"Maybe you could find a way to tell me. I can talk to cops."

"I shouldn't have talked to you tonight, but I wanted to tell you to stay away from Mario. He's been mean since he got out of jail.

Nobody wants to get on his wrong side. If anybody mentions you, he goes wacko."

"I get the message, but I still want to talk to Ernie about the way it used to be. If you want to tell me anything, talk to Ernie."

"Don't expect nothing." Milly finished the drink and stood up, surprised when he stood with her. "It was nice to see you again. I used to wonder what happened to you. Last year there was a thing in the paper about some lady named Sutherland donating money to the Metropolitan Arts Center. It took me a while to realize you were the Andrew Sutherland mentioned in it. Is she really your grandmother? Does she really live in that big house?"

"I'd appreciate it if you didn't tell Mario that."

"I think he knows. He said something about you being the bastard kid of some rich asshole."

"He's wrong. My claim is legitimate." Drew dropped some cash on the table and handed her some folded bills as they walked outside.

Milly shook her head. "You don't gotta pay me. We ain't done nothing."

"I want you to stay home tonight, maybe the next couple of nights. Tell Mario you had to be with your mother because someone is going to tell him you left when I did. Let it blow over."

"Things don't blow over with Mario. He won't forget it. That's why I can't see you again."

"What will you tell him about tonight?" Drew flagged a cab and held the door open for her.

"That I went home to check on Mamma. I do that sometimes."

Drew watched the cab pull into traffic before he crossed the street and started walking in the opposite direction. Two blocks away, Antonio was sitting against a front fender of the grey sedan, frowning at him.

"I didn't know I needed a chaperone."

"That's not where you take hookers."

"I bought an old friend a drink."

"She's a hooker."

"Not tonight. Let's get out of here." Drew reached to open the passenger door and found it locked.

"You think I leave my car open so any bum can get in?" Antonio pushed away from the fender. "I usually put wise asses in the back with their hands hooked together."

"I didn't know I was being a wise ass."

"I was trying to cheer you up. You look like you lost a pissing contest with a skunk." Antonio released the front door locks before he walked around to the driver's door.

Drew sat in silence for a while, thinking about what Milly had said. The stuff about Mario upset him, but not as much as what he'd heard about himself. "You know, Zio, sometimes it's the little things that get to you."

"Like what?"

"Silly Milly, your hair is black, your feet are flat, so take this red heart, cuz you smell like a fart."

"What the hell was that?" Antonio turned to Drew with a disgusted look on his face.

"I guess it was my first love poem."

"Romantic little bastard, weren't you? Are you thinking of selling it to Hallmark?"

"I gave it to Milly in third grade. She said she thought I liked her until I gave her that. It must have hurt a lot. She remembered it for almost twenty years. She said I was mean."

"Kids often are."

"But I did like Milly. It's weird, Zio. I can remember I didn't want to write it. In fact, I remember being made to write it. Jack couldn't write, and he kept threatening to put me in the dark. I understand all the theory. I know all the explanations. But I don't know how it felt back then. I need to try to find out before I can understand what happened to me last winter. I don't like what Milly said about me being a rotten shit. I want to say he wasn't me, but he was me, and sometimes it doesn't make sense."

"A while back I picked up a perp who robbed a delicatessen and assaulted the proprietor," Antonio said. "Then some shrink showed up and tried to tell me I had to let him go because he wasn't the person who did it. I said, pardon me, but that's the bastard I put the cuffs on at the scene and he's not going anywhere until he gets called up for an arraignment. The shrink said it would be useless because the guy in the cell doesn't even know he was in the delicatessen, which didn't make sense to me because he was sitting in the cell stinking like pickle juice from the jar the owner broke over his head. Then I remembered what your father told me about you when he explained why you used to piss me off by telling me you weren't where I'd seen you, or you said you didn't remember what we did when we were together. One day I gave you a book and you told me you couldn't read it. Three days later you were hiding in your room reading a book tougher than the one I gave you. My whole family thought you were a pathological liar."

"I got accused of lying so much I didn't know if I was or not. The shrink was right. But then, so were you. If you let him go, the personality that did the crime would come back and commit another one. But that's all over with me. I haven't been a dissociative multiple since I was about ten years old. And I took full control of myself before I was sixteen. I'm solid there. I have their memories, but I feel I'm still missing something and I won't find it unless I go back to when I was messed up. I have to understand where I came from."

"They're dead, Drew. The ones who messed you up are dead."

"Maybe, but the memories aren't. I have to make sense out of them."

"What memories?"

"I don't know. That's why I have to find them."

"Do you think there's another one in there?"

"There's no sign of that under hypnoses. That's how he found the other alters."

"That French shrink?"

"Yes."

"You talked to him lately?"

"Last winter. He said I'm probably on the right track, that I usually am when I play my hunches." Drew pulled his wallet out of his inside jacket pocket and looked in it. "Damn. You got some money?"

"What do you mean do I *got* some money?" Antonio mocked him. "Sure, I *got* some money."

"I gave what I had in my money clip to Milly. I don't have any cash in my wallet. Oh, never mind, just find me an ATM. I found the right card."

"I thought you didn't pay for it."

"I don't pay for sex. I occasionally give money to an old friend who critiques my poetry. Do you think she'll quit hooking if she finds a better night job?"

"Nope."

"Why not?"

"Probably can't find a better job. Right now, she can make what she needs in a few hours. Schedule is flexible, gets a lot of free drinks, and she doesn't have to pay taxes."

"No medical insurance and bad risks."

"She should be all right, Drew. Milly's selective."

"She says Mario wants a cut."

"I'll ask around and see if I can get someone to keep an eye on her and put some heat on him if it looks like he's pressuring her. He's still twitchy about riling cops."

"Thank you, Zio. She made me feel guilty—like I walked away from those kids I used to know and never gave a thought to what happened to them. I mean, look at what I have and look at them."

"You'll drive yourself nuts with that kind of thinking. We can only use the opportunities we get and make what we can of ourselves. Some of those kids did fine. Milly never tried very hard. She always took the easy route."

Chapter Six

Willow immersed herself in horses as soon as she arrived at the barn the next morning to talk to Roy, who cleaned stalls, fed, watered, and did all that was necessary for the basic maintenance of the barn. Willow's responsibility was to groom, train and see to the performing natures of Mae's horses. Of the fourteen animals at the stable: one was a Dutch Warmblood mare ready to foal; three were mares with new foals; one was a yearling filly.

Two of the riding horses, Bold Venture and King's Knight, belonged to Drew and had been shipped from Europe in early spring. Drew was also riding Rigoletto, the sixteen-year-old Hanoverian stallion his grandmother had trained to international grand prix level before a shattered knee from a fall on icy stairs ended her riding career. Willow was responsible for training three horses: Moonstone, a three-year-old dark grey filly, Donegal, a six-year-old chestnut thoroughbred gelding, and Ko-Ko, an eight-year-old event horse entering preliminary level.

After spending the early morning cleaning tack and familiarizing herself with the stable and equipment, Willow worked with Moonstone, starting with the easy ground lessons Mae had requested. She groomed Shamrock, the pregnant mare, checking for any waxing of the milk bag, a sign that foaling was imminent. Her next job was to lunge Bold Venture. Even though the big, black gelding had been out on pasture all night, he had stored up restless energy since his early morning feeding. Over seventeen hands and close to a ton of leaping, bucking horse on the end of a thirty-foot lunge line almost jerked Willow off her feet, until she thought to hold the line so she could sit back against it like a mountain climber on a rappelling rope.

In spite of a few muttered curses about the understatement in Drew's hang on hard advice, the experience gave Willow a strong respect for Bold Venture and, indirectly, for the man who trained and rode him. Fortunately, the rest of Drew's advice was correct. After his initial bursts of playful enthusiasm, the gelding proved himself a gentleman by settling down to work on an easy circle with good manners and no pulling.

When Willow finished working with Bold Venture and let him out the pasture gate, she thought of Drew's comment about teaching her there were more exciting things than horses. She knew he was talking about sex, which hardly surprised her. After growing up with six brothers, she was well aware of male sexual obsession. It often seemed that every topic of conversation reminded them of sex. Her interest in horses had been a popular issue of speculation that inevitably focused on pointed questions and relentless teasing.

Although Willow admitted she'd allowed horses to take the place of men in her life, she hardly saw it as her fault that the men she attracted refused to understand her obsession with horses and became unreasonably jealous. Since she had no intention of giving up horses, Willow concluded that men were egotistical creatures, who thought they should be the most important focus of her life and she wasn't buying it. However, that didn't mean she never thought about men and sex. In fact, she thought about both of them. A lot.

Last night, Willow had been unable to stop thinking about Drew, even when she was trying to concentrate on what Mae told her about the horses. While his romantic interlude had left her emotionally confused, there was no way she could deny that the feelings he aroused were sexual. Even now, without the magnetism of his presence, the thrill was still there whenever she thought of his enticing kiss, his body fusing with hers in the intimacy of the waltz.

No matter how much Willow wanted to deny it, she knew she had a crush on Drew Sutherland, which both excited and annoyed her. So far, her track record with romance could be summed up as disastrous and she wanted no part of it.

Derek O'Connor had grown up in Ireland and moved to Iowa when Willow was ten. By the time she was fourteen, she knew Derek was the most perfect boy in the world. He was three years older than she was. He was handsome, fun and exciting, and his father Shamus had been on the Irish Army Equestrian team. Willow took jumping lessons from Shamus and fell in love with his charismatic son. But no matter how much she fantasized about Derek, he broke her heart by ignoring her attempts to attract him and remaining staunchly in love with her cousin Bridget.

When Willow was sixteen, Cal Wallace, a swaggering braggart her brothers called the spouting asshole, pulled her behind a horse barn at the state fair and told her he was going to make her day. He pawed at her breasts with hard hands, shoved his tongue in her mouth and forced her hand into his opened jeans to feel his erection. Recoiling in disgust, Willow had twisted away from him, mule kicked his knee sideways and left him bellowing and cursing in pain. When her brother Todd learned about it, he gave Cal a pounding that started a continuing feud between her brothers and Cal's group of rowdy friends.

During her freshman year at Iowa State, Willow attracted the attention of a wealthy senior, who was head of a popular fraternity and a revered campus athlete. She was bowled over by his flattery and thrilled by the thought of being seen as the girlfriend of Larry Peterson, who was fit and blond and gorgeous. Her elation crashed after the first party weekend when she discovered his idea of dating was to get drunk and prove himself a manly lover by refusing to take no for an answer. After more than an hour in a motel room trying to fend him off, Willow lost her resistance and closed her mind to what was happening because she didn't know what else to do and was afraid to fight with him.

When Larry rolled away and stumbled into the bathroom to eject the contents of his stomach, Willow pulled on as many of her clothes as she could find, left a scribbled note telling him to go to hell and walked out on him. During the three-mile trek to her dormitory, she blamed herself for making a terrible mistake she didn't want anyone to know about. As the weeks went by with no contact from Larry and no sign of his success, Willow convinced herself it was no more than an awkwardly botched attempt at drunken sex she hadn't participated in. She had no better luck with a less impassioned romance. Ken Bergman was compassionate, intriguing, and artistic. He painted, wrote poetry, took her to plays and concerts. After filling a sketchbook with horse portraits, he grew tired of sitting on the fence and found someone else.

Willow transferred to an equestrian program at a college in Minnesota the next year, where, between a working scholarship in the school barns, as well as an evening waitress job to help her father pay the higher costs of a private college, she had no time and little interest in social life. Back home in Iowa, Tom Sorenson had been willing to accept her in spite of what he jokingly called her horse affliction. There was little romance in Tom's courtship, but there was friendship and kindness. His attention and affections were genuine and reassuring but they failed to stimulate her. When he wanted sex, Willow panicked and ran to Byron, who helped her understand that marriage to Tom would be a mistake and she wasn't selfish, old-fashioned, or inadequate because she wanted to wait for passionate love instead of allowing sex because it was expected from her.

While she walked to Venture's stall to hang his lead shank on the door, Willow recalled Tom's broad Scandinavian face and the way his laughter built and spilled out like a spring gurgling up from deep underground. She thought about Tom's hands—big, square, blunt-fingered and powerful. He could do precise woodworking with them as well as fix any mechanical device on his farm. And that made her wonder why hands that could be meticulously skillful when he worked with them felt clumsy every time he touched her?

When she thought about Drew, Willow thanked Byron for turning her away from secure thoughts of marriage. After only a few hours with Drew, Willow knew she had never loved Tom and that, in spite of her brothers' often crude analogies, the enjoyment she received from horses, although passionate, was not sexual. The excitement Drew stimulated was sexual and unlike anything she'd ever felt. Even the thrill of starting her job failed to drive him from her mind or quell the feeling of arousal when she remembered his touch. Drew had strong hands, but they were different than Tom's, or those of any other man who'd touched her. Drew's hands were gently stimulating, even spellbinding.

Wanting to impress Drew with her diligence, Willow groomed his other horses before she went home for lunch. She had all afternoon to ride the two geldings. If she could keep herself this organized, she would have plenty of time to keep ahead of the job.

After taking a lunch break and riding Donegal, the young chestnut thoroughbred, Willow was beginning to run down but figured a catnap on the couch in the office would recharge her energy. Teaching a few basic dressage classes at the college and schooling one event horse hadn't kept her in good shape, even with the evening waitress job. She fell asleep staring through the glass windows at an empty arena.

An hour later Willow heard the door open and jerked herself awake. Blinking in surprise, she sat up to see Drew standing beside a tall, unbelievably slender woman with an abundance of red-brown, expertly highlighted curls. The woman wore high-heels that were little more than soles and a few tiny white straps, as well as, of all things, a white skirt and clinging lavender blouse that accentuated a lean model's figure. With her carefully applied make-up and fashionable outfit, the woman belonged on the cover of a magazine, not in a barn. Drew was dressed in the clothes he wore to dinner yesterday.

Willow gaped at them, feeling like a mutt at a Kennel Club show,

"Willow, I'd like you to meet Nicole, who, unfortunately, only speaks French."

While Drew spoke to the woman, Willow forced herself to stand up. She understood her own name and a word she thought meant horse. The rest was gibberish. She had taken French in high school, but Iowa textbook French bore little resemblance to the vernacular language spoken by Drew and Nicole.

"Hello, Nicole." Willow extended her hand and received a cool, boneless handshake. Afraid she might damage or soil the thin, long-fingered hand, Willow quickly released it and gave Nicole a forced smile in answer to a tumble of meaningless sounds.

"I told Nicole about you at breakfast," Drew said. "She says she's glad to meet you but is sorry we disturbed your nap."

"Oh, well, that's all right." Willow answered numbly while her mind grappled with the thought that Drew had just spent the night with this woman and, in a typical display of masculine insensitivity, was thrusting it in her face as if what happened yesterday meant nothing. "I still have to ride Ko-Ko."

With her curt dismissal, Willow turned and grabbed her riding chaps off an arm of the couch. While she pulled the suede chaps over her jeans, she glanced up to see Drew glare at her with smoldering irritation before he curled a hand over Nicole's bony shoulder and guided her toward a wall of framed pictures behind the desk. Willow had looked at them earlier. Most were of dressage horses with Mae, and jumpers with a blond male rider she didn't recognize. A few chronicled the life of a curly-haired, blue-eyed boy as he outgrew a variety of ponies and horses.

While Willow finished zipping closed the legs of the chaps, the French conversation sounded more intimate and Nicole's bell-clear laughter became a sharp stiletto pricking at her nerves.

Pointedly ignoring Nicole, Willow stared directly at Drew until he looked at her. "I lunged Venture and groomed Knight and Rigoletto."

"Thank you," he answered with a tight voice but said nothing more, leaving an unpleasant spot of dead air.

"I'm going to ride Ko-Ko," Willow blurted out to keep the conversation alive. "By the way, why the name Ko-Ko?"

"He's the lord high executioner in the *Mikado*."

"Oh." He continued to look at her with an annoyed expression she saw as patronizing. "Do you want me to saddle your horse before I ride?"

"Forget the groom crap. I know how to do that."

Drew's flat, controlled answer infuriated Willow, and she strode from the room with her jaw clenched so hard it hurt. Forcing herself to control her temper, she quietly closed the door. By the time she reached the tack room, she wanted to rip its door off the hinges. Inside the small room, she gritted her teeth and pulled in a breath of leather scented air. Once again, she resisted the urge to slam a door, plopped down on a show trunk and pounded clenched fists on her thighs until her heart stopped racing. Over and over, she told herself she was overreacting and a twist of humiliation grew into a heavy ball in her chest.

Willow told herself she was a fool, who'd let a few affectionate moments mean too much—a chump who couldn't play the sex game right. Thinking about that made her uneasy and then defensive. Drew was a spoiled womanizer. Both he and his grandmother had intimated as much. And now, like a naive ninny, she had let him sucker her into the oldest con game in the world.

In an indignant huff, Willow decided horses were still the better bargain and resolved that Drew Sutherland was not going to churn up her emotions again. After all, what claim could she possibly have on him? It was a casual flirtation. That's all. Yesterday, there had been a charged attraction between them. Today, something reversed the charge until they repelled each other. Drew was coldly impersonal and she could only blame it on Nicole—an old girlfriend, who'd swept back into his life to stake her own claim.

When she tried to think about Nicole, Willow remembered nothing beyond her first observation of plastic, feminine beauty. After that glaringly surface impression, she had only been aware of Drew. Oh yes, she remembered something else. She remembered the way Drew's hand covered Nicole's shoulder. And she remembered the sound of the French words that purred seductively from a slender throat and glossed lips.

Damn him, damn him, damn him. Willow plucked Ko-Ko's bridle off its hanger and continued her internal tirade while she collected the rest of the tack and brushes. *You can forget your flirting games with me. It's not my way to play. I'm a commonsense realist and I won't play bedroom hopscotch, or patiently wait for my turn on the Tilt-A-Whirl.*

In the aisle by Ko-Ko's stall, Willow swung out the saddle rack and slid the saddle onto it before she scowled at the observation room door. *It would have been much better if you* were *a thirteen-year-old with big feet—and pimples.*

❖

Willow liked Ko-Ko immediately. He was a big boned, muscular, bay gelding—half American Thoroughbred, half German Trakehner. Mae had told her Drew had showed him in dressage and started him jumping when the horse was five. For the last three years, the horse had been leased to a local pony clubber, who gave him up last fall to attend college. Ko-Ko was a little rusty after a winter at pasture that Mae called a needed respite after last summer's show circuit. The break seemed to have worked. He was full of spice today.

After half an hour of quiet, undemanding warm-up exercises, Willow felt comfortable enough to start phase one of the horse's reconditioning program by taking a long ride on the network of trails area horsemen had established on both private and public land. Willow had studied a trail map before lunch, but had left it in the office. Rather than return to the barn and risk running into Drew and Nicole, she decided it was unnecessary. Even if she became unsure of the way home, she knew it was almost impossible to get lost on an animal that knew the location of its feed box.

Listening to the even, three beat cadence of Ko-Ko's relaxed canter, Willow felt warm weather soak into her soul with a comforting embrace and delighted in the smells and sights of a greening woodland. Tiny, pale green buds popped from every branch while ground-hugging displays of white, pink and yellow wild flowers stretched away from the trail like fragrant mists of springtime. From every direction, a lilting symphony of avian music drew her deeper into a mysterious sanctuary protectively enclosed by entwined arms and fingers of towering trees that grew on the hunched shoulders of weathered mountains.

Willow had grown up under a huge dome of endless sky, where vast plains, broken by rugged bluffs, overlooked wide river valleys and gently rolling hills cloaked with a crazy quilt of pastures, cropland, farmsteads and woodlots. Under the open skies of central Iowa, the sun had been a ready compass, a constant reminder of time and direction. Here, in the rising foothills of the Appalachians, it speared through trees in dazzling rays or disappeared in mountain shadows until she lost track of which way the trail twisted between glimpses of the hovering ball of the sun

Slowing to a walk, Willow took a narrow trail beside a switchback brook that tumbled over moss covered stones until she found the spring-fed lake that was its source. A doe and two speckled fawns lifted wet muzzles that dripped sparkling shards of water. For a frozen moment, the animals stared out of round dark eyes before they bounded into the shadowed woods. When the white flash of the doe's tail disappeared behind a thicket of evergreens, Willow walked Ko-Ko into the shallow water and loosened the reins to let him drink. She was trying to catch glimpses of the vanishing deer beyond the dark trees when two hound dogs broke from the brush at the edge of the woods. Ko-Ko reacted with instinctive reflexes by wheeling to the left and throwing Willow forward onto his neck.

If she hadn't taken her feet out of the stirrups to stretch her legs, if the dogs hadn't reacted by barking and charging toward her, she may have stayed on, or the horse may have stopped to graze on the rich grass beside the lake. Instead, she fell off on the second kicking buck, landed on her hip and rolled to avoid flying hooves when Ko-Ko tore down the trail, reins flapping beside his neck, stirrups banging against his sides, dogs running at his heels in full cry.

Sitting up, grass-stained and dirty, Willow took stock of herself: two fingers on her left hand were leather burned from the reins and her right buttock was bruised from a hard landing, but nothing was seriously injured. Except her pride. Her only consolation was that she was wearing comfortable paddock boots, not riding boots. It could be a long walk back to the barn if she failed to find the horse cropping grass somewhere along the trail.

Small orange and white signs marked every trail crossing or branching. Each was marked with a no motorized vehicle symbol, as well as the double horseshoe logo of the Parsons Glen Equestrian Association and numbered to correspond with locations on the map. It was an excellent system—if someone had a map. Sighing, Willow assumed that in view of the way things were going this afternoon she would have to walk all the way back to the stable.

The first branching was an easy choice. She remembered the way the trail curled around a stand of dogwood trees beside a shallow depression filled with a drift of white trillium. At the second trail split, she could see two sets of clear tracks made by a round-hoofed horse wearing new rim shoes on the front. Earlier, while picking out Ko-Ko's hooves, she'd noticed he was newly shod with rim shoes. That was the end of her good luck.

At a three-way split, where all the trees looked the same, Willow started to regret her cocky assurance about not needing a map. She took a guess and walked through a pine forest on a shaky memory, only to find herself in an unfamiliar meadow. Although she'd ridden through several deer meadows, something about this one confused her enough to rattle her. She convinced herself that if she kept moving west, she would find Sutherland land, or at least some houses.

The trail markers had the landowner's name across the bottom of the plate below the marker number. So far, they all said Bucks, which meant she was in the county recreation area south and east of Sutherland Manor. The next marker said Mason. She had no recollection of a Mason on the map. When she found herself in a decaying apple orchard, where a steep slope dropped away to her right, she could see a long valley of farms and homes. None of them looked familiar and the bright blaze of the sun behind her left shoulder told her she was traveling more east than west.

"Damn it!" She snapped a sucker off a dying apple tree and slashed it at the mottled trunk. "How could I be so damn dumb?"

"Pick a bigger one and I might find a use for it."

Feeling as if her heart stopped beating and then expanded to choke off her breath, Willow spun to see Drew glaring at her from Venture's back. For an unreal second, she thought she was facing one of the dreaded Four Horsemen. He towered over her, a huge dark figure, enlarged by the slope of the hill, accentuated by the sun at his back. He seemed bigger, tougher, incapable of the thoughtful introspection she sensed in him yesterday.

"Are you threatening me?" Willow challenged his arrogance like a terrier snapping at a mastiff.

"What were you trying to do, run the legs off him?"

"I didn't run him at all."

"He came back winded and lathered."

"Oh my God. Is he all right?"

"Yes. Roy said he'd sponge him and walk him out." Drew paused to absorb her reaction then added, "We needn't mention it to Gram."

"I didn't run him," Willow answered with relief. "He shied at some dogs. I fell off. When he ran, they chased him."

"Where?"

"At a small lake somewhere up there." She waved toward the hills.

"That would be Harry Trumbull's hounds." Drew frowned. "They run deer, too."

"That's what they were doing until Ko-Ko became easier game. How did you find me?"

"Nemo and I tracked the horse until we found your tracks and followed you." Drew nodded at the wooly black dog that flopped down in the shade of a bush. "Why are you over here? The trail home is that way about a mile." He pointed to where a stone wall edged the orchard.

"I got lost."

"Can't you read the map?"

"I don't have the map." She pivoted on her right foot and set off down the trail with long, determined strides.

After Willow took about ten steps, Drew jogged past her, wheeled the horse and stopped in front of her.

"Get out of my way!"

"Why don't you have a map? Gram and I both told you about them and stressed their importance. These trails are a maze if you don't know them."

"I trusted the horse to know where home was."

"A bad idea, seeing as you lost the horse. Why didn't you take a map?"

"I didn't want to go back to the office to get one. You don't need to tell me I was an idiot. I already know it." Thrusting her chin forward, Willow stomped away from him.

In a continuous flow of motion, Drew vaulted off the horse, caught her wrist, turned her to face him. "Why didn't you go back for a map?"

"That is none of your business."

"I think it is. As is your rotten behavior in the barn."

"*My* rotten behavior?" Willow yanked against his hold.

"I think I just said that. Why didn't you go back for a map?"

"I didn't want to."

"I already heard that answer." Arc-bright eyes stabbed into her. The thumb and bent forefinger of his left hand trapped her chin and forced her to look at him while his right continued to hold her in restraint. "I'd like an answer."

"Because you were there."

"That's what I thought." Drew dropped his hand from her chin but still held her wrist. "And why am I suddenly something distasteful? You couldn't wait to get away from me."

"I can tell when I'm a fifth wheel."

"You were mostly a flat tire. You made a stunning impression."

"And just what was my impression?"

"I can best translate it to: snotty little bitch."

"Bitch?" She recoiled. "Bitch!"

"That was Nicole. I say rude brat."

"Let go of me. Now!" Willow waited about half a second before she simultaneously stamped a boot heel on the arch of his right foot and smacked the apple switch across his denim covered left thigh. The result bordered on spectacular.

"Holy shit!" Gaping at her like a stunned bull halted in mid-charge, Drew seemed unsure of which leg to hop on first. The pain in his stomped-on foot clearly made the decision for him. He released her wrist, stumbled backwards to regain his stance and snorted at her. "What the hell was that about?"

"I told you I was raised tough. So, stop being a macho asshole and keep your hands off me."

As soon as she shouted the victorious declaration that felt almost as devastating as triumphant, Willow turned and ran from him. She ran a long way before she heard trotting hooves striking the hard trail behind her. With her emotions bruised, nerves tightly wound, his pursuit outraged her, made her run faster. Goaded by steady thuds as each pair of hooves hit the ground in an unvarying two-beat cadence that echoed the thumping of her heart, Willow's apprehension grew to fury, then to desperation when the rhythm changed to a pounding gallop and the ground shook from the impact of the gelding's mass.

When the horse swept past her, Willow yelped from the superbly aimed flick of an apple switch across the seat of her jeans. Veering off the trail, she took a wrong step and stumbled. She stayed on her feet but staggered a few strides before she slowed to a weaving walk. Ahead of her, Venture tucked his hindquarters and wheeled on his haunches until he, once again, faced her.

His face sternly unreadable, Drew rode toward her, holding the switch across the horse's withers. "You get tough. Ergo, I return the attitude."

"Stuff it, Drew. And get the hell out of my way." Still feeling the itchy sting of his retaliation, Willow pulled back, then tried to dodge around him.

Venture sidestepped agilely in total obedience to each shift of Drew's weight. No matter which way Willow darted, the horse was in front of her with Drew's stare burning into her. Forward or back, side to side, angled or straight Venture was always there, just out of reach, holding her at bay. There was no way she could outmaneuver him. The horse moved as Drew thought until she was sure she was facing one creature with linked mind and body. Oddly, she started to admire the control he had over the horse and gained an awed respect for his riding skills while he played with her the way a barn cat toyed with a doomed mouse.

Willow knew she had let her temper go too far, as she often had with her brothers. But when she angered one of her brothers, she could usually hide behind another brother, or her father, who could silence any dispute with one bellowing roar. This time she was alone with an irritated man, who was capable of stirring her emotions into a hopeless muddle whenever she got near him. Right now, she wanted to be as far away as she could get; but since she could no longer run, her only choice was to face him with resigned acceptance of what she'd brought on herself.

"All right, you win. It's checkmate." She gasped her surrender and thought: *Checkmate. That's what Byron would teasingly call it: the rape of the queen, the victory of the untouchable king.*

"Willow, a long time ago, humans learned a foot soldier without an appropriate weapon is helpless against a trained cavalry mount. Never take on a knight with a pawn. It's bad chess." He dropped the switch and walked the horse toward where she stood.

There was no desperation now, just a dizzy, helpless feeling that told Willow she'd made a fool of herself by letting Drew get to her emotions. She felt she was going to cry—the absolutely last thing she wanted to do in front of him.

"Get on behind me. I'll take you home." When he dropped his stirrup, and reached a hand across the pommel, Willow shook her head and backed away. She tried to say no but was still out of breath and unable to talk.

"Give me your hand and get on the horse."

"Just go away." The words were pushed out as if they tasted bad.

"I won't go away. I'll make sure you get home without getting lost again. You can continue the stubborn act and walk the five miles while I ride it, or you can be intelligent and hitch a ride with me. One thing you will not do is get rid of me. I won't leave you out here alone. It goes against that code of chivalry you disapprove of."

"I'm not a brainless weakling like your French *femme*."

"The lack of a map argues in favor of brainless." Drew smiled, looking more entertained than angry. "I'll agree you're no weakling. And I've gained a healthy respect for your ability to get your points across. But I take exception to your judgment of Nicole."

When he extended his hand again, Willow started to reject it then looked up at sharply cut features, intense blue eyes. She wanted to kick him. But she didn't want him to see her as a fool.

"I'll take the ride."

"Your common sense is amazing."

After she put her foot in the loose stirrup, a strong hand closed over hers. Once she was up behind him, Drew turned the horse toward the woods and lifted him into an easy canter.

Willow hesitated for a moment before she slid her arms around him and pressed her cheek against the back of his shirt. She told herself it was only to make it easier on the horse since they now moved as one burden. But the feel of his hard warmth and the rhythmic unity of their movements stimulated a pleasant feeling of closeness that destroyed her hold on the tangled knot of emotions trapped inside her. She wanted to go back to yesterday when Drew tempted her with romance that was more fantasy than reality. She didn't want him to act like one of her hardheaded brothers and make her mad enough to smack him. Unable to make sense of her emotions, she let the hurt spill out in tears that tracked down her face in burning lines.

Chapter Seven

On Thursdays Mae taught lessons at the nearby Parsons Glen Equestrian Center and invited Willow to join her so she could see the center. Willow agreed but insisted on driving herself over after she worked her morning horses.

The equestrian center was huge. Two wings with thirty stalls in each reached out behind an oversized indoor arena. Willow found Mae teaching in one end of the arena below an elevated observation room with a mini-bar that offered drinks, snacks, even playing cards. She bought a cup of coffee and carried it toward a cluster of cushioned chairs by the observation wall. Two screened window panels were open, allowing Willow to hear what was happening in the arena.

A short, brunette woman, who looked as if she'd been stuffed into grass-stained breeches, sat in one of the chairs close to the window. Reluctant to disturb her, Willow sat on a couch against the side wall. Mae was teaching a slender woman on a grey warmblood gelding. The horse knew more than its rider. Willow guessed the animal had been trained to third, maybe fourth level, before the woman bought it. The new owner was no more than a first level rider, trying to ride at second level, to catch up to her horse.

Willow had never been able to afford a horse trained beyond her level. Instead, she'd turned a backyard pinto gelding into a dressage horse with hard work and pure determination. After two years of heartbreaking competition at training level, she won a fourth place out of nine and felt it was a gold medal. There were a lot of ribbons after the first one, even some high percentage awards at first and second levels. Packy's hocks started to fail him last year and she had retired him to the farm, where he continued to irritate her father by chasing cattle and outwitting attempts to fence him away from the bovine herd.

About halfway through the next lesson, a slender woman in immaculate white breeches clumped across the tiled floor of the observation room and flopped into a chair beside the brunette. Willow recognized her as the rider of the warmblood and wondered if she'd taken care of her horse or handed it over to a groom—something else Willow wasn't used to. She kept telling herself she was in a different world and would get used to it, but little things like worrying about a sweaty animal hung in her mind.

After pulling a turquoise scarf off her head and shaking her hair into a froth of permed curls, the thin blonde nodded at a tall glass on the table beside the other woman. "Is that mine?"

"I thought you could use a drink after that session. Mae didn't give you much mercy. She had you sit-trot without stirrups for twenty minutes before she was satisfied with your seat."

"I'm not sure she was ever satisfied. It got to where she'd accept it. That's all."

The shorter woman watched the lesson in the arena for a moment before she looked back at the blonde. "Lois, Drew's back."

The statement jumped out at Willow, making her forget she was trying to ignore their conversation. Twisting to look at them, Willow saw she wasn't the only one the words had a strong effect on. The blonde, Lois, tensed as if she were caught naked in a spot light.

"Did you see him, Bonnie?" Lois's hand tightened on the glass.

"No, Sally did. He rode over to talk to Barry yesterday morning. He brought Venture back." Bonnie sighed and made an envious face. "I wish I could afford to ship horses back and forth to Europe the way Drew does."

"Did he ask about me?" Lois's voice was brittle, as if she were trying to sound nonchalant and knew she was failing.

"Sally didn't say anything." Bonnie tipped her glass to finish the drink. Ice cubes and fruit banged into her nose, making her jump and stare cross-eyed into the glass. "I also heard Mae hired a new student. Drew's probably too busy screwing her to think about last year's affairs. If you're smart, you'll forget, too."

"It's easier to hate than forget." Lois took a gulp at her drink.

"What's to hate?" Bonnie poked into the glass with a swizzle stick. "He only took what was offered."

"He took all right."

"Oh, come off it." Bonnie snorted. "You know he has no interest in joint checking accounts or platonic mind-melding. Drew doesn't waste time with women who won't go to bed with him." She succeeded in spearing a soggy round of orange, dragged it out of the glass and held it, dangling, in front of her nose while she set the empty glass on the table. "Drew started seducing his father's French housemaids at sixteen. Seduction is his favorite hobby. And he always finds another one."

"I didn't get so much as a so long and thanks for all the fucks. It was like trying to use a credit card and discovering the account was canceled a week ago and the bank's phone number was disconnected."

"You lied to him." Bonnie examined the rind to make sure it was nibbled clean then dropped it into the glass. Lois frowned at her but remained silent. "You told him your marriage was washed up and you were waiting for final divorce papers."

"I was thinking about divorce."

"You think about divorce every time you want something from Ralph."

"What does the status of my marriage have to do with it? When it comes to women, the concept of future doesn't exist in Drew's mind."

Bonnie frowned at Lois's defensive retort. "But he takes exception to becoming an issue in an adultery scandal."

"That's absurd. Drew was screwing a married woman when he was in college."

"I heard he got careful after her drunk husband tried to shoot him."

"Ralph's too busy computing stock gains to throw much of a scare into anyone. I got the flush from Drew when that darlin' little actress from Atlanta was waiting in the wings."

"Sally saw him at the Zederhaus with a French woman."

"Mae's new student?"

"No. I heard she's just out of college and from somewhere out west."

Lois laughed cynically. "Since he's been through everything in the neighborhood, he has to settle for imports."

"He hasn't been through me, thank you."

"And nobody's likely to. You have a prince in Gary and would never do anything to mess it up." Lois finished her drink, plunked the glass on the table and stood. "I have to see to my horse. I gave Kay's freckle-faced kid five bucks to walk him out and groom him."

"Want to go to Hanson's? It's my turn to treat." Bonnie popped out of the chair and swept the glasses off the table so she could return them to the bar.

"Since I'd rather go to Tennyson's, I'll treat. Burgers and ice cream may be your panacea. I need another drink after news like that."

"It's over, Lois."

"As long as I don't hear him, see him or smell him, I can believe that. In my fantasies, I want to lie naked in the moonlight while he does mind-blowing things to me."

After the two women left, Willow sat very still. She replayed the conversation in her head and tried to analyze how she felt. It reminded her of a concert she'd attended at the Iowa State basketball arena. Her seat was in an upper deck and during the concert, she was enfolded in a darkness that created the sensation of floating in suspension above the rotating, lighted stage. With her attention focused on the singer in the island of lights, the music wove a spell of enjoyment into a gentle cocoon of isolation. She forgot reality, became totally absorbed by fantasy and romance. When the concert ended and applause slacked off like the end of a rainstorm on a porch roof, harsh arena lights shattered the spell and she was surrounded by jostling people, hard steel railings and concrete steps.

The conversation Willow had just heard was like the end of the concert. Blunt, crude reality crashed into her mind and blew away the fantasy she'd been trying to rekindle.

The crudeness of Lois's condemnation and Bonnie's matter of fact acceptance of Drew's insincerity exposed his gentleness and intimacy as the pitch of a con man attempting to add one more name to a long list of suckers. Drew had seemed so sincere. But then, so had dream man Larry.

The humiliating memory of how Larry had conned her and made a fool of her flooded Willow's thoughts until she couldn't decide if she wanted to cry or scream. She refused to do either, but she knew she had to do something besides sit like a woodcarving with a charge of dynamite in her teeth. When she looked into the arena, it was empty. That meant Mae would be looking for her. Not wanting to meet her employer with tragedy stamped across her face, Willow jerked herself out of the chair and rushed through a door tritely labeled *Fillies*.

That afternoon, when Willow rode Ko-Ko in a lesson with Mae, she found she liked the horse even more. In just one lesson, both Mae and Ko-Ko taught her to ride with a shared communication that made lateral work an effortless, circular flow of energy from rider to horse, horse to rider. It had been a rewarding lesson that Willow was rehashing in her mind while she pulled straw bales off a stack in the loft and carried them to the chute over the hay room below.

When she turned with the third bale, strong hands snatched it from her. Startled, she watched Drew hurl it across the floor to where it skidded into the chute and disappeared down the hole.

"Do you need more?" Drew took the bale she yanked off the stack.

"Four more." Willow's throat tightened and she felt as if a thorn bush had lodged in her chest. "I told Roy I'd drop them while he emptied the manure spreader. He's in a hurry today."

Drew fired bales at the chute as fast as she could tumble them off the stack. When she started toward the stairs at the far end of the almost empty loft, he caught her wrist.

Willow tensed but didn't fight his hold.

"Is it possible for you to spare a moment and talk to me?"

"That depends on what you want to talk about." Unwilling to meet his eyes, Willow stared at the word *Tanglewood* on a burgundy T-shirt.

"For starters I'd like to know what the hell I did."

"You didn't do anything. I did it myself."

"Did what yourself?"

"Misunderstood your intentions." She tried to shake her arm free, but he had no intention of releasing her. "I'm sorry I unintentionally led you to believe I want what I don't."

"Willow, I haven't the slightest idea of what you just said. We were having fun. I thought we enjoyed each other. All of a sudden it blew up, and you blamed it on Nicole, who has nothing to do with it."

"Maybe she does. Maybe other people do, too. I wasn't being smart the day I met you. I've become wiser now and see things more clearly."

"Wiser about what?" Drew sat on a bale and pulled her onto his lap before she could resist him. "I like you and want to have fun with you. Is that so terrible?" His gaze captivated her; his hands held her waist in gentle restraint.

"It's not terrible." Her voice felt fragile. "I'm just not interested in the same thing you are."

"What am I interested in?" He moved a hand to her back to draw her closer.

Willow had no idea how to answer without making a mess of it. Drew's free hand cradled the back of her head and his lips brushed across the tip of her nose. She shivered and the lump in her chest expanded until she couldn't talk.

"I'm interested in you, Willow, very interested in you."

At the warm touch of his lips, Willow melted against him the way she had when they danced. The alluring caress of his kiss stilled her resistance, reached into the turmoil of her emotions, touched raw pain like a soothing balm. The tightness in her chest lost its grip and a wave of pleasure replaced the tension with an engulfing sense of detachment. Her lips softened to his; the muscles in her jaw relaxed. When the tip of his tongue traced the lines of her lips, a thrill of pleasure shuddered through her. Her hands twisted in the fabric of his shirt as the kiss captured her breath and ignited a surge of heat that spread through her like a flash of wildfire. Her heart pounded as anxiety turned to panic, made her gasp and push away from him.

"No." Willow shook her head and stiffened her arms. His arms dropped away so suddenly she had to catch her balance to keep from falling off his lap. Her hand closed on his forearm as she steadied herself, took control of runaway feelings.

"What's this about?" Drew stared at her.

"I don't want to be talked about as a conquest who can be sent to recycle when someone new comes along. That's not the way I want to play."

"And how *do* you want to play?"

Drew stood so abruptly Willow slid off his lap onto the straw matted floor. There was no pain, but it startled her and she snapped, "I don't want to play your game, all right?"

"Sure, just tell me what my game is."

"You already told me. It's called seduction. I understand you've been playing it since you were sixteen."

"What are you talking about?" Drew recoiled and shielded himself with a scowl.

"I heard you started seducing your father's maids at sixteen and have turned it into a full-time hobby."

"At least two or three at a time." He retorted with a scoffing huff. "That story gets better every time I hear it."

"Is it true?"

"No." He leaned an elbow on the corner of a stacked straw bale and smiled slowly. "The truth is it was one girl and she seduced me. I was indignant at first. Since I'd broken my leg skiing and was confined to a bed or wheel chair, I felt she'd taken advantage of me. Gabby was a feisty, little minx." He cocked his head and lifted an eyebrow. "You remind me of her."

Willow blinked at him in surprise. "Did your father know about it?"

"Not for a while."

"Did he fire her?"

"Dad figured I could find worse ways to get a sex education. He gave me a lecture on discretion and contraceptives and then ignored it. By then, I was an exuberant accomplice."

"Well, I'm not."

"I rather thought you would be." Drew looked disappointed and rubbed a knuckle on his unshaven chin before he pushed away from the bales and gave her a hard look. "Where did you hear these tales of my licentious past?"

"Does the name Lois ring any bells?"

Drew made a sour face. "It certainly does, but I find it hard to believe she would take it on herself to warn you about me."

"I overheard a conversation she had with someone named Bonnie."

"Her friendship with Bonnie is her most redeeming feature."

"What does that mean?" Willow stood, brushed straw off her jeans.

"Bonnie is a good person. She keeps Lois's neuroses in check and tries to temper her drinking. In return, Lois helps her keep her horse. Bonnie's husband was disabled in a motorcycle accident. With three children and Gary to take care of, she needs an outlet. Lois and the horse are a refuge, the friendship a form of symbiosis."

"Lois said she'd rather hate you than forget you."

"She does like to keep things going." Drew shrugged off the subject of Lois. "I came to find out what went wrong between you and me. Although your answer doesn't make much sense, I gather your only interest in me is in regard to your job and my horses. Is that correct?"

"That's correct," Willow answered in a small voice without conviction. When he made no response, she blurted, "Well, no. It isn't all correct. I mean... I'd like to be able to talk to you about the weather... or something."

"Talking, but no touching? Is that what you're saying?"

"That's what I'm saying."

"Okay, but I don't think I'll be very good at it." Drew strode to the open chute, where he grabbed the edge of a wooden ladder, swung toward it and dropped out of sight.

Chapter Eight

After a long phone conversation with Antonio, Andy Sutherland walked from his home office to an adjacent sitting room with cherry wood paneling and comfortable leather furniture and poured himself a double measure of Glendoncroft Single Malt—a world-famous whisky produced by his Scottish relatives. After two swallows of the smoky peat flavored liquor, he switched on a brass table lamp and sat in a leather wingchair. He stared into the pale gold luminescence of the Scotch for a moment before he took a swallow and set it on a table.

Antonio's concerns about Drew's determination to dig into the years he lived with his mother in Philadelphia stirred unwanted misgivings that had been hanging in the back of Andy's mind since last winter and brought him face to face with a closed door he had never expected to reopen. He wanted to turn away, leave it undisturbed and forgotten, but the anxiety circling in his mind told him he no longer had the option of ignoring that door—no way to avoid revisiting the hellish ordeal that followed his ex-wife's death eighteen years ago.

Andy had suppressed, but never forgotten, the incident four months after he brought Drew from Philadelphia to live with him in Paris—an incident disturbing enough to tell him something was seriously wrong with his son...

After sharing a rare and treasured few minutes nestled together in an easy chair, reading silly stories and laughing, Andy wrapped an arm around his eight-year-old son, hoping that, for a brief moment, his love would penetrate the armor of Drew's rejection. To his surprise, the usually brooding child not only let him hug him but returned the affection and looked up with the charming, lopsided smile of the openly loving boy he'd known before his divorce four years earlier.

Feeling a balloon of relief swell inside him, Andy set his hand on a smooth warm cheek and pressed his son against his chest. Lowering his lips to the tumble of dark curls, he kissed the top of the child's head. "I love you, Drew. Why won't you believe me?"

"I want to lo—" The boy's voice faltered, as if his mouth were unable to form words. He tensed, then went limp and his head dropped toward his chest. An instant later, a shuddering spasm convulsed his body. He stiffened, snapped his head up and forcefully rejected the embrace he had earlier welcomed.

When the child pushed away and stood, he was wrapped in an insulated, surly shield that repelled affection and made Andy think of a feral animal—trapped and fighting for its life.

"Why don't you take the book upstairs? You can read some of it before you go to sleep."

"I don't like your stupid books." He gave his father a defiant look that bent the line of insolence before he backed down and slid his eyes toward the stairs. "I don't know why you try and make me read all the time."

"You said you liked to read." Andy held the book out for him to take.

"I don't like shit like that."

"Give it another try. And watch your mouth."

In a reaction of angry dismissal, the boy snatched the book and headed for the stairs in his irritating way of showing compliance and defiance at the same time that left Andy wondering if his son even remembered the moments of closeness and affection they'd just shared.

Later, as he climbed the stairs toward his office, Andy heard shouting in Drew's room. He couldn't understand the words, but the tone was incensed fury. An instant later, it was answered by a voice of equally intense, bullying torment. It made no sense. Drew should have been alone, but there was clearly an argument going on between two distinctly different voices.

"You're stupid and bad." The bossy, insulting voice stopped Andy in the hallway outside Drew's door. "You can't have it."

"I want to read it." This voice sounded distraught, more pleading than demanding.

"I only let you read because shithead makes me."

"That's because you're so stupid you don't know how to read."

"Reading is what you do, but I won't let you if you don't do what I say. He's an evil shithead. I hate him."

"But I like—"

"Get in the room, you little shit."

"No, please no." The response sounded terrified. "It's dark in the room. I don't know anything when I'm in the room."

"I'm throwing it away."

"No! Please don't—" The plea was a shriek of tearful rage that ended with a crash of breaking glass.

Andy heard a crack that sounded like the firing of a small pistol. Panicking, he thrust open the door and burst into the bedroom to meet a glare of defensive arrogance. His son's left cheek was brightly flushed, as if he'd been slapped. Shards of glass lay on the floor below a broken window.

"What happened in here?"

"The window broke."

"Who hit you?"

"Nobody."

Andy crossed the room and looked into the courtyard. Light from the living room spilled across paving stones where the book he'd given Drew lay on its spine, its pages riffling in a light breeze. There was no one in the courtyard. The driveway gate was closed and locked.

He turned back to his son. "What hit you?"

"I hit him."

"Hit whom? There's no one else here."

"He went away. He can't come back."

"Who went away?" Andy clamped down on exasperation and held his voice steady while he tried to make sense of what he was hearing.

"Nobody."

The answer had a stony finality Andy knew was impenetrable. He could try to force Drew to answer, but it would only result in an explosion of anger he wanted to avoid. The child was evading the question, but Andy sensed that what he heard held more truth than he wanted to accept.

"Can I talk to him?"

"I locked him in the room. He's gone."

"Get the vacuum. You need to clean up that glass."

"I don't want to."

"What you want doesn't matter. You broke the window and have to take responsibility. You will clean it up while I cover the opening, and you will help replace it tomorrow."

"It ain't my stupid house."

"You'll do it, and you know it. Now, how far do you want to push this?"

The boy responded to the question with the irascible absurdity of a face-off between a house cat and a Siberian tiger. He clearly knew he was cornered and going to lose. It was merely a matter of which would win out: his defiance, or his intelligence.

"If I get to three, you'll get spanked and still do it, so get smart." Andy paused for a moment, looking for a hint of compliance. "One." The boy's jaw tightened; uncertainty and indecision flickered in his gaze. "Two." The defiance collapsed and the child stomped toward the hall.

"It was a reprimand," Andy said. "I expect a reply."

His son hesitated, then snarled, "I'll do it."

"Thank you." Andy relaxed with a resigned sigh when his son left the room with stiff strides that were just short of angry stomps.

Common sense had been winning more often lately. Andy felt he was getting Drew to think about behavior control—except for last week, when, instead of capitulating, he shouted, "You can't make me do it, you fucking asshole!"

At first, the boy had fought with loud curses. Then, he shuddered and, as if he turned off a switch, the fight went out of him and he took the last of the punishment with tearful regret instead of defiance. When reminded that he should have remembered what he'd been told would happen the last time he used those words, the clearly repentant child sniffed back tears and insisted he didn't remember the words and there hadn't been a last time. The statement irritated Andy, but he had passed it off as remorseful denial and let it go.

Tonight's incident made Andy wonder if maybe Drew was so far into denial, he actually didn't know whether he was telling the truth or not. The realization made him uneasy enough that after the glass was cleaned up and Drew was in bed, Andy went to his office and called Dr. Paul Reynard, the only child psychiatrist he felt comfortable with and Drew had been willing to talk to at all.

❖

Paul Reynard was a small lively man in his mid-thirties with intense hazel-green eyes and an overgrown mane of ginger hair that defied all attempts to manage it. He had a bushy moustache and chin beard he constantly played with when he thought. He was French, but had been born in Virginia and spent most of the first eighteen years of his life there while his father served in various diplomatic posts in Washington. After receiving a university medical degree in France, Paul had returned to the States for advanced study in psychiatry at Stanford University. He had practiced child psychiatry in both New York and Ann Arbor for six years before returning to Paris with his Michigan born musician wife. His American English was excellent.

Andy was sure Dr. Reynard's success at getting Drew to talk to him could be attributed to his wry sense of humor and the way he both ignored the child and made himself intriguing at the same time. Whenever Andy dropped Drew off, the man seemed to be doing something, or playing with something that caught Drew's attention. Before long, the psychiatrist turned the encounter into a puzzling challenge and waved Andy out of the room.

After two weeks of leaving them alone for two hours a day, Andy was beginning to wonder if he was paying for a psychiatrist or a playmate. All Drew talked about when he took him home was the games they played, or more often, what they constructed out of Lego bricks, an old erector set, or an assortment of other building toys—as if he didn't have enough of that stuff at home. After two more sessions, Andy had an appointment of his own. He showed up with a determined chip on his shoulder looking for more information than he was getting from Drew.

When Andy arrived at Dr. Reynard's renovated nineteenth century town house and entered the old library where he'd been leaving Drew, the psychiatrist was perched on a child size chair straddling a small table with his knees sticking out to the sides. He stared at a chess board while he twisted a hank of beard between his thumb and forefinger.

Andy looked down at the board and said, "You're mated."

"In only sixteen moves. I'm still wondering how he did it so fast."

"I taught him the fundamentals of chess when he was four. He recently told me he often played with an old black man in the park in Philadelphia. He's very good at games. I already know Drew likes to play games and build things. We've been doing it for months. He likes to ride ponies, and he's taking Karate with me. I'm not paying you to tell me what he likes to do."

"What are you paying me to do?"

"Tell me what's wrong with him. As succinctly as possible."

"I can do that, but I don't promise succinctness. Would you like to sit down?" When Andy gave the chair across the table a scathing look, Paul Reynard laughed and pointed to his adjacent office. "My notes are in there."

"Good. I'd rather not pay to play chess for two hours."

"I'm beginning to understand where your son gets his arrogance and pithy sense of humor." The psychiatrist crossed the room and opened the office door for Andy.

"Drew used to have a great sense of humor. In fact, he used to laugh a lot and have fun. He doesn't let it out much anymore." Andy stood by an upholstered arm chair and waited to sit until Paul walked around the desk and sat in a leather swivel chair that dwarfed him. "What did she do? Take the fun out of him?"

"In a word, Mr. Sutherland, yes."

"Please, I'd rather you call me Andy. I have the feeling I'm not going to be able to maintain an impersonal relationship with you."

"You are right about that. However, you may—"

Andy held up a hand to stop him. "Continue to refer to you as Dr. Reynard. You are the professional. The personal exposure is mine. I get that part of it."

"I'm glad you do. Many parents expect me to fix the child without understanding the parents."

"You only have one parent left. I told you as much as I could about the other one."

"And a grandmother. She was an important influence this summer."

"How do you know about her?" The statement startled Andy. "I didn't mention her."

"Drew did. Do you really think all we did was play for twenty expensive hours?"

"That's all Drew talked about."

"It's probably all he wanted to talk about, or remembered to talk about. He didn't want to talk about anything else with me, either."

"What's your secret? All I get is a mouthful of egotistical defiance. I can't get him to talk about himself at all."

"My secret is hypnosis. You signed a form that allowed me to use it as a means of therapy. Drew is extremely susceptible to hypnosis, which, along with his exceptionally high IQ and ability to visualize both logistical and imaginative probabilities, was a significant clue to discovering his disorder. My education, experience and knowledge of recent research supports my diagnosis."

"What is your diagnosis?" Andy felt uneasy about the hypnosis—something his skeptical mind related to trickery.

"Your son exhibits overwhelming evidence of a dissociative disorder that has had a number of labels over the years. It is most commonly called Multiple Personality Disorder."

"Like the schizophrenic nonsense in that *Three Faces of Eve* movie?" Andy frowned.

"For various reasons, the movie was not completely accurate, but it was not nonsense, nor is it schizophrenia, which displays intermittent periods of psychotic behavior accompanied by irrational delusions. Your son is not psychotic, nor is he clinically delusional. He is very sane. In fact, his problem was brought on by his need to protect his sanity from extreme psychological trauma. I surmise it is a result, as you have suspected, of the delusional and obsessive behavior of his mother. Drew's mind learned to dissociate himself from the unbearable sense of helplessness he felt as the victim of her abusive obsessions and vengeful rages. In fact, his dissociative defenses worked so well his mind continued to protect him by creating other children to take emotional abuses he was unable to cope with."

"Other children?"

"In effect, yes. His psyche created them by withdrawing his own consciousness and replacing it with invented personae who could handle experiences that made him feel helpless. Besides Drew himself, there seem to be four other personalities and a shadow of one I'm not too sure about. To avoid confusion, we'll call them by the names that came with them."

"They have names?" The thought startled Andy, who was still trying to grasp what the psychiatrist meant by personae.

"In Drew's case they don't all have what you would call names but they do have identities; and, as far as I can tell, only two of them have reached an advanced enough level of sophisticated involvement that they're demanding to be recognized by names. They are mostly identified by labels.

"The first two to emerge were Dead Boy and Crybaby. They are the children who suffered the distress and horror Drew couldn't handle. Crybaby seems to have appeared at about four or five years old and is undeveloped because he was only present during periods of intolerable stress. Dead Boy is an anesthetic personality, who has the autohypnotic ability to be impervious to pain and trauma, both physical and emotional, while remaining aware in a sort of out of body way. He is basically useless at present because he only had one function: when traumas became intolerable, Crybaby checked out and left it to Dead Boy. Then there's Buffo, who appears to be anywhere from four to six, but it's hard to learn much about him. He hasn't been out for quite a while and only has one role. Buffo is music. All he does is sing. His tonal quality is very good and makes me think music could be an important part of your son."

"His mother was a wonderful singer—before alcohol and drugs messed her up."

"Buffo sang to me in Italian and told me he used to sing with his mother's angel."

"Where did that come from?" Andy gave him a bewildered look.

"I assume it means they shared a love for music and each other when they sang together. He's separated that memory of her and likened it to an angel."

"Carlotta started singing to him when he was a baby. I remember them laughing and singing in Italian when he was a toddler. Drew used to sing to me and I loved it, but he doesn't anymore. He said he forgot how." Andy thought back to the last time he remembered hearing the clear, crystal tones of his son singing. "He was just four when things went terribly wrong in our marriage, and I was gone before he turned five. Are you telling me that's when she started abusing him?"

"That's when he found a way to defend himself against it. I don't know when it started." Paul waved off the irrelevance of the question with a flourish of his hand before he glanced down at the open notebook on his desk.

"The Drew I knew was a brave kid," Andy said. "He took falls, injuries, even corrections, in stride."

"That was my impression, too. And it would take a more serious and terrifying trauma than the irrational physical attacks that your wife's brother, Antonio, informed you about to force Drew to dissociate."

"How could she let herself hurt a child that much?"

"From what Drew implied, I assume that when she lost rational control through psychotic delusions brought on by her indiscriminate use of drugs and alcohol, she was unaware of her child as anything but an outlet for rage against everything wrong in her life. Based on what I've gleaned from Drew, it appears that not long after you started spending a lot of time in Europe, your wife became obsessed with the belief that the body and mind could be cleansed of poisons by fasting and purging."

"I'm aware of that." Andy frowned. "I told her it was a bunch of crap and she'd get better results by staying away from alcohol the way she did when she was pregnant. I never heard any more about it."

"Apparently, it didn't go away. Instead, it evolved into a fixation that told her Drew was possessed by an evil demon that wanted to destroy her soul. Whenever she felt evil was controlling him, she made him fast then forced purgatives into him and left him locked in a dark room until the supposed possession was expelled from his body. Alone, engulfed by shame and dark terrors, he must have feared for his life, to say nothing of his sanity."

"She starved a child and..." Andy recoiled, unable to voice the revulsion assaulting his mind "That's crazy."

"An accurate vernacular label."

"I had no idea it was that bad." Andy clenched his fists and rubbed them into his thighs while he subdued a furious, pointless guilt that hung in his chest like a wad of frozen pain.

"It happened. And you did what you could. Get over it," Paul sharply dismissed the blame. "I doubt if anyone knew how bad it was, except Drew, who was faced with a critical dilemma in which his loving provider was also his torturer, and his psyche found a way to deal with it. It's unusual to discover and be able to treat this disorder at such an early stage. As a rule, such extreme abuse is kept hidden from outsiders by both abuser and victim. About the age of eight, a child begins to gain the ability to separate reality from imagination and starts to sense how he relates to the wider world around him. At that point, if he realizes he is out of step with the norm, he learns to cover his abnormality. I would say another year would have made this much more difficult."

"Do you know how preposterous this sounds?"

"Yes, I do. It is irrational, but it is also true. The human mind is ingenious, and one of the most important functions of a healthy mind is to protect itself from trauma. Unfortunately, some of the ways it chooses to accomplish this create other problems. Drew's psyche carefully, and rather cleverly, boxed off portions of his mind and put other ego states in those boxes to deal with the traumas they contained. However, since those ego states start to believe they are separate people, they strengthen as individuals whenever they are aware. That is what happened with Jack, who surfaced not long after you disappeared from his life. Jack, who is the main problem, insists he's fifteen years old and adopted."

"What?" Andy recoiled and stared at him in stunned surprise.

"Apparently he doesn't want to claim either of you as parents."

"Whom does he claim?"

"No one. Jack doesn't think he needs parents. He was created to be a big brother, an older, tougher kid, who could deal with a mean step cousin, as well as other neighborhood bullies. He not only filled that role; he started to dominate and became the controlling personality. He doesn't know about the earlier ones, any more than Drew does."

"Drew obviously knows about Jack."

"Oh, yes, for at least two years the way I read it."

"You said there may be another one."

"Avenger, but I'm not sure about that. The name could be a recent imaginary fancy, or an older splinter personality—but that's a side issue. The central conflict, which you have exacerbated is between Drew and Jack."

"How did I do that?" Andy straightened in the chair. "And how can I stop doing it and put things back to normal?"

"The last thing you want to do is put things back to what was normal before you reentered his life, but it's a moot point since there is no way you can do that without giving up on your son."

"That I will never do." Andy shot out of the chair, planted his fists on the desk and leaned toward the smaller man in a direct challenge of authority.

"Exactly." Without a sign of retreat, the psychiatrist lifted his furry chin and stared back. "The first thing we need to get straight between us is that this is not my problem. It is yours and your son's, and there is no way I can help without your involvement and cooperation. There are no drugs that will fix it, only an interactive therapy that requires support from you. I have the education and knowledge to treat the problem, but I need you to believe in what I'm doing and give Drew the strength he needs to conquer and control it. Now, do we have an understanding about that?"

Andy battled with his self-protective, dominant nature for a long tense moment before he backed down and returned to his chair. "Yes."

"Accepted." Paul nodded. "Before you reentered Drew's life, Jack was thoroughly in control and only allowed Drew out when he needed him. When you reappeared and won through to Drew, he found the courage to override Jack's control long enough to stand up in court and testify against the man who destroyed his mother. That act of courage infuriated Jack and the result is that ever since then, when Drew is out, Jack can't control him the way he used to. Therefore, he tries not to let him come out." Paul quirked his lips and added, "Jack is the insolent brat who irritates you so much."

"How do you know that?"

"By listening to both Drew and Jack."

"Jack talked to you about himself?"

"Once I let him know I was willing to listen to his bullshit, I couldn't shut him up." Paul smiled at Andy's blank look. "He's an arrogant little bastard who thinks he runs the world."

"He's mostly surly to me."

"He doesn't like you because you're an arrogant big bastard and think you run the world."

Andy tensed and met the hard, olive stare with one that matched its intensity. "He lies; he cheats; he steals. He has a mouth out of the gutter in both English and Italian, no respect for rules and expects me to let him do whatever he wants. You better believe I'm going to run his world. Or is it their world? You seem to be telling me I have five different kids to deal with. Which is absurd."

"You only have two you have to worry about. Buffo is shy and only comes out if he is coaxed out with music. Crybaby and Dead Boy are no longer needed. The abuse is over."

"There are people who might not agree with that." Andy frowned. "I believe in discipline. Some of it hurts."

"I've been hearing about that." Paul glanced down at his desk and closed the notebook before he looked up and smiled at Andy's defensive glower. "I certainly hope you're going to run their world. There hasn't been any meaningful discipline in four years."

"Believe me; I'm well aware of that."

"The way I see it, your discipline sets boundaries for reasonable expectations of behavior that tell him you care who he is. It is based on a logical demand for respect, not an emotional lack of control or demeaning domination. The only thing I'm going to advise is that it would be best if you made sure you punished the right one. It's the kind of dirty trick Jack likes to pull on Drew. He keeps Drew in the dark then pushes him out and abandons him during a punishment in order to avoid facing the consequences for his own behavior."

"You mean I punished a kid who didn't know he was wrong?" Andy looked horrified.

"It's not like he isn't used to the trick," Paul said. "As far as I can tell, it only happened once with you. Something to do with Jack calling you a fucking asshole a while ago."

"That was one of my wife's favorite goads and a button he learned to push right away." Andy grimaced. "He has a habit of mouthing off in front of people and my dignity won't accept it. Since it wasn't the first time he called me that, I did what I told him I'd do. But it was a few swats on his backside with a hairbrush not a beating and didn't do more than sting."

"Andy, he's not afraid of your spankings. It's more that he doesn't like them—"

"He's not supposed to like them." Andy gave him an indignant scowl.

"Consequently, he tries everything he can to avoid them."

"How about obeying? That option is always available."

"He's working on that, but he sees it the same way you see spankings—as a last resort. If it keeps getting pushed to last resorts, you have to win, or your bad boy gets stronger."

"What does that mean?"

"It's a battle, Andy. A fight to the death."

"Not with me." Andy bristled. "I'm strict, not brutal."

"It's about you, but it's between Drew and Jack, his controlling personality. You can't reason them out of it. Neither can I. In order to end this mess, Drew has to win, but he isn't strong enough to do that yet. In the meantime, we have to see them as separate individuals and treat them accordingly. It's vitally important that we accept what's there to keep Jack from covering it up. No matter how you feel about it, don't tell him he's crazy or a freak. His stepfather did and it incensed him."

"I wouldn't do that. Look what's happened because his mother called him bad and evil."

"It gave Jack more power. He doesn't care if he's bad and doesn't believe he's evil. He does, however, use similar accusations to control Drew, who thinks it's true and the abuse was deserved."

"Does he actually call himself Jack? I've never heard it."

"Jack is the name Drew's unconscious mind gave to the persona it created. To strengthen his claim to dominance, Jack insists Drew is Andrew. I suspect it's either because his mother called him Andrew when she berated him, or his first-grade teacher did because it was his given name. When told he's always been called Drew, Jack insists Drew is only a nickname people stupidly use for both of them because they don't know or care who they really are. Right now, I suspect Drew is on the defensive because the loss of the Drew identity would further weaken the personality we need to strengthen. Drew needs our help to defeat Jack."

"By killing him? That's outrageous."

"Symbolically," Paul stated crossly. "In effect, Drew needs to kill off the identity of Jack so he can integrate the personality into his own and absorb Jack's memories—or else make peace with him so they can exist in a shared state of coexistence."

"I don't know as I want him in Drew."

"Of course, you do. Neither of them is complete without the other. I expect the others will fuse spontaneously by the time those two are integrated."

"How can I help? All he wants to do lately is fight with me and hate me. I took him to Pennsylvania this summer to be with my mother because I thought he needed a strong mother image in his life."

"He did, and it worked, with Drew-Andrew." Paul paused and thought a moment before he said. "To make things easier, I suggest we avoid jerking Jack's chain by referring to his counterpart as Drew-Andrew when Jack is out. For some reason I don't understand, Jack is willing to accept the double name identity but stubbornly rejects the name Drew."

"They are both parts of his name." Andy shrugged. "Mother often called him Andrew to get his full attention, just as she still does to me when I try to ignore her. At first, he seemed to like her and we had some good times." Andy thought back to the confusing weeks he and Drew had recently spent with his mother. "Then he turned on her. I brought him here before he offended her."

"Jack turned against her," Paul said. "He didn't know how to deal with her, just as he didn't know how to deal with their first-grade teacher in Philadelphia, so he mostly retreated in their presence. Like your mother, the teacher refused to be intimidated by Jack and was able to encourage Drew's reading and learning skills. The second-grade teacher was a pushover for Jack, so he started coming out more, even in school. By last winter, Drew-Andrew was mostly inactive. It was Jack who refused to behave and was expelled from the schools you sent him to here in Paris. When you stayed with your mother over the summer, she was as openly loving and as consistently firm as you are. It gave Drew more strength. When she opened him up to you, Jack wouldn't stand for it, so he came back and attacked her. He doesn't trust love or kindness, and he sees you as the enemy, just as your wife did."

"I don't know why I became an enemy to her."

"I can't tell you for sure, but I suspect it was because you offered her the wealth she craved, then took it away and became a tightwad when you ran short of money."

"That's probably right." Andy wilted into the chair. "My pride thought she wanted me, but it was more likely my wealth. It wasn't even status with her, just money: for clothes, jewelry, alcohol, good times and, at the end, drugs. That was one of the few things I should have listened to my father about."

"You don't have a good relationship with your father?"

"I had a horrible relationship with my father, but it's a non-issue now because he died two months ago."

"Was he the disciplinarian?"

"No, my mother was. She has rigid rules of ethical behavior. My father had one rule: take what you want and screw anyone who gets in your way. His only interests were being rich and manipulating people with his money. He didn't care if he made money ethically, only that he made it."

"Your ethics are your mother's?"

"Hers and a long line of Scottish ancestors. My father was a distant, American relative eighteen years older than my mother. He married her because she was the daughter of an earl. He was greedy and obsessed with the status symbol of being a descendant of aristocracy. However, he lost all chance of benefitting from the connection when the Scots learned more about him. While my mother and I were warmly accepted as family, he was not."

"Interesting." Paul raised thick eyebrows and gave Andy a probing look. "So, you want to raise your son as an honorable aristocrat."

"Not at all." Andy answered with a scoff. "I want to raise him as an honest man I can be proud of for standing on his own in an honorable way. I don't care how people see my ancestry, but I do care how they see me and my family in regard to integrity and authority."

"You really are arrogant."

"I'm twenty-nine years old and my father's deteriorating health put me in charge of a company that, thanks to his greed, is absurdly out of date and has a reputation for unethical dealings. Instead of rewarding integrity, he fostered avarice. As a result, he was being robbed by corrupt underlings. I'm trying to turn it around. That means I've been upsetting a lot of apple carts and firing the rotten apples. I need all the arrogance I can muster."

Andy leaned back, crossed an ankle over his knee and made a wry face. "Just between me, you and the walls, it scares the hell out of me, but I'm not going to quit because of it. Now you've made me feel guilty for what I let happen to my son." He dropped his foot to the floor and sat forward with his hands grasping the arms of the chair. "But I'm not going to quit on him. I don't want to hurt him, or add to the abuse he's suffered, but I don't know how to be anything but what I am."

"I like you, Andy." A wide grin interrupted the chaos of beard and moustache. "If you can hang on to that determination through this, you'll have a good shot at raising that man."

"If he can ever forgive me for what I did to him." Andy felt his defiance crumble under a weight of regret.

"I think he will." Paul smiled. "He's a nice kid."

"Most of the time I think so, too." Andy relaxed, even smiled. "But there's something here that puzzles me. If Jack is a control freak, how did you get him to let you talk to Drew?"

"Through hypnosis I can hold Jack away, but not for long. He's as stubborn as his father."

"Thanks." Andy frowned.

"Don't take that wrong. You're going to need to give some of it to Drew. He's a little shaky in determination. His self-confidence has been trampled on too much."

"And I hurt him again."

"I doubt if it will make you feel any better, but Drew knows who is to blame for what happened three weeks ago—and it isn't you."

"Which one is the son I used to know?"

"In reality they all are, but the one we call Drew, and Jack insists is Andrew, is the only one who should remember you. We have to get him to do that because to all appearances, he is the center, or birth personality, the most complete person."

"Then why isn't he the one in charge?"

"Because he's the vulnerable one—the one who can love and be hurt by it."

"Why isn't he just Drew to Jack?" Andy asked as the twisted reasoning continued to baffle him.

"I can only surmise about the names. Drew's unconscious mind originally gave the personality he sees as an older brother the name of Jack."

Andy stiffened in surprise before he said, "I think maybe I did it. I used to tease him by calling him a little Jackanapes because he was so mischievous."

"That's possible, because in some ways, Jack was a replacement for you. However, since people predictably called him Drew, not Jack, the dominant personality is trying to take the name away from Drew—or at least I think he's trying to—by insisting his younger brother is Andrew, not Drew. The real Drew is fighting to keep his identity. He wants to reach you but is afraid of his controller."

"Why did he create Jack if he can't control him?"

"Andy, Drew did not consciously create any of this. It was a kneejerk psychic reaction, not a deliberate act. Jack was created to be a psychic tool to fight battles for him. He was created to be hard, fearless and invulnerable." Paul frowned. "However, he is mostly strong-minded, selfish, angry and amoral. The personae grow and become more aware of their internal environments, just as any individual does. The paradox is that the protector often becomes the aggressor and takes on the role of the abuser. Consequently, Jack has gained the power to control Drew, who is starting to believes he's Andrew, and it scares him."

"What is he afraid of? What can Jack do to him?"

"He can continue to make him feel he is bad, and therefore, irredeemable. He can force him into the dark room and abandon him to an unknowing void."

"But if Drew doesn't feel anything in the room, how can he suffer?" Venting exasperation, Andy shot out of the chair and charged back and forth in front of the desk.

"He fears being put in *the room* because he knows it contains what terrified him and he will be alone and helpless." Paul paused until Andy returned to the chair and looked at him with a probing gaze that searched him for clarification. "Drew can't fight him alone. He needs your help. Jack doesn't like you because you make him behave and threaten his control. You don't terrify him, but he doesn't like your rules and restrictions or the inevitable consequences if he fails to obey. He either suffers the punishment or runs away and lets

Drew take it. But that isn't working too well. It exposes Drew to you. Jack is afraid of that."

"Why?"

"The more Drew interacts with you, the more he wants to accept you, which makes Jack's resolve stronger."

"How do you know that?"

"He tried to tell me, but Jack grew furious enough to break my control and then forced him back into the room. You can't change the rules on him now."

"I won't punish him for something he had no control over doing." Andy gave the man a grim stare. "That's totally wrong to me."

"Then you will be letting Jack win." Paul slapped the folder closed. "As you indicated earlier, he pays no attention to anything else. If you want to be in control, you have to be yourself. You have to maintain the structure you have established and live up to your word. Your consistency is the only thing that deters Jack and should make sense to Drew. I surmise it was there before the separation and the traumas he suffered without you."

"When he first came back, I thought I had an undisciplined, disobedient brat on my hands. I told him what I thought of his behavior and exactly how I planned to deal with it."

"That brat is exactly what you do have." The power behind the quiet voice silenced Andy, captured his attention. "You have to deal with it and civilize the wild child, or the lost center of Drew won't have a chance against the dominant brat."

"If I don't feel right about it, I won't do it."

"Do you know when he switches?" Paul asked.

Andy started, then thought back to the incident that had alerted him. "I think so. When he turned cold and I tried to hold him, I felt him shudder. He stiffened for a moment, like a long, drawn-in breath, then snapped his head up."

"Yes, that's when he switches, and it can happen very quickly." Paul snapped his fingers. "Try not to miss it."

"But when he was arguing with himself, there were no pauses. His voice and tone changed in an instant." Feeling as if his mind were running circles around a concept that he was unable to grasp, Andy dropped into the chair.

"They were both out in a state of co-presence, where both are struggling for possession of the body. It's the opening and closing of barriers that causes the shudder. It's like a psychic shock wave to him. The process varies with multiples, but there is always a discernible transition of some sort. Learn to switch with him. When Jack retreats, he gives you a chance to reach the boy you want to find. You probably won't succeed right away. As soon as Jack realizes what's happening, he'll come back and take whatever steps are necessary to keep you from finding the boy who needs you. He will either have to stop fighting you or hurt. As brash and arrogant as Jack is, he isn't very stoic. He never had to be. He could always run away and let Drew suffer, then come back when it was safe."

"You said Drew doesn't know anything when he's in the room." Andy grappled with a logic that was becoming more convoluted all the time. "How can Jack know what's happening when he's in the room?"

"I'll answer that when you come in tomorrow." Paul popped a cassette out of the recorder on his desk and handed it to Andy. "Take this home. Relisten to the session and make notes on what confuses you."

"It's more a matter of accepting than understanding." Andy held the psychiatrist's gaze for a long moment then nodded. "I'll try to do that."

❖

Andy finished a chapter of *Treasure Island*, thumped the book on the table and scooped his pajama clad son up onto his shoulders as he stood and clownishly lurched across the floor. "Aye, me pirate lad, there's a big blow comin' and 'tis time to climb the riggin' and tumble into bed."

Halfway up the stairs, when Andy staggered into the railing, he felt small fingers twist in his hair while loud giggles thrilled him. They fell on the bed and lay laughing at nothing until the giggles stopped and the boy in his arms lay still and quiet with a wary look that bordered on fear.

"Are you hurt?" When the boy shook his head and gave his father a timid smile, Andy asked, "Drew, what's wrong?"

"Why do you call me Drew all the time?"

The sudden question startled Andy. He sat up, pulled his son onto his lap and hugged him. "I've always called you Drew. It's your name."

"My name is Andrew," the child answered with a firm pout.

"So is mine, but most people call me Andy. I gave you the name Drew because I like it and I love you. But if you want to be called Andrew, it's okay with me."

Andy saw a flash of fear in the child's eyes, felt a shudder and held him closer. When the boy relaxed, Andy looked down at a very serious and thoughtful face. "I know your real name is Andrew, but I still like Drew because to me, it means you."

"It's okay. You can call me Drew if you want. Uncle Tonio called me that. I liked him."

"He's a good guy, Drew. I like him, too." Andy smiled, tucked the boy into bed, kissed his forehead and ruffled his dark curls before he turned on the night light that held back the darkness his son didn't like and closed the door.

Yesterday's revelations plagued Andy most of the night and when he, once again, faced Paul Reynard, the chip had fallen off his shoulder and his determination to conquer this new challenge overrode his doubts. He met the psychiatrist's steady green gaze and said, "You win. I concede."

"What did I win?"

"My trust. My son insisted he was Andrew, not Drew. My son is Drew to me and he looked frightened when I told him I gave him the name Drew because I love him."

"Which is exactly why Jack is trying to take the name away from him by locking him in the dark room."

"Yesterday you said Jack doesn't go in the room?"

"The dark room is not real, Andy. It exists in Drew's mind. It's where Jack puts Drew to punish him, just as his mother used to lock him in a dark pantry."

"If Jack doesn't go in the room, where does he go?"

"The answer depends on which one you ask." Paul swiveled the big chair and unlocked a drawer in the long credenza behind his desk. "I think you should hear Drew's response to it. I find it puzzling."

"Will he tell me?"

"Since he's already told me, you can hear it now." Paul closed the drawer and propelled the chair into a corner of the room where he slid a video cassette into the slot below a large monitor. "You may have a better idea of what he's talking about than I do."

Andy started to ask how that was possible. The question left his mind when his son's image filled the screen. He was sitting cross-legged on a beanbag chair with his head tipped down as if he were studying the relaxed hands that rested, palms-up, on his thighs.

"What's the matter with him?" Andy asked. "I don't think he's ever sat that still in his life."

"He's hypnotized." Paul chuckled. "But you're right about his energy. Even when I get him under, it's hard to hold him there without keeping his mind busy."

When Dr. Reynard's recorded voice said, "Drew, I need to ask you some questions," there was no response. After a pause the voice said, "Alright, have it your way. Andrew, are you listening to me?" The boy's body shuddered, then stiffened. When his head snapped up, he wriggled to settle himself into the cushion, leaned his elbows on his knees and rested his chin on clasped hands. "Sure. What do you want to know?"

"You told me Jack doesn't live with you. Where does he live?"

"In a secret room. I got to look in it once before he hid it."

"What's his room like?"

The boy sat up with a grin brightening his face and eyes. "It's full of light from big windows with gold curtains. It has blue walls and smells like ginger cookies. There's a painted horse and gold lions with big yellow eyes. And there are lots of books he can't read. I asked him if I could visit his room and read the books and sit on his horse again. He said he didn't have a horse in his room and wouldn't let me ride it if he did." The child's face fell and he crumpled into the hollow of the chair. "He says horses are dumb. He doesn't like them because they can bite."

The screen went blank and Andy gaped at the psychiatrist until he was able to voice what was filling his mind. "He just described the drawing room in my mother's house. But how could he know that? It was redecorated two years ago. The walls are now light green; the drapes are patterned. The carrousel horse was sent out to be repainted and my mother plans to move it to the conservatory. Only the books and the brass lion andirons are still there."

"Did you ever take him there before the divorce?"

"I took him to see my mother on her birthday." Andy thought for a moment. "She was in the drawing room. But he was only three years old. What does a three-year-old know about drapes and who can read books?"

"Very little, but all he needed was an image within his mind. The words of his description come from now. He said the lions were gold, not brass, because he doesn't know there is a difference, or that the melting point of gold is too low for fire irons. If it was your vision, you wouldn't have said gold because your knowledge of metals would instantly reject that choice. He said curtains while you said drapes. The world he's known doesn't have drapes. He draws on images and knowledge already in his mind to create his alters and their worlds. Drew vividly remembers sensory details and his memory borders on photographic. It is common for a multiple to give his alters a place to stay when they aren't out—what we call an innerscape. Drew's is a large country house, but he says he stays in a playhouse in the garden and never goes inside."

Andy nodded. "That may have come from the picture of Sutherland Manor I had on my desk. There was no playhouse, but there was a gazebo in the garden. He liked to hold the picture and look at it when he was in the office with me."

"When is your mother's birthday?"

"Late November."

"He was almost four, already distressed by his mother's instability and sensitive to tensions in your marriage. That visit to your mother's home must have seemed like an escape to Fantasyland."

"He was excited when he first saw the house last summer, but he seemed disappointed after we went inside."

"There was nothing familiar to him inside because he created his innerscape from older memories and images. However, that drawing room, with its gaily painted horse and brass lions, must have made a strong emotional impression. Do you have any idea why he said he wanted to sit on the horse again?"

"I put him on it. He kept laughing and stroking its wooden mane."

"It was a room with love in it. He put Jack in it because he created Jack as a replacement for you—Jack's as blond as you are by the way."

"How can he be? Doesn't he ever see himself?"

"Only internally. If he was out and, unknowingly, glanced at a reflection in a mirror or window, he would likely see the image of Drew. If he knew he was looking at himself, he would most likely see a blond adolescent."

"That's impossible."

"Maybe to your logical mind. We're talking about a child's mind, and I don't remember saying logic has a whole lot to do with it. It's part of Jack's identity. He sees what he believes he should see. We all do that to some extent. It's what can make eyewitness accounts unreliable. I've known emaciated anorexics who look in a mirror and see a fat person."

"Are you saying Jack is like me?"

"Andy, Jack never knew you, and any role models he had were nothing like you. Therefore, except for memories Drew's unconscious mind used to create him, and a few inherent characteristics of Drew's, he could never be like you."

"Why not? He's in the same mind as Drew."

"Jack has his own consciousness and memories, not Drew's. And they won't share those memories until they are able to form a connection of integrated consciousness. Anyway, Jack says he goes away to a house I suspect was taken from a television sit-com, most likely *Happy Days*. Jack doesn't know what Drew is thinking and feeling. He does, however, have an uncanny sense of what Drew is up to and when he is likely to threaten his control. From what he said, the best explanation I can think of is that it's a neural sensing of threat or danger and then an emotional wariness that's like watching through a fuzzy, sensory surveillance camera to see if he needs to focus in and interfere."

"That's eerie." Andy shivered and shook his head.

"I see it as encouraging. It makes me believe that something about you is causing the barriers to weaken."

"What should I do?"

"What you are doing. Keep the rules reasonable and consistent. Teach him to respect them and you by firmly making him obey.

Whenever you get the chance, try to reach Drew. If they want to fight, let them fight. Stop it only if it gets out of control."

"How do I break up a fight between one person?" Andy's question was exasperated. "I can't send them to different rooms."

"Subdue him until they give up."

"Oh my God." An errant fear grabbed Andy's chest. "What if Jack tells him to run into traffic?"

"It won't happen. Sanity and the body's instincts and reflexes will protect the body they both need." Paul thought for a moment, then said, "Try thinking of him as a set of fraternal twins in one body."

"I'm grasping the concept. I'm having trouble with the reality. When I tried to imagine how he could slap himself and tell me nobody hit him, I felt as if I'd walked into the *Twilight Zone*. How can he not know he slapped himself?"

"Andy, stop trying to fit it into your reality and accept what you witness."

"I'm trying, but I'm afraid of messing him up even more."

"If you stay fair and consistent, you really can't lose. Jack will either learn to obey and act more civilized to avoid restrictions and punishments, or he'll have to risk letting you interact with Drew, who told me he likes you."

"He did?"

"Most certainly. However, he's afraid you won't want him and will leave him when you find out he's bad."

"Didn't you tell him otherwise?"

"He isn't going to believe it from me. It has to come from you."

"I constantly tell him he isn't bad and that I love him."

"He has to feel it, not just hear it, because someone else tells him you're a liar and that you will desert him again. Jack is very possessive and doesn't want you to have Drew or, to him Andrew. Drew-Andrew is accustomed to believing whatever Jack tells him."

"Where does Jack get this stuff?"

"From your ex-wife. It's what she told him."

"If she wasn't already dead, I'd kill her."

"Really?" Paul's eyes widened. "Is that genuine or rhetorical?"

"Rhetorical. I may have been enraged enough to think I wanted to kill a few times in my life, but it was never a genuine intention."

Andy shrugged it off and met the psychiatrist's amused expression. "Can you suggest anything I can do to get through to Drew?"

"Keep him reading. Jack can't and has to let Drew out to do it."

"He can't read at all?"

"At a very basic level, like *MacDonald's* and *Coca-Cola*, but he doesn't like to. This has made Drew more advanced in education. Jack, who associated with older boys, is advanced in social behavior."

"Which ones speak Italian?"

"They all do. Buffo almost exclusively. Drew is more comfortable with it than Jack. Both of them are learning French. It's a matter of natural social adaptation in a child, but Jack is learning it faster because he's out more."

Paul glanced at his watch and closed the file. "I'd like a few more sessions alone with Drew. After that I want you to stay so you can offer the parental contact he needs. I have some tapes I want you to watch alone. They will help you understand the situation. When Drew's ready to trust you, we'll try to get him to accept what he has to do. They are both going to fight this. No matter how much we see the need for integration, Jack will realize that it means he can no longer exist as the person he believes he is. He does not want to die."

"And I don't want to kill him."

"Rhetorically, Andy, the same way you said you wanted to kill your wife."

"Not even that." Andy felt helplessly confused, and after he thought about it, said, "There are things I like about Jack."

"Everything he is will be in Drew, but he won't be as defiant, because the sensible, feeling, moral parts of Drew will be there to temper him. If you feel bad about eliminating Jack, think how Drew will feel. He will be losing a brother. Not the nicest of brothers but still a brother. They don't always fight with each other. Drew will miss him and feel guilty for losing him. You may have to be both father and brother to him for a while."

"How do I do that?"

"It shouldn't be hard. Drew's fun to play with. I think you might be, too. Jack was created because Drew had no father to protect him and no brother to share his life."

"It's a daunting challenge."

"I'll offer you a little advice. You're still young. Don't let that business of yours get in the way of having fun. Ease off on the arrogance and let the humor out. People will like you and trust you more if you're fun—as well as honest and trustworthy and all that other Boy Scout stuff you seem to think is so important. By the way, Drew is very funny and likes to laugh at himself."

"You've gotten to know the son I lost. Do you know how jealous that makes me?"

"I believe I do. It's going to get rough, but as long as we trust each other, we'll get through this. It's not as difficult as treating an adult who has lived as a multiple for a long time. It's a bigger challenge than an imaginary friend that won't go away, or a few other childhood aberrations, but it's very hopeful. His environment has drastically changed and he has a parent he can identify with and understand. You are straight-forward and don't hide anything. Show him you support him and let him know you won't let him down."

"Thank you, but I'm not sure I can live up to your faith in me."

"Bring him next Tuesday. I'm taking a long weekend to chase fish in the Mediterranean."

"Wave at Monte Carlo for me."

"You're a gambler?"

"For fun." Andy smiled. "I learned not to rely on odds about the time Drew was conceived."

❖

During the next month, Andy grew more comfortable with Dr. Reynard's diagnosis, and it started to make sense. It was difficult to watch the tapes and see his hypnotized son undergo changes in mannerisms, facial expressions, attitudes, voices and speech patterns. He could see the years slip away when Drew became Crybaby, the shy and fearful five-year-old, or the emotionless Dead Boy, who appeared to be retarded and spoke in a dull monotone—if he spoke at all. Jack's cocky bravado entertained Andy more than irritated him and he recognized the importance of his conceit as a part of the complete Drew. He was relieved to witness the insatiable curiosity and gentle affection in the Drew-Andrew personality, as well as the teasing sense of humor and questing need for knowledge and fun.

While Dr. Reynard played soft chords on a guitar, a bell clear voice sang in a blend of English and Italian. Hesitant and timid at first, it grew stronger as the personality of Buffo merged with the music. When the child lost himself in the music he was creating, a look of rapture illuminated his face, shined in his eyes. When the guitar fell silent, Andy tried to make sense of the words until he realized there was no sense to be made, only disjointed thoughts and images from fragments of songs that Buffo skillfully wove into complex melodies. The voice was pure and beautiful—both joyful and plaintive—and it ripped open Andy's guilt and pain until he broke down and cried like the unsure, vulnerable youth he was trying not to be.

Andy called his mother that night and tried to explain what was happening, but it was inflated, psychiatric poppycock to her. In Mae's mind, all the child needed was to be loved and held a lot. He needed to be handled firmly, given security and sensible rules that told him someone cared about him and would always be there. Andy didn't doubt his mother was right about most of it and decided it was better she didn't know the truth. He had called to bolster his security, not to upset hers.

Later, when Andy thought about Mae's answers, he realized she may have given him what he needed, a renewed faith in the most important things he could offer: firm consistency and forgiving love that would never go away.

When Andy joined the therapy sessions, he understood why Dr. Reynard had insisted he watch the tapes several times and become familiar with Drew's alters before he witnessed them for real. Andy had been able to maintain some objectivity when he sat in his own office, stared at a television screen and watched the play of a light beam on a crystal prism that rolled and tumbled between deft fingers while the psychiatrist's voice enticed his son into a hypnotic trance.

Watching it happen in front of him was a very different experience. In a quiet, cadenced voice, Paul would ask to speak to one personality or another and then bring it out with a quick clap of his hands. Andy wanted to interfere, tell the man to stop making his son act that way, as if it were an embarrassing stage trick. But he knew that wasn't true.

Most of the time Drew would nod, look down and let the shudder convulse him. When his head snapped up, he would be someone different and Andy never got used to it. And then there were times when it didn't work. Jack would argue and say Andrew couldn't come out because he was being punished. When that happened, Andy could see the struggles reflected in the boy's face. Jack became tense and angry, resisted the quietly insistent voice and tried to break from its control. Sometimes, Jack won and it would take a long time to bring him back under.

The way the psychiatrist accomplished it amazed Andy and he wondered if he could ever develop that much patience and skill. Right from the start, Dr. Reynard realized Jack couldn't tolerate being ignored any more than Drew could, so he ignored him in a way that was constantly aware and enticing. The man was a flame to a moth, irresistible and intriguing in spite of the threat of entrapment. And there were no compromises. If Jack came back to him, he had to accept control and do what Dr. Reynard wanted. It was one of the most valuable lessons Andy ever learned, both for handling his son and people in general. Most of the time, Paul won and Jack retreated.

As the sessions continued, Drew-Andrew began to join the arguments and force himself out by insisting he was more important and Dr. Reynard needed to listen to him. When that happened, Andy knew he was in for a bad time at home. As soon as his son was away from the psychiatrist's control, the alters would fight about it and push Andy's patience to the limit. When they turned destructive or defiantly disrespectful, Andy lost patience and decided it was just fine when they switched. They were both going to pay the penalties. The unexpected result was that they gained a mutual respect for his fairness and often compromised. More importantly, Andy continued his routine of having Drew read to him every evening to make sure they maintained contact.

One evening in October, when Andy set two mugs of cocoa on the table by the reading chair, he noticed Drew was holding a copy of Lewis Carroll poems his grandmother had given him last spring. It was open to the *Jabberwocky* page and he was crying as if his heart were broken.

"Drew, what's wrong?" Andy dropped to one knee and slid the book from the boy's hands. He set it on the floor and rubbed Drew's legs to calm him. "What's so terrible?"

"I want to kill the bad Jabberwock and bring you his head and you can be proud of me and call me a beamish boy and love me."

"Drew, I do love you."

"You can't love me. I'm bad. I want to kill the Jabberwock, but I lost my vorpal sword and can't be a hero."

"You don't have to kill anything to be a hero. You only have to find the strength to be yourself. Besides, you don't have to be a hero to make me love you. I always love you. Nothing will ever change that." Andy lifted his son, held him close against his chest, rubbed tense back muscles while deep sobs convulsed through the child's body.

When Drew stiffened and shouted, "No! I won't go in the black room!" Andy wrapped both arms around him, as if he could hold him back. He felt Drew clinging to him and pressed his cheek against soft dark curls.

"Leave him alone," Andy said. "Don't take him from me."

"Help me Daddy, I want to love—"

"No, damn it!" Andy shouted when he felt the shudder, the rigid stiffness, the snapping change.

Suddenly, Andy was holding a thrashing, angry child. A tight fist collided with his left cheekbone and a hard kick caught him between the legs. Pain swept through him and he bent forward, dropping the boy into the chair. When he straightened, he was staring at an inflamed face and blazing eyes.

"I hate you! I hate you! I hate you!"

Jack kept screaming hate until Andy wanted to shake him, but he bit down on his anger and said, "Give him back. How can you do that to him?"

"I'll never let you have him. I hate you. I hate you!"

While he struggled to gain control over his anger, Andy heard something besides hate in the voice that screamed at him. He heard panic and fear and it startled him. When he reached forward and caught an arm, the boy cringed away from him. Andy jerked him out of the chair, then clasped him to his chest and sat down. He held his son on his lap with tense arms that trapped the struggling body against his chest, clasped twitching legs between his knees.

"I'm sorry you hate me because I love you, no matter who you are."

"You're a liar, liar, liar…" The wiry body thrashed and jerked in Andy's arms. He was amazed by the strength that fought him but he refused to release the struggling boy. "…you're a liar, a fu—"

"Just don't say it." Andy warned.

"I hate you. You can't have him. He's mine. He's—" The voice shattered into incoherent rage. The body shook with violent tremors.

Andy was unaware of the telltale shudder until a hard head snapped up and banged his chin. He recoiled and the body in his arms stopped struggling. When Andy relaxed his clamped knees and loosened his grip, thin arms hugged around his neck, a warm body snuggled against him and whispered, "I love you, Daddy. Where have you been? I miss you. Please take me with you."

"Drew?" Hearing the pleading phrase that echoed in his memory, Andy shifted to let the boy sit astride his lap and clamp strong thighs against his legs. "Please, Drew, stay with me. Let me help you."

❖

The next morning, after sending his son home with Peter Caldwell, the American student he'd hired as a tutor, Andy followed Paul Reynard into his office for what he sarcastically called his after-session battle briefing.

Thoughtfully silent, the psychiatrist poured two cups of coffee before he walked behind his desk and raised his cup as if he were about to offer a toast. "Congratulations, Andy. You found the real Drew. And it was a shock to me."

"You lost me right there."

"This morning, when I asked to speak to Drew, I met a boy who had no idea who I was, or why he was in a foreign city called Paris. Except for a few moments with you last night, his last conscious memories were more than two years ago. He not only has no awareness of Jack or Andrew; I don't think he'd believe me if I told him about them."

"What makes you say he's the real Drew?"

"He told me he was and said he knew you were his Daddy because you smelled right. Are you still using the same aftershave or cologne you wore when he was a toddler?"

"Not still. Again. A few days ago, I bought some Old Spice, a scent I haven't used for years. I opened it and put some on yesterday."

"It appears you unintentionally awakened a sensory memory in an awareness that's been dormant for longer than I suspected."

"Is that supposed to make sense?"

"It explains why we've been stymied in our attempts to get the boy we've been calling Drew to think about integrating."

"What do you mean calling Drew? If he isn't Drew, who the hell have we been talking to?"

"Andrew."

"You said that's only a name Jack calls him."

"I was wrong."

"You're the damn expert." Andy snapped. "Why didn't you know about this?"

"Face up to it, Andy, psychiatry isn't an exact science." Paul flared at the accusation. "Do you plan to sue me because my educated guess was not one hundred percent correct?"

"Depends on whether it's good news or bad," Andy smiled wryly as he threw off the feeling that half his chess pieces had just been swept off the board.

"It's good." Paul relaxed and plopped into his big chair. "It seems Andrew is actually Drew without the awareness or boldness of his true central persona. It's why he didn't remember you and has been unable to access a true memory of the trauma that caused the initial split and brought out Crybaby. I suspect that whatever happened three or four years ago caused Drew to retreat from a life he couldn't cope with and later spawned the emergence of Jack and Andrew: one to fight his battles for him, the other to satisfy his insatiable need for intellectual development."

"But he said he was Drew."

"Both of them respond to the name Drew because that's what people insisted on calling them. If a child is constantly told an imaginary friend or identity does not exist, he eventually stops protesting and goes along with the insisters, even though he knows they are either lying through their teeth or too stupid to see the truth. Andrew and Jack believe they exist in their own right and share evidence that proves it to them. Andy, if you thoroughly believe you have been abducted by aliens, no argument is going to convince you they don't exist. It's the way the human mind works."

"And this is good?" Andy scoffed.

"It's the breakthrough we've been looking for. Integration is only possible through the awareness of the center personality. In spite of Jack's and Andrew's desires to suppress him again, we have to keep Drew aware and get him to understand what happened before we can reunite the three of them. As a starter, I suggest you continue to use Old Spice."

"If an after shave is the cure, I'll bathe in it."

"Not by itself." Paul chuckled. "It's merely a sensory stimulant that opens a path for acceptance and understanding, which is Drew's best chance of staying aware and leading a functional life that resembles normality. In view of both his presently secure environment and the consistency of the expectations you put on him when he was a toddler, the prognosis is good. You cracked through Jack's shell enough that Drew was able to trust his awakening feelings for you and the true center was able to break through the barrier and take control for a short time. It's a significant leap forward and gives us a fair shot at convincing Drew to accept integration of his alters."

During the weeks after what Paul called a significant leap, Andy felt as if he'd been dragged into a private hell, where he had to give his son security while, through the recently emerged Drew, he relived the memories of curling into a terrified ball as he experienced the psyche shattering horror of purgative invasions of his body. As hard as it was for Andy to witness the emotional memories of Drew and Crybaby, it was horrifying to hear the unemotional, factual voice of Dead Boy recounting the extent of his abuses, as if they were being inflicted on someone else.

At first, Andy wanted to scoop his son up in his arms and run away to protect him from what seemed to be no more than a pointless infliction of emotional suffering. But gradually, he understood that Drew had to accept that what had happened was not his fault—that he was the victim, not the perpetrator—that he was neither bad nor evil. It was vitally important for him to know he could not only open locked memories, without feeling guilty for what had happened to him, but could accept them, confront them, and control them. Andy wished he could do the same. But every time Drew exposed traumatic memories, Andy's guilt lashed him raw and he fought to maintain control over his own compulsion to shut it out of his mind and deny it had ever happened.

And then, one morning in late January, while the psychiatrist urged him to refuse to listen to his fears, Drew willingly entered the tiny room in his mind that had once been a pantry with no windows. When its outside light switch snapped off, the only illumination was a pencil line stripe of light below the door—until the kitchen light was extinguished and it turned pitch black. It was here that Andy held his son, while the boy relived the memory of being harshly punished for throwing a pan of hot frying oil on an older, bullying step cousin, who threatened to mutilate him with a knife.

Alone and helpless, with all hope gone, the last of Drew's will to survive failed. As terrifying darkness closed around him, he retreated into unawareness and his mind shattered, spawning the identities of Andrew, his docile twin, who continued to feed his intellectual appetite, and Jack, the tough, arrogant, older brother, who took away loneliness and protected him from horrors buried in his memory, as well as the bullies in his daily reality.

Drew hadn't been old enough to understand that by existing in dissociated separation, he would be living a shattered awareness and there would be no chance of healing. But Paul Reynard, with Andy's support, persevered until they gained his trust and helped him understand he had to absorb the memories he was missing and regain his identity. In order to do that, there needed to be surrender and joining—or at least a mutual compromise, in which he, Andrew and Jack could share a conscious existence.

During the final battles for control, Drew's strength came from the realization that the father he'd blamed for deserting him had always loved him and would never leave him alone again. Feeding off Andy's love and strength, Drew survived the dark and discovered he could use his phenomenal powers of observation and deductive reasoning, along with Andrew's scholarly ability to concentrate and absorb knowledge, to help him accept what he had to do. And then, Drew reached into Jack's experience and reabsorbed some of the toughness and arrogance he'd ceded to him.

This time, when the shudders swept through him, Drew's reasserted center emerged as a more complete Drew with the expanded awareness of both the scholar and the protector. Their memories were intertwined in a jumble of images he would gradually be able to sort out and understand. With a shudder of his own, Andy let go of his anguish and, sitting on the floor of the psychiatrist's playroom, held his son on his lap and joined him in a damn good cry.

Slowly, Andy became aware of soft, pure tones singing: *"Puff the Magic Dragon lived by the sea..."* As the voice grew stronger, he realized it had worked and Drew would sing to him again.

Catching his son's face between his hands, Andy let a laugh bubble up from his chest. *"Come to my arms, my beamish boy. O frabjous day! Callooh! Calay!"* When he pressed his nose against Drew's, they burst out laughing and rolled across the floor, giggling.

There were other memories to relive, other wounds to heal. They were terrifying and painful, but they were never faced alone. Even then, it was more than a year before things were sorted out. The outcome was one neither Andy, nor Paul Reynard expected, but it made sense when they thought about it. After gaining a quasi-understanding of the dilemma they faced, Drew, Andrew and Jack, entirely on their own, decided on a compromise—they would inwardly maintain their individualities, with their own names, while outwardly sharing the Drew identity—all in a mostly constant state of joined awareness.

At this point, Andy inserted his own terms of compromise. He made it clear he personally loved each of them for themselves and accepted their desires to maintain a sense of individuality. However, in the eyes of the world, he only had one physical son. His name was Drew and it was expected that, as his son, he would project a respectful and morally acceptable public image. Since they were sharing the same body and public identity, all of them would be equally accountable for its behavior.

Andy also made it clear that since he was not always aware of what went on between them, the responsibility for finding a sensible way to negotiate and control each other's impulses was also shared—meaning they would all suffer the consequences for misbehavior as well as reap the rewards for sound judgment. And it worked.

By the time Drew was ten, Crybaby and Dead Boy were long gone. Buffo seemed to fade into obscurity not long after Drew realized the importance of music within himself. Drew became a mix of energy and wildness, laughing and crying in turn. He was outrageously cocky, challenging and daring, but also charming and thoughtful, dramatic, full of fun and music. He was still adventurous and temperamental with a quick temper, irritable snits and rebellious streaks that pushed Andy to the end and, occasionally, well beyond the end, of his patience. There had been disagreements, angry arguments, even a few outright fights between two, even all three of them; but for the most part, they all muddled their way through childhood and into the early teen years within what could be called acceptable parameters.

Andrew had been shy, intellectual and introspective—Jack smart, savvy, and arrogant. Drew was a combination of the two as well as a spark of himself that continued to grow and take control. With the approach of maturity, they gradually merged into a coherent whole, until Andy couldn't always tell them apart, or see that it made any difference.

By the time he was sixteen, Drew insisted he had taken all control away from Jack. And after doing extensive research into his disorder, he declared that he fully understood the truth. He insisted he was in total control of all aspects of his life and saw the identities of Andrew and Jack as childish constructs of his imagination—no more than intentional mindsets he could slip into when he felt they were needed.

Two years later, Drew's reaction to the devastating breakup of his first, and as far as Andy could discern, only serious love affair, terrified Andy and worried Paul; but to all appearances, his son showed no signs of dissociation. In fact, after a brief period of emotional chaos, he emerged from the ordeal of desertion with not only his control intact, but a more stable view of himself. He insisted he was cured and it all belonged to a past he didn't want to remember.

And now, after eight years of strongly believing in his adult son's stability, as well as his ability to handle a crisis, Antonio's prediction that Drew was setting himself up for a potentially explosive and dangerous confrontation with an old childhood nemesis added to an apprehension that had been plaguing Andy since last winter.

Drew's uncontrolled outburst and assault of Vittorio Luciani, while not as frightening as past alarms, was more unsettling in that there had been no overpowering trauma, no emotional disaster, no justification for what happened. With all his heart, all his common sense, Andy wanted to believe Drew when he said the incident was no more than an eruption of deeply suppressed anger he'd failed to restrain.

In view of Maestro Luciani's reputation as obsessive, merciless and egocentric, Andy had to admit Drew's explanation made sense and was easier to live with than his fears. But still, the awareness of an emotionally violent black hole in his son's memory haunted Andy's mind like a ghostly remnant of relived nightmares.

Chapter Nine

Drew stopped next to a green lawn tractor and watched John set a plant in tilled ground, press soil around its roots. "Want some help?"

"Would you be expecting me to say no?" John looked up from where he knelt on the grass beside a curving stone path leading to a lattice gazebo by the conservatory. "Grab a flat and start on the far side of the path. Groups of three or five with random space for other colors."

"It's not like I haven't done it before." Drew picked up a trowel and lifted a flat of yellow and brown pansies off the flatbed trailer behind the tractor.

"You interested in my advice, need someone to gripe at, or do you just want to play in the dirt?" John cocked his head, lifted a frosty eyebrow. "From the testiness in your voice, my guess is you want to let go of some aggravation."

"You got that right." After stepping over the flower border John was planting and the one on the other side of the path, Drew plunked the flat on the grass and sat cross-legged beside it.

"Which one's bugging you? Willow or your grandmother?"

"Today? Willow." Drew rammed the trowel into the soft dark soil of the bed and shot a spray of dirt three feet in the air.

"Thank you for volunteering to sweep the path, just keep your exuberance away from me." John brushed dirt off his arm and shot Drew a look of mild disapproval. "What did she do now?"

"Three days ago, when she said no touching, I didn't know she meant **No Touching**." Drew popped a plant out of its plastic pot and caught it before it splattered on the stones. "I can't put my hand on her arm without turning her into a cactus plant."

"Pansies are tough, Drew, but that's no reason to torture them." John stared at the plant in Drew's hands. "Separate the roots; don't rip them apart."

"You think maybe I'm overreacting to being rejected by sweet Willow, the virginal country flower?"

"I would say that was bang on target."

"There's a strong possibility she really isn't interested in me. But either she has an odd way of showing it, or I'm losing my ability to read what she's putting out."

"She doesn't look at you like she's uninterested." John shifted sideways on the grass and continued to set plants at a rate that rapidly moved him away from Drew, who was still on the first six-pack.

"That's my point. She has a way of stirring me up until I want to flirt and horse around with her, but I can't touch her. It's driving me crazy." Drew started talking louder as John moved farther away. "Just being around her gives me a hard-on and I have to get away from her before she notices and looks at me as if I'm a pervert."

"You better start planting faster if you don't want your grandmother to hear you. The conservatory windows are open." John stood and strolled to the tractor for a new flat of plants while Drew hastily stuffed pansies in the ground. "My memory may be fuzzy, but I thought embarrassing reactions like that were more under control and less spontaneous by your age."

"I did too, until I met her. From the minute she backed her sexy backside against me, I didn't want to let go of her. Then she laughed and made me feel I could be zany and romantic with her. It was fun, and she seemed to love it. Then Bam!" He threw his arms up, sending a shower of wet dirt and plant onto the path. "Suddenly, I'm a callus, phony bastard who wants to take advantage of her."

"Do you?" John scowled at the bedraggled plant until Drew picked it up and planted it.

"That's a matter of opinion. I want to make love to her, but how far it goes is up to her. I told her that." Drew crammed one empty packet inside another until the stack crumbled into a wad of splintered plastic. "I don't understand her, and I don't buy the sweet innocence crap. She's a spunky wench, who had the guts to smack me with an apple switch and challenge my arrogance. I want to know what happened to change that." He looked at John, who was shaking with laughter. "What's so funny?"

"She hit you with a switch?"

"Why are you so surprised? You're the son of a bitch who told her to whack me with something."

"That's spunk all right."

"But where did it go, John? She hardly even talks to me now, and I can't get any answers out of her that make sense."

"You don't back down. Maybe you frightened her."

"I don't think so. She went all emotional on me and started crying, but I sensed more thwarted anger than fear, or even disapproval."

"You could give her another switch and see if she wants to whack you again?"

"Like hell. I had a nasty enough welt on my thigh from that one. I paid her back with a swipe across her bum, but I didn't hit her anywhere near as hard as she hit me."

"Is that when she started crying?"

"That's when she told me to stuff it and get the hell out of her way."

"Was that the day Ko-Ko came back in a lather? You were burned when you went after her."

"Trumbull's dogs ran the horse, not Willow. I was pissed because she acted like a rude brat when I tried to introduce her to Nicole."

"Could be she was jealous."

"She sure was." Drew smirked. "But I'm not in the least bit sympathetic. My relationship with Nicole has nothing to do with her."

"Are you going to tell Willow the truth?"

"Not after that. It's more fun sparring with her assumptions."

"Did anyone ever mention you can be cruel?"

"Lots of people. If she wants answers, all she has to do is ask for the truth, not make snide insinuations. I don't respond to jealous jabs. Maybe she'll figure that out some day." Drew looked down at a cockeyed plant he was burying with loose dirt, frowned, then reset it and gently brushed dirt off its drooping blooms. "My problem is I don't know if she really thinks I'm an asshole or wants me to kiss hell out of her."

"You could try that. I remember a saucy flirt who regularly hoisted my boom and then turned away with condescending disapproval until I worked up the courage to corner her in the greenhouse. When I wrapped an arm around her waist, she went stiff, but I kept tickling her face and lips with a rose until she started laughing and let me kiss her."

"And then what happened?"

"I can best describe it as opening the door of a blast furnace."

"Can I ask who it was?"

"I don't think you have to." John's smoky green eyes softened with Drew's understanding smile. "The point I want to make is it wasn't a rejection of me or lack of desire that made her resistant. It was apprehension about betraying a moral code that, in spite of a rebellious spirit, she did believe in. There was also a very real fear of what her husband would do to her and the dread of being left alone to face whatever retribution might befall her. We were young. We were in love. And we vowed to take all those risks together. Things are different with Willow, but she still has apprehensions and fears."

"What are you trying to tell me?"

"You have to let her decide when she's ready to face the perils she sees. One day she won't prick you when you touch her."

"I always wait until they ask, but this is different. I can't touch her."

"Why not?"

"I stuck my foot in my mouth up to my knee by promising I would talk but not touch. I saw it as sexually intimate touching; she saw it as any touching. I'm not a verbal lover and don't express affection well without my hands."

"Not too bright a move from someone who has your gift of touch."

"I told her I wouldn't be very good at it. I didn't know how bad I'd be at it."

"If Willow feels the way I think she does, she'll give you a chance to break that promise."

"And if she doesn't?"

"As you've proclaimed many times, there are a lot of women to choose from."

"But Willow is a compelling fascination and I don't always take my own advice well. I'm obsessed with her and want her. Nothing else will satisfy me right now."

"How about the satisfaction of getting five more flats of plants in the ground?"

"Does that work when you're in your sixties?"

"Priorities shift, Drew. Now keep sticking that tool in the ground and see if you can use your pent-up energy to get something done."

"I get the message. But planting pansies is not what I had in mind for today."

"What did you have in mind?"

Drew gave him a wistful look. "I had a wild hope I could continue a tradition that started my first spring at Princeton when a sexy girl chanted in my ear, 'Hooray, hooray, the first of May, outdoor screwing starts today.' Planting pansies just doesn't hack it."

"Ever missed before?"

"A couple of years I had to settle for leaving the window open and listening to the rain. Sometimes women have no sense of tradition."

"You could ask Willow—for the sake of tradition—then see if she'll rally to your cause."

"I don't think she's figured out the part about sex being fun yet." Drew tamped dirt around a plant. "Actually, I planned to take her for a drive along the Delaware and show her the Gap. But before I had a chance to bring it up, she told me she had all her tack to clean and a lesson with Gram. Whenever I have time to do something, she's either gone or too busy for me. I'm beginning to think she plans it that way."

"You're not around much."

"I have a lot going on right now and I'm trying to catch up on stuff I haven't thought about in a long time. Gram has me tied up with brokers, bankers and lawyers. And Dad has me playing sales rep. I'm driving to New York tomorrow for three days of meetings with two different firms. He can't stand to see me being useless, so he's trying to suck me into the business."

"Andy figures you ought to be doing something by now. Maybe he's trying to show you an alternative. Without him, FiberForms would have gone bankrupt. Andy rebuilt that company. I know he'd like the continuity of being able to turn it over to you when he retires."

"I'm aware of that, but even he knows it won't happen."

"He told me he wants you to find something that gives you as much purpose as his business has given him."

"I thought I had." Drew pulled his knees up in front of him and wrapped his arms around them. "Can we talk about something else? I almost came apart. I can't even think about it without feeling panicked. Paul Reynard says I have to work myself backwards and figure out what I've blocked before I can get through it."

"Don't let yourself lose what you've gained."

"I won't. I keep up my running and exercises. And I practice. According to Vittorio, the technical is fine; the passion is missing."

"Maybe you do need Willow."

Drew looked up and stared at John. "What do you mean?"

"It's your passions she rattles. You usually treat women with cool detachment and see sex as an amusement, a passing dalliance, a physical indulgence. The women don't hold your interest because you're always looking for something none of them can give you. But not Willow. She has you bouncing up and down on an emotional pogo stick."

"What about her!" Drew shot to his feet and glared at John. "She can't make up her mind about whether she wants to be an employee accusing me of sexual harassment or a sexy woman wanting me to screw hell out of her. I can take the spunk and challenge. I love the spunk! I can't stand the shutout."

"I see this talk accomplished a lot. You are right back where you started and still have flowers to plant."

"Can't you think about anything but pansies?" Drew plopped back on the ground and grabbed up the trowel.

"Can't you think of anything but Willow?"

"Not lately. John, I'd rather she smacked me than ignored me."

"That's the story of your life."

"What does that mean?"

"You've been goading people who ignore you ever since I've known you. It makes you very whackable."

"And good at ducking." Drew pressed dirt around a pansy plant and looked up at John with a smug grin. "What if I ignore Willow? I don't think she can stand it either."

"It's worth a try."

"Right now, it's the only way I can sanely keep my promise and save my integrity. I told her the decisions were hers. I could never go back on that and feel right about it."

"And so, we accomplished something after all." John looked at the tractor. "Do you want passionate purple ones, or those perky little white ones?"

Scowling, Drew eyed the remaining flats. "I'll take perky. They remind me of Willow."

❖

After setting two china cups on a round table in the conservatory, Mae turned to where John was holding a vase of pansies.

"Since Drew was kind enough to help with the planting, I'm on time for tea." John handed her the vase and watched her set it on the table before he sat on a cushioned wicker chair.

"What is wrong with Drew?" Mae took the steaming kettle off a hot plate and poured water into an old china teapot when John lifted its lid. "He refuses to talk about why he left Genoa. And he's been sulking for the last three days. I don't know what to do with him."

"May I suggest doing nothing?" John smiled when she looked affronted. "He's sulking because he's falling in love with a woman who doesn't react like the women he's used to."

"If you mean Willow, I think you're wrong. He's hardly been with her lately. Besides, Drew doesn't fall in love. He takes women out and goes to bed with them. I don't think he knows what love is."

"He did once."

"Gabrielle was a long time ago. And she left him. Drew has no intention of letting a woman hurt him again." Mae lifted the lid of the pot and peered at the tea. "I like Willow, but I don't think she would be interested in the type of social life Andy and Drew live. She enjoys art and music and has a brother who plays concert piano, but she told me she feels awkward at receptions and cocktail parties. I can't imagine Willow glibly dropping names and rubbing elbows with self-important nouveau riche in Mediterranean casinos."

"Do you think Drew and Andy take them seriously?"

"They certainly don't, but they know how to... What is the word? Schnoozel with them?"

"That would be schmooze."

"Yes. Yiddish, isn't it?"

"Sounds like it, right along with schmuck, which is what they're likely to feel like after they play poker with Andy while Drew charms their sexy young honeys. It's a good thing your son and grandson are honest and only gamble for harmless fun. They would make a marvelous pair of unscrupulous con artists."

"At least you didn't call the women independent contract hookers the way Drew did." Mae made a distasteful face. "Are all young people as outwardly crude as he is?"

"It does seem to be prevalent these days." John lifted a napkin off a plate of cookies, picked one up and took a bite out of it.

"You're supposed to wait for the tea to brew."

"When I've been smelling Alice's ginger cookies baking, I have no patience for etiquette. You're right about Willow. Next to horses, the biggest concerns in her life are her family and Iowa. She says she wants to experience a bigger world, but that's not where her heart is. She's far too hearth and home to want to live the high life. But then, I'm not sure Drew enjoys it that much lately."

"Are we old fools, John?" Mae smiled at the abrupt bunching of his tangled white eyebrows. "Have I thought of myself and not you? Should I have laughed at the conventions of my social peers and let them shun me by becoming Mrs. Fergusson and openly inviting you into my bedroom?"

"Och, whit ye on aboot?" John huffed and stared at her over the crescent edge of his cookie. "Your peers would have acted shocked and gossiped like a gaggle of agitated geese, but you were too important to shun. If we'd married, you would have insisted I act like a husband and join you at your stuffy dinners and social affairs."

"I suppose it would have been expected."

"Not by me. As for bedrooms, I would say in the last twenty years I've spent more time in yours than my own. And when it comes to last names, you don't fool me. Your Sutherland pride would never allow you to give up the name. I think that's why you agreed to marry that conniving weasel in the first place."

"That and those ridiculous rumors about me and Haimish, the farrier's son." Mae sighed. "My father was very anxious to get me well married and well away from Glendoncroft Hall."

"And the shares of Sutherland Mercantile into his portfolio."

"It was after the war. Even earls have bad times. I suppose you're right about the name. It would have been inconvenient to change it, but we could have married without that. Andy wanted us to."

"I fell in love with Mae Sutherland. I still love Mae Sutherland. But I'm a simple man—"

"You are not a simple man, John."

"I may not be a simpleton, but I am a simple man, a creator of gardens, a Fergusson born and bred. I belong to you and Sutherland Manor, not your social circles. Now pour the tea before I eat all the cookies and disrupt the entire tradition."

"The tradition would survive, but you might not if you eat all the cookies. I've been smelling them baking, too." Mae poured tea into the cups. John added milk and dropped two cubes of sugar into each one.

"It's a pity Americans don't know the value of afternoon tea." Mae sighed. "Andy always grumbled about it ruining his day. Drew just wanted to grab the goodies and run off with them. I wouldn't let him, so he stuffed his mouth, as well as his pockets when I wasn't looking. He would have spread crumbs everywhere, except he usually had one or two dogs following him like shaggy carpet sweepers."

"Mae?" John took her hand when she reached for a cookie. "Why did you ask if we should have married? We talked about all our reasons to keep what we had to ourselves long ago."

"It was what you said about Willow and the way she sees her family. Maybe if we had married, we could have done for Drew what neither Andy nor I could do alone. We could have let him feel the kind of love that makes a relationship last." Mae stopped and thought for a moment. "Am I making sense?"

"No, and sort of. Our love is what it is. It may not have survived marriage. We have our separate worlds, and we both know it. I'm proud of your equestrian accomplishments, but had little interest in your horse shows. You had no interest in my hunting and fishing trips. You have your museum excursions, theater and opera seasons. I go to hockey games; and much to your horror, I used to box, ride motorcycles and get drunk in low places. We have an excellent love affair. I think we would have had a terrible marriage. As they say nowadays, both you and I need our space as much as we need each other."

"I've heard the no. You are absolutely right. What is the sort of?"

"Drew already knows we love each other. We didn't have to marry to show him that."

"Did Andy tell him?" Mae bristled. "I didn't want him to."

"No one told him. He sensed it. Drew's always seen me as a grandfather and you've encouraged it. It just took him a while to figure out the extent of it. I know he knows, and he knows I know he knows, but we don't discuss it because he doesn't want you to know he knows. You might want to bring it up and let him know you know he knows so we can avoid this not admitting what we all know rubbish."

"That makes me feel exposed."

"He certainly doesn't condemn us for it any more than Andy does."

"Andy wanted me to divorce his father and marry you."

"Andy wanted to annihilate his father for the way he treated you. Of course, he wanted you to divorce him."

"It was approaching serious violence between them, which is why I arranged to send Andy to boarding school in Scotland with my brother's sons. I wanted him to go to University in Edinburgh, but his father insisted Andy follow his family tradition and go to Princeton. I was never sure just when Andy knew about us, or how much he understood, but I knew it was more than I wanted to admit."

"Before he was twelve. Andy's the one who ran to get me when the bastard assaulted you."

"You scared me when you burst into our bedroom and threatened him. I was afraid he'd have you arrested and I'd lose you."

"And invite a scandal?" John scoffed. "Let members of his clubs and his business associates know the truth? Not that coward. Besides, he was hiding so much crooked dealing, he couldn't have survived the scrutiny of a divorce that would turn your family's power against him."

"I didn't know that at the time."

"I only knew Giles was afraid of being financially investigated," John said. "But I didn't think about that when I challenged him. I only thought about you."

"You always thought about me, John."

"Not much until I was ten and you kissed the broken nose the stable boy gave me."

"You walloped him because he offended me." A smile softened Mae's face. "And then, you were turning such a lovely shade of purple, trying not to cuss him out in front of me that I thought you were sweet."

"Humph." John lifted a second cookie and dipped it in his tea. "If my father had learned I'd said such things in front of a Lady of the family, I'd have been fork-turning compost for a month."

❖

A week later, after turning Venture out in the pasture, Drew stood by the gate and watched Willow groom Ko-Ko in preparation for a lesson with Mae. The sight of her in form-fitting riding breeches and bent over to pick the horse's hooves, focused his mind on the sensual curves of a backside that drove him crazy. Willow had firm buttocks he wanted to feel wriggling in his hands, or better yet, rubbing against him while he thrust into her like an aroused stallion. The thought of feeling her warm flesh under his palms as he stroked his hands up her sides and filled them with her breasts hardened him and made him wonder why a woman who was so vibrantly hot and had a body that could raise an erection on a cadaver was unwilling to admit to her own sexuality.

Drew had thought about a variety of psychological excuses from narrow-minded parental domination to incestuous abuse, but none of them fit Willow, who talked of a fun, open-minded and passionate family. Willow expressed a down-to-earth view of sex as a healthy part of life that she chose not to participate in—especially with him—which would be fine—if chemistry agreed with opinions. Whenever they were together, Drew's mind turned to the way Willow's nose wrinkled when she was miffed, or when she laughed with sudden bursts of pure enjoyment—the memory of her body molding to his in the movements of the waltz, the inferno of passion that ignited during their brief kiss in the hayloft—how he couldn't get enough of the tantalizing honeysuckle fragrance that rose from her skin and hair.

Drew wanted to make love to Willow so desperately that any thought of her aroused him until he couldn't think of anything except making love to her. He had never experienced a reaction that strong without a reciprocal reaction from a woman. And Willow was no different. He felt it in the flush of her skin when she was close to him, saw it in the brightness of her absorbing, gold-flecked eyes, heard it in the huskiness of her voice when his nearness stimulated her. There had been other times he'd needed to wait until a woman was sure enough to know what she wanted, but he'd never had a woman recoil from his touches and shut him out the way Willow did.

When Willow straightened, moved to the hind foot and bent to lift it, Drew walked forward until he was close enough to touch her. She was concentrating on the hoof and he wondered what she would do if he gave in to his desire and filled his hand with the firm curve of a buttock, gave it a gentle, caressing pat. The sensation would be enjoyable, but Drew doubted her reaction would be one he wanted. His last attempt at an affectionate caress made her stiffen and jump away from him as if she'd touched an electric fence. That had been a gentle squeeze to the nape of her neck. A lingering pat on her bottom would be way too intimate and turn her scarlet with embarrassed anger, or whatever else rose in her whenever he reminded her of the arousal she was clearly feeling.

Deciding Willow could handle it better, Drew settled for a quick swat and continued past her without looking at her. When the horse's hoof thumped onto the floor mat, he stopped, cocked his head, and looked over his shoulder before he turned to meet a lethal glare.

"Why did you do that?" Willow faced him with her raised chin thrust forward, fisted hands planted on her hips.

"Some targets are way too tempting to resist."

"You're as infuriating as my irritating brothers."

"I imagine their motives differ from mine."

"They did things like that to raise my hackles, same as you do."

"I was hoping to raise something else."

"That never seems to be a problem for you." Willow dropped her eyes to his jeans for an instant before she turned back to the horse.

"It was your interest I was trying to raise." Drew turned and walked away from her.

"Mae said you were in New York."

"Did you miss me?" Drew hung Venture's halter beside the open stall door before he turned, leaned his shoulder on the wall and teased her with a slow, appraising smile.

"Sort of."

"At least you noticed my absence."

"It's hard not to. What were you doing in New York?"

"Does it matter?"

"I was just curious."

"Since it isn't related to horses or weather, I'm surprised you care."

"Do you always take things so damn literally?" Willow attacked the horse's coat with short, quick twists of the brush.

"When it's a matter of battle lines, I do."

"It's not a battle line. It's a truce."

"It was a business trip."

"What business?" She eyed him suspiciously. "I didn't think you had a job."

"My father's business. I stood in for him at a few meetings and made sales pitches to construction contractors. I also had some good dinners and entertainment at FiberForms expense."

"Alone?"

"I know too many people in New York for that."

"How many of them are women?"

"A lot of them. They're more than half the population."

"Another old friend you were anxious to see?"

"That was about as subtle as breaking the sound barrier and still isn't your concern."

"I don't know why I'm the one who gets accused of being rude when all I did was get away from where I wasn't wanted."

"I brought Nicole to the barn to meet you and you reacted like a jealous shrew."

"I can't believe you had the balls to expect me to meet your sex life face to face and be polite about it. That's beyond rude."

Straightening, Drew caught the brush Willow threw at him before she stomped into the tack room and slammed the door. He took a long step toward the door, then hurled the brush at it and strode out to his car. He left the lot in a brown cloud of churned up gravel and dust before he squealed the tires on the blacktop lane and sped past his grandmother's car. When he heard a horn blare behind him and saw the red blaze of brake lights in his rear-view mirror, he winced but didn't slow down.

Drew thought of ignoring the turn for the house and heading for Mike Paterno's *Mio Castello,* where he could rant in Italian, while Mike stuffed him with good Italian food and argued with him for the sake of arguing. But his grandmother wanted to talk to him after

Willow's lesson. He figured he was in enough trouble for blowing past her on the road and didn't want any more.

The way he and his grandmother had been tiptoeing around each other lately reminded Drew of the battle of wills they'd waged a few years ago when she strongly disapproved of his choice of lifestyles. Cutting out on an appointment she believed to be vitally important to his future would end the standoff and push her into a state Drew didn't want to deal with.

For some reason Drew couldn't understand, Mae had decided it was important to put her affairs in order before his father showed up in two weeks, and she expected him to be a part of it. Drew not only didn't want to think about a future without his grandmother, he saw it as ridiculous. She was tough enough to be around for a long time and would undoubtedly want to change a thousand more details between now and then. Right now, she was threatening to give him half of Sutherland Manor. He was against the idea because half ownership meant both responsibility and liability he didn't want—especially when he knew it would give her more reasons to rag on him about failing to honor his commitment to his future.

Drew had no idea why a life that seemed so great last fall had turned into such a mess so fast. And who was right? Gram? Who insisted it would only take determination and belief in himself to be the next best thing to God in the opera world. His father? Who wanted him to face the reality of life and do something with purpose that made a positive contribution to the world. Uncle Antonio? Who secretly wanted him to give up the high life so he could help put scum like Mario in prison and make the city a safer place for screwed up people like Milly.

Willow? Who seemed to want the security of a faithful Prince Charming with a steady job, a declaration of undying love and the promise of a wedding ring before she could allow herself to have sex with him. Vittorio? Who told him he was spoiled by premature hype and had years of grueling training before he was ready to even think of being great? Or Paul Reynard? Who said he had no anchor, no steady central identity, no resolution that defined his life.

Drew knew he could do any one of those things if he could find the conviction to stick to it no matter how hopeless it seemed. Or how much better something else seemed. But how could he make a reasonable decision when every one of those roles felt absolutely right when he was living it?

In their talks over the winter, Paul had made Drew face a possibility he'd been denying for years. Although he was no longer a dissociative multiple, Paul insisted he was still analogous to a multiple and was able to create roles, then fit himself into them so completely that any attempt to choose one central goal made him feel he would lose the others and make it impossible to decide who he really wanted to be. Everything Paul said made sense. But, like explanations of his childhood battle with cognitively separate personae within his mind, it was academic knowledge, not true awareness.

Drew knew that, as a dissociative multiple, he'd had no awareness of the thoughts, feelings, or memories of his alters. They were separate individuals with almost no internal control over each other. But that was no longer true. He was every one of those personalities with their intact memories, habits and thoughts; and he was firmly in control.

After wrestling with Paul's hypothesis for several months, Drew had dismissed it as interesting but irrelevant. He was completely in control of himself and believed that if he occasionally reacted or presented himself differently, it was a matter of circumstances and appropriateness—not separate identities.

Drew felt he was unable to decide which career was right for the same reason he was unable to decide which woman was right. He liked variety and wasn't ready to give it up to make his father and grandmother happy. As for his life being a mess, Drew was sure it would be fine if everyone else quit worrying about it and left him to sort it out for himself.

At the moment, that especially meant his grandmother, who seemed to think she had a divine right to dictate his behavior the way she had from the first day he arrived at Sutherland Manor and she told him he wasn't going to get a thing to eat until he sat up properly and kept his fingers out of his food.

After parking in the front drive, Drew jogged up the wide front stairs and headed for the kitchen to see if he could talk Alice into making him a sandwich before Gram showed up. In the dining room, while he stared at a carved walnut chair that sat in a corner beside a marble-topped sideboard, his first clash with his grandmother gelled into a clear memory that filled his mind. He remembered slamming his fork onto a china plate so hard it split in two, and then sitting on that chair in the corner of the dining room watching his father and grandmother eat without him. He also remembered wanting to tell them that Jack, his bad older brother, had broken the plate, not him, but knew they wouldn't believe him anymore than anyone else did.

This memory jolted Drew more than when he'd been with Milly and remembered being forced to write the Valentine verse that upset her. That memory was vague and confused, and he hadn't remembered the excuse of an older brother until Milly mentioned it. This memory was clear and now—as was his fear of a tough, angry boy who controlled him and made other people hurt him.

Jack felt a flash of hate for both the woman, who dared to tell him what to do, and the man who swept him off his chair and plunked him on the one in the corner. At the same time, Andrew felt a swell of desolation clog his chest as he scrubbed tears out of his eyes to keep the one who hated from forcing him into the dark. He couldn't remember the dark. He only knew he was terrified of it and would do anything to stay out of it.

Drew's gaze shifted from the chair in the corner to the one at the far end of the table... *Relief flowed through Andrew when Gram called him to her, asked if he was ready to be the civilized boy she knew he could be and finish his meal on a clean plate. He nodded and felt her smile chase away despair. Afraid to smile back, he held his breath while she hugged him against her. He knew that if he let himself relax and feel her affection, Jack would come back and he would know nothing but dark emptiness.*

Shuddering, Drew grabbed the back of a chair and closed his eyes on the reactive memories that felt so real he wasn't sure he could cope with them. At that moment, he believed it was a mistake to try to understand the past and was sure it had no relevance to who he was now. When the intensity of his feelings subsided, Drew knew he didn't have a choice.

Somewhere inside him there were things he had to know. He'd been running away from them for years, convincing himself it didn't matter if there were gaps in his life. Did anyone really remember what it had been like as a child? Or how it felt? Then he realized what other people remembered or didn't remember wasn't important.

Antonio had said he had almost perfect recall of memories; and yet, he remembered so little of his years with his mother. Whether he wanted to or not, Drew knew he had to find those memories in order to understand what was happening. And this time he couldn't let himself fail.

While he stood on the terrace watching Willow and Ko-Ko trot beside a hayfield on their way to the trails, Drew heard the conservatory door open and close behind him. He supposed he should turn around, but there was a chance he could distract her by getting her to wonder what he was interested in.

"That kind of driving does not belong here." His grandmother stopped beside him and leaned toward him with her hands locked together on the handle of her cane in a firm, tripod stance.

"Yeah, I know. I'm sorry."

"The word is yes, Drew, not yeah."

When her frustration snapped at him, Drew continued to look across the dropping lawn and hay fields at the horse and rider cantering along the lane between the stable and a trail into the greening forest.

"Drew, are you listening to me?"

"Yeah, I'm listening."

"Obviously, you were not listening."

"I heard. I just didn't heed. It's the way I talk; give it a break."

"It is not the way you talk to me."

Drew ignored her disapproving huff and watched Willow disappear in the shadows of the woods before he pulled a cushioned chair away from a table. He held it for his grandmother and said, "She's a good match for Ko-Ko."

"Is Willow a safe subject? Nothing else seems to be."

"She's perfect for the job. Totally dedicated to horses and devoted to you." Drew sat across the table from Mae and poured her a glass of lemonade. "I convinced Alice it was warm enough to make lemonade."

"What did you do to Willow?"

"I didn't do anything to Willow."

"She was upset by something before her lesson. From the way you passed me on the lane, I assumed it was your fault." Mae took a long swallow of the cold drink.

"I dared to smack her untouchable ass." Drew smirked when his grandmother stiffened and reached for a napkin.

"And why did you do a crude thing like that?" Mae drilled him with a sharp blue stare.

"Because it was there."

"That is an unsatisfactory answer."

"Do you really want to hear what was in my mind?"

"Certainly not." Mae plunked her glass on the table.

"Then accept that it's the only answer you're going to get."

"Maybe your father puts up with attitude like this, I don't."

"Dad doesn't treat me like a ten-year-old, or pry into things that are none of his business."

"If you were a ten-year-old, I'd take the hairbrush to the seat of your pants until you remembered how to behave properly."

"I'm not ten years old." Drew gave her a disgusted look. "And I'm behaving fine."

"You are not behaving fine. I see no reason why you can't be nice to Willow. She's a very sweet girl."

"Miss Sweet has the defenses of a hedgehog and I'm tired of getting stuck with spines whenever I try to be nice."

"You have no right to hit her. You've been taught better manners than that."

"I didn't hit her."

"You said you smacked her."

"Oh, for shi—Pete's sake, I gave her a playful swat."

"Why?"

"I already told you why."

"It isn't much of a reason."

"Maybe not to you."

"And obviously not to Willow."

"I suspect she's more upset because I rile up feelings she insists she doesn't have than how mannerly I was raised."

"I will not sit back in silence while you hurt Willow. If you can't be a gentleman, leave her alone."

"I have been leaving her alone."

"It doesn't sound like it."

"Willow is an adult woman, capable of taking care of herself. Since I am neither a ten-year-old, nor an abuser of women, I would appreciate it if you stayed out of it."

"I wasn't accusing you of being an abuser." Mae picked up her glass and sighed. "It upset me because I like Willow and don't want to see her hurt." She paused and stared into her lemonade. "But when I think about it, I don't know if she'd be more hurt by sleeping with you, or by not sleeping with you."

Drew blinked at his grandmother while she took a drink. "I don't believe you said that."

"It wasn't easy to say. I may be an old widow lady, whose marriage turned bad, but that doesn't mean I haven't loved."

"Did you ever love your husband?"

"I told myself I did when we were first married and I made myself believe I meant it. He was handsome and suitable. And he was highly approved by my family. But I never liked him, so I don't know why I thought I could love him. I tried to be faithful to what I called love, but I couldn't even do that for long." Mae flushed and looked away from him at terraced banks of tulip blooms beyond an emerald lawn. "John always protected me and made my world beautiful. I loved him when we were children. I still love him today."

"Don't ever feel ashamed of that, Gram. John is the best thing that ever happened to you. And the best grandfather you could have given me."

"Do you mean that, Drew?" Mae turned her head and looked into his eyes. "Can you understand how we can love each other deeply without proclaiming it to the world?"

"I don't need to understand the details. It's enough that I've been able to feel you are protected, fulfilled, and not alone." Standing, Drew took her hands, bent down to press his forehead against hers and winked one eye and then the other the way he had as a child. When he kissed her forehead and straightened, she was laughing with him.

"You're still a cheeky rascal who knows how to charm the anger out of me."

"Only when you want to be charmed."

❖

After Drew left and Mae remembered him saying John protected her, she realized John had been doing that since she was a girl. There had been the fight with the stable, boy who had bloodied John's nose when he was ten, and the times he took on her abusive husband in his twenties. But when she thought about it, there had been a more dramatic and misconstrued example of his devotion less than a week before she married Giles Thornton Sutherland...

During World War II, every effort, every bit of extra wealth at Glendoncroft had gone into winning the war, either through heavy taxation, constant appeals for donations, or the growing costs of housing American troops. The young, freshly arriving Americans, with their constant source of money and supplies—as well as a brazen confidence in themselves as liberators come to save the old world from tyranny—were living matinee idols to a romantic adolescent girl whose mind was filled with daydreams about peace and freedom from what she saw as a stifling life of propriety, traditions and responsibilities she was expected to dutifully obey.

By the end of the war, Mae was horrified by how many of her friends and neighbors failed to come home or returned maimed in body or mind. And although her older brother Gordon survived his years in the RAF, he had been wounded and burned in a crash that left him scarred and barely walking on a painfully crooked leg.

The Sutherland family had been forced to sell land to meet financial obligations; and although Mae didn't understand just what was at stake, she did realize that if they couldn't find a way to finance extensive renovations to the distillery, they could lose Glendoncroft Hall and its tangible reminders of a heritage that identified who she was. Without the hall and distillery, her family would be unable to support the nearby village of loyal, hard-working families—many of them generations old—who were intrinsically interwoven into the living fabric of Glendoncroft.

Mae desperately wanted to help, but there was nothing she could do. And then, like a miraculous answer to fervent prayers, her father, Lord Ronald, received a handwritten letter from Giles Sutherland, a distant American relative, who had learned about her family from an American Army officer quartered at Glendoncroft during the war. Giles explained that out of curiosity that turned into obsession, he had traced his family back two centuries to Andrew Sutherland, a second son of the third Earl of Glendoncroft, who had arrived in Philadelphia soon after the Jacobite defeat in 1746.

A flurry of exchanged information led to an invitation for Giles to visit Glendoncroft Hall in the fall. Consequently, after what Giles claimed to be a case of love at first sight, he made an extraordinary offer to transfer a large amount of his rapidly expanding shipping corporation's stock to Ronald as an undocumented payment of bride wealth—as well as a token of gratitude to Scottish forebears who, according to his research, forgave a condemned son and supplied him with enough wealth to start an enterprise that now belonged to him.

A short courtship that, to Mae, was more a willing acceptance of family duty than a matter of love, ended with a marriage proposal and formal agreement for a wedding in late April.

Five days before her wedding, Mae set an open book on her lap, leaned back against the intricate latticework of a white, wrought-iron bench in the east garden and closed her eyes against the flashing brightness of high sun glinting off the shifting surface of Moray Firth. The welcome heat of a sunny spring afternoon soaked into her and she drifted into a daydream about sailing to Philadelphia—a city untouched by ugly, bombed-out reminders of war—where she would live in an intriguing, totally undamaged manor house she'd only been able to experience through black and white photographs.

When she heard footsteps on the gravel path, Mae looked up to see Giles striding toward her with a wrapped package and bouquet of white lilies. He was tall and lean; and as soon as she saw his red-gold, chestnut hair and looked into eyes that mirrored the Sutherland-blue that gave life to the clan tartan, she had no doubt about his claim to Glendoncroft roots. Mae knew he was almost twenty years older than she was, but there was nothing about him that showed his age—beyond a man of the world maturity that flattered her and promised a life of extravagance, travel and adventure. Mae wanted to add love; but as a sheltered girl, who hadn't turned eighteen until a month after her engagement, love of that sort was still a mystery and drawn from the pages of idealistic romance novels like the one that slid off her lap when she stood up to greet him.

"Giles, I didn't expect you until dinner."

"We docked earlier than I expected and a train was ready to leave. I brought the gift from home but purchased the European flowers at the village station when I arrived."

Mae had already learned that Giles was quick to take offense at anything that, in his mind, hinted of criticism. She was tempted to tell him that since he had purchased the flowers at the village railway station, they had been grown in a greenhouse at the hall but suspected it would most likely be interpreted as snide amusement at his expense.

"Thank you. They're pretty." Mae dropped her head and sniffed at the blossoms to cover a smirk and then set the lilies and package on the bench. She picked up the book and laid it beside them before she stood, caught his hands and offered her cheek for a polite kiss of greeting. "Was the voyage pleasant?"

"And swift since we navigated in a lull between two storms."

Mae glanced at the package. "Do I get to open it now, or is it reserved for the wedding?"

"It's for now, but there is an important matter we need to discuss first." Giles continued to hold her hands in a restraining grip. "Mae, when I said I wanted to transfer ownership of Sutherland Manor into your name, I saw it as a way to protect it from a possible upcoming litigation. If a lawsuit is filed, there is a small, but unlikely, chance the court may rule against me and I want to save our, and our future children's, home from any chance of seizure."

"That's reasonable, I suppose."

"Unfortunately, when I received a copy of the agreement, which you had foolishly signed, it says the property is to be transferred to you, with your father and brother as additional trustees, in an irrevocable trust, *in perpetuity,* with inheritance rights exclusively reserved for legitimate descendants of our marriage."

"I'd say that would most certainly protect it from being seized as personal property of yours."

"It cuts me right out of the picture." Giles looked appalled and totally stymied by her answer. "It means the only way I can regain possession of my own property is to buy it back from the trust, with your consent, at or above fair market value."

Mae deliberately looked naïve and confused before she said, "So what you're saying is you aren't interested in life-long protection of our family's home, only a temporary evasion of a specific litigation. Is that correct?"

"That's correct. And I want you to inform your father that you made a mistake and refuse to take the longtime liability for it on yourself."

"Giles, that entire thing is between you and my father." Mae held his gaze with an apologetic suggestion of helpless regret showing in her expression. "I have nothing to say about it."

Giles tightened his hands on hers until she winced. "You will insist on the withdrawal of your foolishly implied consent. That's what I want from you. And you'll do it, because if you refuse, I won't sign it, and there will be no wedding."

"I will broach the subject with my father." Mae pulled her hands away when his hold relaxed and then meekly sank a spike in his self-assurance. "But our customs and yours are not the same. My father is an earl, and there is a strict code of respect that goes along with that. I'm afraid it will still be my father's decision, just as it was to accept your proposal in the first place."

With a sudden bright smile, Mae dismissed the entire issue by turning away from his stunned silence to sit on the bench with the wrapped package on her lap. "I'm brimful of curiosity about your gift." She stroked a caressing finger on the smooth, satin bow. "May I open it now?"

"Of course." Giles tight smile returned when she brushed a stray lock of golden hair away from her face before carefully removing the blue bow and wrapping paper.

After setting the box on the bench beside her, Mae pulled aside white tissue paper and lifted out a deep azure-blue chiffon dress with a modest V-neck bodice and softly flared skirt, where a profusion of tall, colorful meadow flowers appeared to be swaying in a gentle breeze as they grew upward from the grassy hemline.

Laughing with delight Mae stood up, held the garment in front of her and twirled across the grass, feeling as if she were dancing amid the blossoms. "It's so light I'll feel as if I'm one of the flowers, wearing nothing but a silken spider web."

With a flush of instant reaction to the erotic image Mae's words conjured in Giles imagination, thoughts of cancelling the wedding struck him as absurd. Mae was beautiful and enticingly desirable. He wanted to possess her with a fervor he'd never felt before. She was young, innocent and sheltered. She would soon learn she belonged to him, not her shrewd Scottish father.

"I knew you liked flowers, so I bought it at Lord & Taylor in New York before I sailed."

"It's beautiful. Thank you so much for thinking of me in that way."

Mae tossed the dress onto the opened box and wrapped her arms around him in an impulsive hug of joy, then stiffened when he clutched her to him with a possessive embrace that made her gasp. A strong hand moved to the back of her head and pressed her mouth to his with a fierce passion that frightened her. Mae had never been kissed like that and could only gape at him when he let her draw back.

"My... my apology." Giles stammered in a tone more irritated than regretful. "I fleetingly forgot you are still an innocent girl. But your beauty arouses me and I want you so much I get impatient."

Giles reached out and caught her arm just above the elbow. His tightening grip pinched her flesh when she jerked free and looked past him with an expression of alarm on her face. His hand dropped away and he twisted to see a heavily loaded wheelbarrow careening down a steep embankment with a distressed teenage boy stumbling in its wake. Ignoring Mae's retreat, Giles panicked and tried to dodge away, but he wasn't fast enough. The barrow crashed into his legs and tipped over against the bench, pinning him under it and dumping its load of manure and compost on him and the bench.

"What have you done?" Mae shouted at John when he pushed himself to his feet behind the fallen wheelbarrow. "How could you be such a clumsy fool?"

"He hurt you." John's voice was low and he looked at her with pleading desperation. "Dinna gang with him, Mae. Please, dinna dae that."

"Just go away." Mae stomped toward the bench, glanced at where Giles was struggling to free himself and then gaped at a piece of the blue dress dangling off the bench below a dark clump of damp compost.

Infuriated, Mae grabbed up the ruined dress, whirled back to John and hissed at him. "Get away from here, ye daftie." When he gaped at her with a devastated face, she lowered her voice to a harsh whisper. "If you just go away, I won't tell him who you are."

"I canna dae that." John strode past her, jerked the empty barrow off Giles and flung it out of the way.

When Mae looked at Giles, he was angrily brushing clots of compost off his pale linen suit and limping on his right leg. Turning away, she saw John's father rushing down the embankment. His face was flushed from exertion and he looked around in confusion until he saw his son locked in a furious staredown with Mae's husband-to-be.

"What's happening here?" Quinn Fergusson demanded with a loud voice that didn't seem to know which one to focus on.

"Does this boy work for you?" Giles demanded.

"Aye, he is my son."

"He's careless, clumsy and defiant. He needs a good thrashing. If you won't do it, I will."

"How did it happen?" Quinn snapped an angry stare at his son.

"Tripped on the brae. Tried tae stop," John answered. "I cudnae."

"Ye be sayin' it were an accident?"

Enraged, Giles cut in before John could answer. "It was malicious recklessness that caused injury and damage. He was negligent and at fault. I demand retribution."

"He hae the right of it, son." Quinn backed down and, with a sour expression of fuming resentment, turned his back on Giles and pushed John toward a garden shed beyond the bench. "Take off yer shirt and put hands on the wall."

When Quinn unbuckled his wide belt, Mae started to protest, then saw John shake his head and look toward the house with an expression that said he wanted her to go home and get away from it.

The first crack of leather on skin cut into Mae with a stab of guilt she couldn't understand; and when she saw her father striding toward her, she ran to him. "Make him stop, Da. It wasn't his fault. It was mine. I betrayed him. Please make it stop."

Mae stared toward John's silent, rigid stance while a blur of tears burned away an innocence she would never know again and heard her father's commanding voice say, "That be enough, Quinn. Take him home. I'll send him on the Dover run tomorrow with the next shipment. It will keep him away until after the wedding. We'll talk about it then."

...Mae hadn't seen John until almost six years later; and when she did, she realized she never wanted him to leave her life again. But it wasn't until now, when she remembered how she'd condemned John for trying to tell her she was making a horrible mistake, that Mae understood why she had told her father she betrayed him.

As Mae looked toward the mowed hayfield beyond the manor's terrace, her vision blurred and tears streamed down her face.

"What did he do or say to you?" A firm, calloused hand turned Mae's head until she was looking up at John's angry face.

"What did who say?"

"Drew, who else? He was mad about something and if he—"

"No. Drew was wonderful. It was just that..." She started crying again. "Oh John, I'm so sorry. I don't know how you ever forgave me."

"For what?" He looked stunned.

"Betraying you to Giles when you knocked him down with the trolley."

After a moment of total bewilderment, John laughed and handed her a handkerchief. "Mae, that was fifty years ago, and you've never betrayed me."

"I insulted you and accused you right in front of Giles. And then you got a beating and I got married and I never said I was sorry."

"There was nothing to be sorry for." He wiped a tear off her cheek with a grass-stained thumb. "I was fair fashed and guilty as sin."

"Are you telling me you did it on purpose?"

"Of course, I did. I was moving compost on the path and saw you together. He was hurting you. I couldn't stand back and let him do that. But mostly, I was so jealous of him when he kissed you, I wanted to flatten him. Since I had the means right in front of me, I did it. That trolley couldn't have dragged me down the hill that fast if I hadn't been pushing it. My father knew that, and I think yours did, too. I was fixing to wallop Giles. That leathering likely saved me from a nastier mess."

"I was too angry with you for spoiling a pretty dress to understand what you were trying to tell me."

"It would have made no difference. Everything was arranged. I knew that, but I hated him and wanted to hurt and humiliate him for what he did to you."

"When Da talked to me, he said he had misgivings about Giles's true motives and asked if I felt safe with him. It gave me a chance to back out. But I couldn't risk Glendoncroft. I told him I thought Giles was spoiled and too full of self-importance but I felt he was sincere and I still wanted to marry him. In the long run, it saved both Glendoncroft and Sutherland Manor. So, I guess I betrayed you then, too."

"Mae, it might have made me happy at the time because I sensed ruthlessness in Giles. But I understand now, as you did then, that no matter how much your father wanted to protect you, he couldn't have done it without a tremendous loss; and most likely a lawsuit from Giles as well. Mae, your father's responsibilities reached far beyond his own family. His sense of honor, like yours, was too strong to let him abandon them. Besides, they would have found someone else for you to marry and there would be no Andy, no Drew, no Sutherland Manor in your life. Messing with the timeline is a dicey business that makes dwelling on past regrets foolishly self-indulgent."

"After what happened, I was surprised my father had no objections to me hiring you?"

"The only conditions Lord Ronald expressed to me before I left Glendoncroft were that I take good care of his headstrong lass and keep him informed about Giles. It was a responsibility I was more than willing to accept. Which I suppose made me his spy in an enemy camp."

"How did you find the courage to come here and face Giles again?"

"I wouldn't call it courage." John chuckled and winked at her. "Just a helpless inability to say no to you. And then, when I came here, Giles didn't even recognize me. No one at Glendoncroft had told him my name, and brash young garden boys change between fourteen and twenty-one. Besides, I was a servant laborer. To people like Giles, servants were furniture. By the time I told him who I was, it was too late for retaliation. It's all water over the dam, Mae."

John smiled at her puzzled expression. "Mae, If you are truly concerned about me, remember the Fergusson clan motto *Dulcius ex* *asperi*s. Sweeter after difficulties. I'm the one who won the prize and sweetened the fearless Mae Sutherland. I do regret you had to suffer his insults and abuses, but you were the ultimate victor over him. I think that makes us even. Don't you?"

"I still feel like a fool for not seeing beyond my own vanity. No pretty dress should ever be worth someone else's suffering."

"I thought a pretty Lady Mae was worth at least that much." He reached out, stroked gentle fingers through silvering hair, conjured up a peppermint drop and popped it from its wrapper into her open mouth.

"You still know how to do that at just the right time."

"That sounds like an invitation to go upstairs and see if I can still remember how to make the bees buzz in the peppermint trees."

"I believe it was." Mae smiled coyly.

Chapter Ten

Dear Byron...

Willow paused to think about how to put her feelings into a letter. *...You were right again—of course, as usual, as you always are. There is passionate love in the world, and I'm up to my pointed elfin ears in it. The downer is I'm not sure there's the slightest chance of me convincing him of it since I, once again, dug in my heels and denied its existence. I told him I wasn't interested in him, which was dumb because I am interested in him.*

Why do I let myself say things like that when I don't really mean them? Unfortunately, he has a special thing for a skinny brunette, who is French and acts ridiculously clingy and helpless around him. Love or no love that's not my way to play the game. Even if I am getting more and more tempted to try it.

His name is Andrew Wayne Sutherland, but he prefers to be called Drew. I have the fortune (or misfortune) to be his groom, which right now he's rubbing in with a scouring cloth. I thought of putting oatmeal in his riding boots, but I'm not sure how he would take it. Retaliation I would welcome, but Mr. Worldly would probably turn a cold shoulder and call me childish. That would devastate me almost as much as his long phone conversations in French.

By the way, did you ever notice that when people are speaking French, they always sound as if they're talking dirty? I don't know what he says to her, but the sound of it makes me want to kill her...

Willow stopped writing when she heard the throb of Drew's car turn toward the stable. It was too early in the afternoon for him to be back, which startled her. Except for the three days he'd been in New York, Drew had been regular in his schedule. On weekdays, he arrived at the stable at nine, worked with Venture for half an hour, then rode King's Knight or Rigoletto. He always left before noon and returned about five to condition Knight on the trails.

Willow was still amazed by the way Drew and Bold Venture worked together. They were like two old friends instead of a man and a horse. Venture came to Drew's whistle and obediently stayed at his shoulder, as if he were attached by an invisible lead. Occasionally, the big horse would rub his face on Drew's arm or nuzzle at his neck with a deftly inquisitive nose. It was possibly just a way to soothe an itch or get Drew's attention, but Willow was sure it was affection and she envied it. She also noticed that the black dog, Captain Nemo, would quietly slip his head onto Drew's lap when he was sitting or push his muzzle into his hand when he was standing or walking. They often played an impromptu game of tag, soccer, or a form of touch football with an old milk jug. Both games seemed to have rules known only to Drew and Nemo.

It seemed to Willow that every living thing on the estate was on intimate terms with Drew, except her. She was sure it meant he didn't like her, until she thought it over and understood what she had failed to put into focus earlier. She had never seen him force himself on an apprehensive animal. He waited until they came to him and asked for his affections—or he met their challenges with firm control.

With a start, Willow remembered Bonnie telling Lois that Drew only took what was offered. When she accepted the statement with the masculine logic her brothers would use, it made sense. Drew had promised the decisions were hers. And they had been. She'd asked him to keep their relationship limited to her job. That's exactly what he was doing.

"I'm the one who's been making an emotional tragedy out of it." Willow blurted at the dim reflection of her own eyes against dark pines beyond the window. She blinked at it, then picked up the pen and wrote…

After a little analytical thinking, I've decided that killing the competition is not a solution. The problem is me, not her. But I don't know what to do about it. I can't take him casually. I'm even feeling jealous of his horse, which will no doubt amuse you, as it should me, but he's making a wreck of me and I haven't been laughing much. I can't keep working with him this way, but it would kill me to be away from him. Oh, Byron, love can be a painful thing. I want him. But I want him on my own terms. I don't want to be his other love. I want to be his only love. I feel my pride weakening until I'm starting to agree with whoever said it's better to have loved and lost than never to have loved at all.

At the same time when I look toward the future, I'm afraid I'll view it differently if I lose. I suspect the hurt I feel now is nothing compared to the devastation I'll feel if I let myself love him and then lose him to his next conquest. Or when he goes back to Europe without me next fall.

I don't know what he does in Europe. For some private reasons of his own, he's unwilling to discuss it, especially with me. But my curiosity is driving me crazy. His grandmother said he has to make some sort of decision before November. When I overheard her mention a commitment to an engagement in Genoa, Drew gave her a hard look that backed her off and gave me a bad feeling. You talked me out of my engagement. How can I talk him out of his?

Help, Byron, I need your brotherly words of wisdom...

Willow nodded over her last sentence before she signed it with a flourish.

...Love from your troublesome sister, Elf.

By the time Willow mailed the letter and reached the barn, she realized the decision to destroy the wall and invite Drew's affections was easier to make than initiate. She could hardly crawl up to him and put her head in his lap the way Nemo did. And she wasn't about to admit she was weak-kneed over him.

She had occasionally caught Drew giving her appraising looks, especially when she wore skin-hugging riding breeches. It rankled her—until she realized she did the same thing. Drew was athletic with well-toned muscles, especially in the chest, shoulders, and arms. She was sure he didn't get them living a life of luxury. There were other things she wanted to know, too: such as where he went every afternoon and at night after his evening rides. He did it with such regularity that it puzzled her as much as the existence of Nicole, his unknown life in Europe and the pending engagement in Genoa.

And why was he growing a beard? When she'd asked him, he said, "Someone told me to," then offered no more explanation—not that he ever did anymore. Drew had become a master of terse responses and blunt questions, making him an extremely frustrating person to talk to lately. In a total reversal from his previous candor, he showed no interest in small talk and was totally reticent about himself.

Occasionally, when it was least expected, he would ask a question about her family, especially Byron. He listened to her answers with interest or laughed when appropriate, filed the information in some cerebral memory bank and let the conversation die. As a result, Willow was finding him an extremely perplexing person. Any attempt to make sense of him was like removing paint from an adulterated canvas to expose an original painting. So far, she'd only cracked the outermost layer and caught teasing glimpses of the true portrait. She knew she was about to make an impatient move that could strip away all the paint and leave bare canvas but she was tired of the flat, impersonal picture.

While Willow sat in the observation room, with her feet on the coffee table, and watched Drew jump Knight over training grids in the arena, she felt the window between them was symbolic of their relationship. She saw no way to reach beyond it without shattering it, which was frightening. The glass wall was painful, but it was also security and insulation against what could be a heartbreaking truth.

Isn't it better to cling to tiny hopes than find out I'm chasing rainbows? The question hung in Willow's mind like a lingering mist until she burned it away by declaring tiny hopes were poor consolation.

When Drew left through the open doors at the end of the arena, Willow tried to think of some openers. She could compliment him on his jumping. She'd already done that. He was properly gracious in his acceptance, then asked if she'd found the check that he had left on the bulletin board as payment for the splint boots she had bought at the tack shop. Conversation was not the answer, especially not his brand of concise conversation.

She practiced: "Seen any good movies lately?" It sounded like a bid for a date. "Would you like to hear some of Byron's CDs?" That might work, even if it was an outright invitation to continue what had started with the waltz. But then, that's what she wanted. Wasn't it?

When Willow thought about the way Drew treated her after she met Nicole and again last week when he swatted her in the barn, she had to accept that her own behavior made her more like an annoying little sister to be taunted than a woman to be courted. Since there was no way she could imagine the worldly gentleman treating Nicole that way, Willow suspected he saw her as an inexperienced teenager when compared to the fashionable socialites he deemed acceptable for love affairs.

Finally, after looking at herself honestly, Willow realized she could never be a Nicole, or a Lois, and it was foolish to try. Reluctantly, she let go of the unrealistic hope that Drew would pull her into his arms, sweep her into a dizzy whirl of romance and confess that he was desperately in love with her and would never see Nicole again.

Ironically, as soon as Willow stopped trying to think of ways to make herself into the sophisticatedly aloof partner she thought Drew wanted, her mind turned to ways to break down the wall and make him laugh with her again.

The clear memory of her brother Owen saying, "Thank God for co-ed roughhouse. It's the greatest sexual icebreaker known to college men," popped into Willow's mind and made her wonder if maybe the intent of Drew's swat was to get her to roughhouse in a way that may not have been as brotherly as she thought.

After watching Drew clear a massive log jump and gallop up the hill toward the trails, Willow remembered him saying he used to play pranks on people in charge of him. A boy who played pranks should have turned into a man who would appreciate the art of practical jokes.

"Ah-ha!" Willow broke into a broad grin. "That's a game I know how to play, Mr. Smug. I come from a family of pranksters. And with eight siblings for targets, I've had plenty of practice."

In order to complete her plans, Willow decided to recruit John as a partner. The gardener remembered a multitude of pranks Drew had played on him over the years and expanded her simple idea into a diabolical masterpiece.

An hour later, stationed in a lawn chair beside the arena porch, Willow watched Drew stroll past her, twirling his car keys on his index finger and whistling to himself with cocky self-assurance. The moment he stepped over a hose stretched across the stone walkway she lifted the handle of a deep-shutoff hydrant that sent cold well water to two lawn sprinklers and two water guns—all aimed at an angled path leading to the silver Mercedes.

The first water gun hit Drew full in the chest. He leapt straight up like an electrified cat just as the second gun caught him in the back and two sprinklers jetted water from the sides of the path. Drenched in an instant, he looked so unbelievably shocked that Willow, convulsing with laughter, found it almost too much of an effort to push down on the handle and shut off the deluge before she collapsed in the chair, laughing so hard tears streamed down her face and her diaphragm hurt.

When she darted a quick glance to where John leaned against a tree, shaking with laughter, he raised a thumb and winked at her before he ducked behind the vegetable garden hedge.

"What in holy fucking hell was that about?"

The bellowed burst of profanity snapped Willow's attention to Drew, who stood rigid while water ran from his hair and dripped from the dark beard outlining his jawbone. His flabbergasted look as he locked eyes with Willow sent her into another fit of laughter and she was too weak to react when he charged forward. His hands closed on her arms and lifted her from the chair, but she was limp and collapsed at his feet, still laughing.

"I didn't know you wanted a swim in the pond so much." Drew thrust cold arms under hers and hauled her to her feet.

"No, Drew." When he bent forward and lifted her over his shoulder, Willow kicked and squirmed in a hopeless effort to get away.

"Your puny attempts won't save you. In my rules, one drenching deserves another."

Ignoring the fists pounding on his back and shoulders, Drew strode toward the old gristmill across the drive. When she increased the force of her blows, he winced, held her legs with one arm and swatted his right hand across the seat of her jeans.

When she pounded harder, he swatted harder and said, "I'll bet I can keep it up longer than you can."

It was a challenge Willow was sure he meant, but she had no intention of going in the pond without putting up a fight. She continued to struggle and shout at him with loud yelping protests every time he swatted her. Realizing she was engaged in a battle she had little chance of winning, a new strategy flashed into her mind just before he reached the end of the wooden dock and lowered her in front of him.

Instead of prolonging the struggle, Willow wrapped her arms around his neck and kissed him full on the mouth. It worked. Drew stopped dead and stood frozen while she clung to his unyielding lips. The stunned resistance lasted for a heartbeat before he responded with an answering kiss that engulfed her with its possession and swept her into a maelstrom of spinning excitement. Willow's lips parted and she breathed in the heat of his kiss; her muscles relaxed as she melted into his arms. Strong hands slid down her back, pressed her against his body.

All resistance, all thought flew out of her mind as the kiss and moving hands claimed Willow's senses. When he slipped an arm under her knees and lifted her in front of him, she was heady with a whirl of pleasure and willing to let him carry her anywhere—as long as he continued to kiss her and hold her against him.

Drew stepped forward, opened his arms, and let her drop.

Willow let out a squawk of alarm when she hit the surface of the pond then gasped in a breath before cold water closed over her head. The instant her feet hit bottom, she shot up and splashed to the short ladder. Stunned and outraged, she stomped onto the dock to see him walking away from her. Burning pain ripped a hole in her when she realized he was leaving her as abruptly as he had when he dropped out of the hayloft and disappeared.

Spurred by fear that it would happen again, she ran to him, caught his arm, jerked him around to face her. He looked furious, muscles rigid, hands clenched into fists. "Don't leave me, Drew." She faltered under his stare and pulled back, stammering, "Pl-please touch me again."

"Why?" His word was a blow, knocking the air out of her. "So you can cut me down by telling me I've offended you? Make up your mind, Willow. Do you want to be an impersonal employee, or are you going to let me make love to you?"

"I don't know." She started to shake from cold and the empty hole he blasted in her emotions. "I want you to hold me again. I don't like it behind the wall."

"Then why did you build it?"

"I didn't mean to."

Drew's arms wrapped around her and she pressed close to him, trying to absorb his warmth through wet clothes.

"You're a book of contradictions, Willow, and I can't read past the introduction."

"It was supposed to be funny." She sniffed and fought back tears.

"It was very funny." His hands rubbed on her chilled arms and back. "Until you kissed me."

"That was supposed to save me from the pond."

"Maybe it would have if it hadn't been so good." He rested his cheek on her hair, hugged her to him. "I don't want the door slammed in my face again. I'm long past hesitant necking in back seats with testing forays against armored virginity. The decisions are still yours, but at least give me a chance to let you make them. I won't force what you don't want to give, but don't freeze me out."

"You slammed the door. You and Nicole."

"You shut it on my foot the first night when you made it clear I was to see you as my groom and could shove my affections. I don't know what Gram told you, but it sure turned you off."

"She didn't turn me off."

"Then why were you in such a hurry to send me to Philadelphia?"

"I didn't want you to be late."

"That's my decision, not yours. The next day you not only slammed the door and locked it, you dropped a bar across it. To top that off, I had to listen to a lecture from Gram on how nice you were and how big a cad I'd be if I failed to respect you."

"I don't know why she did that."

"I guess she felt you needed protecting. I'd rather leave that decision to you." Drew molded her shivering body to his side and walked her across the grass toward her cabin. "You need to warm up before you shake yourself apart."

"I was going to invite you over to listen to one of Byron's CD's."

"Excellent idea. Why didn't you think of it sooner?"

"I thought you wouldn't want to."

"I said I wanted to listen to him." Drew gave her a chastising shake with the arm around her waist. "It would be better if you believed what I said instead of what you think I feel."

When Drew opened the cabin door, his arm dropped away in a withdrawal of shared warmth. "Give me a clean towel. Then take a hot shower. I'll throw my clothes in your dryer."

After a shower that steeped the chill out of her bones, Willow dressed in jeans and a too-large, tailored shirt she had borrowed from Byron and neglected to return. She rolled back the sleeves and left the shirttails out before she walked into the kitchen to find Drew pouring fresh coffee. He was barefoot, wearing grey running shorts and a zippered sweatshirt.

"Where did you get the clothes?" She put away the milk carton he had left on the counter.

"My car. I walked to the stable in your towel, showered and dressed before I drove back." He carried the mugs into the living room and set them on the coffee table beside a sugar bowl and pitcher of milk.

"I was wondering if I'd find you still wearing the towel."

"Wouldn't that be rushing things a bit?" Drew sat on the couch and took her hand, pulling her down beside him. "You're nervous enough. If I met you mostly naked, you'd run like a frightened rabbit."

"Probably." Willow tried to answer nonchalantly but it was no use. "I'm less nervous when I'm arguing with you. Drew, I don't know how to answer the question you asked on the dock?"

"About making love to you?" When she nodded, he lifted her hand to his lips, kissed the tips of her fingers. "Making love is as tender and simple as that, or as passionate and fulfilling as total sexual union. I'd like to start with that simple kiss and see how it grows. I suppose I made it sound like all or nothing, right now, but that isn't what I meant. I have come to believe in your innocence. I respect it. What I don't understand is why."

"I haven't been completely honest with you." Willow stared down at her pale hand in his larger tanned one. "It's something I've never told anyone before."

"Are you sure you want to tell me?"

"I owe you an honest answer." She looked up to meet the deep blue of concerned eyes. "There was someone else. It was my first year in college. He was drunk. It was awful. I don't think he was successful. I shut it out, so I don't know."

"That makes sense." His hand tightened on hers for an instant before he released it and reached for his mug. "Drink some coffee and stop acting as if you're next in the start box."

When she flushed, Drew took a swallow from his mug and eyed her over the rim. "When I retrieved my car, I discovered your accomplice rolling up his hoses."

"John was very helpful."

"I'm sure he was." A crooked smile lifted one end of Drew's new moustache. "I was horrible to him when I was a kid."

"Sometimes I have trouble seeing you as a normal kid."

"I'm not sure I was." He set the cup down. "At least not in most views of normal."

"You haven't said much about yourself lately."

"I don't know why I did before." Drew gave her the same pensive look he had in the garden two weeks ago. "I guess you made me feel you care about who I am, not what I am."

"John didn't say you were horrible." Willow set her cup next to his. He called you a dynamo of mischievous energy."

"I loved John, but my bids for his attention often misfired. When I glued his tools to the shed wall, I pushed him too far."

"I'll bet."

"It's a hair-raising experience to be chased by a raging Highlander." His smile turned to a deep chuckling laugh. "He caught me just before I reached Gram, who had watched the whole crazy chase from the terrace. He sentenced me to hard labor to pay for the time and cost to fix the mess and then gave me a few good whacks on the ass. That man has a hand like a steel shovel."

"What did your grandmother say?"

"She waited until we reached the terrace, then said, 'Drew, you need to learn when your fun becomes someone else's burden. Go to your room until dinner. And you will eat with no sulking or you'll eat alone in the kitchen and go straight to bed.'"

"I thought she spoiled you."

"Not that way. Gram never condoned bad behavior."

"Is that why you're so gallantly chivalrous?" she asked, wondering if he would take offense.

"She was a good part of it. There's a gracious quality to Gram that I admire. She was the first caring, consistent person I remember trusting after my mother died." He gave her a thoughtful look. "I was an uncontrollable brat when I came to live with my father, who brought me to Gram after two months of exasperation. I sometimes wonder why she let us stay here that summer instead of sending us back to Paris posthaste. I suppose she wanted to prevent child abuse by outright strangulation. Dad and I didn't get along very well at first."

"Your grandmother's easy to get along with."

"Most of the time," he answered with a tone of reservation. "My civilized behavior didn't come easily. I spent a lot of time fighting against discipline before I saw sense in it."

When Willow set her empty mug down, Drew slid an arm around her, brushed the hair away from her neck and dropped his lips to the sensitive skin below her ear. "Such a sweet taste makes me want to forget I'm a gentleman now." He opened his mouth, biting with a gentle hold. His tongue tickled against her skin until she squirmed away.

"Do you still want to hear a CD?"

"Sure." Drew sighed when he released her and leaned back on the couch. "But make it Mozart, not 'Turkey in the Straw'."

"How about a compromise. *Rhapsody in Blue*?"

"On a piano?" He gave her an odd look. "Or a fiddle?"

"Byron mostly plays the piano." She sat on an ottoman across from him. "In this case he has the Iowa State orchestra to help him."

"That's a relief. Classically, I much prefer a piano."

As the woodwinds started the composition, Drew lifted bare feet to the coffee table and leaned back in relaxed comfort. At the first piano notes, he closed his eyes and listened with a deep absorption that surprised Willow and she sensed a depth that intrigued her. When the music reached its dramatic and powerful finale, Drew's captivated expression changed from an approving smile to an excitement that radiated approval.

"If that's what Iowa cornfields produce," he said. "I'm going to eat a lot more corn."

"Maybe. We do eat a lot of corn." Willow chuckled then looked thoughtful. "My father never understood Byron very well, but he said that since music was part of a Welshman's soul, he would encourage it in his son." Willow shook her head and started to laugh. "Dad bought a grand piano at a farm auction and rebuilt part of the house to get it into my grandmother's old apartment over the garage."

"I'd say it was a wise investment. He's damn good."

"I didn't know you knew so much about music."

"That's another thing Gram instilled in me." Drew shrugged then shied away from what he didn't want to divulge. "How old was Byron when he recorded that?"

"Twenty-five." She stood to remove the CD. "The concert was this past winter."

"I want to hear him when he's thirty-five."

"Could you please wait? That would make me thirty-four. I'm in no rush."

"You aren't?"

"Why should I be in a hurry to get old?"

"That's when goals are in reach, from thirty-five to forty-five."

"I can wait."

"I'm not always sure I can."

"Do you really want to be middle-aged?" She turned with the CD in her hand and frowned.

"I want the impatience and indecision behind me."

"What planet are you from? This is a country that worships youth." Unable to disguise the tease in her voice, Willow felt a laugh building behind her control. "We're envied for our freedom to enjoy the fruits of a hyped-up, plugged-in, wireless society." The laugh burst out when he made a sour, kiss-Aunt-Agatha face. "Isn't that what we're brain-washed to believe? It's the commercial gospel."

"I'm not convinced."

"I didn't want Mae's grandson to be thirteen. I don't want him to be forty either."

"You would if you were forty."

"But I'm not, and I want you the way you are."

"Then convince me of it. Maybe we can meet somewhere between the innocence of sixteen and the contentment of forty."

"Do you want to hear more Gershwin from *Porgy and Bess*."

"No." His answer was firm. "I don't want to listen to Byron while my intention is the seduction of his sister."

"You have a one-track mind."

"As you said, it's the rites of spring."

"I have that." She reached toward a box by the stereo."

"I'll take anything but your brother."

"*Mary Poppins?*" Willow teased while she sorted through the box.

"Or that." Drew stepped over the coffee table, reached past her and switched off the stereo.

When Willow turned to him, Drew's hands caught her face and the clowning left his voice. "Willow, you've been driving me insane. I wake up desperate for you. You're ruining my sleep by showing up in my dreams, filling them with your alluring eyes, bubbling laugh, firelight hair and unbelievably sexy, elfin ears." He tipped her head and nipped at the tip of her ear.

"Byron insists I have elfin blood and calls me Elf."

"Maybe you do. There's something wild and woodsy about you." He murmured and caught an earlobe in his lips before he brushed his chin against her neck, tickled her with his beard. "You have a power over me that could well be magic."

"When you let yourself go, you have a beautiful way of saying things. I'm sorry I insulted your chivalry. I didn't know it was real."

He gave her a quick wink. "I'm a Miniver Cheevy, '…who, mourned romance… and loved the days of old, / When swords were bright and steeds were prancing…'"

"No wonder you don't have a job. There aren't any openings for knights of the round table these days."

"Like Percival, I came to Camelot ignorant of courtly manners and earned my knighthood. I have yet to find my Holy Grail."

"Wasn't Percival a virgin knight?"

"Only after Mallory's version. I rather fancy myself less pious in matters of love."

"You keep reminding me of Tom Jones."

"The singer?"

"The novel."

"Umm?" He lifted an eyebrow thoughtfully. "An astute analogy. And so, *Cherie*, it brings us back to lesson two of *la valse de l'amour*."

When Drew kissed her, Willow started to answer with the surge of passion she'd felt on the dock, but he held back, tasting more than indulging. He cradled her in the bend of one arm while his other hand stroked down her throat into the opening of her shirt. It lingered at the first closed button and tested her response, before he opened it and several more.

Willow shivered with apprehension that turned to anticipation when, with tantalizing touches, he trailed fingertips across the rounded tops of her breasts, nibbled at her lips, then covered her mouth with a warm, enticing kiss. His fingers continued to caress her neck and the exposed bulges of lifted breasts. His other hand moved on her back, arched her toward the warmth of a firm body that molded to hers in an enclosing caress. A flush of heat whirled into a lightheaded thrill of pleasure, eased her tension, closed out reality, erased hesitations.

"I like the shirt. This is unnecessary." Drew hooked a finger around the center of her bra and pulled it away with a quick jerk.

"How did you do that?" She stared at him with wide, startled eyes.

"A magician guards his secrets." He held up an open hand. "For my next act, I'm going to turn you into Miss May, gorgeous centerfold and woman of my fantasies. Don't move a muscle."

After releasing the clip in her hair, Drew set his hands on the waistband of her jeans, opened the button and zipper before he slowly stripped them down her legs. "Now, shake your hair loose and come to life as a beautiful seductress."

Blushing Willow stepped out of the jeans piled around her bare feet and self-consciously lifted her hand to close the open shirt.

"No, don't spoil it." His fingers slipped around her hand to hold it away. "The effect is sensational. To me, that is one of the sexiest things you could wear. One side of the shirt caresses the peak of a firm breast; the other shows the vague shadow of a tight nipple. The front and back hems barely conceal what the eyes strain to see. If you were May on my calendar, I'd never turn the page."

Drew sighed comically. "Unless in June you turned to me and let the shirt fall away from that spellbinding nipple. If you teasingly exposed a little more with each succeeding month, it would be a summer worth repeated browsing."

In spite of, or maybe because of, the zany way he expressed himself, Willow's apprehensions dissolved. She felt no threat from Drew. He had a way of reshaping reality and pulling her into his fantasy, but she doubted he would force himself on her any more than he did on Nemo. There was no battered milk jug she could offer and she was unfamiliar with the rules of his game. But she wanted to play.

"Is it my turn to create a centerfold?" she asked. "Or do you get to have all the fun?"

"Fun is best when shared." A wide smile lit his face, ignited a spark of laughter in his eyes.

"I'll call it a travel poster for Ancient Olympics." Stepping forward with a boldness that sent her pulse racing, Willow opened the sweatshirt to his shoulders then took hold of the zipper tab and slowly lowered it to expose more of his wide chest with each inch of descent. "You're awesome." She released the words in a husky exhalation.

It was hard for Willow to grasp the reality of Drew wanting to make love to her. She knew it could be a mistake. She also knew that in the split second it took to decide to kiss him when he held her on the dock, she threw away her chance to retreat. Her feelings, even her reasoning, answered his question about wanting him to make love to her and let the kiss on the fingertips grow toward fulfillment. When his hands cupped her breasts, she pulled in a breath and pushed into his hands, straining for what was promised by caressing fingertips that moved closer and closer to the tightness of peaked nipples. He sat astride the arm of the couch, slowly moved the torturing pleasure nearer to her nipples, then sketched tantalizing rings around their tips without touching them.

Willow's hands tightened on hard muscles; her eyes closed while, again, he traced teasing circles that almost touched the centers of sensitivity. The first touch was with his tongue. The gentle flick of warmth on intensified nerve endings was a shock of release before a surging need for more. As sure hands covered her buttocks and massaging fingers pressed into her flesh, Willow arched toward him, thrusting forward into pulling enticement.

"It's fantastic." She gasped.

"In the words of a nameless creator of modern lyrics—you ain't felt nothin' yet—baby." With a gentle kiss on the end of the nipple, he stood.

Willow blinked, then burst out laughing. "Okay, wise ass, what are you going to do about the other one?"

"I'm saving it."

"For what?"

"The second act." He took her hand to lead her to the bedroom door.

"Oh, Drew, it's a mess." She hung back enough to stop him.

"Can we get to the bed without maiming ourselves?"

"It isn't that bad."

"Then stop being silly. I won't see anything but you."

"It's still afternoon." Willow felt trapped, face to face with the leap into final commitment. A tremor of uncertainty became a nervous fist clenching in her stomach like paralyzing stage fright.

"Which gives us plenty of time." Drew pushed back her shirt until the second breast thrust past the material. He touched it softly. "I left something unfinished."

When his hand cupped her breast, lifted it with caressing fingers, Willow trembled with agitation. Unable to understand if it was desire or trepidation, she broke from his eyes and looked past him at the unmade bed. She saw rumpled sheets, remembered searing physical pain deep inside her, along with a bigger, smothering pain of shame. When he covered her mouth with his, she was unresponsive and numb.

"There's nothing to be afraid of, Willow. I won't hurt you."

The words crashed into her mind stiffening her against him. "No. Please, not now." When he backed away, she ran into the bathroom and banged the door closed.

Leaning back against the barrier, Willow wrapped her arms around her chest and held her breath against hollow emptiness. There was silence on the other side of the door. Then the front door slammed with a force that made her recoil from its finality. When tears burst through her fragile control, she slid down the door and sat on the tiled floor while uncontrolled sobs erupted in convulsions. She hated herself for turning him away. Maybe this time he would believe it was forever. Mortified by what she'd done, she dreaded facing him. Drew's withdrawal had hurt before.

Now, after feeling so close to him, after sharing an intimate part of him, after the heat of his passion and stimulating touches, the coldness would be unbearable. She had glimpsed and been captivated by an exciting piece of the portrait. Then, she'd smeared the canvas and it was ruined.

Chapter Eleven

Drew jerked the laces tight on his second shoe and slammed the car's trunk closed before he ran down a foot trail into the woods. Growing anger heated his blood and pounded behind his eyes until he wanted to head-butt a tree or fell one with his fists. But no matter how much he wanted to vent his anger at himself and suffer the pain of atonement, he knew it would never erase the fear from Willow's eyes or take away the intensity of his obsession for her.

"Damn it!" He kicked a fallen branch with a force that sent it sailing down the trail. He hadn't felt like this since dark-eyed, hot-blooded Gabby introduced him to wild, uninhibited sensual expression before she ripped the heart out of him and blasted out of his life like a rocket blazing a white-hot trail of pain into the black iciness of an emotional void. Although Drew knew he would never again love with the callow wonder of adolescence, he could sense in Willow the fun and fire that had been Gabby and wanted to share it so fiercely, he couldn't think of anything else. He stopped running, grabbed a leafy chunk of broken branch and thrashed it against the thick trunk of an old oak until he held a short, ragged piece of green wood.

Hurling the battered stub into the woods, Drew shouted back along the twisting trail, "Willow, what the hell did I do wrong?" His only answer was the memory of her frightened face and the flash of panic that widened her eyes before she bolted to safety behind a closed door.

When empty pain engulfed him, Drew dropped his head, shuddered and snapped his head up.

"You wimped out on me, Andrew?" Jack scoffed as the pouting image of a dark-haired child filled his internal awareness.

Andrew glared at the tall, lean image of his teenage brother, who flipped blond hair away from his face and leaned back against the oak tree. "Drew ended it. She said no when you tried to take over and push her."

"She wants it; I want it; Drew wants it." Jack grinned with arrogant assurance. "So? Let's get 'er laid."

"She's afraid of it." Andrew crossed his arms and stamped his foot in childish frustration. "He won't do that to her."

"Horseshit, she's a virgin with cold feet. Me and Drew can handle it."

"Please, Jack." Andrew whined. "She said no. They have to ask. It's a rule. You can't break Drew's rules."

"She'll ask. Trust me."

"You said that once before."

"I was wrong once." He shrugged. "And she got over it soon enough."

"We have to know why Willow's afraid."

"She's not afraid. She just doesn't know what's good for her." Jack laughed at Andrew's petulant frown. "Face it, little prick, you want her as much as I do."

"Maybe a little more." Andrew muttered as he met the belittling scowl on the fair, beardless face in in his mind.

"What is this?" Jack straightened in surprise. "You never give a shit about sex."

"They're always your kind of girls, all shined up and out to show it off, as if the facade is all that matters. I never liked any of them, except Gabby." Andrew let his thoughts drift to the way Willow asked so many questions—as if she wanted to understand the inside of everyone and everything. "Willow's different."

"Yeah, but she's hot, kid."

"It's not the sex, Jack. I don't like the sex." Andrew twisted his face in a childish grimace of disgust. "I always go away when there's sex. There's more than that in Willow. I care about her. I think I could even lo—"

"We don't go there, Andrew." Jack crossed his arms in mocking imitation of Andrew and looked stern. "That's also a rule, so get it out of your mind and accept what we can get."

"You mean what you can get."

"For shit sake, brainy boy, she just opened the door to fucking rapture and you're moping around like a sulky shithead." Jack laughed at Andrew's offended glower. "Hell, without me, Drew would turn his failures into guilt trips and you'd be fizzling out in your pants."

"Stop being a dickhead. Drew needs her, and I won't let you hurt her." Andrew pleaded. "If you push Drew aside, I'll never forgive you."

"Like I'm supposed to be scared by that?" Jack snorted his question.

"You should be." Andrew stamped his foot to stiffen his resolve. "Jack, listen to me. You know Drew's tougher than you are. If he finds out you're still real and able to come out, he'll get back at you. He's done it before."

Jack bristled, clenched his fists, ready to argue, until fear cowered him. He shuddered and yanked Andrew into withdrawal with him.

Drew snapped his head up, ready to leap forward and punch at nothing. Then he slumped against the oak, letting the anger dissolve into a gnawing irritation with himself for trying to persuade Willow instead of backing off as soon as she hesitated. He felt he'd been too impatient; but then, it had been her decision to change the rules and everything had felt right.

From the moment he picked Willow up and headed for the pond, Drew had sensed a difference in her. Her prank, even her protests, were open challenges in the age-old game of sexual dominance—her kiss a clear invitation to take the game to a more intimate level. Willow had been as eager as he was, totally responsive to his touches, warmly aroused.

"She was ready, damn it." He snapped out at a squirrel that stared at him from a clump of brush as if it were challenging his right to lean against the tree sheltering its nest. "And I wasn't even close to taking her."

When the animal blinked instead of darting away, Drew sighed and shook his head in bewilderment. "What has she got against an inviting king size bed? It's a better playground than the couch or floor."

With no idea of what to expect, Drew pushed away from the tree and headed toward Willow's cabin. Part of his mind wanted to get in his car and drive away without facing her. He had enough failures banging at him. He didn't want to see hurt and mistrust in her eyes or discover that he'd fucked up the only positive thing he had going this summer.

A stronger part of Drew's mind knew he couldn't do that. It didn't matter if she wanted him to touch her again or not. He had to go to her. If ever a woman needed to be held and sheltered, it was Willow. And like a damn fool, he'd reacted with a burst of anger that left her alone with her fear. When he thought about the way Willow looked at him after he turned away on the dock and realized how she must feel now, he broke into a run—in spite of a spiked ball of doubt that expanded in his chest, fought him for every breath.

❖

Willow had no idea how long she sat on the floor, knees drawn up in front of her, arms clutched around them while pain streamed down her cheeks and soaked into the rough towel covering her face. When she left the bathroom, she was stiff from the tense position and sunlight knifed through the bedroom windows. She wondered if Drew had gone to Nicole, the way he had last time she spurned his advances. She wanted to feel jealous but there was no room for it.

After putting away the CDs, Willow turned and caught a flash of reflected sunlight beyond the end of the porch. Her heart jumped, then sank when she looked out the window and saw the silver car parked in the drive but no sign of Drew. Unconsciously drawing back, she pulled the shirt closed over her breasts, fastened a few buttons, and bent down to pick up her jeans. When she found her dismantled bra, she puzzled over how he'd unhooked the straps without her noticing.

Hearing a step on the porch, she dropped the clothing and turned to the door that swung open as if it had been snatched by a tornado. Drew stepped partway in—hand on the doorlatch, eyes bonding to hers. He was still wearing the shorts and sweat shirt but had added socks and running shoes. His face was a frozen mask of stone.

"Where were you?" Willow asked the first thing that put itself together in her mind.

"Running, thinking about bashing my head into trees. What did I do, Willow?"

"Nothing."

"That wasn't nothing."

"I saw... I thought... I remembered..."

"What?" He stepped toward her, then stopped when she shrank back. "What did you remember?"

"He said he wouldn't hurt me. But he did."

Wincing, Drew leaned his forearm against the edge of the door. For a long silent moment, he pressed his forehead on the grey cloth covering his forearm. When he looked back, his eyes absorbed her. "The one who didn't succeed?"

"He did succeed. I didn't."

Drew closed the door and stood with his back against it. "Why didn't you tell me? I would have understood."

"I felt so wrong I didn't want anyone to know. I stopped resisting and let it happen. I was so ashamed of myself I didn't want it to ever happen again."

"We have a problem, Willow. It's as big as a planet and we're going to have to come face to face with it before you send me screaming out of my mind again."

Drew pushed away from the door and strode straight to her. His hands closed on her arms and held her in front of him. "I want to make love to you with every nerve and fiber in my body. I left here in a state of frustration and fury I couldn't control. It wasn't against you. I want you, but I can't have you. It's tearing me apart."

"It's doing the same to me," Willow shouted, as if volume could make him understand, then started to shake. "I don't know why I panicked."

"Willow, you have to face it." His arms closed around her. "You have to accept that it's over and it was never your fault. It was his wrong, not yours."

"I've been telling myself it didn't really happen—that it wasn't important. I remembered and it was important. I said I didn't want you to make love to me, but it was a lie. I've wanted you since I met you. Maybe if you just do it, I'll get used to it."

"I don't want you to get used to it. It isn't castor oil." His face twisted in distaste. "You have to want it and welcome it, not let me take it because I want it. Willow, I don't just want to take my own pleasure. I want to give you pleasure. That's what makes it good."

"I want you so much I hurt from the wanting." She looked into deep blue eyes. "Why don't you just take it?"

"I can't do that. That's what he did. He raped you, Willow, and I'd like to take him apart." His muscles tensed, clasped her against rigid stone, then released and she could breathe again. "It's not that you don't want sex; you're afraid of it. I won't force it on you."

"How do you know that?"

"I could feel what you wanted and I could feel your fear every time you froze up and rejected me. I just didn't understand the reason."

Willow started to shake again and pressed into the shelter of his strength. "I was so ashamed I convinced myself it didn't happen. I was afraid to tell anyone."

Secure and protected by the circle of his arms, Willow let a fresh flow of tears wash away memories of shame and failure until she knew that she, too, wanted to make love to him with every nerve and fiber in her body and would never build a wall between them again. She felt his fingers comb through tangled hair, trace the folds of her ear with a touch that took away apprehensions, made her wonder why she even thought she could live without his touches.

"Don't be afraid of me." Drew stroked his hand on her face, wiped away tears before he lifted her chin. "I won't ever take what isn't wanted and asked for."

"You may have to."

"Not that." He stared out the window beyond the couch then looked back. "It was never hard to get women to offer what I wanted, but I never took anything that wasn't freely given. Do you understand what I'm saying?"

"I think so. Do you always stop when a woman says no?"

"Yes. My father instilled that in me a long time ago."

"How did he do that?"

"He said that although persistence could most likely change a woman's mind, she would always have lingering doubts. I took it to heart and made it a rule that they always had to ask, or at least answer positively if I asked."

"I'll try to remember that when I'm feeling ornery." She flushed. "I say a lot of things I really don't mean when I get ornery."

"I've noticed that." He lifted a teasing eyebrow. "But I think I can tell ornery from genuine apprehension."

"What you're saying is that you don't want to take responsibility."

"You're very perceptive. It's a big problem in my life."

"Responsibility?"

"Living up to it."

"Since we both want it, we'll have to share the responsibility." Willow reached out and slipped her hand inside his open sweatshirt, molded it to his shoulder muscle. "It's a simple way to sidestep our hang ups."

"I don't think respecting your desires is a hang up."

"You haven't been respecting my desires. You've been believing what I said. My desires and my mind have been at war lately."

"Looks as if I'll have to get you to offer what I want."

"I think I'd like that." She looked at his questioning expression and lifted her chin. "In fact, I know I will."

"I'm really a good teacher and it's an enjoyable subject." Drew stepped closer, circled an arm around her. "Especially for a woman."

Willow slid her palm down his arm and lifted his hand in front of her. She pressed it into the warmth between her breasts. "Weren't we about here?"

"No. We were over there at the bedroom door." Drew scooped her up in his arms. "Since I seem to have trouble keeping you at your lessons, I'm going to make sure you don't try to play hooky again"

"Are you a tough teacher?"

"Probably. Most of my education was from private tutors." He carried her into the bedroom and kicked the door closed behind him.

"Is that a better education?"

"Depends on the tutor. It's a one-on-one relationship that can be as demanding as it is rewarding." He set her down then sat on the bed, stripped off his shoes and socks. When she hung back, he stood and took her hands. "I believe we were on lesson two."

His hands framed her face and his eyes searched hers. They were intensely blue, darkening to a deep violet that absorbed her thoughts and stirred up deep feelings until any lingering misgivings were dissipated by their spellbinding depth. With gentle caresses, his hands relaxed the tension in her face and neck. He unbuttoned the shirt, pushed it open and let it fall from her arms. He trailed fingertips down her chest and, once again, touched her breasts with enticing touches that made her skin tingle. His hands were sure, patient, building tension to a peak before he tasted with the slow relish of a connoisseur.

Drew striped away bed covers and, with his arms circling her, lay back and rolled over, pulling Willow with him. "You're ambrosia." He nibbled his way to her neck, chin and mouth. "The more I taste, the greater my hunger."

His kiss was long and deep, drawing her against him. His hands moved on her neck and back, stroked down to her hips, settled her closer between strong legs that shifted and twined around hers. Willow felt surrounded by him and his overpowering nearness ignited a passion that surged between them. Firm hands spread over her hips; strong wandering fingers caressed sensitive skin on the insides of her thighs then gently spread her legs and stroked across the thin layer of nylon shielding the core of her sexuality.

For an instant, Willow's mind seized, then relaxed with a shiver. A deep, tingling sensation grew inside her, made her squirm with a pleasure she'd only known in the privacy of sexual self-expression, where there had been no fear—only a desperate need for a release that satisfied the immediate need but left her feeling unfulfilled.

When Drew rolled her onto her back and pulled away from the kiss, Willow looked up in unfocused abstraction and watched him strip off his clothes. He kissed her again and the roughness of chest hair brushed across excited nipples. Her arms slid around him as she softened to a kiss that held her captive, a passion that challenged her, stole her breath, set her heart pounding. Linked by the kiss, their bodies wound together in a writhing embrace of shared fervor that snatched away time and dimension.

For the first time in her life, Willow experienced the unleashed power of sexual passion. Every feeling part of her cried out for the closeness of Drew, who moved and rolled with her in a turmoil of urgency. He was heat and strength that demanded she fuse with his supple undulations. He stripped away the last scrap of clothing then knelt between her legs, slid his palms up the front of her legs until his hands framed the patch of red-gold at the top of her thighs. His thumbs brushed through it and his lopsided smile slanted up on one side when she shivered at the sensation, bit at her lower lip to suppress a gasp.

"No inhibitions allowed." Drew's smile widened as his eyes appraised her. "You're perfect—a woman of alluring beauty, her hair a rain of fiery embers—just as I knew you would be. This is a calendar page I'll never tire of seeing."

He buried a hand in the fall of her hair until his palm cradled the back of her head, lowered his mouth to hers in a deep, breathing duel of thrust and parry that heated the fire in his groin, left her breathless. The sight, feel, and scent of arousal increased his painful hardness, stimulated a compulsive urge to abandon control. But, knowing this seduction couldn't be hurried, he reined in his impatience.

Drew had been dreading a virgin. This was worse. Willow was not only inexperienced; she'd been hurt and frightened. In spite of anything she said or how brave a front she was showing, he sensed her fear and knew that while her desire trusted him to make it right, her shredded emotions couldn't handle the usual awkwardness of a first sexual encounter. Since he never wanted her to feel fear, or failure again, he knew he would have to arouse and satisfy her so completely the sense of her own pleasure would make it right.

As if her mind read his thoughts, Willow's awareness dissolved into floating detachment, where sensitized nerves made her squirm and purr like a stroked cat. Gentle hands caressed her entire body until she was writhing in a spinning pleasure that wanted more sensation, more strength. When he covered her mouth in a deep, breathing kiss, their tongues tangled and his body slid over hers, hot and rough and strong. She molded to him while they moved together in a building rhythm of pleasure that made her grasp hard back muscles, clasp firm buttocks—as if she could fuse him to her writhing body.

When the warm, hard length of Drew's stiffness touched the inside of Willow's thigh, phantom memories tensed her; but when it rubbed slowly and sensually against her skin, she thrilled to the touch, trailed her hand around his hip to where his groin pressed against her.

"Can I touch you?"

"Do you want to?"

"I need to know..." Willow's breath caught when he rolled away from her and she saw the rigid shaft between them. Her hand tightened on his hip for a moment before she slipped it across tight groin muscles, brushed the tips of her fingers along unexpectedly soft skin. Drew pulled in a breath, then let it out with a low groan when she closed her hand. When he twitched and the swollen shaft moved in her hold, she jerked her hand away. "Did I hurt you?"

"Rapturously." He caught her hand, moved it to his lips, nipped at her fingers. "But unless you want to spring me out of the start box at full gallop, it's best you leave the reins in my hands for this ride."

Rising on one elbow, Drew cupped his hand over her cheek, studied her eyes and face. "Speaking of the start box, you made the decision to enter it. You've sampled the excitement of the run to the finish line. Should I worry about your starting jitters—or pretend I don't know they're there?"

"They're there. But I think it's something more."

"And that is?" An eyebrow lifted quizzically.

"Drew, I grew up on a farm that raises Angus breeding bulls. I've listened to my brothers, even seen more of them than I should have—but never like that. I know how sex is supposed to work. I'm afraid it will go wrong again."

"Lassie," he answered with a gently rolling brogue, "I'm well-endowed with what my Scottish cousins braggingly call a Highlander's caber of prowess. But I can assure you, it isn't beyond the scale of masculine normality."

"But what if something's wrong with me?" Her eyes pleaded with him to understand. "What if the pain and failure really was my fault?"

"There's nothing wrong with you, and you didn't fail."

"Then why did it hurt like I was being ripped apart?"

"You didn't want it and weren't ready for it. It was rape, and your body rejected it. I won't let that happen."

"You'll stop if it doesn't work?"

"I'll stop whenever you want. Just say no. That's my promise. Yours is to trust me as a teacher and enjoy your education." He lifted her chin and gently kissed her lips. "Willow, you have to let me touch you. I can't make love to you without touching you, without sharing all the sensations with you. Will you trust me and take a chance on me knowing how to make it right?"

"I want you so much I have to. What do you want me to do?"

"Relax, soften to me, bend to me, open yourself to pleasure." He lowered his head and murmured in her ear, "Stop thinking. Stop comparing."

Feeling a softening of tension, Drew let go of some of his own apprehension, took a firmer control of the reins. The pressure of his hand spread her legs and gentle fingers caressed beneath a cover of auburn curls. He felt her tense, then relax as he touched sensitive flesh, heard her breath catch. He paused until she accepted it and pulled in a gasping breath, tightened around his touch, exhaled with a soft sigh.

"There's nothing wrong with you, Willow. You're perfect and as ready as a woman can be."

"It feels so good I want it to last forever." When he pulled away from the clutch of her arms and fumbled for his discarded sweat shirt, Willow tried to sit up and reach for him, but her body felt boneless and he rolled away from her and stood up. "Don't leave me, Drew."

"I'm not leaving. I'm keeping it safe." He rolled her onto her stomach, swept her hair away and leaned down to kiss the side of her neck. His lips nibbled at an ear as he lay beside her and rubbed his hand on her with touches that made her squirm beneath him.

While his hands petted and massaged, Drew trailed kisses down her back, tasted the saltiness of damp skin, breathed in her honeysuckle scent and the stimulating tang of her sexuality. "Roll over and relax."

When he saw her moisten her lips and try to speak, he pressed a forefinger across her lips, shook his head. "No thinking. No talking." He shifted closer, let the rough surface of his thighs brush against the softness of hers, and closed a hand on her waist. "Let it all go. Close your eyes and let me really turn you inside out."

Willow remembered what he'd said about waltzing and let the memory of the way they'd molded together and moved as one during the dance fill her mind. She softened to his hand, put her trust in his ability to lead and surrendered body and mind to him. With a smile of relief, she let desire soar until there was no way she could think of anything except the desire possessing her.

"Ready for the really big fences?" Drew's voice rumbled in the blissful vertigo of her senses.

"You mean there's more?" She winked at his teasing smile.

"You bet. And we get to take the ride for the gold together."

"Then go for it." Willow chuckled at his smile, just before his mouth devoured hers with a suddenness that stopped her mind.

Willow wanted to tell him there was no need for caution because she both wanted him and welcomed him. Her words were snatched away in a gasp when, with a quick thrust, he slid partway into her. She tensed, felt him stop, but not retreat. There was pressure but no pain. Relief flowed through her and when he pulled back, she grasped his back, braided her legs around his thighs and felt engulfed by the pleasure of him filling her. A huge bubble of excitement burst inside her and she laughed when it flowed through her in total release from fear and inhibition. She pulled him closer, felt the full pleasure of penetration.

There was no pain, only deep, clutching spasms, heat and exquisite thrills as he retreated and advanced slowly, letting her thrill to the sensation of joining, discover how to move with him, match his rhythm. There was no awkwardness, no confusion. She merged with his movement and he increased the tempo until she dug her fingers into his back, wrapped her legs around his and answered him with a strength that disintegrated self-control.

Rearing up, Drew broke the grip of her legs, entwined his fingers with hers, pinned her hands to the bed beside her head and thrust into her with unrestrained lust.

"Yes, yes, yes!" With laughing relief, Willow let desire soar, arched to meet his force and reveled in the expanding bubble of elation that kept coming and coming until it engulfed her, cascaded through her body in shuddering spasms.

Drew finished with a deep, resonant groan that rumbled up from deep in his chest. He collapsed to his elbows before he slid his arms under her shoulders and lowered his weight. Wanting to remain a part of him, Willow tightened her legs around his, her arms around his chest and hugged him as hard as she could. She was crying and smiling and laughing all at the same time.

"Thank you, thank you," she babbled as tears of release streamed from her eyes. "Thank you for showing me it's wonderful."

"You're welcome any time." Smiling, Drew lifted his head, kissed the warm track of a tear and then the tip of her nose. "I love your laugh."

"I couldn't help it." Willow smiled up at him with a joy that bubbled in her chest.

"Don't ever fight a laugh of pleasure. It makes it more fun." Drew propped his chin on a fist and winked at her. "I knew you would be good. I learned you are fantastic."

"I have a fantastic tutor."

"And you said I didn't have a job."

"How many more lessons are there?" She giggled when he looked down his nose with a professorial scowl. "I wouldn't want you to be unemployed."

"How many would you like to contract for?"

"An infinite number."

"No problem. I like the idea of an open-ended contract. It's like riding, you never know it all and have to practice a lot."

"I'll go for that." Willow released her legs and shifted under him. "Drew, I need to breathe."

"Suddenly you're appealing to my chivalry. I'll consider it."

"If you don't let me breathe, I'll turn blue."

"I like blue."

"Get off me." She poked him in the ribs until he rolled off the bed.

"Good grief, Willow, this room is a mess!" Drew let his dramatic statement hang in the air while he strode to the bathroom.

"You are infuriating!" She snatched his sweatshirt off the floor, balled it up and threw it at him.

When the shirt fell on the hall floor in front of the closing bathroom door, Willow flopped back on the bed and giggled with a thrill that kept erupting from deep inside her. Yes, he was infuriating. And she loved him for it. She positively knew she was in love and was sure he felt the same. In her mind, only two people in love could experience something so complete and wonderful. Willow hugged herself and a huge grin spread across her face. *I love you, Andrew Wayne Sutherland, and I won't let you go. Your commitment is right here, not in Genoa.*

When the bathroom door opened, Willow sat up to see Drew stoop down and sweep something off the floor. The sweat shirt flew at her from close range, giving her little chance to do more than deflect it before he dove at her, crushed her to him and tickled her with darting fingers.

After four older brothers and one almost her age, Willow had developed a certain immunity to tickling. It failed her today. Once she started laughing, she was helpless and he was mercilessly victorious.

Finally, after rolling and kicking all over the bed, she collapsed beside him and sucked in a deep breath. "The roughhouse was supposed to come before the lovemaking."

"Says who?"

"My brother Owen. My plan was to get you to roughhouse as an ice breaker."

"Your choice of water temperature was hardly an ice breaker." Drew lay on his back beside her and pulled her head onto his shoulder while gentle fingers played with her hair.

Willow propped herself on an elbow. She was pensive for a long moment while she lost herself in his eyes. Her other hand teased at his hair, played with its soft curls. If there had been any doubt in her mind about loving Drew, it was gone now. The kiss on the fingertips had grown to a fulfillment she'd never believed possible.

In Willow's mind, they hadn't just made love. They'd shared each other and become a part of each other. It changed her, made her more complete, more aware. Spent passion left a warm ember of happiness inside her. It had no size, no shape, no dimension. It was as tiny as a cell, as large as space, as personal as a dream, as engulfing as life itself. It was love. It couldn't be proven by chemists or biologists, not even by doctors or psychiatrists. It was unexplained, but it was real. And she had it. She was in love with a man who was still an enigma to her, but it no longer worried her. In fact, she looked forward to gradually exposing a portrait that was taking on an exciting third dimension.

"Drew, do you know you create convincing atmospheres that are one step from reality?" She ran a forefinger down his forehead and nose to his mouth, where he caught it between his lips. "Sometimes, I'm not sure if you're being serious, or tongueincheek, or just playacting."

"Would you believe all of the above? We live in a mundane world. Sometimes it helps to create a little magic. And, if we can't see the world with irony, it's a pretty tough grind."

"Do you do that with all your women?"

"No." His answer was sharp. "Most women I know think they're too sophisticated to enjoy the silly parts of me."

"You always keep me one step off balance. One minute you want to be forty. The next you're playing magician. And then, when you transported me into a world of erotic sensation, you had the nerve to crack a joke."

"I plead guilty to absurdity." He looked at her with his mischievous schoolboy look. "Do you know what I first liked about you?"

"Probably the back of my blue jeans when I leaned into my car."

"That was the first thing I noticed." He slipped his hand down her back and laughed at her flush. "I fully admit you have a bonny bum that drives me crazy. But I liked you when you banged your head on the car and made a goofy face. You hooked me when you told me I was supposed to have big feet and a cracking voice."

"I did?"

"You made me laugh, Willow. It fascinated me. Not many things have fascinated me lately. Everything and everyone have been too serious about images, accomplishments, and manipulations."

"And responsibility?"

"That, too."

"What is it you're trying to live up to?"

"I decided to start thinking about it in August." Drew pulled her down for a soft kiss. "But unfortunately, I do have an obligation I have to meet in an hour."

"What is it?"

"I'm having dinner with a stock broker. Then I have a call at seven and an appointment after that." He sat up and swung his legs off the bed. "Keep that kiss warm until I come back."

"I won't lock the door."

"Doesn't matter. I have a key."

"Why doesn't that surprise me?"

Chapter Twelve

It took Drew a while to recognize the solitary man Sal pointed to at the far end of the bar. Ernie Romano held a beer mug in both hands and stared into it as if he were trying to decide if it was time to order another or make the last few ounces last a little longer. The short, chubby kid with a shaggy mop of brown hair that Drew remembered was gone. The man at the bar looked older than twenty-six, but it wasn't his thick-lensed glasses or stubbly beard. Ernie was still short, still overweight, but his vitality had shrunken into him, leaving him withdrawn and uninterested in anything except the beer in his hands.

"Thanks, Sal. Could you refill Ernie's beer and bring me a JD, no ice, when you get a chance?" Drew smiled at Sal's confused reaction to his polite request and walked to the stool next to Ernie. "Hey, Captain Marvel, what's happenin'?"

"Captain Marvel?" Ernie twisted in surprise. "Drew? Is it really you? I heard you was looking for me. I thought it was some kind of bad joke to get Mario pissed at me."

"I don't want Mario pissed at you."

"But dumbass Dominic does. He likes to stir up trouble and Mario's easy to stir up. He went ballistic when he found out you come in here bad mouthing him."

"I heard he was threatening me and laid my response on thick. I mostly came back to see if I can make sense of my life here."

When the drinks appeared, Drew looked up to meet Sal's eyes. The man's confusion had turned to shrewd intelligence that conveyed both understanding and a clear warning when he glanced at a high corner table across the room. Drew followed his gaze to three men, who were eyeing him the way chained pit bulls watched a bold stray piss beyond their reach.

"It's all right, Sal. I already made my point. I'm here to talk to Ernie. I have no interest in Mario's cronies."

"I'm trying to clean this place up and don't want trouble."

"What about them?" Drew nodded toward the corner table.

"They should know. I've called the cops on them before."

"Does Mario know?" Drew paid for the drinks and lifted the glass.

"He hasn't been around much lately." Sal set the change on the bar. "Maybe my luck will hold until you're gone."

"Want to bet double or nothing for free drinks on that?"

"Nope. I don't gamble or drink. It cuts into my profits." Sal walked toward a customer who was pointing into the beer glass in front of him.

"I like that man." Drew turned back to Ernie. "Do you think he has a chance here?"

"I hope so. Most of the neighborhood likes what he's doing. You really come to see me, Drew?"

"I came back to sort out some lost memories. When I heard you were still around, the thing that popped into my mind clear as shit was that night we tried to steal a few bucks from your mother's purse. She lit into us with a wooden spoon and your sister kept laughing and holding the door closed. It was like some crazy chase scene from a slapstick movie." Drew watched Ernie's blank expression brighten as the memory surfaced in his mind. "Christ, Ernie, we trashed the fucking room before I went out the window."

"My mom grabbed your pajama pants to stop you." Ernie convulsed in laughter and thumped his hand on the top of the bar when his attempt to talk was choked off by more laughter.

"That's right. I wiggled out of them and slithered onto the fire escape. I ran all the way home, barefoot and bare assed, with my hands between my legs, terrified I'd run into some girl who knew me."

"I can still see your ass disappearing over the window sill and hear my mother hollering at you to stop before you hurt yourself."

"I was avoiding getting hurt. She was vicious with that thing." Drew laughed with Ernie. "The fire escape was no sweat. I went down ours whenever I wanted to sneak out."

"You used to get me in trouble for stealing and stuff, then act like you didn't know why I was mad at you, or why my mother said I couldn't play with you anymore."

"I'm trying to sort out a lot of those screwed up memories. When I talked to Milly a couple of weeks ago and now, talking to you, I remember some of the stuff we used to do. Remember when we found your father's old comic book collection and pretended to be super heroes? We stapled that hunk of yellow ribbon on a red shirt so you could be Captain Marvel. Who was I?"

"Crimson Avenger. You said you wanted to wipe out all the bad kids." Ernie's laugh died; his face grew uneasy. "But you turned into one of the bad kids, Drew. You got tough and weird when you tagged around with Dominic and his gang."

"That's the stuff I didn't want to remember. I'm trying to be one of the good guys now."

"Why are you after Mario? You still trying to impress Dominic?"

"What do you mean? I hardly remember Dominic." Drew gave him a bewildered look then cocked his head and looked thoughtful. "Was he that older kid who used to get us to start some kind of ruckus at a newsstand so he could steal candy and cigarettes."

"You and his two younger brothers. I was afraid of him and stayed as far away as I could." Ernie dropped his gaze away from Drew and stared into his beer. "You got really weird that last winter. You wouldn't even read the comics with me. You called them stupid."

"Would you believe me if I told you I didn't know how to read?"

"No way." Ernie shook his head. "You was the best reader in the class."

"Do you remember me telling you I was my older brother?"

"Sure do. When you wanted to be tough, you sometimes pretended to be him. You said your name was Jack. Nobody believed you."

"Except me." Drew picked up his drink and took a swallow while Ernie twisted his face, as if he were trying to make sense out of a bad riddle. "I wasn't pretending, Ernie. He was a very different kid, and he lived in my head."

Ignoring Ernie's bewilderment, Drew let an image form in his mind. "To me he was bigger, blond and had his own name. It was Jack. He took over my life little bits at a time and I couldn't stop him until after my father took me away and gave me stability. I don't remember much from my years here, but I know I need to."

"I don't know what happened with your mother. I was only a kid. Nobody would talk about it around me. She was dead and you was gone with a man people said was your father. We hadn't been friends for a while because you didn't want to be."

"Jack didn't want to be."

"He was still you and it scared me."

"Yes, he was. I just didn't know it at the time. Back then, I was as much afraid of Jack as you were."

"You still talk crazy."

"I guess I do. And in that context, I was a little crazy. I don't need you to tell me what happened to my mother. I know about that." Drew drank some of the liquor and let it slide down his throat while he shied away from memories he didn't want to revisit. "I was taken to a very different world. After a while, nothing here seemed real anymore. But somehow, I know there are memories I've avoided too long."

"What can I tell you, Drew? We were best friends. Then you started hanging with Dominic and Mario."

"I hung around with Mario?" Drew gave him a stunned look.

"You hung around him, not with him."

"Mario was a bully. I hated him, even when I was being a dope."

"You kept getting in his face, like you was daring him, but you was always fast enough to get away. And then Antonio, who lived over by the market, stood up for you. Mario was scared pissless of him."

"My mother's youngest brother." Drew smiled. "Undisputed leader of the Eagle Gang."

"Antonio still comes around once in a while to keep in touch. He gets his hair cut at my cousin Joe's barber shop. They played football together in high school."

"Who lives in my old apartment now?"

"It's been vacant awhile. The building was sold and the new owners plan to knock it down."

"What have you been up to?"

"Not much. I work a delivery route for a food service. See a lot of restaurants and bars."

"Got a family?"

"I married Rita Garcia a few years back."

"Should I know her?"

Ernie shook his head "We met in high school. Anyways, we had a little girl, but she died. Rita said she couldn't stand to live with me after that. She ran off with a Cuban who worked on the docks. He got a job in Duluth loading lake freighters. I got divorce papers to sign a year later so they could get married. Maybe she can forget out there."

"You mean better than you can?"

"I loved that little girl, Drew."

"Rita?"

"No, Angela, my baby." Ernie stared at the beer cradled in his hands. "She rode her tricycle into the street and a car hit her. I was watching her, but there was nothing I could do. She went off the curb in front of a parked car and into the street. I tried to stop her, but I couldn't. Why did I give her a bike? Why was I so far away?"

When Ernie continued to stare into his beer and ask unanswerable questions that he had already asked a thousand times and would ask a thousand more, Drew reached out and put his hand over the top of the glass. "The answers aren't in there, only the questions."

Ernie looked up with an expression that looked too tired to care. "I see her at night, lying on the street like a broken doll."

"And you'll go on seeing it as long as you keep drinking yourself to sleep."

"I know." Ernie shifted his gaze away from Drew and looked toward the door at the other end of the bar. "Oh fuck. Get out of here before he sees you."

"I don't think that's possible." Drew glanced toward the door, then drank the last of the whiskey. He thumped the empty glass on the bar top before he swiveled the stool and studied the man confronting him.

In a black satin jacket from a nearby boxing gym, Mario looked much as he had five years ago, but his once slender frame showed more bulk, more age. A flash of panic washed across a bitter face that would have been handsome without the puckered scar that lifted one side of his upper lip and the off-center lump Drew's piece of pipe had added to his hook nose. Mario darted a jumpy gaze to the trio of drinkers across the room, seemed to absorb courage from their presence.

The face that swung back to Drew was a hard mask of unreasoning hate that swelled to rage when Mario met sharp blue eyes that unnerved him with intense, burning dominance—eyes that refused to look away, eyes that showed no fear, eyes of a demonic child, who had poisoned his own mother's mind and then destroyed Gino, the uncle Mario had worshipped.

Suddenly, Mario was face to face with the blue glare of an enemy who had dared to defy him, left him horribly scarred and not once, but twice, humiliated him in front of his followers, thwarted his vengeance and sent him to prison where he'd endured degrading humiliations. Like superheated magma, years of hate surfaced, along with an unreasoning wrath that could only be satisfied by the annihilation of the will that had caused those defeats.

Without losing eye contact with Mario, Drew stood and slipped a card with his cell phone number into Ernie's hand. "It would be real smart for you to get away from me and head for the door as soon as you get a chance."

When Ernie took the card and moved toward the kitchen door in the back corner of the room, Drew stepped away from the barstool and moved toward Mario, who shifted closer to where his three cronies straightened in their chairs and pushed away from the table. Not knowing if they were looking for an escape route or fighting room, Drew stayed close to the bar to keep them in sight. He didn't want any of them behind him if Mario did something stupid.

"I hear you've been looking for me, Pissface. Well, I'm here. What do you want?"

"Your balls in a jar, Sutherland."

"Not a chance. I'm here because I have old friends I want to talk to and you aren't one of them. My deal is you stay away from me and I won't have to knock the shit out of you again."

"You're still a cock-sucking bastard."

"I'm not the one who did time sucking scumbags at a state correctional lockup for bad boys." Drew read fury in Mario's face and eyes, saw his right arm tense when its hand gripped something under the jacket's waist band. "The choice is a no brainer, Mario. You can back off and save your pissface, or make an ass of yourself again."

Ducking under the left fist that feinted toward his jaw, Drew sidestepped, caught Mario's right hand with his left as it swung free of the jacket in a backhanded arc meant to slash a blade across his stomach. With a snapping jerk, he spun Mario and twisted the captured arm up behind his back.

An instant later, Mario slammed into the edge of the bar and gasped for air while his free hand groped across the counter to keep him from sliding to his knees. With a loud thud, Mario's now empty right hand smacked across his left wrist an instant before the sharp point of a switchblade knife stabbed through both sleeves of his shiny jacket and pinned his arms to the wooden surface of the bar.

"Wrong choice, pissface." Drew glared at Mario's cronies, who cautiously settled in their chairs before he looked back at Mario. "Be glad I'm too civilized to put it through your hand as a payback for Jimmy Rice."

"You'll pay for that, Sutherland." The threat croaked out of a dry throat as Mario gaped at the sight of his own knife quivering in front of his face. "You'll pay big."

"In case you don't get it, I'll reiterate. You don't scare me. If you leave me alone, I won't have to keep proving it."

Noticing two uniformed policemen at the far end of the bar with hands resting on loosened guns, Drew walked to where Sal was eyeing him with a scrutiny that seemed to be asking questions Drew wasn't ready to answer. "You didn't have to call them. There was no trouble."

"I didn't. They showed up right after Mario. Maybe you got a guardian angel."

"Don't know why anyone would think I needed one." Drew shrugged. "Sorry about adding another gash in your bar, but it was the only thing I could think of at the time."

Drew looked from the policeman beside Mario to the one in front of him. "It's an old issue. He's a slow learner."

"You willing to answer some questions about this?" The officer nodded toward the street.

"Sure." Drew pushed away from the bar, noticed that the wary policeman moved back then stepped behind him when he walked to the door.

Outside, two patrol cars, with lights flashing, nosed up to the curb, forcing traffic to edge around them on the narrow street. Two more uniforms stood beside them on the sidewalk. One talked on a radio, the other fingered the butt of his gun. The black woman with the radio opened the back door on the first car and motioned Drew into it.

"What is this, an arrest?" Drew balked and gave her a wry scowl.

"Not yet," the man behind him said. "But it could be if you don't get in the car."

"For what?"

"Just get in the car. Someone wants to talk to you."

"I can guess who that is." Drew ducked into the back seat of the patrol car and heard the locks engage as soon as the door closed behind him. When the officers were in the car, the woman turned on the siren, backed into the street, and pulled away from traffic stacked up behind the second patrol car that had backed up to block off the street.

"Could you just take me to my car?" Drew asked. The thought of Willow waiting for him to return to her bed was much more appealing than a face-off with Antonio, which is why he hadn't bothered to tell his uncle about his decision to see if he could find Ernie at Sal's tonight. "I don't want to talk to him right now?"

"Vitale said to pick you up." The older policeman turned enough to look at Drew through the heavy wire barrier between them. "He wasn't in a good mood when he said it."

"I'm sure he wasn't."

In Antonio's driveway, Drew stepped from the car, took one look at the way his uncle glowered at him from inside the open garage door and decided he definitely didn't want to talk to him. The big man looked ready to rip him into small pieces and feed him to the nearest stray dog.

"What did I do to twist your tail?" Drew asked when his uncle marched toward him.

"I'll explain it after I talk to Harrison."

"Don't take too long. There's someone a lot sweeter than you waiting to give me a warm welcome home."

"Then what the hell were you doing in a bar inciting violence?"

"I had some time…"

Drew scowled when Antonio continued past him as if the question were unanswerable, then shrugged and walked into the kitchen. Sitting at the table, he picked up a folded section of newspaper beside a coffee cup. He studied a partially filled in crossword puzzle for a while before he reached for a pencil.

"What are you doing to my puzzle?" Antonio's voice boomed from the door to the garage.

"Fixing it." Drew tapped an unfinished word. "A double bassoon or reed organ stop is a contrafagotto."

"That sounds indecent. Besides, it can't be." Antonio picked up the puzzle grid. "It doesn't start with a D."

"Because something edible should be comestible, not digestible."

"Humph." Antonio dropped the paper on the table. "Explain to me what you thought you were doing at Sal's."

"I was having a friendly drink with Ernie when Mario showed up. I asked him why he was looking for me. I took his answer as a threat."

"So, you goaded him into a fight?"

"Wasn't much of a fight."

"He almost gutted you."

"He did not." Drew shoved the chair back and stood, challenging his uncle's hard glare for a tense moment before he relaxed his stance. "I had the knife before he could touch me. Somebody taught him some dirty tricks, but he's so stupid he advertises them. He doesn't stand a chance against me."

"And now he knows it."

"What does that mean?"

"He won't make that mistake again. You foolishly humiliated him. He'll make sure you can't do it again."

"I wouldn't bet on that. He reacts with dumb instincts and doesn't think."

"You caught him by surprise. Mario isn't as stupid as you think. He'll avoid you until he gets you where he wants you. The next time you see him, the odds will be on his side. It will never be one on one again."

"It wasn't tonight. Three of his buddies were there, but it was over before they could react."

"They also know Sal has no tolerance for fights. A point well made when two uniforms walked in the door."

"Sal said he didn't call them."

"They don't know that. I told Harrison to stay close if you were in the area. He called for backup when Mario showed up."

"For shit sake, Tonio, nobody's going to talk to me if I have a police escort getting in my way. When Sal implied that I had a guardian angel, I thought he was joking. I don't need one, so back off."

"That's my decision, not yours. Ditch the cocky attitude and work with me on this or I'll have Mario run in on a parole violation and hope they put him away until long after you go back to Europe."

"I thought you wanted to use him to catch bigger game."

"I do, but I will not work with a loose cannon who thinks he's invincible. You're good, but it might not be enough. I want to know when you're anywhere near that neighborhood and where you'll be every minute. None of my cops will get in your way if they know what to expect. Now, do we have an agreement?"

"Yes." Drew dropped onto the chair and stared at his unclenching hands. "I don't know why I goaded him like that. It was as if we were kids again. I can't see him the way you do. I saw the bullying coward he always was, and I was the wise ass I used to be. That arrogant cock is still part of me. Sometimes he gets strong enough to blur my commonsense."

"Like you don't remember it?" Antonio gave him a cautious look.

"No." Drew made a sour face. "I know exactly what I did. I'm totally in control. I just get cocky sometimes and go with it. Riles Dad when I do it to him." Drew smiled at his uncle's agreeing nod. "Don't worry about it. Mario brought back some memories. That's all."

"Is that what happened in Italy with that opera teacher?"

"I don't know what that was. Dad thinks I dissociated, but I don't agree with him. I blacked out for a bit, but it was just anger. I'd been holding it in for a long time and it snapped my control. After I blew it out, I couldn't face him, so I ran away. I don't feel wrong about Mario, but I do about Vittorio. Maybe that's why I refused to remember it."

"Maybe." Antonio looked as if he wasn't buying the explanation but was wise enough to leave it alone. "Where's your car?"

"In a safe structure in Center City. I really do want to get home and would appreciate a ride to my car."

"Right after I take you in for a statement about what happened tonight."

"Won't that give him a violation?"

"Not if I don't want it to. Right now, Sal's the only one who actually saw him try to use the knife and he's agreed to keep it to himself as long as we want."

"Ernie says Sal wants to clean up the neighborhood."

"At least his piece of it. He's a retired Jersey cop from Camden. He came back to his old neighborhood because he didn't like what was happening to it." Antonio grabbed two soft salted pretzels out of a bag on the counter and tossed one to Drew before he headed for the garage. "Would this sweet, warm thing at home happen to be named Willow?"

"She certainly would."

"I thought she was sealed in a virginal bank vault."

"She dropped the key to the bank in my pocket this afternoon and we blew the vault wide open." Drew followed him through the door.

"Worth it?"

"Would not being able to get enough of her qualify as worth it?"

Antonio stood on the far side of the grey sedan and met Drew's eyes across the roof. "Same question. With someone like that waiting for you, what were you doing in a bar inciting violence?"

"I need to know what happened to me. All the answers are wrapped up in the years between four and six when I lived in Philly. I know what people told me about that time, but I don't have true memories because it was before Jack and Andrew came out. No matter how much hell I relived in therapy, none of it was from then. It's important. I know it is."

"If you believe that, I won't get in your way but I want to know about it."

"I got that message loud and clear. Just keep your angel corps out of my sight. It makes me feel spied on."

"It's not a tight cover. I just want them alerted to possible trouble."

"Okay, I can handle that. Let's get this over with before she accuses me of cheating on her."

Chapter Thirteen

Willow smiled when she heard Drew's car pull in the driveway and rolled over to face the open hall door. She yawned and stretched before she propped herself on an elbow and tried to shake sawdust out of her head. She'd wanted to stay awake; but at eleven, when her eyelids kept blotting out the book she was reading on the couch, she gave in to drowsiness and went to bed. A glance at the clock told her it was after midnight, which explained why she felt drugged by sound sleep.

When Drew walked under the hall light on his way to the bathroom, Willow rolled onto her back and stared up at the steeply peaked ceiling. She knew she had to tell him about uncertainties that nagged at her while he was away, but her mind was unable to focus on anything but the thrill of knowing he'd come back to be with her. When she heard the shower start, she closed her eyes and floated in a drowsy halfsleep filled with a pleasant reverie about the feel of his hands, the excitement of his kisses, the intensity of his lovemaking.

Willow drifted back to sleep and was unaware of Drew until he slipped into bed and molded to her side, warm and cleanscented from the shower. A gentle hand turned her face and he was kissing her before she was awake enough to say anything. His toothpaste minty kiss was deliciously tender and stimulating in a dreamy way that erased all practical thinking and pulled her into a euphoric state that lost touch with reality.

With a moaning sigh of enjoyment, Willow stretched and arched in somnolent arousal. His hands stripped away her nightshirt and caressed her body with intimate touches that sensitized her skin, made her squirm against him. She could hardly put two objective thoughts together; and when the surge of pleasure swelled, she was unable to think at all—as if a charge of sexuality emanated from Drew and took possession of her whenever she felt his touch.

Tonight, Willow learned the power of her own sexuality and the strength of her sensual need for this man who could reach into her and stimulate her with intense passion. She gave heated excitement free rein, released all restraint, allowed pure sensation to take her on an unbelievable trip that transported her beyond the tangible.

Drew conquered her with power and played to her senses with the skill of a conductor directing a symphonic masterpiece. Always sensitive to her responses, he explored her body and electrified her nerves. His touches and movements kept her heady as he lifted her beyond reality. His hands and body controlled her, giving her what she craved and then drawing back until she pled for more.

With a sudden, deep thrust, he filled her with the hard, searing essence of his maleness and answered her plea with powerful strokes that drove her beyond pleasure into the passionate maelstrom of a firestorm. A thrilling sense of exhilaration expanded inside her, grew with each beat of his demanding rhythm until she could no longer contain it. The tension peaked with a swelling bubble that burst into exquisite splinters of ecstasy. She heard a deep laugh of triumph escape his chest as she clutched at lingering sensations of neural bliss.

Instead of crushing her with his weight, Drew clasped strong arms around her and rolled onto his back with her head nestled on his shoulder. They lay still for a long time, bodies joined, hearts beating together, eyes moist from the power of shared emotion.

This afternoon Drew had been cautious, holding a corner of his mind in check while he tested her reactions. Tonight, he unleashed an explosive lust Willow not only accepted but matched with her own.

"You are a fantastic woman." Drew slowly relaxed his arms but continued to hold her to him with hands that caressed the softness they'd been holding. "You have enough high-octane fuel to accelerate my fires and blast me into orbit."

"I thought a dousing with cold water was supposed to put out fires not fuel them. I'll have to try it again."

"Try it, Lassie, and I'll forget the pond and kindle a fire with the flat o' ma hand on your shapely bum."

"That is a male chauvinist answer." Willow raised her head and poked a forefinger on his chest until he grabbed her wrist. "Men always resort to brutality to defeat wit."

"Arrgh," He twisted his mouth and raised an eyebrow in a cockeyed scowl, "where, me lusty wench, is the wit in ten gallons of cold water?"

"There was a lot of fun in it." She giggled.

"And I would find it great fun to warm your irresistible derrière." He gave her a caressing swat before he rolled away and headed for the bathroom.

Willow was confused. Then relieved. "I'm glad you're such a careful person."

"I never said I had *no* sense of responsibility," Drew shouted over the flushing toilet. "While we're on the subject, I have the address and phone number of an excellent gynecologist. Go to her, so you can make careful a certainty."

"That sounds as if you've been making assumptions." Willow turned on the bedside lamp, found her nightshirt and pulled it on before she straightened the twisted covers and slid into bed.

"Of course, I have." Drew strode into the room and stared at her with an expression midway between consternation and alarm.

"Well, so have I." Willow knew she sounded hard, but she had to force herself to be serious and break out of the spell of contentment that told her nothing mattered except the pleasure they shared. "I don't think they're the same assumptions."

"I don't read you again. It isn't something to gamble with."

"Oh, I don't mean that. I agree with that. It's just that there are some things we need to reconsider if this relationship is to continue."

"We just experienced all out sexual magnificence that demands repeat performances. And you want to reconsider?"

"I did some thinking while you were gone."

"I can hardly wait to hear this." Drew slid into bed, faced her with his head propped on his fist.

"You can't stay here."

"Why not?"

"It isn't proper."

Looking annoyed, he rose on his elbow. "You're saying it isn't proper for me to sleep here, but what we just did is proper?"

"None of it is proper, but what we just did is between you and me." Drew looked so appallingly dense Willow wanted to smack him. "If you stay here, everyone will know about it."

"Who's everyone?"

"John, Roy, your grandmother."

"John will only smile smugly. Roy won't give it more than a passing thought. Neither of them will gossip to my grandmother."

"She'll know you didn't come home."

"I often don't come home. I'm not the thirteen-year-old bigfoot. Besides, my rooms are so far from hers she wouldn't notice if I came home with a marching band."

"How can you be so unconcerned with sexual propriety?"

"Nobody ever told me I'd go blind."

His answer silenced Willow and she didn't know how to counter it. "Well, I'm not ready to commit myself to that kind of relationship."

"Need I remind you we already have that kind of relationship? There's nothing to reconsider."

"It's not a relationship—yet." She sat up and turned to face him with her legs folded tailor fashion, arms crossed in front of her.

"It isn't?" He sat up and glared back at her. "Look, Ms. Sitting Bull, if this is supposed to be some kind of joke, I'm not laughing. It's the best relationship I've ever had."

"Sexually."

"Isn't that what we're talking about?" His voice grew deeper and more powerful.

"It's not what I'm talking about. You can't just move into my house as if you belong here."

"I don't remember saying I was going to."

"You seem to have moved into my bed."

"I was invited here. Aren't you the same woman who told me she'd leave the door open?"

"I didn't mean all night."

"There were no hours mentioned in the invitation." Drew's voice approached loud, but with an obvious effort to control himself, he reached forward to cup a hand around her shoulder. "Willow, look at it sensibly."

"I am." She jerked away from a touch that almost made her resolve crumble. "You're the one not being reasonable."

"What is this?" Drew flared. "Thanks for the fuck and call me sometime? Isn't that supposed to be the callous male chauvinist line?"

"You've got it all wrong." Willow's fists clenched on her knees in an effort to keep from shouting. "I'm not brushing you off. I just don't want you to spend the night here."

"You don't?" He lunged forward, grabbed her arms, threw her on her back, and stared down with dominance blazing in the dark depths of his eyes. "I think it's time for the next lesson when you find out you don't mean that."

Willow squirmed under his stare and felt him slide a leg over both of hers. She was sure he could hear the thumping of her heart as easily as she could. Smiling cruelly, Drew yanked off her lavender nightshirt with a big fuzzy lamb on the front and threw it across the room. One hand caught her chin while the other twisted in a tangle of loose hair until she was trapped, unable to look away from the closeness of his face, the probing intensity of his eyes.

Holding her motionless, Drew lowered his head, gently brushed his lips across hers, pulled back just enough to trace her lips with the tip of his tongue before he teased them with tiny nips. When butterflies of anticipation fluttered through her, Willow tried to freeze against him, but her resolve failed to communicate with her reactions. He tempted her with tantalizing kisses, then pulled back whenever she tried to answer his teases.

In spite of all the will she pulled together, Willow was overpowered by his sexuality, betrayed by her own passion, mastered by attraction for a man who could turn her into a captive of her own emotions. His mouth closed on hers, his tongue thrust between her lips and twisted with hers and his hands softened, stroked her face and throat with enticing gentleness.

Within moments, she was, once again, clay in the hands of a sculptor, a puppet moving as he wished. His caressing hands and exploring lips found countless ways to stimulate her as they moved down her body, inflamed her with arousal. His hand slid between her legs and touched a sensitive trigger of sensation that built to an unbearable peak of excitement before it splintered and sent her into floating euphoria.

It wasn't until he left to wash his hands that Willow knew she could no longer deny the depth of her feelings or hide them from Drew. He had to know she was hopelessly in love with him, intoxicated by passion and totally enthralled by lovemaking skills that showed her just how much he could teach her.

"Do you really want me to leave, Willow?" Drew slipped into bed with her, kissed her and moved his lips to nip at an earlobe. "I want to sleep with you in my arms and feel your warmth snuggled close to me. Can you be cold enough to deny me that?"

"I want you to stay forever. I'll hate being alone in a bed you've shared with me. I'll keep reaching out, hoping to find you beside me. I don't want you to leave, but I don't feel right about something."

"What?" He turned her to face him and settled the sheet over them.

"I need to know more of who you are before I commit myself to a relationship everyone's going to know about. I can't explain it. It's just there, making me feel wrong."

"You aren't making much sense, but what do you need to know?"

"I want to know what you do in Europe. What you do here every day. So much of your life is lost to me."

"That's *what* I am and isn't important to what we share."

"It could be important. For all I know you're an international jewel thief or a mafia hit man."

"I assure you I'm neither of those things." He laughed gently. "My reputation is unsullied by heinous deeds. A few damn stupid ones, but nothing heinous."

"I think you're too assertive and purposeful to be a wastrel." Some of the mischief returned to her smile. "Although your most obvious talents hint at a career as a gigolo."

"Call me a student." He stuffed a pillow on his folded arm and lay facing her. "That's mostly what I am."

"Do you have a degree?" She touched his face, trailed her fingers through the roughness of his beard.

"Princeton awarded me a B.A. six years ago. I was only twenty and not too clear on what I wanted to do. I bounced from one post graduate program to another. A person becomes educated by the knowledge he gains, not by the letters he can add to his name." He caught her fingers with his lips, then let them go with a kiss.

"But they help."

"Only the way advertising helps sell a product. If I were trying to sell myself to someone who thought degrees were important, it would behoove me to flaunt degrees." He reached out and straightened her tangled hair. "Do you want to know about the prince? Or the pauper?"

"I don't know what you mean."

"The prince is blood heir to Sutherland Manor, the son of a wellknown international businessman, who gambles with high stakes and races on the Grand Prix circuit." He rolled onto his back and stared at the ceiling. "The pauper is the tough Philadelphia street kid who watched his mother kill herself with an overdose of heroin."

Willow sat up and stared at him while the shock of his quiet statement thumped in her chest. "You said she died. You didn't say she killed herself."

"The truth is she was killed by her second husband, Gino, who supplied her with drugs, even pushed them on her until she overdosed herself."

When Willow continued to stare at him with a stunned expression, Drew sat up to face her. "It was a hell of a scandal and the trial was a front-page bonanza since it involved a Sutherland, which gave it the aroma of upper-class money. I was a witness. The verdict was guilty of involuntary manslaughter. His sentence was eight years, but he only served four. Not long after he was back on the street, he was found in an alley shredded by buck shot. My Uncle Antonio was suspected, but the evidence for a drug related killing was much stronger. That did not make big headlines. A Sutherland was no longer involved."

Drew sat back against the oak headboard and held her across his lap with her back against his raised knee. "I saw her die, but I couldn't do anything about it. Gino threw me across the room. I split my chin falling against a radiator and was knocked unconscious."

"They beat you?"

"I don't remember much. But I know she smacked me when she drank, and I hated the shots she took because they took her away and left me feeling abandoned and hungry. I mostly ran away from Gino, who would knock me out of his way or wallop me with his belt if I irritated him enough. He didn't treat her much better." Drew looked at her twisted face and held her against his chest. "There's a lot of ugliness in the world. I was fortunate enough to get away from some of it."

"How could your father let you stay with them?"

"He didn't know about it. Dad tried to take me away from her when he divorced her, but it blew up in his face. However, he refused to quit and constantly fought for custody of me. It took close to four years to get it because she and Gino wanted the support money. The social workers always told her when they were coming, which gave her time to clean up her act and portray the ideal mother. The courts preferred to leave a child with his remarried mother, not an unmarried father, who lived most of his life abroad. It was only necessary that he pay."

"Didn't you tell him the truth?"

"They found ways to keep him away from me. She hated Dad and told me he left me because I was bad. Willow, I was such a screwed-up mess I didn't even remember him when I went to live with him."

"You said you didn't get along with your father."

"That was a gross understatement." He huffed, then gave her a slow smile. "Dad expected obedience, manners, good grammar, a clean vocabulary, decent behavior—everything I saw as unacceptable. We had a couple of rough years, but he did get the job done. He found tutors for me when I was thrown out of two Paris schools; and thanks to an excellent French psychiatrist, a firm, clearcut discipline, my animals and some fantastic people as tutors, it worked out all right. But mostly, in spite of my hateful rebellion, Dad never stopped loving me. Once I started to remember him, I found I liked him. We get along great now, except on the subject of opera, which he finds poisonously boring."

"You like opera?"

"Very much. As does Gram." He chuckled. "Dad insists she's corrupted me and Gram thinks it's her duty to drag him to an opera whenever she gets a chance."

"Byron introduced me to some operatic music, but I've never seen one."

"You toured Europe with a classical musician and saw no operas?"

"We went to a number of concerts for piano and orchestra. In London, Byron tried to get me to an opera. I chose a Pantomime instead. It was in English, even if they didn't say much." She teased with the scrunchedup face that always made him smile.

"That sounds like an opera to me." Drew laughed at her confusion. "The words get absurdly monotonous and useless. It's the music that shines."

"If you say so." Willow shrugged. "As far as romantic singers, Byron did get me to fall in love with Placido Domingo's voice, but he didn't take the place of Neil Diamond."

"I could tell that by the profusion of Diamond's golden oldies in your music library. Does my life story help your dilemma?"

"It makes me feel I know you a little more, maybe even understand you better."

"Is that important?"

"It is to me." His question had confused her. "It's important because you're different than I am."

"Not very. I have the regulation number of toes and fingers. I function the normal way. I also need to sleep at night. Don't you?"

"I am tired." Willow admitted when his yawn stimulated one from her.

"I should hope so." Laughing, Drew rolled her off his lap, wrapped an arm around her waist when she tried to stand up. "Where are you going?"

"I need my nightgown."

"Absolutely not." He gave her an appalled look. "There is no way I'm going to sleep with Bo Peep and her damn little lamb."

"That's Mary. Bo Peep lost her sheep."

"I thought Mary was the contrary one, which is more fitting at the moment."

"She was the one with a garden."

"Oh, yes, the madam with the pretty little maids all in a row." He gave her a lascivious smirk and laughed when she scowled at him. "There's a decided deficiency in my nursery rhyme education. I'd just as soon keep it that way."

"My youngest niece gave me that nightgown for Christmas."

"She is not invited to our pajama parties. Now turn off the light and let me keep you warm." When Willow settled into bed, Drew pulled her close against him with a hand cupped over a breast, fingers gently caressing her skin. "I like you just the way you are."

Sighing, Willow gave up the fight for propriety—at least for tonight. She always seemed to lose battles with Drew and understood his comment about having no trouble getting people to offer what he wanted. He had not only seduced her; he'd made her realize she loved him and wanted him forever. She just wasn't sure how she was going to get him to consider the forever part of her scenario.

In the morning, Drew's kiss, just below her left ear, stirred Willow, but it was an uphill climb to awakening.

"A little sore this morning?"

She nodded, then looked up when he lifted her chin. "I didn't want you to know and feel bad."

"I expected it."

"Why?"

"The blunt truth is you're not the first filly I've broken to saddle." He paused when her eyes clouded. "Just the best."

"Do you say that to all your conquests?"

"No, I don't. Most of them were comfortably broken in before I knew them." His face hardened at her scowl, along with his hand. "Stop resenting my past. It is not yours to claim. Accept it as an education you'll be glad I have. The pleasure of ultimate sexual performance does not come instinctively."

"I'm sorry." Willow's voice was husky enough she had to clear it. "I don't know why I said that. It wouldn't make sense to take on a tutor who didn't have an education in his subject."

"That relieves me. I'd hate to lose my job." He dropped his hand away from her chin. "Take a long hot soak in the whirlpool bath."

"I don't know how it works."

"The manual is in one of the drawers by the sink."

"I don't have time. I have to work with Moonstone, and I promised Mae I'd go over my training charts with her at ten."

"Moonstone won't care. Gram is another matter." He glanced at his watch. "I'm a little late myself."

"What time is it?"

"Almost seven. I'm usually halfway to Jared's Mill by now."

"Why?" It made no sense to Willow. Jared's Mill was a deserted sawmill in the county recreation area. It was on a back road that went nowhere. "There's nothing there."

"That's why I go there. I don't like running on busy roads."

"Do you run every morning?"

"I try to. To the mill and back is a five-mile run. Twice a week I double it and go to the picnic area by the falls. You can join me, sweet Mary most contrary."

"I might make it to the mill road." She caught the nightshirt he scooped off the floor and tossed to her. "Did you notice I cleaned the room while you were gone last night?"

"I really didn't think it was a mess yesterday, but it was a good way to rile you. Starting tomorrow, I'll take you running with me. When you can't run any more, start walking. I'll find you on the way back."

"I wondered why you were in such good shape. I suppose you lift weights, too."

"Among other things. I won't subject you to that." He leaned down to give her a quick kiss before he left the room in long, silent strides.

Willow flopped back against the pillow, telling herself she ought to get up and head for the barn, but the thought of a hot bath was more appealing—except she could barely keep her eyes open, her body refused to pull out of its enervated state, and her mind was turning to fuzz. Her last coherent thought before she drifted back to sleep was that loving Drew was proving to be a greater challenge than she expected. It seemed just keeping up with him was going to be exhausting.

❖

Drew watched John park his pickup next to the vegetable garden between Willow's house and the stable and jogged over to talk to him before he started his run. "John, you're a genius."

"I am? What did I do?" John lowered the truck's tailgate. "While you're here, grab a bag of fertilizer and dump it in the spreader." He nodded toward the implement behind the tractor.

"How come whenever I show up, you put me to work?" Drew picked up both bags of fertilizer and followed John to the tractor.

"I'm an opportunist. I see your car spent the night at Willow's. Does that mean something or did you lose the keys?"

"That's why you're a genius. Your idea of dousing me broke her loose."

"Sort of broke you loose, too." John observed drily. "I noticed you forgot the no touching edict, or didn't that apply to smacks on the bum?"

"I took the blast of icy water as a clear release from any former nonaggression pact."

"That's exactly what it was," John said. "but it was Willow's idea, not mine. All I did was supply the equipment. I'd say she got tired of being ignored."

"Ignoring her was getting difficult. Her challenge was impossible to ignore."

"Thought it might be." John closed the lid of the filled spreader bin. "Does she still think you're a callous, phony bastard, who wants to take advantage of her?"

"Maybe, but she likes the advantages I've taken so far. You were also right about something important." Drew leaned his shoulder against a maple tree beside the tractor. "It wasn't lack of interest or desire. It was fear because someone did take advantage of her by refusing to listen to the word no and forcing her to have sex with him. For five years, she saw it as a failure on her part. I call it rape. She wanted me, John, but she was afraid of it."

"How did you solve that one?"

"I don't know. Once she understood what she feared and knew the decision was truly hers, she forgot to say no and turned into that blast furnace you mentioned." Drew flushed and gave John a sideways look. "You realize that no matter what I'd already assumed, your candid confession made me see my grandmother in a whole different light. But then, thinking of Gram's shell of propriety makes me understand Willow's latest hang-up a little more."

"What's that?"

"She's all worked up about me spending nights with her because people might guess we're having exactly the kind of relationship we are. It makes no sense."

"It does to Willow." John held his gaze. "Drew, even today, everyone isn't raised in the open-minded way your father raised you. There are your realities of love and there are Willow's daydreams of love. She believes in her dreams. Don't fault her for it. It has more power than you realize."

"That's what worries me. She's all over me with questions about myself that I don't want to answer. Why can't she just enjoy what's great now and quit worrying about this where I'm coming from shit."

"Because she's Willow. She isn't wrapped up in herself and has a genuine desire to understand what makes people tick."

"Yeah, but she doesn't need to know what makes me tick any more than anyone else does." He looked away from John, let his gaze follow the trail toward Willow's cabin. "I like her John. She's feels like an armful of sunshine and makes my world warmer. There's no way I want to chill that."

"She does have a way of wriggling herself into a person's heart." John smiled. "She has a strong sense of family and wants to find it here. I know she charmed me into caring about her."

"Aren't you a little old for her?" Drew gave him a twisted scowl.

"Not if you're talking about a granddaughter."

"I suppose that means you're going to want to protect her from me the way Gram does. You can relax. I don't think she wants to be protected anymore."

"Why would I want to protect her from what she's wanted since she met you. Enjoy making love. Have a wild summer romance. It's the best thing that can happen to both of you."

"She brought fun back into my life." Drew smiled when he thought about Willow's laughter and the teasing playfulness they shared. "I don't know if she's the best thing to happen to me, but she is the most enjoyable." He winked and pushed away from the tree. "If I don't get my ass in running gear, I'll be late for a lesson with Gram, which will not be cool."

Drew took a step toward the garden fence, then turned back. "John, could you get it through to Gram that I'm not a damn kid and back her off a little? Cripes, she keeps looking at me as if she thinks I'm a temperamental child and need a spanking to set me straight."

John laughed at Drew's snarl. "Try not acting temperamental every time she tries to talk to you about what went wrong."

"I don't know what went wrong, except Vittorio Luciani is a madman and I got sick of taking crap from him. I can't talk to her because every time she brings it up, I feel like hell for failing her. If she could make that go away by turning me over her knee, I'd almost be willing to let her do it."

"Don't push her, Drew." John lifted a thick eyebrow and gave him a warning look. "She certainly won't turn you over her knee, but that head mare can still put down a rebellious colt who forgets his place on her chart of family pecking order."

"I hear you, John."

❖

By the time Willow convinced herself to roll out of bed and test out the relaxing luxury of the whirlpool, it was after eight. Almost an hour later, coffee mug in hand, she headed for the barn to collect her charts and noticed John working in the vegetable garden. Realizing her only route would take her within a few yards of him, she decided to hurry past with a preoccupied expression on her face. Her plan fell apart when John turned and caught her looking at him. Accepting that she had no choice, Willow stopped by the fence.

"Good morning, John." One look at his face was enough to tell her he'd noticed the car in her driveway. "Thank you for your help. We engineered a successful gotcha."

"That we did." John set a foot on a cross rail of the fence and leaned a forearm on the top of a post. "I had me a good laugh. I even received a thank you from the victim."

"You did?"

"An emphatic one. He'd been grumbling around for weeks and kicking himself for offending you. He just wasn't sure how he'd done it."

"Does he tell you everything?" Willow looked away when a blush flooded her face.

"Not everything. You see, when Drew was a lad and complained of boredom or angered his grandmother, she sent him out to pull weeds for me. We did a lot of talking and it turned into therapy more than punishment. It was a good system. Mae got him away from her, I got a good assistant and Drew learned a lot about gardening. Before long, he started volunteering to help, especially when he was troubled about something. He was troubled enough last week to help me set two pansy borders and plant sweet corn."

"Because I wouldn't throw away my pride and fall into his arms?"

John's laugh was sudden, but kind. "I think it was more that you turned your back on the challenge. He said that since he thought you had more spunk than you were showing, you really must have been turned off by something and were uninterested. When you asked me to help you play a prank on him, I knew it would work better than a gypsy's potion."

"Because of my spunk?" She gave him a skeptical look.

"Drew admires spunk. Look at his horses. He controls their spirits, but he doesn't want them broken, or even docile. He doesn't want a spiritless woman either."

"John," Willow squared her shoulders and scowled at him, "women aren't horses."

"That's part of the problem to Drew. All his life, he's had trouble understanding why people didn't do and say what they really felt instead of weaving complex webs of rationalizations and deceptions, then inventing rules so they could break them. Drew's been civilized but not tamed. He can't be shackled or nagged. There's a part of him that's afraid of being owned and it won't let him give up his freedom."

"His grandmother says he's an incurable flirt." Willow blushed again, but only gently.

"He is that, but he doesn't mean any harm by it. He's perceptive and reads feelings, reacts to them and communicates by touching."

"He certainly does." Her blush deepened.

"It's one of his gifts. Enjoy it. My advice is to fall into his arms, but never abandon your pride. He's had enough lasses like that since he was a teenager. And never lose the spunk that loves a good challenge." John pulled his foot off the fence and started to turn away. After half a stride, he turned back. "Sometimes you have to fight to get what you want."

"Who do I fight?"

"Drew, of course."

"I don't know what you mean."

"There's a part of him that won't give in without a fight, lass. It's part of his nature."

On the way to the barn, Willow kept thinking about what John said. She wasn't sure what he meant about fighting Drew, but one issue was paramount in her mind. When it came to love, Drew was going to have to give up some of his freedom, especially the area of freedom that included Nicole and late nights she knew nothing about.

Chapter Fourteen

While Willow groomed Shamrock, the pregnant brood mare, she discovered a telltale waxy secretion on the milk bag, as well as a few other signs of imminent foaling, which meant she may be spending the next few nights in the barn instead of her house. It was something she'd been looking forward to. But now, after what had been an unbelievable night of sexual excitement, every female hormone in her body told her she would rather spend those hours in Drew's arms than cocooned in a single person sleeping bag on a cot outside a foaling stall.

Another exciting thing happened while she was riding KoKo in the large outdoor dressage ring. When she asked the horse for extension at the trot, he dropped into her hands and reached out in smooth, floating strides that glided across the diagonal of the ring. He was balanced, even in rhythm, lightly held in her hands, allowing her seat and legs to release him and send him surging forward with freedom and power. After crossing the center line, she eased the gelding back to a smooth, collected trot and reached the boards with no loss of impulsion or rhythm. Feeling that the flawless transitions, when the horse stretched into extension and contracted into collection, had been spontaneous flowing reactions to subtle changes in the swing of her back, Willow rounded the end of the ring and, again, asked for extension. With an eager release of power, Ko-Ko stretched his strides and accelerated straight down the boards on the long side of the ring.

Willow's thrill at the breakthrough spread into a wide smile as the animal became a responsive part of her physical body, his power a continuation of her will. After she settled into the saddle and dropped the reins as a signal to walk, Willow leaned forward and wrapped her arms around the horse's neck in an appreciative hug. "Fantastic, KoKo. No more work today. You deserve a fun gallop through a meadow and a bushel of carrots."

"Don't I deserve one of those carrots?" Drew's voice startled Willow, and she sat up to see him mounted on Rigoletto just outside the opening of the dressage ring.

"What for?"

"If not for a good performance, at least for teaching you about suppleness of loins."

"Now that's conceit." She stopped her horse beside his.

"I just know what I'm good at."

"For your obnoxious conceit you deserve the carrots after they've been through the horse."

"Since there's no way I can top your fertile wit, I'll have to resort to brutality." Rigoletto sidestepped when Drew reached out an arm and pulled her to him for a kiss.

Willow gasped, then relaxed when her gelding stood patiently headtotail with the bay stallion. The kiss was short, but it was enough to stir up yesterday's excitement.

"I'm ready and willing to resume my job as tutor." Drew pulled his arm away and she straightened in the saddle.

"You may have to wait. Shamrock looks like she'll have the foal tonight." Expecting a frown, she was surprised by his wide smile. "I'm staying in the barn."

"I'm eager to see the foal. Do you know that Shamrock is Venture's mother?"

"Is it the same stud?"

"Venture was begat via frozen spermsicle from a Percheron stud in France." He swatted Rigoletto on the neck. "This is the foal's sire."

"Why did Mae name him Rigoletto? I looked him up in her library. Rigoletto was deformed and not a nice man."

"The horse was named for Verdi's opera, not the character. It is not deformed and has fantastic music."

"It may have good music, but it is definitely deformed." Willow made a sour face. "Rigoletto is a tyrannical father, who hires hit men to kill his daughter's lover. They grab the daughter instead and then give her body to her father in a sack. That's sick."

"The character of Rigoletto is usually described as tormented by life and a fateful curse."

"He's a vengeful tyrant and the story is ghastly."

"I admit opera is often gruesomely tragic; but then, it is more interested in tragedy's effect on the characters than the caliber and firepower of its instruments of tragedy."

"I'm not too fond of shooting gallery films either."

"Actually," Drew smirked and thrust out a clenched fist, "I get a visceral, right-on satisfaction out of seeing no-account morons blown away in a deafening chaos of incendiary percussion."

Willow gave him a scowl she usually reserved for her brothers. "How about we go for a ride?"

"I can't. I talked Gram into giving me a lesson on this beast. She'll chew me out if I'm not ready to do something when she comes back from lunch?"

"I'll try to get back to watch some of it."

The trail ride proved as rewarding as the workout; and although Willow admitted Drew did deserve some credit, she was sure it was more from what he did for her spirits than her loins. After taking care of Ko-Ko, she walked out to sit on the mounting block near the "A" end of the dressage ring to watch Drew's lesson. It didn't take long to notice things were rapidly going from bad to worse.

Drew rode Rigoletto skillfully, but not as freely as he rode Venture, and insisted there was a communication block between them that frustrated him. Willow had seen signs of it before, when Drew lost patience and threw down the reins to avoid a display of temper he would regret.

In spite of romantic tales about willing, fiery steeds, Willow knew stallions were often dominantly stubborn, even bullishly pigheaded, when it came to work and discipline. Watching Drew and the headstrong Rigoletto, she could see the problem was mutual. The horse was resistant and Drew looked ready to detonate when he halted in front of his grandmother, who sat on a large white cube of fiberglass displaying the letter "A" on its faces.

"Drew, you know you can't force a passage. It must grow from the collected walk and erupt beneath you." Mae explained with a firm but quiet voice. "You're making him resistant and inflexible because you're not developing a vibrant flow of energy before you release it."

"He's not responding to me."

"Of course not. You tried to bully him. He's every bit as ornery as you are, but a lot less intelligent. You should be smart enough to recognize the problem and fix it."

"I can't communicate with this horse the way you can." Drew marched the horse through the opening of the ring and halted in front of Mae. "Why don't you show me, Gram?"

"I'm trying to, but I don't know how to make you feel his moment of transition."

"By getting on him and showing me."

"I can't do that."

"Why can't you? Your doctor never said you couldn't ride again. Why did you stop?"

"That's enough, Drew." When her face tensed, Mae showed a remarkable resemblance to the grandson she was facing. It was in the tightness around the eyes, the set of the jaw, the gemlike luminescence in her deep blue stare. "I don't wish to discuss it."

"I do." Drew's vault from the horse landed him smack in front of the startled woman, who stiffened in irritation. "You quit because you were afraid you couldn't produce any more."

"I knew I couldn't."

"You didn't know. You never tried."

"I'm almost seventy years old."

"So, what. There are a lot of dressage riders over seventy. Why should Mae Sutherland run up her stirrups in her sixties?"

"You don't understand." Mae stood and headed toward her car. "We'll try again tomorrow. You are obviously much too upset to do any good now."

"I understand quit, and that's what you did." Drew let go of the reins and cut her off before she passed the mounting block. "You had the audacity to tell me I was a quitter. You said I was throwing away my goals and sulking now that it was getting tough."

Drew swept his eyes to where Willow caught the horse's reins when it wandered to some tempting grass at the edge of the ring. "Willow, bring him here. It's time you saw the way that horse should be ridden."

"Drew, are you sure—?"

"Yes, I'm sure." His stare blazed a warning before it moved back to his grandmother. "When you fall off, you climb back on. When you lose, you try again. When you think you can't do it, you prove you can. Those are your words, Gram. When I was a kid, I believed in you enough to climb back up, scared and in tears. Sometimes I hated you when you wouldn't let me quit. It's your turn to hate me." His hands closed around her waist and firmly assisted her onto the mounting block.

"I don't have boots or breeches."

"You're going to ride for five minutes. Slacks are fine."

"Well, maybe for five minutes." Frowning, Mae waited while her grandson adjusted the stirrups, then slowly swung her right leg over the horse's rump.

"And five minutes tomorrow and the next day and so on. You start with the scales and before you know it you can sing the aria."

"Yes, Drew, that's what I said." Mae sorted out the four reins and took the long training whip he handed her.

"Then prove it to me."

While Rigoletto crossed the grass to enter the ring at a relaxed walk, Drew circled an arm around Willow's waist. He gave her a quick wink before he looked back at the horse and rider.

With the flowing grace of a ballet dancer, the woman on the bay stallion fused her movement with the swinging freedom of the horse's balanced strides until they became a single unit of vibrant energy. Gently, imperceptibly, Mae shortened the reins, closed her legs against mahogany flanks and took control of Rigoletto's surging power. In response to a subtle lightening of her seat, the stallion softened his arched neck, rounded his spine upwards beneath her. His strides became shorter, more elevated and energetic. His hind legs stepped farther under him as controlled power lifted him into collection. The transition to a passage happened spontaneously, as if the impulsion and vibrancy could no longer be contained in the walk. In one upbeat, the cadence of the strides switched from four beats to two.

With powerful thrusts of his hindquarters Rigoletto lifted diagonal pairs of legs in exaggerated elevation and stepped into the passage—a majestic gait that moved him forward with slow, floating grace. With his full black tail swishing from side to side with the accented rhythm of his rising and falling hindquarters, the gleaming bay stallion snorted as he strutted across the diagonal of the ring with regal elegance. There were only a dozen strides of passage, but they were a magnificent display of contained power.

When the horse returned to the collected walk, Willow glanced at Drew and saw the blue of his eyes glisten with unusual brightness while diamondlike glints of tears flashed on curved lashes and a tiny droplet traced a shimmering path to the dark line of his beard. When his vision caught her watching, he tightened his arm around her, included her in his emotion.

"She'll do it, Willow." Drew watched Rigoletto do a smooth turn on the haunches and, with his legs crossing in even cadence, glide diagonally toward the centerline of the ring. "She'll come back to claim what she loves. Maybe I will, too."

"Am I supposed to understand that?"

"No, but I think you're a part of it."

Drew released his arm when Rigoletto came to a perfect, square halt in front of him. Taking all four reins in her left hand, Mae dropped her right arm straight down and dipped her head in a formal dressage salute that Drew returned with a firm nod. Outside the ring, he reached up to catch his grandmother by the waist and lower her to the grass. When her feet touched ground, he closed his arms around her for a long, silent moment.

"We can't let each other quit, Gram."

"Where did you rediscover your incentive?"

"You gave it to me when you brought Willow here. She goes after what she wants. It's contagious."

"Well, it certainly is exhilarating." Mae reached past Drew to rub a hand along the stallion's satiny neck. "It's like being reunited with a long-lost lover. He remembered me and made me feel welcome."

"I think I'll be able to get that passage now that you've reintroduced him to it."

"You could have produced it yourself, but you have to learn to keep your temper in control with horses. They won't accept your intentions the way your reluctant grandmother does."

"You impressed that on me long ago."

"Yes, you do refrain from taking it out on them. But you've been bottling it up lately and letting it upset you."

"Well, I can't seem to eliminate it." Drew gave her a steady look that was part irritation, part perplexity. "I'm not all hardheaded

Sutherland. There's too much Vitale in me. It makes me part volcano. You'll never cool it."

"I don't want to cool it. It gives you the passion you need." Mae rebutted gently. "You defeat yourself whenever you let Sutherland perseverance fight your flamboyant nature rather than direct its energy into positive expression. Don't try to be your father. You are a lot like him, but you don't have the same temperament. We tried to teach you to control the volcano. We never wanted you to deny it—or be ashamed of it."

"Maybe I'm afraid of it," he said quietly.

"I think you fear the wrong thing."

"That makes no sense."

"You need to talk to your father about the rage you fear. It is not Vitale." Mae set her hand on his forearm. "At least you get decisive when you get angry. It can be positive. Thank you. I needed the push."

Mae shifted her gaze to were Willow held Rigoletto's reins. "And Willow, keep going after what you want. It's effective. I'll be here for your lesson at one tomorrow. I'll wear boots and breeches if Drew will see that my horse is warmed up."

"I'll do that any time, Gram." Drew picked up the cane she had left on the block and handed it to her. "Do you really need this?"

"I haven't needed it for a long time, but I'm rather fond of it." Mae leaned on the smooth, worn handle of the wooden shaft. "My father had a walking stick. I used to think it was a foolish appendage, but I understand him now. It gives us oldsters an edge of authority and a decided air of importance. I see it as my swagger stick and will undoubtedly need it when your father arrives next week." She flourished the cane like a fencing foil before she walked toward her car with a satisfied swagger in her stride.

Laughing at his grandmother's clowning, Drew opened her car door. "Do me a favor and leave me out of your squabbles."

"Andy and I don't squabble." She looked offended. "He just needs to be reminded that he's not the CEO around here."

When Mae drove away, Drew laughed and slid his arm around Willow. "Dad always tries to tell her how to run her life and she does the same thing to him. Each, mind you, swears the other is the most controlling, stubborn person in the world."

"I've heard that's a Sutherland trait."

"It certainly is." He gave her a probing look. "I've heard rumors of Iowa stubborn, too."

"And we Roberts are pure Iowa." Willow lifted her chin and wrinkled her nose. "Speaking of stubborn, how much of your temper act was genuine?"

"Most of it. The horse does frustrate me. He's always been a one rider horse. Gram could do things with him no one else could, which makes her come down hard on me. She expects me to bring him back in a matter of weeks. If I had more time to work with him, I'm sure we could become a trusting team."

"Like you and Venture?"

"That I doubt. I raised Venture from a foal. He shared my troubled and volatile teen years when nobody else wanted me. I think that makes him eligible for sainthood along with Gram." He tweaked her nose until she wrinkled it.

Willow lifted her hand to bat his away then looked at his shoulder and plucked at his shirt. "Do you know you have dirt and grass stains on your shirt?"

"The son of a bitch pitched me."

"Why?"

"It was one of those stallion vs stallion things." Drew scowled at Rigoletto's swiveling ear. "Yeah, you. Okay, you won that skirmish, but you haven't won the battle yet."

"What happened?"

"He didn't want to do the damn passage and just plain shut me out. So, I jabbed him with a spur to get his attention. He shot forward, threw his head straight up and dropped his back out from under me. Before I knew what was happening, he snaked his head down, turned into a catapult and launched me." Drew shook his head and started laughing. "It was pretty much hopeless after that. It happened just before you showed up. That was what the lecture was about and you undoubtedly noticed her sympathy toward me was nonexistent."

"And you let your grandmother ride him after what he did?"

"He needed pacifying and she's the one who can do it best. Few stallions will bully a dominate head mare and she's his. Actually, I think both of them were symbolically giving me the finger." He laughed at Willow's startled reaction that turned to one of agreement after she thought about it. "How would you like to take a break from sandwiches and go out to lunch?"

"The offer is impossible to refuse."

"Put on something casual, yet sexy. I'll take you to *Mio Castello*. I have a ravenous hunger for pasta and good Italian Borolo wine. As well as a desire to argue with Mike in Italian."

"What do you argue about?"

"Everything. But usually sports, music or politics."

"You speak Italian as well as French?"

"And German, Spanish, Scots and some Gaelic. I love Italian and learned it along with English. My mother's family spoke Italian and there were a lot of Spanish speakers in the neighborhood in Philly. It was easy to keep it up in Europe because Dad spoke them all and we spent a lot of time in different countries."

"What's your primary accent?"

"For the most part, it goes with the language. I seem to swing with the locality just by engaging in conversation for a while. Dad calls me an innate mimic."

"What do you use most?"

"Depends on where I am. At home, Dad and I almost always spoke English because he insisted that we were first and foremost Americans. We also spent a lot of time with the relatives in Scotland and here in the States. I grew up multi-lingual and, in certain situations, I've been known to carry on a conversation in several languages at the same time. It's all just talking to me." He started for the barn.

"I have an appetizer for you." Willow reached into the pocket of her windbreaker and pulled out a single carrot. "You helped, and the performance merits a reward."

When she held the carrot in front of him, Drew took a bite, then offered her one. He gave the rest to Rigoletto, who nudged between them when he smelled the treat.

Drew locked his hands behind Willow's waist as he slowly chewed the piece of carrot. "Maybe I'll buy a bushel of carrots and spirit you away to a deserted island. You make me want to run away from the world and make love to you forever."

"You're fantasizing again," Willow reminded, with the hope he would think about the forever in a more realistic vein.

"You have that effect on me, C*hèrie*."

Willow sighed at the French endearment that gave her tiny shivers of excitement when he said it with a deep nasal accent. She was beginning to recognize it as the harbinger of an intimacy that, although romantic and exciting, was an evasion of reality.

That night, while she burrowed in her sleeping bag in a hopeless attempt to get comfortable on the narrow cot, Willow tried to remember how the soft brush of Drew's lips made her pulse jump with promise. She was bursting with love for him, but what seemed so perfect when she was with him, filled her with apprehensions when he was gone. Maybe it was the suddenness, the newness, the juggling of feelings that made her feel so alone when he left her. She was in love. Yet she kept sensing something was very wrong. Love was supposed to be happiness and trust but some of it was misery.

In one day, Willow had felt joy and hurt, triumph and helplessness; and now, this aching aloneness made her afraid he would never want her again. A gnawing fear inside her told her tonight, or tomorrow, or the next day, he would find someone else to tease and charm and seduce with his passion. Would it then be her turn to wait alone without even a so long or thank you?

There was no foal that night. There was no sign of Drew either.

❖

The next morning was cast with gloom and the weather complied by drenching everything with three violent thunderstorms. When Mae came to give Willow a lesson on the thoroughbred, Donegal, she wasn't wearing riding clothes and explained that Drew had called from Philadelphia to say he was tied up with something and had no idea when he would be home.

The news pushed Willow into deeper depression. She had to ride indoors and between her bruised feelings and the rain pounding on the roof, they accomplished little. Her excuse of not getting enough sleep because of apprehension over Shamrock was accepted but she sensed it wasn't entirely believed. She knew Mae had seen her radiance yesterday and felt that even if Drew's grandmother hadn't guessed the extent of the cause, she undoubtedly saw the nature of it.

They ended the lesson when a fresh torrent of rain and hail made it impossible to hear and Donegal became agitated by the din. It was quieter in the barn under the hayloft but the horses inside were restless, especially Venture, who wasn't used to spending much time in a closed stall. After putting Donegal out, Willow took a carrot to Venture. He thrust his head over the half door, pushed against it with his chest and banged a forefoot on the wooden barrier.

"You don't like cages any more than your owner, do you?"

Willow scratched under the gelding's chin, straightened the long strands of his black forelock and rubbed her fingertips into the white zigzag on his forehead. The distinctive blaze was the only part of him that wasn't black. Its surrealistic resemblance to a zee had almost named him Zorro. Willow was glad Drew reconsidered. She liked Bold Venture better.

When the big horse pushed his nose against her chest to guide her toward the outside door, Willow gave in and grabbed his lead shank. "You're as spoiled as he is, but it's all right. I know you'd rather be rained on than held prisoner."

In the pasture, gentle lips plucked the last piece of carrot from her hand before Venture wheeled and tore off into the rain with leaping bucks. Willow watched him run for a moment, chuckled diabolically when he sought out the worst mud hole in the pasture, sank to his knees and reveled in a good roll. By the time the horse stood, he was coated with thick brown mud and looked like the clown Drew insisted he was.

At ten o'clock that night, Willow, once again, wrapped Shamrock's tail with a clean cotton bandage, picked the stall clean and banked the bedding to form a sheltered nest of golden wheat straw. The mare looked ready to drop the foal at any minute. Her milk bag was swollen and dripping, the muscles around her tail loose, her huge belly low and angular. Willow was sure the birth couldn't be stalled off another day while Shamrock, totally unconcerned, contentedly picked through her hay and emptied her water bucket.

After refilling the bucket, Willow fell asleep listening to the soothing rhythm of the mare's chewing. She was sure she woke every few minutes to check on the mare, but it was probably closer to an hour between alerts. Unbelievably serene, Shamrock finished her hay, drank some water, then stood facing the aisle and dozed. Willow had been led to believe all mares were restless and paced in their stalls before foaling; and so, at five o'clock, when Shamrock snorted, tossed her head a few times, circled twice and dropped to the straw, she assumed the mare was lying down to do some serious sleeping.

When a sound resembling the sudden gush of a fire hose followed by deep groans from the stall, jolted Willow awake she shook away drowsiness, stumbled across the aisle and looked into the stall. Shamrock lay flat on her side, breathing hard between shuddering convulsions that stiffened her while she grunted with her pushes.

Charged with excitement, Willow ran to the switch panel and snapped on the aisle lights, the office lights and the ones in the stall. When she returned, Shamrock rolled onto her chest, looked back at her tail and whickered with soft huffing sounds that called to the unborn foal. Encouraging the mare with soothing words, Willow opened the door and slipped into the stall where, unconcerned by human presence, the mare flopped back onto her side and strained with the next contraction.

Willow caught a glimpse of a tiny hoof before the push ended and the hoof retreated. She checked her watch. It said ten minutes from the start of heavy labor. Mares delivered quickly. If a foal wasn't born in half an hour, there could well be a problem. With the next contraction, she saw more of the hoof, even a little of a white pastern and fetlock. Ten minutes later, Willow knew something was wrong. The right foreleg was pushed out to the cannon bone, but there was no left foreleg. One leg was often a little ahead of the other, but not that much. By now there should be two forelegs with a muzzle nestled on top of them.

A foal came into the world like a diver, forelegs extended, head and neck stretched on top of them. The forelegs and head should come easily. The biggest effort was the shoulders. After that, it was a matter of letting the foal slide out with its hind legs trailing behind it. The presentation of one foreleg panicked Willow and she ran toward the office to call the vet. She collided with Drew when he stepped through the office door. He was groggy, bleary eyed and yawning.

"I have to call the vet. There's only one leg. It isn't right."

"How long has it been?"

"About twenty minutes." Willow followed Drew down the aisle, impatient with his ambling strides and the casual way he hunkered behind the mare while he appraised the situation. "Should I call Dr. Allen?"

"Just talk to her head. I'll be right back."

He was gone before Willow had a chance to ask anything, and she assumed he was making the call. When Drew returned, he pulled off his shirt and spread a large towel over the straw behind the mare. He slipped on a long surgical glove and coated it with lubricant.

"What are you doing?" Willow asked.

"Fixing the problem. It's purely mechanical. All I have to do is push it back, find the other foreleg and straighten it out."

"What about the head?"

"It's there, but it's out of line. The missing foreleg is twisting the foal."

"Are you a vet?"

"I wanted to be once, so I worked with Mark Allen while I was in college. I started vet school at Penn, but Gram talked me out of it."

While he talked, Drew lay behind Shamrock and gradually slid his hand up the foal's leg into the mare. "This should be a simple job, but mares are always against it. They want to push it out and can't understand why I'm pushing it in."

Drew's face contorted when the mare stiffened with another convulsive effort. When it relaxed, Willow asked, "Why did your grandmother talk you out of vet school?"

"It wasn't hard. I wanted her to do it. She believed in the same dream I did and promised she'd see me through it."

"Is that the responsibility, or the goal that may be unattainable"

"It's both." Drew grimaced and held against the strength of the mare's push. "I can feel the chest and angle of the leg. It's bent at the knee. If she doesn't overpower me, I should be able to draw it forward next time she lets up."

Once he had his hand on the left foreleg, Drew was able to inch the leg forward, but he had to wait until after another strong contraction before he could push the chest back far enough to let him unbend the knee and guide the lower leg forward. When he pulled his arm away and crouched behind Shamrock, the result was dramatic. With one push, two forelegs slid out with a long, dark head laid on top of them. With the next contraction, Drew took a firm hold of both forelegs and gave the tiring mare help with a steady but easy pull toward her hind feet whenever she pushed. The shoulders slipped out and Drew wiped the tiny nostrils clear. Only halfway free of its mother, the foal raised its head, snorted and struggled to stand.

Within seconds a dark, wet colt lay thrashing in the straw, trying to thrust himself to his feet on long, rubbery legs that wobbled like disjointed tentacles. Willow stood beside Drew, laughing with him while they watched the bay colt find his balance and stand. Swaying on spread legs, the foal staggered forward a few steps then banged into his mother when she heaved herself to her feet. The foal plunked down but, undaunted, tried again. After the third fall, he was standing on fairly solid legs and impatiently nosing around his mother until he found what he was looking for—a swollen milk bag filled with nourishment.

After examining the placenta to make sure it was intact, Drew slipped it into a plastic bag and watched the brush of tail swish back and forth while the newborn sucked vigorously at his first meal. "He's a nice one. Could you paint the umbilical with iodine and mop up in here while I duck over to your cabin and take a shower?"

"No problem, Doc. Does Mae have a name for him yet?"

"Not yet. She's big on musical characters and, if it was a colt, wanted to call him Rotten Luck Willie, but I vetoed it. I didn't think the mention of rotten luck was a good idea for a competition horse."

"How about Wee Willie Winkie? Maybe it will entice you to read more nursery rhymes."

"Ask her. I think she'll like it, especially if she knows it came from you."

"When did you get here?"

"About two. You were asleep and I was tired, so I crashed on the office couch."

When he gave her a quick kiss, Willow recoiled with a sour face. "You taste like liquor."

"Not just liquor, very good whisky. It's probably because I was drinking with a distraught friend until about one."

"Were you drunk?"

"Just mildly anesthetized." He broke away and strode toward the office.

"Who were you drinking with?"

"Nicole."

Convinced that she looked as stricken as she felt, Willow was thankful he said the name while he walked away from her. She dropped onto the cot and stared across the aisle while a black hole expanded in her chest.

When Drew came back, the vet was there to check the new foal. Nothing was said about Nicole, nor why Drew had been drinking with her.

While she listened to Drew and Dr. Allen, Willow wondered how someone with the knowledge and skills the vet credited Drew with could throw away a career he would have excelled in. She had learned something else about Drew, but it only confused her and made her determined to learn more. After Dr. Allen left, Drew was happy and in a teasing mood Willow was reluctant to destroy with probing questions. She concealed her wounds; and by afternoon, she'd smothered the hurt and convinced herself Nicole was distraught because he'd told her about his romance at home.

Willow's rationalized hope worked until Drew was gone and she lay alone in the bed they'd shared before he'd *gotten tied up in something* in Philadelphia. The pain turned to a gnawing uncertainty she was afraid to ask about but was unable to forget.

Willow was awake when Drew returned. She was sitting up in bed reading a dressage magazine and wondering how much more of his nonanswering she was going to accept. While he unbuttoned his shirt, she decided she wasn't going to accept it at all.

"Where were you?"

"What do you mean?" He paused with his shirt in his hand and gave her a puzzled look.

"Just what I said. Where were you? Where are you almost every night?"

"If I want you to know, I'll tell you." He balled up the shirt and threw it on a chair as emphasis. "You may never find out if you keep bugging me about it."

"Does that mean you plan on telling me?"

"When I'm ready." He stood beside the bed and emptied his pockets onto the bedside table.

"Is that a promise?"

"Yes, it's a promise." He plucked the magazine out of her hands and dropped it on the floor. "Right now, I don't want you involved.

You'll learn about it the way I want you to learn about it and you'll understand. That's all I'm going to say, except that starting next Monday I to need to take Venture with me. Try to keep him out of mud holes and have him in by four."

"Sure." Her answer was toneless, her mind blank. At the mention of Venture, all her scenarios collapsed. None of them included a horse. "May I ask one more thing?"

"Maybe."

"Is it good?"

"Willow, I believe there are some things that need to be shown, not told, so humor me. I don't want to argue with you tonight. It would ruin all the erotic thoughts I've been having about you."

"Okay, teacher, I'll stifle my curiosity."

"Oh, don't do that." He slipped off his watch and set it beside his wallet. "Don't ever lose your curiosity."

"I'm finding it impossible right now." Willow raised an eyebrow when he opened his belt. "The center fold game was fun, but I like the strip act better." Smiling in approval, she watched him finish undressing. When he turned to toss his pants on the chair with his shirt, she noted his cleanly defined shoulder and upper back muscles, long, supple loins, firmly muscled buttocks. "You have a nice seat off a horse, too."

"You're turning into a sex fiend." Growling deep in his throat, Drew dove at her and rolled her across the bed until she was pinned under him with loose hair fanned across the ivory sheet.

When he kissed her with soft enticement, Willow sighed and slid her arms around him. "There's no sense pretending I'm anything else when you always turn me into a helpless victim of desire."

"You can do the same to me."

"I don't have your power."

"But you do. It's time for the lesson when you find out about things like that."

"But men are different." She gave him a teasing smile. "Men are the aggressive takers. They fight off rivals, tear off women's clothes, throw them on their backs and conquer them with mad, passionate love. I read about that in historical novels."

"Willow," Drew sighed and gave her his patient, professorial look, "you're never going to learn it right if you keep trying to skip ahead of the lesson plan."

"Try it and I'll fight you tooth and nail." She teased.

"I'm sure you will," he answered with a lecherous leer.

"When's that lesson?" Willow eyed him warily until something told her he was baiting her. What surprised her was the way the thought sent a shiver of stimulation through her that rivaled the anticipation of challenge and danger.

"When the time is right." He rolled onto his back, holding her so her hair rained around his face and the tips of her breasts brushed on his chest. "You can turn the act around and make me as desperate as you were. There are no official rules for making love, *amore mio*. It's pure unfettered expressionism."

Willow's first touches were hesitant and unsure. She felt shy about being the aggressor, until he showed his pleasure and let his building passion react to her advances. The heat of their combined fervor engulfed them, entwined them in twisting urgency that crested toward desperation, then rolled back to languid pleasure, only to reignite and surge into powerful excitement.

As Willow learned to play Drew's sensitivities and hold him on the edge of selfcontrol, she discovered he was right when he said she could make him desperate. But he was not helpless.

When Drew lost his balance, male lust controlled him. He captured her wrists, pinned them beside her head and took what he wanted with a sudden possession that filled her with a power that challenged her lust and mastered it with his own, left her sated and glowing with pleasure. She snuggled up to him like a purring cat and spiraled into deep sleep.

Chapter Fifteen

The next morning, Drew kept his promise about taking Willow on his morning run and accepted no excuses on consecutive mornings, not even when she tried the ageold, female complaint of cramps. He insisted that if she couldn't run, she could walk, but she would not stay in bed like a lazy slug. He was heartless and the first four days were killers. And then it was all right.

By the sixth day, it was enjoyable and Willow looked forward to it. She found she could actually run a full mile before she had to drop back to a walk. She felt vibrantly alive with some of the energy that constantly radiated from Drew, who was a physical powerhouse of endurance with phenomenal lung power and breath control. He always left her behind from the start and his five or ten-mile runs included several wind sprints when he spurted ahead until his heart was pounding, his lungs working like efficient forge bellows. Yet, whenever he joined her again, he took up an easy conversation while he jogged circles around her or harassed her into another short run.

Today, Drew had gone on to the picnic park by the falls.

Before he left Willow at the old stone sawmill, Drew told her it had been built by Andrew Sutherland's son Jared in the early nineteenth century to supply lumber for Sutherland Mercantile's flourishing shipyard. The mill continued to operate into the last decade of the nineteenth century.

In 1936, in spite of Drew's grandfather's angry protests, Graham Sutherland donated the mill and four hundred acres of forestland to the county for historical preservation and recreational use. The structure had been preserved as a visual landmark with its doors padlocked or bolted closed. The huge vertical blade had been dulled and, along with its operational mechanisms, become rusted and inoperable.

Willow peered through a dusty, mesh covered window beside a padlocked door identified as the mill office. The brightness of a low sun made it impossible to see much more than shadowy shapes of a massive wooden desk, pieces of office furniture and labeled artifacts appropriate to the mill's period of operation. Deciding it would be better to come back on an afternoon when the light was coming in the side windows, she backtracked to an old wagon road once used by massive draft horses hauling logs into the back of the mill, where they were rolled onto a timber carriage and fed through the tall blade. The sawn lumber was then dried, sorted and stacked in the open main floor until it could be loaded onto four to six horse wagons for transport to the Delaware canal and Philadelphia shipyards.

From the loading ramp, Willow picked her way along a rocky foot trail to a fenced deck cantilevered over a dizzying drop behind the mill. The two lower floors that housed the operating mechanisms between the wheel and the sawblade clung to the rock and mortar face of the hillside beside a stone walled mill race that had once carried torrents of water from a dammed pond to the wooden undershot wheel.

The story of the mill and what it said about the enterprising spirit of a young Scottish rebel, who fled from what he saw as conquering oppressors to create a commercial empire in his new land, awed Willow. But then, hadn't the same thing been true a century later when her great-grandfather Roberts fled the poverty of a Welsh coal mining town and her mother's ancestors left famine ridden Ireland to claim plots of Iowa farmland under the newly enacted Homestead Act?

Every one of them had walked away from all they'd ever known to become free Americans. The only difference she could see was that, while her ancestors had arrived with nothing but a physical and spiritual determination to make a new life, Andrew Sutherland had arrived with, not only rebellious, gritty determination, but sufficient wealth to create a thriving enterprise.

Willow's revelation put the past in better historical perspective and reminded her of when Drew said that although his family heritage was impressive, it came with a price and he couldn't expect it to save his ass if he didn't live up to his respect for it. She wasn't sure what he meant but suspected it had something to do with the responsibility issue he was refusing to talk about.

After poking around the deserted mill, Willow continued along the gravel road to an overgrown two-track leading into the woods. She climbed onto an erratic boulder beside the road and, sitting in the warming sun, pulled in tasting breaths of morningfresh air. Spring was in full vibrancy as it balanced on the precipice of summer. The woods flared with a lush glow of health—the greens so green she was sure they were on the point of bursting into verdant fire.

For the last week, Willow had been floating on a high with few chances to dwell on questions and misgivings. And she had heard from Byron yesterday. His letter created an odd twinge of nostalgia in a small corner of her feelings, where uncertainty lay, and helped her see that she was no longer running from home. It was more that she was growing apart with a detachment that made her miss the good things and dull the sting of discord. She'd even chuckled affectionately at Byron's references to their father.

Not long ago, Willow had been blinded by her view of the man as an ogre and wouldn't have understood the humor in Byron's irony. Now, her more philosophical reaction to the letter made her realize she was growing up and could see it all with Byron's tongueincheek objectivity instead of indignant rebellion. In only a few weeks, Drew had opened her mind to an acceptance of moral freedom that, with the exception of Byron, would have shocked her family.

In truth, Willow had abandoned her battle for appearances so completely that when Drew didn't spend the night, she felt something was wrong. He'd been correct about John and Roy; and if Mae knew about it, she neither mentioned it nor seemed concerned about it. Unlike her own family's small-town world, where everyone seemed determined to mind everyone else's business, Drew's associates seemed determined not to mind anyone else's business. Right now, Willow felt caught in the middle, viewing one side as concerned, gossiping busybodies, the other as aloof, rationalizing hedonists.

Perched on the rock like an Indian sentinel, Willow folded her legs in front of her, pulled the letter out of the zippered pocket of her shorts and reread her brother's words...

Dear Elf,

I have heard broken hearts are good for growing up. However, I have no idea why, so I don't wish one on you. But neither do I wish you an unfulfilled love racked with doubts. As for advice, I don't suggest you play helpless weakling. It would be a false, unconvincing charade and no man worthy of you would want a breakable wimp. Try the oatmeal somewhere, but not in expensive riding boots. Your practical jokes always got predictable rises out of us. If he's a pompous ass, who can't share your high spirits, he isn't for you, sweetWilly. You're tough and lusty and the thing you do best is have fun. It isn't right that you aren't laughing.

As for the French, I thoroughly agree with you. It's a very sexy language, especially when spoken with a true Parisian accent (which makes one wonder if they all need adenoid surgery). During my first stay in Paris, I fell in love with a gorgeous jeune femme, who gave me a hard-on every time she did the weather report on T.V.

When I mentioned there was romance in Pennsylvania, our parochial sire started huffing and puffing again. He's still convinced you will come to your senses and return to Tom, the land, and the production of grandchildren with Iowa tans and farming in their blood. However, Keith and Glenn are doing well in that line. Both their wives are due, once again, to increase the Roberts clan by Christmas.

My dropped comment on your potential love life put me on Dad's sour side. But what's new? According to him, I'm the scoundrel who turned your head with improper notions, which takes some of the heat off you. Since he's already placed your sins on my head, feel free to enjoy your liberation. I've been whipped and condemned for so many sins I'll never notice a few of yours.

It was Alfred, Lord Tennyson who wrote: "Tis better to have loved and lost, / Than never to have loved at all." I quite agree. If you feel it is love, go for it, Elfin sister. While resorting to poets, remember Andrew Marvel: "The grave's a fine and private place, / But none, I think, do there, embrace..." Fuck the savings account, Willy. Spend now while you have the chance, just use discretion and take all necessary precautions. Virtue is not the asset it once was, except to your father and your brother Todd—in his sister, that is.

In regard to engagements, it may not be what you expect and you can't talk him out of anything. You'll have to let him feel his way to the decision you want him to make. Oh, by the way, Tennyson also wrote: "He will hold thee, when his passion shall have spent its novel force, / Something better than his dog, a little dearer than his horse."

I love you, Elf, and miss you.
As ever, your incorrigible brother, Unlordly Byron.

...Willow refolded the letter, glanced at it before she slipped it in the envelope and noticed a scribbled note on the otherwise blank back of the page. It surprised her, until she realized she must have missed it yesterday when Drew pulled in the driveway and she hastily stuffed the letter in a desk drawer with the errant thought that maybe she would show it to him someday. But not now.

After unfolding the letter, she read, *"Andrew Sutherland? All I can say is: Placido—move over!"* The scrawled note confused her until she remembered a lonely winter when she had consistently fallen asleep listening to the Placido Domingo CD of romantic songs Byron had given her for Christmas. He'd accused her of trying to take the singer to bed with her and intimated there were better ways to solve that problem. When she heard Drew coming, she put the folded letter in her pocket and zipped it closed before he stopped in front of her and held his hand out for her to clasp.

"It's a fantastic morning." Drew caught her in his arms when she jumped off the rock, whirled her in dizzying circles before he set her on her feet and kissed her.

"It is. It makes me want to sing." Willow laughed, then frowned. "That is, if I could sing. Byron got all the musical talent. I just got the appreciation part. Why don't you sing?"

"Let's go for a walk in the woods." Drew paused for an awkward moment, then said, "Your appreciation does not need the shock of my singing."

Still clasping her hand, Drew started down the rutted road. "I'll show you the scene of one of the greatest terrors of my life."

"What's that?"

"Zeb Bronson's farm. He was an antisocial hermit, who gave rise to many horror stories, few of which were true."

"But yours is?"

"Absolutely. I was here for summers, scattered stays when Dad was doing business, occasional Christmases and holidays, so I was only a quasiresident and an outsider to the local kids. I was eleven that summer and a cocky little monster, which made me number one target to the older native sons, who didn't want me hanging around them. As a result of their crabbing, Dad told me to leave them alone.

But, being a jerk, I didn't heed the warnings. The kids decided to scare me off by daring me to sneak onto Zeb's back porch and steal a jug of homemade hooch for them."

"Did you do it?"

"Yeah, I did it, or at least I got the jug off the porch. Zeb saw me and ran out the back door, cussing. I was bolting away as fast as I could and didn't pay any attention to him until the shotgun went off and disintegrated a rotten stump ahead of me. When I turned around and saw the ends of those twelve-gauge barrels, I dropped the jug and damn near pissed my pants. About that time my cohorts in crime lit out like spooked rabbits, leaving me—alone and terrified—to face the madman. When he clamped a huge hand on the back of my neck and marched me to the house, I had visions of a violent death at the hands of a maniac, or some horrible occult torture beyond my imagination, which would make it really bad because I had a big imagination."

"What did he do?"

"Sat me on a kitchen chair and called Dad to come get me. He wasn't any of the things the kids said he was. Zeb was an alcoholic, who wanted to be left alone, and a damn good artist when he backed off on the booze. Dad knew him, which stunned me. It also got me in big trouble. My father had no sympathy for disobedience, trespassing or stealing, and even less for the excuse, *they made me do it*. I was so grounded you could have used me for a lightning rod."

"Sounds like a complete backfire to me."

"Actually, it wasn't. The experience reversed my standing with the neighborhood kids, and I basked in a short period of popularity because the stories I invented about my captivity would put Edger Allen Poe to shame."

"So, you really came out ahead."

"I wouldn't say that either." He frowned. "Dad and Gram spent the last week we were here arguing about his restriction, which included riding. I took fuel from her support and turned it into a colossal battle."

"Who won?"

"I would have to say Dad because I sure lost. He never gave in to her, and I defied him by disobeying his orders, which was a sin of the highest magnitude. He could swing a mean strap when he had to. After that, I sure didn't want to ride a short striding pony."

Willow laughed at his hammed expression of agony. "I used to think rich kids didn't get tannings like us farm kids."

"Nobody told my father that. When Dad gave an order, or delivered an ultimatum, it was as if he painted a white line on the ground with huge lettering that said, 'That's the law. Step over it and you'll pay—every time.' I needed to learn my behavior had consequences, good or bad, as directly and consistently as possible."

"Sounds harsh."

"Not really. It made things very clear. And there was wiggle room..." he waggled his hand and smiled wryly, "...for mitigating circumstances. It was like the boundary lines in football. When I was learning the ropes, I could get one foot over and be reminded. Then it turned into pro ball when I had to keep both feet in bounds and reprieves were hard won. With odds like that, I didn't cross his line very often."

"At least he listened to you."

"Sometimes too well." Drew made a sour face. "I wasn't used to that and had a bad mouth and gutsy attitude. Before Dad and Gram, my behavior and opinions never seemed to have anything to do with what did or didn't happen. The only thing I learned from my mother and Gino was how to get away or curl up in a ball to protect the vital parts when the yelling started. With Dad and Gram, I knew what I would be punished for and how. It made life a lot easier to cope with."

"That sounds like home. Only we seemed to know it from birth."

"You lived with consistency from birth."

"Maybe we aren't entirely different."

"Would you stop saying that!" Drew snapped, then pulled in a slow breath before he stopped on top of a hill. With his hands curled around her shoulders, he turned her to face him. "Willow, I'm not different. Except in window dressing, which doesn't matter."

"But we do have differences. And it's so important to me I can't conquer it. Drew, I can't face life with the nonchalance you do." Her voice faltered, but she could no longer keep it inside. "I can't keep pretending I'm enjoying a pleasant interlude. I'm in love with you."

His hands tightened and a shadow of panic swept across his face. "I was afraid of that."

"Afraid of it? Is it something you didn't expect?"

"I don't know what I expected." He turned and stared down the hill at the decaying farm house patched with scraps of tar paper, corrugated metal and odd pieces of wood.

The weather-beaten house below them was deserted and slowly disintegrating. Willow stared at the abandoned structure beyond Drew's straight, almost rigid stance and had the horrible feeling she had just made a similar shamble of their relationship by saying what she had been intuitively holding back.

"Maybe you didn't fully learn the lesson about behavior having consequences." She waited until he swung around to meet her eyes. "Drew, you worked very hard at getting me to fall in love with you."

"I worked very hard at seducing you."

"It went far beyond that. But isn't that love?"

"Yes, and I love you that way. However, I know that's not what you're talking about. I can feel what you're talking about. Sometimes I think it's suffocating me."

He looked agitated, unsure of himself, which was unlike him. When Willow touched his arm, he froze, then shuddered, twisted and jerked away from her. For a long moment, he was a silent wall and Willow had no words to answer him. Then, with a sudden convulsion, he snapped his head up and turned to face her. The agitation was gone. His expression was pensive and troubled.

"I don't know what to tell you, Willow. I can't make up lies or promise what I can't give. I just know I want to keep making love to you."

"I had to tell you. It kept swelling inside me until it hurt to hold it in." Her voice started to break apart and she thought she would cry. His arms folded around her with sheltering strength.

"Please, don't cry. I like to make you happy. I like to hear you laugh. Crying isn't happy." When he tipped her face up, his lips touched the edges of closed lids, kissed away tears. "You mean more to me than any other woman I've known. You fill me up and become a part of my feelings. Don't build another wall. It hurts too much."

"I won't do that again." She pulled in a steadying breath. "I was afraid you were going to run away from me."

"Impossible. I'm hobbled by your bed sheets and a slave to the mesmerizing aroma of your cinnamon rolls." He was laughing again, his eyes bright with a joking sparkle. "Come on, I want to see if I can find that stump he blasted."

"Is he still there?" Alarm tightened Willow's throat.

"Zeb died in March and the county took over the land. I was surprised to learn he was only sixty. He seemed really old back then. Of course, to an eleven-year-old that could be anything over thirty."

When Drew started down the hill, Willow heard a low, threatening growl and turned to face a snarling, rough coated dog slinking toward them from behind a crumbling stone wall. She gasped and her voice was a croak in her throat. "Drew, by the wall."

"I see it. Back away slowly. Don't turn your back on it."

While Willow inched back, Drew moved forward, putting himself between Willow and the dog. He stood still, in a relaxed, loosejointed pose that made Willow wonder how he could take it so calmly. She was clumsy with tension, battling a fear that told her to turn and run away in screaming panic.

When Drew moved forward, the dog leapt. Willow did scream, but she was too terrified to run. The charge was a blur of tawny brown fur, a snarling mouth with white daggers for teeth. Willow didn't see what actually happened—Drew moved too fast and her horrified stare was welded on the leaping animal. She was sure the slashing teeth had torn into Drew's face until she heard a yelp and saw him holding an old leather collar in a clenched fist. The other hand was clamped on the dog's throat, closing off the windpipe until the snarls became strangled cries.

Drew pinned the dog to the ground on its back, shook it, then hurled it away and stood waiting in the same stance of calm readiness. The dog had had enough. Without another look at Drew, it tucked its tail and ran on three legs toward the crumbling building at the bottom of the hill.

If Drew hadn't caught her to him, Willow would have collapsed when she tried to move. "Why did you do that?" she asked when the strength of his body, the security of his arms absorbed her fear.

"I couldn't let him hurt you. It must be Zeb's dog gone feral."

"He's dangerous."

"Unfortunately for him." Drew's face twisted with concern. "It's a wonder no one's shot him."

"Shouldn't we tell someone?"

"I'll take care of it." He started to let her go then slid his hand to the back of her head and tugged her pony tail. "What are my odds for survival if I make a suggestion you may not like?"

"I won't know until you make it."

"Gram is going to her hairdresser tomorrow morning. She's invited you to join her and let Joseph style your hair?"

"It just does whatever it wants no matter what I do to it." Willow bristled. "I thought you liked my rain of fiery hair."

"When it's free and I can bury my hands in it, not when it's hogtied." Drew slid off the elastic, thrust his fingers into the tumbling fall and pulled her to him for a kiss. When he retreated, he bunched her hair in his hands, teased her lips with gentle nips. "Joseph is very good at making hair that does what it wants look good."

"Maybe you ought to go, too." Willow sputtered and raked windblown hair out of her mouth. "You're starting to look like a mountain man."

"Very perceptive of you to notice. It's not a negotiable issue."

"But my hair is?" She tamed her wild mane with an elastic she dug out of a pocket.

"It was a wishful suggestion, not an issue." Drew slid his arm around her waist and walked back along the track with her.

When they reached the road, Drew gave her a sheepish look. "If you're still pissed at me, you'll be ready to smack me for not giving you more warning. We're going to a play Friday night."

"Tomorrow Friday?"

"That's the one." He hammed a wince when she smacked his arm. "It's summer theater. Nothing fancy."

"What play and where?"

"I thought I'd show you some of the area culture. It's opening night at Parsons Glen Barn Theater. Gram always buys season tickets for four. She's going. And Dad, if he gets here in time."

"Why is he coming?" Willow gave up the argument when Drew refused to take part in it.

"It's an annual visit. Memorial Day is the weekend after this."

"So?"

"There's a race in Indiana he never misses."

"Is he driving in it?"

"He's getting too old for Indy cars." Drew chuckled. "Just don't tell him I said that. I can guarantee he has a bundle riding on it."

"I was taught gambling is wrong?"

"By a farmer?" His sudden laugh was skeptical. "Isn't that what farming's all about?"

"I mean deliberate gambling for sport, not with nature or markets."

"If you're gambling with your security, it's wrong. When my mother blew fifty bucks at the track, it was wrong because it was usually the rent. When my father puts up a few thousand on a car race, it's spending money."

"Let's not talk about money. I can't think beyond a hundred and fifty dollars a week."

"You really mean that, don't you? You are totally unconcerned about money beyond your immediate needs."

"I get concerned when I need to buy stereos, fix my car or can't afford to replace my trashed computer."

"That's not money. That's petty cash." Drew laughed at her startled look. "It's one of the things I like about you."

"What?" His reasoning confused her. "That I don't have money?"

"You don't care about it. You only care about me. It's a novel feeling and I'm beginning to like it."

"Drew, you're not making sense. I just told you I love you. Of course, I care about you."

"Well, you're the first woman who ever did. I think some of them compiled a list of my financial assets to see if I was worth their efforts. They checked out the price of the dinner wine to rate me as a lover."

"Your rating as a lover has nothing to do with wine, or worth, except it's more intoxicating than wine and beyond any price."

"And you're happy with that poetic view?"

"Who wouldn't be?"

"If you want to know, I'll give you a list." He made a sour face. "At risk of ruining your inflated image of me as an insatiable Lothario, my sex life wasn't always great. There's something fantastic between us I can't figure out."

Willow wanted to tell him it was love that was fantastic between them, but she held it back. She wanted to say it was not her love that was suffocating him, but his own love, which he refused to accept since it threatened his precious freedom.

"I'm not denying I've had good sex before, but with you it's way beyond good. It defies description. I can't stop wanting you."

"There goes the rest of the morning." Laughing, Willow swung her hip and bumped him out of step.

❖

In Philadelphia, Drew left Sal's bar and walked to the Italian Market, where open stalls, displayed an international array of foods and produce that spread over the boundaries of sidewalks and forced vehicles to crawl along a narrow, beehive-crowded street that swarmed with a global palette of sounds and scents—all reverberating in a sensory mish-mash of entwined languages, both familiar and teasingly alien. An enticingly exotic jumble of aromas surrounded him and saturated his senses with the mouth-watering temptations of herbs and oils, cheeses and spices. After stopping for a moment to absorb sensuous sensations that seeped into a deeply forgotten corner of his mind and took him back to a time he barely remembered, Drew hurried down a side street of old row houses renovated into apartments and low-grade commercial establishments.

With the sounds and smells of the market fading into a background of city noise, Drew stopped in front of a vacant, four story building of dingy red brick. The blank stares of streaked, grimy, or boarded over windows sent a chill through him, as if he were staring at a gaping crypt containing ghostly remains of past demons he couldn't expunge from his mind.

He took a hesitant step forward then looked down at scuffed toes and frayed, knotted-together laces on dirty black and white gym shoes. He shook his head, closed his eyes and breathed in the tantalizing aroma of rich tomato sauce, Italian cheeses, garlic and oregano, then lifted his head and stared up at an open window of a third-floor corner apartment. Filmy white curtains twisted and fluttered beside bright orange and blue pots of herbs and red geraniums carefully lined up on the sill. A clear visualization of a room with gaudy, flowery wallpaper and overstuffed furniture smothered in fringed, maroon and gold throws filled his mind. Dark ornately framed Italian prints cluttered the walls. An old upright piano with yellowing keys dominated a front corner beside crooked stacks of musty books and tattered sheet music.

With the mouthwatering smell of Signora Colucci's cheese and garlic ravioli wrapping tight bands of hunger around his empty stomach, he bounded up the stairs and reached for the recessed door. The instant his hand touched the scarred surface of the barrier, a barrage of anger assaulted him...

"Stop lying to me, Andrew. Tell me where you were. And don't look at me with those demon eyes."

Frozen in silent denial, Andrew thrashed to break the grip of the hand twisted in his hair, felt sharp slaps crack across his face before bruising thumps of a broken towel rod pummeled his shoulders, his back. "You're a lying demon's child and need to be cleansed of the evil he seeded in you."

"No, Mamma, no." Resistance crumbled as he cringed against the door jamb and curled around his knotted stomach. When the dark door to the pantry swung open in front of him, he was shoved onto hard, bare tiles. "Please, no, Mamma, please don't, please don't—"

When the door slammed shut and the hard metal funnel was forced into his mouth, he went rigid, dropped his head and shuddered into dreaded oblivion that left him shivering in a deep, stone laundry tub—sore, naked, and helpless. Sour vomit scoured his throat, intense pain cramped his bowels; the odor and burn of filth assaulted his senses until it was scoured away with a harsh brush and scalding water.

After a releasing shudder racked through him, Drew found himself grasping the handle of a door that refused to open. Realizing it was locked, he backed down the steps and stumbled across the sidewalk to a metal light pole. He stood with his hands grasping the pole, his forehead pressing against its hard surface while he waited for his heart to stop pounding.

Drew snapped back to present awareness with the same disorienting sensation he'd experienced in the manor house dining room when he remembered smashing one of Gram's china plates. He looked up at the third-floor corner window. It was as blind and dark as all the other dirt-streaked windows.

This time, he was aware of losing the control he'd been able to depend on for close to sixteen years. It made him think about other memories he'd relived in the first few years he lived with his father. The thought of there being more of the same hell frightened him but he was able to subdue it by telling himself he was still in control—it was only being so close to reminders of things buried that was causing it to happen. There were no more terrors, only fragments of memories he needed to understand.

And they weren't all bad, just forgotten: Milly and his foolish Valentine; Ernie and the comic books; Signora Colucci, who lived in the front corner apartment, and the meals he shared with her on Sunday nights after her family went home and he stole his mother's key to sneak out and visit her. She always had a plate of leftover Sunday dinner for him—the remains of a plump chicken with scrumptious ravioli or cheesy eggplant parmigiana, a garlic risotto to die for—a dinner served with the never changing lecture on how his mother was starving him and he needed more pasta to fatten his scrawny body.

Smiling, Drew closed his eyes and leaned back against the light pole while lost memories of a tiny woman, who twittered and fussed like a white-capped chickadee impulsively tidying her nest, flooded into his mind. Surrounded by the floral and talcum smell of bath powder, he felt tickling touches of delicate fingers teasing his curls while Italian words flowed over him in the soothing caramel tones of her alto voice. "Come, my little Buffo, sing for me." Her dinner price was always a recital of songs she insisted he sing while she played her old piano.

With a start, Drew realized that by nurturing and shaping the talent and perfect pitch his mother had unwittingly passed on to him with her DNA, Signora Colucci had been his first music teacher and introduced him to a fascinating world of musical magic. She'd been the first to call him Buffo and taught him to identify notes until he could pick one out of the air and give it to her whenever she asked for it. He'd stopped going to her when the music was taken from him by the boy who hated his love of it—the boy who took over his life and detested everything he loved.

Thinking that maybe looking backwards wouldn't always show him trauma and pain, Drew turned a corner and walked north until Antonio picked him up.

"You in a hurry or do you want to share the pizza I bought?" Antonio asked when he parked in his driveway.

"It smells like Bebbe's Pepperoni Supremo, and you better be willing to share it," Drew answered as he stepped out of the car. "Besides, there's something I want to ask you."

After an almost ceremonial and silent enjoyment of the first piece of what Antonio insisted was the best pizza in Philly, Drew handed him an envelope Ernie had given him. "Milly will never testify against Mario, but that's a list of some leads she thinks you can pressure, as well as times he may be meeting with dealers."

"I thought she wouldn't help?"

"Ernie says Mario's been scaring her. She's starting to think she'd be safer if he was in jail. I think maybe Mario would be, too. If he hurts her and I find out, he'll be bragging out of his own asshole."

"Could you explain the physics behind that statement?" Antonio looked astonished. "I don't think such contortions are possible."

"It would take some serious restructuring, but I don't know about impossible. I know a circus contortionist who comes damn close to it." Drew tipped his chair back and sighed. "You're very frustrating, Zio. You always destroy my outrageous hyperbole with reality."

"With you I'm not always sure you won't try. You said you were going to teach a juiced-up loudmouth how to make a facedown snow angel after body-surfing down a sledding hill. And then, you proceeded to do it."

"The art is all in calculating the trajectory and applying the correct impetus." Drew chuckled. "I get a sadistic kick out of teaching acrobatics to idiots who threaten me with bodily harm."

"Like the two guys in Italy last winter?" Antonio gave him a hard look.

"Only they weren't idiots. And I was the one doing the threatening. It upsets me when I lose control of my temper. It's like a red-hot ball expands in the center of my being and detonates like an exploding firebomb. It engulfs me and I lose all cognizance of what's happening."

"You've done it before?"

"A few times." Drew shrugged. "But it was never for something as insignificant as Vittorio throwing a plastic water glass. He was always throwing things when he got wound up."

"How many times did you lose it and when?"

"I don't have an answer for that." Drew took another bite of the exquisite concoction of meats, cheeses and Bebbe's secret, spicy tomato sauce. "But it always seemed to have something to do with an attack on a woman. Maybe it goes back to when Mario was hitting that girl and I attacked him."

"Or Gino."

Drew lowered the pizza before he took a bite. "You may be right about that. I seem to remember feeling that same kind of rage toward him. But I don't remember ever attacking him, only trying to run or curl up to keep his fists away from where they hurt the most."

"Which," Antonio said, "besides the fact that Gino killed my sister, was one of the reasons I didn't hesitate before I let him have it with both barrels."

"Did you go there looking to kill him and then drive by and do it?" Drew gave him a puzzled look. "It doesn't fit with what I know of you."

"The thought was in my mind, but I couldn't just blast him away. After he made his drug sale, I stopped the car at the end of the alley and got out. It was a direct confrontation, not the drive by shooting it looked like. Gino did get in the first two shots. Both of them hit the car."

"So, it was self-defense."

"If you don't take into account that I showed up well armed and Gino couldn't hit a moving target if it was glued to the barrel end of his gun. There was a chance I could have disarmed him. Instead, I dodged, dropped to one knee and blew him away. Is that what you wanted to talk to me about?"

"No, but I'm glad you told me. It was one of the unsettled things in my mind. The one I wanted to ask you about is why you helped Dad win the custody battle. Your family hated him."

"They didn't always. When I first knew him, I thought he was great—a little weird and stuffy but friendly enough. By the time he started traveling, Carlotta was cheating on him with Gino. She turned my family against Andy with some blatant lies about him being the one who beat on her. She even went as far as getting a restraining order against him by convincing some neighbors to testify to witnessing violent fights I now know never happened the way she said they did."

Antonio set down his pizza, held Drew's gaze. "After the divorce, Carlotta and Gino made Andy out to be uncaring, but I knew they were getting extra money out of him by making up stories about things you needed. Since Andy always sent the money, I figured he really did care about you. About then I decided nobody could be a worse son of a bitch than Gino and my sister was mentally fucked up from drugs. I took a more serious interest in you and some of the things you told me made me know that under all the mess in your head, you needed your father."

"It took me a while to understand that," Drew said. "One of the first things he did was tell me my behavior was totally unacceptable to him. Then he dragged me off to France, where he laid out a code of conduct that would put boot camps to shame."

"I remember him saying he'd like to duct tape your mouth shut."

"He gave me one free chance to cuss him out, then said if I ever called him, or any other adult, a fucking asshole again, I wouldn't want to move for a while. After he proved good on his threat, I learned to repeat the epithet in my head like a mantra whenever I wanted to obliterate him. Somehow, it gave me the guts to prove I could meet his challenge."

"I didn't say you wanted him. I said you needed him."

"Do you know what he said when I brought it up years later?"

"Probably didn't surprise him."

"He said, 'I figured as much. I didn't want to break your spirit, just shut your mouth to save my dignity.' I never could put much over on Dad, even when I thought I could."

"Neither could I." A twisted smile shifted Antonio's square jaw. "I was only sixteen when I wrote that letter telling Andy I could help him get you away from my sister and Gino. It was hard to betray my family, but it turned out to be the best thing I ever did for both you and me. Your father turned me around, too, and I fully believe that if I hadn't let him convince me I had to stand up for what I knew was right and testify against my sister, I'd be in prison instead of putting scum like Gino inside. I also believe that if things hadn't changed, you stood a good chance of growing up just enough to get killed in a gang war or do time yourself."

"That's a sobering thought, but I have to agree with you. A few of the neighborhood kids I saw as mentors seem to have met those fates." Drew paused for a thoughtful moment, then smiled crookedly. "You couldn't have been all bad, Zio. You decided to save me; maybe you would have saved yourself."

"Probably not on my own." Antonio shook his head. "When your mother died, I was tempted to blame your father for causing it, the way the rest of my family did, but I knew better. I tried to tell them it was Gino's intent to get rid of her as soon as the support checks stopped and he secured a better source of money, but they refused to believe me. When the court made a deal with Gino and let him out of prison early, I took it as an unforgivable failure of the justice system and knew he would be out for my blood. So, I took him on. When the cops started breathing down my neck, I panicked and called the only man I could trust—Andy Sutherland. I don't know what he did, or how he did it, but the car I was trying to ditch disappeared. Two days later, I had an unbreakable alibi for that night and a full scholarship to Penn State."

"You're kidding!" Drew blinked. "Dad helped you evade the law?"

"Without hesitation. Especially when he learned the full truth of it. Out of gratitude, I studied like a dedicated monk and found out I liked education and law enforcement enough to go on to a masters and into criminal investigation."

"I'm still amazed that he helped you evade the law. I commend him for it, but he was always a strait-laced pain in the ass about things like that, both literally and figuratively."

"His ethics are rock solid, but his sense of justice is stronger."

"When I was eighteen, he let me suffer in a Marseille jail for a goddamn week when all I did was get in a bar fight."

"He told me about that." Antonio burst out laughing. "Consider it his sense of justice."

"Do you know what happens to wise asses in those jails?"

"I know what your father said they couldn't let happen to you."

"I don't follow that." Drew peered at him over a raised piece of pizza. "He wasn't there until they let me out."

"Drew, you still have no idea how much influence your father and his Scottish family wield. Some very important people made it clear to your jailers that if you were severely injured, confined in a dark room, or sexually abused some heads would roll. Andy figured you needed some reality checks, but he didn't throw you into total depravity. It was a good deal. The way I see it, you served a miserable stretch of time, and the charge was dropped to a misdemeanor for time served then expunged from their records. You even got special treatment." Antonio laughed at Drew's skeptical look. "There were two good men watching out for you."

"Watch out for me? They worked the ass off me." Drew looked indignant then laughed with him. "There were a few other things I would have put on his list of don'ts."

"You survived them all, didn't you?"

"Yeah." Drew shrugged. "I definitely learned how the real-world treats what Dad called arrogant rich brats."

Chapter Sixteen

Standing in front of the full-length mirror mounted on her closet door, Willow stared at an image she wasn't sure she recognized. Her trip to Philadelphia with Mae had turned into an experience as alien to her as a trip to Hollywood.

First there had been Joseph, the charming, movie-idol-handsome stylist, who attacked her wayward hair with the zeal of a man with an inner vision. Then, after a sensational crab cake lunch—prepared with ingredients she couldn't even pronounce—at the renowned Fountain Restaurant, Mae took her to a stylish boutique and insisted on buying her a dress for the theater performance. When protests failed to make the slightest impression on her determined employer, Willow recalled Drew telling her there was no way to distract his grandmother once she set her mind on something.

Apparently, Mae's desire to transform Willow into a date worthy of her Sutherland grandson was one of those things. And here she was, wearing an absolutely stunning, silk chiffon cocktail dress in a deep amethyst hue that, much to her amazement, enhanced rather than clashed with her auburn hair.

Willow was slipping the post of a gold horsehead earring through her right ear lobe when Drew stepped behind her. He slid his hand into the deep vee, where gathered shoulder straps crossed her chest, kissed the hollow between her neck and shoulder, moaned in pleasure as he tasted her skin. When she slapped his wrist, he circled his arms around her and, growling, cupped his hands over her breasts, nibbled at soft skin under her ear.

"I like the haircut." Drew buried his face in the softness of loose curls covering the nape of her neck and breathed in their fragrance. "Joseph interpreted my visions to perfection."

"Your visions?" Willow frowned. "I thought they were his."

"After I called and had a talk with him, they were."

"You told him how to cut my hair?" She stared at the reflection of his grinning face.

"There's nothing about how to cut hair I could tell him. I merely suggested the image in my mind." He chuckled at her glower. "Think about it. Is there anyone you would rather please?"

"How about Joseph?" Willow smiled smugly. "I found him devilishly handsome."

"Ha! I could land him faster than you could, which narrows your chances dramatically."

"I'm still getting used to it." Flushing, Willow turned her head to look at the way short hair around her face blended into longer hair behind her ears. Then, shifting her attention, she glared at the mirror's full-length reflection of Drew in jeans and a darkblue Tshirt with wind ruffled hair. It made him look roguish and exciting—not ready to go to dinner and a play. "Drew, you aren't even dressed."

"And you're so stunning it's a shame I'm going to have to stand you up for dinner."

Willow straightened so suddenly she banged his chin with her head. When he backed away, rubbing his jaw, she twisted to face him. "Did I hear you right?"

"Yeah, I think you did." He tried the sheepish schoolboy look, but she was unsympathetic.

"You have the nerve to show up at the last minute," Willow's response grew in volume when he hammed a wince, "and tell me we're not going?"

"I didn't say we're not going. I'm not going to dinner. I'll meet you at the theater. Willow, it's unavoidable. Trust me. I'll explain it later."

"It doesn't happen to speak French, does it?"

"What are you talking about?"

"Is this another tieup with a devastated Nicole?"

"No." He scoffed at her flash of jealousy. "I brought you a standin for the dinner date. He's in the living room, so let's not make a scene out of this."

"A standin?"

"You'll like him. And I think I can trust him with you for dinner." Before she could protest, Drew circled his hand around her left wrist and led her out of the bedroom.

Then it was too late. Willow was face to face with a man of Drew's height in navy slacks and tie, a butter-yellow shirt and open navy blazer. He was strikingly attractive with sharply defined features that were hauntingly familiar yet unfamiliar at the same time. When she met his eyes, she recognized a more mature version of a face that had stared out of black and white photographs of jumping horses in the stable office and knew who he was. The eyes were Sutherland blue; the face hinted of both Mae and Drew. He was slighter than Drew, not as heavily muscled, more athletically lean.

"Willow, my father, the one called Andy. Dad, Willow Roberts."

Willow tried to look composed, but it was hopeless. When she'd tried to imagine Drew's father, she never once thought of him as blond. She certainly had no inkling he would look young enough to be Drew's older brother. Recovering from her surprise, she noticed some of the duskyblond hairs were silver, the lean face showed faint age lines near the eyes. It added credibility, but she had trouble believing he was almost fifty.

Willow hadn't thought of Drew's life away from Sutherland Manor lately. By refusing to share anything with her, except a few scattered memories of a traumatic transition period between opposing childhood environments, Drew had created a comfortable retreat while he sorted himself out and pulled her into it until she'd become encapsulated by the circle of her cabin, the morning runs and the horses. Now, in the presence of his selfassured father, she felt the intrusion of an unsettling outside force. There was nothing neutral about Andy Sutherland, whose arrival felt threatening.

"Hello, Mr. Sutherland." Her smile was as uneasy as her feelings.

"As your dinner date and escort to the theater, I would much prefer you called me Andy."

"All right." The brittleness left her voice when one side of his mouth lifted in a smile that turned on a quiet charm and relaxed the threat. Willow felt she should say more, but the words in her mind were for Drew and verged on profane.

Realizing she forgot the jacket for her dress, Willow used it as an excuse to rush back to the bedroom, where she banged open the closet door and jerked the light garment off a hanger. She wanted to choke Drew for the way he had maneuvered her into a situation she couldn't back out of without being illmannered, or creating a scene that would embarrass them all. She pulled in a breath to steady herself and decided she would accept it for now. But he was going to hear about it when they were alone tonight. It would take more than a few cajoling words and seductive kisses to appease her this time.

When she walked into the living room, Willow tried to relax and be friendly, but her steps were short, her glance at Drew venomous. He was smart enough to say nothing and let his father break the tension.

"Our reservations are for six. If we want to make an eight-thirty curtain, we need to get there on time." Andy took the jacket from her hand and held it for her to slip into. "It's a bit chilly. I think you'll need this."

"Thank you." Willow felt a hand sweep her hair out of the way and started at the caressing touch on neck and face. It was as electrifying and possessive as Drew's. When she saw Andy walk to open the door, she realized the hand was Drew's. Stiffening in rejection, she marched through the open door without so much as a glance at him.

At the car, when Willow reached for the handle on the passenger door, a strong, wiry hand closed on hers and a bluesleeved arm reached past her to open the door.

"Do I have to suffer for his sins? I thought the sins of the father were visited on the son, not vice versa."

"Every time something is going right, he finds a way to sabotage it." Willow plunked down on the door sill and, with practiced skill, swung her legs over it, slid onto the leather seat and swept her skirt away from the door so he could swing it down. When the door remained open, she turned to see Andy holding the end of a seat belt in his hand. They had been later additions to the car and lacked the sophistication of modern seat belts. They were heavy and stiff, awkward to locate after the door was closed. "I don't use it in this car. It's uncomfortable."

"When you ride with me, you'll use it."

Taken back by the quietly firm tone of command, Willow took the tab end of the belt from him and fumbled between the seats for the adjustable end. She clicked the two sections together and left it loose in her lap while she stared ahead of her in a mood that could only be called a sulk.

Willow had been looking forward to tonight as a date with Drew. She didn't even know the name of the play or where she was going to dinner. The excitement had been Drew. Now, at the last minute, he had snatched it away from her and railroaded her into a date with a man who was nothing like the one she'd envisioned.

Willow found it impossible to take Andy casually. He was as dynamic and charismatic as Drew, but in a quiet way that was, somehow, more authoritative and in charge than anyone she'd ever encountered. She'd had no idea how to envision a middleaged businessman, who gambled for recreation and lived with a woman only eight years older than his son.

Willow had expected an older Drew or a flashy, robust, slightly overweight wheelerdealer, even a reckless, loudtalking braggart. She had been all wrong. Andy Sutherland was the image of a British aristocrat, or an officer out of Kipling's era. He was coolly suave with a quiet, commanding manner and the bearing of someone who was used to giving orders and being obeyed. Willow doubted he spent much time arguing when he wanted something done.

Just before Andy let out the clutch to back out of the short driveway, Willow saw his hand move from the gearshift toward her lap. Before she could react, he caught the end of the strap and pulled the belts snug around her hips and across her chest.

She flashed her eyes to him. "It wrinkles the dress."

"Which is infinitely preferable to smashing your face."

"I thought gamblers took risks." Her voice cut with an irritation caused more by the situation and Drew than Andy.

"Only fools and bad gamblers take unnecessary risks."

"I heard you were a good driver."

"I'm not the only driver on the roads." Andy backed out of the driveway and drove toward the main road at a speed even Mae would accept as reasonable. Willow continued to stare ahead with her thoughts locked inside.

"Drew's absence really is unavoidable and innocent." Andy flicked a quick glance at her, then looked back at the road.

"He can make his own excuses."

"That's true." He smiled wryly. "I remember some of them were very creative, especially when he was in trouble."

When Andy stopped at the end of the estate road to wait for an approaching car, he turned to look at her with an expression that was clearly irritated, yet willing to offer a truce. "Nursing your anger may be satisfying to you, but it makes you very poor company. Drew insisted you were a wealth of wit and a barrel of laughs—as well as the best thing to happen to him since puberty. You aren't proving it very well."

"Did he really say that?" Willow felt some of the heaviness lift, sensed the faint tugging of a smile.

"That got your interest, didn't it?" When she nodded, Andy smiled. "The last part is his. The first is paraphrased. It's too trite for Drew, who rarely deals in clichés, unless he can twist them into plays on words."

"I'll try to put the safety on my anger until I can aim it at the right person."

"Good. If we can forget Drew's misfortune, I'm sure we'll have an excellent dinner."

As soon as Andy squealed the tires on the paved road and accelerated through the gearbox at a rate that pressed her against the back of the seat, Willow was thankful for the snug seat belt and grab handle by the door.

Willow had ridden in the same car with Drew on a number of occasions and had been impressed by its speed, acceleration and handling. Compared to the way Andy drove, Drew hardly taxed the machine's capabilities. Andy drove a car the way Drew rode a horse, as an extension of his nervous system. She was stunned when he swept the powerful car around curves, roared into tight turns, always downshifting at the last possible instant to squeal or drift through them. Her heart thudded and her knuckles whitened on the chrome grab handle and the inside edge of the leather seat. It was terrifying and exhilarating at the same time.

When they reached the restaurant, Willow was flushed and excitedly animated. "I thought Drew drove fast."

"Drew drives with his passions, as most Italians do. I rarely drive like that on public roads, but I know this road well and wanted to see what the car could still do." Andy backed into a parking space and twisted off the ignition. "It's a good machine, but my mother keeps it as a museum display for someone who doesn't exist anymore." He released his seat belt and stepped out as the door swung up.

Willow smoothed the skirt of her dress while Andy circled to her door. A month ago, she would have opened her own door, but she'd learned enough about Sutherlands to stall until she gauged the man's intentions.

Inside a restaurant that resembled a Swiss chalet and offered excellent French cuisine, it was obvious Andy had been there before. He was not only remembered, he was treated with an attentiveness Willow knew was genuine respect for a patron, who tipped well, expressed sincere appreciation and expected to be competently served. Her restaurant savoir-faire impressed him and he complimented her on it after the waitress brought their drinks: a whiskey sour for her, Glendoncroft single malt Scotch whisky for him.

"I learned from the other side. I was a waitress in Minneapolis."

"Pretty city. Drew said you grew up on a beef farm in Iowa."

"Mostly beef, corn and hay. Some wheat, soy beans and sorghum. Between my father, two oldest brothers and other relatives, the Roberts own a fair piece of Iowa."

"There's a lot of Iowa to own." Andy looked thoughtful. "I was in Iowa once. The vast openness made me feel I'd been caught naked before the eyes of God. It cleans your soul because there's nowhere to hide. There's a lot of that openness in you. I can see why you have Drew twisted up like a dog trying to devour his own tail. You don't give him any place to hide. You are enough woman to distract any man and enough forever to scare him."

Willow flushed at his frankness. "He seems to have the experience to handle it."

"Humph. He has no experience at all against your kind of woman. Drew usually views women as appetizing diversions and samples what looks good to him. When he turns on the charms, they flock to him. Once he gets his hands on them, they fall all over him. He usually tires of them after a few dates. Drew sees women as he sees a wardrobe. He picks an appropriate bedpartner when he needs one."

"That isn't the Drew I know."

"He isn't exactly the one I know either. In fact, I haven't seen Drew like this since he was eighteen and lost Gabrielle."

The name straightened her. "The maid? Gabby?"

"Maid?" Andy looked surprised. "Her father was process manager at the FiberForms manufacturing plant in Bordeaux. Drew first met her when he was twelve. Four years later, she stayed with us in Paris while she studied at the Sorbonne. They used to joke about her being his personal *servante de la chambre à coucher.* But it was hardly her profession in either connotation."

"Would you have disapproved if she was a maid?"

"Not on that criterion." He gave her a questioning look. "I'm much more concerned with the ethical integrity of both my employees and associates than their social status. Gabby was a captivating young woman, and they were a tempestuous couple for better than two years."

"How did he lose her?"

"Gabby was three years older than Drew and grew up before he did. She fell in love with a Canadian medical student and Drew went to Princeton. He once told me she was the first and only real love he ever had and he's been looking for something Gabby was ever since."

"Maybe he's still in love with her." A heaviness filled Willow's chest and she was unable to keep it from her voice.

"No." Andy shook his head. "Gabby had a lot of trouble handling his possessiveness and temper. They'd about burned it out—although that wasn't apparent from his reaction, which resembled a self-destructive rampage more than a broken heart. Drew wasn't ready to offer the mature relationship Gabby needed."

Willow remembered Drew saying she reminded him of Gabby. "He still isn't." The finality of her insight surprised her.

"That's possible." Andy sipped at his whisky and studied her for a pensive moment. "Life threw a roadblock in front of him last winter. He shied away from it and ran to his grandmother. He knew she'd pamper his ego and let him sit it out for a while. She's spoiled him and let him mark time most of his life."

"He admires her and feels she's responsible for the gentleness in him."

"True. She let me put the backbone in him."

"Drew said she protected him from you to prevent child abuse by outright strangulation." Willow stared directly into his eyes, letting him know she was prepared to stand by Mae and Drew.

"He put it very well. After two months of obscene, screaming temper tantrums, I was a bomb of suppressed anger. It wasn't against Drew. It was against the hate my wife had transferred to him and I didn't want to let my vengeance loose on a child. We spent most of the summer with Mother so she could help me deal with my feelings. Once I understood and confronted his problem, it was easier to cope with Drew. He was always a dynamo of energy with an insatiable intellect, but he had a lot to learn about the rules of civilized living. Mother cracked his shell first. No one had taught him to hate her."

"I can't understand how anyone can let love become hate."

"Willow, there are many sides on a die, but we can only see one of them at a time. In my case, I thought it was love. Now, I see it more as a rebellion into vices that were proscribed in my society. Sort of an: up yours, *mon pere*, I'm tasting the underside of the world. Then she got pregnant. My father wanted to pay her off, but I couldn't give up my child. We married the summer before my senior year at Princeton and rented a garden cottage behind an old mansion. At first, she saw it as a Cinderella ending of happily ever after and was so much in love with the idea of having a baby that she stopped drinking while she was pregnant, even talked about enrolling in music classes while I earned my MBA. But her visions of marriage had little connection to reality."

"In what way?"

"A strange thing happened to me when I had a child who needed me. I became a father, instead of a rebellious son, and saw the importance of all those standards and ethics my mother had instilled in me. My wife saw it as free use of big limit credit cards and ready access to my checkbook. By the time Drew was three, we'd exhausted a trust fund from the estate of my mother's brother, and my wife treated my efforts toward fiscal responsibility as insults. In spite of a good entry level job, I was still in debt for student loans and unable to keep up with her spending habits. To keep ahead of debts, we moved to a cheaper apartment near her parents in Philadelphia. I was forced to appeal to my father for help. He wasn't forgiving, but he did offer me a better job. Unfortunately, it was in France and she refused to go with me. I was away a lot."

"Drew said his grandfather refused to help you."

"It was more an action of revenge than kindness. He gave me a job managing a company that was in deep financial trouble. His underlying motive was to humiliate me when I failed."

"That's an awful thing to say."

"It's the way he was. But my mother's Scottish grit had instilled a strong sense of purpose and determination in me that accepted it as a challenge. When I found solid backers and bought him out, he outright told me I would fail and he wouldn't save me. But I'd already figured out how to turn it around and prove him wrong."

"What did you do?" When Willow led him away from the subject of her relationship with Drew, defensiveness relaxed and interest grew.

"I cut all outdated and failing processes, concentrated on the one area that was doing well and reincorporated under a new name. I then hired innovative construction engineers and process designers, gave them the opportunity to prove their worth. It was a high-risk gamble, but we carved ourselves a niche and proved our reliability."

"What does FiberForms do?"

"We developed patented processes for manufacturing lightweight, recyclable building forms for poured concrete. Given a structurally sound design for anything from a backyard fountain to a public building we'll manufacture the forms, deliver them, supervise the setting and pouring, then take them back and use the material to make more."

"100% recycling?"

"In order to maintain product quality, we run about 40%."

"Is that what you were doing in Iowa?"

"We did the forms for a library outside Des Moines ten years ago. Three years later, the same architect was hired for a community center and hockey rink. I was there to go over the designs and assess the sites."

Andy picked up his glass and stared into it for a moment before he said, "My arrogant vengeance defeated my father, but I lost my family because of it. I no longer had the time or money for the wild life, so my wife lived it without me by going back to old habits and acquaintances. That included Gino Pisano, an old boyfriend, who supplied her with drugs. When we divorced, she refused to give me Drew and used him to get money out of me. That's when things turned bitter. When she taught my son to hate me, they turned ugly. I, and consequently Drew, were to blame for everything that went wrong in her life. He was not only a reminder of me, he was a whipping boy, who had to take the brunt of her vengeance against me. I was too preoccupied with FiberForms to understand what was happening until it was too late to save Drew from years of abuse he never should have had to take."

"But you did save him."

"Not soon enough."

"You let a job and vengeance keep you away from your son?" she asked, unable to accept that a parent could do such a thing.

"A court order kept me away from my son." While his blunt statement slammed into Willow, Andy took a slow swallow of his drink and considered just how much more he wanted to say. "It was the result of the biggest mistake in my life."

"I don't understand." Willow was taken back by his sincerity and candor. He didn't strike her as a man willing to share inner feelings and she wondered why he was doing it with her. Part of her wanted to hear him out; part of her wanted to close her mind to truths she was unwilling to accept. But she couldn't look away from his absorbing gaze or find her voice.

"I came home one night and found her in bed with Gino. When I went after him, she grabbed me and held me back so he could reach the fire escape. He got away; she didn't."

"You beat her up instead?"

"I slapped her—something I'd never done to a woman. Then I told her it was over; I was taking Drew and getting out of her life. She started throwing things at me and ran into the public hallway screaming false accusations that infuriated me. All I wanted to do was subdue her and shut off her lies, but I lost control and slapped her again. Then the police were there and she was shouting her lies to them. By the time it was over, the only way to avoid an assault conviction was to accept an expensive divorce settlement that included a restraining order keeping me away from both her and Drew."

"But she and Gino—"

"They set me up. It was Gino who called the police. I had no proof he'd ever been there. Some of her friends and a few neighbors had been swallowing her lies for months. And I, stupidly, gave them ammunition to use against me."

"Why would she do that?"

"I'd told her that if she went back to drugs, I'd divorce her, take Drew, and leave her with nothing. She wanted the money for drugs. Gino helped her get it. A conviction, even without jail time, would have ruined me. I'd have lost my passport, my business, my reputation and any hope of getting my son back. I figured I had a better chance of fighting for and helping Drew by giving them what they wanted. Unfortunately, it proved to be a tougher fight than I expected. When I finally gained custody of Drew, the boy who came to live with me didn't even know me, except through the eyes of an unstable mother, who couldn't forgive me for growing up and shutting down her pipeline to money."

Willow watched a shadow of regret darken his face and sensed the bitterness in his words. It reminded her of the pain behind Drew's shielded voice when he'd told her much the same thing. It touched on the vulnerable part of Drew that both enticed her and frightened her.

"Drew said his uncle helped you by telling you what was happening."

"After I read Antonio's letter and talked to him, I hired private detectives and the courts had a change of heart. After I officially won the case, the police had to break into the apartment with a court order. We found Drew unconscious and bleeding, my ex-wife dead on the floor from an overdose."

His words stunned her. "Drew told me he was a witness."

"A very credible one. Willow, do you blame him for growing up with insulated feelings?" The thrust of Andy's question went right to Willow's heart and she recoiled.

"At least he didn't grow up callous." Unsure if he was warning her or threatening her, she failed to keep the knife out of her voice but saw no reaction to the jab she gave him.

"He's not old enough and he's been wise enough to use his insulation. Drew is a bit of a romantic, but he isn't a fool."

Fortunately, their appetizers arrived—because his last statement kicked Willow square in her insecurity.

❖

Jean Kehoe Van Dyke

Parsons Glen Barn Theater was a huge, Pennsylvania-style barn. The theater itself was in the old hayloft. Lobby, refreshment area, rest rooms, bar and smoking lounge, as well as dressing rooms, workshops and green room were on a lower level that was partly built into the side of a hill and walled with field stone. It was a large house and totally sold out for the opening night of *Paint Your Wagon*, newly readapted for the stage from the movie version.

They were running late, so Andy rushed Willow through the lobby to an elevator and into the theater where a smiling teenager escorted them to their seats. Mae and the Rutledges, an elderly couple from the hunt club, were there. There was no sign of Drew.

Willow sat between Mae and Andy tightly rolling her unread program in her hands. She tried to listen to Mae but was distracted and kept looking toward the back of the house or at the empty aisle seat on the other side of Mae. Finally, she turned to face the stage and unrolled the program in an attempt to keep her mind off thoughts that told her the reason Drew refused to tell her what he was doing was that he knew she wouldn't like it. She even suspected he wanted her out of his way and knew she wouldn't go unless she expected him to join her at the play. When her thoughts made her angry again, Willow realized they were also getting out of hand. She couldn't make herself believe Drew would be that devious.

When she started to open the program, Andy reached over and closed his hand on hers. "I thought you put a safety on your anger."

The house lights dimmed as Willow looked up at the glow of his eyes. They were the intense blue of Drew's without the darker violet that added to Drew's hypnotic attraction. "I forgot."

"Well, don't forget again." He chuckled. "I don't want a knife in my ribs."

Someone slipped into the aisle seat just as the overture started. It was John with Drew's ticket. When Willow looked at him, he leaned across Mae's lap. "Drew said he'll meet you after the show."

Willow had no chance to answer him, but she was starting to sense that something was awry and she was the only one who didn't know it.

The production was brilliantly staged, the music good enough to capture Willow's attention. In fact, she became so involved in the opening scenes she was unaware of the truth until it stared right at her. When the character, Rotten Luck Willy, moved out of the knot of miners and set his foot on a whiskey keg, Willow's nerves tightened and prickled on her skin. But it wasn't until the actor turned to the audience, looked into her eyes and started to sing the opening solo, *They Call the Wind Mariah,* that Willow knew it was Drew.

His transformation to a suave old west gambler with neatly trimmed hair and beard went unnoticed when his voice, an unbelievably rich baritone, captivated her, held her spellbound. She paid little attention to the words, only to the voice that surrounded her with emotions, swelled in her chest, spilled from her eyes. When he looked directly at her, the power of his voice mesmerized her. She barely realized she was clutching Andy's wrist with a crushing grip, or that her face was wet with tears. It all made sense and Drew had been right—some things were better shown than told.

After joining the sustained applause, Willow took the handkerchief Andy offered from one side while Mae squeezed her hand on the other.

"I feel like a kid at a surprise party," she said lowly. "I'm stunned and want to choke him differently now."

During a later number in the first act, the rest of the puzzle fell into place. While the chorus sang, *"There's a coach coming in..."* Venture, totally unconcerned by the lights and activity around him, strutted onstage in rhythm with the music, then snorted and posed while Drew sang about a pirated stagecoach of harlots approaching the gold rush town of No Name City.

When the house lights came up for intermission, John hurried up the aisle and Willow turned to Mae. "Venture was amazing. And the padded hooves solve the mystery of adhesive on his feet."

"They have performed together many times. Bold Venture has become a local favorite and the theater owners fit him in whenever they can."

"You can read your program now," Andy said before he stood and stretched. "It will explain a lot."

Willow opened her program and leafed through it until she saw a familiar face. Or at least, it was almost familiar. She'd forgotten what Drew looked like without a beard and stared at the picture for a moment before she started to read...

Jean Kehoe Van Dyke

> *Andrew Sutherland as Rotten Luck Willy: Parsons Glen Barn Theater is especially honored to have Andrew Sutherland back for this production. Since his summers with us while studying at Princeton, the University of Pennsylvania and the Metropolitan Conservatory in New York, Drew has continued his operatic training at the Bologna Academy of Music in Italy and has been invited to train under Italian opera maestro Vittorio Luciani in Genoa, Italy. Drew has given us memorable performances in such roles as: Harold Hill in The Music Man, KoKo in The Mikado, Billy Bigelow in Carousel, Judd in Oklahoma, Bill Sykes in Oliver, and Tevya in Fiddler on the Roof. His companion, Bold Venture, appeared in Oklahoma and Fiddler on the Roof. Drew and Venture will be Arthur and his valiant steed in our upcoming production of Camelot...*

Willow looked at Mae's beaming smile and flushed. "Now I know why he said you felt he was a worthy investment. It's the dream you share."

"I believe he'll make it now that he's regained his incentive." Mae slid her hand over Willow's and patted it.

Willow blinked away fresh tears that could have been from joy or love since she felt them both—as well as a dizzy pride that made her feel out of touch with reality. "He told me he couldn't sing."

"He did?" Andy gave her a startled look and a handkerchief. "Drew is a genius at evading questions, but he doesn't lie."

"He said my appreciation didn't deserve the shock of his singing." Willow smiled at the memory. "He didn't lie. It would have been as shocking then as it was tonight."

"That was his plan." Andy admitted. "Only I don't think I want the assignment of keeping you out of the way again. It borders on combat duty."

"I guess it was." Willow flushed. "But why did he hide it from me?"

"He wanted to surprise you." Mae sighed. "But mostly, he wanted you to know him without his talent."

"He said he wanted me to know *who* he was, not *what* he was," Willow said.

"Drew felt his talent was overwhelming him and wanted to separate himself from it." Mae squeezed her hand before she released it. "He was adamant about the deception, so John and I went along with it. Drew came here wanting to give up opera. The discipline of his training is taxing and he felt he wasn't improving as he should. You see, in spite of hard work and long hours, so much depends on time."

"That's why he said he wanted to be forty."

"Male operatic voices don't fully mature much before forty." Mae nodded. "Pushing his voice too soon could ruin its quality for the future. Drew is good, but he's not great yet. Nothing can guarantee he will be great. He hit a plateau, went into one of his blue-funk sulks and ran out of patience."

"That's not the crux of the problem, Mother." Andy cut in. "He rammed headfirst into Maestro Luciani and came out bruised."

"Well, you weren't much help." Mae glared past Willow at Andy, who sat against the back of an empty seat ahead of them. "Your advice was to get out if he believed he didn't have the stuff to make it and settle for what he's good at."

"You said it yourself," Andy said. "There's no guarantee he will ever be great. He can sing the socks off half the world now, but it has to be opera to satisfy you." Andy's features sharpened when his voice hardened, but he didn't raise it. Andy rarely raised his voice. There was enough bite in the way he could turn it as hard as obsidian, as cold as space.

"Good God, Mother, you could convince him he's immortal, or at least you could make him want to prove he is. Quitting may be painful. Being told by Luciani that he didn't have greatness in him was devastating. He's afraid he might fail the ordeal, but he's more disturbed about failing to live up to your dream. I thought he was going to cash in more than a career last winter."

"I think I inadvertently found a cure for that this summer." When Mae smiled, a twinkle sparkled in her eyes.

"I see a diversion." Andy's eyes brushed Willow's face. "And I rarely bet long shots without equalizing the odds."

Mae spoke slowly with a finality that rivaled her son's. "Stay out of it."

"You never understood what Drew and I went through, so you don't see the signs I do. You don't even understand what he's fighting."

"Phantoms, preposterous imaginings."

"We don't see it that way. You may have meddled yourself into something that blows up in your face. I'm going to have a drink with the Rutledges. Do you want to join us?"

"No, thank you. I did a great deal today. I'll keep Willow here for company."

When her son left, Mae sighed as if she'd rid herself of a troublesome problem. "Don't let him upset you, Willow. Andy's too cynical and stubborn to admit he may be wrong."

After the play, while she waited in the lobby, Willow studied rehearsal pictures and read a posted article about Drew. It said he had won a long list of awards. It said he had a master's degree in music. It made him bigger than life. It made him Andrew Sutherland, B.A., M.A. and Doctoral Candidate of Musical Performance under Opera Maestro Vittorio Luciani in Genoa, Italy. It didn't make him Drew.

The article called Drew a New World phenomenon, a baritone Domingo. The name triggered something in Willow's mind, making her catch her breath. Byron's postscript hadn't only been a reference to that old Christmas CD. It told her that Byron knew who Drew was. The revelation stunned her, added to her feeling of alienation.

During the show, Willow had been thrilled. Drew sang to her in a place and in a way she could understand. What she'd just read intimidated her. She tried to relate it to Byron, but she couldn't identify with her brother beyond the farm and Iowa. In the summers, Byron lived in a tiny apartment in Italy, studied at a university. The opera houses and cultured academies of Europe were beyond Willow's comprehension and she felt as if someone had just told her the vase that she had put dandelions in was a rare piece of Byzantine art worth a million dollars.

A lot of other things started to make sense and Willow understood why Drew hadn't told her. She would have been awed, as she was now, which would have destroyed his retreat. It explained why he'd tried so hard to convince her he was no different than her brothers. But he was different. Willow knew almost nothing about opera, but her image of it was daunting. It made her see Drew as a famous man, who associated with the most cultured of Europe's wealthy and influential people. She saw no room in his life for a farm girl from Iowa.

Deep in her mind, Willow believed Andy Sutherland didn't want his son to repeat his mistake by marrying a woman who didn't fit the correct mold. She sensed that even though Andy's wounds had been covered by thick scars, he still felt them. He was hardened, if not bitter, and wary of her feelings for his son. One thing she was sure of was that Andy would not stay out of it.

A shadow fell across the bulletin board and Willow turned to see a smiling, bearded face on a darkhaired man in navy slacks. His white shirt was open at the throat, showing a strong neck, dark chest hair. The sleeves were rolled back on hard forearms and his blue eyes were chips of an Iowa evening sky. He was Drew. And right now, that's all that mattered. A smile exploded out of the thrill inside her.

Willow ran to his arms, hugged him as hard as she could. "When you plan a surprise, you do it right. I can't believe you have that much voice in you."

"I don't. There's a digital chip implanted in my back teeth. It uses my empty head for an echo chamber." He winked. "The hardest part was convincing the director to change the blocking for tonight so I could fade into the background before Mariah. He should stop glaring at me by tomorrow night."

Willow blushed. "I was too mad at you to think about it."

"I noticed that." Drew kissed the tip of her nose. "Dad's taking us out for drinks and I need food. I missed a good dinner. But then, I never eat much before a performance."

"What about Venture?" Willow asked.

"Your charge is safe. John took him home. He's meeting us at Mio Castello." Drew hugged her against his side while he crossed the lobby, only dropping his arm from her to embrace his grandmother.

When Drew ended the embrace, Andy clapped a hand on his son's shoulder, gave him a playful shake and a ribbing smile. "Good show, Drew. I enjoyed it almost as much as my dinner date."

"I told you she was worth knowing, even when she's on slow boil." Drew slipped a hand along Willow's shoulder and held her gaze.

Andy lifted an eyebrow. "You better watch out for that one, Drew."

"What do you mean?" Drew broke away from Willow's eyes to look at his father.

"She's the marrying kind and you're falling so fast you can't find the rip cord."

Although Willow had never seen Drew blush or known him to be caught without a quick retort, his father's quiet observation both embarrassed him and knocked him offbalance. He was mute for an awkward moment before he recovered and said, "What qualifies you as an expert on marriageability?"

"The fact that I'm not. I learned to stay away from her type years ago." Andy laughed at his son's frown, then sobered his expression. "I was impressed with your performance. You rattled my expectations again."

"What does that mean?"

"They are things a parent has. Mine have been erratic to say the least. When you were a toddler, I thought you'd be president of the world. When you first came to live with me, I thought you'd be lucky to survive to maturity. When you were an adolescent, I thought you'd be a convict or Tibetan Monk. When you were eighteen, I thought you were going to join a foreign revolution. During the ensuing years, your forays into wildly changing obsessions and enthusiastic immersions into academia have left me totally confused. But throughout all of it, in spite of the fact that you were always good at singing and performing, I have trouble envisioning you as an opera divo."

"I'm a long way from that."

"With my luck you will become one and I'll have to sit through the damn things."

"Is that your way of saying you approve?"

"It's my way of saying I support you if you truly believe it's what you want."

Drew glanced from his father to his grandmother with a troubled expression and then back to Andy. "That's the hard part, isn't it?"

"If you renew that contract in Genoa, you'll think you've sold your soul to Mephistopheles. The man has produced great performers, but he's a tyrant and a fanatic about it. When you train under Luciani, you are owned by Luciani. He'll dictate how you eat, sleep and breathe—particularly how you breathe." Andy emphasized the phrase with a strong roll of his voice and an expansive gesture that made Drew laugh.

"That's not a bad imitation. I take it you talked to him."

"I let him rant and rave at me."

"That's only mild displeasure. Did he pound the furniture and shake his fists at God?"

"No."

"Then he may take me back."

"But you already have one strike against you for walking out on him. He was volatile about that and called you *un asino burbanzoso,* as well as a few other names I won't use here, even in Italian."

"That's not the first time he called me a haughty ass. What did he call you?"

"Actually, we got along all right once he realized I wasn't there to make excuses for you or buy his forgiveness. I told him if you went back, you would stick it out. You survived my tyranny with your spirit intact."

"It's a very different tyranny. You never wanted my soul." Drew held his father's gaze for a moment then relaxed. "I'm beginning to put it in better perspective."

"You have to put several things in the right perspective." Andy moved his eyes to Willow for a probing instant. "Drew, your ego may not survive him if you aren't totally committed and willing to give to the point of emotional exhaustion. It's a grueling regimen at maximum effort—mentally, physically and emotionally. The man plays God and insists that not only is he the only one who can make you great he believes that almost everyone you've worked with before has been wrong. But he is just a man, who is occasionally fallible and blasts out diatribes with no regard for anyone he wounds."

"He's the only one I want. I'm the one who failed him."

"Bullshit." Andy scoffed. "Find another way over the wall. What makes Vittorio Luciani so important to you?"

"Verdi."

"That's it?" Andy recoiled. "Verdi?"

"He idolizes Verdi. He lives Verdi!" Drew's vehemence filled the lobby making the few people in it look at him in astonishment. "In my opinion, he's the best teacher of Verdi that ever lived. If I'm ever ready to master Verdi, I'll need Vittorio Luciani."

"I see." Andy pulled back for an instant before he answered with quiet finality, "Then you better get those priorities straightened out because he doesn't sound as if he wants to grow much older waiting for you."

Chapter Seventeen

Willow was unsure why Drew had changed, but after a lot of thinking, she blamed it on his father. After the play, Drew spent the night with her. She was floating on a wave of excitement and the long, slow climaxing of their lovemaking made her know she loved him beyond comprehension. Yet, when the swell of emotion flowed from her in a wash of warm tears, a knot of mourning hung in her chest for the intimate part of Drew she'd shared before she learned his life was much bigger than the world of his summer retreat from stress and responsibility.

Sunday night, after the play, Drew took his father to the airport so he could fly to California. Willow had no idea when he returned, since he didn't come to her house. He had a hangover the next morning and did a lot of grumbling about the stupidity of trying to match his father's intake of alcohol. Now that Andy was gone, Willow hoped he would stay gone instead of returning after a trip to Las Vegas and Indianapolis.

Monday afternoon, Drew showed up at the cabin at lunch time in a mood she could only describe as rotten and irritating. He stared into the refrigerator for a while then thumped the door closed and searched through the pantry cabinet. When the cabinet door banged closed, Willow plopped her sandwich on her plate and glared at him. "What has gotten into you?"

"There's nothing worth eating around here. Don't you ever shop?"

"There's bread and sliced turkey. Make a sandwich."

"I'm sick of turkey sandwiches." He backed against the counter and made a sour face. "What happened to the roast beef I bought?"

"You ate it yesterday. If turkey isn't good enough, go eat with your grandmother. Alice or Greyson will make you anything you want."

"I'd rather eat with a porcupine. This is one of those times Gram is not easy to get along with. I've been avoiding her since breakfast."

"Does that mean I'm going to have a bad lesson this afternoon?"

"Should be fine as long as I'm not there. She's not, as she would say, cross with you."

"Why is she cross with you?"

"I'm evading her prying questions."

"About what?"

"There are things in my life that are none of her business. On top of that, she's upset with Dad and I'm refusing to talk about him, which irritates the hell out of her." When a horn blared in the driveway, he frowned and looked at his watch. "Damn. I forgot the appointment with her lawyer. If I make her late, she'll bitch me out all the way to his office and back. Come outside and smile sweetly. Maybe it will soften her up."

"Not if you keep acting like a dill pickle."

"Oh, stuff it, Willow." He pushed away from the counter and strode past her. "I don't want to listen to two of you."

By the time they reached the porch, Mae was headed for the door with her face set in a hard scowl, her cane thumping the flagstone path with every stride. She gave Willow a tight smile that showed no sign of softening before she glared at Drew with the penetrating brilliance of a welding torch.

"I'm sorry, Gram, I got involved in some phone calls and forgot the appointment." Drew offered his apology with overacted charm before he stepped off the porch in a purposeful stride that implied he wanted to waste no more time.

"Just one-minute, young man." The sharp command stopped him, turned him to face her. "You are not going to town with me dressed like that." Mae eyed his worn jeans and faded T-shirt as if they were indecent.

"Blue jeans are the in thing these days. Loosen up, Gram. Adam can handle the fashion shift."

"You can drop the flippancy. I am not amused." Mae planted her cane on the stone walk as if it were a scepter of ultimate authority. "I assume you have some decent clothes here. I'll wait in the car while you change into them."

"Oh, for shit sake!" Throwing his hands up dramatically, Drew strode past his grandmother. "He's interested in my signature, not my fucking wardrobe."

"I've had my fill of that attitude." With a loud thwack, Mae's cane smacked across the seat of Drew's jeans.

"Ow!" He stiffened with a stunned, wide-eyed expression before he spun back. "What the hell was that for? I'm not one of your horses."

"No, you're my grandson, and you can start acting like it. I won't tolerate language like that. What has gotten into you lately? You don't listen. You don't remember what you're supposed to do. And you're insolent. Now straighten up and remember your manners. I know your father raised you better than that."

Drew stood rigid for a moment, then snapped, "Yes, ma'am," strode to the car and yanked open the passenger door for his grandmother.

Willow sputtered into a laugh when Drew closed the car door, without slamming it, and headed toward the house.

"What's so fricking funny?" He stomped past her in a disgruntled huff. "That damn thing hurt."

"You were right. She still sees you as the thirteen-year-old bigfoot." Willow followed him to the bedroom, where he peeled off his shirt and threw it on the bed. "I thought you said she wouldn't chew you out in front of me?"

"I guess you're not company anymore." He kicked off his deck shoes and unbuckled his belt. "Obviously, *my* dignity is not important to her."

"Oh, give it up, Drew. She doesn't like your shitty mood any better than I do."

"Now you know why I have manners." He yanked the belt off his jeans and tossed it on the bed with his shirt. "She never misses a chance to let me know when I forget them, but that was uncalled for."

"Are you going to whack her to get even?"

"What!" He gaped at her with an appalled expression. "Strike the lady of the manor? Commit high treason? Sutherland honor would be desecrated. I could be drummed out of the family, flogged and cast into a deep dungeon for committing such a horrific sin against Sutherland honor." His jeans flew after the shirt and belt before he slid the closet door open so hard it bounced back against his arm as he stripped a burgundy polo shirt off a hanger and then dove into it.

"You certainly do rant well." Willow leaned against the door frame, chuckling at his tirade. "And just who would be the deliverer of this archaic retribution?"

"It was rhetorical." Drew pulled on a pair of tan slacks and snatched his belt off the bed. "But if you want wrathful avengers, my father and John are likely candidates. All we have to do is sign some papers involving a joint investment account. She acts as if it's a formal state occasion." He jerked the belt tight, then backed it off and buckled it.

"Was it the jeans she objected to, or what they reveal?" Willow teased, trying to get him to accept the situation with his usual levity.

"I'm not about to ask her that. But you can if you want." He smirked with his answer and almost laughed when she vigorously shook her head. "Gram sees T-shirts as underwear and doesn't accept them, or jeans, as appropriate outerwear for anything but outdoor recreation or menial labor. Certainly not for business affairs—trivial or not."

When Drew strode past her, he was still grumbling, but he sounded more annoyed than angry. "I may have to keep her in front of me to survive the next few hours without getting any more whacks with her cane."

"What are you doing?" Willow watched him pluck her sandwich off the plate.

"I'm hungry and won't get any sympathy out of her. I was sent to bed without supper enough to know that." He took a huge bite of the sandwich and washed it down with half the glass of milk before he resumed his ranting. "Then I had to risk getting caught sneaking down to the kitchen to raid the larder. I swear that old witch of a cook she used to have had a sixth sense about missing morsels of food and never failed to report it."

Willow scowled when he devoured the rest of her lunch. "You have mayo in your beard."

When she held out a paper napkin, he snatched it out of her hand, scrubbed it on his mouth and chin, then tossed it at her before he stormed through the living room, kicked open the screen door and let it bang closed behind him.

"You're welcome, Mr. Manners," Willow shouted at his back, then followed him onto the porch, where she watched John move away from Mae's window before Drew backed the car onto the lane and drove away at the sedate pace his grandmother expected on the estate.

"I'm glad I'm not in that car." John stepped onto the porch, shaking his head and chuckling. "She is really burned at him. And he's going to hear about it."

"At least you can see the humor in it."

"I'm not the one who got whacked."

"John, what is the matter with him?"

"What do you mean?" He knit thick eyebrows together into a frosty caterpillar.

"He isn't Drew?"

"Sounded like Drew to me." John laughed when she made a disagreeing face. "The problem is there are different facets to Drew and it isn't always easy to figure out which one you're dealing with. He isn't always the charming romantic you've been seeing."

"Are you saying it's all an act?" A hollow pain knotted in Willow's chest and she looked away from John to where Drew's car waited in the drive. "That he's been conning me?"

"It's more the opposite. He's rather smitten by you." John set his hand on her shoulder and turned her to face him. "You muddle up his composure so much I'm surprised this is the first time you've been subjected to one of his contrary snits. He's famous for them—in spite of the fact that he was raised to be a proper Sutherland gentleman."

"Maybe you better sit down and explain what you mean by that." Willow gestured to the porch chairs and noticed that John politely waited until she was seated before he joined her. "John, I get the feeling from Mae there's a lot of tradition involved with being a Sutherland. Drew makes fun of it, but I don't think he really rejects it."

"That's a perceptive and accurate observation," John said.

"Drew said honorable family comportment is one of Mae's eccentricities and she's absurdly old-fashioned about it."

"She can be that." John nodded. "But then, I remember a time when she thought her parents were dreadfully stuffy and old-fashioned about Sutherland propriety. It didn't keep her from growing up to respect it, or from accepting the responsibilities she believes her heritage imposes on her. Glendoncroft Sutherlands have little indulgence for young, rebellious heirs."

"Drew said he was both the prince and the pauper and had trouble trying to find himself in the transition."

"His ability for succinctly expressing himself has always amazed me. And there is more truth in his analogy than I think you realize. Mae is not only a wealthy American widow. She is a titled Lady, the daughter of the fourteenth Earl of Glendoncroft, which is now a mostly symbolic title that her older brother's son holds."

"An earl? Isn't that practically royalty?"

"Yes. And centuries before the earldom, Mae's ancestors were Scottish lairds. Their powers were far from symbolic and often meant life or death to their subjects. Over the years, through wise marriages with local clans and English gentry, they acquired hereditary titles and became absolute rulers of their lands. The Earldom of Glendoncroft was bestowed on Lord Gordon Sutherland by Queen Anne, the last Stuart monarch, in 1706, shortly after the Act of Union that Created Great Britain by uniting Scotland and England. It was not a well-accepted unification in Scotland and was responsible for serious rifts in many families, including the Glendoncroft Sutherlands, which is why the fourth Andrew Sutherland ended up an American industrialist instead of a British aristocrat."

"Drew said Mae's marriage brought the two branches of the family back together."

"What it mostly did was keep the Scottish estate from being broken up and sold piecemeal. Due to a strong genetic tendency to produce healthy male heirs, the family has weathered centuries without a hitch in succession. But changing economics, urbanization and wartime expenses took a toll on the family fortune. The transfer of a significant amount of Sutherland Mercantile stock allowed the family to save Glendoncroft Hall and most of the land by establishing them in profitable enterprises of their own. To their historical and local credit, Glendoncroft Sutherlands ruled justly and believed in a strong code of humanitarian ethics that made them respected leaders. They no longer legally rule but they are still a highly influential family."

"It's sort of mind boggling to think Drew is related to aristocracy."

"Mae, Andy and Drew don't care about titles." John removed his grey tweed cap and set it on the table between them, exposing a balding head fringed with close-cropped white hair. "They are very much Americans and proud of it. What they do care about is the Sutherland code of honor that, in their minds, defines them. From early childhood, they are disciplined and trained in how to present themselves to others, as well as how to behave in public. In Mae's mind, Sutherlands do not engage in inappropriate behavior that could embarrass the dignity or reputation of the family without being corrected for it. And they better accept it with respect."

"Is that why Drew said he'd be drummed out of the family, flogged and thrown into a deep dungeon if he dared to strike his grandmother?"

"Stated in Drew's overly dramatic way, that is correct."

Willow relaxed when she looked into kind grey-green eyes. "He named his father and you as wrathful avengers. Does that make you a Sutherland? And is he right?"

"He's very right. Andy would be outraged that he could do such a thing. I would be infuriated if anyone, hurt Mae. But it won't happen. Drew may occasionally rebel against her authority. He would never violate his own rules of respect."

"As he said, it was rhetorical. I was hassling him because he was being a grumpy ass."

"Which only riles Mae more and turns it into a battle of wills that can go on for a long time if Drew doesn't give up and apologize." John smiled and held her gaze. "You ask good questions, Willow. Am I a Sutherland? The answer is both yes and no. I was born in a cottage on the grounds of Glendoncroft Hall and lived there until I was twenty-one and came to live at Sutherland Manor. I've known and loved Mae Sutherland most of my life."

"You have?" Willow blushed when she felt she was undoubtedly putting the wrong interpretation on the word loved.

"My father was head gardener at the Hall. When I was young, I thought Mae was the most beautiful, desirable and fascinating female alive. She was perfect, and gracious—and totally unattainable. I worshiped her and would have done any harebrained, heroic deed to make her notice me. Since she loved flowers and gardens, I stopped seeing gardening as work my father expected me to do and let it become a labor of love. I was desperate to please her and believed her enjoyment of my creations was an admiration of me. It was very romantic, but totally unrealistic. When she was eighteen, she married and moved to America. I was a heartbroken fourteen-year-old, who had to accept the fact that, although she loved my horticultural creations, she didn't love me."

"But you're here?"

"After six years of frustration trying to get someone to understand her visions for the gardens here, she and Andy spent a summer holiday in Scotland. She noticed me, or at least she noticed my work, and offered me the opportunity to help her build the gardens she envisioned. Her offer was generous; but more important, she seduced me with her visions and I still wanted to please her with my creations."

"Did she ever learn how you felt about her?"

"I think she always sensed it. But she was a Sutherland. I was the gardener's son. Propriety did not allow her to accept me as more than that."

"Is that how she sees me?" Willow looked past him to the manor house and forced herself to speak through a painful constriction in her chest. "Unworthy of her grandson."

With a large, calloused hand, John turned her face to meet his eyes. "No, Willow. Mae has no feelings like that. She never did. I was merely a younger boy with a crush on her. Any thoughts of romantic involvement at that time were in my mind, not hers."

"From what Drew said about his grandfather, I think she made the wrong choice."

"There was no choice to be made. Mae married a man approved by her family. It was expected of her and she accepted it. Seven years later she found out her husband had no respect for the ethical standards she believed in. She fought with him over it. When he physically attacked her for correctly calling him greedy, dishonorable and criminal, she ran to me because she didn't know what else to do. Since I had a personal score to settle with him myself, I didn't have to think twice before I acted. She convinced me not to thrash him senseless, but I knew I wouldn't keep that promise if it ever happened again. That night I made a personal vow to protect her and never leave her."

John gave her a long look before he added, "I had the chance to act on that vow a few years later after a similar incident that ended the marriage in Mae's mind. The next nineteen years were a sham. They remained married but led separate lives. He played golf and spent most of his time on business, gaming, or at his Country Club. She raised and trained horses and made them her life."

"And you never married?"

"I had other women from time to time; but no, I never wished to marry one of them."

"Other women?"

"Sometimes you ask too many questions, Willow. That's not one I know how to answer."

"I'm sorry." She blushed and stared down at her hands for a moment before she looked at his thoughtful face. "I'm always putting my foot in my mouth like that. My mother says my thoughts are like popcorn in an uncovered pot. You should have married and had children. You would have been a wonderful father."

"I was more of a father to Andy than his real one. He spent a lot of time with me. We went on fishing and hiking trips. I taught him how to box and enjoy being a boy. Andy pulled a lot of weeds, too." John lifted his cap off the table, started to put it on, then lowered it to his lap. "I was the only grandfather figure Drew ever really knew. In answer to your question, I'm not a Sutherland. But I'm not an outsider by any means."

"Drew said you were more than a gardener to Mae. He said you were a friend and made it possible for her to stay on the estate and not be alone."

"I couldn't have said it better."

❖

Drew was thankful for his grandmother's silence, until he stopped to turn off the county road and took a long look at her stony profile. This was not a silence of truce. It was the ominous silence that came before a horrendous squall. He knew he could either continue to ignore it and act innocent when she accused him of whatever it was that was irritating her the most. Or, he could attempt to defuse it by apologizing for the temperamental outburst that had provoked her into hitting him with her cane. However, such an apology would signify a willingness to accept that he was wrong about their whole disagreement. He was in no way ready to do that.

Wondering about how he could distract Mae from an inevitable showdown by pacifying her with a leisurely drive along one of her favorite scenic routes, Drew appeared totally unaware of her irritation and stared ahead of him at the gently winding road that followed the historic Delaware River Canal and deeply trodden tow path hugging its banks. He had his answer the instant he reached the speed limit and eased up on the accelerator.

"Drew, I would like an explanation for your outrageous behavior this morning."

"You pissed me off."

"That gives you no excuse to storm away from the breakfast table when I'm talking to you, or persist in using language I find offensive."

"Then leave it alone."

"I certainly will not. You insist your behavior is a private matter and I have no right to concern myself with it. You are very wrong about that. And I want an explanation."

"About what?"

"What you're doing in Philadelphia."

"I'm not doing anything in Philadelphia that has anything to do with you. I don't need your approval on where I go and whom I know."

"You may not need my approval but you are going to listen to my opinions about your disregard for common decency."

"What indecent thing am I supposed to have done?" His tight voice was more snarl than question.

"I have occasionally turned a blind eye on your less than discreet dalliances, but I will not tolerate such a blatant lack of discretion concerning the people you've been associating with in the city."

"What people?" Drew shot a stabbing look at her then stared back at the twisting road.

"Well, I certainly don't want to have to say it when you know full well what I mean."

After a glance at her inflamed face, Drew tightened his hands on the wheel, held his voice even. "Since I don't know what you mean, you better say it."

"I'm appalled that you would have anything to do with a prostitute you picked up in a bar. It's irresponsible, degrading and dangerous."

"I assume you mean Milly and you have it all wrong."

"Is she a prostitute or not?"

"Yes. But that is not what she is to me."

"What else could she possibly be to you?" Mae stiffened and glared at his stony profile with an expression of shocked condemnation.

"A nice girl I went to school with when I lived in her neighborhood. I had a crush on her in the third grade." He chuckled. "I even wrote a valentine poem for her. Milly is still nice and still a friend. Life hasn't been good to her. There isn't much I can do about that, except remain a friend if she needs one."

Drew paused for a moment to sort out the unsettling thoughts filling his mind and let her think about what he'd said. "The important thing I need to know is how you found out about Milly."

"From someone who claims to be your friend. Although I can't believe you can call a person who frightened Roy out of his wits a friend."

"What are you talking about?" Drew stiffened when the worst of his apprehensions solidified into alarming possibilities.

"Yesterday, I saw an unfamiliar black car drive toward the stable. Later, I went to the stable and had a talk with Roy about it. Although he was agitated, which makes it hard for him to express himself clearly, Roy told me he saw the man standing by the lane fence shaving slivers of wood off a post with a long, sharp knife while he watched Willow ride in the outdoor dressage ring. Apparently, when Roy asked him to stop cutting the post, the man told him he was a friend of yours from Philadelphia and only dropped by to see if you were home. Then, the man scared Roy by holding the knife in front of him while he asked a lot of questions Roy couldn't answer. At that point in his story, Roy became upset with himself and kept telling me he was sorry."

"What was he sorry about?"

"When the man asked if Willow was your sister, Roy told him she was your girlfriend. The man said that someone with such a..." Mae paused before she said, "... attractive girlfriend should stay close to her instead of spending time with a whore he picked up in a bar."

"Why was Roy frightened?"

"As you should know, Roy was cruelly picked on by bully's like that because he was easily confused and couldn't find the words to communicate with them. I assume he was afraid the man wanted to hurt him."

"Or Willow." The words slipped out before Drew could stop them and his mind froze on the thought.

"I think you could be right." Mae's face paled at his implication. "Roy was agitated about the way the man looked at Willow and said it gave him bad feelings. Do you know who it could have been?"

"I certainly do. And he is no friend of mine."

"I want you to stay away from those people."

"I'll take care of it," Drew answered with a hard tone of finality and turned her attention away from Mario. "And I'll talk to Roy myself."

"Roy didn't want to tell me, but I insisted. He's so loyal I know he told the truth. I asked John to talk with him. Roy worships John, who is very good at settling him down when he's upset."

"Actually, I'm glad I found out. But I'd rather Roy or John had told me instead of you."

"It will upset Roy to talk to you. He's afraid you'll be angry."

"He's right about that, but I'm not angry with him. It's all right, Gram. I know how to talk to Roy," Drew answered with a firmness he hoped would prevent further discussion of the topic.

Relaxing when his grandmother leaned back in her seat, Drew turned the car onto a tree-lined back road that swung away from the Delaware River and meandered through farming country surrounding the village of Parsons Glen. Straight white fences stretched away from the road and undulated over rounded hills, delineating lush pastures and hayfields of picture-perfect, designer farms with large white barns and towering stands of hardwoods.

"How is the play doing?" Mae asked after a prolonged silence.

"Very well. We're almost sold out for the entire run."

"How is Willow reacting to her discovery of your talent?"

"Exactly the way I was afraid she would."

"She was thrilled and totally enthralled by your voice."

"Yes, she was. She still is. That's the problem. She's awed by my voice, my purported fame, and the perceived grandeur of it all."

"Drew, after the play all she could talk about was how much she loved your singing and how proud of you she was."

"That's true. She was caught up in the wonder and I was high on the euphoria of a good performance. It was great. But excitement fades. She's been looking reality in the face. It's changed her somehow. I don't know what to do about it, nor do I want to talk about it."

"Are you willing to talk about what went wrong with Vittorio?"

"I'm willing to admit Vittorio is right when he says I'm not as great as I thought I was." He saw her face cloud but continued before she could say anything. "Vittorio shot the legs out from under me when he told me the awards and rave reviews were mostly media smoke and mirrors to promote concerts or programs."

"That's absurd."

"No, it isn't. He never denied I have talent or potential. What he did was tell me it wasn't enough on its own. He said I was enamored by hype and glitter and pushing my voice too hard, too fast, without spending enough time on basics."

"How much time is he talking about?"

"More than I want to give." Drew glanced at her frown before he continued. "I don't think I have the patience, or dedication, to spend ten or more years searching for the Rigoletto Vittorio wants me to be."

"Does it have to be Vittorio's Rigoletto?"

"Now you're sounding like Dad." He darted a quick, reprimanding glare at her. "I know that pleasing Vittorio is the closest I can come to pleasing Verdi himself. I could never be satisfied with a Rigoletto that was not what he wanted. It's been a dream inside me, but I have to decide how much of my life and soul I'm willing to risk on a dream that may be unattainable."

"For whatever help it gives you, I want you to know that my dream is only that you find reward in the journey, no matter where it leads."

"Thank you for that." Drew reached over and squeezed her hand. "Now leave it alone. The proposed embarkation of that journey is a long summer and autumn away. I don't need to book passage yet."

By the time they reached Doylestown, Drew had concluded there was nothing he could say that would change his grandmother's determination to force him into what she saw as fiscal responsibility and he saw as fiscal encumbrance. He did, however, accept the inevitable and magnanimously offered a truce by holding back his objections and signing a thick folder of documents he didn't even try to keep track of. Since everything would be sent to his financial advisors for review and become the headache of several accountants, he wryly wondered if Mae's latest round of reshuffling assets wasn't just a complicated scheme to keep them gainfully employed.

Right now, the only benefit he was grateful for was the solidifying of his truce offer and hasty conclusion of the session with her lawyer.

As a result of Drew's desire to slake his overwhelming hunger, and his grandmother's strict rule of avoiding any hint of discord in front of nonfamily, they managed to get through a pleasant and satisfying dinner at a tastefully decorated Pennsylvania Dutch restaurant Mae was particularly fond of—without straying into any mine fields.

On the drive home, he was able to keep her talking about the meal, horses and her approval of the way John had repaired the steps and opened the view on the path to the lake. As soon as they reached the house, Drew looked at his watch and announced that if he wanted to catch Roy, who was extremely punctual about his routine, he had to hurry to the stable before Roy finished his afternoon chores.

When he reached the stable, Drew heard the rattling sound of the diesel tractor beyond the machine shed. With Nemo bounding beside him, he jogged toward it in the hope it was Roy, not John. He was rewarded by the sight of a bright orange ball cap skimming along the top of a brushy fence row as it returned from the manure piles. Years ago, a hunter's shotgun pellets had spattered into the side of the equipment shed while Roy was working near it. Ever since, no matter what season or what type of hat he chose to wear, every one of them was a brilliant blaze-orange that could be seen bobbing around the grounds like a signal flare.

As soon as the tractor cleared the fence row, Drew let out a shrill whistle to catch Roy's attention then signaled for him to stop and shut off the engine.

"Is something wrong, Drew?" Roy met Drew's gaze with the confused look he always showed when his routine was interrupted or he wasn't sure of what was happening around him.

"I need to talk to you."

"It's about that man, isn't it?" Roy's broad shoulders rounded, as if he were shrinking into himself and he shifted his eyes to where his big hands engulfed the steering wheel. "I didn't like him. He shouldn't have come here."

"No, he shouldn't have." Drew leaned an elbow on the tractor hood and waited until Roy looked at him. "I don't like him either. And no matter what he said, he is not a friend of mine. You were right to tell him to leave."

"John said I should go get him if I see that car again." Roy tightened his grip on the wheel. "I'm sorry, Drew. John told me to stay near Willow. She rode Donegal away before I could stop her."

"There was nothing you could do about that. It's alright." Drew gave Roy a reassuring smile before he looked toward the woods, where black storm clouds scudded in from the west. "I doubt if he's still around, but if she doesn't get back fast, she's going to be damn wet and have her hands full of skittish horse. It looks like we're in for a drenching; and if I remember right, Donegal gets his nerves in a twist when there's a storm brewing."

"I tried to call her back but she was too far away."

"I understand that. You tried. And it's alright" Drew set his hand on Roy's knee to recapture his attention. "If the man comes again, find me. If I'm not here, get John, not Mrs. Mae. I don't want that man near her, or Willow."

"Yes, Drew, yes, yes." Roy nodded with the emphatic movement of a pecking chicken.

"Thank you, Roy."

Drew pushed away from the tractor fender and stiffened when he heard the pounding beats of a horse at full gallop. He turned toward the sound just as Willow and Donegal emerged from the shadowed woods beyond the shed. The young thoroughbred's bridle, or at least the reins, bit and broken cheek pieces, dangled in front of him, banging and twisting around his forelegs. Willow clung to the horse's mane with her head between her forearms, her face pressed against his neck.

"Whoa, Donegal, ho-down…" Drew sprinted into the horse's path and extended his arms while he continued to repeat soothing words that he knew the horse had been trained to respond to.

As the sound of Drew's voice eased the gelding's panic, Willow used her seat and balance to settle him, but he was still head high, snorting and blowing through flared nostrils. Drew ran beside the wary animal's left shoulder and grabbed the still intact nose band. He jerked the horse's head down and spun him in a tight circle until the horse was distracted from the stimulation of flight instinct by the more urgent problem of keeping his feet underneath him. In a few seconds, Donegal relaxed his neck, dropped his head in winded submission and stood still.

Drew slipped the reins of the broken bridle off the gelding's sweat darkened neck and tied them to the nose band as a makeshift lead shank before he handed them to Roy and looked up at Willow. Her shirt was torn. Welts and red scratches marked her face. When she slid off the horse into his arms, she was trembling, unable to do more than utter unintelligible sounds he barely recognized as words. All Drew could glean from her gasping attempt to talk was: car, madman, scared me, crazy horse saved me, tried to kill me, ran away.

"Stop trying to talk." Drew lifted her in front of him and, with Nemo trotting beside him, carried her to her cabin, sat on the couch and cradled her in his arms while the trauma shuddered through her. When she tried to sit up, he stood and set her down with a cushion behind her back, her legs stretched out on the couch. "Get your thoughts together. I'll be right back."

When Drew returned with a pan of warm water, washcloth, and towel, Willow wanted to tell him she was all right and didn't need pampering. The deep concern on his face changed her mind and she gave in to his sense of chivalry by letting him sit beside her with the pan on the coffee table and gently wash away dried blood and dirt.

"They looked a lot worse than they are. I think you'll live." Drew leaned forward and kissed the end of her nose.

"I feel stupid for panicking but runaway horses have always terrified me. When he bolted down a game trail, all I could do to get away from the branches was hang onto his neck and hope he stayed on his feet until he ran himself down."

"Once he lost the security of your rein aids, there wasn't much else you could do, except bail off him. At that speed, it would have been an insane thing to do." He dropped the cloth in the water and lifted her hand to his lips. "I'm more interested in the rest of what you said. Who was the madman? What did Donegal save you from? Who tried to kill you?"

"Donegal tried to kill me by running away like that. The man scared me and Donegal saved me from him."

"Start at the beginning and tell me what happened."

"I'll try to get it straight." Willow pressed her lips together while she sorted her thoughts. "I was trotting along the trail that follows the stream below the mill pond when I heard a horn blaring up on the lookout. I saw a car with its hood up and a man waving at me for help. When I rode up to talk to him, he grabbed my thigh and talked crazy."

"What did he say?"

"That he'd been watching me and was going to take me where he could fuck me whenever he wanted." Her face twisted when Drew's hand gripped hers. "When I tried to tightened the reins, he jerked them out of my hands. I grabbed mane and dug my heels into Donegal, who crammed him into the railing. Then the jerk did a stupid thing. He hooked the looped reins over the post at the end of the railing and tried to pull me off the horse. I kicked Donegal until he hauled back on the reins. When the bridle broke, he plowed the man over and bolted down the bank into the woods."

"What did the man look like?"

"All I remember is an ugly scar on his upper lip, a crooked nose and creepy black eyes that were never still." She shuddered. "He was wearing a dark, long sleeved shirt. I remember thinking it was weird on a such a warm day."

"He always wears long sleeves." Drew clenched his jaw and watched her eyes widen. "His left arm was burned with hot oil when he was a kid. He hates the scars."

"You know him?"

"He's Gino's nephew, my step-cousin. We lived in the same neighborhood as kids. His name is Mario and he doesn't like me very much. He'll like me even less after he answers to me about this."

"Stay away from him, Drew. I don't want you hurt."

"Willow, he knew who you were and did it to get to me."

"Then don't give him want he wants. Can't you just let it end at that?"

"He won't stop until I have it out with him. We've been through this before: he attacks; I take him down; he lays low for a while; then he starts building up resentment until it repeats."

"Drew, you're not the tough street kid anymore. Don't take on someone who is."

"I can handle him, Willow. He likes to scare people who are weaker than he is. I don't scare. It makes him back down fast."

"Are you sure?" She looked at his hard face and realized her objections would have no more effect on him than they had on Todd when he went after Cal for what he did to her at the fair.

"Yes, I'm sure. I'm more worried about him coming after you again."

"I'm not helpless, Drew. I am capable of fighting back. In fact, I already did, which should back him away from me, too."

"You had over twelve hundred pounds of horse for a weapon. Although it is basically true that most rapists and muggers who pick on women are looking for easy victims and will avoid a fight, that does not apply to Mario. He isn't looking for any victim—he wants you and he can be damn persistent about things like that."

"Are you trying to scare me?"

"Yes. He hates me and is irrationally obsessed with revenge. He won't stop until he gets it—or I stop him. I've been trying to get him out of the way legally, but his attack on you just changed the game. I need you to trust me and protect yourself by doing what I say."

"You don't want me to fight him?"

"If he gets a hand on you, I want you to fight and scream like a cornered wild cat in the hope you can escape to a place of safety or attract help. But unless you're hiding skills I don't know about, or are damn lucky, chances are you will be helpless against him. Therefore, I want you to make sure he can't get anywhere near you. If I'm not with you, lock your cabin at all times. Stay close to home, preferably near John or Roy. Call my cell phone if you so much as see him. And always keep Nemo with you."

"Nemo?" Willow looked at the wooly, black dog sprawled on the cool tiles of the kitchen floor, snoring. "He'd lick him to death."

"Don't underestimate Nemo."

"All right. You scared me enough I'll feel better with a warm, furry bodyguard." Willow frowned when she tried to imagine Drew's big, loveable bear of a dog intimidating anyone for longer than the few seconds it took to get over his size and notice his wagging stub of a tail. "What's Nemo's breeding?"

"Bouvier and standard poodle."

"He mostly got the Bouvier."

"In bulk. But his coat's curlier and he has a lot of cleverness from the poodle. He's one of the sharpest dog's I ever trained. Once he learns a command, he never forgets it. If Mario comes near you again, point at him and say: 'Nemo, take! Hold!' Mario will be flat on his back until I come and let him up. I'll let you practice with him tomorrow."

He started to stand, but she caught his hand and held it. "Mario said he already paid Milly back. Do you know what he meant?"

"That I have two good reasons to take him down." Stiffening, he shook her hand away and strode toward the door.

"Drew, who is Milly?"

"A hooker I should have walked away from."

"What are you talking about?" He yanked open the door as if he didn't hear her. "Drew, where are you going?"

When he twisted to look at her, he was rigid, his face hardened in an expression that made Willow feel she was facing someone she didn't know and couldn't communicate with. "What's wrong with you?"

"Nothing. Something is very wrong with someone else."

"Drew, talk to me!" Willow shouted when he charged out the door, slamming it behind him.

Willow heard the roar of the Mercedes as she jerked open the door. She watched the car disappear beyond a grey curtain of wind driven rain and knew there was no way to stop him.

"Damn you." She kicked the door closed and thudded the sides of closed fists on it. "How could you do such a thing?"

The only answer to Willow's anger was a booming roll of thunder that, like Drew's departing car, rumbled off to the east, leaving her with a sinking feeling and wild thoughts. *Oh, God, I'm in love with a man who's involved with a prostitute. How does he know her? He could have something terrible. No, he would have told me. He loves me. He wouldn't do that to me. But why does he know her? What has he done with her? When did he do it? It could be something from before I knew him. He goes to Philadelphia a lot. Who was he seeing when I thought it was Nicole?*

Willow tried to tell herself she was overreacting. Drew didn't lie or deceive. She knew that and believed it. She had to believe it. Anything else was too horrible to think about. Her thoughts calmed when she remembered him telling her his Uncle Antonio was a policeman in Philadelphia and he often went to baseball games with him. Maybe Milly had something to do with his uncle.

Thinking of Drew's uncle reminded Willow she had one of Antonio's business cards. Drew had told her about Antonio when he emptied a pocket and left the cards on the dresser, along with a mess of receipts and spare change. She knew she couldn't change Drew's mind. Maybe Antonio could. Everything Drew told her about his Uncle implied he admired and respected him.

Chapter Eighteen

The gleaming scythe of Drew's stare sliced through the smoke-heavy haze of Sal's Bar, focused briefly on the unchanging tableau of Mario's three cronies hunched together behind the high corner table—chugging down mugs of beer, feasting out of baskets of fried food—then swept to the bar. It stopped when it reached Sal and was returned by a challenge as intense as his own.

"Are you looking for good American sour mash?" Sal took in Drew's L.L. Bean shirt and Docker slacks. "Or highbrow Scotch?"

"I'm looking for Mario."

"Not in here. I threw him out last night when he went on a rampage and busted up a TV."

"What was the rampage about?"

"Somebody told him Milly followed you out of here and he's been asking around about it. Last night, somebody else told him he saw her leave a hotel with you and get in a cab."

"How is she?" Drew clenched his jaw, balled his fists.

"She was pretty beat up when she got home this morning. When she started pissing blood and passed out, her sister called emergency. She's in the hospital and must have talked because an hour ago two cops were here looking for Mario. Nobody's seen him all day. The rumor is he's gone to ground near the Navy Yard, which is kinda dumb. The place is crawling with guards."

"Think they know?" Drew looked into the corner and three pairs of eyes drown themselves in beer foam.

"Probably not. They hang with him but not thick enough he trusts them."

"I think I'll find out. You may need this." Drew tossed a five-dollar bill on the bar.

"Why would I need five bucks?" Sal caught Drew's wrist before he turned away.

"You'll figure it out."

"No fights."

"Just a demonstration. Trust me." Drew glared down at the hand on his wrist until Sal let go.

"I don't know if it's wise, but you stirred my curiosity enough I'll go for it."

Drew crossed the room in long strides, smacked flat hands on the round table and lunged forward menacingly. When the three toughs reared back in their chairs, he grasped the rim of the table, shoved it into the corner and leaned into it. The heavy wood top tipped all three chairs back against the walls, trapping the gasping occupants with their feet off the floor and the edge of the table jammed under their ribs. A swing of Drew's hand smacked down the beer pitcher to crack it and an immediate downward chop smashed it.

"I could do the same to your faces with either hand if you don't cooperate and tell me what I want to know. Where's Mario?"

"He didn't say nothing about where he was going." The answer came from the heavy man in the corner, who was just as trapped but less effected by the table's hard edge. The other two were busy trying to squirm closer to him—away from the crush of the table and out of Drew's reach.

"What did he say?"

"Jest that he had things to settle."

"Like what?"

"Like Milly messing where she shouldn't."

"What else?"

"Nothing else."

"How about you?" Drew snapped his stare to the younger punk to his right and lifted a stiffened hand in front of his chest. "You got a better answer?"

"He called a while ago. Said we was to get some stuff for him."

"If you do anything for him, or try to warn him, it makes you an accomplice. You don't want that." Drew snatched a cell phone off the table and stuffed it in his back pocket. "Where's he meeting you?"

"He ain't said yet."

"What did he say?"

"Just some shit about squaring with a mouthy bitch that ran him down with a horse."

Drew stiffened and shoved the table tighter into the corner. "When did he call?"

"Half an hour ago." The answer was a weak croak.

"Son of a bitch!" Drew thrust the table deeper into the corner, then spun away, almost colliding with Sal, who held a nightstick in a way that said he knew how to use it. "Thanks. I wondered why they didn't try to get away."

"Impressive, but gutsy. And you overpaid for the pitcher."

"You owe me a drink sometime." Drew started toward the door, then turned back and handed him the cell phone. "It could be evidence, so do me a favor. Keep them here and don't let them near that or any other phone. Call Antonio, maybe he can get a trace on it."

"Where are you going?"

"Where I should have had the sense to stay."

As soon as he reached his car and headed out of the city, Drew dug a cell phone out of a pouch below the doorsill, punched a number and left a message: "Tonio, I just left Sal's. I think Mario is at the manor. I'm going after him."

After a quick call to Willow's answering machine, Drew tossed the phone onto the passenger seat and sped up a ramp onto the expressway with anger, guilt and fear pounding through him in a turmoil of panic that threatened to rip away his control. Sucking in deep breaths, he grasped onto the leather covered wheel and expelled the panic by burying his vulnerable self and slipping deeper into the role of hardened arrogance he had developed to reject fear and apprehension when he was with the police. With an almost imperceptible shudder, uncertainty and fear disappeared, leaving a grim, calculating mindset that balanced on the edge of merciless vengeance.

❖

Willow's brief conversation with Antonio, who understood her concern without adding to her alarm, had calmed her. The depth of his voice and the way he talked reminded her of Drew. Listening to him made her smile, told her he knew a lot about her and liked her. Somehow, the thought of Drew telling his uncle good things about her reined in runaway thoughts about Milly. Antonio's reassurance that Drew was well able to handle a confrontation with Mario and come out on top relieved the worst of Willow's fear, but not enough to erase the uneasy feeling that Drew may not be thinking as rationally as Antonio believed.

The call ended with the promise that either he, or Drew, would call her back in an hour and tell her what was happening. When Antonio hung up, Willow thought about how much he sounded like the tough, in control part of Drew and suspected his return call would be more to check up on her than update her. Drew had a habit of withholding apprehensions. She doubted his uncle was any different.

After channel surfing for a program or movie that would take her mind off Drew, Willow felt she needed to concentrate on something that would absorb her mind. That meant getting her recently neglected training charts up to date. The problem was that both her charts and scribbled notes were in the stable office and she'd promised Drew she would stay inside. She knew it would upset him if he called and she wasn't there. But then, it would only take a few minutes to run to the barn, get back and check for messages.

With a twinge of regret that this would be a good time to own the cell phone she insisted she didn't need and couldn't afford, Willow headed for the back door. She looked for Nemo in the kitchen and then saw him asleep in the bedroom with Drew's sweat shirt rumpled under his head. The sight made Willow smile and understand that, even though the dog lived with John most of the year, his deepest loyalty was to Drew. Instead of disturbing the dog's contentment, she stepped outside and closed the door behind her.

The sun had dropped below the hill, turning the rain-soaked pines into a dark gathering of murmuring, long armed giants. For an instant, she felt they were watching her, waiting to surround her, cage her, smother her with a pungent fragrance and heavy branches. Shivering, she took a step backwards before she shook away the feeling and chided herself for letting earlier fears stimulate imaginary dangers. They were trees, not monsters, and there was still more than enough light to follow the trail to the barn.

Finding everything she needed and stuffing it in a plastic shopping bag Willow found in the trash took longer than expected. When she left the barn, it was nearing full dark. A bright moon played a game of hide and seek behind dark, fleeing clouds, but the range of the pole light at the edge of the parking lot reached well down the trail and she could see the reassuring glow of her kitchen window beyond the cleared area of the vegetable garden. With the bag clutched in her hand, she jogged toward the trail and home.

Almost past the garden, with only a short dash through dark pines to her back door, Willow heard movement behind her. She stopped and turned, expecting to see a raccoon, possum, or worse yet, a skunk trying to dig under the wire fence around the compost bins. The figure that materialized out of deep shadows by the garden shed and blocky humps of bins was taller and larger than any of those animals.

Willow went cold the instant she made out the outline of a head and shoulders. Her skin tightened and her muscles froze until her mind locked on the belief that the apparition wasn't real and would disappear as soon as she stared it down and understood what bush or tree created it. The paralysis shattered when the apparition moved toward her with scissoring strides and the glow of the pole light touched a scraped, bruised jaw and hook nose then glinted off a dark jumpy eye. She screamed and hurled the bag at Mario's face before she bolted toward her lighted window.

Willow knew the trail better than her pursuer and was able to dodge around, or leap over rocks and roots that tripped him and slowed him. At the end of the trail, she heard Nemo's deep baying bark and hoped it would stop Mario long enough she could get behind a locked door and call Drew and John for help. She was twenty feet from the back porch when a hand caught her hair, jerked her head back and slammed her to the ground. Air rushed from her lungs, left her whirling in blackness, gasping for breath. She was vaguely aware of being yanked to her feet and it took her a moment to realize the sound she thought was in her head was the ringing of her phone. By the time she could breathe, a hard forearm pressed across her throat. Her right arm was wrenched up behind her until her shoulder burned.

As the dizzy whirling faded to an awareness of Nemo barking and banging against the back door, Willow's brain was working enough to tell her she had to break away, reach the door and let Nemo out. Twisting, she jammed an elbow into Mario's ribs. When the arm across her throat slid away to grab her upper arm, she surged forward as if she were fighting his hold, then threw herself backward hard enough to make him stumble and release the wrist trapped behind her.

Spinning left, Willow broke Mario's grip on her arm, bolted toward sounds of frantic clawing on the wood below the kitchen window and a ferocious growling that filled her mind with violent images of an enraged bear. She screamed when an arm locked around her waist. Blinding pain exploded against the side of her head. The next blow knocked her against the side of the cabin. The last one blacked out her senses and she crumpled to the ground.

When awareness returned, Willow was stumbling along the gravel lane that led to the chained gate separating the estate from the road to Jared's Mill. Her wrists were lashed behind her with a thin cord that chaffed her skin whenever she tried to wriggle free. A strong hand clamped the back of her neck and her legs were hobbled by the green and yellow shock cord that had secured the lid on her trash can.

Willow raised her leg to stamp back on Mario's foot, but the elastic cord jerked it forward and made her stumble sideways. Shaking away from the hand, she threw her head back to scream for help. It ended in a choking gasp when the hand shifted to her throat. The glinting blade of a sharp knife lifted in front of her and she shrank back against a hard, unyielding body.

"Nobody will want you without that pretty face, especially not that rich cocksucker you been fucking. I told him he'd pay big. You're just the start."

"You won't get away with it, you ass!" Willow stiffened and glared at the knife as if the heat of her anger could melt it. "Drew knows it was you yesterday. If you do anything to me, he won't quit until you're locked up."

"Shut up, bitch." Mario slapped the flat of the knife against her cheek and slid his other arm across her throat. "You get to pay what Sutherland owes for taking free tricks from a whore who should have known better."

"You're wrong!" Willow gasped when a line of fire crossed her cheek and her defiant shout crumbled into a shaky plea. "He wouldn't do that."

"You lie just like she does. I owe that son of a bitch for four years of hell. I watched him head toward the city, so you and me are gonna hole up while he looks and I set my trap. If you're smart and do what I say, give me what I want, you won't get hurt so bad."

"You won't get away with it."

"I told you to shut up." Mario stepped around her, tightened a hand around her throat and shook her. "My car is on the other side of the gate. You can shut your mouth and keep walking. Or you can stay stupid and get sense beat into you. Don't matter which way to me."

Willow wanted to spit at him, but the moonlit glint of jumpy black eyes unnerved her, told her that pushing him further could topple him over the edge of madness. Without the defense of rational argument or enough strength to get away from him, Willow collapsed into herself and understood what Drew had been trying to tell her about being helpless against Mario. He was evil, or insane, or both. The realization that what she saw as civilized behavior, even right and wrong, were meaningless to Mario crushed her resistance.

"I'll walk." Willow shuffled forward when he pushed her ahead of him.

❖

Drew banged on the cabin's locked front door only moments before John's pickup jolted to a stop on the road from the manor house. Lights blazed in the living room, bedroom and kitchen. Nemo was barking excitedly. He twisted his key in the lock and thrust open the door on a scene of chaos where items from the shelves beside the back door lay strewn across the kitchen floor. Nemo alternated between barking at him and slamming his paws against the back door.

In the kitchen, Drew stared at a churned together mess from spilled canisters and jars, mashed cereal and cracker boxes, splinters of wood and fresh blood. His mind froze until he saw the clotted-over cut on one of Nemo's forelegs and looked at the window beside the back door. Desperate to get outside, the dog had left deep claw marks in the heavy wood of the door, broken one of the small panes of glass in the window. He'd ripped away part of the sill but failed to make a large enough opening to free himself.

The instant Drew opened the door, Nemo streaked past him, circled a patch of lawn. With his nose tasting the air just above the grass, he ranged back and forth between the bathroom wall of the cabin and the opening of the path to the barn. Trash spilled out of the tipped over trashcan on the back porch; groundcover plants beside the cabin lay crushed and broken.

Putting together what he saw and the dog's tracking pattern, Drew assumed: Willow stepped outside to put something in the trash can; Mario grabbed her; she tried to fight him off, and one, or both, of them had fallen beside the wall before he overpowered her and carried or forced her into the pines. And yet, something didn't feel right about his scenario. If Mario had been able to get to Willow during the brief time that she was outside, Nemo would have sensed him and barked. She would have had time to open the door and there would have been no way for Mario to get her away before Nemo caught him. When Drew heard Nemo barking farther down the trail, analytical thinking flew out of his mind.

With the beam of John's flashlight opening the trail from behind, Drew ran into the pines in panicking dread of what he might find. They found Nemo by the garden, barking at a white plastic bag. Willow's notes and charts were scattered around the bag as if it had been thrown, rather than dropped.

"Damn it." Rising from where he'd been examining scuffed foot prints on the open ground, Drew snapped his fingers, pointed at the tracks, then back along the trail. "Nemo. Seek."

"What happened?" Clasping the hastily stuffed bag, John fell into step with Drew.

"He has her. Are you sure no one drove in the main drive?"

"Positive. The system was on. It recorded your gate remote. That's why I knew you were here. Since you were driving like a bat out of hell, I followed you."

They found clear signs of a struggle when they reached the gate across the lane then two distinct sets of footprints on the damper surface of the running path around it. The trail ended just beyond the gate where tire marks showed that a car had backed up to the gate then headed south along the gravel road towards Jared's Mill. There were no tire tracks heading back toward the county road.

"John, do you have your key for the gate?" When John nodded, Drew said, "Open it. I'll be back with the car," and took off running.

When he returned, Drew stopped at the open gate and popped open his door. "Only one car has been down here since it rained. There's no other way to drive out of there. I have him cornered." He scooped his phone off the seat and handed it to John. "Take this and keep pushing redial until you get my Uncle Antonio, not his voice mail. He should be on his way out here. Tell him what happened. Then meet him at the end of the drive and follow me so he can scrape up what's left of that bastard and arrest him."

"I take it that bastard is the old friend Roy told Mae about."

"Never a friend—a dark piece of my past I want eliminated." Drew reached for the door strap, yanked it down the instant John backed away.

The tires of the Mercedes bit into damp gravel and spewed it out behind them. Jumping away from a pelting shower of gravel, John let go of Nemo's collar and helplessly watched the dog tear after the car that hurtled down the dark empty road like a relentless juggernaut of destruction.

"Nemo, no! Come!" John's shout was answered by dark silence.

❖

"Slow down, dickhead!" Andrew shouted at his internal vision of Jack's sharply shadowed profile, the gleam of silver moonlight on golden hair. "You charged in and took over before you listened to reason."

"There's no time to reason." Jack snapped at the voice that pleaded with him. "Drew thought those tracks were made when the road was wet. They could be more than an hour old."

As he approached a tight curve, Jack stamped on the brake pedal without a thought about the clutch and impatiently crammed the accelerator to the floor. The car bucked as the engine started to stall, then tires dug into gravel and the Mercedes shot forward on the two-mile-long, rising stretch of road before the millpond.

"Slow down!" Andrew shouted. "You don't know how to drive. Let Drew out before you kill us all."

"Are you stupid enough to think Pissface has been talking to her that long?"

"What do you care? You don't even love her."

"She's the bitchinest thing he's ever had and that fuckin' asshole Mario ain't gonna take her from me."

"Then think, damn it!" Andrew screamed his protest against the fury emanating from his stubborn older brother. "If we top that hill and roar toward him, he'll hear us a mile away. Mario knows he's cooked for what he did to Milly. That makes him desperate and crazy enough to kill her and wait to get us."

When the accelerator backed off and the roar of power softened to a deep rumble, Andrew continued to assault Jack with logic. "We have to rely on Drew's training or we all lose. So, back off and let Drew out now. Is that a deal?"

Jack's jaw tightened, then relaxed. "It's a deal."

Drew shuddered, then snapped his eyes to the curved road ahead of him and eased up on the accelerator. Still in the cover of woods, he slipped the gearshift into neutral, switched off lights and ignition, let momentum take him to a narrow crest, where the road leveled before it dropped down a steeper slope between the mill pond and moonlit structure of Jared's Mill.

When a flashlight beam moved inside the office, then swept across the road in front of the building to glint off a car's reflector in the parking area beyond the porch, Drew angled onto the wagon road and let the silent car roll to a stop in front of wide double doors at the back of the main floor of the mill. He was out of sight from the porch, but clearly visible to anyone farther up the hill.

If Mario saw him, Drew knew there wouldn't be enough time to get to him before he either reached his car or locked himself in the building with Willow. Drew knew he could easily chase Mario down if he tried to flee, but the more likely scenario was that Mario was afraid of a one-on-one confrontation and would go back in the mill. He was already on the run for his assault on Milly. If it came to a standoff, Drew hoped Mario would be rational enough to try using Willow as a bargaining chip for a chance to escape, instead of as a target for his vengeance. But then, from what he knew of Mario's deranged obsession for revenge, he couldn't be sure of anything. That meant he had to stop Mario before he could hurt Willow.

Tensing, Drew watched the flashlight beam move along the underbrush beside the road then probe into the woods. It paused on the bushes near the opening of the wagon road, jerked back towards the crest of the hill in time to catch a gleaming eye, russet flank and white tail flag of a bolting deer. A moment later, the light disappeared. Quick steps on the mill's wooden porch were cut off by the thump of a closing door.

Thoughts of what could be happening, or could have already happened inside the mill, clawed at Drew's stomach. An image of Willow's pale face when he pulled her off the horse filled his mind. Fear caught in his chest, threatened to break through his control. He pushed it aside with the hard, calculating role that kept him focused on what he had to do instead of what he might find. From the information extracted from Mario's cronies, Drew knew Mario expected he would be looking for him—but in Philadelphia, not in a deserted mill in the woods.

It was hard to second guess Mario, who was driven by impulse more than logic, but it made twisted sense that the man had some kind of scenario of his own and planned to take his hostage where he felt more protected before he carried it out. But whatever scenario it was, Drew had no intention of letting it happen. He had his own agenda, which centered around taking Mario down himself, then letting the police have what was left.

Drew suspected Mario had broken into the mill office by prying the hasp out of the rotten wood of the door frame. He also knew there was an iron deadbolt Mario could use on the inside and vandal proof screens on the windows. Although Drew knew his prey was cornered, he had to find a way to get inside before Mario had time to hurt Willow or use her for a shield.

Aside from the office, there were only two ways into the mill. The first was a hazardous climb up the wheel itself and then a balancing act along its shaft into the building. Drew had done it once as a boy in a new kid initiation to prove his courage. But it had scared the hell out of him and he wasn't keen to try it again. The other was in front of him—two wooden doors he knew were padlocked on the outside and barred by a two-by-four on the inside. He also knew the floor inside was clear, as well as sturdy enough to support two to six horse teams of heavy draft animals pulling logs and loaded wagons.

With a clear plan filling his mind, Drew calculated the force he would need to break through the doors as he started the car and sped backwards up the hill. Without a trace of hesitation, he released his doorlatch, crammed the shift lever into first gear, then floored the accelerator, let out the clutch and speed-shifted with the rapid acceleration.

With a roar of released power, the one ton, fuel-injected sports car passed 60 mph before it reached the doors. They held for a split second, then parted and flew apart in ragged hunks of boards that pelted down on the car and the figure rolling away from its thrust open door. The Mercedes hit the stone wall on the far side of the mill floor with a sickening crunch that made Drew cringe before he rose to his feet and sprinted across heavy plank flooring marked by distorted light and shadow grids of moonlight streaming through high, wire covered windows. He was halfway to the office when he heard a scream.

The latch on the inside office door gave out with one solid kick and he was through it before it crashed into the wall. Willow sat with her arms lashed behind the back of a heavy wooden office chair. Mario stood behind her: one hand twisted in her hair; the other held a knife in front of her face.

The instant Drew saw them, his mind locked on an image of blood running from dark hair, disappearing into a cleavage between heaving breasts. Red rage exploded and all awareness blacked out as he snapped his head up and charged toward the horror filling his mind.

"Do not hurt her!"

"Back off, Sutherland, or—" The threat cut off when hard hands threw Mario into the wall before he could do more than raise the knife.

Reeling, Mario bolted for the door. Strong hands spun him and pounding fists drove him backwards across the open floor of the mill until he crashed into the rusted gears and levers of a mechanism that had once connected the millwheel to the blade. A toothed gear grabbed his shirt and held him on his feet while hard blows hammered at him.

As powerful hands closed on his throat, Mario lifted the knife still clutched in his hand and swung it toward Drew's back. A blur of black ferocity latched onto his wrist and the weapon fell to the floor. Strong hands shifted to Mario's arms as Drew ran him backwards across the floor and slammed him into a support post. Mario pitched forward when his attacker was snatched away from him.

"Stop it, Drew." Antonio jerked Drew away from Mario and spun him toward the far wall. The face that swung around and stared past him was stone hard, the eyes dark cold disks of blued obsidian. "Are you trying to kill him?"

"The pig bastard will not get away." The stony command froze Antonio an instant before Drew's straight-armed blow shoved him aside.

"Get away?" Antonio shouted. "He can't even get up."

Antonio grabbed at a rock-hard arm when Drew strode to where Mario scrambled across dusty floorboards. The back of a clenched fist thudded into Antonio's stomach and sent him staggering sideways before Drew reached down to grasp a handful of Mario's hair, haul him to his knees.

The right fist that connected with Mario's jaw knocked him flat on his back an instant before Antonio drove his shoulder into Drew's back and ran him, face first, into the wall. The jolt that should have been disorienting had almost no effect on Drew, who spun to face Antonio and surged forward with the power of a charging bull.

"What the hell is wrong with you?" Bellowing straight into a stark, unfeeling face, Antonio grasped at unyielding shoulders and banged Drew back against the wall. "You're freaking me out, damn it!" He thudded him back again. "Come out of it and talk to me."

"He hurt her. I will stop him."

Slamming into Antonio with a full body block, Drew sent his uncle staggering backwards as he charged forward. He froze when he saw Willow in the office doorway. The moment she stepped toward him Drew went limp; his head dropped forward and his body shuddered. When his head snapped up, he looked confused then scowled at where his uncle's hands were locked on his upper arms.

"What are you doing you big ox?"

When Antonio stepped back warily, Drew glanced to where Mario lay on the floor—out cold, unmoving. He stiffened, shook his head and looked irritated. "Thanks for the help, but I really wanted to do that myself."

"You did."

Drew stared down at bruised, painfully swollen knuckles for a long, uncomfortable moment before he raised his eyes to Antonio's wary face. "I lost it again, didn't I?"

"You sure did."

"At least this one deserved it." Drew turned away and crossed the floor to Willow. She was wearing John's flannel shirt and shivering. He couldn't say anything, could only close his arms around her and hold her while adrenalin and the horror of what had happened flowed out of him.

"I told him you would come for me, Drew. I never doubted it."

"He could have killed you." Drew traced gentle fingers along the lines of dried blood on her left cheek, kissed the bruise near her ear.

"It was you he tried to kill. I was terrified when he swung the knife and Nemo grabbed his arm."

"Nemo?" Drew lifted his head and looked along the line of her gaze to where his dog lay, panting, with a protective paw firmly planted on Mario's knife.

"He was with you, Drew."

"He must have followed me and spooked the deer."

"What deer?" Willow looked confused.

"In the woods when Mario went outside with the light."

"He thought he heard something. Then he came back and said it was just an animal."

"What did he do to you, Willow?" Drew's hands held her face, his gaze searched into her eyes.

"He mostly talked about what he would do to me in front of you and then what he would do to you with his knife. After a while, when I realized he was doing it to scare me, I told him he was wrong and would never defeat you. He started yelling at me to shut up. But it upset him, so I just kept saying it. When he heard the car, he looked scared. The crash panicked him. He was terrified when you broke in the door."

"He had reason to be." Drew touched the cut on her cheek. "I saw you bleeding and lost all control."

"I screamed when he grabbed me, but I wasn't bleeding anymore. I just knew you were there and it was all over."

"Are you all right with this?"

"You're here and you're holding me. Of course, I'm all right."

"I'm always here for you." Drew kissed her then relaxed his arms when his uncle walked up to him. "What's going on?"

"I notified the locals as soon as John told me where you'd gone. Mario's still out cold and, I hope, unaware of my presence. It would blow a cover I need to maintain"

"You don't want him?" Drew asked.

"Don't worry. We'll get him back. We have more against him than they do. It should be enough to lock him up and keep you and Willow out of it. I talked to John. He knows what to say." When the wail of sirens approached on the forest road, Antonio crossed the open floor and disappeared through broken doors.

After Mario, still unconscious, was handcuffed to a stretcher and loaded into an ambulance, Drew saw a deputy head for the knife with a plastic evidence bag in his hand. He set a hand on the man's chest to stop him. "Let me do that." He felt the man pull back when he heard a deep growl from Nemo. "Believe me. You don't want to try to pick it up."

When the man handed him the bag, Drew crouched, snapped his fingers and pointed at the knife. "Nemo. Pick it up. Give."

Nemo sat in front of Drew with the knife delicately held between his teeth while, looking as pleased with himself as a dog could, he gently set the weapon on the inverted bag in Drew's hand.

Reaching forward, Drew scratched the dark, wooly head. "He led me to where Mario's car had been parked, then ran for better than two miles to save my life. The least I can do is respect his dignity and let him finish his job with pride."

When it was all over and the police were gone, Drew slid his arm around Willow's waist and walked to where John and Antonio were examining the carcass of his car. The entire front of the Mercedes was a crumpled mess of steel and aluminum. The driver's door had been ripped away from the body and dragged across the rough wooden floor by a twisted lift arm. The steel frame had survived the impact without distortion, but anchor bolts were sheared off, allowing the engine to break through the firewall into the cockpit. A tangled rat's nest of wires sprouted from a section of dashboard lying across the passenger seat. The articulated steering wheel drooped onto the driver's seat.

"How did you get out of that unscathed?" Antonio stared at Drew with the look of a man staring at a ghost.

"Once I lined it up and gained enough speed, I popped it out of gear and dove out the open door before it hit. But I wouldn't say I was unscathed. My skidding slide seems to have left tread marks on the back of my left shoulder and ruined a good shirt." Drew looked back along the car's path. "It held a good straight line for a rudderless juggernaut."

"What are you going to tell your father?"

"I'm going to have it towed to the mechanic who works on it and let you or John tell Dad. The last time I wrecked one of his cars, I saw murder in his eyes. I'd rather not repeat that."

"Didn't he say you'd be doing him a favor if you drove it off a cliff?" Willow looked at him with a puzzled expression.

"That's what he said, but I knew he didn't mean it literally. Dad wanted his bitter memories over the cliff, not the one thing he'd dreamed of owning for years and then had snatched away from him because he did the honorable thing and gave me life."

John set a large hand on Drew's good shoulder and squeezed it, "Andy will see it as a small sacrifice for saving Willow. You'd more likely see murder in his eyes if you hadn't used the only means available to get to her."

"It will still hurt. We're looking at the battered remains of what's been named the car of the century. There aren't many of them left."

"So, what?" Antonio gave Drew a disgruntled look. "I know Andy would have done the same thing. It's the way he is."

"I know that. I just don't want to have to say—Hey Dad, I wrecked another one of your favorite cars."

Chapter Nineteen

When Antonio's kitchen door stuck, Drew thumped his shoulder into it. The heavy barrier gave way, sending a case of empty beer bottles rattling across the floor into a table leg. He heard a television blaring from the den and strode across the empty kitchen. "Where the hell are you, Antonio?"

"I'm right here." A hard voice answered from just beyond the cracked open door to the dining room an instant before it jerked open. "And don't you ever bust in here again."

Stiffening, Drew stared at the barrel of Antonio's automatic. "Looks to me like you're ready to get out of the cop business."

"Not yet." Antonio stuffed the gun into his belt while Drew moved the case of bottles against the wall. "How'd you get here?"

"The stable's pickup. It smells like horse shit so nobody will steal it. The garage door was open and there was a big tool cart in the way."

"I was working on the Buick, but I wanted to catch a weather forecast for the game tonight." Antonio walked past Drew to pour coffee. "I didn't expect you so soon."

"I have a lot on my mind." Drew sat next to the mug his uncle set on the table. "Like what the hell happened last night?"

"You tell me." Antonio stood at the end of the table, holding his coffee in front of him.

"I hurt all over. What did he do to me?"

"Nothing." Antonio frowned when Drew recoiled in disbelief. "When I ran through the mess you left of the doors, you were slugging Mario like he was a sack of rats. I had to bounce you against a wall a few times to get through to you. You don't work like that and you know when to stop."

"I don't remember that. I just know I needed to save Willow. She was bleeding, damn it."

"That's a lie. She wasn't bleeding."

"I'm not lying. She still has a mark on her face."

"He nicked her long before that and it was dried up by the time you got there."

"She was bleeding. I saw it. You didn't."

"Willow said he was holding a knife when you burst into the room, but there was no blood."

"I saw blood on her face, in her hair and I…" Drew froze for an instant, then slumped back against the cabinet. "Oh, God, why does it keep happening like that?"

"Happening like what?"

"I get mad and see blood. Then the red rage burns away my control and I do things I don't remember."

"Maybe Jack does them the way he used to."

"Even when he was around, Jack never did things like that," Drew said. "Jack spent more energy running away than attacking."

"Then who does?"

"No one!" Drew shouted then clenched his fists and fought down the panic. "It's a repeating abreaction of hate and fury, but I don't know where it comes from. I could never hate that much, never. It just isn't in me."

"Who is the pig bastard?"

"What are you talking about?"

"You said the pig bastard will not get away. You called Gino that. Did you hate him enough?"

"Not like that." Drew lifted his mug, then set it down. "Paul tried that angle this winter. It didn't get anywhere. Hell, I ran from Gino. All I wanted was to stay away from him—far away."

"You didn't look angry. I don't know what was driving you, but you weren't you, and it wasn't anger."

"It's way beyond anger. It comes and then it goes away as if it never happened. Dad calls it primitive battle rage, a form of self-preservation I need to find a way to control. He's probably right. But if I don't know where it comes from and what triggers it, I won't know how to control it. It scares me, Tonio. I have to find an answer before something terrible happens."

"Like what?"

"I don't know. But I'm terrified it will happen again and won't go away soon enough."

"Soon enough for what?"

"I could have killed him." The admission ripped out of Drew's throat, left him horrified. "That was never my intention. I never wanted to kill anyone." When his uncle continued to stare at him without responding, Drew felt his control crumble. "It's the reason I quit the police. I was afraid I might have to kill someday. I couldn't accept that."

"I guessed that. And maybe that reluctance would have made you stop if I hadn't been there yesterday."

"What if the rage doesn't listen to it?"

"Killing is harder than you think. You have to develop a sixth sense that tells you when a situation changes from defensive to retaliatory, when right becomes wrong. I can help you with that because I've crossed the line myself and know what it feels like."

"How can I do that when I'm not feeling anything?"

"I don't know, but we have to find some way to disarm the charge before the trigger sets it off. Have you talked to Paul about this?"

"Not yet." Drew shook his head and pulled in a deep breath. "I need to think it through, but I had to know what happened first and you're the only one who could answer that." Drew took a few swallows of black coffee before he straightened and squeezed his hand on Antonio's hard forearm. "Thanks for backing up a loose cannon who thought he was invincible."

"You didn't have much choice. Sometimes you have to go with your instincts. That was one of them." Antonio frowned when Drew headed for the door. "Leaving so soon?"

"I have some stuff to do." Drew paused before he opened the door. "And I have to talk to Willow about things I should have told her a long time ago."

❖

That evening, Drew walked into the cabin with Zeb Bronson's tawny, underfed dog tagging at his heels. Willow took one look at the amber eyes, remembered the low growl, the leaping attack with sharp, white teeth. She froze by the kitchen table with her left hand clenched around hard flatware.

"What are you doing with that dog?" She pulled back behind the corner of the table. "He tried to kill you."

"I tried to kill him, too. Neither of us was serious about it."

"What do you mean?" Willow relaxed a little when Drew stopped on the living room side of the doorway. The dog sat beside his leg and pushed his nose into Drew's hand while his feathered tail swished back and forth on the wood floor.

"Friday morning, I picked up a syringe and euthanasia solution from Mark's vet clinic then went to Zeb's to find him. He remembered me enough to be wary of me, but when I crouched down beside the bowl of dog food I'd brought to lure him, I didn't have to wait long. He wasn't vicious, just hungry and scared. He had an infected wound on his foot from a muskrat trap and infected cuts from a beating with a chain. I suppose he was raiding traps to eat and someone didn't like it. He probably had a stash of food nearby and thought we were going to steal it from him. I couldn't kill him. He's only five and deserves another chance."

"You've been feeding him since Friday?"

Crouching, Drew rubbed behind the dog's ears before he looked up at Willow. "I took him to Mark's clinic. His wounds have been treated. He's been neutered and had a flea bath, as well as all his shots. He doesn't even have heart worms. Mark said Zeb brought him in every spring and traded off some of his homemade hooch in payment."

Standing, Drew chuckled. "I should have gone back when I was older and tried for another jug. Mark said it was great stuff."

"Maybe Zeb would have aimed better the next time."

"That thought crossed my mind whenever I got near the place." When he stepped into the kitchen, the dog moved with him, then sat, pressed close to Drew's leg and looked up at Willow with deep, golden-brown eyes.

"What are you going to do with him?"

"John will keep him. Nemo needs a play buddy. He's a nice dog, Willow."

"I'm still afraid of him." When Willow looked down, the dog was sitting still, but trembling. "What's wrong with him?"

"He's afraid, too. He wants you to pet him. When he finally let me touch him, he couldn't get enough love."

"Are you sure?"

Drew nodded and Willow carefully reached out her hand. With her first gentle scratch on top of the head, the dog's tail swept across the linoleum. When she moved her hand down his neck and rubbed behind his ears, he sighed and wriggled toward her.

"What's his name?"

"Zeb called him Friend. I've been calling him Gascon."

"Gascon?"

"It's an old French word for a cocky braggart. It was a teasing nickname my father gave me when I was a kid. He still slips it in when I hassle him."

"Is that why you brought him home?"

"He reminded me of myself." Drew slid his arm around her. "I attacked out of fear, too, but when I finally cried it out in Dad's arms, fear went away and I knew he loved me. Since then, I've never doubted it. It's sort of weird, but no matter how much my mother and Gino whaled on me, I never really cried. I hollered a lot, but I didn't cry—not until I had someone who loved me enough to care if I felt wrong and needed to cry away hurt and guilt."

"You're really touchy about your past, aren't you?"

"I have been lately." Drew took the utensils from her and set them on the table. "Are you cooking anything that will burn in the next half hour?"

"No." Willow recognized the vulnerably pensive expression she'd first glimpsed in the rose garden the day she met him. "Is something wrong?"

"Only with me. And I want to try to explain it." He led her to the bedroom and closed the door before the dog could follow them, held her for a long moment before he relaxed his arms and let her step back against clasped hands. "I guess it's no secret to you that I ran out on something I'd worked for years to achieve. It was like climbing to within the last stage in the ascent of Mount Everest. Then running away without making the final assault."

"Why did you run?" Willow set a hand on his chest, felt the hardness of tension through his knit shirt. "Drew, you wouldn't have gotten that far if you weren't good enough."

"That had little to do with it." His fingers dug into her arms for an instant before he dropped his hands and moved away from her. "Vittorio told me I had a technically perfect voice and excellent technique. Then he proceeded to tear me to shreds every time I sang anything."

He strode to the window and stared into the forest with his hands on the frame, grasping the wood trim so hard Willow was afraid he was going to tear it off the wall.

When Drew pushed himself away from the window, he was agitated and flushed. "I couldn't take the irrational ranting that blamed me for him being a crazy man—as if it was my fault that he couldn't control his temper—as if I committed blasphemy by not being what he wanted. He would shout *Appassionato,* Andrew! *Appassionato! Fieramente! Impetuoso! Maestoso! Maestoso!* until I wanted to shove his majesty up his scrawny ass!"

The side of his clenched fist slammed against the log wall.

"Son of a bitch!" He recoiled, shook his hand and scowled at it as if it offended him.

"Todd ended up in a cast after he punched a block barn."

"Been there; done that." Drew knifed his stare at her then shuddered and relaxed. He lowered his hand and met her eyes. "According to Vittorio, I was dead. He said I had no passion in my singing, that I was singing with my head and body, not my heart and soul. He wanted me to bare a buried part of me and I couldn't do it."

Drew closed his hands on her arms and sat her on the bed. When she scooted back against the headboard and faced him, he sat beside her leg and absently stroked his hand on it as if he were letting the gesture calm him while he sorted through a tangle in his mind.

"In less than a week, that madman cut through every barrier I'd constructed until I lost all that was rational to me. Those few weeks with Vittorio were an intense hell of violent emotions I thought I'd smothered years ago. When he's riled, he shouts, he curses, he pounds on walls and furniture. He throws things."

Drew snatched his hand away, stood up, and paced while he talked, as if he had to keep moving and gesturing to let the words out. "When he's excited, he isn't much different, except it's exuberance instead of fury. And when he's depressed, he broods and glares and cuts. We got along like two enraged tomcats. It made me a shattered wreck. It made him exultant!"

"Sounds like he's the one with a problem," Willow said.

Drew stopped to stare at her. His mouth smiled at her statement. His eyes didn't.

"Willow, I hadn't fought like that since I lived with my mother. It brought it all back: the screaming, the cursing, the violence—as well as the irrational tantrums and hysterical freak-outs. Vittorio reached into my emotional guts, jerked them out and mangled them." Drew clenched his right fist, twisted it violently and jerked it up in front of him.

"Did Vittorio ever call you Drew?" Willow asked quietly.

He dropped his hand and blinked at her. "Never. That would be calling an aria a tune."

"So, you left because Vittorio angered you?"

"It was way beyond anger. I lost my hold and attacked him in rage. I…" He started to say something then backed away from a vision that flashed in his mind and was gone. "I was out of control and terrified of what I might do if it happened again. I ran to my father, who was my stability, so he could put me back together."

Drew sat beside her on the bed and picked up her hand. "Dad took some time off and we spent most of it sailing and playing. He tried to get me to remember why and what actually happened. I couldn't." He set her hand on his thigh and caressed the shape of it with restless fingers. "I wanted to give up opera, but I feel I owe Gram more than that. Vittorio may take me back in November, but I have to know I can take it."

"Your father told you to quit if you couldn't take it?" Willow caught his hand and held it when the sensation distracted her.

"That's the way Gram interpreted what I told her. Dad, in his down-to-earth way, said that since I was rejecting excellent offers for other musical roles in order to do the opera thing, I should back off and take the fame being offered to me while I sorted out my priorities. That's why I took the booking with the Barn Theater. It was here and familiar to me."

"It's professional?" Willow let go of his hand and looked at him in surprise.

"Did it seem amateur to you?"

"Well, no, I mean…" His question flustered her. "I thought it was just local summer theater."

"It's a blending, where locals have the opportunity to be extras and stage hands without running into union restrictions. Around here, professionals view summer theater as a way they can get out of New York and still earn a living."

"Then you do have a job?"

"I have a career. But I'm not union and can't work in New York." He smiled at her question. "And right now, I'm actually being paid."

Willow laughed at his reply, then remembered there was more she wanted to know. "Your father made you think about it again, didn't he?"

"No, you did." Drew pressed a finger across her lips when she drew in a breath to protest. "All Dad did was listen to me in a bar near the airport. I was finally able to talk with him about some of the things I've been remembering lately. My mother twisted him up, too, so he understands better than Gram."

"What was your mother's name?"

"Carlotta." He gave her a startled look. "Why?"

"Everyone talks about her as if she were a nameless disaster." Willow frowned. "For God's sake, Drew, even hurricanes have names."

"I was a kid. I called her Mamma." A shimmer of pain tightened his features, then softened. "She used to call me Buffo when we sang silly songs together. A neighbor gave me the name when I was a little kid. I didn't know what it meant until years later."

"What does it mean?"

"A male opera singer who plays comic roles. I've done some."

"Your mother sang opera?"

"No. The hidden story is that she was the bastard daughter of an oversexed, ne'er-do-well tenor. The man who married her mother to legitimize her unborn child emigrated to America to get his wife away from shame and her lover. Antonio's father is not my true grandfather."

"Who was the tenor?"

"All I know is he was from northern Italy and had blue eyes. His name and identity were left in Italy." He reached forward and stroked his fingers along her cheek and lips, letting her nibble at them before he tipped her chin up and kissed her with a tenderness that surprised her. "Carlotta Vitale was my mother and part of me loved her as a mother. But you used a good metaphor. It was like living in a hurricane and hoping you could stay in the eye forever.

She gave me the volcano that's threatening to blow the top off the mountain I've built over it."

"Mae said the volcano wasn't Vitale."

"Gram said the temper I fear is not Vitale. She was referring to an ancient barbarian trait that Dad likens to primal battle rage that can overpower reasoning. I think it's what happened last night and with Vittorio last winter, but it's fueled by passions Vittorio is trying to force me to release. If I go back to Genoa, I need to use that volcano, but I have to learn how to control it and direct its power. It could control me. I'm terrified of it destroying me."

"How can it destroy you?"

"When the rage explodes, everything goes red, then black, and I lose myself." His eyes jumped away from her then looked back with anxious vulnerability. "Willow, if I can't stay in control, I'll come apart and won't know who I am."

"Come apart? How will you come apart?" Drew tensed, seemed to be looking through her for a moment before he shuddered and came back to her. "Drew, how can you not know who you are?"

"I don't know how to answer that anyway but clinically and that isn't good enough anymore."

"Why not?" Willow felt him pull back—watched his anxiety ebb away as he retreated behind his shield of control.

"It's only theories and in the past. They don't make sense out of what's happening to me now."

Drew looked down at her hand for a moment before he said, "I never could understand what Vittorio expected from me. I was giving him the best I could but it was never enough. And then, last week, I discovered what I think he meant." He lifted her hand and nipped at her fingers. He kissed the palm of her hand and closed her fingers around the kiss. "Last week I had someone special to sing to."

"What do you mean?"

"I've always impressed an audience with my voice. Last Friday, I enthralled an audience. I stopped listening to the technically perfected voice of the music inside me and sang from me to you. I don't think I'd ever done *Mariah* so powerfully. I touched what Vittorio was talking about by reaching into my emotions, shaping and painting the words with my feelings. It took more out of me, but it was stimulating, too. Vittorio makes me feel my passions, but he's never satisfied and badgers me until I turn against his invasions. Even though Dad was demanding and strict, he accepted my emotions and helped me channel them into acceptable outlets. But Dad was always firmly in control of himself, not an irrational fanatic like Vittorio."

"Didn't you fight with your father when you didn't get along with him?"

"No one *fights* with Dad. Every time I tried was like attacking that log wall. He stood up to my fury and let it bounce back at me until I got tired of fighting with myself. The violent energy was all mine. If I kept shouting at him, nobody wanted to be around since he gave me ample opportunity to let it out and develop my lung power until I ran out of venom and accepted the irrational futility of it. Dad listens to reasonable arguments then makes up his mind and doesn't budge. Finis. Done. Over with. If he's proved wrong, which isn't often, he admits it. And he rarely holds a grudge. My father is as steady and predictable as magnetic north. That isn't perfect, but it's about as close to it as you can get."

"You have to find your own balance, Drew."

"That's for sure. Just when I thought I was on solid ground and in control enough to make rational decisions, you burst into my life."

"Me?"

"You've been churning me up since I met you. You threaten the same barriers Vittorio does, but in a much deeper way."

"All I did was fall in love with you."

"You stir up the volcano, but it doesn't scare you. Most women in my life wanted surface lovemaking. They took and I took. It was pleasant and satisfying. But you want so much more. With you, I can share both the fire and the sunshine, the ridiculous and the sublime. But you frighten me, Willow, because you want my soul and I can't risk that."

Drew held her face in his hands and looked into her eyes with hurt agitation before he pulled her against him, crushed her in a tight embrace, as if he could absorb her inside him. "You're a drug I crave and fear at the same time."

Willow was unable to answer him. She knew what he was saying about the power of their love, but she had no understanding of what he feared. "I only want your love."

"You want more than I can give. It frustrates me until I feel I'm going to explode if I don't make love to you."

"Can you hold back the explosion until after dinner?" Willow covered his wrists with her hands, moved his hands down to her shoulders. "I turned down the oven when you were late. It's hard to destroy my mother's tuna noodle casserole, but it's reaching its limit."

"Just give me enough time to feed Gascon and settle him in the kennel at the stable."

After supper Willow carried the dishes to the sink then looked back to see Drew picking at the crusted edge of the casserole dish. She laughed until he looked up at her. "Sometimes I don't understand you."

"What do you mean?" He looked baffled.

"It's just a thrown together mess of everyday ingredients Mom fed the mob of us when she was in a hurry. We used to groan and gripe and say things like: 'Not tuna casserole again.' Or 'Why didn't someone hide the can opener?' How can a person who's used to gourmet cooking and international cuisine like it so much?"

"Maybe that's why. There's nothing sneaky about it, no hidden chef's secrets I'm supposed to pay through the nose for." Drew leaned the chair back against the wall and smiled wryly. "All I have to do is eat my fill and kiss the cook to get a hot roll in the sheets."

"My answer to that is…" Willow turned to the sink, pushed the faucet handle to full cold and spun around with the spray nozzle in her hand. "…that you, Mr. smart ass, need your ardor cooled."

Willow burst out laughing when the jet of cold water flattened Drew against the back of his chair with the same wide-eyed, drenched cat look she'd seen when John's water guns hit him in May. Hearing the chair legs bang on the floor, she threw the sprayer in the sink and tried to run as far from it as she could. An arm wrapped around her waist before she finished her first stride.

"What did I tell you would happen if you did that again?"

"Don't squirt me with that thing." She struggled in his grasp, desperately trying to keep him from reaching the sink. When he reached past her swatting hands to shut off the water, she remembered what he'd actually threatened. "No way will you spank me. That's not fair."

"All's fair in love and war, my daring little wench." He trapped her arms and, walking her ahead of him, strode into the bedroom.

"But it was only a little bit of water." Willow protested.

"Amount is immaterial. It was cold; it was wet; it was intentional provocation. And I always keep my promises." Drew released her long enough to yank her shirt and bra up until they trapped her arms above her head, then stripped her shorts and panties to her ankles. While she struggled to disentangle herself and peel off the shirt, he sat on the edge of the bed, pulled her across his lap and closed a strong hand on her waist.

At the first teasing swat, Willow reared up against the firmly restraining hand sprawled across the small of her back. The second made her sputter in indignant protest. "Drew Sutherland, you are a—hummumm."

Willow wriggled on his lap when he withdrew his hand just enough to brush his palm across her flesh in a circular pattern that stimulated a radiating heat that she realized had nothing to do with pain and everything to do with a sensual urgency that made her squirm against his legs. When he swatted with a gently teasing hand, she giggled, then purred as he caressed sensitized skin.

"Willow, you're not taking this seriously." Drew gave her a quick swat before he slid his hand between her legs.

"I'm taking it very seriously." She continued to squirm on his lap, rubbed her hip against his groin and smirked at the touch of growing hardness. "And I dare you to keep doing exactly what you're doing now."

"I thought you might say that." Drew moved his hand in caressing touches until she flamed in heated desire and he swelled to unbearable discomfort. "Good grief, woman, get off me before I explode."

When his hands lifted her and rolled her onto the bed, Willow grabbed his wet tee-shirt and tried to jerk it over his head while he grappled with the waistband of his jeans. Laughing hysterically, they wrestled off the last remnants of clothing and coupled together in a thrusting embrace that made Willow pull in a gasping breath and move with him in an undulating dance of pleasure that left them entwined like fused branches of windswept trees.

"You think that's going to stop me from drenching you again?" Willow purred in his ear.

"That was never my intention." He chuckled. "I said I would get great pleasure from warming your delectable derriere, I never said you wouldn't enjoy it, too. Willow, I will never seriously hurt you, but you do ask for retaliation and I can't resist your baiting."

"How many other rapturous sources of wicked pleasure are you hiding?"

"A few, but I object to the wicked connotation. Nature supplied us with a sumptuous smorgasbord of sensual pleasures. As long as they are mutually enjoyed, why should any one of them be more or less acceptable than another?"

"Do you know everything about women?"

"I have intimate knowledge of the basal urges and needs of their desiring bodies. But alas, I am an unevolved male and vastly ignorant of the mysterious intricacies and contradictions of their minds."

"Unevolved?"

"É vero!" He flamboyantly tossed his hands in the air. "Fight rivals; make babies; hunt game; make babies; annihilate predators; make more babies. Is there more?"

"I may need to keep you away from my brother Todd."

"Why?"

"You just described him."

"Ah!" Drew held up an index finger. "A man who knows his place."

"Todd's hopelessly obnoxious." She gave him a withering glare. "Just as you are right now."

"How did I go from rapturous to obnoxious so fast?"

"It's one of those mysterious contradictions of my female mind." Willow yawned and snuggled against his warm furry chest. "Is it too early to go to sleep?"

"Not if you want me to wake you up later and introduce you to more wicked pleasures."

"Is that a promise?"

"Absolutely. And I—"

"Never break a promise." Willow twirled her finger around a nipple and giggled when he smacked a hand over it. "I'm counting on it."

While Drew stroked the softness of Willow's face with gently soothing fingers, an elusive aroma teased at his mind, then grew in his awareness until he pulled in a tasting breath of its alluring fragrance. Reaching beyond her to the night table, he picked up a palm sized cloth bag with an intricate Celtic design embroidered on it.

"What's this?" He held it in front of her when she lifted her head.

"It's a sachet. One of my O'Reilly great aunts makes them and keeps giving them to us for every occasion she can think of. Mom threw a plastic bag of them into my trunk before I shipped it. I just found them and thought I'd put that one in my underwear drawer."

"What's in it?"

"I don't know." Willow sniffed at it. "I'd say lavender, maybe a little jasmine. She mixes up all kinds of scents. Why?"

"Don't put it in your underwear drawer."

"Why not? Don't you like it?"

"I do like it, but it reminds me of someone I don't want to think about when I'm anywhere near your underwear."

"A bad romance?"

"No. My Italian grandmother."

"What was she like?"

"I don't really remember, but I'll try." Closing his eyes, Drew turned the cloth bag with his fingers, inhaled its scent. "She was soft and round, black-haired, like my mother, but more olive skinned with jet-black eyes. She had red hands with big knuckles. Dad said she worked in a laundry. Her hands were very strong. I remember her grasping my arm and yanking me away from the street when I tried to catch a stray cat." A look of amazement washed across his face. "I couldn't have been more than five. She and my mother stopped talking to each other when Gino moved in with us."

"That's a lot of not remembering."

"It's been happening like that lately. Probably because I'm trying to remember the parts of my life I blocked."

"Why did you do that?"

"I guess I thought it was all bad. More likely, I was afraid of what it would reveal about me."

"Did you think you were bad?"

"I was told I was…" Drew let the thought go and slid behind his shield. "I was just a kid who didn't understand what was happening to me, and around me."

"Did smelling this give you those memories?" Willow took the sachet from his hand and set it on the table.

"Must have. I often relate images and people to scents. Dad is peaty, single malt Scotch and Old Spice. Gram is heather, roses, or fresh mountain thyme. You're honeysuckle, nutmeg and cinnamon rolls…"

"I thought I was mostly horses and barns."

"Often, but there's nothing uniquely you about horses."

"Is there some scent I should avoid?"

"Don't ever wear gardenia."

"Why?"

"My mother doused herself with it to cover the stink of drugs. It sickens me."

"I'll remember that."

Chapter Twenty

Willow and Drew went to a cocktail party the next Saturday afternoon. It was given by the Van Dussens—neighbors Willow had met once when they visited the stable after a Sunday dinner at the manor house. Except for a few friendly waves when she rode by their house on her trail rides, that brief encounter was the extent of her contact with them.

Mr. Van Dussen, a natty little man in a bottlegreen sport jacket, was a hospital administrator. Mrs. Van Dussen, who pursed her lips spastically and laughed disjointedly while she patted people on the arm, owned a boutique in a nearby shopping mall. Willow had never seen the hospital, or the boutique. Both the Van Dussens were obsessively concerned with the decoration of their lives and Willow found it impossible to talk to them. She didn't know the right kind of small talk or any of the names they, casually, dropped.

The cocktail party was before a barbecue for a neighborhood group that was going to the show. Willow and Drew attended out of politeness and planned to leave in an hour. Willow was now trailering Venture to the theater and then back to the stable after the first act to give them more time to themselves after the show.

There were no definite plans for tonight, but Willow assumed that, since Drew was always hungry after the play, they would go to Mio Castello for a late supper. Willow had been impressed by Drew's professionalism and the almost casual way he accepted his role as a celebrity. He did, however, have a routine and refused to eat anything but V8 juice and soda crackers during the two hours before a performance. An hour before curtain time, he closed out the world to concentrate on his warmup routine and put himself into the role he was playing. If he was disturbed during that hour, he was likely to snap or roar, even trigger what Mae and John called an annoying Drew-snit.

Within minutes of arriving at the party, Willow noticed Drew was in constant conversation with one person or another, most of them women, which left her with Ted Ramsey, a short, selfcentered stock broker and bachelor horse owner, who'd already found too many reasons to visit the stable at Sutherland Manor and pester her for advice about his two horses. Not knowing what else to do, she let Ted get her one of Mr. Van Dussen's locally acclaimed daiquiris before she sat on a redwood chaise beside the pool and watched Drew while she listened to Ted on a level of consciousness that undoubtedly made the man question her intelligence, or stability, when she kept forgetting what he was saying.

While Willow watched Drew, she began to recognize the man his father had talked about. He was casually aloof and outrageously charming, especially to Marjorie Van Dussen, the twentyeight-year-old daughter, who was visiting for the weekend and throwing everything she had at him with a familiarity that told Willow they knew each other well. Marjorie seemed very interested in renewing their relationship, while Drew coolly parried her flirts. He didn't encourage her; but then, he didn't discourage her either. He was clearly flattered by the tall, leggy blonde's advances, even enjoying them—particularly after Willow started giving him cutting glances.

When Drew drove Willow home in the used Mustang convertible that had replaced the Mercedes, he told her he needed to rush off. The blunt, almost patronizing, way he told her Marjorie was going to meet him at the theater for a backstage tour before the show twisted a barbed thorn into Willow's insecurity and made her snappy.

"She's more interested in a back-seat tour if you ask me." Willow jerked on the door handle and shoved the door open as soon as he stopped the car.

"I didn't ask you." Drew returned her sharpness, lunged across the car and grabbed her left wrist before she could get out. "I'm fully aware of what's on Marjorie Van Dussen's mind. It's been there for years."

"And you've never sampled it? Somehow I can't believe that." Willow pulled against his hold, but it was as strong and restraining as a manacle. "Let me go before you're late for your date."

"I've sampled it a number of times. I've sampled most of the local offerings. Get over it."

"I don't want to see it. Is that all right with you?"

"Believe me, you won't see it. There are some things I don't do in front of an audience."

"There are some things you better not do at all."

When Drew raised her hand to pull her toward him, Willow snaked her head forward and bit into the back of his hand. Startled by sudden pain, he bellowed in surprise and let go of her wrist long enough for her to jerk her arm away and bolt from the car. By the time Drew turned, released his seat belt and opened his door, she was in the house with her back against the closed door. Willow knew there was no way to keep him out if he really wanted to force the door, but she doubted he would go that far.

After a tense moment, the powerful engine roared his reaction. Willow spun to look out the window in time to see the car back out of the driveway and then accelerate ahead as spinning tires dug into the lane with a crunching whine that spewed geysers of gravel out behind the fleeing vehicle. Backing away from the window, Willow cringed at the sounds and the intensity of anger that caused them. The only other time she had made Drew really angry was the day he rode out to find her after she fell off KoKo. Compared to the flash of fury she glimpsed when he recoiled from the pain in his hand, that earlier anger was only a flicker; and, once again, Willow realized she had foolishly let her temper control her. It was something she usually regretted when she had time to think about it, as she did now; but when she was fired up, her mouth refused to stay closed, even when wisdom dictated it should.

Before the show, Willow saw Drew when he mounted Venture. They said nothing to each other; but then, they rarely did. He was locked in his role and she was occupied with the horse. She heard him sing from backstage. It lacked the power and fullness that could be felt in the house, but there was no difference in his voice. In spite of a tight fury crackling between them from an unfinished argument that had intensified while they were apart, he was doing his job and she was doing hers.

After the stagecoach scene, Willow took the horse from him in cold silence and concentrated on removing the padding from his hooves for the trailer ride home. When she sent Venture into the trailer and latched the door, she saw Drew stride toward her from the stage door. She hurried to the cab and slid inside before he reached her. His expression stayed locked in irritation until she tried to slam the door in his face. He caught the handle and yanked it open so hard she almost fell out of the truck.

Steadying herself by grasping the sill of the open window, Willow met a blaze of blue flame in a face hardened by contained fury. She glared back, expecting a roar of anger, but Drew was silent and visibly forced himself to control his temper. He slammed the door closed and strode away without so much as a word or gesture in answer to her defiance.

There was no sign of him after the show, or all-day Sunday. The earlier Sunday evening performance was no different than Saturday's, except he was harder and colder while she was short-tempered. He was locked in an *I won't apologize until you do snit*, while she was set in an *I won't budge from my injured martyrdom until I get an apology snit*.

Willow saw no reason to apologize. After all, he was the one who ran off after a woman who practically crawled all over him at a cocktail party.

After caring for Venture and parking the trailer and pickup truck beside the big horse van at the end of the stable's parking lot, Willow knew she could no longer live with distrust fermenting inside her. In the shower, she thought about what John had told her and decided that if she had to fight for what she wanted, this was the time to do it.

Willow's resolve and the dilemma of what she could actually do about it kept plaguing her until—sweeping away all objections—she threw on a clean pair of jeans and the toobig shirt of Byron's. Before she could reconsider, she ran to her station wagon, drove to the theater and parked in the employee's upper lot by the backstage loading door, where she could look down at the theater, the emptying main lot and the dark blue convertible parked near the lower-level backstage door.

Although Willow had no idea what she expected to see, or what she would do if she did see something, she fervently hoped she would see Drew leave the theater alone, get in his car and drive away. Then she would drive home slowly and find him at the cabin wondering where she was. She thought about telling him she went to see Ted. Since Drew had little good to say about Ted, some intimation in that direction would show him she was capable of a little getting even of her own.

The first part of her scenario was correct. Drew strolled out the stage door alone. By the time he reached his car, a white Lincoln crossed the lot and stopped, effectively trapping the Mustang between it and a low wall of railroad ties. With his departure blocked, Drew sat back against a fender of the white car with his hands in his pockets and waited for Marjorie to walk to him. They were too far away for Willow to see his facial expressions, but she could clearly see what was happening and read his body language.

When Marjorie stepped up to Drew and set elegantly tapered hands on his chest, he remained in the same relaxed stance. There was no change when she moved them to his shoulders, stroked them across strong muscles to his neck. He showed no reaction when she moved closer, slipped a leg forward until their thighs rubbed. Willow couldn't decide if the fingers Marjorie buried in his hair guided his head forward or if Drew made the move; but no matter how it happened, they were kissing—or, more accurately, he was being kissed since, so far, he hadn't moved. Willow knew Drew did not kiss without moving.

As if it were the most important thing in the world, Willow watched Drew's hands. While they stayed relaxed, still partway in his pockets, she hung on the edge of dilemma. When they tensed, she felt her chest compress. When he set them on his thighs, she stopped breathing and stared at hands that had held her, caressed her and introduced her to exciting pleasures. Even now, from across the narrow parking lot, Drew's hands were intensely expressive. They stiffened on his legs while Marjorie moved against him, worked her fingers into his back, moved them to his hips.

Willow's hands grasped the steering wheel while she willed him to stop playing a foolish game and shove Marjorie away. He seemed to draw back, then glance toward where she was parked. When he looked back at Marjorie, his hands moved with sudden possession, covered her slim back, rumpled the material of her dress. Willow's trance shattered like a smashed mirror. He may have once been disappointed in her refusal to fight back with spunk. Not this time. She planned to let him know exactly how she felt.

While Willow had conceded that she could accept a love affair without a commitment to forever, she would in no way accept a love affair that included more than two people—one male and one female. If he wanted Marjorie and/or Nicole, he could have them, but he was not going to have her at the same time.

In the ensuing moments, Willow was surprised by how calm she felt when she started the car and drove toward the embracing couple. She was even more amazed that her little, front wheel drive station wagon could churn up such a huge cloud of dust and gravel when she floored it in second gear and skimmed past the white Lincoln. In fact, there was so much dust that when she looked in her rear-view mirror before she turned out of the backlot onto the paved entrance road, the pair of them was totally engulfed by a swirling brown fog. Frowning, Willow wondered if she had created so much dust it would be impossible for Drew to recognize her car, but she doubted it.

Willow was barely in the house when the convertible crunched to a stop in the driveway. When the front door flew open, then slammed with a bang that made her wince, she stood her ground in the kitchen doorway and met the arcing flash of his eyes with the hard darkness of her own.

"What was the meaning of that asinine display?" His voice wasn't loud but it was powerful with a resonance that infuriated her.

"Just the fact you have to ask shows how ignorant you are."

"And how naive you are." He took two long strides toward her.

Willow pulled in a breath but refused to retreat. "Yes, I have been naive, but not anymore. I can tell when I'm not wanted."

"Not wanted!" His voice roared as he took another stride that put him right in front of her. "If that's what this is all about, I'll damn well show you how wanted you are."

When his left arm snapped around her waist, Willow gasped, then stiffened against the strength holding her. "You want me. You want her. You want anyone you can get. Well, you've had me, so let's end it at that."

"End it?" Drew recoiled with disbelief scarring his face. "Willow, you're being foolish."

"I believe in love, Drew, honest, open, one-to-one love. I will not be another woman to anyone. If you can't honor that, take your affections elsewhere. I'm not a selection from your wardrobe. I won't be hung in the closet while you wear someone else."

"She's hardly an ember next to you."

"I don't want her next to me. I don't want her in my life. I don't want you in my life."

"I don't believe that." His hand caught her chin and he clamped her against him so firmly her struggles were useless. "You want me. We want each other."

Willow wanted to shout at him, but a tight throat squashed her voice. The brilliance of his eyes sliced into her, weakening her until she felt she'd crumble if she didn't fight back. She stiffened, tried to push away from him but his arm was a vise, his hand a shackle. When she felt his mouth come down on hers, she twisted her head to bite at his lip. He was ready for it and strong fingers dug in at the hinge of her jaw and defeated the attempt by preventing her from closing her mouth.

"Oh, no, you don't." Drew's head jerked back and he relaxed his hold on her chin, slid his hand to the back of her head where it twisted in the tumble of her hair and tipped her head back. "You're not getting away with any tricks tonight. I don't like getting stamped on, switched, or bitten every time you lose your temper."

"Then let go of me." Willow swung to slap him, but the back of a hand swatted the inside of her forearm just hard enough to brush away the slap.

"I won't take it, so don't try. You've been spoiling for a fight since that party. Only there isn't anything to fight over. She's unimportant."

"I told you I didn't want to see it."

"Then why did you come looking?"

"I... I was looking for Ted—"

"Don't lie to me. And please, don't insult my opinion of you." Drew stroked his hand on her throat while his stare burned into her like a laser beam. "You have as much interest in Ted Ramsey as you do in a night in the manure pile."

"You went chasing after someone else, not me."

"Did I?" His voice was a cold blade slicing through the heat of her anger. "Or was I sent after someone else?"

"She wiggled her ass and you took off after it."

"You not only accused me of planning to cheat on you, you dared me to do it. When I didn't fight back, you let your distrust stick its nose where it didn't belong. That was enough to make me mad. Your stunt with the gravel pissed me off."

"Go away before I piss you off again."

"I'm not running out on any more of your dares. You just come up with bigger ones."

The way he kept hammering her with an accusation Willow refused to accept disoriented her. "I didn't dare you."

"Shall I quote? 'There are some things you better not do at all.' That's not a dare? I don't take orders like that. Slamming the truck door on me came close to starting a fight that would have been a public spectacle. And your parking lot exit was a clear dare. Things like that tell me you want a reaction."

"You're not going to make me want you." Willow shouted her challenge without thinking and struck out so suddenly Drew only had time to intercept the slap by raising his arm. Her hand cracked on his forearm and the hardness of his tensed muscle left her palm stinging.

Drew recoiled then shuddered as Jack snapped his head up and a thinner, sharper voice answered her challenge. "I'll accept that dare."

"You'll lose it."

"Keep daring, Willow. You're very good at it." He backed her into the kitchen, closed his right hand on the front of her shirt and yanked down. The buttons popped onto the floor before the shirt slid up her raised arms and sailed over her head. Before she could react with more than a gasp, he pressed her against the end of a row of kitchen cabinets. The hand in her hair twisted harder, arched her backwards over the end of the cabinet until her elbows were pinned to the Formica with her breasts thrust up at him. His right hand unsnapped her jeans and aided by her struggles, stripped them to her ankles.

"What am I not going to do?" His voice was hard and taunting.

"You're not going to seduce me and make it all right with your charms." Willow tried to kick free of the jeans and shoes that hobbled her, but they continued to cling to her feet with the inside-out garment flapping harmlessly against his legs.

"I don't feel charming. I don't even feel like seducing you. I just want to take you, kicking and hollering if I have to."

"You may have to."

"You can't stop daring, can you?"

"I'm not daring!" She tried to jerk away from him with an effort that took all her strength, left her out of breath and flushed with heat.

"I hear dare and dares don't stop me. They excite me. You are mine, Willow, and I won't let your irrational jealousy destroy that."

When Willow looked up at him, she was awed by the harsh look on his face. She had not only touched his vulnerability, she'd bared it. The portrait was exposed and some of it was raw from abused emotions. She had reached a part of Drew she didn't know. She felt the hard, commanding authority she'd sensed in his father. It frightened her; and yet, with a flash of clear insight, Willow knew that if she ever wanted Drew to love her without restrictions, she had to shatter his control, reach the primal center of his emotions and take them. She had to be the one woman who could match his possessive intensity and continue to love him.

In spite of the pounding blood of arousal, a chill shivered through her as he slowly raked his eyes down her body and his tongue and teeth played with his lips. It felt as if he halted time and intensified the static tension while he studied every detail of her exposed and forcefully offered body. The touch of his gaze made her tremble and squirm with an impatience that was half expectation, half dread. She had no idea what he would do and the wait made her tremble with arousal.

A firm hand touched her hip in a painless touch that felt like a searing brand. She winced and her flesh flamed. He rubbed his palm across her stretched belly, down her thigh; his mouth lowered to a breast. At the same time, his hand slipped to the inside of her thigh, forced her legs apart so he could sense the heat of an arousal that flamed beyond her control.

Stepping back, he grabbed her wrist and strode from the kitchen, dragging her behind him without a care for the trailing jeans that made her stumble after him. In the bedroom, he threw her onto the bed. She tried to roll away, but he grabbed her by an ankle and dragged her back to him. Rough hands stripped off pants and shoes before he moved onto the bed and clamped her between his knees.

When hard lips crushed down on hers and his tongue invaded her mouth, Willow understood how passion could be love and hate at the same time. She wanted him with an aching fervor that made her hate him for defeating her resistance and exposing a helpless lust for his possessive dominance. At the same time, she wanted to be his woman, his only woman. Forever.

Aroused by the heat of her anger and his passion, Willow grasped his shirt and peeled it off over his head. Her nails raked on his back and they rolled together in a grappling embrace. There was no sanity left, only a demanding need for his volcanic lust.

"What do you want, Willow?" He pushed away, holding her at arm's length.

"Damn you." She reached for him, but he rolled to his feet and backed away from the bed. "I want you."

"How much?" He taunted as he backed away. "Enough to fight for it?" He was too slow and her hand caught the loosened end of his leather belt.

"Enough to know how to get what I want." She yanked him to where she knelt on the bed and jerked open the buckle. When he recoiled, she stripped the belt out of his jeans, grabbed both ends and flipped it over his head. Holding, the strip of leather across the back of his neck she pulled his head down for a kiss.

His hands closed on her fists, pried them off the belt, snaked it around her waist and used the encircling strap to pull her against him as he rolled her across the bed. He grasped her upper arms and held her away for a split second while his eyes knifed into hers. His hand slid to the back of her neck and pulled her mouth to his.

"Kiss me, woman, take off my pants and make me love it."

Willow moved her hands and mouth down his chest and hard muscles to the waistband of his jeans. She opened the button and zipper, gradually inched down jeans and briefs, caressed each new area of exposure until he groaned with a desire that set him on fire. Smirking at his arrogant acceptance of victory, Willow tossed his clothes on the floor, slid cool hands up his legs. She paused for a long moment to taste, caress and tease until he was a sealed boiler, slowly building up pressure she knew would blow apart with action and strong possession.

Willow reveled in the blasts of passionate action that sated her craving for challenge and excitement; but this time, she was reluctant to give in to him. He may think he'd mastered her without losing his control, but he was going to discover her spunk wasn't all that easy to conquer. When it came to sex and lust, she'd learned to enjoy his love games; but more than that, she understood his need for challenge and was determined to become a competent opponent, maybe even the best opponent he'd ever challenged—the one he wanted for life.

"I'm willing to fight you, Drew." Willow pushed away from him and knelt back to sit on his legs with her hands resting gently on his thighs. "But you don't seem to be fighting anymore." Her fingers moved on him with tantalizing touches and then twisted the hair on his legs until he jerked from the sharp pulls.

"Ow!" He shuddered then stiffened, snapped his head up with a dumbfounded look on his face and snatched at her hands, but she jerked them away.

"I'm not your helpless wench." Willow's voice rose to a shout as she let out an anger that flared whenever she remembered the way he clasped Marjorie to him and answered her kiss. "I want you, Drew, but I'm still mad enough to want to pound on you!"

"Then go for it, damn it!" He grabbed her by the waist with strong hands and lifted her above him until she was infuriated. "Throw a good tantrum while you're at it." He tossed her above him, caught her with spread hands, then held her away from him while she flailed at him. "Just get it over with."

"Damn you, Drew. You're as bossy as my brothers."

"You said they raised you tough." He smirked. "I think they used kid gloves."

"Let go of me."

When Willow planted a knee on hard abdominal muscles, Drew lost the last shred of control in the internal battle of wills over his identity and reacted with startling strength. He arched up under her like a bucking horse and threw her away from him, which made her so mad she could no longer reason with herself. When he rose to his knees, Willow saw the belt lying on the bed, grabbed it and swung it with the same instant flash of wild impulse that had made her smack him with the switch, bite his hand. Only this time she was horrified the instant she heard the tongue of leather crack against his side and snake around to bite into his back. Jack reared back in stunned pain, dropped his head forward, then shuddered and snapped his head up as a sudden flash of triumph blotted out his control.

A strong hand grasped Willow's wrist, yanked her to him. She thrashed and kicked as she tried to keep Drew from taking the belt from her clenched fist. When he broke her grip with a quick wrist pinch and wrenched the strap out of her hand, Willow thought her pounding heart would choke off her breath. He jerked his arm back while she yanked against his hold. The next instant hung in a block of suspended time. She wanted to scream or fight to break away, but she was paralyzed by the horror of what she'd done.

When Drew's arm snapped forward, Willow held her breath. His body stiffened as he fought for control. Then he shuddered and the belt flew across the room, crashed against the closed door. Willow was heady with relief when he clamped his right hand on the back of her neck and fell forward trapping her under him. She threw away rationality as his passion ignited hers and pulled her into the seething mouth of the volcano.

If there was pain, it was lost in the wildness of lovemaking as they fought to devour each other, outlove each other, satisfy deep desires for each other. All Willow sensed was a twisting, arching exhilaration of heat that carried her crashing over the top of her emotional peak. She clamped herself to him and rode with the power of his thrusts until he broke free and flipped her onto her knees.

Drew satisfied the last of his lust by grabbing her hips and plunging into her with a power that drove her into grasping hands, rocked her forward and backwards until, with simultaneous shouts of release, they collapsed on the bed. Enervation and the pleasure of complete satiation soaked into their senses. When he was able to breathe steadily, Drew rolled beside her so she could move into his embrace and hold him with clasped arms and legs that linked their bodies together in exhaustion.

Caressing hands rubbed on her back, hips and buttocks. He kissed her hair, her closed eyelids, her lips. "I'm sorry, Willow. I lost hold. I went crazy." His voice was uneven, deep and rough with emotion.

"I know," she answered in a soft voice while she reached up and laid a gentle hand on his face. "It was great."

"It was what?" Drew pushed up on his elbow and peered down at her. "I was afraid I hurt you?"

"What do you think I am, a breakable wimp?" She wrinkled her nose in a teasing face. "I was raised tough, remember?"

Drew flopped onto his back and stared at the ceiling. "I used to hear Gino rape my mother. I wanted to stop him, but he always locked my door. I swore I'd never do anything like that."

"You didn't rape me, Drew. I never said no because I knew that would end it and I wanted to find your volcano." Trailing her fingers up his chest, she caught his beard and tugged until he rolled onto his side and kissed her. "Drew, I don't want to do battle with a volcano every time I make love to you, but it has an awesome power to it. It made me feel we were fused by a force greater than both of us."

"You may be more right about that than you think." He was puzzled by what he'd just said then let his denial shrug it off and smiled while his fingers played with Willow's jumbled hair. "We did the impossible. We created an energy force greater than the sum of its parts."

"I don't know. There's a lot of love in me, Drew. I think there is in you, too. Why did you even think you could be like Gino? He sounds like a selfish brute."

"I'm more afraid of being like my mother." He sighed at her questioning expression. "Gino was an abusive pig, but she was the one who had no control of her violence. People have tried to convince me her instability was from alcohol and drugs, but to me she was insane. It's part of me, too."

Willow laughed and shook her head. "If you're insane, my whole family is insane. Sometimes, it sounds as if we want to kill each other. We don't. We love each other and are only angry and loud, not insane. You never do more than give it back and you don't overdo that. I'm the one who needs to apologize. I wasn't thinking when I hit you with that belt. It was a terrible thing to do." Blushing, Willow leaned over and kissed the red mark on his side.

"Actually, it was well timed. I was having a hell of a control issue with myself and it snapped it right out of me. But I think it was a little more stimulation than I needed."

"I'm not always so resourceful." Willow giggled and wriggled against him.

He gave her a skeptical look and kissed her on the end of the nose. "Somehow I find that hard to believe. Your contrition has a short life."

"You made me mad. Your meaningless flirtation was a nasty kick. And why, why, did you kiss her back?"

"I just did." He looked repentant and then confused. "It wasn't smart, and I'm sorry I did it that way. Please, don't ruin the truce."

Willow purred in contentment while she snuggled her back against his chest. He kissed her on the neck and then slipped a gentle hand up her leg and body, caressed her breasts and held her in secure encircling arms.

"I do love you, Willow. You make me feel good." He yawned. "And very, very sleepy."

"I love you, too."

"Uhhuh." He closed his eyes and smiled with his boyish look of innocence.

Willow knew he was already asleep. The way Drew could instantly fall asleep, or wake up, amazed her. She always had to sort her thoughts, get herself comfortable and drift into deep slumber. Tonight, she approached sleep with confused feelings. He said he loved her, and she felt the strength of his love. It made her glow with soft pleasure—except for a twinge of uneasiness over the way he cut her off about Marjorie and called tonight a truce.

Willow remembered Andy saying Drew could evade any question but didn't intentionally lie. It told her that if she wanted the truth about Marjorie or Nicole, the only way she could get it would be to ask him directly and force it into the open where she could confront it. Her mistrust was a spreading infection she knew she had to resolve before it contaminated their love.

Chapter Twenty-One

Exhausted, with Drew's arms cradling her in warm strength, Willow slept soundly, but she woke up troubled because he had, once again, covered her insecurity with the excitement of lovemaking and avoided talking about the most important issue—what had actually happened with Marjorie. To Drew, it was no longer an issue. It was a big issue to Willow, and she refused to push it out of the way.

"Drew, we have to talk about this weekend." Willow sat on the bed in shorts and a Tshirt, tying her running shoes while he did stretches by the window.

"What is there to talk about?" He straightened and gave her a perplexed look. "It was a misunderstanding blown out of proportion by my spoiled pride and your jealousy."

"There's a lot to talk about. Me, you, Marjorie, Nicole, us."

"You, me, and us are the only ones we need to talk about. Nicole isn't part of it. Marjorie is a dead issue." He looked away and stretched down to touch the floor between his feet.

"She was doing a good job of rising from the dead when I last saw her."

"You're at it again." Drew's fist thumped the top of the high dresser before he spun and drilled her with arcing blue eyes. "Your caustic accusations fire my temper faster than a torch in tinder. All right, I let her flirt and try to revive an old issue. I don't remember giving you or anyone else exclusive rights to me."

"That depends on what rights we're talking about." Willow faced his arrogance with her hands gripping the edge of the bed.

"Willow, I don't need this hassle."

"But I do. I know I've acted like a starry-eyed teenager in the throes of a first love, but I'm not so bedazzled anymore. I learned more about you. It awed me and made me see I'm no more than an unimportant interlude in your life—" Willow held up her hand to stop him from saying anything and watched his expression cloud in protest. "Please, let me finish. I was willing to accept that. I can see there is no place for me if you decide to take advantage of the opportunity in Genoa. In view of your career, you would be a fool not to, and I can understand why you don't want to make any long-range commitments. But there is one commitment I do insist on." When his eyes slid away, Willow was surprised by the defensive crust that hardened his features.

"I get your drift." With his voice edged by testiness, Drew looked anxious to get away from her, or at least out of the conversation. "You're still on your jealousy kick."

"I need honesty. I can't live with non-answers about something like that. If you can't be honest and faithful, I can't let it continue. It is love to me and love is faithful."

"What am I supposed to do play true confessions, spill out all my past sins and repent?"

"I want the full truth about Marjorie because it eats at me."

After a long, sober look, he said—coldly, factually, "We went out drinking after the play Saturday night and ended up in a casino hotel in Atlantic City."

His answer drove a tombcold spike into the pit of Willow's feelings, but she clenched her jaw and asked what she had to know. "Did you sleep with her?"

"I woke up with her."

"Did you make love to her?"

"She says I did. I don't remember."

"How could you not remember?"

"Because..." He pulled his eyes away, looked past her at the open door. "I drank too much. It was lousy, Willow. It had no more meaning than a casual social obligation."

"I don't care *how* it was, only *that* it was." Painful tears welled up from deep inside her. She sat very still and looked down at hands that twisted in her lap.

"I told her I wasn't interested in a repeat last night, and then..." Drew paused, pulled in a steadying breath. "...I saw your car and stupidly gave you the finger by kissing her. You can stop worrying about her. After you left, I told her if she didn't move her car, I'd take it and she could walk home. I'm dog meat to her right now."

Willow remained silent. She sensed him step forward before she felt his hand caress her face, touch the wet wash of her tears, but she couldn't look at his eyes. She was afraid they would be hard or cynical.

"Willow? Willow, stop it." He dropped to one knee in front of her, cradled her face in gentle hands. "It meant nothing. I really don't remember it."

"Just leave me alone. I don't want you here right now." When she met his eyes, he looked hurt and confused. He also looked agitated and unsure, like a colt ready to spook at any sudden movement. "Please, go away."

When his hands slid from her face, she felt cold. When he crossed the room, she held her breath. When the front door closed, she started to shake. Pain broke loose in catching spasms. It was grief she was unable to explain and a deep hurt that engulfed her. Drawing her knees up in front of her, she lifted clasped hands to her mouth and bit into the knuckle pressed against her teeth. Her body rocked with the rhythm of her sobs. Willow told herself she could stop loving him. It was futile. She loved him so deeply she felt ripped open.

After a shower and breakfast that had no taste, Willow felt she could face Drew. She was bruised but had absorbed the worst of the hurt. The blue Mustang was still in her driveway, but Drew wasn't at the barn. When she took KoKo for a ride, she saw him by the maintenance barn, sitting against the tailgate of the pickup, handing tools to the Scotsman, who was lying halfunder a huge mower deck. When she came back from her ride, John was mowing the lawn and the white Lincoln was parked by the manor house. Drew's car was no longer in her driveway.

On an impulse, Willow called her mother from the barn phone at one o'clock on a Monday afternoon and had nothing to say. No one else was at the house, so she pumped her mother for news in the hope it would take her mind away from Drew. She learned that Byron would be at the farm until midJuly when he left for Italy; Gwen was working toward her R.N. by interning in a hospital outside Des Moines; Beth had a part-time summer job at Cole's Dairy Ice Cream Parlor; greataunt Edna died at the nursing home last night and the funeral would be Wednesday; Matt's graduation party would be next Saturday at the annual family reunion.

Willow never said anything was wrong, but it was unusual for her to call during the day and she sensed her mother knew better. She tried to cover it by talking about the show and Drew's career, then suggested her mother should talk to Byron since he probably knew more about Drew's musical accomplishments than she did. Talking about Drew made her impatient to get off the phone. She used the excuse of time and money to end the call.

After the phone clicked off in Iowa, Willow knew she should have said more, but her mother's voice had been a serene harbor she was reluctant to trouble and it had refused to come out. She knew her mother would understand if she could really talk to her. Unfortunately, her mother could keep very little from her father, who wouldn't understand at all.

Lloyd Roberts had properly courted Maureen O'Reilly in high school and married her at nineteen. As far as Willow knew, he'd never had desires toward another woman during the thirtythree years of their marriage. He probably never had anything to do with another woman during his entire life and had no complaints about it. Within her family, divorces and affairs were scandals—or at least embarrassments nobody openly talked about. Failed marriages were exceptions, not the rule. Infidelity was a moral wrong committed by dishonest people.

Willow was still sitting at the desk staring at the phone when Drew walked into the office and closed the door with a quiet, but purposeful, thump. When she looked at him, she wanted to feel repelled. She should have known it was impossible. He was as magnetically attractive as ever. There was no slackening of Willow's physical desire for Drew. His body still excited her, but she preferred to keep her gaze away from his face. She dreaded meeting eyes that could pull her into the vastness of their depths and draw out her most private feelings.

Drew stepped past the desk and swiveled her chair to face him. When he set his hands on the chair's arms and leaned toward her, Willow pulled in a steadying breath and shrank back as far as she could but his eyes were unavoidable. They captured her feelings, held her stare with compelling intensity.

"Do you really want to end a truly fantastic love affair over a foolish one-night stand?"

The deep roll of his voice was as entrancing as his eyes. It was carefully modulated with resonant power but little volume. It was tenderness that expressed humility without being penitent. He'd been so right when he told her he knew how to get people to offer what he wanted. Willow wanted to offer an apology and go back to the fantasy world of last week, when their love had been an emotional high. But she resisted. Willow knew how she had to answer him. It was not with capitulation.

"I don't want it to end at all, but if it's going to continue, we need to make a few promises and believe in them."

"It's over. I told her that."

"I noticed how well it worked."

Drew stood with a huffing scowl and sat against the corner of the desk. "She came to see my grandmother, who invited her for lunch out of politeness. Knowing Gram, I suspect she wanted to get a feel of things and watch me suffer."

"I suspect Marjorie was more interested in sharing dog meat with Nemo."

"Obviously she doesn't discourage easily. But I'm not interested. It won't happen again."

"With her, or with anyone?" Willow watched her question hit. His eyes shifted away; his face clouded. "Drew, I don't ever again want to feel the way I did this morning. I have a strong faith in my creed of love. I felt as if it had been torn out of me."

"What do you want, a pledge of lifelong fidelity? That sounds like marriage to me."

"No." Her answer was soft. "I want you to promise I'll be the only one as long as it lasts. If you want someone else, you're free to do it. You just won't have me anymore."

Drew stared at the pictures on the wall behind the desk while he chewed on her words. When he looked back, there was sincerity in his expression as well as the chagrined, spoiled boy.

"It should be an easy thing to promise, shouldn't it?"

"No, Drew, not for you. You already told me you can't make up lies or promise what you don't feel, which is why I know I can believe you. I love you and I'm willing to give myself to you but I need more of you in return."

Drew stood with his hands thrust into his pockets and stared through their ghostly reflections in the glass wall at the brightness of sunshine beyond the open door at the far end of the arena. "You're a hard woman."

"No, but I'm a stubborn one when I'm backed against a wall."

"Why do I feel you're asking for more than you say you are?"

"I don't know." She focused on his pale reflection. He remained silent. "I just talked to my mother in Iowa. My Aunt Edna died last night. I'm going to ask Mae if I can fly home for the funeral." The idea had been a shadow in her mind until she said it. Now she knew it was exactly what she needed to do. "Dad will reimburse me for the ticket."

"You're going to Iowa?" Drew whirled to face her, clearly stunned by her decision. "When?"

"Tomorrow. The funeral is Wednesday."

"When will you be back?"

"I want to stay for Matt's graduation party Saturday—and a little longer." She stood abruptly and took long strides toward the door, but he moved faster and caught her by the shoulders. His hands were firm restraints that made her long for their caresses and possessive touches.

"Is that it? You're walking out of my life?"

"That's up to you, isn't it?"

"I want you. I don't want anyone else. Willow, you can't make me believe you don't feel as desperate for me as I do for you."

"No, I can't. You've proved that again and again."

"Isn't that enough? We need each other."

"It isn't enough for me."

Drew looked fragile as he searched her face, looked for a softness she refused to show. Willow was unsure where she found the strength; but somehow, she was able to remain rigid and harden against him.

Recoiling, Drew dropped his hands and stepped back. "You remind me of my father—rock ass stubborn. Are you two in a conspiracy?"

"No. In fact, I suspect we're in opposition."

"You're not. He's the one who blew it all up with his wise cracks about you being the marrying kind. Then he spent the rest of his visit making subtle comments about how he wished he'd met someone like you twenty years ago. Well, *he* can marry you if he thinks you're so goddamn great!" Drew pivoted and strode from the office in a way that snatched away Willow's chance at a dramatic exit by stealing the scene with a finality that bordered on melodrama.

Willow stood still for a moment, while she sorted things in her mind. She was unwilling to accept that Andy wanted their romance to succeed. His subtle remarks were undoubtedly meant to do exactly what they had—make Drew see her as a threat to his freedom. Since she was reluctant to run into Drew, who was still in the barn, she sat at the desk and dug in a drawer for a phone book. She was looking for a travel agency she could call about a flight home when the phone rang.

"Sutherland Stable," Willow answered automatically then scowled at a voice thick with a French accent. "Just a moment." She dropped the receiver on the desk before she crossed the office to shout into the barn for Drew.

Willow understood none of the French conversation, but there seemed to be a lot of emotional inflection in Drew's voice. When he hung up, he looked upset and preoccupied, but he was gone so fast she was left with a numb feeling. He hardly glanced at her after he let Knight out in the pasture and hurried to his car. At that moment, Willow knew she was going to Iowa as fast as she could—maybe for good.

❖

When they left for the airport the next morning, Willow asked John to stop at the main house so she could say goodbye to Mae and leave the journal she kept on the horses she rode. She found Mae on the terrace by the rose garden and set the notebook on a glasstopped table beside a glass of iced tea. "It's up to date and thank you for letting me go home like this."

When Willow pulled her hand away, Mae caught it with a grip she couldn't break. "When will you be back?" The hand tightened when Willow tried to pull back. "It's only attainable if you don't quit."

"I need to think about it. I need to talk to someone at home."

"His behavior is outrageous."

"He's protecting his freedom. I fell in love. He didn't. You tried to warn me."

"You were different. I think you still are. Don't run away, Willow."

"I have to come back. I'm leaving a lot of me here."

"More than you realize."

"Thank you, Mae." Bending suddenly, Willow hugged the woman and kissed her on the cheek before she turned and hurried away.

Turning from where John waited in the circular front drive, Willow dug in her purse for a tissue to scrub the salty wetness off her face. When she blew her nose, something beside the gazebo in the English garden caught her attention. She looked more closely and saw Drew standing by the reflecting pool with his arms around Nicole, his face buried in tousled curls. When his hand rubbed on the woman's narrow back, hurt clutched at Willow's throat and twisted like a coil of barbed wire. Biting down on a flood of emotion, she pivoted and marched to the car. Numb shock, too cold for tears, clamped around her.

When Willow slipped into the front seat beside John, she started to shake; her breath caught in spastic convulsions. A large, sunbronzed hand closed over hers and held it while the car swept around the circular drive and headed for the bridge at the end of the exclamation point lake. When an iceberg in her chest broke apart in a gush of tears, John released her hand and pulled a red and white bandana out of his pocket.

"I don't think all those tears are for your dear departed Aunt."

Willow was unable to answer, could only shake her head in response.

"He just up and ran from you, didn't he?"

"Uhhuh." She controlled the sobs and blew her nose again.

"He clammed up on me when I told him he wouldn't know spring water from a cesspool if he was swimming in it."

"He's just proving you right by refusing to give up his freedom. He never talked about anything that could be taken as a commitment. But I had to, John. He can't be caged and I can't be uncommitted. I want simple things. I want love to be what it's been to my family. That's weddings and children—and a lot of anniversaries."

"Now that isn't what Drew's seen, is it?"

"What do you mean?" Willow looked across the car at his round face with its full grey sideburns and thick, snowy eyebrows.

"The nearest Drew has been to a long-term marriage was his grandparents, and that became a sham when Andy was a lad. The old man was eighteen years older than Mae and about as bitter a man as I ever met. He wouldn't hear about divorce, so Mae agreed to stay married in name as long as he stopped trying to break the trust that gave her ownership of the stable and Sutherland Manor. He never forgave Andy for his marriage, or for Drew."

"Drew said it was hard on his father."

John thought for a moment before he said, "The first time Drew was here and threw a childish temper tantrum, the old man said, 'You should have done what I told you and had that bastard aborted when you had the chance.' Andy was so incensed I thought he was going to kill him, but he controlled himself, turned his back on his father, and rarely spoke to him again. A year later, when Andy discovered his father had been paying Carlotta and Gino to keep Drew away from him, the rift became irreparable."

"That man was sick."

"He had no compassion. When Andy defied him, he saw it as just punishment."

"He didn't even love his son?"

"Giles Sutherland possessed. He loved neither his son nor his wife. I'm sure Drew sensed it. He has always been able to sense more than he understood. Could be you're asking him for something he's a wee bit afraid of."

"I can't imagine being afraid of love."

"It's not the love he's afraid of. It's an inner distrust of his ability to cope with the risk and responsibility that goes with commitment."

"I tried to be happy with sex, but the alone times were too empty." Willow sniffed when the tears started again. "I always felt he was shielding himself from me—like there was a big piece of him I couldn't reach."

"I can try to talk to him again. Or, if you'd rather, I can give in to my strongest desire and punch him out." John winked and gave her a cajoling smile. "There was a time I paddled his britches good. Maybe I could get away with one good punch now."

"Just talk to him, John. It's what you're best at." Willow gave him a partial smile. "I'm afraid I'll have six brothers and a father wanting to punch him out."

Jean Kehoe Van Dyke

❖

Willow saw him as soon as she entered the terminal. At sixfour, Byron was tall enough to stick up in a crowd and there was no mistaking the thatch of windblown auburn hair or the full moustaches drooping beside his wide mouth. Her brother wore faded jeans and a worn shirt that meant home and the farm, not culture and academia. She felt a swell of emotion crest in her when she ran to the security of strong arms, breathed in the summer aroma of freshly cut hay mixed with grease, man and Lava soap.

"Oh, Byron, hold me tight." She pressed her face against his chest and hugged her arms around him while tears broke loose again. Strong, sensitive hands rubbed her back as Byron retreated from the crowd into a relatively private corner.

"I knew something was wrong, Elf. Since you haven't seen greataunt Edna in six years and she hasn't known anyone for almost three, it didn't make sense you would fly home for her funeral."

"Mae Sutherland doesn't know that." Willow relaxed her hold and stepped back to accept the red bandannaprint handkerchief her brother offered. She blew her nose then wrinkled her face and scowled at him. "It smells like stale sweat."

"We're haying and it's hot out there."

"I thought you always planned an important seminar or left for Europe at hay season."

"My best laid plans *gang aft agley* this year." Byron slid an arm around her shoulders and headed her toward the baggage claim. "I have a concert scheduled for early July and already subleased my apartment in Ames for the summer semester. I needed somewhere to live."

"And Dad won't house you if you don't work."

"Brilliant observation."

At the baggage claim, Byron took Willow's luggage stub and sent her out to flag down Todd, who was supposed to be hovering somewhere outside the terminal in his old blue pickup. Todd must have seen her first and pulled into a loading lane when she spotted him striding toward her.

Todd was four inches shorter than Byron, but he made up for it in the breadth of his burly, muscular body. He had huge hands that could tear a piano apart but never play it. Todd's jeans were greasespotted with a back pocket flapping loose. The sleeves were ripped out of his faded, olive-green Tshirt. He'd made less of an effort to clean the farm off him than Byron, which was no surprise to Willow. Of all her brothers, Todd was the least concerned about anything except the farm. Todd's muscles weren't sharply defined and sculptured the way Drew's were. They were massive knots of power. His dark brown hair was a tangle of loose curls on a round head with broad features and a wide mouth. He had high O'Reilly cheekbones and jade green eyes. The rest was all Roberts—stout, powerful and fierce-tempered.

When Todd stopped in front of her, he gave her a serious, scrutinizing look that made her laugh.

"What are you looking at?" Willow asked when he gave her a bear hug that threatened to cut off her breath.

"Lost some hair and weight." Todd proclaimed in a deep voice that thrummed out of his chest like a plucked bass string. "You look good."

"As a matter of fact, I've gained five pounds. It's just distributed better. I ride a lot, and I've been running for the last few weeks. I'm almost up to three miles."

"Got any luggage?" He looked around her.

"Byron's getting it."

"Jump in so we can take off when he gets here." He turned toward the front of the truck.

"I was waiting for you to open the door." Willow smirked when he swiveled his head and stared at her.

"Something wrong with your arms?" Todd scoffed as he marched toward the driver's door.

"I got used to gentlemanly manners in Pennsylvania."

"Well, this is Iowa. I'm your brother, not a gentleman."

"That is probably one of the truest statements you've ever made." Willow opened the door, hopped up into the high cab of the four-wheel drive truck and slid next to Todd when Byron sauntered out of the terminal.

After setting Willow's suitcase in the truck bed, just behind the cab, Byron swung into the truck and thumped the door closed while Todd pulled away from the curb. Squirming his long arm out from between them, Byron laid it across the back of the seat to let Willow move closer to him and avoid Todd's elbow as he shifted with the subtle movements of King Kong.

"So how did you find out what your Andrew Sutherland does in Europe?" Byron asked.

"I went to a musical with his father and grandmother. Drew was in it. I read about his background at the theater. It was a jolt, especially when I realized you knew. But why didn't you tell me?"

"Your letter implied he didn't want you to know. I figured he had his reasons and left it at that."

"But why did you say Placido move over? Drew won't take his place. Placido Domingo is a tenor."

"How many other operatic names would you recognize?"

"Pavarotti?"

"He's a tenor, too. But if you want to get technical, Domingo started as a baritone. Andrew Sutherland is an Italian baritone, which is lighter than a German baritone. However, he has a better than two octave range, which makes him extremely versatile."

"Mae said Drew is a Verdi baritone."

"Yes, and in that light, the predecessor I would give him is Piero Cappuccilli."

"You're right, I've never heard of him. I don't even know what Verdi baritone means."

"It means his range and skills are suited to Verdi's operas."

"Like *Rigoletto*?" she asked with a wrinkled nose. "He wants to do *Rigoletto*. I think it's an awful story."

"It's a difficult role, both musically and physically. The character, Rigoletto, is a twisted, hunchbacked jester. It's damn hard to sing in that position and the old pillow in a shirt trick is unconvincing."

"I'd rather he did romantic leads."

"They are usually tenors." Byron laughed at her chagrined face. "I imagine Drew sees Verdi's larger roles, such as Rigoletto, which is the epitome of perfection to a baritone, as a goal. The tessitura, which translates to texture, but really means range, reaches from G or A below the stave, which is in the bass register, to A flat and A natural in the tenor register—"

"I'm really stupid about opera, Byron." Willow snapped in frustration to shut him up, then cocked her head and asked, "How did you know about him?"

"Nobody in the classical music world who was in Italy last summer could not know about him. When Vittorio Luciani invites someone to train under him, it is big news. Luciani takes many students, who pay through the nose. Most of them last about a month before he throws them out. He only takes the exceptional as protégés. Your Drew is the first American he's ever taken an interest in, and I can see why. Andrew Sutherland's voice belongs on Mount Olympus."

"You've heard him sing?"

"In Bologna last August. He did some Rossini for a recital."

"I've never heard him sing opera," Willow admitted, then amended, "except once when we were doing dishes and I bugged him about it. He let loose with some crazy thing about a Figaro that was awesome. I don't know how to judge it, but my cabin wasn't big enough."

Willow remembered the simple scene when Drew flourished a dishtowel and burst into a fragment of an aria that overfilled her kitchen and made her step back in astonishment. It had all dissolved in laughter and the memory twisted the hurt again. She hardly heard what Byron was saying.

"That was undoubtedly 'Largo al factotum,' Figaro's first aria from Rossini's *Barber of Seville*. If it was, I've heard it. He's very good."

"That's what he said about you when he heard you play *Rhapsody in Blue*."

Byron looked startled then smiled smugly. "I think I might like him after all."

"He doesn't talk about his singing much." Willow shrugged while she fumbled John's cleaner bandanna out of her purse. "And I don't want to talk about him right now." When the tears started again, she felt Byron's arm move from the back of the seat and slide around her shoulders. "He tore a hole in me, Byron."

"Did I give you some bad advice?"

"I acted on my own before I got any advice from you. I let myself fall so much in love I couldn't help believing he felt the same way. I didn't expect he was going to rush out and buy an engagement ring, but I didn't expect him to have an argument with me then run off to a hotel with someone else and shrug it off as unimportant."

"Was this the French woman you mentioned in your letter?" Byron asked with more than a little confusion.

"No. I never quite knew what was between Drew and Nicole. She just hovered in the background. I thought he'd broken up with her, but I guess he was with her last night. It makes me wonder how he spent other nights he wasn't staying with me."

It wasn't until the truck jolted to a stop at a traffic light that Willow thought to look across the cab to where Todd was glowering at her.

"What does, *staying with you,* mean?" Todd growled.

"For God's sake, Todd, stop looking like a raging gorilla. I'm not your virginal little sister anymore."

"That's a nice piece of news. Is it gentlemanly manners to sleep with any girl handy? What did this bastard do? Seduce away your morals along with your virginity? How long you been sleeping with him? Only been two months for shit sake."

"Has it really been so little time?" Stunned, Willow thought about his pronouncement. "Nine weeks, but I feel I've known him so much longer. How could he become so complete a part of my life in so short a time?"

"Hey, Todd." Byron reached over and punched a fist on his brother's arm. "The light's been green a while. If you don't move, someone is going to get angry."

"Someone is angry. Me!" When Todd stomped on the accelerator, the truck squealed across the intersection, just as the light changed to red and horns blared around them. "If I get my hands on that son of a bitch, he'll need a body cast and a new face."

"Why do you always try to solve every problem with brute force?" Willow shouted.

"It's not a solution. It's a fucking payback."

"He hurt me, not you."

"Yeah, well, I take it personally when the son of a bitch did it to my sister."

Willow looked up at Byron, who made a comical face and winked at her. Both of them knew it was useless to argue when Todd was juiced up with macho outrage. It was similar to reasoning with an enraged bull.

Chapter Twenty-Two

Three days after Willow went to Iowa, Andy returned from his trip to Vegas. His mother was on the terrace reading and Drew was hacking at an overgrown bush with a pair of hedge shears. The glowering scowl on his son's face gave Andy the impression Drew was trying to mutilate the bush instead of beautify it.

"Hello, Mother." He leaned down and kissed Mae's cheek before he nodded toward Drew. "What's his problem?"

"I reminded him he promised John he would prune those shrubs last week."

"Looks more like he's trying to obliterate them." Andy scowled. "What did you say to put him in a snit like that?"

"The snit was already there." Mae gave him a sour glare. "He seems to think you have something to do with it. I suspect he's right."

"What did I do?" Andy straightened to face an accusing frown.

"You didn't stay out of it the way I asked."

"You mean the way you told me. I don't remember it as a request."

"Now Willow's gone."

"Gone? Literally gone?"

"She said she had to go to a great-aunt's funeral but I'm sure it wasn't the real reason. Drew treated her horribly."

"What did he do?"

"You'll need to ask him about that."

"I think I will."

Stunned by what he'd just heard, Andy crossed the terrace and a short strip of lawn until he stood beside Drew with his hands in his pockets while he watched chunks of bright green foliage pop into the air as sharp shears attacked the defenseless shrub.

"What have you got against that bush?"

"You don't want to know."

"Actually, I do."

"She acted like I tried to kill her." Drew glared at the bush as if he intended to deck it.

"Who? Why?"

"I flirted with Marjorie a little. Willow turned it into a war by accusing me of planning to cheat on her—then dared me to do it. Where does she have the right to tell me what I better not do?" Drew took another swipe at the bush. "She doesn't own me."

"Am I missing something here?"

"I got drunk and fucked Marjorie because I was mad at Willow. We had a hell of a fight."

"What did you do, throw it in her face?"

"She didn't know about it then."

"Then what was the fight about?"

"She made me mad and wouldn't leave it alone."

"What did you do?" Andy felt Drew's anger building like pressure in a steam pipe.

"I lost my temper and gave it back to her."

"Did you hurt her?"

"No… Yes… Maybe… But she didn't care. It started as a quarrel and ended up the wildest sex I've ever had. And she loved it! We blew the top off the volcano and it was great. Everything was great." Drew looked exultant for a moment then the grumbling, sulking anger returned. "Until the next morning when she started on her jealousy thing again. She asked me straight out what happened with Marjorie. I told her the truth. I also told her it was lousy compared to her. She just cried and said she didn't care how it was, only that it was. What the hell kind of answer is that?"

"One that means I love you and feel betrayed."

"She told me she wanted me to promise she'd be the only one. Then she went to Iowa. How could she do that?"

"Do what?"

"Leave me like that." Drew lopped off a huge hunk of bush.

"Put those damn things down before you decapitate the poor thing and have John out for your head."

"He already is. He wanted to slug me." Drew threw down the shears, sinking the blades into the ground about six inches from his father's foot. "Gram acts as if I desecrated a vestal virgin. Willow has six brothers, who are probably thundering east like an avenging posse. All because of one lousy fuck I don't even remember."

When Drew shouted loud enough to reach his grandmother, Andy grabbed his son's arm just above the elbow, turned him, and strode around the corner of the conservatory toward the gazebo. "I think we need to go for a walk before I want to slug you."

"Just let go of me." Drew tried to pull his arm away from the strong hand that grasped like a steel clamp. "Everyone's out to avenge poor Willow—except you, who wants to marry her!"

"I do?" Andy let go of Drew's arm when they were well away from the terrace.

"That's what you said." Drew stepped back and glared at him.

"If I was twenty years younger, I'd challenge you for her." Andy's dare was a dart, aimed straight at the heart.

"If you were twenty years younger, I'd take you up on it!"

"Why don't you take her up on it?" The quiet question hit Drew with the force of a shock wave. He stiffened and looked as if he'd been shot. "She stated her terms, Drew—grow up or get lost."

"I don't even know what I want to do with myself. What the hell would I do with a wife?"

"What's the matter, Jack?" Andy shot the question like a well-aimed harpoon. "Can't you admit to the possibility of there being someone in this world more important to Drew than you are?"

"There is no Jack!" Drew glared at his father.

"Then why am I hearing him? Why don't you remember what he did?"

"You're full of shit."

"Stop listening to him, Drew. He drove away Gabby. Don't let him get control again."

Drew stiffened in angry denial as his father's words slammed into him. He opened his mouth to argue then stared at him with a stunned expression.

"As I see it, you have a choice." Andy nailed his son with a glare that offered no quarter. "Save your arrogance and keep having lousy fucks or admit you're in love with the best woman you'll ever find and make a commitment." After delivering his challenge, Andy picked up the sheers and walked away.

Turning from the house, Drew stomped into cool shadows in the gazebo and stared down the hill at the churning cascade below the exclamation point lake. His father was wrong. He hadn't split in years. There was no separate Jack, no Andrew. That had all been a childish way of dealing with contradictory impulses and lack of control—nothing more than an elaborate replay of old cartoons, where tiny angels and devils sat on a character's shoulders: one trying to entice him into trouble, the other guiding him along the path of good intentions. He was cured—armed with a solid background of knowledge—too smart and too old to fall for what his childhood imagination had created. There was no longer a Jack to blame it on.

Drew was sure his father knew that as much as he did and only used it to jolt him into thinking straight, make him accept the awful truth that he'd reacted to Willow's dare with an angry retaliation that went way too far. He told himself he hadn't remembered what happened with Marjorie because he felt wrong. Then he wondered why he still couldn't remember it. He had told Willow he was drunk. But this morning, when he tried to use that same excuse to tell Marjorie it had all been a regrettable mistake, she countered by saying he hardly had anything to drink. Already convinced Marjorie was lying, he had ordered her to get the hell out of his life and walked away from her. His righteous indignation had lasted until he checked his credit card receipts and discovered that not only did the bar tabs agree with Margery, other receipts showed a sex shop purchase of erotic lingerie, a useless suede flail and silk bondage rope—as well as a drugstore charge for condoms he didn't remember buying.

Much as he wanted to blame someone like Jack, none of those things was unfamiliar to him when Marjorie's kinks were involved. The answer was simple: he felt guilty and didn't want to remember his night with her—anymore than he wanted to remember what had happened with Vittorio.

"Damn! I really stuck it in shit this time!" He smacked his hand on a support post, grimaced and, shaking the sting out of his hand, sank onto a cushioned bench. *And then, on top of all that, my father has to show up and rub my nose in what I did to Willow.*

Drew's mistake appalled him. Not remembering unnerved him. There had been other incidents of missing time when he'd been upset and not known how to resolve a problem. He always convinced himself they were nothing more than episodes of self-induced meditative trances that allowed his subconscious to work out solutions to unsettling quandaries. He always came out of them with a clearer view of a situation—a better insight into its solution. He saw them as needed anxiety checks that tapped into his common sense and reset his mental balance. But none of them had lasted longer than a few minutes. Nothing had ever happened during them and, as far as he knew, never included anyone else.

How could I have done that to her? Curling in on himself, Drew dropped his head to his hands and fought against a pain that threatened to engulf him.

There are so many things I want to tell her, but I can never say them. Dad's right; she means more to me than even myself. And now it's too late; she doesn't want anything to do with me.

Lifting his gaze, Drew focused on flashing kaleidoscopic images of sunlight dancing on the rippling surface of the narrow lake then shuddered as emptiness blotted out the pain.

"She has to be told the truth about us." Andrew snapped to his feet like a petulant child and stomped back and forth across painted floorboards in the octagonal gazebo.

"Like hell she does."

"I don't see any other choice." Andrew turned to where Jack's image leaned against the support post beside the steps to the lawn. "Now that he knows what you did, his conscience will torture him and he won't be able to keep it from her. You know he's like that."

"Part of being honest is knowing how much to tell and he already did that." Jack's image shrugged it off. "And when it comes to us, there's my unbreakable rule. Nobody tells nobody the way it is with us."

"Drew broke the rule by trying to tell Gabby after you got possessive and beat up that drunk student who slapped her and threw her onto a bed at a party."

"Drew blew his temper, not me." Jack flared.

"Convenient excuse since no one ever claimed to remember it," Andrew grumped.

"It had to be Drew. He's the one who doesn't want to remember things, not me. Gabby dumped us because your egg-headed bullshit and Drew's dumb-ass revelations sounded so crazy she wanted out.

Accept the truth, nerd brain. Common people don't want to be tied to a weirdo. It's why we made the rule to keep it to ourselves." Jack flipped his head to toss a wayward lock of hair away from his face. "You think Willow would take it any better?"

"They're not like Gabby. Willow's different, Jack. She's more determined... more... more... just more perceptive." Andrew nibbled nervously at his lower lip while he pleaded with Jack to understand. But he could feel his conviction drain away and leave a feeling of hopelessness that knew Jack was right. "I want to believe her love is big enough to understand."

"She doesn't need to understand." Smiling, Jack cocked his head and thought for a moment. "She only needs to be loved."

"What are you saying?" Andrew eyed Jack with suspicion. "You don't love her. You tried to dump her by running off to play sex games with Marjorie."

"That was before she challenged me. How could I not want a chick like that?" Jack laughed and punched air in front of him. "We don't need to break our rules, Squirt. All we have to do is accept her terms without taking the stupid risk you and Drew did with Gabby."

"You're willing to do that for her?"

"Yeah, I'm willing to do that if it's the only way I can keep her. I sure haven't found anyone better to play with."

"Jack?" Andrew asked with a pensive look of innocent hope. "Do you think it will ever be right again? I mean the way it was before Drew trashed our pact and stopped talking to us?"

"Can't say as I care." Jack shrugged. "Look on the bright side, dork, he's willing to take all the blame on himself and doesn't get so bossy."

"And all the credit." Andrew pouted. "I don't like being referred to as an insignificant figment of his imagination when I'm the one who busted my ass doing all that studying and research. It makes me feel used."

"That's because you're a pisser and moaner." Jack laughed then looked annoyed. "But now that you bring it up, with all this studying and opera shit, life was getting boring. He needs to quit sulking so we can get Willow back and have some fun."

Drew shuddered, snapped his head up and, totally unaware of leaving the bench, pushed away from the support post with new determination filling his mind: to hell with getting beat up by a screwed-up conscience; if there was any chance of Willow coming back to him, it would be foolish to hurt her with mistakes like Marjorie—or confuse her, even frighten her, by dragging her into a situation he was able to handle himself. Life was hell without her. It was time he let go of the guilty crap, took control of himself, and did something about it.

❖

That evening, when he returned to the manor after a visit to Antonio, Andy crossed the main hall to the drawing room bar. After pouring a double shot of Glendoncroft, he sat in one of a pair of reading chairs that faced the empty fireplace. Bathed in the golden glow of a Tiffany floor lamp, he sipped at the whisky and stared at the gleaming eyes of the lion andirons that Drew, as a child, had placed in an imaginary room he created out of scraps of memory from a single two-hour visit to the manor house when he was three years old.

Last January, when Vittorio called from Genoa, Andy thought about a past that had worn a ragged hole in his emotions. Later talks with Drew and Paul Reynard eased his apprehensions and he gratefully backed away. Until now—when a ghostly remnant of the past resurfaced.

Rising from the chair, Andy walked to the bar cabinet, thought about refilling his glass then set it down and fished a cell phone out of his hip pocket. It wasn't until the call was answered by a somewhat annoyed voice that he remembered what time it was in Paris.

"Paul, it's Andy Sutherland. Do you have time to talk?"

"You mean aside from the fact that it's after one o'clock in the morning and I'm standing in my underwear wondering if this is going to sabotage thoughts of disturbing my wife's slumber?"

"I'm in Pennsylvania and didn't think about the time difference."

"Since that's uncharacteristic of you, I'm forced to accept that something is upsetting you. Keep talking while I locate a robe and head down to the office."

"What about Sharon?"

"The night is yet young. What prompted the call?"

"I think your phantom nemesis is real." Andy waited for a moment before he said, "Are you still there?"

"I assume you mean Avenger. Tell me what happened to make you say that."

"He did it again. Only this time he picked someone who deserved it and he wasn't as easy to stop. My brother-in-law Antonio had to yank him off Mario and slam him into a wall a few times to get through to him."

"It's out of character but that doesn't necessarily mean what you suspect." A door thumped closed on the other end of the connection before Andy heard the creak of the big chair in Paul Reynard's office. "I want to hear why you suspect it."

"Antonio knows Drew very well," Andy said. "He insists the person he was fighting with was not Drew."

"Or wasn't acting like Drew. There's a difference."

"What do you mean?" Andy picked up the bottle of Scotch and eyed it for a moment before he splashed some into the glass and walked back to the chair.

"He's still doing it, Andy. He's been using his ability to focus his behavior all his life. You've taught him emotional control and he's learned to use it to understand Jack's wildness and channel it into harmless fun instead of malicious violence. Drew and I have talked about it. He knows what he's doing and he doesn't split."

"Just what do you mean by focus his behavior?"

"He still uses old alters as roles, but he is in control and aware enough to understand what they are—and he remembers what they do."

"Are you saying he's still a multiple?"

"Yes. In spite of what he chooses to believe, I feel we have never fully exposed the inciting incident that caused the initial split. That condition allows a continuing state of controlled co-existence with traces of his alters' behavioral traits. However, his intellect has matured beyond the point of believing it is a reasonable state of existence, so he merely uses skills he developed as a multiple to create roles and behave as they would."

"I've heard that excuse, but I can't get a grasp on it."

"Andy, Drew's acting ability goes beyond any school of acting I know about. It's an inborn talent, not a skill that can be taught. He studies every nuance of a role intently before he creates it—then he becomes the role and grows within it. When he puts himself into a character, he is able to exclude the parts of him that would interfere with the role he is portraying. When Drew performs a role, he reacts as the character, not himself. It's very deliberate and self-absorbing, which is why he has to jerk himself out of a role much as he did when he switched personalities. The difference is that he controls the process. It does not control him and it is not dissociative."

"You're talking about a stage role. I'm not."

"Neither am I." Paul's voice sighed. "Drew uses personae whenever he feels he needs them. Sometimes he steals from roles he developed for acting. Some are his own creations. It's the way he is and that isn't going to change."

"I still don't buy it, Paul."

"When you are faced with a situation you have misgivings about—or are afraid of but know you have to face—you create a mindset that allows you to act against those misgivings or fears. Drew is capable of taking it way beyond mindset. He literally turns himself into a person without those misgivings or fears. You've seen it yourself when something triggers his rage. I remember you telling me you couldn't believe it was Drew. You were mostly right."

"You told me the intensity of his anger overrides his sensibility."

"It does. When his sense of righteousness is violated, his reaction is to eliminate conflicting emotions by slipping into the role of an avenger, who has no compassion. It's what happened last winter. His rage overrode his sensibilities."

"But he didn't remember doing it."

"I suspect he didn't want to remember. He accepted the fact, not the memory."

"Paul, I don't think this was a role. That may not have been either."

"His roles are very convincing. His portrayal of Bill Sikes in *Oliver* terrified the actress playing Nancy the first time he let loose with the full power of it."

"I remember that and it makes me wonder why Vittorio says he has no passion in his acting."

"He doesn't say that. He says Drew has no passion in his singing. When he becomes deeply involved in the music, Drew takes on the Buffo role and loses the character. It works in musical theater because the music is basically outside the character. In opera, it *is* the character. In fact, it is everything, which leaves him caught between the two. Andy, I've talked with Vittorio, who says it's because Andrew was taught to sing but allowed to act. There's truth in that, but I don't agree with it as a complete explanation."

"What do you think it is?"

"He's not a child anymore. There's a confidentiality issue here I won't violate."

"I know that. My apology. I'm still a concerned parent."

"Then ask him. It's his privacy, not mine."

"Drew isn't talking beyond the theoretical aspect of it."

"He hasn't figured it out yet, but he is trying." There was a long pause before Paul asked, "Is he in legal trouble over this?"

"The law places all culpability on the man he attacked. Mario is in a hospital and under arrest for a more serious assault and will likely be put in jail for a long time. I'm concerned about Drew, not what he did."

"If it's the Mario I've heard about, I'm not surprised."

"It is and it hasn't mellowed a bit," Andy stated.

"I'm aware of that, but I need to start with why he did it?"

"It involves a woman."

"There's nothing unusual there. Drew has zero tolerance for abusive bullies, especially when it concerns women or children. Most, if not all, of his avenging outbursts have been provoked by that type of behavior. He can get a little carried away, but he does stop when he feels he's eliminated the threat."

"Not this time. But then, Willow is a very special woman."

"How special?"

"He fell in love with her."

"Drew constantly falls in love." Paul laughed. "I once asked him if he belonged to a romance of the month club. He said he didn't pay much attention to duration as long as there were frequent bonus selections."

"I mean really in love." Andy let himself smile and sat back in the chair. "To the point where bonus selections have lost their appeal and he's an emotional powder keg without her. It's Gabby on a power of ten."

"And someone hurt her?"

"That old nemesis Mario threatened her and then abducted her to take revenge against Drew. He would have raped her, probably disfigured her, if Drew hadn't stopped him."

"And you question why Drew lost control of his rage?"

"I don't question that at all. I fully understand it. I question who it was who did the avenging."

"Why are you so sure what happened wasn't Drew in his avenging role?"

"It doesn't fit what Antonio told me."

"And what was that?" Paul asked.

"Antonio is well aware of the way Drew can project an attitude. He insisted this was entirely different and described it as robotic—as if he were listening to an android, or an extremely stilted amateur reading from a bad script. He likened it to comic book writing—an old Batman show without the nuance of ironic humor. Antonio said Drew attacked with pure vengeance and a total lack of the skills he knows Drew has. He didn't even disarm the assailant and that is the first thing Drew would do. In fact, if it hadn't been for his dog Nemo, he would have had a knife in his back. Antonio is sure Drew was unaware of who anyone was until he jerked himself out of the rage. That's almost the same story I got from Vittorio. And there was the thing with the blood again. Willow had a small cut on her cheek that was already dried up, but he insisted she was bleeding and it was in her hair."

"You're right; I need to talk to him—and Antonio, even Willow."

"That may be a problem. I know he's as seriously in love with her as she is with him, but he hasn't admitted it to himself. When he rebelled against making a commitment and tried one of those bonus selections, Willow gave him a choice of faithful or nothing. Then went home to Iowa."

"That explains the powder keg and your reference to Gabby. We can only hope he's grown up enough to cope with it better than he did when Gabby left him. Although Drew adamantly denies it, I still suspect he let Jack take control, and it scared her."

"It looks that way." Andy said. "Willow left three days ago and he hasn't stormed off seeking a life at sea yet. As far as anyone here knows, he hasn't done anything but run and ride and sulk. He's doing the show tonight so he is sticking with his commitment to the theater. Where he goes after the performance and with whom is unpredictable."

"I have a vacation planned for next month." Paul said. "I can spend a few days in Pennsylvania then fish in the Rockies just as well as the Pyrenees. Before I arrive, I want you, John and Antonio, maybe even Antonio's mother, to search your minds for anything that might be of help, even if it is obscure. In fact, there is a strong chance that obscurity is hiding what we need to know."

"Like what?" Andy asked bluntly.

"Something traumatic that happened when he was very young. The hard part is that what may have been traumatic to a pre-school child may seem like nothing to an adult or older child. I'll sift through my notes and see what I can find. Am I correct in assuming that you'll supply the transportation?"

"FiberForms flights go back and forth on a regular basis. Let me know when you want one."

"As far as Drew is concerned, I would rather you let him see my visit as a spontaneous side trip from a fishing vacation."

"Be better for my mother, too." Andy nodded. "While she accepts you as a friend, she suspects you as a psychiatrist."

"That tenacity is one of the things I adore about your so very regal mother. One more thing I'm going to mention is that ever since we decided Drew was old enough to handle the truth about his MPD, he's extensively studied the disorder. As far as academic knowledge, he is probably as well informed as I am. But his only clinical experience is with himself. With that bias, he's formed some strong and, in my mind, dismissive opinions about how it relates to him."

"And you don't agree with him?" Andy quipped as he picked up the short, crystal glass and took a swallow of the smoothly satisfying liquor.

"I agree with his knowledge, not with his rationalizations, which is why I encouraged him to expand his clinical knowledge by looking into lost pieces of his life in Philadelphia."

"I don't know as I'm comfortable with that, Paul. His presence there disturbed an old hornet's nest that led to the attack on Willow and his recent instability."

"The hornet's nest was unfortunate, but the instability was already there and has a lot more to do with what was happening within Drew before he went to Philadelphia."

"And that is?"

"Drew's pretty lax about what I tell you, but you're pushing at my ethics again. Besides, I'm a psychiatrist, not a fortune teller."

"Why not? I've probably paid you enough by now to buy a fail-proof, rechargeable crystal ball."

"Keep that up and I'll charge you for this phone call—that means triple time for after hours and a penalty fee for disrupting my sex life."

"I accept no liability for derailing mid-life fantasies. And, as a side note, when the hell was last the time you sent me a bill?"

"I think I lost your address about the time I started seeing it as a family matter."

"Good. I like that excuse better than the one about it being a freelance research project." Andy drained the glass and held it in front of him while he watched the last drop of whisky slide down the inside of the glass. "I don't expect a prediction, but I know you wouldn't have mentioned that possibility if you didn't have some thoughts about it."

"I had them last winter. Drew adamantly denied the possibility."

"And you believed him?" Andy scoffed. "Paul, I learned a long time ago that when Drew adamantly denied something, it was because he was guilty as hell and refusing to believe it."

"And there was no way you could convince him otherwise, right?"

"Exactly."

"I introduced a few contrary points then left him to work it out for himself."

"I just did the same," Andy said. "I hope I get better results than you seem to have. I'll be heartbroken if he bottles it up and walks away from the best woman he's ever found."

"I'd like to say she's exactly what he needs, but I'm afraid you're hoping for a leap of faith he isn't ready to take."

"Why not?"

"I'm not ready to answer that. I should have a better hold on it when I get there."

"Just tell me he isn't going to try joining the French Foreign Legion in the next two weeks."

"He isn't going to join the French Foreign Legion. Does that make you feel better?"

"Actually, it does." Andy relaxed with a laugh. "I keep telling myself I'm overreacting, but your mention of instability stirred up memories of a weeklong panic that ended with a call from the police in Marseille."

"When I said instability, I didn't mean a return to what he now sees as damn fool adolescent insanity."

"Mostly he was lucky I was far enough away I couldn't get my hands on him." Andy frowned at the empty glass.

"I seem to remember that when he was fourteen, he stole your keys and wrecked a brand-new race car. I thought you used great restraint when you slammed him against a wall, grounded him and told him if you heard one word of complaint or he took one step over the line, he wouldn't want to move for a week."

"Interesting you should mention that. Maybe his memory of hitting a greenhouse at more than a hundred kilometers an hour paid off because he just rammed my old Mercedes through a set of barred doors to get Willow away from her abductor."

"Ouch. How's the car?"

"Questionable. Mother wants it restored. My first reaction was to junk it; but in spite of my bitterness, I wanted to cry. I'm reserving a decision until I get the estimate."

"Go with your heart, Andy. It's your saving grace."

"Merci, Docteur Reynard."

"Pas de quoi, mon ami."

Chapter Twenty-Three

Willow heard the mumble of her parents' voices in the living room while she finished cleaning the kitchen after Sunday dinner. She supposed they were talking about her again. In the last five days, her shattered romance with Drew had become an episode in a family soap opera. Willow loved her family; but right now, she wondered why. She had obviously said too much in front of Todd, who said too much to her father, her brother Owen, and Tom Sorensen.

None of them saw themselves as gossips, but as concerned people who wanted to help, which was worse. Their idea of helping was to discuss it amongst themselves then offer sincere advice on what she should do. They were all on her side, of course, and all too eager to condemn Drew as a heartless cad who took advantage of her. She wanted to choke them all, except for Byron and her youngest sister. At thirteen, Beth saw it as exciting. Byron felt her hurt and empathized without judgment.

Willow was wiping down the counters when her father walked into the kitchen on the pretense of getting a beer from the refrigerator. She knew it was a pretense since he would normally have sent someone else for the beer. She turned away from the refrigerator and busied herself at the sink. When she heard him clear his throat, she turned on the water in an attempt to discourage him. Her diversion was a failure and only made him talk louder.

"Now that you are home, I think you ought to look into a job at the feed mill." Lloyd made his announcement as if the issue of her remaining at home was already decided. "Henry wants to broaden his retail store to include more horse supplies. He could use someone who knows about horses."

Willow twisted off the tap and turned to face him. "I did not get a degree in equestrian studies so I could work in a feed mill."

"It will be good temporary income until you find something better."

"I have a job," Willow answered in a firm tone that left no doubt about what she meant and expected that would be all she would have to say. Until she turned and saw his face redden.

"You will not go back to that man."

"I'm going back to my job." As she watched him grow taller, harder, broader, Willow told herself that if she could challenge Drew and face down his dominance, she could certainly stand on her own against her father. "I won't be a quitter just because I was burned by something that has nothing to do with the job."

"You're not going back. That's my final word on it. Todd will get your car and other belongings."

"He will not. Todd wants an excuse to pick a fight and Owen would love to go with him."

It seemed to Willow things had been that way all her life. She and Byron had always been caught between Todd and Owen, the nononsense, down-to-earth pragmatists, who believed subtle hints were delivered with ten-pound sledge hammers. They could have been clones in looks, and Owen had always been a shadow of Todd—a little quieter, a little less volatile, but just as hardheaded.

"If I want someone to come get me, I'll call Byron."

"Byron!" Her father roared the name as if it were an oath. "I should have whipped some sense into him a long time ago."

"Well, it wasn't for lack of trying." Willow's face flamed and her eyes burned into him with the vehemence of her accusation. "All he wanted to do was live by his own creeds, which are as good as anyone else's."

"Not to me. He's not only shamefully sharing his apartment with a college girl, he's talked you into immoral behavior, sent you chasing after daydreams and encouraged you to disgrace yourself with some singer when you had a good man here."

"In the first place, Sarah is a graduate student, not a college girl. Secondly, he didn't talk me into anything immoral or send me chasing after anything. Thirdly, I don't love Tom. He's nice, but I don't love him."

"But you love this singer?"

"I do. He may have broken my heart but he showed me I could never love Tom or be happy with Tom, no matter how nice he is."

"He took you to his bed. That's what he did."

"No, he didn't." Willow watched dark brows cram together with the glowering wrath that rose when he suspected one of his children was lying to him. Squaring her shoulders and raising her chin, she met his anger with defiance. "It was my bed. And I let him into it."

"He took his pleasures from you and anyone else he wanted then left you." Anger stiffened Lloyd, hardened his face. "Maybe I'll go set him straight myself."

"Drew gave as much pleasure as he took. Things are different with women now." When the man recoiled in outrage, Willow pulled in a long breath before she snapped with a sarcastic tone that pushed his control. "We admit to our enjoyment. It isn't our sacrifice anymore."

"Not my daughters. You're staying right here where you'll behave decently until you get properly married."

"I'm getting on a plane to Philadelphia Thursday and you aren't stopping me."

"I made that mistake once. I won't do it again. I'm still your father and still know when you're being foolish."

"I'm going, even if it is foolish."

"You're not. And if I catch sight of your Andrew Sutherland, he better take to his heels before I let him know how I feel about pushy rich boys who think they can buy or take whatever they want."

"Drew isn't like that."

"Good con man is what he is. He used you and lied to you. I won't allow you to go back to that shameless place."

"Oh! You are so unreal!" With rage clenched in tight fists, Willow spun away, stomped through the mudroom and banged out the back door.

Willow halted on the large back porch when she saw Byron sitting on the railing with his back against a corner post—one foot on the floor, the other on the railing in front of him. It was one of his favorite reading poses and allowed him to either see his father coming in from the barn or hear him crossing the kitchen. Byron had been able to drop off the railing and disappear within seconds when his father sounded as if he had work on his mind. But Byron had always been around whenever there was food to be eaten, or his favorite sister needed him.

"Arguments like that taught me how to run," Byron said when she scowled at him. Rolling to his left, he dropped to the ground and stood looking up at her. "Let's go for a walk. You look as if you need to get away from your wrathful sire."

"I'd forgotten how unreasonable he can be." She jogged down the steps and took the hand Byron offered.

"Willy, have you forgotten the way this family conjugates? I am persistent; you are stubborn; he is a pigheaded ass."

In spite of her lingering anger, Willow smiled. "No wonder I fell for Drew. He can be so much like you it's uncanny."

"You've decided to go back? Or was that just a rebellious front?"

"I've decided to go back. I never felt right about leaving Mae the way I did."

Willow followed her brother by ducking under a pasture fence he easily vaulted over and walking along a cow trail through lush, kneehigh alfalfa. They squeezed between the slats of a sagging wooden gate into a copse of cottonwoods growing up around the spring house, which was little more than a peaked, shingled roof set over a pit lined with moss-covered fieldstones and filled with cold water.

"Thirsty?" Byron opened a door at one end of the low structure, lifted a battered tin cup off a bent nail beside the door, and dipped it into the spring water.

"I'm always thirsty when I come here. Water from the spring house rates an excellent in my memory." Willow sat on the newer, flattopped cover of the pump pit while she sipped the clear water.

"Our greatgreatgrandfather had to protect his homestead claim by arming his family and workers," Byron said. "He named his claim Sweetwater Farm because of this spring, which made it the most coveted claim in the area. Four men were killed fighting over Roberts Spring. Actually, three men and a boy of twelve, since he lost a son here. Now we only use it to water stock when they're on summer pasture and to irrigate the house gardens during dry times. We have three deep wells and only use the windmills for irrigation. Yep, things do change." He took the cup back and filled it for himself before he sat on the concrete sill of the open door with his long legs stretched out in front of him. "Maybe he'll figure that out."

"He sure hasn't with you."

"Don't come down on him too heavy an account of me. I got into some bad messes with drug kicks in high school. It could have been a lot worse if he hadn't found out."

"He almost drove you away, Byron." Willow grabbed his wrist and held it while she stared into his eyes. "I hated him for that."

"Don't hate him, Willy. Stand up to him, but don't hate him."

"He's intolerant."

"He's scared."

Byron's answer stunned her and she had no answer.

"There's a big, bad world out there and he doesn't want it to eat us up." Byron winked at her. "He believes morals are safety rules and wants us to play by those rules."

"His rules."

"They're the ones he believes in, Elf." Byron drank the rest of the water and returned the cup to its nail. "Is the job the only reason you're going back?"

"No." Staring at tiny purple flowers on a tall clump of dusty green alfalfa that had strayed from the hay field, Willow hugged her arms around her raised knees. "I think Drew needs me, and I want to be there if he wants me again."

"That doesn't sound like the pride you rode home on."

"It's more honest. I love him, Byron." She looked into the absorbing brown depth of his eyes and sensed understanding. "Right now, it hurts to be near him, but I feel empty all the time without him. I'd rather hurt than feel part of me had been amputated."

"I can't argue with that, but I don't like to know you're being hurt."

"It hurts no matter what I do. I thought he loved me and I'm afraid he won't ever see it if I stay here. I want you to keep Dad or Todd or anyone else from going after me. It would humiliate me. I don't know what it would do to Drew. I guess he'd see it as barbaric."

"They think it's chivalrous."

Willow gave her brother a puzzled look and thought for a moment. "Drew likes chivalry, but I don't think he sees it the way Todd does. Drew would see honor in a fencing foil, not a fist fight."

"Probably because neither his head nor his fists are made of cement the way Todd's are when he gets offended. He feels Drew betrayed you, dear Elf."

"Drew didn't do anything I didn't want. He made sex a beautiful experience, as well as an exciting one. And a fun one."

"Is that what you're in love with?"

"Only if it's with Drew. It's so powerful, Byron. I want him so much I ache inside."

"I'd call that love—a serious case of it." He lifted a rusty eyebrow. "Now, how am I supposed to convince those boneheads? Todd and Owen would understand if he'd been faithful to you. But you clearly let Todd know Drew ran around on you. Todd's reasonable enough to know some of his girls were somebody else's sisters, but he never ran around on them."

"Drew never promised he wouldn't."

"That only makes it worse to Todd, who sees making love as a binding vow of fidelity for the duration of the relationship. It doesn't rest well with me, either, but I'm more concerned with what you want." He pressed a hard finger on her breastbone. "It's what you feel in there that's important, not what I feel. I'll get you on that plane and do what I can."

"They'll be mad at you, Byron."

"Don't worry about your outraged siblings. As I see it, most of their machismo is show. There's more crowing and strutting than actual confrontation."

"You're right." Willow smiled. "Remember when we used to bet on the cock fights in the chicken yard?"

"They mostly fizzled out after an instant flurry of feathers."

"Todd doesn't fizzle out, Byron."

"Willy, I doubt if anyone will go chasing after you. It will just make for some bad feelings for a while. They should cool down before Christmas."

"Thank you, Byron. You're being my hero again."

"Only because I know I can still outrun both Todd and Owen if their hackle feathers go up."

❖

Deciding the thumping sounds that awakened her were nothing more than a restless cow bumping the water tank in the south pasture, Willow stared out her open window at the bright, silver disk of a nearly full moon peeking through the lacy silhouette of an ancient oak in the front yard. A leafy branch moved in a light breeze and a dark crater-eye winked at her. Sighing, she wondered if Drew was looking at the same moon and thinking of her. Then she glanced at her clock and knew he would be asleep at four o'clock in the morning—if he was alone.

Rejecting a line of thought she didn't want to follow, Willow rolled over to stare at moving branch-shadows on the wall. With her second pillow hugged tight to her body, she closed her eyes and rocked herself to sleep the way she had as a child when she felt alone and sad.

> "A way out here they've got a name/For rain and wind and fire.
> The rain is Tess, the fire's Joe/And they call the wind Mariah.
> Mariah blows the stars around/And sends the clouds aflyin';
> Mariah makes the mountains sound/Like folks are up there dyin'."

When she first heard it, Willow accepted it as a remnant of a dream. Then she realized she was fully awake, and it was not only clear, it was captivating, and wrong. She was at home in Iowa, but it was Drew's voice, and it was coming in her open window. Without a pause, she threw back the sheet and rushed to the front window. He stood below her in a silver wash of moonlight with one foot on a picnic bench, a relaxed hand resting on his raised thigh. Byron sat astride the wide board seat of the tree swing, playing an acoustic guitar.

> "Before I knew Mariah's name/ And heard her wail and whinin',
> I had a girl and she had me/ And the sun was always shinin';
> But then one day I left my girl/ I left her far behind me;
> And now I'm lost, so goldurned lost/Not even God can find me."

The caressing fullness of Drew's voice rolled up to surround Willow with its power. Caught in a flood of excitement, she was barely aware of lights snapping on and splashing angular patterns of light on the shadowed lawn.

"Out here they've got a name for rain/For wind and fire only,
But when you're lost and all alone/There ain't no word but lonely;
And I'm a lost and lonely man/Without a star to guide me;
Mariah, blow my love to me/ I need my girl beside me."

Tears streamed from Willow's eyes; and when Drew stepped forward and added still more power and mellow depth, she was sure the swell of emotion would explode in her chest.

"Mariah, Mariah, blow my love to me."

While the last clear note hung in the quiet night, Willow grabbed her bathrobe, bolted from her room and, with her heart leaping wildly, rushed down the stairs without noticing the steps. She heard the rumbling roar of her father's voice from the master bedroom at the back of the house as well as thumps overhead as she ran through the living room and out the front door. The porch floor felt rough under bare feet and then she was on cool dewwet grass. The arms that caught her were strong and welcoming. They wrapped around her and lifted her off the ground in a crushing embrace. His kiss churned up her feelings and spun her into a euphoria where time was held captive.

"Come back to me, Willow. Spend your life with me." Drew glanced past her shoulder. "Answer fast. I don't have time for a wordy proposal. Will you marry me?"

"Yes, I will."

When Drew straightened and thrust her away, Willow was stunned until she turned toward the porch and reality crashed down on her. Todd and Owen were thudding across worn floor boards like two shirtless gladiators in faded jeans and bare feet. Too angry to be sensible, she stomped forward, only to feel two hands clamp on her arms and pull her backwards—away from Drew and her charging brothers.

"What are you doing?" Willow twisted and glared up at Byron's shadowed face.

"They won't listen to you. Leave it to Drew."

"They'll clobber him."

"I warned him. He said he could handle it."

When Todd and Owen reached the opening in the porch railing, Drew faced them in the relaxed, unassuming stance Willow recognized from the day they were charged by Gascon at Zeb's farm. When she remembered how Drew moved to grasp the dog by the neck and throw it to the ground, she started to wonder how much of it really had been luck. He looked the same now—casual, arms slightly flexed at his sides. He appeared loose and nonchalant; Willow suspected he was tense and alert.

"Okay, Romeo," Todd bellowed. "Tuck your tail in your ass and get off this farm before I stuff your fucking teeth down your throat."

"I wouldn't advise trying." Drew warned as the shorter, burlier Todd advanced on him. "I won't retreat, but I will suggest negotiation."

"I don't negotiate with a son of a bitch who mistreated my sister." With a sudden lunge, Todd swung his right fist at Drew's face.

A solid left forearm deflected the punch a split second before a strong, right hand circled Todd's wrist. With a sudden burst of speed, Drew spun, jerked the captured wrist down over his shoulder. In a smooth flow of motion, he twisted, dropped his upper body and thrust up with his legs. Todd flew. Like a clown doing an awkward cartwheel, he flailed his arms at empty air, bounced on his ass, then flopped flat on his back with a grunt of expelled air.

Drew dodged sideways and thwacked the back of a clenched fist into Owen's stomach. The blow failed to stop him, but it staggered him, made his swing clumsy. Drew snatched a fist out of the air, snapped it down and twirled his attacker in front of him with his right arm bent up behind his back. When Todd, now on his feet, churned forward like a battle tank, Drew shoved Owen at him. The brothers collided with a thud and simultaneous grunts.

"That's enough!" Lloyd Roberts bellowed from the porch as he closed a powerful hand on the waistband of Matt's jeans and watched his older sons sort themselves out and square off against Drew, who was standing in the same pose of relaxed readiness. When Todd and Owen pulled back a few steps, the burly farmer swung his eyes to Drew and raked him with a judging stare. "What in holy hell are you doing here?"

Drew stared back at him without a falter. "I came to ask if I could marry your daughter."

"You mean make an honest woman out of her?"

"Mr. Roberts, she's never been anything but honest."

"Which is more than I can say for you. I ought to punch you in the mouth myself."

"I admit you have a stronger case than they have, but I get damn protective about my mouth." Drew answered calmly and locked eyes with Lloyd in a tense moment of confrontation that could only end in stalemate.

"Why do you want to marry her?" Lloyd withdrew his threat and Drew relaxed his defensive stance.

"I love her."

"Humph." Lloyd snorted. "Sounded to me like you loved half the women in Pennsylvania."

"I think someone exaggerates." Drew made a pained face and took Willow's hand when she stepped beside him. "There was only one and only once."

"Two," Willow answered firmly while she held up two fingers. "Or doesn't it count in French?"

"One." Drew caught her hand and bent down the index finger.

When Willow glanced at her hand, with its still extended middle finger, she snapped her fist closed.

"You have it all wrong about Nicole."

"Do I?" Willow lifted her chin and glared at him. "The last time I saw you by the gazebo she was wrapped up in your arms."

Catching her chin between thumb and bent finger, Drew backed her toward Byron and said firmly. "She has a husband she loves very much. He came to the States for brain surgery and learned the risk of severe complications was high. Last week they did the surgery and he went into a coma. Nicole is also thirty-eight years old with big investments in cosmetics and plastic surgery."

"You spent the night in her hotel room."

"I spent the night in my own hotel room because she had an early appointment at the hospital and I was needed as a translator. Nicole needed help and support from me, not sex."

"Why didn't you tell me?" Willow's anger wilted as the words caught in her throat.

"You never asked for truth. When you finally did, I told you and you ran away." Drew glanced across the wide stretch of moonlit lawn and driveway at a frozen tableau of confused faces, then back at Willow. "After you stonewalled Nicole, I was miffed enough to let you stew over it. She and I share strong feelings for Peter. He was my favorite tutor and means a lot to me."

"Is he the friend you want to name a son after?"

"Yes. Marjorie was a stupid attempt to convince myself I didn't love you and want you forever. It didn't work." With his arm around Willow's waist, Drew looked to where her bewildered, but still glowering, father stood at the top of the porch stairs, and raised his voice. "Willow said yes. That leaves it up to you."

Lloyd cleared his throat, glanced sideways at his wife, who was standing on the porch with a smug smile that implied things were turning out the way she wanted. When he looked back at Drew, he was clearly uncomfortable. "It isn't a question I'm ready to answer at three in the morning. You can stay with Byron. I'll talk to you when I've thought it out."

"Thank you, sir." Drew slid his arm around Willow's shoulders and rubbed his hand on her arm with an affection that sent her blood racing.

"Willow, I want you in your room alone in ten minutes. You aren't even dressed." Her father gave her a stern glare before he turned and strode toward the house.

"Yes, Dad."

The rest of the family melted away. Her mother, Byron and Beth looked pleased; Matt looked confused; her father looked stern; Todd and Owen looked annoyed.

Willow sighed and tilted her face up to Drew's. "Are you serious about letting my father make the decision?"

"It's the proper way to do it, isn't it?"

"What will you do if he says no?"

"Convince him to say yes. I won't give up, Willow. I'll keep working on him, even if I have to commute to Pennsylvania every week to do the show. Gram isn't the only persistent one in the family." He walked to the porch, where he sat sideways on an old, steelframed glider and held her in front of him with her back snuggled against his chest, his arms wrapped around her. "I only have ten minutes to tell you there isn't another woman in the world who could stop me from loving you. I guess I loved you right from the start. I could sense it, but I couldn't say it, or stop it."

"Why did you want to stop it?"

"I was afraid of it. You became so much a part of me I was terrified that if I let myself love you completely, I'd be owned by it. I felt responsible for you and to you. I wasn't sure I could handle that."

"Why not?"

"For the first time in my life someone else was more important to me than I was. It panicked me, but losing you was worse than terrifying. When John said I'd be the biggest ass in the world if I didn't go after you, I knew he was right. Both he and Dad riled up my rebellious streak by telling me what I already knew but refused to accept."

"Does your father really want me to come back?"

"Desperately. He says I need a levelheaded compass, who can force me to make decisions. But he knew if something didn't kick me into accepting the inevitable, I'd let it drift in indecisive limbo until you gave up on me. I don't know if he coached you or not, but you blew my control to hell and delivered a kick that took me back to when someone else told me she wasn't my property."

"Gabby?" She watched him react with surprise. "Your father told me you loved her."

"With the reckless abandon of first love—totally absorbed and too smitten to even think I wasn't her whole life." He pressed his cheek against her hair. "I don't think I could take the aftermath of that again. I'm sorry, Willow. I know what you meant when you said I tore a hole in you."

"I didn't want to hurt you, Drew, just get you to think about what I meant to you."

"The reality of you not being there was hell." He hugged her with a strength she thought was going to crush her, then he relaxed and kissed her hair. "But this time there was something I could do about it and, aside from my display of arrogance when you, in effect, told me to grow up or get lost, I was no longer self-centered, eighteen and totally irresponsible. It devastated me as much, but I didn't go on a drunken rampage that almost killed me."

"You?" His confession startled her and she turned to face him with her legs folded in front of her.

"That was one of those damn stupid things I referred to. I was full of offended belligerence and got some fool idea in my head about running off to sea as a swashbuckling merchant marine. All I did was antagonize some of them in a bar in Marseilles. It was a miracle I got out of it alive. Those gorillas had very big knives and huge fists." He grimaced. "And then I spent a hellish week in a French jail because my father wouldn't bail me out until he decided I'd learned a crucial lesson."

"What was that?"

"Humility. It took a few reminders, but I finally got the message. It was a bad summer and Princeton started to look good."

"Is that what he meant by putting the backbone in you?"

"That was part of it." Drew laughed at himself. "The old school British fortitude shit. It runs in the family."

"Except for you."

"Don't bet on that. I was raised by that man with no softhearted mother to assuage my wounded ego. He was both father and brother to me and we understand each other."

"But you like fun."

"He does, too; but there are rules. And they are rigid."

"He intimidates me."

"Dad can have that effect."

"I thought he disapproved and was trying to turn you against me."

"John said he told you that you had to stand up to me, and Dad made sure you did by provoking your stubborn streak. He manipulated both of us. He's good at it." Drew gave her a contemplative look. "The way I see it, we can react with stubborn indignation and get back at him by dumping each other to prove him wrong—"

"You can't mean that." Willow looked devastated.

"—or we can be ourselves, swallow all the stupid pretensions and jealousies we've been battering each other with and accept that we love and trust each other."

"I like that plan." She grinned at his spreading smile.

"Me, too. Willow, I'll meet your demands but I can't change who I am. Since you issued the ultimatum, it's your call. I'm giving you your last chance to take me as I am or run like hell. You blasted me out of my funk and I feel whole and alive again. It's only fair to warn you. I can be wild and hard to take when I get rolling."

"I'll accept that challenge."

"You're on." Drew tapped her on the jaw with a closed fist. "And maybe I'll be forgiven at home. When I said I thought I'd go to Iowa tonight after the show, Gram looked ready to clobber Dad with her cane if he didn't rush me to the plane. John said he'd take care of Venture after the show, and Dad tried to break the sound barrier getting to the airport. If I don't come back with you, I may find I'm locked out. We all love you and want you to stay a part of us."

"I was going to go back. I feel I'm important to Mae."

"It's me you're important to. If I go to Italy, I'm not leaving you in Pennsylvania."

"Are you going to Genoa?"

"I don't know, but it's looking less frightening with you in the picture."

"Will he take you if you're married?"

"It's a music conservatory, not a monastery."

"Not if you have anything to do with it." Willow giggled at the thought of Drew living in humble, or any other form of celibacy, then sobered and asked, "Did you tell them you were going to ask me to marry you?"

"Nope." Drew tweaked her nose when she wrinkled it in confusion. "I figured it would be better to find out if you wanted me first."

"You mean I was the first to know?" She looked smugly pleased.

"That was my intention." He looked impishly repentant. "Until Byron demanded I tell him what my intentions were. I couldn't lie to him."

"How did you get with Byron anyway?" The question popped out when Willow thought about his sudden appearance.

"I called him before I landed to ask directions to the farm. He said he'd pick me up and had a few things to explain to me."

"Such as Todd and Owen?"

"From his concern, I deduced you hadn't told him about the tough street kid."

"That was a long time ago."

"He's there when he's needed. Martial Arts training was part of Dad's rehabilitation program to build self-confidence and teach me discipline. I started at eight and memories of feeling helpless against bullies kept telling me I wasn't good enough, so I kept at it. I admit I was first snagged by the aggressive side of it and rejected the rest. Then, as I continued, I found the Oriental discipline of seeking inner strength was a complement to the Sutherland discipline of projecting outward self-assurance."

"You have a black belt in karate?"

"Fifth degree. But that stuff I just used was judo. When Byron said Todd's and Owen's idea of a fight was to throw the hardest punches, I told him I could handle them without his help." He cocked his head and gave her a perplexed look. "For some reason, I never doubted I would get his help if I needed it. I thought brothers stuck together right or wrong."

"Not when one of them is wise enough to know the others are acting like jerks." She leaned forward for a kiss. "Byron was always on your side, even when I wasn't." Willow giggled. "Especially after I told him you were impressed by his *Rhapsody in Blue*."

When Willow kissed him, Drew slipped a hand under the overlapped front of her bathrobe, enticingly caressed a breast and then pulled away before the heat of the kiss fused them together.

"I need ten hours alone with you, not ten minutes." Drew nuzzled at her neck, kissed it softly then nibbled her ear lobe. "Use some elfin magic and transport us to a woodland bower where we can make love in the moonlight."

"I wish I could. But if you want to keep things proper, you'll have to wait." Willow slid a hand over his and pulled it out of her robe before she sat up.

"Your father is a cruel man." Drew dropped a foot to the floor and let her stand.

"He thinks he's doing what's best for me."

"Fathers are notoriously misguided. Mine used to say things like that when he froze my assets or grounded me. I know what's best for you, *Chèrie*."

Standing, Drew caught her face in his hands. His kiss started as a gentle brush of sensitive lips, until she slid her arms around him and melted into his embrace. When he pulled back, Willow was dizzy with happiness and weak with need for him. "Drew, we don't have to stay here. I'll be forgiven if I run away with you now."

"No." He shook his head and backed away from her. "It's my chivalry showing up again."

"Then I think we need to keep at least six inches apart to honor your chivalry."

"That's not a bad idea." He looked past Willow to where Byron leaned against the door frame. "Are you my friend or my conscience?"

"I thought I'd show you where you get to sleep. I'm housed in the garret over the garage. It has its own stairway."

Drew smiled wryly. "And there's no way into the rest of the upstairs, right?"

"Right."

❖

At seven-thirty in the morning, Willow stormed into the kitchen where Todd and Owen were devouring breakfast before heading out to grease and check the equipment needed for raking and mowing the last two hayfields. When they looked at her with guarded expressions, Willow knew the issue was far from over.

"Do you know where Drew is?" Willow scowled at Todd with the righteous zeal of an inquisitor.

"He dragged Byron out of bed to show him where he could go running. Probably gave the lazy slug a reason to question what side he's on. They headed for the river road."

"Good. This is my gripe to voice, not his. Where's Matt? I'd like him to hear it, too."

"He and Dad are at big brother Keith's farm," Owen answered. "He has a problem with a cow stuck in a culvert,".

"What are we supposed to hear?" Todd focused a jade green stare on her. "Maybe an explanation for your change of attitude."

"I didn't change anything."

"You got conned by a rich womanizer you knew was running around on you. Now you want to marry him? Still doesn't sit right with me."

"Or me," Owen supported his older brother.

"I didn't actually know he was running around on me." Willow's belligerence crumbled when they gave her silent, penetrating stares—one green, the other brown. "I just thought he was, and I heard things about him that made it easy to believe."

"Not the first time you've done that." Todd rumbled in his gruff morning voice and Owen nodded in agreement.

Willow gave them a glare but refrained from taking the bait and letting them bring up an old issue of false tattling she wanted to avoid. "Drew just plain refused to talk about it, which only made me more suspicious."

"He lied to you when you asked if he was running around?" Owen gave her a hard look.

"Drew said I never asked for the truth, and he's right. I just kept stabbing him in the back with accusations whenever I got mad at him. Then he took my rejection literally and ignored me. I was miserable without him and told him I wanted him to make love to me."

Willow dropped onto a chair and read consternation in the way they looked at her. "It wasn't what he did to me that made me run away. It was what we did to each other. Drew was afraid of losing his freedom and my jealousy drove him to someone else. When he apologized and admitted he was wrong, I wouldn't listen to him and he walked away. I thought he didn't want me as anything but a handy bedmate. But after last night, I think he was as devastated as I was. He found the courage to come out here and face his accusers, you could at least give him credit for that."

Todd stared at her in his silent, calculating way that said he was choosing his words carefully. "He didn't have to look very hard for courage. That man is an army in himself. And you could have warned us before Kung Fu showed up."

"I didn't know he could do that. I knew he was a cop for a while, but he was a canine cop. I thought they just handled tracking dogs."

"I thought he was an opera singer." Owen looked bewildered.

"He is now, or at least he's training to be one. He said he was a tough street kid in Philadelphia when he lived with his mother. Drew's a lot of things and he's led an interesting life, but you need to hear it from him. He thinks he needs to shield me from things like that."

"What do you expect us to do about this?" Todd's question was more demand than query.

"Get to know him before you judge him. I kept trying to categorize him but I could never get it right. Then I decided it was easier to just love him and, as he said, take him the way he is." Willow shrugged then added, "But I will warn you about one thing."

"That he holds grudges?" Owen looked uneasy.

"I don't think so, and there's nothing underhanded about him." Willow paused for a moment before she decided there was a more important thing they needed to hear. "Someone did have a grudge against him, but Drew ended it by saving me and taking down an old enemy of his, who did this with a knife," she pointed at the thin scar on her left cheek, "and threatened to rape me."

"You said you didn't know he could do that." Todd challenged.

"I didn't know about what you call Kung Fu. Only that, he crashed a car through barred doors, then kicked in another one to get Mario away from me. The police took the bastard away in an ambulance."

"That's enough warning for me." Todd stared at her with wide eyes, then thought about it and smiled. "And I guess we owe him a debt of gratitude at the same time."

"I didn't think I needed to warn you about Drew being tough. You seemed to have already gotten that message. I wanted you to know that he doesn't like being ignored so don't put up a silent wall. He'll keep poking holes in it until he gets you to laugh with him, or at him. He doesn't care which, as long as it's in fun."

The two brothers looked at each other for a while then nodded with tacit agreement before Owen said, "Sounds better than getting thrown across the lawn." And Todd seconded it.

❖

After an enlightening day of physically taxing labor that shifted from a monotonous routine of stacking hay bales in a loft to crisis management intensity following the bellow of a destressed bovine and a final banging and screeching surrender of a huge piece of greasy dust-encrusted farm equipment, Drew experienced a startling revelation about the realities of farming. But he was too exhausted to dwell on the ramifications of it and crashed into the oblivion of deep sleep as soon as he hit the extra bed in Byron's two room apartment that resembled a cross between a musical recording studio and a rummage sale.

A few hours later, the sound of stomping feet on the stairs roused Drew from oblivion. The thud of a fist on the door, accompanied by Todd's booming bass voice, sat him bolt upright while a clear vision of a rerun clash with half naked gladiators filled his mind. When he saw the ghostly, long-legged form of Byron stride toward a door that was already swinging open, he bellowed, "Lock the damn door and tell them I already gave at the office."

"It's a little late for that." Byron snapped on an overhead light and faced his two brothers with a scowl that added to the drooping chaos of a disheveled moustache. "It's five o'clock in the morning, Todd."

"That gives us just about enough time."

"For what?"

"Me and Owen figured out how to pull it off. But we need Drew's help."

Deciding it wasn't another confrontation, Drew sat up and joined Byron in confusion. "Since I get the feeling that you're trying to sucker me into something, I'd like some details."

"Sure." Todd tossed a mound of clothes off a chair, swung it in an arc, then straddled it with his arms crossed on the back and faced Drew. "Byron says Willow's been complaining that you never sing to her."

"I sang to her every time she slipped into the back of the theater during a performance."

"But it was always the same songs. Right?" Todd leaned forward. "I imagine even you can get boring after a few weeks of the same shit."

"I get the point." Drew laughed. "What's your problem?"

"Willow's also been nagging Byron because she wants you to hear his fiddling. In order to shut her up, we decided to give her a little surprise." Todd glanced from where Byron sat dozing on his bed to where Owen perched on a mostly clear dresser top that had suffered the same swift denuding as the chair, then back to Drew. "There's this bar we like and Wednesday night is pretty dead there. We figured Byron could get his band together and get Willow off our backs."

"It's a good idea." Drew perked up. "She'll like that. And surprising her is one of my favorite games. I'll even pick up the tab."

"That's not the kind of help we need."

"What kind of help do you need?"

Todd gave him a long, calculating look before he said, "There's this local collection of annoying, big-mouth assholes who think they own the bar on Wednesdays. We don't want them there."

Drew recoiled and stared at Todd's impenetrable expression with a wary look. "Just wait a minute. I don't think you fully realize what happened last night. You two charged at me with the expectation that I was going to try to get away from you. I just let you keep coming, then used the old *objects in motion tend to remain in motion law* and turned your own strength and momentum against you."

Drew smiled at their conceding nods. "It was merely agility against aggression. I'm not a hit man for hire. I like to see it as defense, not assault and battery."

"That's not what we need either." Todd waved his hands in denial.

"That's good because I want to take Willow back to Pennsylvania, not spend time in jail talking to her through a bulletproof Plexiglas wall. Mug shots do not fit my idea of publicity posters."

"Cal and his bunch learned not to mess with us that way a long time ago." Todd brushed it off with a flick of his wrist. "The feud's turned into a one-upmanship thing to see who gets the most skunked-you points. We're way ahead of them, and the assholes are too stupid to realize we get laughs out of it while they take it as a personal attack on their collective manhood, which hasn't changed much since they got out of high school."

"I can relate to all of that." Drew nodded in agreement.

"Drew," Owen said, "you need to know something else. Willow doesn't get it. She thinks we're bigger jerks than they are because we goad them and then play along with them. To us, it's merely a form of entertainment that keeps things exciting in our Podunk environment."

"I can relate to that, too." Drew laughed. "I suspect you get as much fun out of jerk-baiting and riling your sister as I do. I guess she was right when she said you raised her tough."

"We tried, but we've looked out for her, too." Owen smiled. "It's sort of like mastiffs raising a terrier puppy."

"You nailed it perfectly." Drew cracked up at a vivid visualization of Owen's simile.

"Welcome to our pack of bone-headed, jerky mastiffs." Todd laughed with the enthusiastic resonance of a kettle drum. "Just don't let out our secret. We're waiting for her to figure it out for herself. Gwen did that a long time ago and she's turned downright boring."

"This has been an enlightening visit." Drew drilled Todd with an impatient stare. "But it's late and I still don't know what you want me to do."

"Ride a bull."

"Wh-what?" Drew's impatience turned to total disbelief.

"I heard you say something to Byron in the loft about being in rodeos."

"I messed around with it for kicks when I was in college. But my thing was bareback broncs. I watched those crazy bull riders and wanted no part it. Those damn animals spin around and do impossible contortions while they're in midair."

"This one won't."

"Did it sign a no dirty trick affidavit to that effect?"

"It's an electric bull in a bar," Todd said. "We have an ongoing betting rivalry with the rowdy bunch. Part of it is a silent agreement that the winners get to tell the losers to suffer some sort of consequence. Our intention is to tell them to clear out. Problem is I heard they found a ringer I suspect is better on the bull than anyone we have."

"And you think I'm going to be a better ringer than he is?"

"I asked Willow about your riding skills," Todd said. "She said things like awesome and a bunch of shit I didn't understand. But she also said: sticks to a horse like he's part of it; moves with it like they're one being. That sounded right to me because moving against it always got me a face full of safety mat."

"I like the safety mat idea." Drew said. "I got tired of bruises and sand in my mouth. But I'm not a shoo-in. My grandmother's horse pitched me clear out of the dressage ring a few weeks ago."

"Your grandmother rides a bronc?" Todd gave him a stunned look.

"Rigoletto would never do that to her. I got mad at him and jabbed him with a spur, which he hates. His back is so supple he can hollow it then use it as a catapult. When he threw his head up, then shot it down and bolted forward, I wasn't expecting it. Hell, I flew farther than you did and got zero sympathy from Gram." Drew thought for a moment then jabbed a pointed finger at Todd. "But you're risking a lot on a dark horse. If I lose and we have to leave, there's no surprise for Willow and I desperately want that surprise because I know what I can do with it."

"We won't know until it's over," Todd stated. "But I don't see them demanding that. They'd rather tell us to do something stupid they can gloat over. And then, when they get obnoxious enough, we can all play bouncers and pitch 'em out the door with the bar owner's support. Harvey doesn't like 'em either."

"Does that mean I'm not really needed?"

"You're needed for pride of victory and a chance to collect on the bets." Todd looked at Drew as if he were an idiot. "I just like to have a fallback for important risks. And because I know how music freaks need a lot of practice, we arranged for a little rehearsal time."

"When?"

"Now."

"We're going to break into a bar so I can ride a fake bull at five in the morning? I still don't want to look at Willow through a plastic wall or whatever system you have out here."

"We have a better plan than that." Todd scoffed. "There's a pen full of rebellious steers out behind the main barn. Some of those suckers still think they're bulls."

Drew thought about it for a while to keep Todd guessing, then burst out laughing. "Why not? I've done stupider things. But don't mention it to Willow. I don't want to hear her objections for two days."

"If we have it our way," Byron's firm voice cut across the room. "she isn't going to know anything until it happens. Isn't that what *surprise* means?" He stood up and looked at the trail of clothes strewn across the floor. "Damn it, Todd, you made a mess."

Drew took a quick survey of the room and shook his head. "Byron, how can you make a mess out of something that's already a mess?"

"Because it was my mess and he messed with it." Byron pointedly looked out the window and announced, "It's starting to get light out there. Let's get this show on the road."

Chapter Twenty-Four

By Wednesday afternoon, Lloyd still had no answer. Willow knew her father well enough to suspect he'd already decided but was holding it back to consider all the possible ramifications. Important decisions were rarely impulsive; and once Lloyd made up his mind, it was almost impossible to change it. Since Monday morning, he had been a silent wall of non-expression or not home, which left Drew to work with her brothers. The one thing none of them did was leave him alone with her. After three days of hay baling and farm chores, Willow was beginning to wonder why Drew didn't just snatch her up and take her to Pennsylvania. They could get married without her father's permission; and even though Drew's insistence on doing it right pleased her, she was willing to bypass what she considered outdated nonsense.

Willow, who tended to view farm work from Byron's viewpoint, was flattered by Drew's sacrifice and decided to offer condolences during one of the rare times they managed to be somewhat alone with each other for a few minutes. She was out by the main barn, feeding carrots to Packy, her retired pinto, when Drew clanked down the elevator from the hay loft, helped Byron shove the wagon away, then followed him to the hydrant by the corner of the barn.

Watching Drew douse himself with a hose, then dry his face with the T-shirt in his hand, Willow remembered how she had looked at him the first day she met him and tried to see him on the farm against the openness of Iowa with the eye-squinting blue of a summer sky behind him. Now he was here, drawing their worlds together. It threw her off balance and she realized her earlier vision had left out some of the realities of working men on a hot Iowa day: the gritty tang of salt on his skin; the sharp musk of sweat mingling with the heady, fresh scent of curing hay; the wrung-out look when emerging from a sweltering, dust-clogged hay loft after throwing around seventy-pound hay bales.

Drew was sweaty and dirty, his forearms covered with scratches from hay stems, his tanned, shirtless torso coated with a film of hay dust and streaked by rivulets of well water dripping from his head. His wet hair was a tangle of hay scraps and unruly curls; his beard sparkled with water droplets. He smelled of man, hay, grease and diesel fumes all tangled together in an aroma that meant home, summer and her brothers. Yet under it all, he was still the man who excited her and turned everything else in her life into trivial, background noise. Which startled her.

Willow had been seeing Drew and Sutherland Manor as a refuge, an escape from the farm she had seen as stifling, provincial and dull. Since returning home, especially after Drew arrived, Willow knew it didn't matter if they were in Pennsylvania, or Iowa, or Europe. If he could suffer through hay baling, she could make it through operas, maybe even learn to understand them and like them. Drew believed there was room in his life for a farm girl from Iowa and it thrilled her.

After picking up the hay hook that he'd dropped by the hose, Drew swaggered to her and slid the smooth metal down her cheek and neck into her opened shirt. He hooked it around her bra and pulled her toward him. "Arrgh, I've caught me a lusty wench to warm me bunk or walk the plank."

"I'll take your bunk, brave buccaneer. Are you ready to blow this slave camp and head back to luxurious living?" Willow watched him drape the damp T-shirt around his neck and lean back against the board fence. "Have you had enough of how the other half lives?"

"Are you kidding?" Drew laughed at her ribbing question and hung the hook on the fence. "I haven't enjoyed myself this much in years. No wonder you captured me. There's some of the plains in you, some of its openness and freedom, the sense of being able to stand on your own and live by sweat and determination. People are self-sufficient here. They don't need a clutter of civilization and pretense. No wonder your family is so tight together. You grew up needing each other."

"My god, they've made a farmer out of you." Willow stared at the enthused sparkle in his eyes and burst out laughing. "And I was feeling sorry for you."

"Well," Drew grabbed her hand, pulled her to him and gave her his innocent schoolboy look. "You can give me a little sympathy.

Todd and Owen are determined to find out where my breaking point is. I feel I'm being challenged to prove I'm as indestructible as they are."

"If you let them show you up, they'll ease up."

"No way." Drew bristled. "Remember the kid who braved the old hermit to steal his booze? He's still there. If they win the bout fair and square, I'll accept it, but..." He screwed his face into a punch-drunk expression. "I don't take no dives for nobody, lady."

"Then they'll probably work you into the ground."

"I'm getting that message, but I'm still stubborn." Drew caught her face between gentle hands and pulled her to him for a kiss.

He was salty and sticky but Willow was unconcerned as he molded her to him with hands that knew how to touch her and control her.

"I hate to break up the love scene, but we have more hay." Byron hung up the grease gun he'd been using on the elevator and pointed to the tractor Matt was driving into the barnyard with three wagons of stacked hay bales behind it.

"I thought you'd gone to those big round bales?" Drew nodded at the huge rolls lined up beside the barn.

"We have for the cattle," Byron said. "It's made haying much easier. However, we still put up about 5,000 square bales to sell to backyard farmers and crazy horse people like you two."

"But I've seen wagons like that." Drew argued. "They pick up the bales by themselves and then stack them in the barn. So why are we doing it the hard way?"

"We already filled two sheds the easy way, but that wagon won't climb into a hayloft and Dad figures as long as we're hanging around eating off him, we're cheaper than a new shed." Byron set a hand on Willow's shoulder and squeezed it. "You found a great man, Elf. But get him away from the farm and back to Italy. I want to see him taking bows on an opera stage, not sweating on a farm. This fascination with work makes me question his sanity."

"If she gets determined enough, I'll end up wherever she wants me." Drew shrugged. "She doesn't have much more patience with indecision than my father does."

"She takes after her mother. Mom could always get what she wanted out of Dad, no matter how much he blustered or denied it."

"Byron?" Drew gave him a pleading look. "Is there any way I can get her alone for more than fifteen minutes at a time?"

"Dad, Todd and Owen are going to an auction tomorrow morning. I'll see what I can do."

"You're a lifesaver. Now, let's see if we can work Todd and Owen into a lather."

"Drew," Byron scowled, "I've spent most of my life trying to get out of work not make it worse."

"I thought it would be a good idea to even the odds."

"Do you realize you're destroying an image I've taken years to create? I've painstakingly created this myth that says people with musical talent are dangerously allergic to manual labor."

Sitting on a corner of the wagon's loading deck, Willow smiled as they continued to banter while they scrambled up the elevator. She'd known Byron and Drew would like each other. She was amazed by how well they fit together.

Willow had exposed most of Drew's portrait now and some of it surprised her. It was not only brushed with a texture that belonged to Byron, there were strong accents that reminded her of Todd and Owen. Then she realized it shouldn't have surprised her. Her life had been surrounded by those three brothers. As four children in as many years, Todd, Byron, she, then Owen were bunched together in the middle of the family and grew up with a closeness that bonded them together and set them apart from the rest of their siblings. Now there was Drew, dovetailed between Todd and Byron and not as different as she tried to make him.

"Excuse me, Princess, are you going to sit around spinning daydreams and getting in my way or are you going climb up that stack and throw bales down to me?"

With a start, Willow looked up to see Matt's dark brown eyes staring at her with a chiding expression, as well as an amused quirk of a smile that reminded her there was another annoying but loved brother. "I think I remember how to do that."

A few hours later, while she was helping her mother with dinner, Willow was starting to wish Drew didn't fit in so well. He seemed to be having so much fun with her brothers that he was talking about going to a cowboy bar with them. It wasn't the way she'd hoped to spend the evening, but she doubted she would get much of a say in the matter. When Drew came in a while later, she made one more attempt to change his mind. He laughed at her objections and told her she could stay home if the planned entertainment wasn't good enough.

"It's always full of rowdies and the weekday atmosphere is loud and awful."

"That's what my father says about Wagner." Drew tweaked her nose then dodged her jab and swatted the seat of her shorts before he headed up the back stairs to Byron's room.

"Drew Sutherland, do you ever listen to me?"

He turned on the landing. "How about one to three on Wednesdays and Thursdays?"

"It's Wednesday."

"But it's after three. Besides, I have to go. I'm buying."

After he bounded up the stairs, Willow turned to her mother with a sour face. "He should be in farce, not opera."

"He certainly isn't what I envisioned as an opera singer. He's so unpretentious and fits in so well."

"Too well. He's just like them." Willow smiled at the amused look on her mother's face. "As the saying goes, you won't lose a daughter, you'll gain another pain in the ass son."

"I wouldn't say he's just like them." Maureen arched an auburn eyebrow. "None of my sons ever showed me how to prune roses or volunteered to help me pick vegetables. Drew not only offered to carry them, he opened the gate and the back door for me."

"When was this?"

"Early this morning. Drew was out running while everyone else was asleep. When I went outside, he was crouched down examining my rose bushes. He showed me a new way to prune them and gave me a prescription to pep them up."

"If he absorbed enough from his grandmother's gardener, you'll have beautiful roses. Mae used to put him to work helping John in the gardens."

"John must have taught him a lot. While we picked and weeded, we had an extensive horticultural discussion. It was very enjoyable talking to a knowledgeable, attractive young man with such pleasant manners, and good-looking legs."

Willow burst out laughing with her mother and sighed dramatically. "He's a real hunk, isn't he?"

"Yes, Willow, but there's something more important that makes Drew special. He's fascinated by everything, wants to learn everything and experience as much of life as he can grab. I don't think he'll ever be dull or sit in one place for long. Tom would have given you a secure life and been kind to you forever, but he would have stifled you, put blinders on you, and never offered you a challenge."

"That's what Byron told me." Willow gave her a wry look.

"I'm not surprised. Neither you nor Byron will settle down and be content in one corner of the world—doing the same things, dreaming the same dreams. But at least you and Byron have a place you identify as home. Drew said he has no specific corner of the world he can call home. Remember to always carry a part of your family and Iowa within you and call that feeling home."

"I love you, Mom." Willow sniffed back a swell of emotion, circled her arms around her mother and relaxed in the warmth of her hug. "I knew you'd understand, but what about Dad? I'm going to marry Drew. Why doesn't he realize it and stop being so stubborn?"

"He's not just being stubborn. Drew did an unexpected thing. It's made your father do some thinking. Give him time to sort it out and answer the way he wants."

Willow finished setting the table with Beth, then took two six packs of cold beer onto the front porch. After opening a beer for herself, she offered a can to Todd, who held out a cupped hand when he walked out of the house.

"I thought you were going to destroy him." Willow ribbed her burly brother.

"He's hard to destroy." Todd gave her a scowl that turned into a slow smile. "Has a sharp wit, too."

"What did you think I'd fall in love with, a dull wimp? Honestly, Todd, you could give me some credit for taste."

"Matter of fact, I'm impressed by your serenading lover. Good match for you. Clever enough to keep you in hand without being a brute about it."

"He's an infuriating tease about it." Willow screwed her face into a grimace that was mostly for effect.

"Can't fool me, little sister. You were always looking for a skirmish. He took us on with a laugh. Finished on his feet still laughing."

"Todd's being kind." Drew slipped the open beer out of Willow's hand and collapsed on the glider. "I remember finishing flat on my back after he threw a bale that hit me smack in the chest."

"But you were laughing," Todd said.

"Who wasn't? I was too tired to move, let alone get up. When that hot shower hit me, I thought I was going to slide down the wall like it was the inside of a lava lamp. Every hay scratch stung like sin. Farming could replace both health clubs and S&M parlors."

"Probably why there ain't any in Cottonwood Forks." Todd leaned back against the porch railing.

"You have a point there." Drew admitted. "I was also worried that if I didn't get the hay dust out of my lungs, I was going to lose an octave and start sounding like you."

"Got a place for me in opera?"

"As soon as I find a basso profundo role with a three-note range, I'll let you know."

Willow sat next to Drew when Byron and Owen joined them. They were followed by Matt and Beth, who was starry-eyed over Drew and usually blushing, since he kept giving her teasing smiles that flustered her. It didn't surprise Willow when she looked at Drew, who was much more himself—barefoot in blue running shorts and an open-necked polo shirt. In fact, he was much too stimulating—as she sensed she was in shorts and another shirt swiped from Byron's clean laundry.

Todd studied Drew for a moment before he asked, "Can you teach me whatever Kung Fu magic you did when you wiped out me and Owen?"

"Sure, but it's not as simple as learning a few magic tricks. I've had almost twenty years of training in martial arts. You can know how to do it and lose if your reflexes don't take over. If you want to know how to do it right, take a course and drill with it."

"Never was keen on the pajamas," Todd said. "Always thought there was a lot of cult ritual to it."

"There's discipline and courtesies and a certain amount of ritual. The pajamas are comfortable and allow for free movement. I'll show you some basic moves when my body recovers from the torture inflicted on it in the hayloft. But I have a warning." Drew held Todd's eyes for a moment. "Don't get cocky about it. It makes you a target. All it takes is one flung beer mug to knock you dizzy enough you can get the crap beat out of you when they gang up on you."

"Had experience with that?"

"At a roughneck bar when I was in college. I view it as humility training."

"I keep learning more about those damn fool stupid deeds." Willow sat next to Drew. "What jail did you end up in that time?"

"I was unceremoniously deposited in a campus dumpster near my dorm."

"Why do you guys think that's funny?" Willow scowled when her brothers laughed with him. "What's humorous about getting beat up?"

"It's one of those man things you keep screwing up." Drew slid his arm around her and teased her ear with his fingers.

The conversation stimulated a spate of jokes about Todd's flying act the night Drew arrived. Adding his own embellished account of the entire confrontation, Todd laughed as loud as any of them and Willow knew that no matter what her father said, Drew had been accepted as a member of the family.

When Drew folded his legs in front of him and ignored Willow to talk with her brothers, she smirked, set her hand on his knee and casually trailed her fingers along the inside of his thigh. He straightened with a jolt and, smacking his hand over hers, continued to swap outrageous macho stories. She looked up at where Byron sat on the railing with his back against a post. He laughed at her then took a closer look and frowned.

"I think I recognize that shirt. What happened to the one you stole before you headed east?"

"Someone ripped it." Willow glanced at Drew and worked her fingers loose until she could twist the hairs on his leg.

"That someone may rip another one if someone else doesn't stop playing with his leg." His voice low, but carrying, Drew reached over, grabbed the front of her shirt and pulled her face to face with him. "You're pushing for a hot blast of trouble."

"Why don't you steal his shirts?" Byron asked. "Maybe he won't rip them."

"I wouldn't put any bets on it." Drew muttered. "She can make me very impatient."

Jolted by a harsh snort, Drew released Willow's shirt and glanced toward the doorway at a gruff face set in a glowering frown. He looked stung and, for the second time, Willow saw him blush. Matt gave up the rocking chair for his mother as Drew stood in a smooth reaction of trained manners and continued to stand until Lloyd sat on a bench facing Willow, who carefully studied his face. Her father's features were masked with the stern expression that could be disapproval or a put-on to keep her guessing.

"The rest of you can get lost." Lloyd waved them off the porch before he focused a probing stare on Drew and cleared his throat. "First, I'm going to explain my side of all this. I'm sure you know you aren't the first man to want to marry her."

"Yes, sir." Drew was politely charming and relaxed.

After a rub and tug on his right ear, Lloyd said, "I knew Tom well enough to put my approval on him with no hesitation. It's possible all of us put so much approval on him we didn't give Willow a chance to voice her misgivings, except to Byron, who's always been the renegade in the family."

"Pretty good renegade as I see it," Drew said.

"Oh, he turned out all right, but some of the getting there was shaky. Be that as it may, Byron convinced her not to marry Tom just because everyone else thought she should. None of us took it very well or tried to see it from Willow's viewpoint." Lloyd paused for a moment and seemed to chew over what he was going to say next.

"It wasn't until you gave me the chance to make a decision that I not only stopped and thought about it, I had a talk instead of an argument with Byron. While I had no misgivings about Tom, I had so many about you I couldn't voice them all. Most of them can be blamed on a father trying to protect his daughter from hurt long after he has the right to do it. She is my first girl, and you hurt her in a way I see as wrong. I wanted to thrash the stuffing out of you."

"I can understand that because I deeply regret hurting her."

"You have every reason to." Lloyd nodded, then continued to explain, "When Willow defied me by saying she still loved you, I was too hardheaded to realize I'd lost. I wanted to keep her safe and that meant here, where you couldn't hurt her again. When you had the nerve to brazen your way through that middle of the night fracas, I liked something about you. You had the guts to come out here and fight for her. After watching you together, I'd have to be an ass not to see you're in love."

"Dad, why don't you just say yes and get it over with?" Willow blurted with impatience.

"Because it's not my permission Drew wants." Lloyd seemed to receive some sort of confirmation from a quick glance at Drew. "You don't need that. He wants my approval and blessings. That's not so easy."

"Why not?"

"I have misgivings that won't go away." Lloyd lowered dark brows and stared at Drew as if he were a judge grilling an inept lawyer. "Do you have a steady job?"

"Dad, you have to be kidding." Willow huffed.

"Willow, I don't know anything about him, except he wants to be an opera singer and his grandmother hired you to help train horses. I know a lot of people who put on a show of wealth when what they have is debts. And in spite of Byron's biased view of Drew's talent, I don't believe in the financial stability of entertainers. There seem to be more unemployed entertainers than there are successful ones."

Willow flared, but Drew squeezed her hand to stop her from answering. "Relax, Willow. He has a point."

When Willow clamped her mouth shut, Drew looked at her father. "Mr. Roberts, I don't have a steady job."

"It doesn't matter, Dad." A flush of embarrassment and anger stung Willow's face. "Drew is a great singer and I can work while he trains his voice."

"Willow, I'd like to answer for myself." Drew calmed her and, feeling miffed, she sat back with her arms crossed in front of her.

When Willow looked resigned, Drew said, "I've never discussed the subject with Willow. She's refreshingly uninterested in money, which may or may not become my headache. She also has an amazing confidence in her own ability to succeed at whatever she wants to do. Willow sees money as a commodity needed for survival, not as a goal in itself. Although I don't show much interest in money either,

I do have the means to support her almost anyway she would like to be supported."

"What are sufficient means to a man with no income?" Lloyd demanded.

"I didn't say I had no income."

Drew looked uncomfortable and Willow worried about how her father was going to accept the fact that his grandmother supported him. But she kept quiet and let Drew continue.

"Mr. Roberts, I didn't bring a prepared financial statement and I'm a little hazy on some of it. The best I can do is put it this way: if I wanted to purchase this farm, you could have the money in your bank by tomorrow afternoon; if I wanted to buy your new combine, I could write you a check on a money market account now and it would clear."

"That combine's well over a hundred thousand dollars." Lloyd looked as if he'd been swatted with a two by four.

"Neither purchase would cut into my stock investments. My shares of Sutherland International alone provide me with an annual income in excess of two hundred thousand dollars. I can support her."

Willow gaped at Drew while she tried to absorb and digest what he'd just revealed. "That's mind boggling."

"I told you my grandmother made sure I was solvent."

"I thought she just gave you money to live on." Willow stammered.

"She gave me stock portfolios, trust accounts and joint ownership of Sutherland Manor when my father wasn't interested in it. For tax purposes, Gram started turning my inheritance over to me when I turned twenty-three and seemed to have, in her words, settled down enough to be reliable. It made me independently wealthy. It also forced me to manage it. I found that if you ignore money, it gets itself into a tangled mess that makes a large number of accountants cross-eyed. I also have some properties and assets in Europe."

"Such as?" Lloyd reacted to Drew's casual statement with a look of astonishment.

"A small stud farm in France, a sailing yacht, a chain of small art galleries, a small ski resort in the Swiss Alps, which my financial advisor calls diversification and I call a liability I would like to get rid of. I also own a number of what I guess would be translated to refuges for abused, runaway, or unwanted children in Italy. Although I own the properties, the non-profit foundation is run by an order of Catholic nuns. About three years ago, I found a boy of eight hiding out in my basement. He'd been stealing food because he was hungry and afraid to go home. It hit me where I was tender, so I looked into what I could do to help him as well as other kids like him."

Drew paused when Lloyd blinked at him, then added, "I really don't mean to be vague about my wealth. I just don't pay much attention to it. My idea of managing it is to put it in the hands of trusted experts. And although my father nags me about taking a little more interest in what's happening with my money, it seems to be doing fine without my interference."

Drew looked at three stunned faces and shrugged uneasily. "The truth is money has always been there, like air or water. I use what I need when I need it and let my brokers and accountants worry about details. After all, that's what I pay them to do."

"I would say you had sufficient means." Lloyd stated drily.

"I assure you Willow will never be left destitute. And as long as we keep loving each other, she'll never be left at all. I'm beginning to like her ideas of marriage, children and anniversaries. I'd even like them to have an Iowa farm to grow up on. I feel very real here."

"How many children do you want?" Willow's question popped out of the confused jumble of thoughts in her mind.

"More than one." Drew contorted his face and looked at her as if he thought she was deranged. "You?"

"Fewer than nine."

"I guess I can work within an octave range."

A low building laugh rumbled out of Lloyd's chest and he shook his head with the same bewilderment of her sidebar as Drew did. "When do you want to get married?"

"Sometime in October," Drew answered. "As soon after *Camelot* closes as possible because there's a chance I'll need to be in Genoa by mid-November. The details are up to Willow."

"Will you get married here?" Maureen asked her daughter. "In our country chapel?"

"I hadn't really thought about it." Willow looked at Drew.

"Sounds fine. You have more family to invite than I do."

"Do you want a big wedding?"

"Willow, I want to marry you. I'm not fussy about how, but I shudder at the thought of facing Gram if she gets cheated out of a chance to see me thoroughly and properly hogtied. Of course, she'll also insist on a catered reception at Sutherland Manor at some point and expect your family to attend. And Dad will throw some sort of soiree in France after the honeymoon and hope they will attend that, too."

"Honeymoon?" The sudden reality of it hit Willow with a barrage of disconnected thoughts. "Where will we go for a honeymoon?"

Drew laughed at her bedazzled expression. "Right now, that bushel of carrots on a deserted island sounds good."

"Well, Maureen," Lloyd stood and reached for his wife's hand, "I think we should break out a bottle of the good wine so we can toast a new member of the family."

Squealing with a thrill that continued to expand inside her, Willow bounced off the glider and hugged her parents. There was an awkward moment before her father clasped Drew's offered hand and her mother responded to his hug. And then everything was relaxed and she was in Drew's arms, wishing they were alone on a mountain top, or that deserted island, or anywhere but on her front porch with dinner ready.

Chapter Twenty-Five

The Bucking Bull Bar and Grill, where ambiance was created by a hovering haze of cigarette smoke illuminated by a plethora of neon beer signs, did not meet Willow's idea of a location to celebrate her engagement, but no change of plan had been suggested. Thoughts of a romantic, intimate interlude with Drew vanished when they entered the combined dance hall, dining room and bar to join Todd and Owen at a large round table that was far enough away from bar and band platform they would be able to hear each other without shouting. Drew was casually introduced to a group of Todd's and Owen's friends at a nearby table and greeted with cursory banter and nods.

Willow knew most of them and was flattered by the way both the men and women seemed to be sizing up the bearded stranger sitting beside her with his arm across the back of her chair, hand possessively caressing her shoulder. Even in fairly new jeans and an open neck western shirt he'd borrowed from Matt—Byron's were too tight in the chest and Todd's hung on him like worn out feed sacks—Willow believed Drew stood out like a masterpiece at a Grange Hall craft fair.

Todd's droll observation that she'd see a shine in shit if Drew was wearing it, surfaced in her mind, but the acute interest in the faces around her bolstered her opinion. Worries about the rough wood tables, scuffed dance floor and loud, beer drinking patrons being below Drew's sophistication fled under a secret swell of pride Willow felt in showing everyone that she'd stepped beyond Cottonwood Forks and found cultured sophistication.

Todd signaled a blonde waitress and ordered pitchers of beer as well as the bar's specialty—baskets of hot pretzels and spicy mustard. "Put it on one tab, Cindy. Willow's classy eastern boyfriend's shelling out tonight."

Todd's boasting announcement annoyed Willow. She wanted to show Drew off, but not by crassly embarrassing him. Before she could say anything, Drew met Cindy's questioning expression with one of his boyish looks of innocence. "He promised a good time as long as I was willing to pay for it."

"From him I believe it." Cindy swatted Todd on the back of his head. "He took me out three times. Forgot his wallet once and met me here twice because I get a discount on food."

When Cindy walked away, Willow scowled at Todd. "What a clod."

"I work the angles." Todd shrugged and looked at Drew. "Ever ride an electric bull, Drew?"

"Nooo." Drawing out the word, Drew followed Todd's gaze to the bull riding machine in a corner at the bar end of the room.

"Want to give it a whirl?"

While Drew stared at the black devise and the padded floor area around it, Willow grabbed his arm and dug her nails into it. "Don't even think about it."

Drew settled back in the chair and shook his head. "You promised a good time. You didn't mention I could get hurt."

"Afraid of a little pain?" Todd sat sideways at the end of the table with his legs stretched out in front of him, the heels of his boots resting on the floor.

"Stop it, Todd." Willow glowered at her brother. "You're talking so loud people are staring at you."

"It's something we do here." Tod crossed his arms, leaned back in the chair and continued to talk in his deep, carrying voice. "Gals make us dance when the music plays and guys dare each other to ride the bull when it doesn't. Did you forget?"

"That's what *you* do."

"Relax, Willow," Drew said when Cindy returned with pitchers of beer and baskets heaped with thick salted pretzels. "I'll test the beer and pretzels."

The casual way Drew dismissed Todd's baiting challenge surprised Willow, but she accepted it as a mild victory over masculine posturing and put it out of her mind.

Byron, as usual, showed up in time for food. When the band arrived, he stood up and Willow caught his wrist. "That's *Salt Lick*. Why are they here?"

"I asked them to play tonight," Byon answered.

"Harvey's willing to pay them on a Wednesday when there's no cover?"

"We worked it out." Byron excused himself to talk to the band, and Willow grinned, knowing he would play with them and give Drew a chance to hear the down-home fiddling he kept asking about.

While the members of the band were busy setting up, recorded Western dance music blasted out of speakers. Willow jumped up and grabbed Drew's hand. "It's my turn to teach you dancing—country dancing."

After years of musical theater that included extensive dance training, Drew was a quick learner and Willow found herself trying to keep up with him. When he tossed her in the air, she yelped, but firm hands caught her waist and lowered her for a kiss.

While Willow blushed with discomfort at being the center of attention, Drew thrived on it, which made her realize she was either going to get used to it or spend a good amount of her life red-faced and mortified. And then, when he missed a step and stumbled into her, she met sparkling eyes and was instantly snared by his passion for fun.

Laughing at Drew's clowning efforts to get back in step, Willow let his uninhibited enthusiasm sweep away her embarrassment until she stopped caring what anyone else thought. He was Drew; and since she'd agreed to take him the way he was, her only choice was to enjoy the wildness of the ride.

They returned to their table exhausted and laughing. Willow sat next to Byron, and Todd plopped full mugs in front of them.

"Didn't catch me after you flung me." Todd stated in his gravelly monotone.

"Wrong trajectory." Drew downed half a beer without pausing.

"Are you trying to get drunk?" Willow asked.

"I'm thirsty." Drew took a few more swallows before he looked across the table and met Todd's eyes. Nothing was spoken but something was clearly communicated.

"Drunk enough to ride that bull, Drew?" Todd asked in a booming voice.

"Why not?"

When Willow caught a glimpse of Owen talking to Cal Wallace and his gang of friends, she realized what was happening. "Leave Drew out of it, Todd."

"Of what?"

"Anything between you and Cal and his bunch. They don't like us Roberts."

"Probably cuz Cal's an asshole and we keep proving it." Frustrated with her brother, Willow grabbed Drew's beard and pulled his face to hers. "He's setting you up so he can bet against you."

"You have that backwards." Drew growled in a low but firm voice.

"What do you mean?"

"Do you know what a ringer is?" He pried her hand away, stood up, and followed Todd across the dance floor at a slightly off-balanced gait.

Fuming, Willow elbowed Byron, who was building a tower of pretzels on an upturned basket. "Go tell him he's a jerk."

"You tell him." Byron scowled at his toppled pile of pretzels. "I'd rather watch."

Willow stewed over her lost victory and Byron's desertion as an ally long enough to decide that if Drew was going to be a jerk she might as well let him. When the first rider slid off the far side of the gyrating machine, she said, "He leaned forward. Bad move."

"How will he do?"

"Byron, if any of those suckers ever saw Drew on a horse, they'd keep their mouths and wallets shut."

"And if they weren't so sloshed with beer, they may have noticed that Todd and Drew aren't as drunk as they look." Byron picked up a pretzel and looked, one-eyed, through a loop at Willow.

"You knew about this?"

"It's a payback. Cal cheated Todd with a rigged bet."

"Does Dad know about all this betting?"

"Todd's a big boy and, as far as I know, he and Owen haven't had to sell any of their restored tractors, yet."

"I think he's a jerk and so is Drew for helping him, but I'm not going to argue with him tonight." Willow sighed and watched Drew play a convincing reluctance act while Todd clearly goaded him. "He and Todd are still trying to sort out this man-to-man thing. I guess I have to let them."

"Oh, they have it all figured out," Byron said. "And as far as staying out of it, you're being wiser than I sometimes give you credit for. Saves me having to hold you down again."

"What?"

"Take my word for it. There's method to their madness."

Willow and Byron reached the knot of spectators in time to watch Bill Turner, Cal's ringer and the clear favorite in bets. He lasted fifteen seconds before he over balanced too far to the right. The next twist increased his angle and he started to roll off the right flank. Flailing attempts to recover threw him away from the machine and he fell into a crumpled pile on the mats. But he'd lasted eight seconds longer than anyone else. When Bill stood up, he gave a condescending nod to Drew, who was the last rider. Willow chuckled at Bill's confident smirk and Drew's diffident shrug.

From the moment Drew vaulted onto the machine his ride was anticlimactic. He just sat there, leaning back, with his free arm relaxed at his side, his seat glued to the metal beast's center of gravity. His lower body moved with the motion of the machine while his upper body maintained a constant upright orientation to the plane of gravity. After a buzzer signaled Bill's time, Drew waited out the next two seconds that would clinch a win instead of a rematch, kicked his legs up behind him, clicked his heels together and vaulted clear of the machine to land on his feet.

Willow walked up to him and he kissed her with a relish that thrilled her. When he let her go, she looked up at him. "You're a jerk."

"For once I agree with you." He walked toward their table with his arm around her.

"How did you know you could do it?"

"Well, there were the wild couple of summers I spent riding bareback broncs with the Penn rodeo gang. That put Gram in a lather and bolstered her opinion that I wasn't responsible enough to have her money. Every time I limped home, she gave me that serves-you-right-jerk look." He laughed at her agreeing smirk. "The bar's insurance carrier seems to agree with you. I had to sign a release before they let me on that thing?"

"That thing isn't a horse, even a bronc."

"That's what Todd said before he had me practice on some of your smelly steers."

"When?"

"At the crack of dawn."

"You spent a lot of time playing with my brothers."

"It kept me from climbing in your window." He hugged her against his side. "You never told me farm boys have so much crazy fun."

"I can't believe you rode steers." Willow shook her head.

"Except for the one that stood there looking stupid until Todd smacked it with a tree branch. It kicked out at him then dropped to its knees and practically stood on its head. When I bailed off, it butted me in the ass and splatted me in a pasture pie. That T-shirt will never be the same."

His sour face made her laugh. "You can throw it out."

"I think I'll frame it as a trophy. I can hang it in the stable and let Gram wonder if I've reverted to being a brainless asshole."

"Mae wouldn't say that."

"It takes the right provocation."

"Why do you do such dumb things?"

"They always seem like good ideas at the time and doing is more fun than watching." His voice lowered to a soberer tone. "Besides, Todd had good reasons and I felt I owed it to him."

"Why?"

"For making his sister cry in front of him."

"What?" Willow halted and twisted her head around to look at him. "I cried on Byron's shoulder. What do you owe him?"

"Byron isn't Todd."

"What does that mean?"

Drew set his hands on her shoulders and turned her to face him. "Willow, your big, tough brother Todd loves you and can't stand to see your heart broken."

Willow was quiet for a moment while she thought about how twelve-year-old Todd had spent all his savings to buy her a new puppy when Rascal was killed. She remembered Todd fixing broken toys for her. And when he was eight, he walked more than three miles in a late-night thunderstorm to find a doll she'd lost at a picnic. Her father had said they'd go back the next day, but there was lightning and Willow cried for her lost doll friend. Todd got a tanning for going out at night. She cried for him and saw him as her hero.

Willow had trouble answering around the lump in her throat. "How do you know these things?"

"I can't answer that. I just do."

"But you didn't know how I felt about you."

"Oh, I knew. I just didn't want to accept it." He hugged her to his side and walked toward the table. "Don't let Todd know I'm on to his soft heart." He winked at her confusion. "It's one of those man things."

When Drew sat down, Todd clasped his hand and shook it. "Got a gyroscope up your ass?"

"I hope not. It would make it damn hard to turn a corner." Their elbows dropped to the table and their grips changed in a simultaneous shift from a handshake to arm wrestling. Drew's face tightened with agonized effort just before the back of his hand thumped onto the table. He shook it when he raised it. "Damn, he does it every time."

Todd turned in his chair and stared toward the bar. "Ever been in a bar fight, Drew?"

"Too many of them." He scoffed and looked around him. "We're not in Marseille, are we?"

When both Drew and Willow laughed, Todd gave them a strange look. "Would that help?"

"Not a bit." Drew frowned.

"Then wherever it is, we ain't there." Todd watched Cal, Bill and four others stride toward him. "We got Owen on our side. Maybe even Byron if the mood strikes him."

"Todd, you boneheaded jerk—" Willow froze when he threw his head back and laughed. "What's so funny?"

"You. Cal's pissed but knows when he has to pay up and get the hell out of here." Todd pushed out of the chair and strolled toward Cal.

"I thought I was good at mind games." Drew slid his arm around Willow and kissed her neck. "Todd is a master."

"I don't follow you."

"He settled a score and cleared out the unwanted rowdies with one ingenious gambit."

"That's what Byron meant. Why didn't he just tell them to leave?"

"He didn't have the right until he skunked them."

Willow stared at Todd's back with a thoughtful look then snuggled her head against Drew's shoulder. "I still don't have the man stuff figured out, do I?"

"You do better than most women. I got bitched out a lot for crude insensitivity—and political incorrectness."

"I always felt cheated for not being a boy. Until I met you."

"Thank you. I don't do that with boys." He trailed his fingers along her jaw and held her gaze with his. "Willow, do you Roberts ever let up on each other?"

Willow thought over his question before she said, "I don't think so. At least not Todd, Byron, Owen and me. They act like they raised me."

"I think they did." Drew kissed the top of her head. "Are there usually so many people here on a Wednesday night?"

"No." When Willow noticed the tables were filling and heard more people clumping in from the door, she smiled. "Unless it's because Byron and *Salt Lick* are here. It means he'll have to play to appease his fans."

"You're right. Come on." Drew took her hand and led her to a table near the bar and closer to the band.

When Byron stepped into the lights illuminating the band platform and plucked a microphone from its stand, the overall hubbub of noise faded to a smattering of applause, a few whistles and shouted demands that he put down the mike and grab a fiddle. Byron waved them to silence and lifted the microphone.

"For any of you who haven't been around here much in the last few years, I'm Byron Roberts. Glad to see you. And for you folks who heard about tonight via the Roberts/O'Reilly grapevine or the Cottonwoods Forks hearsay grid—which puts the internet to shame with its speed of information transfer—thank you for coming to celebrate with us."

When a burst of enthusiastic acknowledgment made him pause, Willow straightened in her chair and caught Drew's hand. At the same time, she saw Keith and Glenn, her oldest brothers, sitting with their wives. Her sister Gwen was with them. So was Tom Sorensen and an attractive brunette she didn't know. Looking around the room, Willow started to recognize friends, relatives and neighbors. When she saw her parents, as well as Matt and Beth, she knew this was no coincidence. Harvey Anderson wouldn't let anyone underage in his bar after eight without special arrangement.

The noise ebbed and Byron continued. "I guess you all know by now that my sister Willow took a job out East. She came home a few days ago, and while everyone was still trying to sort out what was going on, some love-struck nut showed up on the lawn at three o'clock in the morning, serenading her and asking to marry her. Of course, anyone with the good taste to use music in courtship and the balls to rouse a houseful of Roberts in the middle of the night is my kind of man. It took a while to convince a few others, but he did it. He mostly answers to the name Drew, but his professional name is Andrew Sutherland. That name doesn't mean much around here but in a few minutes, you'll know why it does in other parts of the world." Byron turned to the bar and waved Willow and Drew over.

"Did you know about this?" Willow clasped Drew's arm when she stood.

"Byron said you complained about me not singing for you so I agreed to do some songs with him. I didn't know it was going to turn into a party."

"I feel like a heifer at an auction." Willow grumbled and took his hand before she stepped onto the platform.

"Get used to it," Drew muttered. "You're going to get presented a lot."

The presentation was mercifully brief. Leaving Drew with Byron and the band, Willow retreated to the table near the platform. Owen, Todd, and Cindy, joined her. "Do you know what he's going to sing?" Willow asked Todd.

"Some. Practiced with the band this morning after Mom dragged you out shopping."

The room went silent when Byron picked up a fiddle and faced Drew across the open front of the platform. He held the silence long enough to build a static tension before his bow zinged across the strings and Drew's voice snapped out like a cracking whiplash, "The devil went down to Georgia…"

The choice startled Willow, but she was yanked into its intensity until she almost believed she could smell brimstone and see smoke curling away from Byron's racing bow. The power in Drew's dramatic stage voice, the blaze of his eyes and the intensity of his delivery reached into her emotions, ignited a zealous fervor that held her entranced. The final words hung in the mind for a few heartbeats before they were lost in shouts, whoops and applause.

When the din peaked and then started to taper off, Drew held up his hand to recapture the audience's attention and Byron moved to the piano. "To keep the mood going and prove to Willow that I know about her secret idol, we've revived a Neil Diamond favorite of mine, *Brother Love's Traveling Salvation Show*."

Drew took hold of his audience like the gospel preacher he was singing about and pulled them into his spell so completely they joined in the final chorus and its reprise with rhythmic clapping and stomping. After loud demands for more, Drew sang an emotion grabbing version of Diamond's *Cracklin' Rosie*. His boastful invitation to a store-bought night of imbibed pleasure enticed and delighted Willow. When he dropped into a lower register with an appeal that built back up in pitch and power, his voice twisted a deep desire in her. This wasn't just a performer—this was Drew—and his appeal was deeply sensual.

When Drew left the stage to let Byron play his fiddle with the band, Willow rushed to him the way she had three nights ago and felt that if his closing arms didn't hold her tight enough, the excitement would blow her apart. He backed her away from the lights into a dim hallway leading to an office where, fueled by heightened passion, the kiss swirled her into a state of whirling excitement that bubbled out of her like an effervescent geyser.

Willow was still spinning when she pressed her cheek against his shirt. "You made me want to fall to my knees and shout in tongues. You should be an evangelist."

"In effect, I am. So is Diamond. We're entertainers." He chuckled. "And *Cracklin' Rosie?*"

"You know what that made me want to do." She made a cross-eyed face and then sobered her voice. "After that, I don't see how Vittorio can say you sing without passion."

"I didn't sing like that for Vittorio."

"Why not?"

"I was too busy being perfect." Drew twisted his face while he thought about it. "The problem with opera is that its scale is so huge, its delivery so technical, it removes me from my feelings and my audience. I don't think it will now." He winked at her. "My sabbatical worked."

"How?"

Drew caught her nose between two knuckles. "I found you and a family in Iowa that made me feel the way it was with my own brothers—" His jaw clenched, abruptly cut off his words.

"Brothers?" Willow tightened a hand in his beard to keep him from looking away. "You have brothers?"

"No." He answered quickly. "I meant they take me back to visits with my Scottish cousins Alex and Duncan—"

"But you said brothers." Drew looked more vulnerable than Willow had ever seen him. Then, with a shiver, it was gone, as if it had never happened.

"It's nothing important." Drew hesitated, as if he were grappling with something he didn't know how to explain. "It was just a silly slip of the tongue."

"It didn't sound silly." When he touched her face, she caught his hand and held it still.

"It also resurrected an embarrassingly childish thing. My life fell apart after Dad left me and I invented imaginary brothers so I wouldn't be alone. It took me a long time to put them into proper perspective."

"Well," Willow looked down the hall at Todd's profile. "Now that you've been saddled with a new crop of them, you might find that real brothers aren't as agreeing and easy to control as imaginary ones."

"As I recall, mine were rarely either of those things." Drew looked puzzled then chuckled. "They did, however, give me someone else to blame things on, even if I could never get anyone to believe it."

"That doesn't work too well with real ones either." Willow flushed then said, "Blaming someone else always got me in more trouble than confessing."

"Mostly, being with your brothers brought back those fun vacations in Scotland and made me realize how much I missed by not having real brothers. Your family is so real it renewed me."

"How did we do that."

"By dragging me into the open emotions you all thrive on. I let go of my shields with you, then found my balance here and learned to accept that I am the sum of my life, even the wild parts of it."

"Those are the take my breath away exciting parts." Willow teased.

"To rehash one of my bad quips, you ain't seen nothin' yet—Baby."

"Your performance stunned me. I thought you were going to sing an aria."

Drew pulled back with an appalled look. "Why would I do that?"

"To show them you really know how to sing."

"I just did and they liked it."

"But you can do better. Why don't you show them what you can really do?"

"Am I detecting a little snobbery here?" Drew frowned.

"I'm not a snob." Willow recoiled from his accusation.

"Then why are you trying to get me to do what my audience doesn't want?"

His answer startled Willow and she didn't know how to answer.

"Why doesn't Byron play Tchaikovsky's First Concerto here?"

"Because no one would appreciate it."

"No. Some of them probably would appreciate it. He doesn't do it because it doesn't belong here. People come here to enjoy dancing, rock and country music in an atmosphere suited to it."

Willow understood what Drew was saying but wasn't ready to accept what he was implying. "There isn't much sophistication in it."

"Au contraire. Sophistication is awareness of complexity through education and experience. It has damn little to do with class or culture per se."

"Would you stop sounding like a professor." Willow wanted to say she'd gotten the point but it hadn't come out that way.

"Willow, you're trying to run away from who you are."

"I want to fit in your world."

"You fit with me. That's what's important. I love you in any world." He laughed and hugged her against his chest. "Some of these people may also enjoy Mozart or go to operas. It doesn't matter. They came here for a rousing good time and that's what we gave them. When I'm on an opera or concert stage, I sing classical. In a bar, I sing what fits. I try to do my best at both. It's a matter of appropriate, not better."

"I think I just witnessed an example of sophistication." Willow looked up at him and felt a numbing hole of humiliation in her chest. "And snobbery."

"It took me by surprise. I've never sensed it in you before." Drew held her face between his hands and studied her expression, asking for a truth she needed to express.

"I was proud of you and wanted to let people know I found something better than Cottonwood Forks."

"It staggers me to think of beating out a whole town." Drew pressed his nose against hers until she was looking into one huge blue eye. "But I can't do that. I just want to be the best for you."

"You are."

"That's good enough for me." He kissed the end of her nose. "I have one more song. Let's get back."

Drew stepped onto the platform, where the band left him alone with Byron. While the applause tapered off, he said something to Byron, who handed him the microphone.

Holding the round, black ball in front of his face, Drew gave it a wry, scrutinizing look before he turned it off and slipped it into its stand. "If I use that you'll all be running for the parking lot. I assume you can all hear me." When the projection of his voice carried across the room, a chorus of affirmation answered him.

"Okay. I've been out of touch with Country for a while, so bear with a little shift in style on another oldie. Fortunately, Byron has been at this long enough he knows just about everything." Drew turned to where Byron sat at the piano then looked back at the audience. "I want to keep this guy. He's a perfect accompanist. Give him any instrument and he can play the fool thing."

"I'm not too good on an accordion," Byron said.

"*Incredibile!*" Drew threw his hands in the air. "No squeeza da box!" He looked toward the ceiling with an imploring look and shook spread hands before he snapped his eyes to Willow and let loose with a barrage of operatic Italian. The sheer power of it was even more awesome than when he'd fired Figaro at her in Pennsylvania. Suddenly, he stopped, snapped his fingers and pointed at her. "Okay, you got another taste of Rossini, but that, *amore mio*, is all you're agonna get."

Willow pulled in a gasping breath then burst out laughing with everyone else while Drew stood with his hands on his hips, tapping his foot and scowling with exaggerated pomposity. When the laughter died down, he transformed from melodrama to casual.

"That's to let you know opera singers aren't stuffed shirts. They just make us wear them."

Drew looked over at Byron, who was bent over laughing so hard he couldn't breathe. "Let me know when you're ready to plink that thing. I'm running out of improv comedy."

With a few deep breaths, Drew composed himself. "It's time for the gushy part when I get soft and sentimental and Willow gets dewy-eyed and emotional." He smiled at the sound of a D major chord behind him. "If I do it right, she won't be alone in her feelings, which will save her a lot of embarrassment."

To Willow, John Denver's *Annie's Song* was a beautiful love song. When Drew sang it to her, she felt it was the most perfect love song she'd ever heard. The rich timbre of his operatic voice, the clarity of pitch and the way he enriched the words with meaning wrapped around her as securely and gently as an embrace. When she saw Todd pull Cindy closer and noticed a glint of moisture in his eyes, she knew Drew was doing it right.

Willow felt both alone with her private feelings and part of the palpable emotion surrounding her. She wanted to feel Drew holding her and touching her. At the same time, she never wanted the song to stop, never wanted the lights to come up and return her to reality. Drew's image shimmered in the wash of tears streaming from her eyes but she was held helpless by the intensity of his gaze.

When Drew ended the song, held out his hand and said, "I love you, Willow," into the silence, she ran onto the stage and into his arms, let his kiss hold off reality for a few more moments while the applause died down.

Sliding his hands down Willow's arms, Drew dropped to one knee and reached into his shirt pocket before he lifted her left hand and slipped a ring on her finger. "I have a little more time for formality now than I did when I first arrived at the farm, but my question is the same. Willow, will you marry me and spend your life with me?"

"Yes, I will." When he stood, she fell into clasping arms, squealed with excitement.

After two hours of non-stop hugs, congratulations, advice and ribald teasing from friends, relatives and neighbors, Willow was able to wind down and sit with Drew, Byron, Todd and Owen to share the remains of a last pitcher of beer and basket of pretzels in the emptying barroom that, for a few brief hours, had shimmered with diamond dust, sparkled with excitement. She was still smiling, but the thrill had mellowed to a warm feeling of contentment and a huge curiosity about how it had all come about.

"What did I do to make you think so hard?" Drew gave her a probing look.

"How do you know I'm thinking about something you did."

"I can sense the tumblers clicking into place in your mind and you keep giving me that look you get when you think I'm up to something."

"Actually, I've been thinking of a lot of things that a lot of people have been up to. First off, how did you know to call Byron before you even met him?"

"See? You really do know more than you're supposed to."

"That sounds like one of your slippery answers to avoid telling me the truth."

Drew gave her a long look before he said, "After listening to you for more than two months, I figured if you were going to tell anyone how you felt, it would be Byron, so I went through your desk to see if I could find a way to contact him without calling the number Gram had for your parents. I found his cell phone number in your address book." He hesitated when she gave him a worried look, then confessed, "I also found a letter from him and I read it."

"You read my letter?" A bright flush heated her face.

"I read Byron's letter, not yours, but it wasn't too hard to interpret what had prompted his replies. It not only told me Byron was being a lot kinder to me than I deserved, it made me feel he might be willing to talk before he tried to punch me out."

"Why did you think he wanted to punch you out?"

"Because I would have wanted to punch me out. Willow, I came out here ready to do battle with your brothers and father then tear you away from that damn farmer who wanted to return you to the land and produce children with Iowa tans and farming in their blood."

"I didn't come here with the intention of marrying Tom." Willow huffed.

"I especially liked the poetry Byron used to make his points." Drew ignored her indignation. "It made me think about things. Like, how much you mean to me?"

"And what answer did you come up with?"

"It's not easy to answer, but I'll give it a try." He leaned back in the chair and studied her with a perplexed look on his face. "For you, I trashed a car worth more than half a million dollars—which means you are worth way more to me than any amount of money. I've been stalked and vamped by salon pampered sex kittens in mesh stockings and silken thongs, but I was bewitched by a sassy country redhead in a shapeless purple nightshirt with a big fuzzy lamb on the chest—which means a night with you is more exciting than erotic fantasies. I gave up a playboy life that men foolishly dream about to make you my only woman—which says you're worth more to me than any other woman ever has, or ever will." He lifted her chin and traced his thumb along the lines of her lips. "But things start to get dicey when it comes to my dog and my horse."

"You know, Drew..." Willow wrinkled her nose while Byron groaned and Todd and Own looked confused. "...for a moment, a very, very brief moment, I was deeply touched by the depth of your loving sincerity, only to find out it was one of your jokes."

"A joke?" He looked stung. "You wound me. After all, Nemo and Venture have been around much longer than you have. They don't ask probing questions and expect me to explain things I'd rather avoid. And above all, they are much more obedient."

"If your desire is obedience, I suggest you sleep in the barn with those who are obedient." Willow stuck her tongue out at him, then leaned crossed arms on the table and glared at her laughing brothers. "Okay, you guys. I can't stand the suspense any longer. How did you manage to pull off such a great party on such short notice?"

"Started planning the party three days ago." Todd stood up and looked across the room to where Cindy was wiping down tables.

"How could you? We didn't even know there was a reason for one until this afternoon?"

"Maybe you didn't know. Byron did." Todd plunked his empty mug on the table. "He can explain it. I got something else on my mind."

"How did you know?" Willow shifted her attention to Byron when Todd walked toward Cindy. "If Dad told you his decision and you didn't tell me, I'll choke you."

"He didn't tell me anything, but his answer was inevitable. Even Dad knows better than to thwart love when it stares him in the face."

"But that wasn't what convinced him."

"Of course, it was." Byron scooped a gob of mustard onto a hunk of pretzel and jabbed it at Willow while he talked. "He just had to come to terms with his protective pride and swallow a nasty wad of trumped-up resentment that had been gathering force for over a week. Besides, I'd already heard what he called rational objections and knew they were bullshit."

"How?"

"Well," Byron looked uncomfortable and glanced at Drew before he said, "It goes back to when I picked Drew up at the Ames airport. There were no scheduled flights from anywhere near Pennsylvania, so my first thought was that Drew got his airports mixed up and was coming into Des Moines like you did. But he sounded too sure for that. I started prying around and found out the only plane coming in at the time he'd given me was private. When Dad said he was worried about Drew being able to adequately support a marriage, I figured anyone who flew himself here in a private turboprop wasn't going to fail the financial scrutiny."

"I wasn't sure you noticed exactly how I arrived," Drew said, "but don't take it too far. It's not my plane."

"That was confirmed by the corporate logo with the name Sutherland in it, which told me you were either a remarkably accomplished skyjacker, or someone with big bucks trusted you enough to let you fly that machine." Byron ate the chunk of pretzel he was still holding and frowned at the glob of mustard that had dropped into his beer.

"It's owned by my father's business, but he keeps it in Pennsylvania for when he's in the states. If I have a good enough reason, he lets me borrow it. He clearly thinks Willow is a good enough reason." Drew picked up a piece of pretzel and studied it. "Now more importantly, can you explain to me why a bar in Iowa has such good Pennsylvania pretzels?"

"Probably because Harvey's from Pennsylvania and he missed them?" Byron shrugged. "He says it's an old family recipe, but he never says whose family."

"Is Byron right?" Willow ignored Drew's pretzel diversion. "Did you actually fly here by yourself?"

"It was the fastest way to get here after the show."

"Does that mean I wasted money on a round trip ticket?"

"Probably not. Your insignificant weight won't make a difference in my fuel costs, which makes it a moot point. However, if you're determined to play a Katy-bar-the-door game by stubbornly sticking to your battle plan, in spite of my unconditional surrender, you better remember to call John to pick you up because he expects you to be with me."

"I could just wait for you to arrive." Willow argued, purely for the sake of annoying him.

"That would be tricky because I'm going to Quakertown, not Philly. It's where the plane lives."

"But I have a perfectly good ticket and I know the pilot is certified."

"I have a valid international license and if I have to listen to much more of your orneriness, I'll be certifiable as well as certified."

"Well, if your father trusts you with his airplane, I suppose I can, once again, trust you with my life. Especially if it means I don't have to rush to the airport in the morning." Willow leaned over and kissed him on a furry cheek.

"That's good because I have much better plans for tomorrow morning."

❖

After Lloyd, Todd and Owen left for the auction the next morning, Drew led Willow to the top of a hill that overlooked a rumpled valley of cropland and pastures dotted with the black shapes of cattle. The open land stretched away from them to where a serpentine creek etched a sinuous path toward the distant bank of the West Fork of the Cottonwood River. "I've been running up here the last two mornings and the vastness of the land and never-ending sky overwhelms me."

"Your father told me Iowa's openness made him feel he'd been caught naked before the eyes of God with nowhere to hide."

"It frees me, Drew said. "And makes me feel at peace with myself, the same way the sea does."

"It's the way it's always been to me: cows and corn and home. But you're both right. There's no escaping the land and sky. It shapes so much of our lives we can't ever forget it." Willow pointed down the hill at an oxbow in the stream. "I used to ride Packy down there and splash my way across the narrow sand bridge to the island it makes in the spring then eat a picnic lunch under the trees. We could go there on our run."

"We're not running today. Byron had a much better idea." Drew took her hand and they turned back along a trail that ended at a small calf barn in the west pasture.

Willow climbed a wooden ladder to the straw loft of the barn, poked her head above two rows of bales and stepped away from the square hole in the loft floor. When she turned and stopped suddenly, Drew pushed away from the ladder and bumped into her.

Drew chuckled, slid his arms around her and hugged her. "Byron's touch of decor is marvelous."

The end door was open letting in a spill of sunlight that swept across golden wheat straw to a cozy nest of stacked bales. There was a large comforter spread across loose straw; a cut-off milk carton filled with daisies sat on a straw bale beside two jelly jars on a red and white bandana, a corkscrew and stainless-steel milk bucket full of ice. A bottle of champagne poked out of the ice beside a bunch of bright orange carrots with a white satin bow. The card propped against the champagne read, "an Iowa engagement party for Drew and Willow from your siblings: Keith, Glenn, Todd, Byron, Owen, Gwen, Matt and Beth." Byron's scrawled note on the carrots read, "Drew, I won't even try to speculate on why you asked for carrots."

After reading the note, Willow sat on the comforter with her knees bent in front of her, her arms hugged around them and watched Drew open the champagne bottle. "How can I have sex with you?" She laughed. "They made you another nutty brother."

"I think I can make you feel the difference."

"Probably without even a dare." She jumped at the pop when he removed the cork and expertly wiped the lip of the bottle with the bandana. "After last night your fame is established. You charmed my entire family and received the longest standing ovation the Bucking Bull has ever witnessed."

"Ah, La Scala is a mere side show in comparison." Drew handed her a jar of champagne and sat facing her in the same position with his hard, bare thigh touching hers. "It was certainly the first time I ever received a standing ovation for a kiss. I took it as an Iowa mandate that I better take good care of you, little Elfling."

"You called me Elf. You never did that before."

"Byron gave me permission. I was crushed when you told me he came up with it first."

"I like it from you." Willow made a wrinkled nose face. "Do you have a house in Genoa?"

"My father has a villa near there. I think I can work something out with him."

"What you want most isn't unattainable, Drew."

"No, it isn't. It's right here."

"It is?"

"It's us, Willow. I thought what I wanted most was to sing Rigoletto at the Met. I'd still like to do that, but it's not what I want most, and it would be an empty accomplishment without you to share it with me."

"And just what is it you want right now, great impresario?"

"Willow," his voice chuckled, "I want to sing operas, not produce them."

She flushed. "Drew, your worldliness scares me. I'm afraid I'll humiliate you by saying dumb things like that."

"Never. Sometimes you get the details wrong and it amuses me. But your innocence of pretensions is one of the endearing things I love about you." He lifted his hand and caressed her cheek. "What I want right now is your beautiful body joined with mine in neverending waves of rapturous lust. As long as I have that to return to every night, I'll be a tower of strength and more than a match for Vittorio."

"Bravo!" She raised her champagne in front of her.

"You're learning already." Drew lifted his jar and clunked it against hers. "It lacks the ring of crystal, but it works as well. Let's capture today in our memories and keep it forever so we can always pull it out and remember the fun in life." He smiled with a touch of irony. "I've seen wonders of the world. I've lived in places that were lavish with treasures and luxury. In my opinion, none of them can compete with this tiny, sundrenched corner of today."

Drew filled his hand with her hair and let a glitter of sunlit strands tumble from it. "The sun sets it on fire and makes your skin glow. I want to make love to you in the sunshine when you're warm and brushed with gold."

"I don't have your touch with words, but I want to remember with you, make love in the sunshine, see your face and feel your strength."

They finished the champagne with their eyes locked together in a lover's gaze that pulled them away from reality and wrapped them in the fantasy of their love. Willow felt the caress of his fingers when he took the empty jar from her hand. The deep, midnight blue of his eyes drew her closer until their lips met with a soft touch. His hands held her face with a tenderness that stroked down her throat and around to her back while the kiss grew from tasting pleasure to hungry yearning.

When Drew cupped his hands over her shoulders and lowered her to the thick, quiltcovered bed of straw, the shaft of warm sunlight painted a golden path from behind her head, down the length of her body. Unbuttoning her shirt, he moved the material away from her breasts. After tasting each one, he undressed her with slow hands and teasing kisses until she lay below him, glowing with sunshine.

"I knew I'd find her again—my creature of fire and grace—hair falling like a rain of fiery embers." He stripped off his clothes and winked at her. "I just didn't know it would be in an Iowa cow barn."

"Can you ever stay serious?"

"I think I'm about to."

Willow studied his bearded face with its chiseled triangle of nose and violetblue eyes edged with dark curled lashes below bold black brows, all framed with loosely curled dark hair that contrasted so strikingly with his vivid eyes. She lowered her eyes to wide shoulders and a broad chest that contained the power for a voice that could enthrall her with its tone and fullness.

The passion started slowly then grew and built while they touched and kissed with entwined bodies moving in a fiery dance that fused them together with powerful surges of desire. She was breathless for his touches, his kisses, sensitive hands, teasing mouth. Heat and want flowed through her while her eyes and face begged for the fulfillment he was holding just beyond her reach. And then the bubble of building pleasure erupted in her with splinters of ecstasy and his sunsplashed face tightened as the last spasms of release swept through him. He smiled with a look of pure, boyish happiness before he lowered himself on strong arms, rolled beside her and kissed her.

"Drew, I'm so full of love I can hardly contain it." In a dreamy glow, Willow tightened her arms around him and closed her eyes, felt him stroke her face, lift her hand and kiss her fingertips the way he had before he first made love to her.

Chapter Twenty-Six

The moment Willow stepped into the nine-passenger, turbo-prop airplane its luxurious interior gave her the disorienting feeling of being out of place. Anxiety clenched in her chest then wormed itself into her mind like a malignant virus. For an instant, all she could think about was running down the carpeted stairway and through the terminal before Byron reached his car. But the feeling was all wrong. She loved Drew more than life itself, belonged with him, couldn't imagine life without him. She felt his arm hold her firmly, saw confusion on his face, concern in his eyes.

"Willow, are you alright?"

"It's not what I expected." She shook off panic, relaxed in the security of his embrace. "I mean it's unreal, like something out of a movie."

"It's a corporate plane. Dad travels a lot and doesn't have the time or patience to contend with commercial schedules."

"But it's so… luxurious." She stroked a hand on the high back of a seat, felt the warm softness of fine leather.

"It's the way they come." He raised an eyebrow and gave her a slow crooked smile that was pure Drew and banished her misgivings. "It impresses customers when he flies them to jobsites or on inspection tours of existing projects to butter them up before he hits them with a big bid."

"Well, it impressed me." She sighed. "What's your big bid?"

"My bed for the rest of my life. I believe we already sealed the initial stage of that contract." He lifted her left hand where his engagement ring sparkled in the light from the open doorway, held her palm to his lips for a moment before he let her turn it to the sunlight.

The flawless, blue diamond flashed back a spectrum of color chips that stunned her with the purity of the gem's fire. "It's so beautiful."

"When I found myself in a jewelry store Friday morning and saw this ring, there was no uncertainty left."

"How did you know the size?" Willow touched the warmth of the intricately entwined band and Celtic lovers' knot that formed the stone's setting. "It's perfect."

Drew smiled slowly. "I had a store full of women who wanted me to feel their fingers."

"I'll bet." She sighed and shook her head. "Drew, please keep your hands away from other women. It just gets you in trouble."

"I'm not giving up all my fun." He looked stricken, then shrugged and gave her a teasing look. "Of course, there was also the pair of leather riding gloves you left in my car. But to ease your apprehension, I will reiterate my promise to always make love to you and only you."

"No hedging, no caveats?"

"Not a one."

"Then, Sir Andrew, let us ride into our future together on your prancing steed."

"I already tried that approach." Drew grumbled. "All I got out of it was a wet shirt."

"Just shut up and kiss me."

Still reeling from a kiss that reminded Willow of how much she belonged to Drew, she helped him stow bags in a roomy luggage compartment before she followed him to the cockpit and belted herself into the empty co-pilot seat.

While Drew went through a clearly familiar procedure of starting the twin wing-mounted engines and taxiing toward the runway, Willow studied the intent expression on his sculptured face, smiled at the dark beard and collar-length hair that was styled for his summer theater role. It made her wonder how many other guises she would have to get used to if he continued to pursue his career as an actor and singer. Of course, it didn't matter. The first moment she saw him perform, the power of his voice wrapped around her and she was drawn into its spell by the way he sculpted musical tones and shaped words into feelings that twisted inside her.

Willow admitted she was awed by Drew's talent, but she knew it was the man she was in love with—a man her mother described as fascinated by everything, wanting to learn everything and experience as much of life as he could grab. Yes, that was Drew in an Iowa nutshell and she had agreed to accept him as he was, grab onto his hand and go along for the ride.

"How long have you known how to fly?" Willow asked.

"I got a license right after I turned sixteen, but the first time Dad let me get my hands on the controls was my eleventh birthday. As his business grew, the planes kept getting bigger and faster. Later, when FiberForms became more global, Dad and the Glendoncroft Scots formed the subsidiary company of Sutherland Ayre. It owns the planes and provides air service for FiberForms, Glendoncroft Highland Distillery, or most anyone else willing to pay for it. Some of its planes are long range corporate jets flown by professional pilots. I'm not licensed for them, but I have flown as a co-pilot when there were no paying passengers."

A sparkle of adventure brightened Drew's face. "It's an awesome experience to be in control of that much power and speed—sort of the closest I've ever been to feeling invincible—almost made me want to enlist in the Air Force, or was it the Navy, so I could get my hands on the controls of a jet fighter."

"Why didn't you

"It's that responsibility thing again." Drew looked uncomfortable for a moment, then shrugged. "I was just out of college and it came with a long commitment that wouldn't be easy to get out of. I opted for a different kind of adventure and became a canine cop sniffing after drugs."

"That explains your relationship with Antonio." Another piece of Drew's portrait puzzle clicked into Willow's mind when she thought about his big bear of an Italian uncle. "And Nemo."

"Nemo was later. Some bastard drug dealer shot Heracles, my working dog, before I got to him." Drew's jaw hardened and his eyes started to mist before he caught himself and closed off the glimpse of pain. "I found Nemo in France and trained him myself. He tracks and protects, but he doesn't do drugs."

Willow wanted to ask more, but without a warning they accelerated at a speed that stunned her. She'd never experienced a takeoff from this perspective and her thoughts froze on a vision of barreling off the end of the runway into a rolling crash. She gulped when, little more than halfway to the end of the concrete strip, the scene in front her dropped out of sight and they climbed into clear blue sky.

"Relax." Drew reached over and ruffled her hair. There's way more pavement here than needed. Quakertown has a shorter runway and landing is a steep dive with a full flap run toward the end."

"I wish you hadn't told me that."

"No sweat. It isn't like I haven't done it before."

"Drew, is there anything you can't do?"

"A lot of things." He gave her a startled look. "Like cook. Once we reach cruising altitude, you can search the galley and see if you can scrape up something better to eat than chips, dips and booze."

"Sexist." Willow wrinkled her nose and stuck her tongue out at him. "Sometimes I think you decided to marry me for my cooking."

"That's a good part of it, but it's more a matter of life preservation than being sexist. Trying to exist on my cooking would be a gruesome experience."

"You could always learn."

"I see cooking the way you see singing and plan to stick with the appreciation part."

While she watched Iowa's summer-green croplands give way to the dense needlepoint-richness of Wisconsin's dark green forests and jewel-bright lakes, misgivings pricked at Willow's mind like an itch she couldn't quite reach. By the time the blue depths of the Great Lakes slipped away and the wide, rising and falling spine of the Appalachians stepped down toward the east coast, her uneasiness had grown to a feeling of uncertainty she was unable to define. Willow wanted to mention it to Drew; but since she had no idea how to explain what didn't even make sense to her, she pushed the sensation out of her mind and stared out the side window at a mosaic pattern of woods, farms and rambling subdivisions.

"Drew?" Willow turned to see him looking at her with a puzzled look on his face and wondered how he could always tell when she was becoming apprehensive about something he saw as trivial. "Maybe we should have stayed in Iowa. You said you felt real there."

"Maybe you could do that. I don't have that option right now." He laughed, stood up and, with his hands on the arms of her seat, leaned down to kiss her. "I still have an obligation to be at the theatre for a performance tonight; and Dad wants his plane back."

"For God's sake, Drew." Paling, Willow pushed him away and stared at the empty sky in front of her. "You're supposed to be driving."

"It's a deluxe model. It can fly itself, and there isn't a plane within miles in any direction." Chuckling at her alarm, Drew pointed at a light on the panel. "If you hear beeping and this starts flashing, yell for me. I have to take a piss."

"You can't leave it with me. I don't know where the brakes are."

"Believe me, brakes don't work when you're airborne. I had an experience with that and ended up in a greenhouse full of hedge plants."

"You crashed a plane into a greenhouse?"

"It was a car and it flew like a chunk of granite. If it makes you feel better, you can hold your wheel and stare at the instruments. I'll be right back."

North of Philadelphia's sprawl, the plane dropped out of the sky to open a sweeping panoramic view of the Parsons Glen valley before it zoomed in on Southerland Manor in a low pass that Willow saw as more of a collision course with the mansion's unyielding stone facade than a scenic flyover. Suddenly, in what she was sure were the last seconds of her life, she was thrust into the back of the seat and the plane rose above a forest of chimneys in a banked turn that took them over the stable and woods at a more comfortable altitude.

"What were you doing?" Willow gasped. "Trying to kill us?"

"I thought it would be a good idea to let someone know we're back." He gave her a teasing wink. "Besides, you were looking too serious. I thought a little excitement might perk you up."

"You think wetting my pants would perk me up?" She shot him a sizzling glare.

"You peed in my father's plane?" He gave her a look that was half horror, half amusement.

"Not quite, but for a frozen moment I thought you'd found an insanely overdramatic way to avoid your family's reaction to our engagement."

"I'd be more worried about Dad's reaction to me making you desecrate his newest toy."

"Convincing me to come back to my job is not the same as telling your grandmother that you're bringing me into the family." Once expressed, Willow's anxiety tumbled out in rush. "Do you have any idea how she's going to react to that?"

"Sure." Drew shrugged with casual indifference. "Gram will do what she always does when I pull a one-eighty and drop a bomb on her views of proper protocol—she'll look at me as if I've gone daft and either blast me for being an impulsive jerk or look as if she can't believe I actually made a sensible decision."

"Well…" Unconvinced by his dismissive answer, Willow asked, "Are you being an impulsive jerk?"

"Yeah, I am." He lifted her chin and smiled. "But I've never felt so right about anything in my life."

"Neither have I." His kiss pushed away uncertainty, until a loud beep stiffened Willow and she twisted to stare at a pulsing instrument light. "Aren't you supposed to be doing something—like steering?"

"It knows where it's going." Drew patiently shook his head and glanced at the light. "It's just the GPS system telling me we've reached the location I set."

At Sutherland Manor, Andy charged onto the terrace and glared at a rapidly receding view of his plane dancing away in wing-tilting flamboyance. Hearing footsteps behind him, he pivoted to face his mother. "What in hell does he think he's doing?"

"Letting us know he's home." Mae met the irritated blaze of her son's eyes with a frown meant for him rather than her grandson's dramatic action. "Since I also assume it means he has successfully convinced Willow to return to her job, I applaud his enthusiasm."

"That is not a barnstorming, stunt aircraft and things like that are routinely frowned on by the FAA." Andy huffed at her, then shrugged it off and pulled out a chair so she could sit at the table. "Besides, he didn't need to do a harebrained thing like that. I already knew she was coming back."

"How did you know that?" Mae stiffened and glared at him as if he'd just violated a sacred trust. "We haven't heard a peep out of him since he left."

"He left a message on my cell phone late last night."

"And you didn't tell me?"

"I didn't see you until I walked in the house ten minutes ago."

"Well, what did he say? Why didn't you call him back?"

"Drew said, 'We'll see you after the show,' and then shut off his phone. I've been trying to call him all day."

"Why would he do that? What does he mean? Is she going to stay? Has he apologized to her? Are they still speaking to each other?"

"Mother, when Drew doesn't want to tell me something, there is no way I can get him to do it. He said we. I assume he meant Willow because I can't think of anyone else it could be."

Drew found his Mustang at the airport and the rest of the afternoon was a grabbed burger and a rush to the stable that would give Willow enough time to get Venture ready while he drove to the theater. The familiar routine of the show restored a sense of security that lasted until just before midnight when they stepped into the formal opulence of the drawing room at Sutherland Manor.

In spite of Drew's attitude of indifference, Willow suspected he had intentionally hung around in Iowa long enough to stall off the inevitable ordeal of facing disapproval of what his grandmother would interpret as an impulsive, even blatant, violation of proper Sutherland protocol. The conflict with her own father's stubbornness had frustrated Willow; but not once had she sensed a flicker of doubt that she was doing the right thing. But that was home, with people she understood, and Drew, with his uncanny ability to adapt, had become so much a part of her family she'd felt totally secure about their love and future. That was no longer true.

When actually faced with the reality of Sutherland wealth and social prominence, Willow saw herself as a one-legged duck trying to swim with a flotilla of elegant swans. She imagined herself awkwardly floundering in their wakes, bumbling into one humiliating disaster after another until her uncertainties convinced her she didn't belong with these people, didn't know what she was getting herself into.

A quick flash of reflected lamplight made Willow glance, for perhaps the thousandth time, at the sparkling diamond on her left hand—just to reassure herself that last night and this morning weren't an intoxicating daydream spinning out of control. Her heart was racing in her chest and her hand clamped on Drew's as if it were the only thing keeping her from bolting out the door.

The radiant glow from tall, antique Tiffany floor lamps drew Willow's gaze to the two imposing figures standing side by side

Slaying the Jabberwock

in front of the fireplace with their sapphire stares riveted on her in a united front of authority. They looked both expectant and coldly severe, which crumbled her resolve and convinced her the impulsive decision to marry had been hasty and ill timed.

Then, without as much as a hint of hesitation or doubt in his voice, Drew announced that they were engaged and planned an Iowa wedding in the fall. Willow's lungs froze on an inhaled breath and her knees threatened to give out. She felt Drew's arm mold her to his side. It was hard to breathe.

An instant later, relief, more disorienting than her earlier dread, turned Willow into a rag doll in Drew's steadying embrace. Andy was beaming, as if the riskiest wager of his life had paid off in his favor. Mae was so overjoyed her excitement rocketed from crushing hugs to enthusiastic plans for an engagement reception that went so far beyond the impromptu family celebration at the Bucking Bull Bar and Grill in Iowa that it rivaled a royal garden party.

Willow tried to say she only wanted a simple announcement and family celebration; but before she could find the courage to voice an objection, Mae rushed to a phone and called John so he could join them and share the news. Andy walked to the bar to open a bottle of Glendoncroft and Drew muttered, "Don't even think about protesting. She's never forgiven Dad for marrying without proper pomp and circumstance. I'm in no way brave enough to scuttle her glory."

"But—"

"You'll live through it."

"If you stay right by my side."

"Doesn't that depend on how many indignant old girlfriends show up. Oomph!" He winced away from the force of the elbow that jabbed into his side.

"Over your dead body."

"Isn't that supposed to be your dead body?"

"I'm not self-sacrificing."

"You already proved that, my dear. It brought on the ignominious downfall of my carefree life."

❖

For the next week, life settled into a comfortable rhythm of Willow's horse training job, Drew's summer theater performances, thrilling cross-country gallops on forest trails and exciting nights of lovemaking that ended with her snuggled in his arms while a warm glow of happiness radiated into a wide, impossible-to-suppress smile. Although Willow had no idea how it happened, she sensed, almost from the moment she accepted Drew's proposal, a new depth of self-assurance and affectionate gentleness in him that continued to grow between them until she knew that forever was no longer a hope in her mind, but a safe haven of reality they shared.

With the arrival of Noel Stafford, the Englishman hired to direct *Camelot,* Drew's summer hiatus from stress was rudely interrupted by hard reality. Instead of having Monday to Thursday evening free, Drew had rehearsals five days a week, as well as weekend performances of *Paint Your Wagon.* Willow rarely saw him during the day and it didn't take long for her to realize that the difference between the minor role of Rotten Luck Willy in *Paint Your Wagon* and the lead in *Camelot* was astronomical. By the time he came home, he was either elated or frustrated by his struggle to appease both the demanding director's vision of Arthur and the one developing in his own mind. And there were times when Willow wasn't sure if she was facing Drew or a medieval King of England, who, incongruously, looked like a slightly shabby gambler in a goldmining boomtown, wearing Dockers and designer polo shirts.

Concerns about Drew's stress peaked one afternoon when, after pulling a pan of baked chicken out of the oven, Willow shouted into the living room that supper was ready. She was answered by a prolonged silence that was finally broken by an angry blast of vulgarity that had nothing to do with her or supper. Tension erupted when she strode into the living room and jolted Drew out of what looked like a stare down with a brightly highlighted item on a list of director's notes in his hand.

Willow had barely opened her mouth to speak when Drew vehemently proclaimed, "I can't just act like Arthur—I have to be Arthur." With no idea what he was talking about, she shouted, "What are you trying to do rewrite the play?"

"No." He twisted to face her and looked appalled, as if she'd accused him of committing a crime. "Lines belong to the playwright. I can only interpret how they are said, not what they say."

"Well, excuse my ignorance, your majesty, but for the third time, supper is ready."

His laser glare froze her for an instant, then he shuddered and looked back at the list crumpled in his fist. "He has the reaction right. The delivery he wants is all wrong."

"Drew, did you hear me?"

"I guess not." He tossed the wad of paper into a waste basket. "It wasn't a good day."

"What happened?"

"Noel and I had a shouting match over his idea of how I should play a scene and the way it feels right to me."

"Is this another Vittorio thing?" Remembering Drew's description of the way he'd violently lost his temper and walked out on Maestro Luciani, Willow crossed her arms and gave him a wary look.

"That would be comparing a flash fire to a nuclear detonation." He tweaked her nose. "Did I ever tell you loving me would be easy?"

"No, but I thought it would make sense."

"Noel directs a role from the outside in. He expects to tell me how to present a surface and get the result he wants. I don't work that way. I build a character from the inside out, then slip into its skin. He's good and knows what works for an audience. He's just rushing too far ahead of me. Noel has directed Arthur before; and right now, he wants me to put his Arthur on like a secondhand suit, then adjust it to fit me."

Drew stepped forward and pulled Willow into a firm embrace then relaxed his arms and softened his voice. "Our visions are not so different. It's our way of bringing them to life that clashes. I'm sure that once my Arthur becomes a living part of me, Noel will have something worth directing and it will be all right."

"So, if Noel is the person you're upset with, who is this Jack you were shouting at?"

"What?" Drew recoiled and stared at her with an expression that shifted from blank vulnerability to a stumbling explanation. "I... I was arguing with myself over how to handle the clash with Noel."

"Well, I doubt if calling Noel an egotistical dickhead is the way to do that."

"I didn't call Noel that." Drew looked aghast, then awkwardly muttered, "I think you misheard me. I probably called myself a jackass. And a dickhead. I felt like one."

"I can accept that." Willow sighed and tugged his beard until he gave her a quick kiss. "How come you weren't such a crab during *Paint Your Wagon*?"

Drew laughed. "Rotten Luck Willie is a singing part. Arthur is a role." He caught her chin and looked into her eyes. "I'll give you fair warning. Developing an opera role will be like Arthur on steroids."

"Just don't take it out on me."

"I wish I could promise that, but there will undoubtedly be times you'll need all your Iowa grit just to put up with me." He gave her a quick kiss on the nose. "Now, when will supper be ready? I'm starved."

Sighing, Willow frowned and said, "Ten minutes ago."

With an elusive persistence she couldn't ignore, the incident stuck in Willow's mind like an unsettled foreshadowing that eluded her. The way Drew seemed totally unaware of supper being ready when she'd practically shouted it at him made her feel she was missing an essential insight into her portrait of him.

As long ago as the first day she met Drew, there had been instances when Willow felt him reaching out to her for understanding and she still couldn't shake the feeling there was something crucial he wanted to tell her. But each time, as soon as she touched his vulnerability, he shifted away from the contact and slipped behind a shield of self-assurance that seemed totally unaware of the moment of indecision.

A week later, the tug of war between Drew and Noel ended when a totally convincing, fully believable King Arthur emerged and took control of the role as if he were born to it. The opening of Camelot was a tremendous success, especially Drew's robed and crowned entrance on Venture with the shimmering sword, Excalibur, at his side. The beard was still there, but shorter, trimmer and, in Willow's mind, more majestic. Willow was, once again, trailering Venture to the theater and their life relaxed into a familiar and peaceful routine.

Chapter Twenty-Seven

When Paul Reynard arrived from Paris, he didn't share Andy's elation over Drew's impulsive decision to turn a love relationship into a lifelong commitment. In fact, he was troubled enough by it he insisted it was necessary to find out how much Drew's denial was hiding from Willow before he had a chance to talk to him. On the trip from the airport Paul and Andy decided that tonight, when Willow returned from the theater with Venture and without Drew, would be a perfect time for a serious talk with her.

After dinner when it was too late for his mother to do anything about it, Andy excused himself and Paul from her concert invitation by explaining that Paul had reminded him they were committed to a meeting with an old friend of Paul's in Doylestown. He then kissed her on the cheek and packed her off to the concert with the Rutledges.

"Do I have an old friend in Doylestown?" Paul asked when he sat in one of the four wing chairs clustered near the fireplace in the drawing room.

"As a matter of fact, you do." Andy chuckled at the psychiatrist's baffled look. "He graduated from Princeton with me and you met him when he visited in Paris five years ago. He's a history professor at Penn and obsessed with countercultures during the late renaissance period. I'm sure your hour in his presence gave you enough insight to convince Mother you know him."

"Right. How could I forget longwinded Harold what's his name?"

"Barkley, but it doesn't matter. Mother thinks he's progressed from an overindulged hell raiser to a pompous ass, so she won't care to hear about our evening." Andy handed Paul a glass and sat in a matching wing chair.

"Ah, Glendoncroft." Paul held up the Scotch and admired the play of light on the pale gold whisky. "My reason to bless the survival of your aristocratic Scottish forebears."

"That means you've run out and I need to send you two cases next Christmas." Andy lowered his glass and looked at Paul. "I take it you don't think Drew has told Willow he was a multiple?"

"I'm damn sure he hasn't told her he *is* a multiple. No matter how much he insists it's no longer a relevant issue, I'm now totally convinced there's no *was* in the description of his disorder. Willow has to know the truth in order to understand and cope with him." Paul's scrambled eyebrows pinched together with his stern frown. "Even you deny it by referring to it in the past tense. And you know full well it's something he has to control, not forget."

Andy started to argue then thought better of it. "I think he knows that."

"It's what he should know, but it isn't what I've been hearing from him."

"You may be right." Andy slumped into the chair and tented his fingers together. "Last winter when I asked him why he dissociated, he insisted he hadn't and that he was no longer a multiple. I let myself accept it because it was what I wanted to hear."

"As did I, but with strong reservations." Paul relaxed his frown. "It was a professional blunder that comes from liking him so damn much I have trouble keeping my distance."

"Well, he won't accept another psychiatrist now any more than he would then, so, as you once told me—get over it."

"I'm not used to patients old enough and educated enough to beat me at my own game." Paul smiled wryly when Andy nodded his agreement. "Drew used Freud's sometimes a cigar is just a cigar gambit and then made a good case for last winter's angry outburst being a regrettable loss of control over his temper. And I have to admit he certainly had enough provocation for it to be just that. Drew admitted he was upset because he felt like a failure and then overreacted to being beat over the head with it. For the most part, he was right. Incidents like that can happen to almost anyone. Out of respect for his rationale, I gave him the benefit of the doubt, just as you did. However, I felt uneasy enough after I talked with him last winter that I've spent time reviewing case notes, as well as watching and listening to old recordings of his sessions with me."

"You still have them?" Andy set his glass on the table.

"He's still my patient, even if the lines are blurred and we prefer not to word it that way. Drew has been a fascinating enough example of positive control that I've transferred everything to external hard drives and DVDs to keep the bulk down. And I've made use of it in published papers and lecture tours."

"Does he know this?"

"In typical Drew fashion, he said that if any of it can help someone else cope with the disorder, he's all for it. But he's sensitive enough to widespread misunderstandings, skepticism, even outright disbelief—as well as the social stigma associated with MPD—to distance himself from it and insist on total anonymity. In view of the magnitude of both his and your family's public reputations, it's a wise choice. There is a persistent and, unfortunately, much substantiated belief in the inherent instability of multiples, even among professionals. Drew is very aware of that view, but strongly denies its possibility in relation to him. He has convinced himself he was cured before the disorder took full control of him; and therefore, it is no longer a relevant issue. However, in spite of the reassurance of his denial, I know the incident last winter has shaken him. He doesn't know what caused it; and although he insists that he wants to find answers, part of him is terrified of what they might reveal."

"You mean there's a chance he may split again?"

"Andy, I'm beginning to think it's an ongoing condition with Jack and Andrew. Drew blocks it with denial while Jack and Andrew tread carefully because they don't want him to suspect it. I discovered it last winter whenever I tried to reach them and only sensed footprints, or reflections, as if they had left ghostly images of themselves in his mind. I'm not sure what that means; but since I have to go through Drew to reach them, I suspect his denial is the cause of it."

When Paul paused, the implication of his answer jolted into Andy's mind and he absorbed the possibilities—or at least tried to. Unable to get a grasp on the concept, he said, "Paul, I still have trouble trying to mesh theory and actuality. I understand everything you say, but I can't get my mind around the reality of it."

"I'll try to give you a simple, up-to-date analogy in terms you will probably understand better than I do. Drew is a super computer with a faulty operating system. He has a phenomenal memory capacity with a retrieval problem. As well as a multitude of excellent programs that can't communicate with each other."

"Sounds easy." Andy quipped. "Just call Micro-Soft to upgrade his operating system."

"It would be better to contact Intel about a new processor." Paul shot back at him. "The point is: we are stymied because access to a vital part of his central processor is blocked; and until we find a way to eliminate the command that created the block, instead of spending time tweaking programs with trivial patches, nothing will really change."

"Thank you." Andy looked at him with a bright, pleased expression of enlightenment.

"However, since neither of those companies is in the brain business, we'll have to do it my way."

"I get that." Andy frowned.

"The upshot is: I'm now convinced that what he did in Genoa and again two weeks ago when he defended Willow against attack were clear disassociations. After talking with you, I had a very lengthy phone conversation with Antonio, who is a remarkably believable firsthand witness. As a result, I'm willing to stake my reputation on your gut feeling of it being my old nemesis—Avenger, the phantom splinter."

"Is this happening because he's afraid he can't control Avenger?" Andy asked.

"Drew is totally unaware of Avenger. It's happening because he's losing his grip on a shield that has been protecting him from a deep subconscious guilt, or fear, or both."

"Like what?"

"I have no idea." Paul turned his hands up and gave Andy a baffled, wide-eyed look. "But, after talking with Drew last winter, then rehearsing, and again experiencing, some of my earlier sessions with him, I became aware of breaches in his protective barrier I hadn't been able to detect in the child, adolescent or recent adult. His preoccupation with reaching back to discover missing pieces of his childhood undoubtedly stems from an unconscious suspicion that alters he locked out of his awareness in his teens are still with him. I surmise Jack and Andrew are not only still there but gaining strength every time Drew gets stressed and loses control of his denial, which allows them to emerge for short periods of time without his awareness."

"I think I've seen it happen," Andy said. "He seems to lose interest, then he returns with the excuse he was lost in errant, unimportant thoughts."

"That fits." Paul said.

"But that doesn't explain Avenger or what happened with Vittorio."

"I assume his mind is still protecting him from something he was unable to cope with and has been locked away since he was a child."

"What else could she have done to him?" Andy snapped.

"I suspect Avenger is more related to Drew's helplessness to protect his mother than fear of her abuses."

"She's dead, Paul. He knows there's nothing to protect."

"Drew knows that. But does Avenger?"

Although Paul's question set Andy back, he chose to listen rather than respond.

"As Drew matured," Paul continued, "his intellect expanded and he became better and better at using his knowledge, maturity and self-assurance to maintain firm control of his behavior. This is good; this is what we want. Unfortunately, his psyche became so adept at denial he was able to convince himself, and us, that Avenger's occasional appearances were nothing more than eruptions of anger. When you consider the triggering circumstances of those incidents, it is a logical explanation."

"There were no justifying circumstances with Vittorio." Andy argued. "All he did was throw a plastic water tumbler at Drew. The fact that it hit Elise was a mistake."

"Which alerted you and perplexed me even after I accepted his excuse that he was too distraught by the frustration of failure to control his temper."

"I visited Vittorio's conservatory and witnessed one of his tirades," Andy said. "It made Drew's excuse believable—except for the wine and blood. That bothers me."

"I think I have that figured out." Paul lifted his eyes to Andy's. "What did your ex-wife drink?"

"Just about anything she was offered."

"What about when she was alone and had to buy it herself?"

"Cheap white wine because red left stains she couldn't hide from me." Andy sat forward as it started to make sense. "You think he related Elise to Carlotta?"

"I'm hoping he did. It gives us our best chance to break through to Avenger."

"How?"

"I'll explain my strategy after Antonio and Willow get here."

"Paul, I'm sure he hasn't told Willow about any of this. Is it wise to involve her?"

"I don't want him to face it alone, which makes her cooperation as important as yours was when you brought him to me."

"I'm still here for him."

"You've been his anchor for eighteen years." Paul sat back and said, "Don't you think it's time you let him move beyond you?"

"He needs to find an anchor within himself."

"I don't know when he'll be capable of that. In the meantime, you have to face the simple fact that he's maturing beyond the father/son relationship you've had. In view of that, who can better help him find that anchor than the woman he loves?"

"No one." Andy let out a slow breath as he accepted the wisdom of Paul's words, but he wasn't ready to transfer his responsibility for his son's stability to a woman he wanted to protect from hurt. "What if she isn't able to accept it?"

"You're underestimating Willow's belief in the power of love."

"Is that a scientifically sound statement?"

"No." Paul shook his head and stared into the gleaming topaz eyes of the fire irons. "It's a gut feeling I've had since I talked about Willow with John before dinner. Drew is determined to find the truth behind his demons. My plan is to help him do that, and I'm asking the rest of you to trust that I'm right."

❖

Less than an hour after returning from the theater with Venture, Willow felt as if her carefully pieced-together portrait of Drew had been slashed and twisted into chaos. It had started when she returned to find Antonio and John waiting for her. With little explanation John took Venture from her and Antonio escorted her to the manor house drawing room, where they joined Andy and a dynamically energetic, ginger-haired man named Paul Reynard, the psychiatrist friend Drew had often mentioned.

After close to an hour in which Willow had been able to understand the gist of Andy's and Paul's rudimentary, and somewhat clinical, account of what they claimed was Drew's disorder and the way he had coped with it, she was still unable to accept its reality. She asked a lot of questions, even argued with answers she didn't understand until nothing seemed to make sense. Finally, not knowing how to express what she was feeling, Willow lost herself in a jumble of contradictory thoughts and let her mind glaze over.

"Thank you." Willow accepted the refilled glass of lemonade Andy held in front of her. "I'm sorry. I—"

"I understand, Willow. We hit you with a truth that's hard to accept, no matter how it's presented." Andy paused while she took a swallow of the cold beverage and set the glass in its coaster on the table beside her chair. "But at the same time, you seem to understand it better than I expected."

"Psychology was my minor in college. My instructors felt a strong understanding of human psychology would be a valuable asset for working with both horses and riders." She smiled at Paul's and Andy's agreeing nods. "I learned about several disorders, including MPD, in psych classes. I know what it is, but I can't believe it about Drew. He isn't anything like those cases I read about."

"From what I've gleaned over the years, there is no schematic diagram for a multiple," Andy said. "They are frustratingly individual."

"He's normal, not... not... insane."

"You're right; Willow, he's not insane." Paul pulled her attention back to him. "Drew has a disorder that makes him experience the world in a different way than most other people do. Whether it becomes a curse or a blessing is a matter of how well it is understood and accepted by the multiple, as well as those who have to relate to him on an emotional level.

"Willow," Paul set a hand on a knee she was bouncing up and down and helped her relax when she met his gaze. "I know it's not an easy thing to accept, but it is real and we have to cope with it, just as Drew had to do at the age of eight when he learned two other fully aware children were sharing his consciousness."

"Two other children?" She pulled back and wrinkled her nose. "How is that possible?"

"At the time it was easier for him to see them as children, or brothers, than as personae, or personalities."

"He told me he made up imaginary brothers, so he wouldn't be alone so much."

"That's true; although they were more spontaneous creations of his unconscious mind than deliberate creations of his imagination."

"Did they have names?"

"Of course, even dogs have enough awareness of themselves as individuals to recognize they have names. The intellectual one was Andrew, a physical twin of Drew. The other was a bold, cocky teenager named Jack."

Willow stiffened and sat forward in the chair. "I heard Drew shouting at a Jack. He called him an egotistical dickhead."

"Did it sound like Drew?" Paul asked.

"Mostly." She thought for a moment. "It was a little high and whiny, but he was really frustrated."

Both Paul and Andy burst out laughing and Paul said, "That sounds typical, and tells me that rather than hearing Drew, you heard Andrew shouting at Jack. Dickhead is Andrew's favorite insult."

"He told me I misheard when he called himself a jackass and that he was acting like a dickhead by getting worked up about Noel trying to tell him how to play Arthur."

"That's a common reaction." Andy made an exasperated face. "And his denial will swear to its validity."

"Does he know everything you told me about MPD?"

"He knows way more about it," Paul said. "Drew has extensive knowledge about MPD in general, as well as in relation to himself. However, in spite of evidence to the contrary, he prefers to see it as a disorder that, once understood, is cured and provides him with future immunity. The truth is that knowledge does not offer immunity. MPD is an integral part of him he's been holding in good control for the last twelve to fifteen years."

"How many people know this about him?"

"You're talking to three of the five people who know the truth," Andy said. "But only Paul and I know the extent of it."

"I didn't know until Andy talked to me eight years ago when Drew was coming here to college," Antonio said. "And then, I only wanted to know enough that I could help Drew through rough spots when he was away from Andy."

"Actually," Andy said, "Antonio did way more than that. He helped Drew regain his balance after the trauma of losing Gabrielle and gave him a purpose he could believe in."

"Is that when he joined the police?" she asked.

"Yes," Andy answered. "After sorting out the blowup over Gabby, Drew declared himself alter-free and fully in charge of his own life. He then headed off to college and launched himself on a rocket ride of internally induced behavior that bounced from the extremes of an intellectually insatiable Andrew, who gobbled up education as if it were a smorgasbord of gourmet banquets, and a barely controlled Jack, who, short of addictive substances he knew would destroy his control, was out to experience every wild escapade he could latch onto." Andy shook his head and made an exasperated face. "That's when I started calling him Jack Rabbit and Randy Rooster."

"Randy?" Willow blinked at him. "There was a Randy?"

Andy gave her a startled look. "Willow, you may not be familiar with the term randy, but as a farm girl you should have enough knowledge of roosters to know they have a habit of jumping on any clucking hen that gets near them."

"Point taken." Willow flushed and backed away from the subject. "Is his grandmother one of the other ones?"

"I tried to tell her once," Andy said, "but she rejected it out of hand. In her opinion, it was psychological poppycock."

Antonio made a wry face. "She wasn't the only one who felt that way."

"I had trouble with it myself," Andy said. "It isn't an easy thing to wrap the mind around. In my case, experience created belief. You don't have that option, Willow, but you need to believe us. It is real and it is Drew. The others who know are Drew's childhood tutor, Peter, and John, who needed to recognize stress fractures so they could either reason him though insecurities or give him the strength to stay in control until Paul or I could get to him. Things were shaky after the trauma of losing Gabrielle. He needed a lot of support to set himself right again."

"Did he..." Willow stumbled around in her thoughts as she tried to sort through the tangle of psychological babble in her mind. "...dissociate when she broke up with him?"

"That's not an easy question to answer," Paul said. "I'm convinced he did at one point, even though he adamantly denies ever losing awareness. In a simple summary of what happened, you have to understand that Drew can be fearless and charge ahead aggressive when he feels wrongfully challenged. On top of that, he was emotionally devastated and most likely had both violently retaliatory and suicidal thoughts, which panicked Jack enough he took control in order to save his own life. However, Jack's reaction was not heartbreak, but intense anger over being rejected by what he saw as betrayal and desertion. He lost his temper and Gabby reacted by telling him to get out of her life. Jack complied by running off to Marseilles."

"I don't know this Jack." Willow scowled. "But I'd like to tell him to get out of Drew's life."

"Oh, you know him, Willow." Paul smiled at her appalled look. "He is the dominant and irascible, alpha male in Drew. He reacts with intense, possessive passion, but he lacks the caring tenderness and commitment Drew feels and exhibits. As I see it, Jack is no longer in control of Drew but he is still the ultimate protector of a body that is essential to his existence and he is very possessive about that."

Paul hesitated until Willow thought over what he'd said, then continued. "To a great extent, Jack has been the persona responsible for Drew's cavalier attitude toward women ever since Gabrielle. When her betrayal destroyed Drew's trust in love, he smothered emotional sensitivity and retreated the way he did as a child. Since then, whenever Drew was hurt, unsure of himself, or emotionally vulnerable, Jack gained control long enough to convincingly rationalize away Drew's conscience, sensitivity and better judgment with a self-centered logic that rejected those weaknesses.

"Fortunately, Jack, who was an incomplete substitute for a loving protector, could never break the reestablished bond between Drew and Andy, his true protector. This meant that whenever Drew regained control of his mostly whole and integrated personality, his guilt kicked in and his sense of right and wrong sent him to his father for strength."

"But he hasn't done anything to feel guilty about." Willow puffed up in prickly defense of Drew, then deflated when Andy lifted an eyebrow and nailed her with a hard stare that demanded the truth. She faltered, then added, "Except for his little mistake with Marjorie."

"It was a little mistake to Jack," Paul said. "It was a huge violation of moral honor to Drew."

"Drew told me I was overreacting to a foolish one-night stand."

"The Jack in him told you that."

"You mean Drew didn't know about it? He wasn't himself?"

"Not exactly." Andy scowled and Paul's nod agreed with him. "It's more that he didn't want to admit it, so his denial chose not to remember it. As far as I can determine, Drew doesn't completely dissociate anymore, but he has an annoying habit of pulling his awareness back enough that he doesn't resist participating in things his better judgement doesn't want to do but the Jack part of him does."

"That doesn't make a whole lot of sense."

"It will. After a while the term Jack-shit will take on a whole new meaning to you." Andy laughed at her recoil. "If it gets too deep, it's important to jolt him out of it and get him to use his commonsense to control it."

"You mean when he starts acting like a jerk?" She gave him a puzzled look. "My brothers often act like jerks but it doesn't make them multiples."

"That isn't exactly what Andy means." Paul broke up laughing. "Although it is related. There's being a normal jerk, which is an expression of hasty enthusiasm with little thought, and being an irrational jerk, who doesn't stop to think about any ramifications of his jerkiness. There is still a tug-of-war going on in Drew between what used to be separate personae. Andy has always been able to sense when Drew is bothered by something enough that, instead of coping with the problem, he retreats and lets the Jack part react for him because it's a lot easier than admitting he was wrong. Drew uses what Andy calls Jack-shit as a convenient escape from responsibility. It is hardly irrational or unusual behavior in adolescents or young adults, but it is the antithesis of Drew's nature. With his fluid ability to discover and adapt to new lifestyles, Drew walks a constantly shifting pathway between an intellectual, self-absorbed Andrew, compassionately sensible Drew, and arrogantly irresponsible Jack. None are whole without the others, but unlike the mood swings of normal people, Drew's personae are fully capable of behaving as separate individuals."

"Where am I supposed to fit into this?"

"You need to be the consistent anchor that defines the centerline for him." Andy stated bluntly.

"How can I do that? Drew has never let me control him. I doubt if he ever will."

"He will control himself if he has someone to trust who will remind him of that responsibility."

"What makes you think I can be that person?"

"I think you already are that person." Andy set his hand on her arm to keep her looking at him. "Drew's commitment to love you without reservations tells me he is willing to trust you with his most vulnerable feelings, but I want you to understand that it carries a burden of responsibility that was once mine and will become yours."

"What if Jack made that commitment? How can I trust it?"

"I assure you that Jack is not capable of offering that commitment." Paul stated. "Although he may want to possess you, he would never take on an ounce of responsibility. And believe me, you would have absolutely known it was not Drew. As for Drew, you can disagree with him; you can fight with him; you can express open, honest emotions with him. In fact, you can do almost anything but treat him indifferently or withdraw your love. You can't let him down by withholding the emotional contact he needs to keep trusting his love for you. In order for him to maintain the control he needs, you can neither fail in your responsibility to him, nor let him fail in his to you and himself."

"I love him and would never let myself fail him."

"We're betting on that," Andy said. "I'd just feel surer about it if he'd already told you about his MPD."

"I think he wants to tell me." Willow thought back to all the times she'd felt Drew reaching out to her. "I think he's wanted to for a long time, but he keeps pulling back before he says much."

"The hurt child in him is afraid the truth will drive you away." Paul set his hand on her arm. "Just as it did when he told Gabby."

"And what if he finds out you told me and resents my knowing?" The fear of Drew running away clawed a ragged hole in her feelings. "Wouldn't it be better if you'd just give him time to tell me himself."

"Time is a luxury we don't have." Paul set his empty glass on the table with a firm thump. "Drew came here to confront unresolved traumas in his past and kicked open a door he tried to seal off years ago. If he doesn't come face-to-face with it and hold it open long enough to accept what's behind it, it will remain an armed bomb that could send him to prison or end his life."

"For what?" Paul's prediction slammed into Willow, left her cold and numb.

"Assault, possibly manslaughter. At worst, he could be defeated and killed by his next victim."

"That's crazy." Drew isn't like that. He would never do something like that."

"No, Drew wouldn't," Paul said. "But Avenger would."

"Who is Avenger?"

"An alter Drew knows nothing about. Avenger has no conscience, no humanity. He has no purpose beyond violently eliminating what he sees as evil."

"I don't believe that. He saved me from violence."

"Willow." Antonio spoke up and captured her attention. "How much of the attack on Mario did you see?"

"Drew burst into the room and knocked Mario away from me. I saw Mario try to stab him, but Nemo grabbed Mario's arm and made him drop the knife. Then Drew shoved Mario away from where I could see what was happening. I heard shouting and Antonio's voice; and then John cut me away from the chair. When I went into the mill and saw Drew, I ran to him and he held me."

"That would explain why you can't believe what Paul just told you." Antonio looked uncomfortable before he said, "Drew almost killed Mario, Willow. He didn't disarm him; he didn't subdue him; he attacked in stone-cold rage. When I tried to stop him, he fought with me. He had no idea who I was or who anyone else was. His only intent was to kill Mario."

"No, no, no! That isn't Drew." Willow bolted out of the chair with her arms wrapped around her stomach and shouted her rejection of what she was hearing, "He was fine. He was strong and protected me. I don't believe you. I can't believe you."

"It's true, Willow." Andy closed his arms around her and held her against his chest while she cried. "But it wasn't Drew. It was an alter that has been locked inside him since he was a child. We have to bring him into the open so Drew can accept the truth of him. Paul believes he can do that. It's why he's here, but he's going to need help from all of us. Are you willing to accept the truth and help Drew through what will undoubtedly be the worst moments in your life?"

"I don't know what you mean."

"The only way we can hope to keep Avenger from doing it again is by giving Drew the chance to know him and absorb him into his awareness. He has to confront what created Avenger. It will be hard on him but leaving things the way they are is a tragedy waiting to happen."

"No, I won't let you hurt Drew. I won't. Just leave it buried and let Drew be himself."

When she pushed away from Andy, Paul set his hands on her shoulders, sat her back down and met her eyes with an absorbing, hazel-green stare that pinned her to the high back of the chair. "Avenger in a child's body was no serious threat. In Drew's adult body, Avenger is dangerous and grows stronger every time he is out, making it harder to stop him. I have long suspected the presence of a shadow alter that none of my probing efforts were able to verify. But after listening to recounts of what happened in Jared's Mill and researching information from Drew's past, I believe an episode in Marseilles caused him to dissociate long enough for Avenger to start the brawl that led to Drew's arrest."

"He said he was arrested for assault?" Willow stared at Paul in confusion. "But he wasn't convicted of anything."

"Fortunately, enough witnesses testified that Drew was defending a woman and he was acquitted of the assault charge. The point is, I'm now totally convinced Avenger exists. And although it is nothing more than a splinter persona created for one purpose only, it is more developed than I expected—which supports the belief that it's been out a number of times before." Paul shifted his attention to her with an intense, almost entreating expression on his face. "We have to find the what and why of this deeply buried splinter, and we need your help to do it."

"What can I possibly do?" Willow stared at him while a feeling of helpless fear tightened in her stomach. "I can't believe how any of this can be true, and I don't understand what I have to do with it."

"You have almost everything to do with it." Paul's quiet voice softened the grip of her fear. "From what I've gleaned from Andy, John and Antonio, Drew is more deeply and dependently in love with you than he ever was with Gabrielle. When you went to Iowa, he, once again, found himself in an internal battle between Jack's outrage and his guilt."

Paul watched her absorb what he'd said before he continued, "Fortunately, he's matured enough by now, he was able to understand that the love you share is more important than his pride and accepted the responsibility of its future demands. In order to be able to live up to that commitment, he can no longer depend on his father as his source of stability. He has matured enough intellectually and socially to know he should be independent of his father. He is not, however, emotionally secure enough to break that dependency. Andy was able to help him find the strength to take control during his original therapy. But Drew has grown up and needs to step beyond his need for a parental protector. In order for him to do that he needs to accept that he may never be capable of emotional independence and transfer his trust to you. In turn, you have to be willing to accept it as your responsibility."

"How can I protect Drew? He's the one who protected me."

"I'm not talking about a physical protector. Drew is perfectly capable of doing that on his own. You need to protect him from the helplessness that once defeated him. Drew can be a determined fighter when he believes in what he's fighting for, but he needs someone to believe in him enough to keep him from giving in to his fears and quitting."

"If loving him is what's needed, I can do that with no reservations."

"There will be times," Andy set his hand on her shoulder to draw her attention to him, "that loving Drew will not be easy."

"He told me that."

"There's a lot more that only he can tell you. The most important thing I can tell you is that I want you to be strong and there for him, no matter what happens."

"As long as that doesn't include sex with another woman. I've already told him that's one of his damn freedoms I won't accept."

"That's understandable," Andy said. "And there is no way we would ever ask you to violate your beliefs on something like that. As for Drew, I think keeping your love is important enough to him that he won't revert to old sexual digressions."

"Which were?"

"Nothing morally unacceptable in today's society." Andy smiled at her unconvinced look. "When it came to women, Drew was like a man possessed with collecting. He grabbed up any woman who caught his interest. Then, as if she were a new toy, he tried it out, fondled it, showed it off, then tossed it on a shelf and found a new one. I think it's about time he weeded out the useless clutter and settled on the only treasure he can truly appreciate and cherish."

"And you think that could be me?"

"I'm hoping it is you. The question is: are you ready to accept all the baggage that comes with him?"

Willow let out a long breath and sat back in the chair to set her thoughts straight. When Drew cheated on her or, from what they were saying, let this Jack persona cheat on her, she ran home to Iowa in a reaction of injured pride and pain, but she had never stopped loving him. "I don't know if I'm strong enough, but I'll try because I love him and don't want to share him with anyone, even if they aren't real."

"To us, Jack and Andrew are not real, only disconnected parts of Drew." Paul said. "But they are very real to themselves and do not want to give up their awareness, which would mean, in their understanding, nonexistence. Simply put, they don't want to die."

"How can they die? They aren't real."

"They are part of Drew's psyche and, if integrated into his personal awareness, will remain part of it, along with some memories he is not currently aware of, but they will no longer have specific identities. That may give Drew some things to come to grips with; but, thanks to Andy's efforts in raising all three of them to be morally acceptable, neither Jack, nor Andrew did anything to be truly ashamed of, or feel guilty about. I've known and liked all of them. If we're successful and they integrate with Drew, I expect you will, too."

"I like him the way he is. Why does he need them?"

"To be complete and in total control of his own life," Paul said. "You see, while Drew is the birth personality, or what is called the center, he was virtually unaware of and totally missed two or three years of his childhood. During that time, while Jack was the controller and Andrew was Jack's subordinate, both were capable of not only sharing awareness, but of coming out as themselves.

"At eight," Paul paused while Willow absorbed his words, then continued, "Andy was able to reach the latent Drew personality and, together, we were able to coax him to come out and face the trauma that created Jack and Andrew. But Drew was not very secure and needed Andy's strength and determination to remain cognizant of his importance. At that time, he wasn't ready to accept total integration and the three of them continued to exist in a state of co-existence and internal awareness of each other. As Drew grew stronger, he gained enough confidence to challenge Jack's control but it wasn't until he was about fourteen or fifteen that he was willing to accept the possibility of eliminating them. At sixteen, he seemed to be fully in control and insisted his alters were no more than aberrations of the past and no longer relevant."

"Doesn't that mean he was cured?" Willow asked in confusion.

"It's what we hoped; however, it was a false hope." Paul frowned. "Drew was firmly in control, but the alters were not gone. I don't know how Drew gained this control because I have found no substantiated example of it happening, but I suspect that since he refused to recognize them, they, in order to protect their existences, have kept themselves hidden from him and only come out when he is distressed enough to release his control. Since then, whenever Jack and/or Andrew are out, Drew's awareness is blocked by denial so he has little or no memory of what happened. I have now come to believe that Jack has taken full control of Andrew and is clever enough to keep intrusions brief enough that Drew easily passes them off as lapses of memory he can rationally explain."

Willow recoiled then blinked at Paul for an instant before she slumped against the back of the chair. "I've heard those explanations.

You're trying to tell me Jack had sex with Marjorie, not Drew. I don't think I can accept that as an excuse. It was still Drew."

"It was Drew's body, not his intention or full awareness. The impetus was undoubtedly Jack, who was created out of Drew's childish and somewhat skewed awareness of teenage boys. Jack is still an immature portrayal of an impulsively precocious and self-centered teenager within a man's body. But you do have a point, and if your relationship is going to survive, we have to do something about it."

"Yes, we do." Willow pulled in a long breath before she said, "And I'll help you because I don't like the alternative."

❖

When Andy and Antonio left to find some information that Paul had left in his room, the psychiatrist met Willow's gaze with a deeply questioning look that made her uneasy enough she pulled away and looked past him to study her reflection in a dark window pane.

"Relax and look at me, Willow. Stop resisting what you don't want to understand and open your mind to what I need to tell you."

"I'm confused enough. I don't know if I can absorb any more."

"You don't need more technical explanations of what is as much suppositional as tangible. But I want to help you understand the essence of the man you love."

"What do you mean?" Willow met his gaze with a defensive glare. "If you think you're going to help me by hypnotizing me the way you said you did with Drew you can stop right now."

"Firstly," Paul said quietly. "I can't make you think, or say, or do what you don't want through hypnosis. It's not a mystical power I can invoke to take over people's minds. It's a tool that can help a receptive individual connect with his unconscious mind through relaxation and enhanced imagination that's related to highly attentive daydreaming and a child's innocent freedom to play let's pretend.

"Secondly, there is no way I can hypnotize you the way I do Drew because you are not Drew, who, as a multiple, often lives in trance and is highly susceptible to both induced and self-hypnosis. I've worked with Drew for a long time. For the most part, he willingly submits to hypnosis because he trusts me and wants my help. If he doesn't want to submit, or I try to make him respond in a way that goes against his will or ethical beliefs, I can't make it happen. And on the bright side, if we succeed in our efforts to integrate him, I probably won't have need to, or even be able to hypnotize him in the future."

"What do you want me to do?"

"Just listen and let your inner feelings and imagination guide you. Willow, if you want to understand Drew, you have to understand his world. The best way you can do that is to empty your mind of doubts, questions, errant thoughts and opinions and let my words create a mental movie in your mind." He held up a hand when she started to speak. "No deep hypnosis, no tricky mind control. Just relax, close your eyes and pretend you're alone in a dark, quiet theater. The seat is comfortable. You're warm and safe, willing to lose yourself in a world unlike your own."

Closing her eyes, Willow let out a long breath, settled into the upholstered chair, allowed his low relaxing voice wrap around her.

"Imagine a warm placid sea that's rich with sensual stimuli and nourishing energy with nothing in it but a floating infant brain. But it isn't just any brain. It's a developing brain that contains a highly creative mind with intellectual and imaginative potential so far above the norm that it borders on scary—a brain that already has the ability to decipher the tactical possibilities in a game of chess, as well as the mathematical intricacies of music, and reproduce them as original creations of harmony and beauty—a brain that is capable of absorbing and retaining vast amounts of sensory and intellectual data—a mind that is sensitively intuitive and imaginatively rich—a mind with the ability to recreate memories with photographic detail.

"Now, put that mind in an active human toddler with a mother he sees as a beautiful angel, who fills his life with music and fulfills his every need. Add an affectionate, dynamic father he sees as a steady, protecting hero, who feeds his intellect, delights in his whimsical creativity and challenges his skills. His environment is a cozy, garden cottage surrounded by the sounds of nature, the scents and textures of flowering gardens and thick green lawns that are full of peace and adventure. He laughs and sings with his mother and plays games with his father. I would say his start in life was damn good."

"And then something went wrong." Willow let the words slip out in anticipation of what he was going to say next."

"They went terribly wrong; but, as is usual in human matters, it didn't happen overnight. His environment changed to an apartment in a noisy city; his father was absent for extended periods of time. Then his father was gone and his mother, unable to cope with adversity, turned to alcohol, drugs and resentment. She moved to a cheaper apartment and became unbalanced and delusional until her son became the scapegoat for all that went wrong in her life. Even when he tried to appease her, she refused to let go of her obsession that he was a demon child and needed to be cleansed of the evil possessing him."

"Was it a religious thing?"

"Not in the way of any accepted religion I'm aware of. If there was any outside influence, it came from a brief encounter with members of a cult that practiced bodily cleansing by fasting and purging the body of poisons. At that time, I suspect a past exposure to the movie *The Exorcist* may have influenced an already disillusioned mind enough that she perverted the concept into a method of expelling evil from the spirit."

"And that caused his MPD?"

"There was a time I thought so, but over the years, I found I couldn't justify it as the initial cause. I feel that, not long before the purging started, something unconsciously more terrifying shattered his psyche and, in a defensive reaction, fragmented his sense of identity into separate streams of consciousness. In effect, it buried the trauma and opened the door to an avoidance mechanism that allowed his mind to protect his vulnerability by avoiding or embracing different, even new, streams of consciousness. Can you follow that?"

"Yes, I can." Willow gave Paul a plaintive look that indicated she wished she hadn't.

"Believe me; you were a lot easier to convince than his father was." When she smiled, he winked and continued. "When reality became impossible to face, the vulnerable, innermost center of Drew's consciousness retreated to protect itself from a terror it couldn't cope with. But most of his mind was still aware and, being the resourceful thing that a mind is, it fashioned a world he could live in. Drew's alters were not just cardboard constructs, but thinking, sensing entities, and each was created to serve a purpose."

"What purpose?"

"Good question. We'll pass over the initial ones because they were no more than automatic shields against fear and suffering. They felt either nothing, or a persistent sorrow that couldn't be understood. Buffo, you might say, was a savior. He was music, pure and simple. He could fill the mind with beauty, soothe fear, express hope and offer joy. There was no sense, no meaning to his music. It just made me happy when I heard it." Paul smiled. "In many ways, I think I liked Buffo the most because he made me feel good and released my own inner child."

"I feel that in Drew's singing now."

"I can too, when he isn't trying to make it perfect."

"And the others?"

"Andrew was his intellect and his purpose was learning. But he was also kind with a quirky sense of humor and phenomenal insight."

"Drew can be like that."

"Andrew is Drew without the maturity and grit. And Jack was the older brother, who could deal with other children without being bullied. He was tough, wild and arrogant, but loyal and recklessly daring—until he got scared, backed out and dumped the aftermath on Andrew or Drew. Every one of them had a sense of humor and a love of fun. I liked them all, but I would rather see them as merely facets of Drew. It's where they belong."

"And what about Avenger? Why do you want to bring him out?"

"I want to bring him out, so I can eliminate him. He is a false and incomplete persona based on a child's ruthless concept of evil."

"Do you know him? Have you ever met him?"

"I know him through what he has done. I haven't met him and I really don't want to."

"Then why do it?"

"Because Drew has to absorb him and defeat him."

"What if he can't defeat him?"

Paul laughed, then sobered when she looked appalled. "When Drew confronts Avenger and understands what it is and where it came from, Avenger will vanish."

"I hope you're right. I don't think I could cope with knowing there was a killer in Drew."

"There is no killer in Drew. In fact, Avenger is a contradiction of everything Drew is. Willow, if Drew had been consciously capable of being Avenger, there would have been no need for Avenger. That degree of violent vengeance is not a true part of him."

When Andy and Antonio returned with Paul's laptop computer and a large plate of ginger cookies, they set them on a coffee table and moved it closer to the chairs. While Paul skimmed through some files, the cookies became a diverting center of interest until he brushed crumbs off his keyboard and looked at Andy. "We need a location that will create unsettling memories. Can you think of somewhere here at the manor that could do that?"

"Not really—"

"What about the actual location?" Antonio sat forward and stared at Paul. "The building is empty, waiting for destruction or renovation."

"Who owns it?" Andy asked."

"I can find out." Antonio looked at Andy. "And probably pull a few strings to get you in touch with an owner you may have some clout with."

"It's unsettling enough to me and I was only there one time." Andy shuddered. "When I showed up with the police to claim my son, I found him bleeding and unconscious and my ex-wife dead on the kitchen floor. I can't even guess what memories Drew has."

"Those are the sort of memories I need to find." Paul held Andy's gaze. "Will you be alright with that?"

"Yes, but I don't think I want to be part of it."

"You need to be there at the beginning because I don't think he'll go inside without you. But you can't be part of the intervention because you weren't there when it happened and there is a small chance that could distract him."

"I accept that."

"Another thing I want to do is load up sensory stimuli. Drew's memory is very susceptible to smells. Andy, can you think of a scent that would help recreate that time in his mind?"

"I can think of a lot of them from when I lived with her, but I don't know about when she lived with Gino. The only smells I was aware of when I picked up Drew were accumulated grime, charred cocaine, stale cigarette and marijuana smoke. It permeated everything, but that's not the only place Drew's been exposed to that."

"What about you, Antonio?"

"Like Andy said, dead smoke and the usual cooking smells: olive oil, garlic…" He smiled wryly. "And charred food. She used to burn things a lot."

"Gardenia." Willow smiled at Paul's surprised start. "Drew told me never to wear it because it reminded him of his mother."

"Excellent."

"Darkness," Andy added. "Open fires. Drew always stayed away from their heat, and he's never liked being in the dark, even after he learned it was a reaction to being locked in a dark room. And you can add confinement to that."

"Since we will need to see and I may need a light source to capture his focus, darkness is out and confinement is not an option."

"There's no electricity in the apartment," Antonio said, "but there are windows in the front room that get good afternoon sun."

Paul nodded. "That means late afternoon on a clear day."

Chapter Twenty-Eight

While his father closed the apartment door, Drew drifted into the kitchen and scanned across the back wall, noticing that the stove and sink were new and the small potbelly stove in the corner had been replaced by a cabinet that didn't match the older ones. Hearing Andy behind him, he turned and leaned back against a counter.

"It's changed." Drew pulled in a few quick breaths then looked back at his father with a sour look on his face. "It's creepy, but bleak enough to be another dead-end. Thank you for your efforts, but I think you went to a lot of trouble for nothing."

"How do you know that? You've only been here four minutes." Andy closed the door to the front room of the apartment and leaned a shoulder against the wall blocking Drew in the kitchen. "You came here to learn things about your past. I think it's a good idea to start at the beginning."

Sighing, Drew put his hands on the counter, lifted himself up to sit on it. "Dad, I don't really remember living here, so what's the point?"

"You noticed it had changed."

"I've had flashbacks from the memories of Jack and Andrew, even Buffo since I've been in Philly. All they've done is show me what it was like for them. I need to find my own memories and I don't feel them here."

"I think you can find some of them here. We just have to try."

"How do you want to try?" Drew answered with a shrug of forced indifference.

Sensing that this would go nowhere if he couldn't find a way to distract Drew's wariness and open his mind to the past, Andy locked onto his son's gaze and held it. "By talking about something you've been avoiding."

"What's that?"

"I want to hear what it was like with Vittorio and why it went wrong."

"Vittorio?" Drew stared at Andy as if he thought he was nuts.

"Yes. You told me a lot about his self-centered arrogance and offensive tirades of criticism, but I'd like to hear about the other side of the experience."

"I can't argue with that, but it doesn't have much to do with here." Drew relaxed and leaned his head back against the upper cabinets. "It started out all right. Vittorio worked with my voice and pointed out things no one else ever mentioned. He has a sense of fine tuning I'd never run into before. Things started to go bad when he told me I had to stop singing to myself. It didn't make sense. I've always let the music sing for me. I just let it fill me and flow out of me."

Drew paused and met his father's absorbing stare. "Vittorio said I didn't take instruction, but I thought I did. I'd learned how to use breath control, how to alter my vocal cords, how to shape sounds and enhance them. That wasn't natural. It was taught and practiced. Vittorio said that is only technique and my voice is technically perfect. Then he said I can't sing a role for shit. He says my connection is good in light recitative, but it falls apart when I sing an aria. He says that's when I lose the character and sing to myself."

Drew straightened, grasped the edge of the counter and drilled his father with a hard glare. "No wonder he loses students. That's the way most operas are performed. You play the role, then get trapped in meaningless repetitions in a lengthy demonstration of vocal hyperbole. That is what he calls singing to myself."

"You didn't sing to yourself. Buffo sang to you."

Drew started at the comment, then laughed and shook his head. "There ain't no separate Buffo anymore, mio padre."

"Are you sure."

"Very sure."

"Who is Avenger?"

"What?" Drew looked at his father as if he still thought he was nuts, then screwed his face into a stormy scowl. "That tells me you've been talking to Paul. He had a hang-up about the name Avenger that never made sense to me. After I met Ernie a while ago, I remembered where it came from. It's not important."

"I'm not too sure about that."

"Dad, he was a comic book character. Ernie's Dad had a box of old comic books he let us look at. I..." Drew stopped and looked confused. "Now there's the problem. Technically, I should have said I was Andrew then; but after we shared consciousness, a lot of their memories became a part of me and I can't always separate them or put a timestamp on them."

Drew thought about it some more and smiled slyly. "Ernie couldn't read yet, so I read them to him as best I could. I made a lot of it up from the pictures, but Ernie always believed me. I used to pretend to be Crimson Avenger when we played super heroes. Ernie was always Captain Marvel because he loved to say **Shazam**!" Drew shot his fists up in the air and burst out laughing. "Some of the older kids in the neighborhood found out about it and harassed us by calling us uncool girl babies playing dress-up. It humiliated me enough I didn't want to tell anyone, Paul included, that I was guilty of playing at being a comic book super hero in red tights. Well, actually, baggy red pajamas."

"You were an imaginative kid; they do things like that."

"Maybe most six-year-old kids. Fifteen-year-old toughs on the street had different role models and I was too preoccupied with being my own older brother to accept that stigma. No matter how much we denied it, we were judged as one. But at that time, neither of them understood why."

Drew stopped again, then said, "Wait a minute. The comic books *are* a time stamp because Paul and I worked it out that Jack and Andrew weren't around that early. They came out that next winter after I burned Mario with the hot oil. After that, it was Andrew who was Ernie's friend—until Jack's rotten behavior made Ernie's mother tell him he couldn't play with me anymore." He looked startled, then shrugged. "That means those earliest memories of the comic books *were* mine."

When Andy felt the silent vibration of the cell phone in his pocket, he moved to the door and opened it. "So? Was coming back here a good idea or not?"

"It was good to clear that up because it will make Paul happy when I email it to him so he can dovetail it into his ongoing time charts. It also makes sense out of what Millie and Ernie said awhile back about me turning into one of the bad kids." Drew dropped off the counter and glanced around the kitchen taking in bare walls, chipped countertops and dented, rust-spotted steel cabinets. Everything was dingy, reeked of old tobacco smoke, covered with layers of grime. His gaze skipped past where the pot stove had been, focused on the closed, scarred door to the old pantry.

Shuddering, Drew shifted his gaze to his father. "And Milly was good, until Mario got involved. I could have done without him."

"He won't bother her anymore."

"That's the only thing that makes me able to live with what I did."

"If it hadn't been you, something else would have turned Mario against her." Andy leaned on the wall by the kitchen doorway.

"I wish I could believe that." Drew looked at his father's quizzical expression. "Mario is a sadistic son of a bitch, but his hatred of me goes way deeper than that. He'll never let go of it, and I'll never feel free until one of us is dead. I know how it can happen because it's the way I felt toward Gino. But I was a helpless kid and too afraid of Gino to do anything about it. Fortunately, Antonio ended it after I went to France because I honestly don't know how I would have dealt with it if I'd ever seen Gino again."

"You stood up to Mario to protect yourself and other kids. But you didn't instigate the attacks."

"To Mario I might as well have. I physically disfigured him and exposed him as a coward in front of his gang. He will never let it go." Pivoting, Drew took a step toward the open door. "I've seen enough. Let's get out of here."

"Not yet." Andy caught his arm, turned him back. "I pulled some strings with important contacts to get you in here. I'm not letting you run out on me yet."

"I don't want to be here any longer. It's full of bad stuff I've already dealt with. I've felt all the ghosts and don't want to disturb them." Drew glared at the pantry door as if he wanted to burn it away with his stare. "I have a new life to live with Willow. She isn't part of all this and I don't ever want to go there again."

"It isn't that simple." Andy stepped in front of his son, blocking Drew's view of the darkness filling his mind. "You know you have to find some answers. You've known it since the incident in Genoa."

Turning away, Drew took a stride toward the front room then halted at the doorway when his father failed to move away. Light from a low sun illuminated a haze of dust motes and a knot of flies buzzed against a bright strip of dirty glass above the boards covering one of the windows. The other was a blind eye in an empty wall marked with cleaner patches where pictures and furniture had protected aging wallpaper from sun and grime.

"I don't want to know them anymore. I want to start all over. Willow doesn't know what I was. I can forget it with her, put it all behind me. As if it never happened."

"That's a delusion. You can never let yourself forget it."

"That's what Paul used to say, but it's different now. I conquered it, Dad. I understand what it was and won't let it control me again."

"Stop lying to yourself. And Paul didn't used to say it. He still does. That's why he's here and it's why you have to talk to him now, here, where you don't want to be."

Drew pushed past his father then froze when he saw Paul sitting in the front room on a padded, metal armed chair that didn't belong there. "I don't want to be here, Paul."

"You said you wanted to open the past." Paul held Drew's gaze. "Are you backing out so soon?"

"It doesn't feel right here. Can we talk somewhere else?"

"This is fine, but let's make it easier." Paul watched Drew's eyes flash toward the bedroom hall, saw his tongue wet his lips before he pressed them together. When Drew looked back, Paul gestured to a chair that matched his. "Sit down, Drew. Slow your thoughts, stop trying to anticipate, focus your mind and concentrate on my voice."

While he spoke in a low, calming voice that pulled Drew's gaze back to him, Paul opened his hand to let a beam of sunlight strike the tumbling prism and fracture into a twisting spectrum of flickering colors that captured Drew's attention and stilled his mind.

"Will you listen to me, Drew? Will you help me find the answers you need?"

"Yes." Drew let out a slow breath and relaxed into the chair. "What do you want to know?"

"You're five or six years old. You're in the front room. Are you alone?" Paul pressed a button on the cellphone in his pocket.

"I don't know."

Drew looked confused, glanced around him with growing agitation. He heard a terrified scream, twisted toward the bedroom hall behind him, saw a large man clasp the arm of a dark-haired woman and smash something on her head. He stiffened when streams of red liquid ran from dark hair, streaked down a terrified face. His head dropped forward; he shuddered and snapped his head up.

"Do not hurt her!" Drew shouted and bolted out of the chair so fast Antonio was almost too late as he shot across the room, grabbed Drew from behind and spun him back to face Paul.

"Avenger, don't go away. I can help you if you talk to me." When Paul asked, "Who sent you out?" a cold, emotionless face turned to face him.

"I was called." The voice was loud and deep, but monotone, lifeless.

"Who called you?"

"The need."

"What need?"

"To protect."

"What do you protect?"

"Carlotta."

"Do you protect Drew?"

"Who is Drew?"

"The boy. The child."

"I do not know Drew child."

"How do you know when to come out."

"I come out when there is need."

"Do you feel it? Is there a voice?"

"I take away red pain."

"Who are you?"

"Avenger."

Andy tensed as he faded back into the kitchen, pulled in a deep, steadying breath and grasped the door frame with white-knuckled hands.

Seeing Andy's retreat, Paul nodded his head but continued to hold Avenger's attention with his absorbing gaze. "Who do you know?"

Avenger looked confused then said, "I was called. I know what I need to do."

"What do you need to do?"

"Kill the pig bastard. Save Carlotta."

"Who told you to kill?"

"My prime directive is to save Carlotta. I go away when Carlotta is saved."

"Where do you go?"

"I go to Hell. I come back when I am called."

"Where have you protected?"

"In the bedroom. The glass cut her. There was blood. The pig bastard hit her with his fists and his cock. I hit him with a stick. He fell down. He took the stick and hurt my arm. She was saved. I went away."

Avenger paused for a moment, then continued his stilted recitation. "In the alley. The pig bastard hit Carlotta and ripped her underpants. There was blood. I hit him with a pipe. A man stopped me. She was saved. I went away. In a bedroom. The pig bastard tore Carlotta's dress. There was blood. A boy she called Tonio made him stop. The pig bastard went away. She was saved. I went away. In a party place. The pig bastard pushed Carlotta onto a bed and jumped on her. She screamed. There was blood. I punched him. She was saved. I went away."

The monotonous, mechanical voice hesitated, then continued the flat chronological recitation of the events of Avenger's entire existence. "In a dark place with smoke and shouting. Carlotta was yelling. There was blood. He ran away. I chased him. She was saved. I went away. At a piano. The glass cut Carlotta. There was blood. I hit him. She was saved. I went away. In an empty stone place. The pig bastard had a knife. There was blood. Carlotta was saved. I went away. In this room. The pig bastard cut Carlotta with a glass. There was blood. The big man stopped me."

Avenger went silent and stared at Paul in blank confusion. "You cannot stop me. I must kill him."

"I need to talk to you."

"I come to protect."

"I need to know who you are."

"Avenger. I come when I am needed. I protect Carlotta from the pig bastard."

"They weren't all Carlotta." Paul shouted at him.

"The pig bastard is here. I will kill him." Avenger stiffened, jerked away from Antonio's grasp and pivoted toward the hallway. "It is my prime directive."

"That's bullshit!" Antonio roared and stepped between Avenger and Paul. "I've had enough of this egotistical crap."

Ignoring Paul's startled gasp, Antonio glared at Avenger's stony expression, twisted the front of his shirt into a wad and spun him back toward the chair.

"I will kill the pig bastard." The body in Antonio's grasp exploded with adrenalin-fired strength, that smashed a fist into Antonio's jaw, then jerked free and stumbled toward the man still holding the frightened, dark-haired woman across the room.

"The hell you will!" In a flash of angry reaction, Antonio wrapped his left arm around Avenger's throat, pulled a gun from his jacket pocket and fired it at the large figure in front of them. The horrified man jerked as two more shots shattered the heavy silence. Clutching at his chest, he fell back against the wall, wrapped an arm around the woman and dragged her down into an oozing red puddle that spread across the floor boards.

"I killed them," Antonio shouted. "That makes them both dead. You can't kill a dead man or save a dead Carlotta. That makes your prime directive useless bullshit."

Avenger stared at the bodies in the hallway. "Where is Carlotta?"

"Gino killed her. She's dead." Antonio jerked Avenger backwards. "The pig bastard is dead."

Drew's face went slack. He sagged in Antonio's grasp, then slumped onto the chair he was shoved into.

"You better hope Avenger believed you." In a rare burst of fury, Paul pushed Antonio out of his way and moved his chair closer to Drew. "Because if he didn't, this was all useless."

Ignoring Antonio, Paul captured Drew's stare. "I need to talk to Drew. Talk to me, Drew. Talk to me."

The eyes closed, the body shuddered, and the head snapped up with a suddenness that made Willow stand up and drop the catsup-streaked wig in her hand. She felt Andy's arm slide around her shoulders and back her into the hallway as she continued to stare at a profile that resembled an angular drawing of a lifeless Drew. "Is he alright?"

"I said it would be hard." Andy held her against him in the dark hallway, but you have to stick with it and be here when he needs you."

For a moment Drew looked frightened and vulnerable then he was drawn into the deep, penetrating gaze in front of him, captured by tawny green eyes and a calming voice. "Don't fight me, Drew. Listen to me and think about what I tell you. There's someone you have to accept in you. He's been with you a long time."

"No." Drew tried to shake his head but couldn't break contact with the compelling gaze. "There's no one else. You said there was no one else."

"You don't need him anymore. You can protect better than he can. He's vulnerable now and you have to control him. You have to open your mind and remember when he came to you."

"Who is he?"

"He calls himself Avenger."

"Crimson Avenger was in comic books. I used to read them with Ernie."

"Your mind created Avenger to protect your mother when Gino raped her." Paul held Drew's attention, captured his mind, held the trance with his voice. "Avenger comes out when he thinks he is needed. He protects women in need of his protection. But you don't need him. You're old enough, strong enough and skilled enough to protect them yourself. Think of the wine glass and the blood. It was your mother, Drew. Think about Carlotta with wine and blood in her hair. Think about what happened to your mother. There was blood in her hair. She was frightened. The blood ran down her face with the wine."

Drew's face tightened; his hands clenched into fists. He became agitated; his breathing grew shorter. He saw dark, tangled curls matted together by red blood that welled from a pale scalp, mingled with streams of white wine that ran down an ashen face. "Do not hurt her!" He yelled suddenly. "Don't hurt her! Please, Gino, don't hurt her."

When Drew went rigid, Antonio gripped his shoulders from behind and held him on the chair with firm hands. The restraint failed to distract Drew, who was so deep in memory he was unaware of anything but the vivid images in his mind and the voice holding his awareness, telling him to keep listening to it and not let it go.

"What did Gino do? What happened Drew? Don't lose control. Listen to me. Let him come. Absorb his memories. Remember who you are and take him in, let him become a part of you. See him for what he is then reject him."

A shudder wracked through Drew almost throwing him away from Antonio's grasp.

"I'm here, Drew, stay with me." Paul grabbed at flailing fists until Antonio dropped to his knees and wrapped powerful arms around Drew's chest, grasped the metal chair arms to pin Drew's arms to his sides. "Don't let Avenger control you. Remember when he first came to you."

"Mamma..."

Gino's fist connected with Carlotta's abdomen, collapsed her like a straw dummy cut loose from a pole. Strong hands closed on thin upper arms and shoved her, stumbling, through the bedroom doorway. Drew clutched the ball stick, felt it in his hand as he ran across the cluttered front room. In the bedroom, a hair-cloaked forearm lay across his mother's throat; her dress was jerked up around her waist, blood was clotting on her face and eyelids. Gino was between her thighs, spreading them with his knees. His pants hung off one leg, still caught around his ankle.

"Don't ever say that rich, fucking bastard was more man!" Gino plunged into the struggling woman, stopped her scream with a punch that split her lip, added more blood to the stream flowing from her scalp. He reared up when the stick hit the back of his head. Then the worn wood smashed into his jaw and he rolled to his feet.

Drew felt nothing—had no sensation of what he was doing—could only see the stick, thwacking against a head and body. When Gino lunged toward him and stumbled over the pants trailing from his foot, the stick swung up between the man's legs, hit with an impact that contorted his face.

With a bellow of pain, Gino clutched at his groin, and staggered backwards, fell against the wall. In pain, but not completely down, the man lurched forward and grabbed the stick. "I'll send you back to hell, you damned, demon. And you can close the fucking hole after you."

Shuddering, Drew gaped up in terror as Gino wrenched the stick from trembling hands, slammed it down on the arm that had wielded it.

Drew shrieked in pain, then shuddered and snapped his head up. With his right arm flopping uselessly beside him, he broke Antonio's hold and dove forward as if he were hurled from the chair. His head turned sideways with a twisting jerk and when he hit the floor, he was limp, pale and barely breathing.

"Help him!" Willow pulled against Andy's hold, saw Antonio start toward Drew then stop when Paul held up a hand and shook his head.

"What did you do to him?" Willow shouted. "He looks dead."

"He's not dead now because he wasn't dead then." Paul crouched beside Drew and rolled him onto his back. "Drew, come out of it. Listen to me. I need you to come back to me. It's not real. The pain is in your mind. It will go away when you come back to me."

When Paul sat back on his heels and clapped his hands, Drew rolled his head back and forth, then sat up and stared at Paul's steady eyes.

"It's over, Drew. You're alright, but I need you to relax, open your mind and trust me." Paul moved the flickering prism in his hand until Drew stared into it and dropped his head.

"Avenger, I need to talk to you." Paul gestured for Antonio to kneel behind Drew and hold his arms. "Talk to me, Avenger. I know you're still there. Talk to me. I can help you."

Drew convulsed, as if he were paralyzed and struggling with a power he couldn't control.

"Avenger. Talk to me. Don't let him stop you."

The shuddering snap of the head was followed by the flat android voice saying, "Who are you?"

"Your guide. I can take you out of hell."

"I failed. I go back to hell."

"That's a lie. You belong in Drew. He will free you and take your memories as his own."

"I do not know Drew. I am Avenger. I come when I am called."

"You aren't needed anymore. Carlotta and the pig bastard are dead. You saw them die. You saw the blood. The need is gone." Paul held the blank stare until it faltered and he could sense a deeper mind trying to take control. "Come out with him, Drew. Don't let him go away. See him for what he is."

The shuddering snap ended with a shouted, "No! I don't want him. He's not a hero; he's a monster."

"You have to control him. If you let him go and forget him, he will control you again. Defeat him, Drew."

"You cannot destroy me." The voice was flat and cold, the blank face hard. "I need to protect."

"He doesn't, Drew. Avenger is nothing more than an empty apparition of a childish concept. You don't need him anymore."

"I need to protect." Avenger's strong voice bounced off the bare walls. "I need to protect."

"There's nothing to protect." Drew shouted back at the echoing words. "Carlotta is dead; the pig bastard is dead and gone. Go away and never come back. You aren't needed anymore. I can do my own protecting."

Throwing himself backwards, Drew twisted then jackknifed forward to break from his uncle's hold. He staggered to his feet, almost crashed into Paul, who shoved him away from him. Confused, Drew bent forward and stood swaying with his legs spread, his arms wrapped around himself as he tried to make sense out of where he was and what was happening. He was lost without the voice, without the steady gaze that held him. Powerful arms crushed him, wrestled with him and plunked him back onto the chair. The eyes were back, the voice calming him again.

"It's over, Drew. Close your eyes. Think of Willow. Think of your love for her. Think of Willow and come back to her."

Drew's eyes closed and his head dropped for an instant before the deep shudder convulsed him and his head snapped up. Clear, startled blue eyes gaped at Paul for a moment while deep guilt shuddered through his body. He crumpled in on himself, slid off the chair onto his knees and toppled onto the floor.

Wrapped in a tight, shivering ball, Drew absorbed the horrifying memories of what he'd done as Avenger. He tried to deny them, but they flared up like punishing flames that defeated his resistance and broke through a black wall in his mind, allowed him to absolve a childhood guilt for failing to protect his mother and defuse a hatred he had long ago transferred to Avenger and locked in a deep, inaccessible corner of his mind that he'd once seen as a flaming hell.

He started to shake uncontrollably, then gradually sensed warmth beside him, breathed in the scents of honeysuckle and Willow. Enclosing her in his arms, Drew pulled strength from her warmth, held her tight to his body. Exhausting spasms racked through him while he sheltered her trembling body and let his tears mingle with hers.

When Drew emerged this time, it was Willow who gave him security, not his father—Willow's love that gave him purpose and a reason to put it all behind him. He had found his anchor, a missing piece of his puzzle, a completion that made two into a whole that swelled greater than the sum of its parts.

When he sat up with her, they were alone in a musty, hollow shell of an apartment. He kissed her, then looked around him. "Even the ghosts have left us."

"That's what ghosts do." Willow whispered. "They've all gone and left me to answer your questions."

Willow pulled her knees up in front of her and sat facing him. "Paul insisted we had to banish Avenger before you could fully gain control of your life. I hope it worked because it was horrible."

"It worked. I remembered what Avenger was hiding from me, or more truthfully, what I was hiding from myself."

"Did you feel wrong about what you did? Drew, you tried to protect your mother. That's not a sin; it's a good thing."

"I was a child with a child's view of good and evil. They called me a demon child and I believed them in a way that was much too literal. That's something I need to think over and talk about with Paul."

Drew shuddered, sat straighter and met her eyes, felt strength in her commitment. "A lot of it is confusing. What convinced Avenger to go away?" He shook his head then stared at her with a horrified look. "I saw my mother and Gino. They were dead. But they weren't dead back then. Who was the dead man? Who was the dead woman?"

"Antonio shot Sal."

"Shot Sal!" Drew stiffened when she nodded then gaped at her in stunned disbelief. "The bar owner? No, Antonio shot Gino, but not then..." He stopped and looked confused."

"It was a setup, Drew—what Paul called a charade to make you react and bring out Avenger. I stood in for your mother and Antonio's friend Sal for Gino. When Avenger broke away from Paul's control, Antonio took matters in his own hands and shot Sal, who took me down with him, which Paul said would take away Avenger's purpose."

"Antonio shot Sal!" Drew echoed his earlier reaction to her statement.

"There were blanks in his gun. It wasn't supposed to happen exactly that way, but it had the desired effect, which is what really matters. Sal was taken by surprise, but he played his part well and said the shock is forgiven if it helped you."

Drew stared at her for a moment before he started to make sense out of it and let out a relaxing breath. "I owe Sal big time for that. Who came up with the scenario?"

"Paul, mostly. But shooting Gino, who was really Sal, was Antonio's suggestion, in case Paul couldn't get through to you in time. We had a planning session a few days ago and sketched it out. They planted a lot of what Paul called sensory stimuli to make you sensitive to what was going to happen."

"I'd say they worked. I was a wreck just being here." Drew ruffled her damp hair and hugged her against him. "Willow, I feel as if I've been run over by a cavalry charge. Can we go home and crawl into a cozy bed? I'm suddenly very tired and need to hold you."

"We certainly can. Your Dad and Paul left with Antonio and Sal. So, I'll drive."

"That's a good idea. I need to sort myself out and accept what this means. I don't want to deal with Philadelphia traffic at the same time."

Chapter Twenty-Nine

Willow was watching a serpent of overlapping crust drop away from the knife blade she moved around the edge of a pie when Drew peered over her shoulder, sniffed in the sweetness of fresh raspberries and ran a wet finger across the counter to coat it with the cinnamon and sugar she'd used to dust the surface of the top crust. He'd been at the manor house with Paul since lunch and she wondered how much he was willing to share. From the pointedly flirtatious way Drew looked at her as he sucked the sweetness off his fingertip, she guessed not much. Before yesterday, his charm would have pleased her, even flattered her. Now, after what they'd been through, it insulted her, made her feel he was intentionally excluding her from things she needed to know.

"How did it go?" Willow tossed out her question as she finished pinching a pattern of perfectly balanced fluting around the rim of the pie.

"It was rough, but we got through it." Drew shrugged. "I have it under control."

"I don't." She carried the pie to the oven and slid it onto the rack.

"Don't worry yourself over it. Now that I know the truth, I can handle it."

"Well, I only know enough of the truth to be upset by it. I'd like more explanation."

"You weren't supposed to know anything." Irritation snapped out before Drew caught himself and stepped back against the cabinets. "I don't even know how they managed to get you into it?"

"I learned a lot about you from Paul while you were at the theater last weekend."

"That would certainly explain your recent preoccupation."

His answer startled Willow. She wanted to deny it, but knew it was true. Even while they'd made love, she somehow felt she was deceiving him by hiding apprehensions.

"But it's all right, Willow. I understand why you couldn't say anything. It would have raised my hackles against it and made the intervention useless." Drew gave her an uncharacteristically anxious smile and lifted her chin with a strolling finger. "It was a messy business that I'm sorry you had to witness. When Dad said he'd arranged to get us into the apartment, I didn't see as I had a choice. If there were answers there, I wanted to know them so I could be free of some ghosts I've been harboring."

When Willow remained silent, Drew frowned and withdrew his touch. "But they should have left you out of it. If I'd known about that, I would have refused to go."

"They said that. They also said you would need me afterwards."

"I did need you and I needed you with me last night. I still need you now." He cupped his hand on her jaw and searched her eyes before he dropped his hand and opened a space between them. "But they should have left you out of what they did."

"It was scary, but I still love you and want you forever. It didn't change that."

"Just how much did they tell you?"

"They told me about your disorder, explained about the alters and told me things about Andrew and Jack. Then they said they suspected the presence of an alter you didn't know about. It was Avenger. They said he was a lethal time bomb that could destroy you."

"Or at least everything I wanted to be." Drew admitted quietly. "About that they were right and I understand what they had to do, but they still shouldn't have put you through that or upset you with things you didn't need to know."

"Why not?" Willow caught his hand and squeezed it until he looked at her. "I can't love you if I'm only allowed to see the outside of you."

"I wanted to protect you from it. Some of it is ugly. You deserve the sunshine side of me, not the nightmares."

"No, Drew. Don't you understand? It wasn't your Prince Charming quality that made me love you more than life itself. That happened when we fought each other with a passion that burned us together. Some of that was ugly, too, but, as you said, it's what made us truly more than the sum of our parts. I've earned the right to share that side of you. And I won't settle for anything but the whole truth."

"You only say that because you don't understand the reality of it, even I tried to forget it."

"All I can say to that is you may find I have more grit than you think." Willow watched him recoil and grasp for an argument she wasn't about to let him voice. "I want the truth from you. I want to know your side of it before you run away from me with the lame excuse that you did it to protect me."

"No normal person can possibly know my side of it." He answered defensively.

"Even what you call normal people have ghosts and ugliness they don't want to see."

"That doesn't matter. You can't accept what I am."

"Try me. That's all I ask. Try me before you judge me."

"I'm afraid to."

"What can you lose?"

"You." He answered in a fearful voice.

"Loving only part of you would undermine my love more than anything I can think of. Open truth is something I can deal with. Deception by omission, no matter how noble and chivalrous your motive may be, is not acceptable. I know what you are. It confuses me, even frightens me. It doesn't stop me from loving you."

"You're good at ultimatums, aren't you?"

"It seems so." Willow watched the defensiveness melt away as Drew slumped against the cabinet and stared beyond her with a pensive, vulnerable look that seemed to take away his awareness. It made her wonder if he were merely sorting his own thoughts; or, in view of the vision Paul had seeded in her mind, touching the thoughts of his alters to sense their responses.

He came back with a quick shudder, circled his arm around her waist and walked her into the living room. "If I'm lucky we'll get through this before the pie burns up."

"Through what?"

"I suppose we start with the first question you asked."

"I don't remember what it was." Willow flushed and sat on the couch, leaving him free to do the pacing she knew was inevitable.

"How did it go?" He stated more than asked. "I suppose you meant it is as more than a casual how was your day?" When she nodded, Drew sat on one arm of the couch and she settled against the other with her legs folded in front of her. "Paul brought us all out together. Since I've been refusing to let that happen for a very long time, it was an eye-opening experience."

"Did that include Avenger?" Her question was hesitant.

"No." Drew scoffed cynically. "He was a dumb robot and as useless as Crybaby and Dead Boy now that his absurd prime directive is gone."

"That's a relief." Willow felt tension leave her jaw, relax her shoulders. "I didn't like him very much."

"Who could?" Ranting in disgust, Drew paced in front of the couch. "Avenger was a shallow fragment of childish nonsense whose only substance was vengeance. Paul showed me the video of that."

"He videoed it?"

"He always makes a video. He started showing them to me as soon as I was old enough to understand the truth. It regularly cut the feet right out from under my denials. I'm surprised he didn't tell you. He's usually very careful about things like that."

"Actually, he did, but I forgot about it." She flushed. "I even signed something about being a willing part of that whole thing. Did the video shock you?"

"That's one way to put it. Feeling like a self-deluded ass would be more accurate. Mostly, it made me regret I ever watched *Star Trek* reruns and heard about the prime directive. What the hell kind of depraved imagination did I have as a kid?"

"Does that mean Avenger's gone for good?"

"His prime directive is gone, and his stilted presentation." Drew stopped and looked thoughtful. "He, or more truthfully, *it*, is gone as a viable alter, but I don't know about the role. He had an obsessive black and white passion for justice that I might find useful someday."

"You can't mean that?" Willow stiffened.

"You said you wanted the truth." His retort was a sharp cut, his stare far from apologetic.

"I don't like you wanting anything to do with Avenger."

"There are probably a lot of things about me you won't like. Now, do you still want the whole truth?"

"I do." Standing face to face with him, Willow met his indignant challenge with determination. "Tell me what happened with Paul."

"Andrew was pompously pissed at me for calling him a childish figment of my imagination and taking credit for his intellectual superiority. But he had a change of heart when I told him it was his name on the damn degrees not mine."

Drew paced away from her then turned back, still ranting. "Jack bitched about the way I wrote him off as an egotistical expression of overblown escapism. They both accused me of cutting them out of my consciousness as if they were irrelevant nobodies. Buffo's too preoccupied with sulking to care about anything."

"Sulking?"

"I don't know what else to call it. He's always been there when I sing, as if he's the personification of the music itself, but there isn't much to him. I can't talk to him. But when he's out, I can sense his presence." Drew thought for a moment, then said, "The unsettled state of my musical ambitions seems to have affected him."

"But you want to go back to opera. Isn't he happy about that?"

"He won't know that until I come to terms with it. Buffo is a splinter identity, who feels my music; he doesn't know my thoughts, just as I don't know his, or if he even has any. Our only communication is through music."

"Okay..." Willow smiled uncertainly. "That's a little on the other side of my reality. I mean, I can understand the term being in tune with a talent, a muse, an ability. It's the concept of there being a living and recognizable human identity that baffles me."

"Buffo is personal and not really a muse. He's childlike, but I'm not sure he has a strong human identity. He was a fragment of me I was reluctant or unable to express. But since it refused to remain unexpressed, my mind created an alter to express it, and it took on a noticeable identity. You may never understand the actuality of it. I'm not sure I do. I tried to deny the truth myself. It didn't work. All I can ask you to do is accept what I am and keep loving me." He paused, then asked, "How much did Paul tell you about what created Avenger?"

"Only that it was a dissociative reaction to a traumatic event your mind couldn't cope with. Both he and your father felt it would be a violation of your personal privacy to tell me anymore. They said it was something only you could do."

"Gino raped my mother in front of me when I was about six."

"Drew that's horrible." She gaped at him with round eyes, a devastated face.

"Yes, it was. I wanted to stop him but was too terrified to act. Avenger came out to save her, then went away when Gino went after me. His purpose was to protect her, not me." He looked at her perplexed expression. "Maybe someday I'll be able to understand it all; but not yet, because I don't know what made me like that anymore than Paul and Dad do." His arms circled her and he held her against his chest until his heartbeat slowed and his body relaxed.

"Was what started it something brutal and horribly painful?"

"I don't see or feel things from the same perspective now. At the time, I didn't have words or concepts to understand what terrified me; but somehow, I can sense it was neither brutality, nor pain. It was something much deeper, more primal and it took away my faith in love and decency, left me abandoned and helpless."

"Drew, I'm having trouble trying to accept how one horrifying incident can change a child's life forever."

"Willow, I don't know when it started. I only know some of it was ongoing and Jack is the one who stopped it and saved me."

"How did he do that?"

"I was too helpless to do anything but withdraw from it. When I wanted to die, Jack refused to let me. He didn't feel wrong and wasn't afraid of the dark. He wanted to live. It made him strong enough to resist the terror and hold it away from me. I owe him for that and it sometimes makes me feel he has a right to exist."

"If you integrate, won't he still exist in you?"

"Not with individual awareness. Willow, we chose to have a joined consciousness that makes us all part of me. But just as every conscious being that exists has its own uniqueness, so do we. There's a small piece of each of us that is not part of the shared consciousness. It's what gives us each an identity that makes us truly different." He paused and let a nostalgic smile quirk his lips. "Those were the private thoughts we only felt when we met and talked as brothers."

"You told me you loved your mother. I don't know how you could."

Willow's quiet statement surprised him and he turned to face her. "Something in me refused to face the truth and wanted to save her from craziness so she would love me. But I wasn't around much back then. According to Paul, my center wasn't strong enough to deal with her unbalanced mind. I withdrew from total awareness for about two years, which left Andrew and Jack to take my place. As for my mother, it was Buffo who loved her with a child's faith. He saw her as an angel, not a real person; but then, she only came into his life when he sang. And then, Jack, the cynical pragmatist, took away Buffo's music. It was gone until after I bonded with Dad and rediscovered Buffo as my own."

"That sounds so weird to me."

"To a rational adult it is. To a child with no stability and no way to understand the conflicting emotions and needs inside him, it's a rather sensible way to handle trauma. Instead of trying to make sense out of disparate characteristics within me, I turned them into separate people and made them replacements for my dysfunctional family."

Drew paused for a thoughtful moment before he said, "Jack was an older brother and protective father figure but he was flawed and could never compete with Dad. Andrew was my obsession for learning and imagination. Buffo was my music and what was left of love without disillusion. Crybaby was the pitiful remains of childhood dependence on maternal nurturing. Dead Boy was numbing and all that was left when there was no hope. And I now realize that Avenger was an embodiment of hatred. He was pure, cold vengeance with no sense of compassion or conscience. I condemned him to oblivion because I abhorred the very essence of his purpose."

"His purpose was to protect your mother. What's wrong with that?"

"It would be easier to live with that if were the truth. His ultimate purpose was to kill Gino, a force I saw as evil personified. Even though my mother kept telling me Dad was the demon whose evil seed was in me, a vestige of memory refused to believe it and I sensed there was no true evil before Gino. Willow, at that age, there was enough confused logic in me to believe that all evil would go away if Gino was dead. But, deep inside, I knew I wasn't strong enough to do it myself. That was the birth of Avenger. He would kill the evil and I would be free of it."

"But you were a child and couldn't kill him."

"Avenger didn't see himself as a child. He was an invincible machinelike super hero with a mission and refused to stop trying, even after everyone else knew Gino was dead. Paul and Dad were right. My mind created a time bomb and buried it so completely even deep hypnosis failed to dislodge it."

Drew stiffened, pulled in a long breath, then relaxed with a relieved shudder. "Unfortunately, Avenger's directive was not specific enough to set his aim on only Gino. For all I know, everyone Avenger attacked looked like Gino to him. All I remember him seeing was red blood and an evil enemy. Avenger's directive was simple and never changed, so he failed to see the difference between Gino attacking my mother and any man attacking any woman. At first, his attacks were not life threatening and were easily defeated because he was in a child's body and he always went away when he was subdued and/or the triggering violence was stopped. But later, although Avenger never acquired my martial arts skills, the body he was in grew stronger and harder to defeat. Later attacks became more serious. I don't know what he would have done if he hadn't been stopped."

"Could it happen again?"

"He's gone as a persona because his prime directive is no longer valid and that is all he existed for. Avenger had no reasoning ability. He was a simple android personality and his purpose was literal. Therefore, Antonio, Paul and I were able to convinced him there was no Carlotta to protect and the pig bastard was dead. You could say his program was deleted when the evil he was created to destroy no longer existed. When an alter has no purpose, his individuality is expunged."

"Do you still see Avenger as a person?"

"Avenger never was a viable person. He was the construct of a precocious child too smart for his own good, which is a bad pattern of mine that Paul just knocked into my head with a big hammer." He made a sour face and shook his head. "I have never seen Paul so furious."

"At you?"

"Yes. But mostly at himself for letting my adamant denial make a fool out of him for ten years." Drew hugged her to him and kissed her hair. "Willow, I don't actually remember feeling separated. I only know I was because Dad and Paul have never let me forget it."

"Maybe they should have."

"Absolutely not." He pulled back and scowled, but kept his arms locked around her. "It was important that I understood what I was, so I could recognize the triggers and keep it from happening. Obviously, it didn't always work."

"Paul said you didn't believe it could happen again."

"I denied it could happen again. In fact, I totally convinced myself that it was not a serious disorder, only imaginary delusions brought on by a hunger for the loving parental relationship I blamed myself for destroying. Since denial is a strong force that gratifies pride and absolves guilt, you can't let me forget it either. It's something I have to live with and control because Paul is right. It doesn't go away until the initial root of its cause is exposed. That is a fact of the disorder I vehemently denied for years. I accept it now and know I have to control it, or it will control me."

"I thought there was a therapeutic cure."

"Willow, the only known cure is to discover the buried trauma that caused the initial dissociation so it can be exposed as no more than the reaction of an immature mind to a terror or guilt the child could not accept or face. Paul and I have tried to discover such an incident, but all we've found are later incidents that automatically produced splits because the protective mechanism was already established in my psyche."

"How old were you when this happened?"

"Antonio remembers a change in me not long after I turned five. He said that before that I was an energetic, imaginative, fun-loving and loveable kid, who never slowed down. Dad had been gone awhile and because I cried a lot and started to withdraw, Antonio figured I was depressed because I missed Dad and would get over it. That's when he started to spend more time with me and it seemed to work because I wasn't as depressed after I went to kindergarten and by the winter after I started first grade, I seemed to be back to being myself. Through therapy, Paul discovered that's when Jack and Andrew appeared. Further probing showed a hole in my memories at about the time Antonio first noticed I was depressed."

"Thank you for including me." Willow let him hug her to him for a moment before she said, "I've been trying to form a portrait of you in my mind ever since I met you; and now, I see it's more like a four-dimensional jigsaw puzzle."

"You're right. Time is an important aspect in understanding it. Paul and I have seen it the same way. But he wants to find the missing pieces, while I'd rather leave them lost." He held her face between his hands and looked more vulnerable than she'd ever seen him. "Willow, I never should have asked you to marry me without telling you the truth. I was so afraid it would drive you away that I avoided exposing my weakness and pulled you into a relationship I have no right to ask you to take on."

"I love you, Drew. And I promised I would take you as you are. That means everything you are. It isn't a weakness if we don't let it be. I won't let you down; I won't let you quit; I won't let you lose control. And I won't ever stop believing in you. We'll be so much stronger together than we could ever be apart." Willow smiled at the glint of relieved tears in his eyes. "We found a way to equal more than the sum of our parts. Let's keep doing it for the rest of our lives."

"I accept that and promise you the same. Without you I could never feel whole again. With you to hold onto and love, I feel there's nothing I can't do."

"That's not true." Willow smiled at his wary frown. "You still can't cook worth shit."

"I can't birth babies or sing soprano either. That's why I need you to be my other half."

"After what I've just accepted, I think I'll be a lot less than half of our marriage."

"No. Never accept me as anything but one person with one vote and never let me forget it."

"You're being serious again, aren't you?"

"Very much so." He slid his hand down her throat and opened the front of her shirt before he looked up with a devilish smile. "At least until I get your clothes off and give that disreputable, disillusioned sex fiend Jack one hell of a vicarious ride."

"Why not?" She wrinkled her nose and giggled at his startled look. "He is the one who conquered me. Drew, the thought of loving you without Jack's wild, bad boy excitement is not acceptable."

"That's not exactly right." He flushed with a sheepish expression, then admitted, "It *was* me, Willow. Jack did try to take over, but alone he's more talk and braggadocio than action or mature passion. He really doesn't know what he's doing, but he does have latent stirrings of desire and a persistent way of riling me up and taping into my libido until I throw away nagging inhibitions and pull out all the stops."

"Even with Marjorie?"

"No. I did the checking out on that one, so I don't know what really happened." He looked chagrined. "Except she wasn't thrilled about what she called an awkward and impatient adolescent performance."

Drew paused at her look of confusion that turned into a smile. "Don't look so forgiving, Willow. I was really pissed off at you, and my intentions were far from noble. I just didn't have it in me to follow through. We learned from Dad that wrong is wrong and copping-out by dumping the blame on someone else is still wrong. A long time ago, we made a pact with each other and Dad. We were one person to anyone but Dad and Paul. If one of us did something wrong, we were all responsible because that was the way the world saw us. It was something they never broke. I did that and it was a big mistake. Since I'm the one who is supposed to be in control, I feel I failed you. I'm sorry and I know it won't happen again."

"Unless Jack wants it to."

"He won't because I know he's there now and I won't let him. I defeated and dethroned Jack a long time ago. Besides, I learned today that both Jack and Andrew accept you, each in his own way of course, and do not want to hurt you." Drew blinked and looked thoughtful then muttered, "That's what Jack meant."

"What?"

Drew looked at her in surprise, then laughed. "He said he was yours now. Willow, Jack didn't conquer you. You conquered him."

"I did. How?"

"He took over and scared Gabby away. But when he tried it with you after that debacle with Marjorie, he couldn't scare you. In fact, when you fought back and physically hurt him, he lost control. Since he couldn't fight both of us, he backed down and accepted you as a partner of me in the control game."

"But he'll still be a part of our sex life?" She frowned.

"Probably. In his own vicarious way. But there's no one he can tell, so it'll be as easy to ignore as thin walls in a motel."

"Isn't it illegal to marry more than one man?"

"Not when they come in one body and one mind. Legal systems aren't capable of dealing with things like that. And in a few minutes, you won't be able to either because every part of me is going to ravish you, love you, and make you mine forever."

"Can I make a request?"

"Of course."

"Can I talk to them? Can I try to understand who's sharing you with me?"

"Talk to them?" Drew looked stunned. "I'm not sure I know how to do that. I never brought them out. I never wanted to bring them out. It just happened."

"Well, if I'm going to be a part of this community of Drew, I'd like to know who I'm dealing with."

Drew sighed and then shrugged. "Okay, see if you can get one of them to talk to you." He sat on the couch, settled back against its cushioned back, stretched out his legs and crossed his ankles. "I'll let down the defensive wall and meditate while you give it a shot."

"You're starting to irritate me." Willow scowled at him. "I want to accept this and I don't know how else to do it."

"Andrew's too shy. Try Jack. It might take a little of the sting out of his defeat. Just try not to get in an argument with him. It'll drive you nuts."

"How do I get him to talk?"

"I said I don't know. Between the three of us, it was mostly an internal thing. But sometimes, Paul or Dad would just straight-out ask to talk to one of us."

"You were hypnotized."

"No. We had accepted it as our reality until I denied it." He closed his eyes and relaxed into a state of meditation.

"Jack? Will you talk to me?" Willow frowned when nothing happened. "Jack, are you there? It's Willow. Come out and talk to me. Please?" Her eyes widened when Drew's head dropped forward. She gasped when, with a shudder, his head snapped up and she met a face that was Drew's with a brash expression that wasn't Drew.

"Ho there, Willow. What's up?"

"Are you really Jack?" She suddenly felt embarrassed and tongue-tied, as if she had made an awful mistake or been caught in a cruel practical joke. "Or are you Drew pulling my leg?"

"He ain't here. So, he ain't pulling your leg." The voice that answered lacked the resonance of Drew's, sounded younger, came from his throat rather than his diaphragm.

"What do you mean he's not here. I can see him."

"That's the weird part to people like you." Jack straightened, thrust himself to his feet and tapped his forehead. "If you was in here with me, things would be different, but you can't do that, so accept what you get." He took a book off the end table and looked at it. "This yours?"

"Yes, it's a novel I've been reading." Willow watched him riffle through the pages and sensed that he felt as awkward as she did.

"Geez, it sure has a lot of big words in it." Jack flipped his head, dropped the book back on the table and turned to look at her. "Whatta you want to talk about?"

"Drew said you knew about me. And I wanted to meet you."

"Why?"

"Because you're a fragment of him and I want to know all of him."

"I've heard that shrink talk, but it don't make me a nobody." His brow lowered; his jaw tensed. "It don't even make me less real."

"But you're not real. You're just a piece of Drew's mind." Willow watched a flash of indignant anger narrow his lips and knew she wasn't looking at Drew. "I'm sorry, Jack. I just don't understand."

"*Cogito, ergo sum: I think, therefore I am.* That gives me identity according to some philosopher Andrew's always dribbling on about."

"Wasn't that Rene Descartes?"

"Yeah, some smart Frenchman who didn't have his head up his ass." Jack shrugged and said, "I'm sorry I got cheesed off. I know the way it is with us, Willow. I don't know how it is with you, so maybe it's you who ain't real."

"I can't argue with that viewpoint. I'm not in your shoes."

"Neither am I." Jack looked down at bare feet and chuckled. "You're a cool chick, Willow. And, like Andrew says, keep being good for Drew. You're bitchin' sexy and put the fun back in his life."

Jack clucked in his cheek, winked at her before he dropped his head and shuddered.

When the head snapped up, Willow started to answer, then cocked her head, looked at Drew's questioning face and flopped back on the couch with her hands holding her head. "Like he said, that was weird."

"I guess it worked." Drew looked surprised. "I don't remember getting off the couch."

"Is it always like that?"

"Like what?"

"Finding yourself somewhere else." She wrinkled her nose and gave him a puzzled look.

"It used to be, but not for a long time." He looked thoughtful then sat on the couch arm and crossed his arms. "There were however, times I stayed out late when I had studying to do or a paper to finish and ended up conking out at my desk. I'd wake up in the wee hours and find myself fifty pages ahead of where I thought I was or looking at a draft on the computer screen I didn't remember finishing. That kind of thing should have told me Andrew was not as gone as I proclaimed, but my denial had too many good excuses."

"Such as?"

"Too much to drink, absent mindedness, distraction, immersed in deep concentration…" He tossed a hand up in exasperation. "There were way too many ways to avoid a truth I refused to accept. Paul just managed to gob smack me with that one, too."

"So, it sounds as if you do owe Andrew an apology for taking credit for his efforts."

"We were kids. Apologizing wasn't a big thing between us. Besides, I fixed that. He only accepts me as Drew, so if it says Andrew on it, he can take credit for it. I don't care."

"Well, you're not kids now."

Drew looked at her scolding face, thought for a moment then said, "Willow, I grew up; they didn't."

"But Jack knows about sex."

"Jack is emotionally a child. But, because of his early associations with older kids and teenagers, he is cognitively an early adolescent male. They all know more than everyone else about sex. A lot of it is wrong or ego-inflated, but they're full of assumptions about it." Drew smiled at her nod of reluctant agreement. "Andrew is a precocious child with a genius complex and is much better at getting into my knowledge center than Jack is. Don't let the body they're in fool you. As far as emotional and developmental maturity, they are still children."

Drew paused then drilled her with a hard look. "And who really wants a child who doesn't grow up? They'd be better off with a dog. As for me, I'd had it with them and had a life of my own to live." He paused to collect himself, but the rant refused to simmer down and he strode across the room. "Now I'm stuck with them again and I don't want them."

"Drew, I talked to Jack. I liked him."

"Willow, if you're still looking for the thirteen-year-old bigfoot, you just talked to him." He swung his hand out and pointed to where Jack had been standing.

"I still liked him."

"Paul and Dad liked him. Most times I liked him. But they know I'd be better off without the separation. And I do, too. We just can't find a way to do it." He looked at her stricken face and pulled her into his arms. "Willow, if you want children, I know a much better way to give them to you."

"We're not ready to think about that yet."

"You're right, but when you decide we are, let me know, and I'll give you all the help I can."

"I'll remember that."

Chapter Thirty

Andy knocked on the door to the upstairs rooms Paul was using, then entered when a voice answered, "Come in, I'm mostly ready."

Andy walked through the sitting room, to look at the scattered array of clothes, notebooks and fishing gear covering the spread in the bedroom. "That's almost?"

"I found a sporting goods store and bought a back pack, some hiking clothes, fishing gear and cases." Paul scratched his head as he stared at the jumble on the bed. "Now I have to figure out how to get it all packed."

"That's something you can take up with John. He's fanatic about fishing and knows those mountain streams like a native."

"Maybe I should take him with me." Paul looked at Andy with the bright-eyed expression of a fox with his ears pricked up. "I've never been in the American wilderness."

"John will take you into the backcountry where he swears the trout are big and shrewd and delicious. He'd be as good as any guide you could hire. A lot cheaper, too."

"I'm willing to pay him."

"You can pay the expenses, but I can say for certain, he won't accept anything more."

"Can he leave on short notice?"

"I would say so, but it might not be as short as you think."

"What does that mean?" Paul gave Andy a look that questioned his motive. "The hotel reservation is for tomorrow night."

"I'd like you to change it."

"Did something happen with Drew?" A mix of excitement as well as panic flashed across Paul's face.

"A little agitated with himself, but we expected that." Andy smiled at Paul's agreeing nod. "Antonio called to tell me he was finally able to have a productive conversation with his mother, who has been much more willing to talk about the past since her husband died. He says he gleaned some information he needs to share with us. He also said he had some things to show us that may provide the motivation we need."

"What does Antonio have?"

"He didn't say, but from the sound of his voice I feel he believes he's on to something significant. He indicated it was important enough we should be at his house about seven."

"I'll cancel the hotel—the whole trip if I have to." Relief and enthusiasm washed away Paul's tension. "I trust Antonio's hunches, and I would like to find a breakthrough before Drew marries Willow."

"She's accepted it very well, Paul."

"She's in love, but reality can be a nasty surprise."

"I remember that. But Drew was my only child. I loved him and learned to accept him the only way he could be. I'm sure I can help her do the same."

"There's a good chance you could, but wouldn't it be better if we could end it now? I want to save her from the agonies you went through. I want to protect you from what you may have to face if he loses her."

"I thank you for that concern. Now, let's hope Antonio's right, and he's found the magic talisman."

"Don't get too optimistic, Andy." Paul frowned. "Drew's wall is sealed with primal dread and I don't have a sorcerer's wand up my sleeve."

That evening, after settling into Antonio's living room with pizza and beer, Andy kicked his feet onto an ottoman and studied his brother-in-law's enigmatic expression. "You have that I've-got-your-number-gleam in your eyes."

"That's why I'm a detective. At the precinct, I'm known as the master of stings. I learned the importance of an airtight setup and possess eviscerating interrogation techniques, but you..." he pointed at Paul and lowered dark eyebrows "...leave me in the dust when it comes to sucking in a victim and going for the gonads."

"Thank you, Antonio," Paul returned the stare. "But I prefer to think of it as finding a chink in the darkness of a broken psyche rather than a blow to the vitals. And in Drew's case, I need to let the light of truth penetrate a black hole of terror that repels rational thought."

"That's a little beyond me." Antonio blinked at him, then laughed at Andy's look of sympathy. "And that trick of hypnotism you do with the prism blows my mind away. Drew is a strongminded person. I find it hard to accept the way he drops right into it."

"I reject your label of trick, even though it has way too often been presented that way," Paul said. "It merely directs the focus of the mind inward, as does meditation. However, with someone conditioned to the process, it goes deeper into an absorbing trance that opens the mind to dormant memories and emotions. A functioning multiple often lives in a trance state." Paul lifted open hands and gave Antonio a questioning look. "How else could he see the world, even himself, from entirely different prospectives and points of view?"

"Paul, that makes more sense to me than all the psychological blather I've been trying to absorb."

"I've been hypnotizing Drew since he was eight years old. He allows me to do it because he trusts me. And the prism does not hypnotize him, it merely captures his attention and concentrates his thoughts so I can direct them."

"Since I've seen it work, I believe you, but it still gives me a chill inside to think of someone taking over a person's mind."

"Someone takes over Drew's mind quite often. It's what I want to stop, but I can't do it until he is able to understand what terrified him enough that he shut off the center of his awareness. I'm confidently risking my reputation on a gut-feeling that what terrified him as a vulnerable child will be seen as absurd by his adult mind. However, since Drew can't reach the memory as an adult, he has to retrieve it as a child and then review it as an adult while it is still vivid in his trance state."

"Won't it go away again when he comes out of the trance?"

"I certainly hope not." Paul rebuked him. "When he comes back to full awareness, he should know it for what it is. It may shake him, but I'm hoping he'll be able to regain an essential part of him that's been locked away for more than twenty years."

"That's wacko." Antonio shook his head while he tried to put what Paul said into focus.

"The human mind is, if nothing else, wacko; and at the present time is mostly unexplainable. Extreme fear, whether real or imagined, often creates phobias. In Drew's case, it happened at an age when reality is not yet a solid concept and the terror reached the primitive center of his psyche. In essence, he went away and restarted with a new awareness that created other personae to stand in for him."

Antonio nodded as he thought about what Paul said. "That makes more sense out of what my mother told me and what I found in her attic."

"And that is?" Paul raised a frost-flecked russet eyebrow.

When Antonio reached into a large shopping bag and pulled out a painting, both Paul and Andy straightened. Andy looked surprised while Paul looked shocked. "I found it in the attic where my mother said she put it twenty years ago because Drew was afraid of it and she didn't like seeing him upset."

"I remember that painting." Andy said. "It used to hang in your parents' living room. I looked it up once. It's an old copy of a thirteenth century oil by the Florentine painter Giotto. I've forgotten its title."

"It's commonly known as: *Hell, and Sinners being dragged into the Fiery Furnace*," Paul said. "I imagine it would be upsetting to a lot of people, but only if they knew and believed in its symbolism. Drew was five years old. Why would it upset him?"

"That's sort of what I told my mother." Antonio nodded. "I always saw it as ugly and in bad taste, but not very scary. Then, as they say in bad drama: she told me the rest of the story. She said that one day she walked into the living room and saw Carlotta in front of the painting, holding Drew by the arm. She was shaking him and telling him he was an evil child, who would be dragged into the fire and burned for his wickedness if he didn't let her cleanse the demon from him. Drew started yelling back. He kicked her, then jerked away, ran into the bathroom and locked the door. My mother was furious at Carlotta and told her to get out of the house. Then she kept Drew for the night."

"How was he?"

"She said he was fine after she held him for a while and, in the Italian way of mothering, made him a good supper."

"I'm sorry, Antonio," Paul shook his head. "As awful as it was, I don't think it caused him to dissociate."

"I don't either," Antonio said. "It was what she told me after I asked why she thought he was afraid of the painting that made me find it and call Andy. She said that when she saw Drew again, he seemed different—quiet and docile, as if his spirit was broken. About a week later, my mother took him shopping, then stopped at our house before taking him home. When Drew walked into the living room and saw the painting, he started screaming hysterically and yelling, 'No fire! No fire!' When he calmed down, he cried and whimpered for a long time before he fell asleep. That's when she put the painting in the bag and stowed it in a locked trunk in the attic."

A look of relieved excitement enlivened Paul's face. "What we need to do is find out what happened between the time Carlotta told him about the fire in the painting and the day your mother took him shopping."

"That was my take on it, too," Antonio said.

"I apologize for doubting your instincts, Antonio. You were right to get the painting. It may be the stimulus we need."

"Shortly after that," Antonio said. "Gino married Carlotta and started giving her stronger drugs. My father was furious and my two older brothers vehemently supported him. He told Carlotta if she ever came to the house again, he'd have her arrested for being a user and Gino for dealing. We were all forbidden to have anything more to do with her. It broke my mother's heart to turn away from Drew, but she didn't have it in her to defy her family. I was a teenager and tried to follow his edict for a while, but I'd always liked Drew and kind of looked after him when I could."

Antonio glanced at Andy for a moment then added, "I have something else, too." He reached into the bottom of the bag and took out a stuffed toy horse about six inches high. "She told me that not long after Andy went away Drew asked her if he could leave his pony at her house because his mother said he was too old to sleep with a baby's toy. Carlotta had thrown it away, but Drew took it out of the garbage can and hid it until he could take it to my mother's house."

"I gave him that toy when he turned four." When Andy took the brown and white horse from Antonio, his eyes misted and he had to catch his breath before he could talk. "I bought it in France after Drew and I visited my mother on her birthday and he became fascinated by the carousel horse in the drawing room. It was his favorite toy. He didn't like going to bed without it."

Paul set a hand on Andy's shoulder to steady him. "If I can find that little boy again, I may get the chance to put him back into the man he's become."

"You have to do that." Andy tightened his hand on the soft toy and continued in a broken voice, "I don't want to lose him again."

"I'll do whatever I possibly can." The psychiatrist tightened his grip on Andy's hard shoulder. "But the ultimate effort has to come from Drew. You once told me he was a brave child, who took falls and injuries in stride. I'm betting he can do it again if you give him the incentive."

"You turned that over to Willow," Andy said quietly. "Do you want her in on this, too?"

"No. He needs to repair his initial, childhood bond with you before he will be whole enough to step away from the lost child. And that toy may just do it."

"Paul, why wasn't I there?" Andy blurted out. "Why didn't I just take him with me? I could have stopped it."

"Don't go there, Andy." Paul grabbed his attention with a sharp voice. "Or I'll have to find you a psychiatrist. You've devoted your life to helping Drew, and you well know regrets and self-castigation make it harder on both of you."

"I know all that." Andy met the absorbing gaze with a stricken expression. "I'm scared, Paul. What if he dissociates again and you can't get him back?"

"He won't do that."

"How do you know that? What's to stop him?"

"Love." Paul answered flatly. "He loves you; he loves life; he loves his family; and he loves Willow. No matter how terrified he was as a child, no matter how terrible it will be to relive that terror, the Drew he is now will accept it and choose love over despair."

After pulling in a deep breath, Andy shuttered and controlled the runaway sensation of panic that raced through him. "There really isn't any other choice, is there?"

"Only more of the same for the future. And if he ever wants a stable life and family, I see that as untenable."

"I've always trusted you before, so I'll say it's a go. But I'm still scared. When do you suggest we do it?"

"I have tomorrow off," Antonio answered. "And it's a Wednesday, so Drew doesn't have a performance."

"He probably has a rehearsal call in the morning." Andy thought for a moment. "How does six o'clock sound? And where?"

"I suggest right here." Antonio looked into the kitchen and started to chuckle. "Tell Drew we're having a sendoff get-together for Paul to introduce him to Bebbe's Pizza."

"That'll work," Andy said.

"If it means more of this pizza, it's a yes vote from me." Paul turned to Antonio. "One other thing. I don't want Drew to have any alcohol. It could add an element I don't want to run into."

"Pizza and no beer?"

Andy laughed at the aghast look on Antonio's face. "You can do it, big man; and since Drew only drinks alcohol as a social gesture or tradition, he won't care. In fact, when it comes to beers, he often prefers root beer."

"I have some of that." Antonio nodded. "But I don't prefer it."

The following evening, Antonio opened the pantry door and shouted into the living room. "I'm out of beer. We'll have to drink root beer."

"Tonio, it doesn't matter." Drew laughed at his uncle's disgruntled face. "By the time you go get beer, the pizza will be cold. Besides, Dad's preference comes out of a Scotch bottle and Paul is too French to truly appreciate crude American brew."

"Is what he said okay?" Antonio looked at Paul and Andy, who, tight-lipped, gave him a thumbs-up reply before he strode out of the kitchen with a six-pack of chilled root beer. "I always keep a pack cold for Harrison so the crisis is averted."

When the pizza was gone and to Drew's relief, the fish stories dried up, he looked at the clock and hinted that Willow might want to go to bed before midnight for a change.

"I think that's a possibility." Pausing, Andy focused on reaffirming a willpower that, in the past, had pulled him through what seemed to be hopeless situations. "But Paul thought of something he wants to talk to you about. Since he's supposed to leave tomorrow and you're both here, Antonio and I will clear up the debris while you two have a talk."

"What else is there?" Drew gave Paul a surprised look. "You already know what Willow did with Jack. It surprised the hell out of me, but I think it put it in better focus for her."

"Willow is a very brave and determined woman, never doubt that." Paul leaned forward in his chair to face the couch Drew was sitting on. "There's something I've been missing and I want to try to find it."

"You've been saying that for years. It never goes anywhere."

"I think it might this time. Are you willing to trust me on that?"

"I always trust you, Paul." Drew gave him a helpless look. "It's just that after finding out I blatantly deceived both you and me for ten years, I don't have much faith in myself anymore."

"I have infinite faith in your strength and resilience. I want to find that missing puzzle piece and I think I know where to look his time."

"Okay. Cast out your bait and see if I bite." Drew relaxed, emptied his mind of distractions and stared into the prism and its spectrum of colors.

Continuing to hold Drew's attention with the tumbling colors, Paul reached into the shopping bag beside his chair and put the stuffed horse in Drew's hand. "What do you have in your hand?"

Drew looked down at the toy and smiled. "My pinto pony. Daddy gave him to me."

"You're five years old, your father is away. Do you miss him?"

"Yes. I don't know where he is." His voice was small and uncertain as he stared at the toy and stroked a hand on its shaggy mane. "Mamma won't tell me. She said he went away because I was bad and he didn't love me anymore."

"He's always loved you, Drew."

"He's gone and I can't say I love him." He stared at the toy and looked sad. "It makes Mamma mad."

Paul pulled in a long breath before he slid the framed print out of the bag and held it in front of Drew, who dropped the toy and stared at the scene with frozen terror contorting his face.

"It's a picture, Drew. It's not real. Think about the fire, not the picture. Look for the fire. Think about the fire. Tell me about the fire."

"It's hot, it's hot, no Mamma, no, no, please." Drew shook his head back and forth; his face flushed; his eyes rounded; he started to tremble and cry. "I can't do it I can't I can't I can't kill it… No, please no."

Drew stared down at his cupped hands with a horrified look on his face and resisted the blackness. Suddenly, he jerked upright and threw his hands forward as if he were ridding himself of something terrifying. Shrieking in pain and terror, he thrashed against a force that seemed to be pushing him forward then clamped his hands over his face and thrust himself backwards. His face went blank and he slumped into the corner of the sofa with his head tipped forward, his blank stare focused on nothing.

"Drew, it's Paul. Come back to me." Paul dropped to his knees in front of Drew, grabbed a handful of his shirt, pushed him back against the cushions and held the flashing crystal in front of his lolling head. "Drew, remember me. Come back to me. Drew, listen to me, look at me." With a shudder, Drew's head snapped up and he stared at Paul in confusion for an instant before he again lost himself in the shifting colors.

"Drew, I want you to remember the fire and tell me what happened by the fire."

Paul dropped the prism and brought his hands together in a clap that made Andy rush through the kitchen doorway until Antonio held him back. Drew shook himself and sat up with his gaze intently focused on Paul.

"Drew, tell me about the fire. Where was the fire? What happened by the fire?"

"The pot stove in the kitchen." Drew looked confused as if nothing was making sense to him.

"What were you doing by the fire?"

"Mamma said to throw it in the fire. But it was hot. It hurt. I was afraid of it

"Throw what in the fire?"

"The thing in the bread basket."

"What was the thing in the basket?"

"It was… it was…" Drew's voice was strained and hysterical, his eyes wide in horrified guilt. "…the fire burned me and tried to pull me into Hell."

"Tell me what was in the basket?"

"A towel and blood, a little puppy with a big head and eyes and stubby paws. A snake was eating its belly button."

"It wasn't a puppy, Drew. Tell me what it was. You know what it was. Tell me."

"It was... It was... a demon child like me." He screamed at Paul. "She made me kill a baby and burn it in hell!"

"It was not a demon and you didn't kill it; or burn it in hell. You didn't kill it, Drew. You know better than that. It was already dead and couldn't live outside the womb. You're an educated, adult man and don't believe in false images like that. Think about it with your commonsense and tell me what happened when you come back to me."

When Paul clapped his hands again, Drew's head dropped and the shudder racked through him. His head snapped up and he stared at Paul with a look that was horrified, but no longer hysterical.

"Tell me what you remember from just before the fire."

Drew closed his eyes until an image filled his mind. "A woman, a skinny woman." His voice was sure, strong and adult with an edge of confusion and apprehension. "She had a big handbag with clinking metal things in it. She gave my mother pills and told me to go in my room before she took Mamma into her bedroom. She was there a long time and made Mamma scream. After she left, I heard Mamma crying. My door was locked. I couldn't get to her."

Drew froze for a moment, then shook his head. He was clear-headed, no longer looked confused or vulnerable. "She had an abortion. I heard her tell someone she lost Gino's baby, but I didn't understand what she meant and wondered why she wasn't looking for it."

"Do you remember anything else from after the fire?"

"No. I don't remember back then. Paul, you know I only remember things that happened after Andrew and Jack came out."

"Then how did you remember what you just told me? I don't think Jack and Andrew were there yet. Were they?"

"No, they couldn't have been." Drew looked confused then said, Gino wasn't living there yet. I remember he moved in while I was in school."

Paul smiled and, in a surprising, uncharacteristic reaction, caught Drew's face between his hands and kissed him on the forehead. "You're back, Drew, and I hope with all my heart you are all one person."

"I don't feel any different. Just more confused."

"It will take some time. There will be more things to remember. And some of them will be good."

"This is good. Where did you find this? Drew looked down at the toy horse laying on the couch beside him. I'd forgotten all about it."

"My mother had it," Antonio said.

"I remember that." Drew looked surprised. "I asked Nonna to keep it because my mother wanted to throw it away." He looked up at where Andy stood in the archway to the kitchen. "I remember when you gave it to me. I loved it because I loved you, and it's all I had of you."

Seeing Andy step toward him, Drew met him halfway across the room. There was an instant of awkward hesitation before they clasped each other in a rough, man-to-man bearhug before it turned into an emotional embrace that lingered while they shared bonded strength and Andy's tears of relief.

After the emotions settled, Drew stepped back and studied Paul's questioning expression. "You have that look that says you want to ask me something. What is it?"

"Something you've always avoided talking about and I really want to know because it's one of the things that gave you the strength you needed to make this happen. Just when and how did you take control away from Jack? It's something you shouldn't have been able to do."

"When I was fourteen."

"How did you do it?"

Drew looked reluctant, then let out a breath and shrugged. "Very deliberately. With a big dose of teenage arrogance that told me I knew more than you, Dad, and libraries of psychological data." Drew smiled at their not so surprised expressions. "By that time, you'd clued me in enough that I knew it was all an abnormal construct of my own imagination, which made me think that if I made it happen, I could make it unhappen. But in order to do that, I had to be the one in control. I'd been battling with Jack off and on for five years and was damn sick of the way he used Andrew and I as his whipping boys. I was also aware of the fact that I was ahead of him in experience and maturity. I then, presumptuously, decided I deserved to be the one in charge instead of hotheaded, unpredictable, self-centered Jack. I just had to work out a strategy plan. Since Jack had no concept of strategy beyond bullying, I figured I could take him out."

"What was your plan?" Andy asked.

"There were a number of them." Drew made a sour face. "Most were dumb failures, but a few were promising enough to give me an edge as well as encouraging enough to keep me at it. I studied both of them to learn their fears and weaknesses. For the next few months, I tested out the chinks in their armor. Andrew was terrified of the dark and weak in self-esteem, which made him easy to bully and dominate. But Jack had a grip on him I couldn't break.

"Jack confused me because he bounced back and forth from hero to tormenter, friend to foe, helpful to selfish, with not much in between. His biggest weaknesses were selfish possessiveness and an insatiable need for admiration. He was also amoral and lazy. Chores, reading, studying, martial arts and other learned skills were too much work, effort and discomfort for him. Since his basic philosophy was to pawn as much off on others as he could, he left that stuff to Andrew and me.

"Then, after I made him really mad one day, he punched at me with my own fist and hit a bookcase. I noticed not only did we both feel the pain, it seemed to hurt him way more than me and he kept sniveling about it. That's when it dawned on me that our co-presence was capable of a deeper bonding. Like most bullies, Jack was big on threats and bravado because he was a coward. He couldn't tolerate criticism, ridicule or physical pain, so he always cut out on anything that hurt and dumped unpleasant consequences on Andrew and/or me while he gloated about his superiority."

"I fully agree with that," Paul said. "But you shouldn't have been able to defeat him until you found your own balance and center."

"I didn't care about bullshit like that." Drew answered indignantly. "I just wanted to stop him from mistreating Andrew. I had a problem to solve. Like how could I subject Jack to enough pain and fear to break him and make him accept me as top dog when I knew he could opt out whenever he wanted? Once I learned how to push Andrew out of the way and close him out while keeping Jack totally linked into my physical senses, I figured out a way to win. The snag was I couldn't hold Jack unless I stayed focused on him, which meant I had to split my awareness, join part of me to him, and get a mental grasp on his control before I could hold onto him and make him share the pain."

Drew looked at Andy's and Antonio's totally blank faces and Paul's captivated expression. "Since I didn't like the risks involved in some dangerous stunt or accident, I picked fights with bigger, older bullies. That didn't work because my targets had no concept of a fair fight. Hence, my defense training would kick in and I'd lose my hold on Jack. That's when I knew I had to find something that would be predictable, limited and under enough control that I would have no reason to panic or retaliate and could fully concentrate on keeping Jack out and aware."

Drew looked at his father's confused face for a moment then said, "You often said I was tough, foolhardy and had enough guts to hang myself. That's what I used, but I couldn't do it alone because, like most sane people, I have a built-in reflex against inflicting severe pain on myself. And I knew you weren't up to helping me with it because I'd already tried it with you. So, I waited until I was in Scotland and used Cousin Jamie, the Earl, instead."

"That makes no sense." Andy said. "Jamie didn't know much about your disorder."

"He didn't have to know. He just had to be himself."

"In what way?"

"What I call the old school British fortitude shit." Drew laughed at his father's startled reaction. "I baited Jack into sneaking into the distillery one night. We smashed a lot of bottles and made a hell of a mess. I made sure we were caught by a watchman and Jack thought it was great fun until we faced Jamie, who picked up his damn cane.

"That's when Jack learned I'd turned the tables on him, but I was so locked into him he couldn't check out. I latched onto and melded into his awareness, then refused to let him go. It was nine strokes of godawful pain, but the hardest part was mustering enough control to clamp my mouth shut, retain my calm and keep Jack's howls and blubbering internal so Jamie wouldn't think I was a wimp." He laughed at their startled expressions. "After all, I had a reputation to live up to. And if his son Alex had heard me yowling, he'd still be razzing me about it."

Drew laughed at three stunned faces, then looked pensive for a moment. "There was always something about Alex and my attachment to him that Jack didn't like so he avoided him. Anyway, when it was over, I was so pissed I really made my point by keeping Jack aware until it quit hurting. That gave him a long time to internally whine and cuss at me while he got the message and I got the satisfaction of victory."

"I've never heard of anything like that." Paul looked stunned. "But then, I never heard of any center with as much grit and will to win as you had."

"You probably never will again." Drew laughed. "I don't think anyone else would be dumb enough to try it. And I straightened up my act at Glendoncroft after that because I sure as hell wanted no part of it again."

"But how did you learn to push Andrew away and hold onto Jack?" Paul asked.

"Andrew was easy. I'd just distract Jack by enticing him into trouble then bully Andrew a little. I'd tell him to go home and he'd withdraw to his playhouse and sulk. Jack did it to him all the time, but he put him in the black room too much. I didn't like that because it took any chance for developing courage right out of him. And Jack didn't care if I pushed Andrew away because he thought he had me to boss around."

Drew gave Paul a long look then said, "Jack was a tougher problem until I remembered you saying I had already absorbed enough of his identity to have a strong effect on him. So, my solution came partly from internally mimicking the way you manipulated him, partly from Karate and Martial Arts training that taught me how to focus and remain calm under stress and partly by willing myself to share more of his mind and awareness. But mostly, it came from the bold assumption that if he could do it to Andrew, I could do it to him."

Drew smiled at their blank stares. "I told him if I ever found out he came out when I wasn't with him, he'd get it again, or maybe something even worse. Jack knew I meant it and was afraid of me after that. Whenever he tried to cross me, I'd tell him I was thinking about taking a trip to Scotland. He backed down every time. He never tried to come out at Glendoncroft again, or anywhere near Jamie or Alex for that matter. After that, he and Andrew withdrew from co-presence with me and left me alone. In my awareness, they never came out after that and I declared myself cured. That was a totally wrong and self-centered assumption I made myself believe and now regret."

"But mostly," Antonio clapped Drew on the shoulder. "you had the grit to win the most important battle of your life. But then, I've seen you in action. Pain was never a great deterrent to you so it doesn't really surprise me."

"We can credit Dad for most of that grit. And it wasn't until now that I realized Dad trained me to do exactly what I did. He raised me to take active control of my life, not leave it to fate or someone else, real or not." Drew smiled at his father's knowing look and Paul's nod of agreement. "Neither of you ever let me forget I was the true center, and the battle was mine to win."

Drew paused and thought for a moment before he looked at his uncle. "I always said I was unaware of what happened while I first lived with my mother and Gino, but that was wrong. I remembered I always felt safe when Uncle Antonio was there, just as I did later when I was with Alex, who showed me how to be a winner and stand up to Jack's bullying."

"You always were a merciless victor," Antonio said.

"Only against bullies and assholes. Jack could be both." Drew made a wry face, then sobered his expression. "I suppose it scared Andrew away from me, too. He couldn't handle shakeups and was still dependent on Jack, but it did save him a lot of grief, which was a big part of my motivation. Not long after that, I convinced myself it was all over and felt very proud of inventing my own cure."

Drew stared at three puzzled faces, then frowned and looked chagrined. "Obviously, I was wrong about that, too, but my denial made life a lot easier for the last twelve years."

"Jamie told me about that," Andy said. "It upset him and worried him because, although he knew you were impulsive and a bit too wild, he never judged you as destructive."

"Were you upset about it?"

"With you, yes, but not with Jamie. He had his rules and you defied them. I'd never felt wanton destruction in you either, but I had in Jack and felt it was well deserved. Besides, since Jamie and I survived caning both in school and from his father, I figured you could take it from him. But I don't understand what you meant about trying it with me."

"I wish you hadn't picked up on that because it was the worst of my failed attempts and keeps coming back to haunt me." Drew winced. "That was the time I stole your car."

"You wrecked my car to get a reaction out of me?"

"I *took* the car to get a reaction out of you. Jack *wrecked* the car because he loved the thrill of speed but couldn't drive worth shit. He stamped on the accelerator and blocked me out before I could stop him. All I knew was that I was on a clear straight road that suddenly turned into a tight curve on an embankment with no guard rail and that damn greenhouse was closing in on me."

Drew laughed at their shocked faces. "I knew you'd be mad at me and thought I could probably goad you into taking me down a peg or two while I held onto Jack. But it failed because Jack was gone before the crash. And when I saw the rage on your face when you slammed me into that wall, I knew there was no way I could have remained calm enough to hold onto him, or anything else."

"You could have asked for my help."

"Dad, I realized then that it was too much to ask of you. Besides, it was my battle to win, not yours, or anyone else's."

Paul nodded and gave Drew a long thoughtful look. "I'm glad you told me about that. It gives me a lot more confidence in your future and befuddles some of my educated assumptions."

"Thanks, Paul. But, even if this worked, you're not getting rid of me. I plan on keeping you around as part of the family." Drew reached out to shake Paul's hand and ended up hugging him.

"Well, I guess that wraps it up." Andy exchanged a firm fist bump with Antonio before he started for the door. "Let's bury the head of that damn Jabberwock and go home, my beamish boy. O frabjous day! Calloo! Calay!"

"One, two! One, two. And through and through…" Drew waved an imaginary vorpal blade and thrust it at the painting leaning against the couch. He stopped, glared at the painted canvas, kicked it across the room, snatched up his lost toy and headed for the door.

❖

"No! Don't take it. I need it."

Willow jolted awake when Drew shouted and smashed an elbow into her chin as he sat bolt upright and stared past her at the glowing nightlight in the hall. "Drew, what's wrong?"

"Don't take it. Give it to me. Daddy gave it to me. It's mine." He looked terrified, then blinked at Willow in confusion, shook his head, rolled away from her and stood up.

When Willow switched on a bedside lamp, Drew was standing in front of his dresser, looking into a top drawer. "What am I supposed to give you?"

"This." He relaxed and lifted a hand holding a brown and white toy horse. "It was all I had left of Dad. She took it away from me. And then, I stopped remembering him."

"But you have it. Who gave it to you?"

"Paul, but he only handed it to me. When I was five, my mother took it from me and threw it away. I dug it out of the garbage and gave it to Antonio's mother to keep it safe, which she did for over twenty years. A couple of days ago, she gave it to Antonio."

"That's what woke you up?"

"Not by itself. I was bombarded by dreams, memories, illusions, and regrets until I felt torn apart. I have to see Paul now."

"It's two o'clock in the morning, Drew. Can I help you?"

"Yes, you can go with me."

"Can it wait?"

"No, it can't."

At the manor house, Drew unlocked a delivery entrance near the kitchen and they took an elevator to the second floor. When the door opened, Willow stared down a carpeted hallway at tall, diamond-shaped window panes that looked out over a mystically blurred image of the moonlit English garden sprinkled with colorfully refracted fragments of outdoor lights. "Maybe I should have taken your grandmother's tour. The views must be wonderful."

"We'll stay here tonight and you can do it in the morning. She'll be thrilled." He stopped at the last room on the right and rapped on the door. "That way you won't have to make breakfast."

"Isn't that a bit imposing?"

"We're part of the family, Willow." He pounded the door with the side of a closed fist. "You get it the British way here."

"What's that?"

"Alice starts coffee and tea at six-thirty and sets a buffet at seven. Gram, John, Dad and Paul are already here. Two more won't matter." Drew scowled and lifted his hand to pound the door again when it jerked open and a wide-eyed, wild haired Paul blinked at him as if he were expecting the fire brigade or a police raid.

"What are you doing here?" Paul yanked his eyes away from Drew's raised fist and saw Willow standing beside him. Composing himself, he pulled his robe tighter around him, then glanced at the darkness beyond the tall window. "What time is it?"

"Sometime after two. I have to talk to you."

"Now?" Paul glanced at Willow, who shrugged and gave him an apologetically helpless look, then took a closer look at Drew, read anxiety in the tautness of his features. "Alright, come in and sit down. I'll find something more to wear."

In the sitting room, Willow sat in an armchair and watched Drew stare out the window then look down at his hands. He picked at his fingernails and clenched his hands as if he wanted to punch something. Just about the time Willow realized he was ready to use his own reflection for a punching bag, she heard Paul behind her.

"Drew. Turn around. Now." Paul didn't shout, but his commands stiffened Drew, who pivoted to face him. For a tense moment they faced each other in a frozen display of confrontation.

Drew blinked first and sank into himself with a stricken look on his face. "Paul, I wanted to be free of them. I didn't want to kill them."

"You didn't kill them."

"They're not there. Nobody's there. I'm alone."

"They are there. It's just different because they are you."

"Why don't I know that?"

"Because they've always been you, just disconnected, like faulty wires that only work right when they're wiggled." Paul knit his fingers together and jiggled them.

"Do they know what I did to them?"

"No. They have no individual identities beyond residual memories in your conscious mind. There was nothing to kill because no matter how you perceived them, they were never real. You've known that for years."

"I knew it as a learned fact. I didn't feel it that way." Drew moved away from the window and met Paul's absorbing gaze with a helpless look. "I could see them, Paul. Jack was lean and blond and he had a cocky way of looking as if he were king of the world. Andrew had new teeth that looked too big for his mouth. He looked like a scolded puppy when he pouted. And Buffo created wonder and magic with his musical imagination that shunned the mundane."

"Drew," Willow put a hand on his cheek and turned him to face her. "I haven't seen lean and blonde or teeth too big, but I have seen the cocky king of the world look. I called the puppy-pout your chagrinned schoolboy look. And I clearly remember questioning the rationality of a man spinning a daydream that turned my brother's old shirt into a calendar portrait of sensuality. They are you, Drew. You haven't lost them. You just put the lost parts of you back where they belong."

"Is she right?" Drew turned to Paul with a bewildered look on his face.

"Yes, she's very right." Paul looked as if the biggest wish in his life had just come true. "They were pieces of you that were out of place. You can mourn for them if you feel you need to, but there's no need to take on a misplaced guilt about killing illusions in your own mind."

"So, you're saying I've been having battles with myself all these years?"

"Isn't that what you've been using as an excuse for a long time? You just didn't see it in the right perspective." Paul smiled at him and then looked at Willow. "It still won't be easy, Willow, but if anyone can handle him, it will be you."

"How long will I keep being plagued by this?" Drew asked.

"I don't know," Paul answered. "I'm a pretty good listener, and I have a lot to say most of the time, but I'm still not a soothsayer. We'll talk tomorrow. Can I go back to sleep now?"

"If I can." Drew stated as if it were an edict.

"Make love. It always worked for me."

Drew chuckled and gave Willow a cock-eyed look. "Shall we take my Doctor's prescription?"

"Every four hours." She nodded.

"Now you're fantasizing." Drew opened the door and turned back to Paul. "My rooms are across the hall. Knock on the door when you're ready for breakfast."

Chapter Thirty-One

On the evening before the wedding, Willow stopped just inside the open double doors of the hotel banquet room Mae had reserved for what she breezily called a get-acquainted gathering of the clans and most folks in Iowa called a rehearsal dinner. But then, it had been an unusual rehearsal without a groom or best man because Drew was somewhere in the sky between Pennsylvania and Iowa, transporting wedding guests after a six-hour, weather-related grounding at the Quakertown airport that Drew had strongly insisted wouldn't have any effect on him. But the regulations were written for the airport, not the plane and arguing with officials had proved useless.

Crossing the room, Willow looked out toward the Ames airport but could only see the shape of the tower against a dropping sun in a bright October sky. She felt his arms circle her, sensed the warmth of his breath on her neck when he nipped her just below the ear. When he kissed his way to the hollow where her neck and shoulder joined, she shivered and melted against him. Turning, she let his lips capture hers in a kiss that made everything right again.

"I missed you," she murmured when he pulled back enough to nibble her bottom lip.

"I was only gone for five days."

"Five days of our forever." Willow smiled when he shook his head and chuckled at her overly dramatic sigh. "Drew, have you seen your grandmother?"

"I just flew in with a plane full of boisterous Highlanders and a brogue-befuddled Italian uncle. I haven't seen anyone but you since I walked in the door."

"Mae was at the church with your father and John, but I haven't seen her since then." Willow glanced around the hotel's banquet room. "She's the one running the dinner tonight and no one on the hotel staff will make a move without her approval."

Drew looked at set tables, each displaying an arrangement of Scottish heather, wild thyme, blue bells and purple thistle. He took in the bar across the room, noticed it was well stocked with distinctive thistle-topped Glendoncroft Highland Single Malt bottles. "I see she's already made her statement and John's floral creations survived Dad's high-altitude flight in a company jet. But when it comes to Gram you never know what will happen next."

"She could be in the office. She said something about braving a piper."

"You just solved your own problem. The piper came with me. Gram must have waylaid him as soon as he showed up."

"You're kidding."

"Nae, Lassie," Drew rolled his speech like a Highlander. "He's one of those relatives I've met but don't really remember. But I think his name is Colin and he's good on the pipes, I'll gie ye that." He laughed at her chiding frown and dropped the brogue. "That is if he keeps away from those wildcat-squalling battle charges. They are a long-ago Highland idea of weapons of mass destruction. If they don't destroy the ears first, they scramble the brain, which explains why their foes fled like they were being chased by howling banshees."

"Did everything but the weather work out all right?" Willow gave him one of her patiently impatient looks.

"Mostly. Well..." he gave her one of his schoolboy/Andrew looks. "... except for one glitch."

"The wedding is tomorrow. I don't want to hear about another glitch."

"It's only a little one." Drew relaxed his arms so she could lean back against his clasped hands. "Tell me you won't be upset if I don't wear a tux."

"What?" Willow looked as if she didn't know whether she wanted to swat him or cry. "It's a little late, but if you forgot to pack your tux, we can rent one?"

"I have a tux. That's not the issue."

"Why don't you want to wear it?"

"I have no objection, but my best man does. He insists—"

"It's not Alex's wedding." Willow lifted her chin and drilled him with her damn the consequences glare. "It's ours and I'm not going to—"

"Would you slow down and let me talk?" Drew pulled her against him and tightened his arms when she tried to wiggle away.

"Alright, talk." Willow's mouth clamped shut, but the tension in her body said she wasn't ready to capitulate.

"He insists it's a matter of tradition for a Sutherland to—"

"To what? Look like a misfit—"

"Do *you* want to challenge him?"

When Drew turned her toward the appetizer table, where a trio of casually dressed men in sports shirts and dark-blue chino slacks talked with Byron, Willow's gaze locked on three of the most strikingly attractive, fit and well-built men she had ever seen. "Which one is Alex?"

"The biggest one, with the red-gold locks. The older chestnut-haired man is his father James, the Earl of Glendoncroft, who is Gram's nephew. The dark one is Alex's brother Duncan and the tousle-headed teenager by the punch bowl, who's ogling your sister Beth, is Ian, the unexpected bairn. I learned a long time ago that, except for Ian, arguing with any one of them could be life threatening. Taking on all of them bordered on suicidal insanity." He laughed at the helpless look on her face. "But I will challenge them if you'll calm down and convince me I have to."

"How do I do that?" Willow looked at Drew with a wary look on her face.

"By honestly answering an important question." He paused until she nodded. "Would it deeply humiliate you in the eyes of Cottonwood Forks, if you married a man wearing a skirt?"

The question stunned Willow so completely, she couldn't make sense of it and only one absurd thought filled her mind. "Are you for real? Or am I talking to an unmerged alter you forgot to tell me about?"

Drew blinked and gave her a blank stare before he burst out laughing. "Since I don't remember anyone ever accusing me of exhibiting feminine inclinations, I can unequivocally say, no."

"Then how could you even think of wearing a skirt?"

"In Scotland it's called a kilt and there's nothing feminine about it."

"That does make it more acceptable, but won't you feel a little out of place when every other man in the wedding party is wearing a tux?"

"That would be every man whose last name isn't Sutherland—or Fergusson."

"They all have kilts?"

"Although formal clan attire is normally only obligatory at ceremonies that take place in Scotland, I have been decisively informed that the tradition applies to all Glendoncroft weddings, no matter where they are."

"That better not include me." Willow gave him a glare sharp enough to level a cornfield. "Not after I gave in and accepted my Aunt Rhian's choice of a wedding dress that cost enough to make my father ask me how many times I expected to use it."

"Since I have no intention of ever letting go of you, the answer to his question is—once." Drew raised an index finger and waved it in her face. "The answer to clan tradition applying to you is a simple no. Since you are not yet a Sutherland, you are not entitled to wear its tartan at a ceremonial occasion until you are one." He chuckled at her unusual silence. "The wearing of the plaid is to make sure we know who not to slaughter if a riot breaks out."

"That's ridiculous."

"Maybe now, but old traditions die hard in Highland hearts."

"What about your grandmother?" Willow gave him a withering look.

"I imagine she will wear attire of her choice, but I guarantee the Sutherland plaid will be a part of it, most likely as a sash and a brooch displaying the clan crest with the motto *Sans Peur*."

"What does that mean?"

"Without fear."

"Well, that fits." Willow screwed up her face and looked back at the three men and two equally eye-catching women who had joined them. "Who are they?"

"The Countess Caroline and Alex's wife, Eileen."

"Will they be wearing kilts?"

"The men will be."

Willow sighed and looked up at him with a crooked smile and a laugh in her eyes. "It's alright with me and my mother will like it. She told me you had good looking legs."

"And if we don't have the requisite iron calves, we can always wear padded socks."

Drew glanced at the clustered tables and noticed John tweaking a centerpiece before he looked to where his father and grandmother were standing with a hotel man, who kept nodding his head while Mae pointed at a list in her hand and Andy purposely stared the other way—toward where a growing crowd of friends and relatives clustered around the appetizer table and bar, or checked-out tartan rimmed place cards on the tables.

Chuckling, Drew turned back to Willow. "The lost sheep has returned, and I think that poor man with her is getting the full force of regal charm and persuasion. It's sort of like being backed into a corner by an irresistible force field with a velvet touch."

"I've felt it." Willow thought back to the hair salon and shopping trip before Drew's opening night performance at the barn theater—as well as what happened when they were at the rehearsal meeting at the church earlier. "Drew, what is handfasting?"

Startled, he gave her a probing look. "Where did you hear about that?"

"From your grandmother. I didn't really catch all she was saying because my Aunt Rhian kept going on about a bunch of unfinished details, but I heard Mae ask our pastor and my parents if it could be done just before the actual wedding ceremony."

"There endth our short and simple wedding plans." Drew huffed. "Do you remember when I said that when Gram's involved, you can never tell what comes next?"

"But what is it?"

"It's an old Celtic ceremony of intent to marry that was usually done soon after the betrothal. However, in today's jet-propelled world, it is often inserted as an introduction to the wedding vows. During the reciting of handfasting vows, the couple's clasped hands are bound together with one strip of the groom's clan tartan for each of the vows."

"Do we have to memorize them?"

"No. They will be read to us by your pastor, if he agrees to do it. As I remember from Alex's wedding, our family uses a somewhat abbreviated version of the old pagan ritual. Our simultaneous replies consist of one yes, and four we-wills."

"It sounds nice. Why didn't she tell us about it before?"

"I suppose she didn't want to listen to my objections."

"Do you have any?"

"Only one. I feel it's yours and your family's decision to make, not Gram's."

"That's what she said."

"She did?" He looked surprised.

"Drew, Mae was very gracious about it."

"As gracious as an incoming tide—gentle, steady, unstoppable."

"Like her grandson."

He looked startled for a moment before his deep laugh rolled out. "I think you'd be more right calling me a riptide."

"Drew, she expected you to be there, just as I did. Since you weren't there, she talked to my parents and Pastor Wilson." Willow smiled with a touch of teasing in her eyes. "Then she suggested I introduce the subject to you to avoid one of your snits."

"I can never best her at that kind of manipulation." Drew scowled. "I don't even know why I try. So, what was the conclusion?"

"Pastor Wilson said he knew the ceremony and thought it was wonderful. Mom fully agreed and Dad said, 'The family already has the Welsh and the Irish, let's welcome in the Scots.' And I said, done."

"That doesn't leave me much choice, does it?"

"Nope, and from the way you described it, I don't think you really have an objection."

"Oddly enough, I don't. In spite of my sarcastic harangues about the eccentricities of my Highland progenitors, I am proud to belong to them."

"I'm glad to hear that and I already have a copy of the vows. I think they're perfect." Willow kissed him on a smooth chin that was finally free of a beard. "Any other news I should hear?"

"Yes. With Dad's help, I took care of some stuff that was bothering me."

"What kind of stuff?"

"A couple of simple things, and a big one that's been nagging at my conscience." When Drew saw her face tighten, he smiled, caught her hands and backed behind a screen that blocked a service door to an outside patio. "It doesn't have anything to do with you, but I want you to know about it."

Willow's wary look told Drew she still hadn't been able to come to terms with everything they'd been through, which reassured him that his recent decision to stop shielding her from parts of his life was absolutely right. "It's about Milly and Ernie. I messed up Milly's life this summer and the wrong of it wouldn't let go of me. I also put both of them in danger by accepting some information she gave Ernie and I turned over to Antonio. The chances are slim that anyone effected by it will find out where it came from, but it kept hammering at me, until I talked to Ernie, who said he and Milly have been doing a lot of talking and he wants to help her find a better life. When I explained it all to Dad, he agreed to get them both jobs at a FiberForms plant in Albany. He also found a good nursing home there for Milly's mother, who has Alzheimer's beyond what Milly can handle. They both need to get away from Philly for a while."

"That's a good thing, Drew. Do you think it will work?"

"I don't know; but since I can't reverse what happened, it's the best I can do for them."

"At least your conscience isn't telling you to get Mario out of jail."

"Not a chance." He snorted. "Since Pissface doesn't have a conscience or a sympathetic thought for anyone but himself, I don't care if he rots in the damn place."

"What are the simple things?"

"Your job."

"You want me to go back to my job while you're in Genoa?"

"Absolutely not." He scowled at her. "However, after seeing how well Gram related to you and the way you see riding as an essential part of who you are, instead of as a path to prizes and money, I convinced her to look at it that way, too. And I found the right person, practically living on Gram's doorstep."

"Who was that?"

"Bonnie Cassidy. She's a lot like you, Willow. Horses are people to her, and her dream is to be able to teach children to have fun riding and see horses as partners, not as a means to gain fame and fortune."

"What about her symbiosis with Lois?" Willow asked with a touch more bite than she wanted.

"Ralph got what Lois called a stupendous job in New York. They moved to Connecticut two weeks ago, which left Bonnie desperate to find a place to keep her horse next month. I heard about it and convinced Gram to give her a try."

"Will it work?"

"I think so. She's already told Bonnie to start searching for good-tempered ponies and lesson horses."

"I can see them both enjoying that." Willow smiled. "Now, are you going to drop the other shoe or keep me wondering?"

"Peter came out of his coma and is doing well. He was medevacked to Paris two days ago."

"I should have been there to apologize to Nicole."

"I sort of did that. Let's face it, we both screwed that one up and need to put it behind us. We'll see them in Europe when Peter's back to himself." He smiled at her emphatic nod. "Oh, I did one other thing. I sold Knight."

"It was always your intention. Is he gone? I'd like to have said goodbye to him."

"Not yet. After he's been passed by their vet and the money is in my bank account, my responsibility is over and they can pick him up. You can say goodbye on our stopover at the manor before we head for the Mediterranean."

"What price did you get?"

"Thirty-five."

"Is thirty-five hundred a good price? I thought he'd be worth more than that."

"You're missing a zero." He twirled a finger in front of her.

"Thirty-five thousand." Willow stared at him in astonishment.

"He was highly rated in Europe and his breeding supports the price." Drew watched her think it over, then accept what he said. "I was asking forty-two and had two internet buyers considering it, but it's a nice local family, and I really liked the girl."

"Don't you always." The sarcasm came out unbidden and Willow wanted to snatch it back when she saw the look on his face.

"Give me a break, Willow." Drew's retort hardened his features. "She's fifteen years old, and that's a path I have never taken."

"I'm sorry, Drew. I just get a twinge inside when I hear you say things like that."

"And I get a twinge of guilt whenever you react that way. Don't keep making it harder to bear."

Willow looked into his eyes for a long, thoughtful moment. "Did you always feel that way?"

Drew reacted in surprise, then returned her thoughtful look. "I think you just hit on a truth I didn't understand before now. I could always push my regrets away as irrelevant and get on with my life without them coming back to haunt me. Dad and Gram gave me a good sense of right and wrong, but I think my sensitivity to deep remorse and guilt was buried, right along with my true center."

When he hugged her to him, Willow pressed her face against his chest then lost control when a surge of relieved tears washed away the tension that had been inside her ever since he'd accepted that his alters were gone. "Oh, Drew, you're whole and it's real. I can feel it."

He lifted her chin with a bent knuckle, kissed her then handed her a clean handkerchief. "Come on, Elfling. This is no time for tears. I think there's a crowd of happy people out there who expect us to be a joyful part of this party."

"I'm happy, too. That's why I'm crying."

❖

While her Aunt Rhian fiddled with the placement of a silver tiara headdress that, after Drew's firm statement about wanting to see Willow not a blur, had no facial veil, Willow watched her sisters. Gwen and Beth, in simple cocktail style dresses of sunlight yellow and autumn bronze, giggled and chided each other as they fussed over Willow's bouquet of fall flowers, trailing ivy and, of course, Scottish bluebells. Glancing into a mirror, Willow had to admit that her minimally adorned wedding dress, which was actually a pale, subtly frosted blue rather than white, was as perfect as Rhian had promised.

...And that made her think back to when she'd been in Iowa two months ago and her father's eccentric younger sister arrived, unannounced, at the farm and insisted on taking over the creative details of her niece's wedding.

Irritated by her aunt's assertiveness, Willow had pitched a fit, then stormed upstairs and called Drew on a cell phone she hardly knew how to use.

With a total lack of sympathy, he said, "Willow, it's impossible to run everything. Find good people and let them do their jobs."

"But what if she makes a mess of it."

"Don't hire her again."

"I only plan to get married once. And I'm not hiring her. She's free."

"Just a minute. I'll be right back."

Willow plopped herself on a desk chair with the dead phone against her ear and bounced her heels up and down while her irritation shifted from Rhian to Drew's lack of sympathy. She almost dropped the phone when it blasted out a ringtone that she had no idea how to change. "Drew?"

"Who else? I don't think you gave anyone else your number."

"I gave it to Byron. Why did you cut me off?"

"I looked Rhian up on the internet."

"She's on the internet?"

"If her name is Rhian Roberts and she's a stunningly attractive brunette with dark eyes and your chin, she is definitely on the net. Most event designers are if they want to make a decent living."

"I didn't know she was an event designer."

"You might want to check up on your relatives once in a while."

"I don't even know where she lives right now. She isn't big on keeping us informed."

"Virginia. The point is I like what I saw of her work, and she has good references. Respect her knowledge, use her skills and get the hell out of her way. But do remind her that Byron and I are taking care of the music at the wedding and have already arranged for the reception venue of my choice."

"Are you really serious about having the wedding reception at a cowboy bar?"

"Absolutely."

"But the wedding is on a Saturday. It's Harvey's best night."

"Believe me, Willow, Harvey was very glad to accept my offer, and he plans to post that the Bucking Bull will be closed on the second Saturday in October for a family celebration. And like his pretzel recipe, he has no intention of saying whose family until after the invitations go out. While we're on that subject, please remember to say well wishes accepted but no gifts. We want family, friends and good fun. We don't need money or more stuff."

"But what about your relatives? Isn't the Bucking Bull a little below the taste of an Earl's family?"

"Obviously, you have never been to the Highland Wildcat Pub at Glendoncroft. It's a lively tourist eatery by day, but at night the Wildcat howls like angry bagpipes. Is there anything else I can do for you?"

"Yes, but we can't do it on the phone."

"I'll take care of that when I fly out after the show Sunday. Get your sister Beth to help you with the phone. She's a teenager. They're the experts…"

Finally, after it had all come together, Willow was thankful she had taken Drew's advice and surrendered the project to her aunt. She was not only impressed by Rhian's attention to details, she was blown away by her aunt's ability to turn vague images in her head into a vision that blended the reality of nature with the illusion of fantasy.

Smiling, Willow looked out the window of the small bride's room next to the church's vestibule and watched Colin, the tall, kilted and bonneted piper, as he welcomed arriving guests to her wedding with a medley of Scottish and Irish folk music with spritely lilting melodies that in no way resembled the wildcat squalls Drew had joked about. She started to wonder if Colin's repertoire included melodies from other locations, until she recognized a Welsh tune her grandmother used to hum. And then, as if Colin knew her thoughts, she heard the melancholy strains of *Shenandoah* and felt the rolling power of the Missouri River in the low drone of the pipes. The piper was gathering a large crowd of smiling listeners and Willow let the music, the autumn scene and familiar faces from her childhood wrap around her mind like a homemade quilt.

When her father walked into the room and stopped to look at her with an expression that radiated pride, Willow stepped up to him, slipped her arm under his. A strong hand enclosed hers for a moment before his gravelly voice said, "I'm giving you to a good man, who needs you, and I'm alright with that."

"I found my love, Dad, but I am sorry I was so rotten to you."

"Humph." Lloyd gave her a stern look then smiled. "If you hadn't, we wouldn't have Drew in the family. And that would be a shame."

"You like him, don't you?"

"Right from the first moment he challenged me and asked to marry you."

"Have you seen him? How does he look? Is he nervous?"

"Nervous?" Lloyd looked at her for a stunned moment, then snorted. "Triumphant would be more accurate. It makes me think you gave him as much sass as you gave me."

She flushed. "I'd say a lot more."

While Todd opened the bride's room door to let in the sounds of shifting people that quickly subsided to a low murmur and then silence, Byron sat at the piano and slowly played individually lingering notes of *Amazing Grace*. The purity of the melody made Willow pull in a slow breath and tighten her hand on her father's arm. With the strength of his support to draw on, she knew she was ready to step into a new future. She pulled in a steadying breath when Beth and Gwen left the room and then followed them into the foyer where five of her brothers formed a subtly protective corridor to the opening of the aisle between the rows of pews. Byron added a complex left-hand accompaniment to the expanding melody as Gwen, then Beth, started down the aisle.

After an impatient, jiggling wait until Beth reached the center of the church, Keith's youngest daughter and Glenn's son stepped away from their fathers and headed for the aisle with Megan's hand firmly clamped on Joey's belt to stop the five-year-old from charging ahead without her. Watching the tug-of war in front of her, Willow felt a laugh bubble up inside her and dissolve her tension. It was a wedding, a family wedding; and in spite of all the fuss and apprehensions, it was an occasion to savor and enjoy, not fret over.

When Megan, whose one-handed basket-shaking left clumps instead of scattered flower petals down the aisle, and Joey, whose terrified reluctance refused to let him get anywhere near Drew and Alex, reached their mothers in the first row, Gwen, Willow's always practical sister and patient maid of honor, calmly walked over, retrieved the rings and handed one to Alex.

Sensing how five of her brothers formed an arc behind her, Willow wondered if they were still trying to protect her or just making sure the deed was done and all was squarely and properly resolved. She chuckled at what she saw as totally family, looked up at her father's confused expression and whispered, "They know he's not going to back out, don't they?"

"They should." Lloyd nodded as they stopped in the aisle between the now standing guests.

Stunned by the sight of a church packed with people, who were all looking at her with expectant faces and wide smiles, Willow froze for a moment, then remembered something Drew had said and realized they weren't judging her, they were sharing her celebration—and perhaps, remembering their own. As the piano music grew stronger and fuller, Willow looked toward the altar where Drew and Alex stood shoulder to shoulder like two highland warriors wearing Sutherland blue and green kilts with red and white accent stripes. They wore sporran pouches and ceremonial dirks at their waists, high socks, white shirts, black ties and short formal black jackets that blended perfectly with the tuxedos worn by her father and brothers.

When Drew stepped to the center of the aisle, Willow locked her eyes on his and, engulfed by the tones of his deep, resonant voice, took a first step toward her future.

> "Amazing Grace, how sweet the sound,
> That saved a wretch like me....
> I once was lost, but now I'm found,
> Was blind but now I see.
>
> Through many dangers, toils and snares...
> We have already come.
> T'was Grace that brought us safe thus far...
> And Grace will lead us home."

While the last word lingered in a long, rising note, the church was silent, except for the slow, individually played notes of the melody that faded away when Lloyd set Willow's hand in Drew's. As a couple, they turned and stepped up a level to face the broad smile on Pastor Mark Wilson's kind, walnut-brown face.

"Absolutely, stunning. I think I was just upstaged." The quiet voice turned to a chuckle before the man glanced at the paper in his hand, raised his eyes to theirs and spoke with a deep carrying voice that equaled Drew's projection.

"Willow and Drew, know now before you go further that since your lives have crossed in this life, you have formed eternal and sacred bonds. As you seek to enter this state of matrimony, you should strive to make real the ideals that give meaning to this ceremony and to the institution of marriage. With full awareness, know that within this circle you are not only declaring your intent to be handfasted before your friends and family but to speak that intent to your creative higher powers. The promises made today and the ties that are bound here will greatly strengthen your union and guide the years and lives of each soul's growth."

The pastor paused and held their attention for a brief moment of reflection. "Do you still seek to enter this ceremony?"

"Yes." Willow and Drew answered together.

"Drew and Willow, I bid you look into each other's eyes." When they faced each other with hands still clasped, the deep voice continued, "Will you honor and respect one another and seek to never break that honor?"

"We will."

Pastor Wilson lifted a strip of tartan and draped it over their clasped hands. "And so, the first binding is made. Will you share each other's pain and seek to ease it?"

"We will."

"And so, the binding is made." A second strip was added. "Will you share the burdens of each other so that your spirits may grow in this union?"

"We will."

"And so, the binding is made." A third strip joined the others. "Will you share each other's laughter and look for the brightness in life and the positive in each other?"

"We will." A fourth strip of Sutherland tartan was added and Pastor Wilson deftly tied them the way Mae had shown him. "Willow and Drew, as your hands are bound together now, so your lives and spirits are joined in a union of love and trust. Above you are the stars and below you the earth. Like the stars, your love should be a constant source of light, and like the earth, a firm foundation from which to grow."

When the man stood silent and Drew and Willow continued to face each other, Byron played a complex introduction while a couple Drew had studied music under in New York stepped beside the grand piano. The tenor/soprano duet of Leonard Bernstein's *One Hand, One Heart* from West Side Story filled the church with an emotional awe that reached into even the hardest of hearts and left a silence that was poignantly tangible and shared.

To Willow, the rest of the ceremony was more traditional and comfortably uplifting. And then, when all the vows were spoken, rings exchanged and the declaration of man and wife proclaimed, Drew gave Willow the kiss she had been waiting for. A thrill flashed between them as they met each other's eyes for a frozen moment then exploded with a burst of exuberant laughter. Waving streamers of Sutherland plaid, the newlyweds marched and danced, hand-in-hand, side-to-side, even forward and back all the way up the aisle to Bryon's triumphant playing of Verdi's *Grand March from Aida*.

After ducking into the bride's room while the chapel emptied, Drew gave Willow a kiss that made the one at the alter seem like an innocent peck on the cheek then held her for a long moment of shared stillness before she stepped back and asked, "Is it really true? Are we really married?"

"I certainly hope so." Drew gave her a hammed look of panic. "Because if we aren't, we just hoodwinked a whole lot of people into believing we are. I sure don't want to have to tell them it was all a theatrical hoax."

A sharp rap on the partly opened door turned them to face Pastor Wilson, who was trying not to laugh. "I have the authority to tell you that you are definitely married in accordance with your spiritual beliefs, and as soon as you sign these papers, it will be equally true in accordance with the State of Iowa."

After the papers were duly signed and Willow accepted a hug from her pastor, Drew reached out and shook a strong, warm hand. "Thank you. I'm impressed with you as a man with true dedication and wisdom and I'm very grateful for the way you accepted my grandmother's Scottish meddling. I grumble about her a lot, but I'm really not very good at successfully resisting her."

"There was nothing to resist. As your new father-in-law pointed out when he convinced the chapel's parishioners to hire me, this is a non-denominational chapel where we look for God and inspiration within ourselves, where the gracious offering of fairness and understanding toward all living beings is more important than the worship of dogmas created by humans for the intent of controlling other humans."

"Abou Ben Adhem (may his tribe increase!)" Drew quoted. "That philosophy fits Willow's father and, like the poem, rings true to me."

"Yes, it does. Lloyd Roberts' wording may have been slightly different, but that's the essence of what he said. I think it was the longest speech I've ever heard from him, or probably ever will." He smiled at Willow's nod and thoughtful expression.

"I like the fact that you don't have a church organ." Drew grinned with comic glee. "They're hard to compete with."

"We have exceptional pianists." The pastor smiled. "Byron when he's around; my wife when he isn't. And by the way, when it comes to the Scottish thing. "I have Scottish blood myself."

"That certainly doesn't surprise me. There are a lot of Wilsons in Scotland, and we Scots do spread around a lot."

"Some is recent, but my family connection goes back a long way. My ancestors were owned by a Scottish family of planters in central Virginia. As often happened in those situations, there was a fair amount of mixed blood over the years. However, the Wilson's were an enlightened family that offered freedom and the last name of Wilson to any slave who gave honest labor and made the effort to improve and educate him or herself. During the Civil War, my great-great-great-grandfather and his brother moved to Minnesota with their mixed families to be legally married in a state that had no laws against it. We've lived in the mid-west ever since."

"It certainly breathes freedom and offers enough room to make the most of it." Drew stared out the window at the people gathering between the door and the rented Town Car at the curb. "It looks like the running of the gauntlet is forming and we do have to keep moving with Rhian's schedule." He looked at Willow. "Are you ready to get pelted with rice."

"Birdseed, Drew, it keeps the lawn fertilized with guano."

They made a dash to where Owen held open the back door of the black car, shook off excess seed, slid into the back seat, then started laughing when Todd pulled onto the road and a desperate Owen leapt into the passenger seat and slammed the door.

"Where are you going in such a rush?" Drew bellowed at Todd.

"Rhian wants pictures at Medicine Bluff." Todd huffed. "She speaks. I obey."

"It was my idea, Todd." Willow snapped. "It's one of my favorite places because it has beautiful views of the valley and the farm."

"I thought it was just a way to waste time so everyone can get to the reception before you make your grand entrance."

Chapter Thirty-Two

Three steps into the Bucking Bull, Willow stopped so suddenly she jerked Drew off stride and tripped him enough he banged into her and made their grand entrance more of a farce than a celebratory debut of marital bliss. Unaware of the eruption of laughter surrounding her, Willow gaped at what seemed to be a total transformation in ambiance, until she decided it was more a case of a good airing out, brighter lighting, rearrangement and decoration than a sweeping renovation. And then she realized that everyone in the room was staring at them and Drew's arm was wrapped around her waist holding her upright while he chuckled at her stunned expression.

Still trying to smother his own laughter, Harvey Anderson stepped beside them and pulled in a deep breath before he swept a measured gaze over his audience and said, "It has fallen on me as your delighted host to announce the arrival of Mr. and Mrs. Sutherland. A remarkable blending of a strong-minded young woman I have been fond of for several years and a bold young man, who burst into town about four months ago and left an indelible impression on a good many local people."

Harvey paused for a moment, while a wry smile grew on his face. "And now, as advertised, here they are: Drew and Willow Sutherland, the Bucking Bull's newly famous slapstick act."

Snugging his arm around Willow, Drew laughed and with a loud popping sound, pointed a finger gun at Harvey. "You got me, Harvey. But I'll find a way to get you back."

Before they reached the long head table, Willow caught Drew's hand and stopped him. "I didn't know you were friendly with Harvey."

"I liked him in June, and I've been communicating with him a lot lately. I suspect there's more to Harvey than people here realize. And I sense that in some way, it's connected to entertainment, but he's reluctant to talk about it."

"Why do you think that?"

"From the way he casually understood the jargon I used. And he has a feel for true talent. Why else do you think he's supported Byron and Salt Lick the way he has?"

"Because they bring in customers." Willow stated.

"Because they're good musicians and he knew it soon enough to help them find their feet when they were barely more than teenagers."

"How do you know so much about people?"

Drew looked at her for a long moment. "I suppose it's because I've always been able to absorb feelings and invent believable people."

"That was when you were a child, but they're gone now."

"No, I've always studied people and then blended parts of what I observed into the roles I need to play on stage and in life. That ability was born into me, Willow. And it's probably why I became a multiple instead of a defeated child. I couldn't cope with the life I was forced into. Hence, I unconsciously created what I felt would be a better one. It was far from realistic, but I plead innocence: I was only five or six and only had the world I knew at the time as inspiration." He turned her head and stroked her cheek while he held her gaze. "I lost my child's unfettered creativity when I was about nine, the way most children do; and now, I do it with full awareness of who I really am."

When he kissed her and it was acknowledged by a burst of applause, Willow realized they were still the center of attention and flushed in a totally appropriate way she didn't want to admit to, and Drew winked at her. "You're the star tonight, Elfling."

"That's your job. I don't know what to do."

"Enjoy it. It's your due and they grant it because your happiness will make them feel good. There's something about a wedding that makes people joyful. It's our job to give them what they want. I plan on having a blast. Are you with me?"

"Just don't get drunk."

"Not a chance. I gave that up when I discovered it took away more fun than it created. When it comes to partying, I learned from Dad that I'd rather make teasing fun of a drunk then be one."

When they were finally seated at the center of the long head table and Pastor Wilson had said a few words in blessing, Alex Sutherland stood and waited quietly for the hum and buzz to settle. "First, an obligatory family toast that has its origin in the darkness of our past."

Alex spit into an empty glass, then raised it and glared toward the heavens. "Here's to Freskin, the ruthless old bastard of a Flemish knight, who was hired by the Normans to subdue the land by slaughter and fire and became the progenitor of the Sutherland Clan." Upending the glass, he plunked it down on a napkin. "We at Glendoncroft owe him much, but like him **not**."

No one drank, but Alex was answered by a loud, "Well done!" from every Scot and Irishman in the room and a strong thumbs-up from Willow's father, who remembered tales handed down from his Welsh ancestors about the subjugation of the Celts following the Norman conquest of 1066.

Willow smiled when she realized a few brazen words spoken by the son of a titled aristocrat had just ended a tense edginess about social differences and proved that Drew had been totally right: his down-to-earth, titled relatives were real people, who openly welcomed all folks and customs into their lives.

Turning to look at Drew, Alex tipped his head and arched a thick coppery eyebrow. He seemed to ponder what he was going to say, then nodded with firm conviction. "You finally figured it out and made the right choice. You found a jewel among the paste, which is grand in itself. That she agreed to marry you is a bloody miracle."

After scanning the expanse of tables, Alex held his audience's attention and tossed an open hand toward Drew. "This cheeky, reckless and impudent example of daredevilry and evil schemes— Is the best and truest friend I have ever had. We were an adventurous pair; and although we weren't able to be with each other often, our times together mark high points in my life. We battled foes together, and often each other, but mostly we laughed, and I missed his outrageousness every time he was gone." His gaze caught Willow's attention and held it. "Now that he's yours, lass, I'll gie ye a little advice. When he starts gettin' uppity twist his ear. He hates it."

"Did you have to tell her that?" Drew gave his cousin an indignant look. "She already has enough weapons in her arsenal. Don't give her anymore."

"Oh, I think it's deserved, don't you? I mean you asked me to be your best man and you know the best man always wins."

"I do remember saying that when our roles were reversed," Drew said.

"And there's one other thing I owe ye." With a resounding laugh, Alex stepped beside Willow, picked her up, chair and all, then moved it back, pulled her into arms and gave her a lengthy kiss before he returned her to the chair and table with a stunned look on her face that slowly turned to a beaming smile before Alex looked at Drew with wide-eyed innocence. "You told me it was an American kissing cousin ritual. And since I am a Viscount, I'm diplomatically honor bound to uphold native customs in foreign lands."

"Alex," Drew gestured toward a table in front of them. "You need to meet my new brother-in-law Todd. He's a wicked match for your vindictive tenacity."

Alex took in Todd's nonchalant, but calculating expression. "I ken I'm going to like him."

"Of course. You can show him how to throw a tree and he can show you how to throw a steer. But I'll warn you, a steer is smellier than a caber." Drew made a sour face. "But at least steers don't foul themselves in piss and muck the way some bulls do."

"I believe that was also true of some of our ancient ancestors," Alex said. "They were a barbaric mob."

"And nowadays women seem determined to convert us into steers." Drew shot back.

"Not mine." Alex recoiled. "Eileen enjoys laughing at my barbaric foolishness." He looked down at his obviously pregnant, dark-haired, emerald-eyed, head-nodding wife then stepped back to his place.

"In a more serious and traditional finale to the ridiculous malarkey we just subjected you to, I will put it this way—we're having a wee lad and I thought of naming him Drew, but there is only room for one Drew in my life and I want to keep it that way. I shared enough of what he endured as a young lad to know he is the bravest person I've ever known. I love him and no one else will ever live up to my image of him." Alex blinked a few times and paused to pull in a quick breath before he lifted a filled glass of champagne. "With those thoughts filling my heart, I offer a sincere toast to Willow and Drew and wish them many, many years of happiness and success—all wrapped up in love and spiced with Drew's indomitable spirit of adventure and laughter."

When everyone in the room raised a glass and drank, Drew circled his arm around Willow held her against him while a surge of emotional memories swept through him with enough force to weaken him:

...The image of a naked, laughing, twelve-year-old Alex racing ahead of him through a sunbeam-streaked woodland and launching himself off a ten-foot-high cliff sent a wave of fear through Drew's mind before he conquered it with blind faith in the fearless, older cousin he loved and trusted. The sudden plunge into a deep, cold loch snatched away his breath and he barely had time to clamp his mouth closed before he submerged. He felt a strong hand grab his hair and haul him, sputtering and gasping, to the surface, where a startled voice boomed, "Cannae ye swim?"

Drew tried to shake his head but it was anchored by Alex's grasp and his effort only made him wiggle like a worm on a hook before he was dragged to a rocky shore and crawled onto a small spit of sand between eroded sculptures of ancient red sandstone.

"Dinnae jump in a loch if ye cannae swim, laddie."

And then they were away and climbing the cliff—Alex like a wildcat that knew every notch, crevice and claw hold, Drew groping and stubbing bare toes—until Alex grabbed his hand and popped him up the last few feet before they raced to where their rugged highland ponies were tethered. After hastily pulling on clothes, they vaulted onto the animals' broad, bare backs and thundered back to the Hall before Alex was late for his three-hour shift of packing and sweeping at the distillery's distribution center...

When the image of Alex's flabbergasted reaction to a boy who couldn't swim faded from his mind, Drew knew Alex was right about them being best friends. But it was much more than that. He'd been ten years old that summer when Alex became the first true friend, who was real, he ever had.

"Drew, are you alright?"

Drew heard Willow's soft question and nodded. "Willow, he was so right about our times together. Alex showed me adventure and awakened my courage, saved my life, taught me how to swim. I felt complete at Glendoncroft, just as I did when I found your family in Iowa."

"You were lonely, but it's hard to be lonely in a large, loving family." Willow kissed him because she knew that's what she was expected to do at a wedding, then whispered, "And I promise you, we will never have an only child. It goes against our natures."

When the haunting images in his mind settled into composure, Drew looked away from Willow and saw Alex's father watching him with an inquiring expression that lingered on his face until Drew mouthed the word, "Wow."

Jamie smiled, then stood and tapped his glass with three unhurried tings that stilled the murmur of conversation. "While listening to my son, I felt compelled to share some thoughts on the wild lad of my American cousin, who first came to stay with us for a month when he was ten. I don't believe there was a square inch of the castle he didn't explore or try to scale. In fact, if it hadn't been for Gryphon, the Aberdeen Terrier we'd given Drew for Christmas, I think he would have been lost for hours, mayhap days at a time."

Jamie paused just long enough to absorb the tenor of his audience before he continued. "Drew tried my patience, drained my brain, baffled my mind, insulted my dignity, and challenged my authority by constantly refusing to heed the phrase: **"Dinnae dae that!"**

The Scotsman's projected bellow froze his listeners for an instant before his rolling laugh released them. "But on the backside of the coin, he showed me how to laugh at myself and constantly bewildered or amazed me with his perceptive insights, oft lopsided way of viewing the world, and audacious displays of pluck and determination. When he was thirteen, he challenged me by boldly proclaiming he didn't need to obey me because he was going to be famous and sing grand operas. I told him it was a good idea because maybe then he could pay back the five quid I leant him."

Lord James Sutherland shifted his gaze to Drew and nailed him with a dark-blue stare. "So, when do I get ma five quid?"

"When I sing a grand opera and not a minute before. You set the terms, Your Grace, I didn't."

"When are you going to get it straight, Yank? I am an earl, not a duke, a distinction I'm eternally grateful for. And a simple Jamie is sufficient." Dropping into a thickly overdone Scottish brogue, Jamie glared at Drew and commanded, "Git yer arse a-movin' laddie. *Mak saut tae yer kail,* and earn me ma five quid."

After a slow swallow of scotch, the Earl of Glendoncroft looked out at a more relaxed, laughing audience, then recaptured its attention with a subtly controlled straightening of his posture.

"Forgive me if I turn sentimentally Celtic and admit that I came here with a sense of unease about the fleetness of Eros's deadly arrow. But then, like a morning breeze clearing mist off the firth, my uncertainties were swept away by Willow, a bonny lass, who is not only comely, but strong-minded, brave and a challenging match for that wild lad I welcomed into my heart so long ago. I have since discovered that Drew not only found a soulmate, he had become part of a remarkable family that welcomed him as one of their own."

With a graciousness that was profoundly sincere, Jamie focused the power of his compelling self-possession on Willow's family and smiled at their captivated attention. "We Scots are a clannish lot and our extended family bonds give us our greatest strength. I speak, not only for myself, but for all of Glendoncroft when I offer kinship and the open hospitality of the Hall to both Willow's and Drew's kith and kin."

There was a moment of surprised silence before a round of applause that Jamie waved away. "I've stalled our highly competent host long enough and the enticing aroma of what I've been led to believe are the best barbequed ribs in Iowa is fair makin' me weak." He made a broad, openhanded gesture toward Harvey, who was standing by the kitchen door with an awed look on his face. "Bring on the feast, ma gweed mon. We're at your mercy and fair starvin' for good chow."

Drew looked at Willow and gave her a firm nod. "Now you've met the Earl. Jamie can size up and take over any room and have them eating out of his hand with nothing but this own brand of charisma that is captivating and impossible to type."

"Was he serious about his invitation to visit the Hall."

"Definitely. In case you didn't notice, he loves to entertain. And in spite of its name, Glendoncroft is not a hall as such. It's a thirteenth century stone castle north of Inverness that's mostly supported by the distillery and tourism, rental of agricultural and grazing lands. Most residents in the village of Glendoncroft are hired by the Hall and/or its subsidiaries. Its success has beaten a lot of odds because it is no longer a home for idle aristocrats. They work for their money and they work hard, starting with short hours at the age of twelve. I can vouch for that because I had no exemption when I stayed with them. It's a successful family business and ambitious Scots are very good business people."

With a flurry of activity, long tables were filled with platters of barbequed ribs and chicken, steaming sweet corn, salads and a variety of dishes that made a country potluck into a feast. And, of course, there was a large tiered cake topped with a groom on a rearing black horse, his bride on a prancing pinto. Jackets became chair decorations, uncomfortable shoes cluttered together under tables. As Drew had predicted, the wildcat howled and the blast began. There was singing and dancing that alternated between the downhome country of Salt Lick, the ballads, jigs and reels of a hired Celtic band from Ames, even a piano/bagpipe duet by Byron and Colin.

And, of course, Alex, Duncan and Ian insisted on challenging the yanks in a bull riding contest that turned into an intense four round elimination bout that pitted Drew against Alex for the final round. It ended with Drew maintaining his championship title by four seconds with third going to a grinning Matt, who hung on for three seconds longer than Ian, who looked thoroughly annoyed when Alex took an ale out of his hand and replaced it with a Coke and the warning that he may be able to cheat on eighteen at home but nobody would accept he was twenty-one. Shrugging, Ian joined Matt, then let his scowl turn into a bright smile when he realized Matt was walking toward Beth.

Drew watched them with an intent stare until he felt Willow slide an arm around him. With a wink, he picked her up, then spun her around before he set her back on the floor. Startled, she looked around uncomfortably and asked, "Drew, are you wearing anything under that skirt?" When he recoiled and looked totally flummoxed by her question, Willow said, "I've heard stories about kilts and they said men don't wear anything under them."

"I think that custom was a way to avoid embarrassing aftereffects during intense battles, or maybe not having to worry about lacing and unlacing while chasing down prey and flirtatious lassies. Besides, I'm an American, not what's facetiously termed a true Scotsman. We Yanks aren't keen on running around bare-assed. And," he winked at her, "to protect your reputation, I will refrain from upending any Scotsmen to satisfy your curiosity."

"I watched that whole bull riding contest wondering if something awful was going to happen." Willow caught his hand and looked across the room. "I think we're supposed to roam around and be sociable."

"And I think we owe a few people some very sincere thanks." Drew looked at where Andy sat with Willow's aunt Rhian. "And she's one of them."

"Your father seems to have taken quite an interest in my aunt."

"He says she intrigues him."

"What about Kate? We invited her."

"She's in Australia. And he knows it's not research that's keeping her there."

"Is he upset by that."

"He's not happy about it but he's hardly devastated." Drew looked at her confused face. "Kate's much younger than Dad is, and he's practical enough to know he doesn't want what she needs."

"Well, I don't think Aunt Rhian wants it either. What is it about weddings that make people want everyone else to share the love they symbolize?"

"I have no idea." Drew gave her a baffled look. "I've been to a lot of weddings and I never had that feeling."

"It's that man/woman thing again isn't it?"

"I won't argue with that." Drew looked across the room at the two singers talking with Jamie and Caroline. "Right now, we owe *them* a big thank you before they leave for the airport."

"They're not staying?"

"They have a concert in New York tomorrow."

"All I know about them is that their singing is beautiful."

"Leon Cavetti is from Bologna, his wife Maria from Argentina. Leon was my professor in Italian Operatic History. He gave it life and made it not only fascinating but extremely entertaining. He's also an internationally acclaimed tenor, but he's important to me because he recommended me to his father, who is not only on the board at Bologna, but a longtime friend of Vittorio."

When they joined Jamie, Caroline and the two singers, Jamie was saying that Glendoncroft hosted an extensive, weeklong music festival every summer. Since he was interested in expanding its scope, he wanted contact information from not only Leon and Maria but from Byron as a pianist as well as a member of Salt Lick.

"You'll get it, Jamie," Drew said. "And I'll make sure they get some CDs recorded before they get there."

"That offer includes you as well. If I can't get my five quid for a while, I can at least get some honest work out of you." He turned to Leon. "Is there such a thing as a soprano/tenor/baritone trio you three could do?"

"There are several. It would be fun. We'll work on it." Leon took in Drew's smile before he shook Jamie's hand. "And if you'll all please excuse us, I want to have a talk with Drew before I run out of time."

Intrigued, but puzzled, Drew followed Leon to an empty end of the bar and ordered lemon and club soda to flush the taste of liquor out of his mouth. "Do you disapprove of me going back to Vittorio? I know you were disappointed, but not surprised when I left him."

"I don't disapprove, but I'm still apprehensive. When I knew I was coming out here, I flew to Bologna to talk about it with my father. It turns out he's been seeing a lot of Vittorio lately. He says it's been frustrating because everything he gets from him is contradictory and unproductive at best."

"I heard he was looking into a baritone at Bologna." Drew said.

"Is that a big problem to you?"

"I don't think so. I know the man and I'm sure Vittorio won't take him."

"Why not?"

"He has a range problem."

"In what way?"

"He has a slight quaver in the higher register. And he can't project the lows in true pitch." He covers it well but it won't pass Vittorio's notice."

"My father agrees with you, but not necessarily because of the range."

"I'm sure he noticed it. Your father's ear is still sensational."

"Yes, he did. But it's mostly a moot point. Vittorio has rejected every baritone who's applied or been sent to him for the last year. He wants you, but he's too stubborn to admit it. And too bitter to let go of a tragedy he's never recovered from."

"Are you talking about the plane crash that killed his wife, his son and his son's family?"

"Yes, but he refuses to talk about it. How did you learn of it?"

"Not long before I left Vittorio, I told him I wanted to fly to Scotland for Christmas. He launched into a scathing tirade about the criminal incompetence of pilots and airlines. When I said I planned to pilot myself, he went ballistic and called me a number of things from insane to suicidal. His utter obsessiveness about the danger I was facing confused me enough I got on the net and started searching newspaper articles. The crash was five years ago."

"The son who was killed was a developing baritone about six years older than you are now. Vittorio once believed his son was going to reinvent Verdi's image for the modern world. He still says he wants someone who can kick tradition out the door and release the true emotional sensitivity of Verdi's music through the freedom of modern human expression."

"I'm not sure I know what that even means." Drew twisted his face.

"Drew, it's not the perfection of musical competence he's looking for. It's the soul of the character he wants." Leon lifted a hand and gesticulated with Italian vehemence. "Verdi was a man ahead of his time, who was often thwarted by censors and pompous public morality, but his Rigoletto triumphed in spite of the protests because, beside musical magnificence, it was a deeply human composition, not a polished exhibition." Leon dropped his hand on the bar with a loud bang. "That, clear and simple, is what Vittorio wants to reproduce."

"That's an eyeopener, Leon. But it sounds as if he wants me to be a reincarnation of his son and I can't do that."

"I don't think that's it. He admitted to my father that, even before the accident, he suspected Gianni was incapable of the depth he wanted and he may have to keep looking. Losing Gianni was a devastating blow. Losing faith in his vision of bringing Verdi's most enigmatic character into light took the zest out of him. As an opera, Rigoletto is a masterpiece in itself and opera viewers flock to the performances no matter who the singers are. Hence, no one has paid much attention to the true depths of its emotional possibilities.

Vittorio won't stand for that. He wants a way to bring that emotional power to completion and let it be felt. Gianni was an excellent singer; but like most singers, he was only capable of bringing the music to life."

"Isn't that what it's all about?" Drew asked.

"That's what most operatic singing is all about. But you are foremost an intuitive actor, who gives a character a vibrant identity that reaches all the way to the depths of a living soul. And that, in my opinion, is what really hooked Vittorio's interest in you. I'm not sure he's figured it out yet, but I've felt the way you act and I see it as your strongest asset."

"Leon, do you know how hard it is to concentrate on both at the same time?"

"Do you always concentrate when you act?"

"Only while I develop a role. Once I become it, I own it as a part of me." Caught up in Lean's fervor, Drew joined him in gesticulating fervor. "But I can't do that if he won't let me experience the role, which is impossible when he keeps jamming the music in my face and jumping me all over the damn libretto, which doesn't let me feel comfortable with the identity. He keeps demanding passion when I'm not ready to feel what to be passionate about, or where it comes from."

"You need to talk to him about that." Leon held up a hand when Drew bristled. "I know. He's too preoccupied with his own vehemently profane oratorio to listen to you. My advice is to shut up and not add to the performance. Then make him listen to what you want to say."

Drew stiffened then burst out laughing. "Why the hell didn't I think of that?"

"Because Vittorio can rattle a turtle into a frenzy and you're a prime target because you can't resist returning it. You're an emotional mirror that reflects his vehemence right back in his face."

"He revels in it."

"Of course. You not only feed his zest for overblown theatrics with your own, you reciprocate in kind, which intensifies the intensity until it becomes a battle of vehemence that has nothing to do with what started it. My father has witnessed it and said it was like fire blindly feeding fire until it devoured any substance it ever had."

"I didn't know you knew me so well." Drew gave him a wide-eyed look of astonishment.

"I'm Italian, too. Just weathered enough to develop the patience part. Stop charging after a goal you're not ready to meet. Vittorio is right to hold back the prize you're thundering toward like a knight with a lowered lance. Drew, if he finds a way to save his pride and swallow his egotism long enough to take you back, you do need to get him to understand the way you act. But you also have to let him be the master and follow his plan for the future. It will take you where you need to go. Believe me, Vittorio knows the progression you need to follow before you can be musically worthy of both Verdi and the Rigoletto Vittorio envisions."

While Drew stared at the singer with an uncharacteristically blank look of chagrin and dawning understanding, Leon looked toward where Willow was sitting with Maria and Caroline then back at Drew. "Slow down for God's sake. You have a lot more to fill up your life than a bullheaded charge to fame. On that front, I suggest you take a lesson from your father, who calmly refuses to feed the fire. Your father has Vittorio totally confused because he likes and respects Andy but can neither inflame him, nor discredit him."

"Dad's been doing that to me most of my life." Drew relaxed his defensiveness. "I admit I get obsessive and impatient; but Leon, there's so much out there to experience and I've always wanted to do it all at once."

"As the clichés go: enjoy the roses, enjoy your wife, enjoy living and absorb the scenery along the way. Opera is experiencing a worldwide rebirth. Rigoletto will still be there waiting for you when you're ready for him."

"I'll think about that."

"Don't think about it. Do it. That's my last assignment for you."

"When do I get the grade?"

"Call me in about eight years. I should know by then."

"That's a long time."

"Maybe in your twenties. Time has a different feel when you're approaching forty."

While they walked over to join their wives, Drew thought over what Leon had said and was surprised to find that the usual sense of tension that always seemed to tighten in him when he thought about

Vittorio and Rigoletto at the same time had loosened its grip and settled into just another challenge to deal with in its time.

After Leon and Maria said their farewells and went to offer the same to Andy and Rhian, Drew ruffled Willow's hair and laughed at her scowl. "Willow, I need to talk to Jamie alone. Can I leave you to talk horses with Caroline?"

"Sure." Willow took a swallow of her drink before she said, "Maria thrilled me with thoughts of galloping across the Pampas; and then, Caroline made me want to explore the highlands on a horse."

"We will, but not in the winter. It's cold and damp and dark."

Jamie chuckled at Drew's sour face. "Spoken by a man who spends his winters uselessly lolling about on the Mediterranean coast having fun and getting into trouble."

"After listening to Leon, I think I'll avoid the trouble and introduce Willow to the fun stuff instead."

"What's on your mind?" Jamie asked as they walked toward an empty corner.

"I was recently reminded about something I did that Dad said upset you. I'd like to apologize for it. At fourteen, it never occurred to me that my self-centered act of disobedience would cause you any stress beyond expected and deserved anger at irresponsible behavior. Now, I'm uncomfortable just knowing you saw me as destructive. I regret that and apologize. I deliberately caused costly damage, that will in no way be compensated by five quid. But it wasn't out of lack of respect for you. I did it for a personal reason that had absolutely nothing to do with you but was selfishly important to me." Drew was surprised by Jamie's slow smile.

"Your father told me; and although I'm not sure I understand it very well, I do commend you for your, so to speak, trust in my consistency. However, you did commit the crime and I won't apologize for the consequences." The Earl raised a thick eyebrow and smiled wryly. "I suppose you can call that my defense of the old school British fortitude shit, which I might add, you have always had in abundance."

"Maybe it came with my genes." Drew gave him a thoughtful look. "Or, more likely, by learning from the men I admired most."

"You're forgiven, Drew, and the five quid is an entirely different issue. I also realized a long time ago that you weren't a destructive person, just too damned fired up with wild energy to slow down and think ahead."

"Well, you did put some brakes on that." Drew nodded. "My risk analysis skills improved about that time in my life."

Jamie looked over to where Salt lick and the hired Celtic band were deep in discussion. "Where did you find the Celtic ensemble"

"I didn't. Byron did. He's fiddled with them a lot."

"He's very talented."

"I noticed that the first time I heard him play piano. The remarkable thing about Byron is he's a natural and was mostly self-taught when he won his first scholarship at Iowa State. Unfortunately," Drew paused, thought for a second, then smiled, "or maybe fortunately, Byron does it because he enjoys it in the now and isn't obsessed with future accolades."

"I sensed that in him."

"Byron says he likes accompanying me because he can play as loud as he wants and it doesn't overpower me." Drew laughed. "He's an odd bird, who fascinated me from the minute I met him. Trying to make sense of Byron Roberts is like trying to analyze Lewis Carroll. He's absurdity and genius all scrambled together. And he doesn't even need the drugs."

"Well, right now they're working on a musical finale we often do at the pub to pull everyone together and send them home in love with the highlands. You're expected to join them."

"Do I know it?"

"Probably in the core of your heritage. And," Jamie paused to let Drew's curiosity peak. "the singer may surprise you and show you that you aren't the only Sutherland who can sing."

"Well, I know it isn't Alex. He has the lung power as well as a captivating, melodic lilt to his speech. Musical tonality is nonexistent. But it could be your wife. She has a lovely voice."

"Join them and see. I'd like to hear your response."

After the combined bands—with Byron holding a guitar as he talked with the Celtic fiddler and Drew standing off to the side—sorted themselves out, Ian walked onto the stage with a microphone and waited while tables and chairs near the stage filled.

Jean Kehoe Van Dyke

With a spreading smile that brightened his youthfully handsome features, Ian captured attention with a devilish lift of a dark eyebrow. "My name is Ian Sutherland and I join my father in his open invitation to Glendoncroft. So saying, I hope to tempt you with a taste of what—besides making good homemade hooch—we do at Glendoncroft to entertain our visitors. The following song is, in our hearts, as beautiful and old as the hills we call hame and is known by several titles, the oldest being *The Braes o' Balquhidder*, but we offer the more popular *Wild Mountain Thyme*."

While the band played an intro, Ian scanned the faces in front him, located Beth's rapt smile, winked a teasing blue eye and started to sing in a clear, tenor voice that, after the first verse, was joined by a growing chorus of voices that grew to fill the room on each repeat of the chorus.

> "O, the summertime is comin', and the trees are sweetly bloomin',
> And the wild mountain thyme grows around the purple heather;
> Will ye go, lassie, go?
> "And we'll all go together to pluck wild mountain thyme,
> All around the bloomin' heather; Will ye go, lassie, go?
>
> "I will build my love a tower by yon pure, crystal fountain,
> And it's there that I will bring, all the flowers of the mountain;
> Will ye go, lassie, go?
> "And we'll all go together, to pluck wild mountain thyme,
> All around the bloomin' heather; Will ye go, lassie, go?
>
> "If my true love will not come, I will surely find another,
> To pluck wild mountain thyme, all around the purple heather,
> Will ye go, Lassie, go?
> "And we'll all go together, to pluck wild mountain thyme,
> All around the bloomin' heather; Will ye go, lassie, go?
>
> "Oh, the autumn time is comin', and the leaves will soon be fallin',
> And the blossoms o' the summer, will wither on the mountain:
> Will ye go, lassie, go?
> "And we'll all go together, to pluck wild mountain thyme,
> All around the bloomin' heather; Will ye go, lassie, go?"

During the conclusion of the last chorus, Drew came in below the pitch with deep tones that echoed the last phrase and stretched it into a fade like a dissipating mist that rolled across the blooming heather.

Willow was still floating in a glow of happiness from the beauty of the song and too much alcohol when Todd sat beside her and nodded across the open room to where Drew had backed Ian into a corner and was clearly badgering him about something.

"What's with Drew?" Todd asked.

Willow looked at her husband's squared shoulders and snickered. "Todd, you have to understand that Drew's getting two things he never really had before."

"That would be?"

"A huge dose of responsibility. And a little sister."

Todd let out one of his low, booming laughs. "That's a formula for trouble. And he deserves every bit of it."

With an impish grin, Willow nodded in agreement. "As for me, I think Ian's cute, and he has certainly put a flutter in Beth's shyness." She looked up to see Drew drop into the chair next to her. "What were you hassling Ian about?"

"I told him to stop messing around with the bad amateur rockers he was involved with when I saw him last winter and get the vocal training that's necessary to make something of a good voice. He's a natural with folk ballads and when he hit that last legato slur between the words 'go' and 'Lassie,' he set a benchmark he has to meet all the time. His tenor is still a little high and weak, but once he puts age on it, the timbre will strengthen and the pitch will come down a few notches."

"Like what you just did?"

"No." Drew gave her an odd look. "That was low register bass-baritone. Ian is not a baritone; any more than Todd is a soprano."

"Do you think he'll do it?"

"Maybe. If he gets around to thinking about it. Ian was always lost in some weird fantasy world of his own and unconcerned with reality. I also told him to stop embarrassing your sister."

"Drew, I really don't think Beth minds all that much. She's just annoyed because he insists on calling her Lizzie instead of Beth."

"What's wrong with Lizzie? I kind of like it."

"Matt always called her *Lizzie the Lizard* because she used to stick her tongue out at him when he teased her. But Ian has her starry-eyed and she's reluctant to tell him to stop because she's afraid it will turn him off. Beth's always been reserved and doesn't know how to handle him. While I chose to challenge my brothers and Gwen chose to ignore them, Beth was in awe of them, except for Matt, who always sheltered her."

"Willow, there's an enormous difference between his sixteen and her almost fourteen. He's sexually way over her head and I think you need to clue her in on the wild side of randy Highland lads."

"It doesn't matter." She shrugged indifferently. "He's going back to Scotland tomorrow. If they ever see each other again, she should be old enough to have figured it out. Let her enjoy her little crush right now. It's part of turning fourteen." Willow grinned at his skeptical look. "And maybe it will shift her fantasies away from you."

"What are you implying?"

"They're daydreams, Drew, and daydreams are free."

"If you say so." He made a wry face "Boy/girl thing, right?"

"I won't argue with that." She looked at where Alex, Eileen and Duncan were talking with Byron. "I'm enthralled by all the Scottish brogues. How do you do it?"

"It's all in the flutter of the tongue against the hard palette. It puts the birr in the brogue. It also makes us great kissers."

"I noticed."

"Thank you."

"I was thinking about Alex."

"That son of a bitch." With a dramatically indignant huff, Drew snapped his attention to his cousins. Then, grabbing Willow's hand, he marched across the floor, swung a rigidly straight right arm and smacked Alex in the back of the head.

Stiffening, Alex whirled to face Drew and spluttered. "What you be doin' that for?"

"For kissing my wife too well. Every time she looks at you, she gets that rapturous smile on her face."

"Well, two years ago I had to put up with sighs about the passionate ecstasy of Italian lovers."

"I'll accept that excuse." Drew brushed the issue away with a flip of his wrist. "This time."

While they walked away, Willow started giggling, then blushed when Drew gave her a puzzled look. "I think I drank too much. I'm getting so giddy I want to hug everybody because everybody made it such a great day."

"I heard that." A deep laugh turned Willow to Antonio, who caught her in an engulfing bear hug that took her breath away. "And if he doesn't take good care of you, give me a call and I'll straighten him out for you."

Antonio chuckled at her startled look before he sobered his voice. But I do have a serious request. Make sure he takes you to meet my mother before you leave the continent. She needs to feel his love and forgiveness, not just hear it from me."

"We'll do that." Drew smiled. "And maybe she'll make me a good Italian supper and tell me her angels are watching out for me." He paused and looked pensive. "And then, maybe they were."

"She'd love that more than anything else in the world." Antonio flicked Willow on the nose with an index finger then kissed her on the forehead. "Now, go hug everybody and giggle, so they can share your happiness."

Willow did exactly that, especially with Mae, who looked ready to cry but forced it back and held her for a long time before she regained her public composure. And John, whose warm hug engulfed her like the grandfather she wanted him to be. Finally, when a lightheaded sense of contentment started to wrap around her, Willow leaned against her husband and looked around the room with a confused expression. "I seem to have misplaced Rhian. Do you think she went back to the farm?"

"Nope." Drew hugged his arm around Willow's waist and smiled at her naivety. "She and Dad took Leon and Maria to the Des Moines airport. We may see her at the hotel when they get back."

"She stayed at the farm last night."

"She was working, but her job's over now."

"She's leaving already?" Willow gave him an odd look before the truth hit her. "Is she sleeping with your father?"

"Looks that way. I think she's going to skip Virginia and go visit France for a while."

"Oh, my goodness." Willow blushed. "I didn't expect that."

"I thought it was rather obvious all weekend. But then, I've witnessed the subtlety of his affections for a long time." When Drew felt her slump a little in his hold, he laughed and scooped her up in his arms. "It's time to leave and if I'm really lucky, I'll get to spend my wedding night doing something besides tucking you in bed and listening to you snore."

"I am tired but I do want to make love with you. Maybe after a little nap."

When Willow's head drooped onto his shoulder, Drew heard a bagpipe melody behind him and, like a triumphant highland warrior with his captured bride, dramatically marched out double doors held open by Todd and Owen.

Recognizing the melody and looking toward the waiting Town Car, where Duncan stood by the back door, Alex by the driver's, Drew burst out laughing at what he realized was a combined cousins and brothers-in-law re-enactment of an old Glendoncroft ballad titled *Crossing the Clan Barrier*—a romantic tale that told of the dramatic ending of an ancient feud with a marriage between bitter enemies, who became lovers and crossed the battle lines to unite two long-splintered factions of the clan together in peace.

Its message made Drew wonder if introducing those four to each other would become a blessing or a curse. Then he shrugged and decided that if nothing else, it promised a challenging future of laughter and adventure.

Drew slipped into the back seat just as Duncan set a hand on Willow's head to protect it and barked his knuckles on the door frame. Willow stirred and opened her eyes when Duncan let out a burst of Gaelic that would have shocked her if she'd been able to understand it. She merely blinked at him in confusion, then smiled coyly, snuggled into Drew's arms and went back to sleep.

As the car moved away, Duncan leapt into the front seat, punched Alex on the arm and pointed toward the exit from the lot instead of the entrance they were headed for.

Drew settled back in the seat with a fervent hope that if Alex remembered what side of the road to drive on, he and Willow would make it to the hotel and consummate their marriage without any more drama.

Chapter Thirty-Three

Three weeks after the wedding, Drew swung the bow of his single-masted sailing yacht in line with the direction of the waves rolling towards the city of Genoa. He cut power to the auxiliary engine and tossed out a sea anchor before he led Willow onto the foredeck and pointed northeast to jagged rocky cliffs that had been thrust up from the earth's mantle, shattered into irregular chunks of angular rocks and haphazardly toppled into the sea like the strewn remains of ancient dragon bones. Above the pounding force of the surf, a maze of brightly colored buildings clung to clefts and crags of jagged bluffs that rose toward rugged hills densely cloaked in the dark green foliage of coastal forests and ancient olive groves before they spread northward toward the towering up-thrust peaks of the Italian Alps.

"You can't see it without binoculars, but that long, bald cliff that juts out of the hillside is the general area of Falcon's Rest—our villa."

"Is it one of those luxurious modern villas with pools and spas and glossy luxury I don't really want?"

"Not at all." Drew smiled when relief flooded her face. "There is a pool, but thanks to the miracle of FiberForms it's disguised as a natural adjunct to a stream that once powered an eighteenth-century olive oil processing mill. The villa is the restored, two-story stone home of the mill owner and its adjacent office building. The structures are joined by a walled, glass-roofed atrium, and the old office building has six guest suites; and yes, a gym and spa area at the pool end."

"Did your father restore it?"

"Since it was in bad shape and about as off the tourist track as you can get around here, Dad picked it up for a good price about fifteen years ago and restored it in as close to its original appearance as he could. But it's more open and practical now with the bright, fresh feel of the Mediterranean Provincial style. He's talked about selling, but he likes it enough he keeps putting it off. I could rent it from him, but I'm tired of renting and like the idea of owning my own home."

"Are you going to buy it?"

"I offered to trade a ski lodge for it. But that would mean I'd come out financially ahead of him and he doesn't like deals like that. He's still mulling it over; so right now, I'm renting it."

"Maybe he'll give it to us for a wedding present." Willow teased with the hopeful expression of a child wishing for a pony under the Christmas tree.

Drew tipped his head and gave her a pensive look. "I think our Sutherland creed of family principles says things like: love your children, enjoy your children, guide your children, discipline your children; teach them good manners; help them learn to think and know right from wrong; keep them safe from harm; *do not* over indulge your children or destroy their capacity to become honestly respectful of others, responsibly independent and conscientiously productive."

"That's pretty good. Does it really say that?"

"It's not written dogma." Drew chuckled at her perplexed look. "That was an inflated version of what it is to me. The most important thing about it is that each of us has the freedom to absorb it and express it individually. Willow, my key point in all that philosophical drivel is the *don't overindulge* part. Giving me the villa is a little beyond Dad's parental generosity. Besides, if he did that, I'd still be stuck with the damn ski lodge. Dad started teaching me how to make the best use of my capital when I was a child. He set limits and helped when I made mistakes, but he never bailed me out without using it as a lesson to learn from and demanding repayment at a rate I could handle. But I do wish he would make up his mind on this one. I have a use for the money and it beats hell out of high maintenance costs—plus insurance against the liability risks of a ski resort."

"What are you planning to buy with the profit?"

"Sutherland financial policy would prefer you had said, 'Where do you plan to reinvest it?' But in this case, I see my gain as more personal than an investment opportunity because I don't plan to sell it—maybe not even use it for a very long time." Drew looked at her puzzled face. "I plan to buy a specific tract of land near a very special town in Iowa, so you will always have a real piece of Iowa to go home to."

"You've been talking to my mother, haven't you?" Willow tried to hold back a swell of emotion but found it impossible.

Drew closed his arms around her and held her while she soaked his shirt with happiness. "I always talk to your mother. She knows most of your secrets."

"Mom told me to always carry a part of my family and Iowa within me so I could call that feeling home."

"That's one of the secrets. And it works for me, too." Drew turned her and steadied her with an encircling arm while he strolled across the rising and falling deck as if it were as solid as a paved sidewalk. Stopping at the rail, he pointed above a colorful row of beachside dwellings below a steep, tree-smothered hill. "Up there, almost on the edge of the cliff. Do you see the white domed building with the wide stone steps leading up from the cliffside parking lot?"

"Yes. What is it?"

"Vittorio. The area beneath the dome is his museum to Italian opera and a large section of that is his tribute to Giuseppe Verdi. The rest is his *musica conservatori* and concert hall."

"Did you perform there?"

"Willow, I was only there for two months before Avenger blew it to hell. I never got out of a classroom or practice room." He stared at the wide marble steps leading to the entry of the domed building. "It was a dream I shattered. And right now, no matter what Leon said about Vittorio wanting me back, I have trouble holding onto it. Just by being here, I can feel him. And what I feel most is unforgiveness."

"Could that be because it's what you feel toward Vittorio?"

"Maybe I did when it was easier to put the blame it on him than accept my failure to live up to what he expected from me. But not now. Part of me wants to crawl back and beg forgiveness but my intuition says that would be a mistake. I still don't know if it was my loss of control that he can't forgive, or that I gave up on the challenge and ran away."

"When will you see Vittorio?"

"I'll contact him as soon as we get to the villa. If he still wants me, we'll go see him."

"Are you sure you want me to go with you?"

"Absolutely." He gave her a wide-eyed stare of surprise that she would even question a point she had earlier been so adamant about. "He's Italian; and therefore, much more agreeable when a beautiful woman is present. You get to charm him, while I get to look meek and mild."

"Meek and mild will never happen."

"I can try." Drew gave her a helpless look. "I was more than half the problem. I do owe him some humility."

After leaving the boat at a Marina, the newlyweds rented a car and followed a steep switchback road into the hills to a terraced valley of new and ancient olive groves where the village of Falconeria spread out along a jagged hillside. Beyond the village, Drew turned onto a smaller, steeper road that twisted its way to a grassy clearing where the villa that would become their home overlooked a slate patio and sloping lawn. When the drive curled around a copse of trees and faced a contour-hugging stone wall at the edge of the cliff, the world opened into a breathtaking panorama of the distant Mediterranean coast and sunset reddened sea.

"Drew, it's fantastic. I feel like Cinderella going to the ball."

"Don't keep bringing up the Prince Charming bit. It makes me feel like a con artist." He stopped the car and looked at her confused expression. "Willow, I was born to wealth, and you innocently married into it. Just accept that it's both the reality and responsibility of our lives. Then, get over it, and go back to I love you for better or worse because it isn't a fairytale and it won't always be happily ever after. When it comes to the happiness quest, I'll side with love as a clear winner over money's corrupting allure every time."

Drew reached over, tweaked her wrinkled nose then pointed to a blue Lamborghini sports car in the drive. "It looks like we have company already."

"Do you know whose car it is?" Willow gaped at the sleek, powerful looking car.

"Yes. It's mine. But I remember leaving it in France. I think our landlord is looking for a payment."

"It's a good thing we don't have a family to try to stuff into that thing."

"A family was not in my mind when I bought it." By the time Drew swung around the circle of the drive and parked behind his car, Andy had opened Willow's door and was hugging her. "I'm not trading her or the car so don't get any ideas."

"Right now, one Roberts woman for each of us is more than enough." Andy set a hand on Drew's shoulder, gave it an affectionate shake.

"Where is Rhian?"

"Inside, making dinner."

"I didn't know she could cook," Willow said.

"As long as there's a microwave, freezer and take-out she can."

"I guess I came out ahead on that one." Drew laughed at his father's agreeing nod. "Have you thought about my offer lately?"

Andy held Drew's gaze for a silent moment before he said, "Don't you think it would be wiser to find out if you're actually going to stay here before you take on property?"

Drew looked startled, then faced reality. "I guess I've been expecting I would. Because it's what I want to happen."

"I'll give you four months to get your act together so you can make it happen instead of want it to happen. Then we'll talk."

"Sounds fair to me." Drew nodded. "Why are you here so early? We expected you next week."

"Your grandmother sent a shipment that came early. Instead of disturbing you, we drove down yesterday to intercept it." Andy gestured beyond a stand of trees toward a fenced field where Venture and Ko-Ko grazed and a curious bay colt stuck his head between two rails of the fence and snorted at them.

"That's Wee Willie." Willow stared at the colt she and Drew had helped bring into the world last spring. "We were only expecting Venture and Ko-Ko."

"The lady of the manor had different ideas." Andy shrugged. "Willie is her welcome to the family gift to you, Willow. But I suggest a better official name to put on the registration papers before you sign them because he's his daddy's clone and isn't going to stay wee for long." He looked at Drew. "The local haulers I hired didn't like the road out of the village so Enrico, my groundskeeper, brought up the paraphernalia that came with them. He took us back, then Rhian and I played cowboys and rode the horses up here."

"Rhian doesn't ride." Willow gave him an odd look. "She wouldn't even get near a horse."

"She did yesterday," Andy said. "I ignored her reluctance and plopped her on Venture. Hell, he's so wide she'd have to fall out before she could fall down. I continued to ignore her loud protests, gave her two handfuls of his mane before I grabbed his lead, vaulted on Ko-Ko and started up the road."

Drew gave him a startled look. "Sounds like an abduction to me."

A smile cracked Andy's composure and he broke up laughing. "It was the craziest two-mile ride I've ever had. That damn colt that I expected would docilely follow us ran everywhere and Rhian yelled at me to slow down every time Venture moved faster than a stroll. When he snorted and kicked at a fly on his belly, she shrieked and cussed me out with words I didn't think she knew. The cool, unshakeable woman of the world façade blew apart with a flamethrower temper that kept reigniting because I couldn't stop laughing."

"Is she speaking to you yet?" Drew asked.

"I think we literally laid it to rest last night, but every time I'd start to laugh, she'd jam an elbow or knee into me. I may never get her on a horse again, but I think I found someone to make my life more exciting."

"My father called her cantankerous," Willow said.

"That would describe it." Andy nodded. "But I sense more spirit in it than malice."

"I recognize that feeling." Drew looked at Willow's wrinkle-nosed frown. "Do you still think your father's comparison between you and Rhian was totally off target?"

"Well, maybe not. But I do know bossy men need to be set on their asses every now and then." Willow pivoted and strode to where Rhian was standing on the porch looking confused. "I understand you had a riding lesson yesterday."

"Is that what he called it?" Rhian glared at where Andy was laughing with Drew, jerked open the screen door and stomped inside.

Willow trailed behind her aunt, trying to take in the sunny openness of a huge living room/lounge area with a stone fireplace, clusters of comfortable furniture, game tables, a bar and corner entertainment area.

When they reached the kitchen at the back of the house, Rhian closed the door and twisted the latch. "I thought I was going to die when I was on that monstrous creature, and all Andy did was laugh at me."

"That's because he knows Venture is a gentle monster, who wouldn't let you fall off unless you did something really stupid. He's all power and spirit when Drew rides him but put a beginner on his back and he will plod along like what I call a babysitter mount."

"Mr. *just do what I tell you* didn't tell me that." Rhian strode to a corner dining area and stared out a window at the stable and pasture. "He just threw me on the damn horse and told me to ride it."

"Would you have listened to him if he had?" Willow sniffed at the air, wandered across a modern, commercial kitchen to a large stove that fascinated her then turned off one of the ovens and peeked in its door.

"Probably not." Rhian relaxed, even let a smile tease at her mouth before she turned back to see Willow staring down a service area hallway toward the closed door to the main dining room. "I don't like horses. You know that, Willow."

"You never gave them a chance." Realizing that her self-centered aunt wasn't going to let her leisurely explore her new home, Willow sighed and turned to face Rhian across a center prep island. "And from what I've observed—and used to admire about you—you've been the same way with men."

"What are you saying?"

"I think you've been so intent on playing the independent, *I am woman hear me roar,* game that you've forgotten life is more than a showcase for egos and vanity. It may work for some people, but I don't think it's working for you. And it certainly won't work with Andy Sutherland."

"How do you know that?" Rhian tensed. "I've made something of myself. It was hard work, but I did it without the help of a man. I can stand equal with him any day."

"I know it because I'm in love with his son, and they aren't as different as they may seem, except when it comes to temperament." Willow made a wry face. "In that regard, Drew is a roman candle exploding erratically in all directions, while Andy is a cool, brilliant sparkler shining like a pole star that is infallibly consistent." Willow saw a startled look of surprise in Rhian's expression and smiled. "As for your career, you've done exceptionally well. I admire you for it. I'm sure Andy does, too."

"He said he did."

"Rhian," Willow gave her aunt a stern, but sympathetic look, "I don't know what's hardened you recently, but you're so protective about your image of what you are that you've forgotten the most important things."

"And what are those?"

"Love, laughter, fun, foolishness, open feelings, the importance of being family. It sounds corny; and maybe it's out of date, but it's what bonds people together and you can't stand equal with any one of them if you don't share being human with them. Andy wasn't laughing at you, Rhian. He was trying to get you to laugh with him. And if you don't figure out how to do that, he won't be part of your life for long."

Rhian started to say something then stopped when she realized she was seeing her younger niece in an entirely new way. "Either you've been brainwashed, or you and Drew have discovered a truth I could never find."

"What do you mean?"

Rhian let out a breath of frustration and looked surprisingly humble. "I've planned and supervised a lot of weddings, anniversaries and other family events but I have rarely experienced one like yours."

"In what way?"

"It was a mix of people with a huge diversity of backgrounds. And all of them actually enjoyed being with each other. You wouldn't believe how many times people would tell me to make sure I didn't place certain people near certain other people; or how often guests would cling together in tight cliques to ignore or prejudge other people, then nitpick about their flaws. Drew's insistence on a cowboy bar and pot luck meal that included farmers, small town tradespeople and laborers, wealthy corporate executives, highly educated Metropolitan Opera stars—and, of all things, a Scottish earl, complete with a family piper—was a recipe for disaster in my mind. And then, that fascinating earl and his dynamic son pulled everyone together with humor and emotions until they were all enjoying themselves and laughing with each other as if they were old friends at a family reunion."

"Drew calls that Jamie's own brand of charisma. He also told me that Jamie can put down self-important snobs like a striking viper when he has to."

"I don't doubt that."

"Sutherlands do rule, Rhian, but they choose to do it benevolently. To them, even to your own family, none of those labels you used mean anything. Everyone there was important to either Drew and me or our families, and they were all there to have fun and share our happiness. Drew is an entertainer and he insists that entertainers and hosts are only worth their salt when people are willing to share feelings with them and each other. At first, I was as reluctant as you were, especially about the location and pot luck country dinner. But Drew was right when he said, 'If you put people on isolated islands and give them no reason to bump into each other or contribute to the atmosphere, they will stay isolated.' Rhian, I don't know if you noticed it or not, but, at Harvey's suggestion, the entertainments, even serving tables, condiments and dessert carts were placed in different areas to encourage movement and circulation."

"I was too busy being miffed about Drew taking over the reception to think about that."

"Rhian, he didn't take over. Drew, Byron and Harvey had the music and reception in hand before you were part of the picture. And it was Drew who told me to let you do the wedding because he liked what he saw on your Internet site. Your planning and artistic presentations were sensational. We wanted to thank you after the reception, but you left early and I fell asleep from too much to drink."

Willow chuckled at Rhian's startled look. "Drew had to carry me out and I would have been mortified if I hadn't been so tipsy. He stripped me and put me to bed like a zonked-out kid."

"Interesting wedding night." Rhian gave her a curious look.

"Well, it wasn't like we hadn't been sleeping together all summer." Willow smirked at Rhian's startled look. "I woke up at five in the morning when I heard a deep voice saying, 'Good morning, Mrs. Sutherland. Welcome to our forever.' It was quite wonderful to realize Drew really was all mine forever."

"So, he really is a romantic."

"Definitely." Willow laughed. "With a chuckle in his voice and a tongue in his cheek."

"I never wanted to be ruled—or owned." Rhian announced with a self-assurance that wasn't reflected in her body language.

"That's sad because it's a matter of one plus one makes one. Or, as we like to see it, it's a matter of the whole being greater than its parts."

"I don't think Andy wants togetherness."

"You'll never know if you keep putting up a barbed wire fence."

"It's been there so long I don't know how to take it down."

"That makes me wonder why you're here with him." Willow gave her aunt a wry look. "Surely, all this time off must be upsetting your career."

"I didn't really have anything lined up that seemed important to me." Rhian answered glibly, before her shell cracked and she looked vulnerable. "I've never met a man like Andy before. He *is* like that sparkler you mentioned, beckoning and steady, but he scares me, because he's so… I don't know how to word it."

"How about intimidating? That was my first impression."

"That works."

"As Drew once said, 'Dad can have that effect.' But Andy's a lot more than that, Rhian. He's firm and controlling, but he's also fun, totally open-minded and caring. And I suspect he's a very good lover." Willow smiled slyly when her aunt gave her a shocked look that made her laugh. "Rhian, I grew up this year. And do you realize that at times you really are a lot like your big brother Lloyd."

"I certainly am not." Rhian stiffened.

"When I told Dad, I was the one who let Drew into my bed, Dad looked at me exactly the way you did when I brought up the subject of sex and me in the same sentence. Except I think I smelled smoke coming out of his ears."

"I can believe that." Rhian sighed and dropped her shields. "You're right. Andy's a very good lover. That's mostly why I'm here."

"I think it runs in their family. Drew describes it as pleasing a partner before oneself." Willow heard a rap on the door, started toward it, then walked over and hugged her aunt. "Why don't you start by letting Andy laugh at you? It's a funny story the way he tells it. I think it would give you a laugh, too."

Willow turned the doorlatch, jerked open the door and looked up at Drew. "Can't two girls have a private girl-talk without some busybody man poking his head into it?"

"We're hungry." Drew stated.

"You're always hungry."

"Oh no!" Rhian stared at them in horror. "I put a frozen pie in the oven and forgot to set the timer."

"It's all right," Willow said, "I shut it off."

"How did you know it was done?"

"It smelled done."

"You can do that?" Rhian relaxed at Willow's reassuring nod. "I really am the world's worst cook."

"No, you aren't. He is." Willow pointed at Drew. "He decided to make rice one night and ended up cementing it to the pot." She and Drew both burst out laughing.

"Then she made me clean the pot." Drew made a sour face. "I attacked it with a wire brush on an electric drill and sent the damn thing flying across the kitchen spitting rice and crashing into a jar of spaghetti sauce that splatted on the floor."

"Willow," Andy stood in the doorway shaking his head. "Don't ever let Drew get his hands on an electric tool. All he knows is full speed ahead and damn the consequences."

Rhian stood by the table and stared at their hilarity for a few heartbeats before a giggle rose from her diaphragm then erupted in a loud hoot as she collapsed onto a chair and laughed at a mental image of a pot spinning through the air in a swarm of flying rice.

"Feels good, doesn't it," Willow grinned.

"Yes, it does. And someday I might even be willing to get on a horse again. If you can find one about this high." Rhian held her hand out at table height. "With a seat belt."

"That's not a good idea, but I think you could learn to like riding if you'd let me teach you." Willow smiled at Rhian's doubtful look before she grabbed Drew's hand and towed him through the service area into an openly spacious dining room with a massive oak table and upholstered-seat chairs, a marble-topped buffet, china cabinet and two Italian crystal chandeliers—but best of all a wraparound corner view of the front yard and Mediterranean Sea.

"Drew, it's beautiful, but how are we supposed to raise children in a place like this?"

"It's sturdy stuff and they'll learn to respect their environment, not destroy it."

"Did that come from the same person who trashed an antique table?"

"I was a feral kid in a jungle without rules. They won't be." Drew lifted an eyebrow. "But you're right. Careless and enthusiastic accidents will occasionally happen. Now, what's really on your mind?"

"Did you call Vittorio?"

"He's in Bologna, but Stephen, his personal assistant, said he left a memo saying he expects me in his office at nine Monday morning."

"That's it?" She gaped at him. "No greeting. No hint of intention."

"Willow, Vittorio is only verbose when he's ranting in Italian. We'll show up at nine and I'll face the ranting."

"And you'll beg?"

"No." He shook his head. "I have decided that is absolutely the wrong thing to do. Everyone I heard about who played that card lost. He said I needed to grow up. I plan to show him I have. And your presence will be important to my approach. But no matter what you hear or think, don't get your hackles up. For once, be a beautiful, dutiful, old-fashioned wife and stay out of it."

"That won't be hard. I won't understand anything either of you say."

"I'm hoping you'll understand most of it."

"What are you going to say?"

"I don't know yet, but I have an idea of what will work. How it unfolds depends on how he reacts, not what I think should happen."

"That isn't very encouraging."

"Vittorio's either set his mind on telling me to stuff it, or he hasn't. If he hasn't, demeaning myself won't gain me points, neither will criticizing him. The only sane approach I have is to keep myself in control and convince him he has a reason to give me another chance."

"What if he offends me? I know how you'd react to that and it scares me."

"That he will not do. Vittorio's behavior is often irrational, but under all the surface dramatics, he is a gentleman with a great respect for women." Drew lifted her chin and held her gaze. "You're right about me standing up for you but the uncontrollable scary one is gone."

"I was more concerned about an offended, irritable macho one named Drew."

"Good because that's all you're ever going to have to contend with."

❖

Inside Vittorio's office, Drew took Willow's hand and stepped toward a short wiry man whose luxurious mane of white hair, beard and tangled eyebrows encircled a pair of intense black eyes above a narrow bridge of a nose that flared into magnificently rounded nares. Drew remained silent as the older man faced him like a gnome king, who was the equal of giants in both presence and achievement. He answered Vittorio's stare with a calm self-assurance that locked them together for a silent moment of tension before Drew nodded in respect of the maestro's authority.

"Good morning, Vittorio. I want you to meet my wife, Willow. She does not speak Italian, so I will speak English. And since I know you are proficient enough in the language, I, for her comfort, request you do the same."

"Ah!" Vittorio gave Willow a long appraising look before he said, "Another one of your beautiful women."

"No." Drew gave him a sudden, hard look. "She is definitely beautiful, but she is not *one* of my women. She is my wife."

"Perhaps my English is not so good as he thinks." Smiling at Drew's irritated reaction to his opening barb, Vittorio took Willow's hand, lifted it, and gently touched his lips to her fingers. "Good morning, Willow. Welcome to Genoa."

"It's a beautiful city." Willow smiled in flattered astonishment. "I think I can grow to like it here."

"That is in Andrew's hands, not mine. He is the one who broke a commitment and ran from the challenge of greatness."

"We saw it differently." Willow answered in confusion.

Vittorio released her hand and stared up at Drew's startled expression. "And why is that?"

"Because what I did is unforgivable, even to me."

"And just what did you do?" Vittorio met Drew's eyes with a stiletto sharp stare. "Besides lose your temper and behave very badly to two innocent men who tried to control you."

"I lost more than my temper. I lost my hold on reality because I…" A flash of blood and terror flashed in Drew's mind and disappeared. "I believed you attacked Elise and I tried to protect her."

"Why would I attack Elise?" Vittorio looked appalled.

"You wouldn't." Drew admitted. "The truth is it had nothing to do with you. The thrown glass triggered a memory of seeing my mother abused when I was six years old. I didn't run from you. I ran from myself. At the time, I had no memory of what actually happened, but I knew deep in my mind that there was something terrible in me I couldn't face."

"Is it still there?"

"No. With the exception of Willow and some very strong people who took me back to face my buried past, it was a very bad year."

"That is what your father insisted was your truth to tell, not his. I thank you for it. Andy Sutherland is a very complex man, who knows his son well."

"I want to learn from you, Vittorio. Do you still want to teach me?"

"I want you to renew your original commitment. But I am still myself, and you are still yourself. It will not be…" Vittorio smiled wryly. "…*facile*."

"With you, nothing is easy." Drew turned to face his wife. "He's right. I promised him a year and I still owe it to him."

Willow looked at Drew for a long moment then said, "Will you promise me the same?"

"The same what?" Her unexpected question startled Drew, rattled his composure.

"The commitment you already made. You won't quit, and I won't let you quit. It's your responsibility thing against my Iowa stubborn, isn't it?"

For a moment, Drew looked as he were going to explode. Then he pulled in a deep breath and glanced back and forth between the two of them. When he saw Vittorio staring at Willow with an awed look of admiration, he lost all pretense of self-possession and sputtered at her, "Is that how you stay out of things?"

"Since we all want the same thing." Willow gave him an innocent look. "I suggest we all commit to the same thing."

"And what the hell is that?" Drew gaped at her in total frustration.

"That you'll live up to the commitment you already made." Willow repeated flatly.

"I was going to suggest renegotiating the ramifications of those terms. I didn't expect to get run over by a stubborn wife driving a bulldozer."

When Drew glanced from one patiently blank face to the other, he knew he'd lost all control; and what rankled him the most was that he was the one doing the ranting while Vittorio was calmly supporting his turncoat wife.

"All right! I know when I'm cornered. I accept the terms."

"Thank you, Andrew." Vittorio nodded to him. "When should I start scheduling for you?"

"I left stuff here in storage, so we have some moving in to do. My father and Willow's aunt are visiting through the weekend. Any time after that will do."

"You may attend to your stuff, whatever stuff is. Stephen will send you the schedule. Is your e-mail the same?"

"Yes." Drew paused and studied Vittorio's face for a moment. "You baited me with that beautiful women comment, didn't you?"

"*Certamente*! I was looking for the fire under..." He waggled his hands in dramatic frustration before he said, "...under the, as you would say, cool dude façade. I apologize for my error. Your wife is in no way like those *other* beautiful women. She is a..." Vittorio thought over his words for a few seconds before he said, "...perfect match for your tinder."

"That's just plain corny. Go back to Italian." Drew grabbed Willow's hand and led her out the door.

"Andrew!" Vittorio's bellow echoed in the hallway. "What is this thing called corny?"

Drew spun back and threw a hand in the air. "Research it! That's the solution you always gave me."

The drive back to the villa was silent and it wasn't until Drew stormed across the spacious lounge toward the open library doors that Willow grabbed his arm and shouted, "Why did you get so sassy with him at the end?"

"He thrives on sass. It's the most exciting part of our relationship."

"Then why are you still mad at him?"

"I'm not mad at him. The battle terms are the same as they were before I left."

"Well, you're brooding and mad about something."

Drew glared at her, then shouted, "What the hell didn't you understand about *stay out of it*?"

"I didn't see anything to stay out of."

"I had a perfectly good battle plan and you swept the whole thing into the trash."

"There was no battle. You didn't need a plan."

"My main reason for getting him to speak English was to out-rant him and get the upper hand so I could get him to listen to me."

"You said it was for my comfort. And what does language have to do with it?"

"It's very simple. I learned English, Italian and French as a child. They're natural to me. I think in them. I dream in them. Vittorio didn't learn English until he was much older and rarely uses it. He still thinks in Italian and has to do some mental deciphering thing I don't understand to get the words right. It's really hard to rant and rave when the words don't fluently leap out of your brain. After a few seconds of babbling out incoherent, Porky Pig nonsense, the rant self-destructs and it becomes *th...th...that's all folks* and the battle is over. I know Vittorio has experienced this phenomenon because I could rarely sucker him into that trap long enough for him to make a complete fool of himself."

"Why did you want to do that?"

"I didn't. I just wanted to keep his mind busy with the deciphering part so I could get him to listen to me."

"Well, it came out alright, so what difference does it make?"

"My ultimate objective was to get him to accept a simple concept that says it's his obligation to teach me how to sing while mine is to act. And I need to do it my way."

"You'll have plenty of time to bring that up."

"But you just gave him the upper hand. Now, he's one up on me."

"I didn't know it was a frickin' competition."

"Isn't everything?"

"Just go away and punch a tree or something. And to make me happy make sure it hurts."

A sudden eruption of loud masculine laughter froze them both and they turned to see Andy standing between the open library doors.

"Does this mean the honeymoon's over?" Andy looked at them with calm composure and a touch of needling irony in his voice.

"I told her to stay out of it." Drew blustered. "And before I could make my point, she sided with him and backed me into a corner I couldn't get out of."

"I see." Andy nodded. "You obviously used the wrong verb."

"Wrong verb? When?"

"I've found that *asked* usually works better than *told*." Andy glanced down at the dark jeans he was wearing, then back at Drew. "Go change your clothes. I think we need to throw each other around the yard for a while."

"That's a good idea. And it beats hell out of punching a tree." Drew pivoted and strode toward the stairway.

"What's that about?" Willow gave Andy a strange look.

"Drew has never been good at conceding defeat when his often less than brilliant schemes fall apart, especially when they're doomed to failure from the start. This time he's pitted himself against a master tactician; and right now, I expect his aggression level is at breakaway altitude. He needs to channel it somewhere and an exhausting martial arts drill works better than anything else. It always worked for me, which is the reason I got him into it in the first place."

"What do you mean?"

"Willow, Drew had to learn control and I certainly didn't want to punish a child for having too much energy and the aggressive drive he would need to conquer the challenges ahead of him."

Willow smiled with enlightenment. "I think my father saw farm work the same way."

"We have him back, Willow. Now we have to deal with him. In that view, what happened with Vittorio?"

"Nothing." She shrugged in bewilderment. "Vittorio said it was Drew's decision to either leave or come back with the same terms of commitment. I figured it was all over; and since we all seemed to be on the same page, I asked Drew to make a commitment to me that said he wouldn't quit and I wouldn't let him. Isn't that what both you and Paul expected me to do?"

"It's what we hoped you would do. But it might have been wiser if you had refrained from doing it in front of Vittorio." Laughing, Andy pulled her against him and gave her a reassuring hug. "It's why I didn't tell him I asked my mother to send the horses early. I needed an excuse to be here if it went wrong because I had no idea what ultimate failure would do to him, or how you would cope with his reaction."

"It worried me, too." Willow met his understanding gaze. "And, I'm grateful you're here. But I will never let that happen."

Later, when Drew and Andy returned, they were sweaty, grass stained, dirty, barefoot and ribbing each other about who scored more points on whom. The rant was gone and Willow was smiling when Drew took her hand and led her into the library.

"Forgive me, Willow, I'm not very good at having my best laid plans blown out of the water with no chance to retrieve them. And you were right. I will have ample time to voice my views."

"Thank you." Willow gave him a quick kiss, then stepped back with an innocent smile and asked, "So, who got the most points in the Kung Fu competition?"

"Why are you so damned intent on asking questions I don't want to answer?"

"I wanted to see if it worked."

"It worked. And he won because he has hair trigger reflexes and moves fast, which always gets me a kick in the ass." With a quick duck, Drew lifted her over his shoulder and headed for the stairs. "And I know exactly what works between us."

"It's lunchtime."

"That can wait."

❖

Less than a month after resuming his training in Genoa, Drew's clashes with Vittorio escalated into loud, explosive shouting matches when Vittorio's badgering set off eruptions of Drew's irritable snits. He didn't always have them under control when he came home, which made him pick senseless fights that turned his frustration against Willow instead of himself or Vittorio.

On other days, Drew arrived home riding on ecstatic highs that swept into a whirlwind of excitement and wild lovemaking that left them drained and breathless. Before long, the swings from fury to elation created an unbearable exasperation when Drew was unable to suppress the roiling passions of the volcano. He lost control of his emotions, his ability to make sensible decisions, even his determination to master his talent.

One night in mid-January, Drew slammed into the bedroom and declared that he was getting the hell out of Genoa, out of Italy and out of opera. Willow sat up in bed and blinked at his furious face for a moment before she shouted, "You can't do that!"

"Why the hell not? I dared to say I wanted to sing his sacred Verdi. He says it will be a miracle if he can teach me to sing Rossini as it is meant to be sung. According to him, I sing of love like a foghorn and my boastful pride sounds like the braying of a jackass!"

"You can't leave him because you promised me you wouldn't."

"I can do whatever the hell I want," Drew shouted then stopped beside the bed and glared at her as if he expected her to back away from him. When Willow lifted her chin and glared back, he lost some of his arrogance. "You're not the one who has to put up with that son of a bitch."

"No, I have to put up with this one." When Drew stiffened, his wife added firmly. "You said you'd stay for a year. It's only been six weeks."

"I was out of my mind!" Drew threw his hands up dramatically and let the fury turn to exasperated ranting. "He wants me to live the persona of the role and be the music at the same time. How can I do that when he won't leave me alone. He could let me sing the whole fucking thing, then tell me what's wrong instead of shouting, *Basta!* at me, then make me start and stop and stumble around in the score like a fool. As soon as I start to feel right, he distracts me and jerks me away from it. When I lose my temper, he calls me incompetent and hammers me for not doing what he's telling me. Even when I know what went wrong, he keeps badgering me until I'm totally lost and can't even hear the damn piano."

Drew pulled in short breaths as his anxiety built and his voice choked up in his chest. "I can't do it that way. That's not the way I become another person."

"Drew, what are you saying?"

"I don't know," he shouted then doubled over with his arms wrapped around his stomach as if he were in pain.

"Drew, what's wrong?" Willow stared at him, frozen with indecision.

"I can't make it happen. I can't control it and keep it inside me."

With shuddering spasms, the husband Willow believed to be the most courageous man she knew, broke down and collapsed on the bed, curled into a ball and cried with broken sobs that wracked through him. "Hold me, Willow, help me."

"I love you, Drew." When he uncurled, she held him in her arms, felt him press his face against her breasts. "I'll always hold you, but I can't let you quit. I can't betray you that way."

Willow held him for a long time, while he cried out his helplessness and failure; and then she made slow, gentle love to him, resurrecting the man out of the lost child.

After that night Willow started to feel that if Drew truly believed he had failed to live up to Vittorio's visions for him, he would not only walk away from Genoa, he would leave opera all together and abandon a dream that had first been embedded in his mind by Senora Colucci—a tiny bird of a woman, who nurtured his talent, showed him how he could identify notes, pick one out of the air and give it to her whenever she asked for it. The kind, old woman had taught him how to shape it, encouraged him to let the music fill him and turn despair into hope.

With a resolve she didn't question, Willow knew she couldn't let Drew lose the dream. He had promised her he would give it a year, and she constantly promised herself she would make him keep his word. It shouldn't be too hard: his father already had, in his own words, put the backbone in him and tested his son's mettle with his own. Knowing that Drew's Sutherland pride and honor were more on her side than his, Willow told herself all she had to do was plant her feet and stand up to him with ornery Roberts grit.

For the next month, she absolutely refused to let Drew renege on his promise. But it hadn't been easy. Thanks to status, wealth, intelligence and talent, Drew had been able to use his determination and charms to accomplish or have almost anything he wanted without exerting tremendous effort. His father had been secure and rewarding in his love and strict in his demands, but they were clear and understandable demands based on unchanging rules of behavior. Andy had shaped a tough, arrogant brat into a strong, sensible and loving man. Vittorio broke down the strong and sensible to expose the tough and arrogant. And Willow had to deal with it.

Before Vittorio Luciani, no one had told Drew that honors and acclaim, no matter how hyped or widespread, were not greatness. No one ever told him his best was not good enough and that almost everything he did was wrong, wrong, wrong!

Vittorio told Drew he hadn't taken him as a protégé because he had greatness in him, but because he believed he could create greatness in him. Vittorio admitted Drew's voice had all the potential he needed, but it wasn't the voice that would make him great. Greatness would come when Drew could use his magnificent voice to release the full emotional and linguistic complexity of a great operatic role. In order to do that, Vittorio insisted Drew stop thinking about almost everything he had been taught, free his passions and sing from his soul by allowing the music and character to come from within and take control of him. And only he, Vittorio Luciani, could make him do that.

As Willow saw it, the problem was an issue of control alright; but it was between Drew and Vittorio, two egotistical control freaks, not between Drew and his emotions. The longer they were together, the more alike they became and the battle for dominance was like two mountain sheep bashing heads. Drew wouldn't capitulate and Vittorio wouldn't relent until Willow wasn't sure they even knew what they were fighting about.

There was nothing Willow could do to stop it other than give up on her commitment. But she refused to surrender by standing up to Drew and accepting every emotion he hurled at her, by loving him fiercely and deeply. She was angry with him, disappointed in him, frustrated by him but she never stopped loving him and never doubted he loved her. Together, they used the strength of their bond to rebuild his belief in himself.

Slowly, one day at a time, Drew found the courage to keep facing Vittorio's challenge. The battle ended in late February, just before Drew's non-existent twenty-seventh birthday. Without even realizing what happened, Drew responded to Vittorio's verbal flogging by giving up the fight for control. When he could no longer hold onto himself, he let go of his intense hold on the music and let his developing Figaro absorb it, let it flow through him. As the language, the music and the libretto merged into the spirit of the growing persona, it became complete.

Just as Willow had once goaded Drew into releasing the full force of his volcanic sexual passion, Vittorio, in his own way, forced him to relinquish control of his intense emotions, free his inborn creative powers and banish a buried fear of their power to control him. Vittorio then taught Drew how to use them, not only to express the passions he needed but make them a part of his Figaro and take him into himself as he had the conflicting personalities he had absorbed into his awareness as a child.

One afternoon, halfway through Figaro's opening aria, a disturbing sound caught Drew's attention and a quick glance at Vittorio tightened his throat, froze his voice, jolted him out of the role. The man was sobbing; and when he met Drew's startled stare, he was speechless. Vittorio was never speechless, especially when his concentration on the performance was interrupted by the slightest flaw. Expecting a blast of rage for allowing himself to be distracted, Drew was dumbfounded, frozen in a state of disbelief.

Vittorio sprang off the chair, grabbed Drew by the shoulders. After a vigorous shake, he threw his arms around his student, pounded him on the back and shouted in Italian, "I felt Figaro. I heard Figaro. I saw Figaro. I wanted to say: Ho, Figaro, how are you this fine day?"

Recovering, Drew burst out laughing. "And I would have answered—fine, absolutely fine—and never realized I wasn't Figaro."

It wasn't until after Drew told Willow what had happened, that the truth hit him. "Willow, I was wrong. Vittorio knew what I had to do, but he didn't know about Buffo."

Drew smiled at the startled look on Willow's face. "I had absorbed the character over a year ago, but Buffo held the music in himself and refused to give it to Figaro. And then, when Buffo was gone, I continued to hold it back so it would be solely mine and no one could take it from me again. Vittorio kept telling me to let it go, but I didn't know what he meant. Today, I stopped fighting it, and Figaro came to life with the music inside him. It became his—as well as mine—and it was magnificent."

Willow burst into tears that turned into wild laughter. After they celebrated with exhilarated passion, she sat up in bed and without hesitation, said, "Since you're gone most of the day and I only have the horses to keep me busy, it's time we had a baby."

Willow's statement stunned Drew, as so many of her out of the blue announcements or questions did, but when he thought about it, he had nothing against it.

Finis

Sutherland/Roberts Series
by
Jean Kehoe VanDyke

Book One
Slaying the Jabberwock
2020

Book Two
Taming the Muse
Coming

Book Three
Seeking Rigoletto
Coming

Brotherhood of Misfits Series
by
Jean Kehoe VanDyke

Book One
Jason of Kilpatrick
2019

Book Two
Rise of the Argonauts
2019

Book Three
Whispers of Foxbridge
Coming

Wegwas Books: P.O. Box 332, Trout Lake, Michigan 49793

jkvandyke@aol.com

wegwasbooks@aol.com

CPSIA information can be obtained
at www.ICGtesting.com
Printed in the USA
JSHW021706030621
15488JS00001B/2

9 781952 302466